P9-AOV-083

Harlequin® is proud to present

Escapade

four complete novels from four fabulous series

A romance to fit your every mood

Looking for...

Suspense, adventure, intriguing people
and mysterious situations?
Choose *Harlequin Intrigue®*

Sensuous stories and sexy men?
Choose *Harlequin Temptation®*

More drama, more emotion, more pages?
Choose *Harlequin Superromance®*

Steamy romances and provocative relationships?
Choose *Harlequin Presents®*

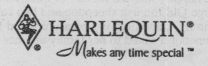

HARLEQUIN®
Makes any time special™

Rebecca York, one of the most recognizable names in romantic suspense, is the pseudonym of Ruth Glick and Eileen Buckholtz. Between the two of them, they have authored over sixty books, including this, the second title in the tremendously successful 43 Light Street series, published by Harlequin Intrigue. Rebecca York has been honored with a Career Achievement Award in Romantic Mystery by *Romantic Times Magazine*. The two-time RITA Award finalists live in Maryland with their respective families.

Vicki Lewis Thompson, a bestselling author of more than forty books for Harlequin, loves the process of creating romantic stories as much as ever. In her fifteen-year career she's collected awards from *Romantic Times* and *Affaire de Coeur.* She's also a six-time finalist for Romance Writers of America's RITA Award, including a 1998 nomination for *Mr. Valentine.* She lives in Arizona with her husband, and has two grown children.

Margot Early's first Superromance novel, *The Third Christmas,* was a RITA Award finalist for Best First Book. *The Keeper,* the novel showcased in this volume, was a 1996 finalist for the Janet Dailey Award. Her next project for Superromance is a miniseries entitled The Midwives, appearing in 1998-99. Margot lives with her husband and son in Colorado within sight of the San Juan Mountains.

Lynne Graham has been a fan of romance novels since her teens, and now has written over twenty of her own for Harlequin Presents. A native of Northern Ireland, she is the happily married mother of three children, and a very large Old English sheepdog and two cats round out the family. Gardening is a pleasure saved for any spare hours not devoted to her family and her writing.

Escapade

REBECCA YORK
VICKI LEWIS THOMPSON
MARGOT EARLY
LYNNE GRAHAM

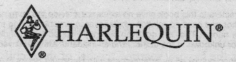

HARLEQUIN®

TORONTO • NEW YORK • LONDON
AMSTERDAM • PARIS • SYDNEY • HAMBURG
STOCKHOLM • ATHENS • TOKYO • MILAN • MADRID
PRAGUE • WARSAW • BUDAPEST • AUCKLAND

ISBN 0-373-83408-X

ESCAPADE

Copyright © 1998 by Harlequin Books S.A.

The publisher acknowledges the authors of the individual works as follows:

SHATTERED VOWS copyright © 1991 by Ruth Glick and Eileen Buckholtz

LOVERBOY copyright © 1994 by Vicki Lewis Thompson

THE KEEPER copyright © 1995 by Margot Early

THE VERANCHETTI MARRIAGE copyright © 1988 by Lynne Graham

Printed in U.S.A.

CONTENTS

CONTENTS

SHATTERED VOWS
by Rebecca York

Shattered Vows originally appeared as a
Harlequin Intrigue® novel, a series of dynamic
mysteries with a thrilling combination of
breathtaking romance and heart-stopping suspense.
Four new Harlequin Intrigue® novels appear at your
bookseller's every month. Don't miss them!

HARLEQUIN®
_____

I N T R I G U E®

CHAPTER ONE

EDDIE CAHILL flexed his leg, feeling the reassuring taut-ness of the knife nestled between his sock and his clammy flesh. The weapon had cost him plenty, plus a few promised favors once he was on the outside. Which was going to be in twenty minutes if things kept clicking along according to plan.

In the prison kitchen the weapon had been a harmless butter spreader. Long, clandestine hours of sharpening had given it a deadly edge. But the knife was only part of the elaborate sequence of moves Eddie had been mak-ing since the day they'd locked him up.

His glance strayed from the soap-filled sink where he was washing pans from dinner. For a fraction of a sec-ond he caught Lowery's eye. The man nodded almost imperceptibly.

The poor geek. In a world where inflicting pain and suffering was a major recreational activity, Lowery came in for more than his fair share. But Eddie had seen the advantage of becoming buddies with a man who suffered from grand mal epileptic seizures. Now he was so piti-fully grateful that he'd do anything for his one friend.

"All right, you bums, finish up so that you can close the place for the night," a guard barked.

Eddie began to scrub harder. He looked sullenly in-dustrious, but every muscle in his body was tensed for flight. Rinsing the pan, he set it on the drainboard with a noisy clatter.

Behind him Lowery moaned. That was the signal, and Eddie's heart began to pound inside his chest. It was now or never.

A guard started cussing. With everyone else in the room, Eddie turned toward the disturbance. Lowery was already on the floor. His arms and legs jerked violently. His eyes rolled back in his head. His jaw opened and closed. Eddie had seen his fits a couple of times before. Only this evening it was all a put-on.

"Quick. Get somethin' under his tongue," he shouted as he edged toward the door to the garbage room. "'Fore he bites it off."

Nobody looked at Eddie. All eyes were riveted to the man on the floor.

"Jeeze," someone muttered.

Two guards knelt beside Lowery. One held his head; the other inserted the handle of a wooden spoon between his teeth. Eddie didn't stay to watch. In an instant, he was out the door and into the garbage area.

The guard inside whirled at the unauthorized entry. But Eddie was ready for action. Before the guy could unholster his gun or push the alarm buzzer, he plunged the knife into the man's heart. The guard went down with only a gurgle. Eddie took the gun and stuffed the body into the dumpster. Then he climbed in after him and began pulling refuse over both of them.

All the time his ears were tuned for the sound of the garbage truck. If it didn't come on schedule, he'd just iced a man for nothing. Too bad the odds of getting another chance were about a gizillion to one. For several heart-stopping moments, he was sure he'd lost the bet. Then the truck came grinding to a halt.

He waited in the foul-smelling darkness while the dumpster was lifted onto the huge truck. Then the vehicle was rumbling down the service road in back of the kitchen.

He almost blew his supper as he waited for the gate to open. Finally it did. Then the truck was speeding down Route 175. Eddie let out the breath he'd been holding and settled back to wait. He was out. That was the important thing for now. But he had plans. The first thing he was going to do was get even with the women who'd put him in the cooler.

SOCIETY PARTIES weren't exactly her scene, Jo O'Malley thought as she backed her Honda Civic out of the garage and pressed the remote control to close the door. Actually, she conceded with a little laugh, she'd really rather be on a stakeout wearing beat-up clothes with a hat to hide her red hair. Tonight her strawberry-gold ringlets had been coiffed by the Beauty Connection. She'd even sprung for a fifteen-dollar manicure to shape and polish her short nails.

She looked down at the Royal Persian polish, thinking that if Abby Franklin weren't one of her best friends, she would have politely declined the party invitation—except that you could hardly back out of the prewedding festivities when you'd already agreed to be the matron of honor.

As she headed up the Jones Falls Expressway, she turned the radio to her favorite country station, hoping the music would occupy her mind. WPOC was just starting a newscast, and she almost turned the dial. Then the name from a lead story leaped out at her like a ghost from behind a gravestone.

Eddie Cahill.

Jo's foot bounced on the accelerator making the car shoot forward and then slow. Behind her, a truck horn blared, and she struggled to proceed at a steady pace while the newscaster wiped out her sense of security.

"...both Cahill and a guard are missing from the maximum security penitentiary in Jessup, Maryland. Cahill may be armed and is considered extremely dangerous."

Realizing her hands were fused to the wheel, Jo made an effort to unclench her fingers.

Eddie Cahill. She'd thought he was safely behind bars. Now she remembered the terrible scene in the courtroom just after the judge had pronounced sentence. The prisoner had swiveled around, and his glittering black eyes had sliced into her, making it impossible to move. Then he'd fixed his wife and the prosecuting attorney, Jennifer Stark, with the same menacing look. A hush had fallen over the courtroom as every spectator caught the tension.

"No prison can hold me, and when I get out, you three bitches are gonna pay," Eddie had snarled with the voice of a witch doctor delivering a curse.

Jo was rarely spooked, but the absolute confidence of the threat had made her blood run cold. She'd never been so relieved to see a man handcuffed and hustled off to prison.

Now Eddie had made good on the first part of the promise. He'd escaped. Was he going to come after her first? Or was it going to be Jenny or poor Karen?

It had all started when Karen had hired private detective Jo O'Malley to prove that her husband was cheating on her. He'd been cheating, all right. But the infidelity had been like an oil slick floating on top of a polluted river. Eddie had been deep into drug distribution. When the police had closed in on him, the evidence Jo had uncovered had played a crucial role in his conviction.

Jo sucked a shuddering gust of air into her lungs and willed her pulse to slow. She would not let this get to her. Eddie couldn't know where she was. Not so soon. Not tonight. Yet all at once the prospect of spending an evening in the middle of a noisy crowd was very appealing, she realized as she turned in at the long driveway that led to the estate the Franklins used when they weren't at their retirement home in Florida.

Tonight the two-story Moorish-style house was ablaze with lights, and baroque music drifted into the night. Probably there wasn't a parking place near the front door, Jo decided with a sigh, as she pulled into a space near the gate.

She'd assumed her velvet suit would be warm enough. She hadn't counted on a long, cold walk up the tree-lined driveway. Jo folded her arms and hunched her shoulders against the November wind. Above her the remaining leaves on the tall oaks rustled ominously like dried-up decorations left over from Halloween.

A perfect place for an ambush, she reflected with a shiver, as she quickened her step. Someone who wanted to pop out from behind the boxwoods and grab her wouldn't even have to muffle his footsteps.

Her mind clicked back to Eddie Cahill and the evil look on his face that day in court. Only now he was waiting in the inky blackness beyond the circles of light that lined the driveway.

Jo managed a feeble laugh at her overactive imagi-

nation. With any luck, the police had already recaptured
the man. Escaped criminals didn't stay on the loose for
long. She let her mind spin out pictures of roadblocks,
squads of uniformed officers on a manhunt, the final capture in a field near the state prison.

"Can I help you, miss?"

The movie in her mind vanished and private detective
Josephine O'Malley jumped several inches off the
ground. As she came down, she realized she was being
addressed by a man in a maroon uniform.

Sheez. He probably thought she was some kind of
loony. "I'm here to attend the Franklin-Claiborne
party."

He looked around in puzzlement. "Did you arrive by
taxi?"

"My car is at the end of the driveway."

"I would have been glad to park it for you, miss."

Jo realized she'd already made her second faux pas in
less than a minute. The Franklins had hired parking attendants. But how could you expect a girl from the
mountains of western Maryland to know that?

"I'll let you get the car when I leave," she promised
as she started up the steps. Moments later she was bathed
in the sparkling light of the crystal chandelier that graced
the Spanish tile foyer. Stepping out of the night into the
brightness had a transforming effect on her mood.

Or perhaps it was her first sight of a radiant Abby
Franklin. She was standing with a not-quite-so-com-
fortable-looking Steve Clairborne greeting guests. Her
sweater-topped sequined gown seemed as natural on her
as the tailored suits she often wore to work. While her
fiancé was ruggedly handsome in a tuxedo, Jo sus-

pected he'd like to rip off his bow tie and open the stud at his neck.

When he saw her, he grinned and shook his head. She smiled back and gave him a thumbs-up sign. Probably they were the only two people here who wished the Franklins had thrown a crab feast instead of a formal party. Except that it was the wrong month for crabs.

They embraced warmly. Jo had helped Abby save Steve's life six months ago when he'd come back to Baltimore from the Far East to investigate his sister's mysterious death.

He pretended to do a double-take as he inspected her expensive outfit, makeup and hairdo.

"Who is this mystery woman?" he teased.

"You didn't think I had it in me, did you?"

"Of course we did," Abby interjected.

"It's a lot different from your usual tomboy-next-door image. But I like it," Steve continued. "I think Cam will, too."

"Who's Cam?"

"Our best man. I'll introduce you later," Abby promised.

After a few more minutes Jo moved aside so others could talk to the happy couple. As she wandered from drawing room to conservatory to dining room, Jo looked for Laura Roswell. She, Abby, and Laura all had their offices downtown in a turn-of-the-century building at 43 Light Street. Abby was a psychologist, Laura a lawyer. The three women often helped each other out on tough cases. More than that, they were the kind of friends who could be counted on in a crisis.

Jo was on a first-name basis with very few of the glittering society crowd who filled the elegantly furnished rooms. But she'd seen a number of the faces on TV or in the newspapers. Most were in small groups talking and enjoying the hors d'oeuvres being passed on silver trays by elegantly dressed waiters.

She couldn't help feeling more of an observer than a participant as she snagged herself a tiny quiche. Finally she spotted Laura and was heading across the drawing room when she felt the fine hairs on the back of her neck prickle. Someone was watching her. She could feel it. Like the malevolent eyes of Eddie Cahill boring into her the last time she'd seen him.

It took all of her willpower to keep from whirling around and confronting the menace behind her. Instead she turned slowly and casually surveyed the room. A waiter gave her a half smile. No one else seemed to be paying her any special attention.

Stop it, she told herself sternly. *The Franklins didn't invite the bogeyman to the party.*

With a too-bright smile plastered on her face, she grabbed a glass of champagne and took several swallows before starting back toward Laura. But her path was now blocked by a knot of men recounting the details of a golf game.

She was debating another route when she felt something hard press into the small of her back.

"Don't make a move, sister," a sinister voice hissed. "I've got you covered."

Her body, already tensed for action, jerked. The champagne she was holding splashed onto the front of her green velvet suit.

"Oh, brassafrax," came a muttered exclamation. "Jo, I'm sure sorry." She recognized the voice, and relief flooded through her. Turning she found herself staring into the apologetic brown eyes of Lou Rossini, the former shipyard worker who was now the superintendent of 43 Light Street. His gnarled index finger was extended like the barrel of a revolver.

"Lou. What—?"

"Just a stupid joke. You ain't usually so jumpy."

When he tried to dab at the front of her suit with a cocktail napkin, she shook her head. "That'll just make it worse. I'd better go see what I can do."

A hair dryer would take care of the wet mess that spread across the front of her green jacket, Jo thought as she went to seek out her hostess. She met Abby first, who directed her up to the master bedroom and told her she'd find the appliance in the vanity in the dressing area.

After a quick thank-you, Jo scurried up the stairs. At the end of the hall, she stopped for a moment to gape at the elaborate bedroom that looked as if it had been transported from the royal palace in Madrid.

The hair dryer was in one of the deep drawers of the marble vanity.

Although Jo had never been particularly domestic, she had some dim idea that she should try to get the stain out with water. Wetting a hand towel, she dabbed at the front of the jacket and succeeded in making the nap of the velvet look like a cat after a swim.

Behind her in the bathroom, someone else was also running water. When the door opened, a tall, dark-haired man stepped into the dressing room.

In the mirror, her eyes collided with those of Clark Kent behind a pair of gray-rimmed glasses. He was the image of Christopher Reeve. Did Abby's family know him? They hadn't mentioned it, but it could be possible.

As she studied his reflection, she began to pick up differences. The features were a bit more angular. The hair was a little curlier. The eyes were gray instead of blue. Yet the face had that same irresistible quality that had made her heart flutter when Superman had taken Lois Lane for that first magical flight over Metropolis. She wondered if this guy would look as good in tights and a cape.

He seemed just as intrigued with her face as she was with his. Then his gaze dropped to the inland sea that spread across the front of her jacket and the washcloth in her hand. "You're going to ruin that."

"No kidding."

Reaching briskly inside his tuxedo jacket, he pulled out something that looked like a slightly flattened flashlight. Instead of a light bulb behind glass at the end, there was a cone-shaped opening.

"What's that?" Jo asked.

"The prototype for an ionization spot remover. It lifts out foreign matter by changing the charge in the fabric from negative to positive. Want to give it a try?"

"Do I get a money back guarantee?"

"Sure." He threw a switch and the device began to purr.

She'd expected him to hand it to her. Instead he crossed the three feet that separated them and began to run the cone-shaped end of the gadget back and forth across the front of Jo's jacket.

"Turn a little to the side." His other hand went to her shoulder. Both hands were long and tapered and almost graceful for a man. As he moved the device back and forth a quarter inch above the suit front, he pushed a rapid combination of buttons on a key pad along the top of the instrument.

"What are you doing?"

"Augmenting the rapid recovery factor. But I'd better separate the alpha and the delta functions."

"Right. Sure."

Jo rarely sat by and let other people take charge of situations. Now a combination of curiosity about the device and curiosity about the man kept her immobile.

Clark Kent's gaze was intense as he bent to the work. In fact, his absorption was total, as if his mind was capable of filtering out any extraneous elements—like the fact that his face was now in close proximity to her chest.

Searching for something to occupy her own attention, she noted that his nose was perfectly proportioned with the rest of his features. His lips were narrow and pressed together as he concentrated on the task at hand. Through the glasses, she saw that his lashes were long and dark, quite striking really.

Wondering why she'd gotten caught up in such details, she shifted her regard to the suit jacket. To her astonishment, she saw that the wet spot had almost vanished and the velvet fabric had recaptured much of its former luster.

"Hey, that thing really does work. Where'd you get it?"

"I invented it."

The strong fingers on her shoulder shifted her to a different angle, bringing her body more tightly against his. She was starting to feel hot. In the next moment she realized why. The fabric over her chest was steaming.

"Ouch."

"Sorry. Let me get it away from your skin." His attention was still on the stain removal operation. Without hesitation, his free hand slipped inside her jacket.

Jo was rendered temporarily immobile as his warm flesh came in contact with the silky fabric of her blouse. As his fingers shifted to press against her breast, she sucked in a quivery breath.

The other hand, which was still moving back and forth with the stain removal instrument, paused in mid-stroke. He raised his head, and his gray eyes locked with her green ones. For several heartbeats, neither one of them moved.

Clearing his throat, he withdrew the offending hand. "Sorry."

Was he?

"Listen, uh—thanks. It's almost as good as new, really," she was surprised to hear herself stammering. Snatching her evening purse from the vanity, she turned and made a swift exit from the dressing room.

Jo was halfway to the stairs when she remembered she hadn't planned to go directly back to the party. Now that her jacket was back to normal, there was a call she should make. Hopefully it would set her mind at ease. If it didn't, she'd know what she was up against.

She found a phone in the upstairs den. The number she wanted was in the address book she always carried, even in an evening bag. One of the things Jo had learned from her deceased husband, Skip O'Malley, was that the right contacts can make the difference between cracking a case and going down in flames.

Now she thumbed through the well-used book and found Sid Flowers's number. A senior administrator in the Maryland prison system, he was bound to know what was going on.

"Flowers here," he answered crisply.

"This is Jo O'Malley."

"Jo, where in the hell are you? I've left messages on your answering machines at work and at home."

"I'm at a party."

"I assume you know about Cahill."

"Can you give me the scoop, Sid?"

"The details are confidential."

"Understood."

"As near as we can figure it, he persuaded a fellow inmate to fake an epileptic seizure in the kitchen. Then, while everybody was watching the Academy Award winning performance, he slipped into the garbage room and killed the guard. Unfortunately, the truck went right to the Howard County dump. If we'd intercepted it fifteen minutes earlier, we would have had him in custody again."

"Then he's still on the loose, I take it." Jo was amazed at how steady her voice sounded when she could feel her nerves jumping like bullfrogs on a hot plate.

"It's only a matter of time before we pick him up."

"Meanwhile, I'd better watch my back." There was an electronic click and the line was suddenly stronger.

"Did someone hang up your extension?" Jo asked the correction officer.

"I'm here alone."

"Well, maybe somebody here picked up the phone and got hooked on the Cahill drama."

Flowers laughed. "If they're still on the line, they're under arrest."

Jo laughed too, but she felt the hairs on the back of

her neck flutter again. Had someone been deliberately listening? No. Why would they?

"If anything else breaks, I'll let you know."

"Thanks."

"Jo..." Sid's voice was edged with concern. "Maybe you ought to consider taking a vacation until they catch up with Eddie."

"Don't be silly. I've got a business to run."

"Guess you do. This will probably blow over in a few days anyway. Either Cahill's in Wilmington by now, or they're gonna scoop him up PDQ."

"Have you talked to Karen Cahill or Jennifer Stark?"

"I'm working on it."

There were more reassurances proffered and accepted. But when Jo got off the phone, she closed her eyes and took several deep breaths. No matter what Flowers said or how tough she tried to sound, she wasn't going to stop looking over her shoulder as long as a psychopath like Eddie Cahill was on the loose.

Right now, however, her immediate problem was getting through the evening without any more mishaps. Piece of cake, she assured herself. How bad could an engagement party be compared to a killer on the loose?

CHAPTER TWO

THE GROUND floor was even more crowded when Jo came back down. For a moment she stood near the foot of the spiral staircase surveying the guests. Which one had been listening to her conversation with Sid Flowers, she wondered. Had it just been an innocent mistake? Or was someone interested in her personal business?

Laura Roswell's voice broke into her thoughts. "Jo. I've been looking all over for you."

"Likewise." They smiled at each other, two women from very different backgrounds who were closer than family now.

The blond lawyer was wearing an ice-blue beaded gown that could have been part of the Nancy Reagan designer loan program. With Laura's long legs and gentle curves, it looked much better on her than it would have on the former first lady. But it wasn't a loaner. Jo was pretty sure that Dr. William Avery, Laura Roswell's husband, invested in his wife's clothing as a reflection of his success.

"Where's Bill?" Jo asked.

Laura's expression tightened. "He's known about this party for weeks, but he decided at the last minute that he just had to attend an Internal Medicine meeting in Atlanta."

Jo heard the mixture of annoyance and hurt in Laura's

voice. Were her friend's marital problems building to some sort of crisis? She'd mentioned several times that things weren't going well with her and Bill.

"I'm sorry," Jo responded.

"One way or another, things are going to shake out," Laura predicted. "But I'm not letting it get me down right now. This is Abby and Steve's night."

Before they could continue the conversation, Abby's mother joined the pair. A tan, slender woman in her late fifties, Janet Franklin looked fit and attractive. If her mother were any indication, Abby was going to age gracefully, Jo thought.

"So there you are," Mrs. Franklin said. "We're taking a few pictures in the library. And we'd like to photograph Jo with Steve's best man, Cameron Randolph."

With that name he was undoubtedly another Baltimore blue blood, Jo thought. Was he a maverick like Steve, or had he carved himself out a comfortable niche with his silver spoon?

The matron turned to Laura. "We'd like shots of everybody who's going to be in the wedding party."

When they entered the room, the photographer was just finishing a series of romantic poses with Steve and Abby. The bride-to-be looked relaxed. Her intended looked as if he'd rather be back running guns into Afghanistan. When he saw Jo, relief washed over his face. "Your turn," he called out, stepping out of the lights and tugging Abby along with him. The photographer was about to object, but she shook her head.

"I think he's reached his limit."

Steve gave Abby a grateful hug.

"Okay, we can move on to the matron of honor and best man."

Jo quickly glanced down at the front of her jacket. It would pass inspection. As she positioned herself in front of the fireplace wall, a tall, rangy man who had been standing in the shadows stepped into the light. When his gaze encountered hers, she knew he'd been aware of her from the moment she'd stepped into the room.

Her stomach did a triple somersault.

"Jo O'Malley, I'd like you to meet Cam Randolph," Abby made the introductions, not realizing she was already twenty minutes too late. "I'm sure the two of you are going to get along famously."

"We've already met," Cam told Abby. "She was a reluctant guinea pig for one of my new inventions." When he spread his expressive hands, palms up, Jo remembered the feel of his warm flesh against hers.

"As a matter of fact he took the stain off the front of my suit," she added hastily. "Otherwise I'd be running away from the camera."

"Sounds intriguing," Steve interjected. "Are you going to tell us about it?"

"No," came the simultaneous response.

Abby looked from Jo to Cam. Before she could comment further, the photographer interrupted.

"Stand right here." He maneuvered Jo and Cam together. She slid him a sideways glance. His tall frame was stiff, his hands awkwardly clasped in front of him. So he wasn't quite as cool as he was pretending to be, she thought, secretly pleased.

The photographer stepped behind the camera and snapped off two shots. "Come on, you guys. Make it look like you're having fun."

Jo turned to Cam and gave him an exaggerated grin.

"Play like you just won the Nobel Prize for stain removal."

He grinned back. "Right."

The photographer was able to snap off several pictures of a smiling couple. "Much better. Thanks, guys."

"Don't go away," Abby said as they stepped out of the lights. "We need you for the group shot."

They moved to a quieter corner of the room while the photographer selected his next victims.

"So how do you know Steve?" Jo asked, making an attempt to normalize diplomatic relations.

"We were at McDonough together."

Well, I was right, Jo thought. One of the city's most prestigious prep schools. Cam Randolph was definitely out of her league.

He must have read her doubtful expression. "I promise I won't spring any more inventions on you tonight."

"It's not you. It's the guy who escaped from prison this evening that I'm really uptight about." It was sort of a relief to joke about the danger.

"What are you talking about?"

"Eddie Cahill. A drug dealer I got mixed up with last year. Apparently the prison system couldn't hold on to him."

"How did a nice girl like you get mixed up with a drug dealer?" Cam sounded as if he suspected she might be pulling his leg.

"On a case. I testified against him."

"Are you with the police?"

"Private detective."

"Oh." His eyes narrowed and his expression closed. Jo suddenly wished she'd kept her big mouth shut. It had a habit of getting her into trouble. "You have something against private detectives?"

"It's nothing personal." He cleared his throat. "If you're worried about escaped criminals, you should have a good home security system."

"I have one of the best. The Centurion from—"

"—Randolph Enterprises," he supplied.

Jo realized her mind hadn't made an important connection. "Your company?"

"Yes. And my design."

"Well, I love the auto-delay feature. And the tone sequence selector."

"It definitely gives you more for the money. But I try to build special features into all our products."

"Have you always been in the design department?" Despite herself, Jo was impressed. She'd seen the Randolph Enterprises catalog and knew the company offered a wide range of innovative merchandise.

"I had to take over management for a couple of years."

Jo caught a hint of tension in his voice but suspected he wasn't going to elaborate.

She was right. He changed the subject. "I'm back in the lab now."

"Do you have a lot of inventions?"

"Thirty-seven patents."

Jo whistled. "Maybe we weren't joking about the Nobel Prize."

"Not likely. Only a small percentage of inventions can be brought to market as profitable products. Since we don't have unlimited resources, sometimes I have to rely on Phil Mercer's judgment on where to put our priorities."

Again she caught an undertone of acerbity. "Who's Phil Mercer?"

"Our CEO. He was my father's right-hand man."

"Your father retired?"

"He died a few years ago."

The answer was clipped, and Jo understood why he might not want to pursue the topic. When you loved someone, it was hard to reconcile yourself to never seeing them again. Even after three years it still hurt to think about Skip.

They were called over for the group shot of all the participants in the wedding. Then dinner was announced. Jo pretended she'd agreed to eat with friends and joined a group of young professionals. As she picked at artichoke hearts vinaigrette she couldn't shake the tension headache Eddie Cahill had generated. Only a desire not to let Abby down kept her at the table, barely holding up her end of several sporadic conversations. Finally, just before dessert, she gave up the struggle and slipped away.

Outside Jo gave her keys to the parking attendant. Once he had a description of her car, he disappeared, and she was left standing alone under the arbor that spanned the circular drive. A tiny circle of light enclosed her. Beyond it the concealing darkness hovered. At least she didn't have to march out into the night again.

It had gotten colder during the evening, and the wind's icy fingers probed through her jacket. Once more she wrapped her arms around her shoulders to ward off the chill, yet she knew the wind and cold weren't the only reasons she was shivering. It was impossible to shake the awful sensation of being watched. She'd felt as if someone had been keeping tabs on her all night, playing hide-and-seek in the crowd.

Last time she'd played it cool. Now she whirled around, her eyes probing the windows on either side of the door. No one was peering back. But that hardly lessened the tension in her neck and shoulders.

She felt some of the strain melt away when she saw twin headlights cutting through the dark. As her car pulled in front of the door, she hurried around to the driver's side. Once behind the wheel, she gunned the engine and roared off down the drive.

She thought of Abby and Steve wrapped in the warmth and love of friends and family. But more importantly, they had each other. She remembered the feeling. Just for a minute she let herself wish there were someone around to take care of her—or someone at home who would breathe a sigh of relief when she walked in the front door. Then she shook her head. Except for the few years she'd been married to Skip, she'd always taken care of herself. There was absolutely no reason she couldn't continue.

Not until Jo was several blocks away did she stop to consider the uncharacteristic panic that had sent her hurtling down the Franklin drive like the Tokyo Bullet. She never acted like this. She was a woman who was perfectly capable of handling dangerous situations. That was what she did for a living. But something about the house or the party or the company had thrown her badly. Or perhaps it was just the threat of Eddie Cahill hovering over the proceedings.

As she drove back toward Roland Park, she went over each element of the evening but couldn't draw any firm conclusions. However, her mind kept coming back to Cam Randolph.

He was part of what had thrown her. In a man-woman way. But she wasn't looking for a relationship. And if she were, it wouldn't be with someone like him. They were worlds apart socially. Not to mention that he was one of the smartest guys she'd ever met. What in the heck were they going to talk about until the wedding was finally over?

She was still trying to puzzle that one out when she turned onto her street and reached for the automatic garage door opener. After the door had shut behind her, she got out of the car and punched in her I.D. code on the security system's key pad. The box played back a little tune that told her everything was as she'd left it. Suddenly she realized she wasn't going to be able to hear that melody without thinking about the inventor. She wasn't sure whether she liked that or not.

THE STASH HAD BEEN right where he'd left it, in the Eternal Friend Pet Cemetery on Route 1. Early Sunday morning had been a good time to disinter the grave marked Rambo. Back when Eddie had buried the little casket, he'd said he was putting a beloved poodle to rest. The watertight box had really contained twenty thousand dollars in small bills. Eddie had put the bread aside for an emergency when he'd been riding the crest of a wave of successful drug deals. He hadn't had any specific catastrophe in mind, but now he was damn glad he'd had the foresight.

Last night he'd stolen some coveralls off a Howard County clothesline and hitched a ride with a trucker to Jessup. At the cemetery he'd found a shovel in the groundskeeper's shed and dug up the dough. Then he'd checked into a rundown motel in Elkridge, where he'd scrubbed the garbage smell off his body. After that, he'd watched accounts of his escape on the evening news and gone to sleep with the guard's gun under his pillow.

The next morning he was feeling rested, refreshed and ready to settle a few scores. As he watched the news again, he chuckled. The money was going to make all the difference. Without it he'd just be a poor schmuck on the run. With it, he could buy what he needed and lay low until some of the heat was off.

Over an Egg McMuffin and a cup of black coffee, which he brought back to the motel room, he considered his options. First on the agenda were some decent clothes and some wheels. Then he'd think about the tools he needed. He already had a gun. Adding an assault rifle to his arsenal wouldn't be a bad idea.

Jo O'Malley woke up determined to look on the bright side. As she retrieved the fat Sunday paper from the front walk, she counted her blessings. She owned her rambling old Roland Park house free and clear, thanks to Skip's mortgage insurance. She was self-supporting. And the police had probably already recaptured Eddie Cahill, although she wasn't going to spoil her Sunday morning by calling them until she'd eaten breakfast— just in case.

On weekdays Jo just grabbed a bowl of cereal and instant coffee in the morning. On Sunday she continued the ritual that she and Skip had started. Baking-powder biscuits, country ham, fresh ground coffee. They made her think of home and warmth and love. She did so in a positive way. There was no point in dwelling on what was missing from her life.

First Jo whipped up a batch of biscuits, then she opened the *Sun*. Since she'd been a kid in western Maryland, she'd always read the comics first. Usually her only concession to adult responsibility was to scan the headlines when she opened the paper, but this morning she read the article on Eddie Cahill. It had less information than she'd gotten from Sid the night before, so she turned to her favorite comic—The Far Side. Talking cows again. She grinned.

Her good mood lasted through two cups of coffee and a plate of biscuits smothered with butter and her mother's wild raspberry jam. Not a very low cholesterol breakfast, she thought as she went out to empty the trash. But one of the joys of living alone was eating what you wanted.

Halfway down the steps to the backyard, she stopped and uttered a rather unladylike imprecation. The trash cans lay on their sides, and the refuse looked as if it were scattered as far as the Baltimore County line.

Standing with her hands on her hips, she did a slow burn. Then she got a pair of garden gloves out of the toolshed and started picking up the debris from her well-tended yard. After Skip had died, she had assumed the upkeep of the three-quarter acre that surrounded the house would be a chore. Instead she discovered she liked pulling up weeds and planting flowers. She even had a garden down near the alley where she grew tomatoes and zucchini.

Muttering under her breath, she pulled a soup bone out from under the forsythia and a wad of clothes dryer lint off her favorite tea rosebush.

Mac Lyman, the retired postman who lived next door, came out to commiserate. Jo liked Mac. He reminded her of the honest, hardworking folks she'd grown up with in Garrett County.

"I guess those good-for-nothin' dogs got you again," he said as he began picking up scattered papers.

Jo stuffed a juice carton back in the can. "'Fraid so. Did they mess up your yard, too?"

"Not this time."

"You're lucky." Trying not to get her bathrobe dirty, she edged under a hydrangea to retrieve a plastic meat tray.

"Funny thing," Mac mused. "Usually I hear barkin' or somethin'. Not this time."

"You didn't see anything?"

"Zippo. No details." He waited for a moment. "Don't you get it? Details. Tails."

She forced a laugh. "Yeah. Right." She hadn't heard any barking, either. And she hadn't slept particularly soundly. Maybe it hadn't been dogs. But what else could have made such a godawful mess?

Jo tightened the belt of her bathrobe. All at once it was easy to picture a short, wiry man with Eddie Cahill's ferretlike face prowling around her house.

Come on, O'Malley, she chided herself. *What's happened to your deductive reasoning? If Eddie Cahill came after you, he wouldn't get much of a kick from scattering a little bit of garbage. He'd be scattering buckshot at the very least.*

With Mac's help, the trash was cleaned up in less than fifteen minutes. Jo thanked the old man warmly and went back inside to shower. Hot water washed away the outside chill, but it couldn't quite reach the cold feeling that had sunk into her bones.

WHEN CAM was deep into a new project, he couldn't stay away from the lab, even on Sunday morning. So after his regular five-mile run, he showered and pulled on a pair of jeans and a sweatshirt.

The outfit was modest. His Cross Keys Village town house was small but comfortable. The sleek red Lotus in the garage was one of the few luxury items he'd acquired. Although the Randolph fortune would have bought a life-style full of upscale perks, in general, material items didn't mean much to Cam.

He cared more about intellectual challenge and about having built Randolph Enterprises back up the Forbes' hot list.

Electronics was one of his true passions. So was maneuvering the Lotus down narrow Baltimore streets with the skill of a race car driver.

He hummed along with the radio as he made the twenty-five-minute ride from Cross Keys to Owings Mills. Pulling into the executive parking lot, he noticed Phil Mercer's Mercedes nearby. So the CEO was catching up on business again on Sunday, too.

Cam sighed. With any luck he wouldn't run into him. Phil was a good manager, excellent at handling day-to-day operations. It was just that the man had strong opinions about which projects to push. Often his decisions were driven by monetary considerations rather than the love and challenge of innovation.

In the workroom behind his private office, Cam brought up the computer specs for the little electronic spot remover. The thermostat was definitely out of whack, he thought as he typed in instructions for a two-minute simulation of the cleaning cycle.

While the results plotted themselves out on the screen, he realized he wasn't thinking about the temperature curve. He was recalling the soft curve of Jo O'Malley's breast under his hand.

Randolph, you've been buried in the lab too long, he told himself sternly, *if all it takes is a little inadvertent canoodling to make you react like a teenager at his first strip show.*

But even as he mentally tossed off the self-deprecating thought, he acknowledged that the response had been more than a case of overloaded circuits. There had been something very appealing about Jo O'Malley. The bouncy red curls, the impish blue eyes, and the slightly sassy manner. Most of the women he met were impressed with his money. He'd known instinctively that Ms. O'Malley didn't give a damn. In fact, the Randolph millions probably meant as much to her as mildew in the corner of the shower. He hadn't met many women like her, and he hadn't been sure how to parry her thrusts. Yet he'd enjoyed her unpredictability and the natural sex appeal she projected.

Being with her generated the same excitement as the start of a new lab project. You had a definite result in mind, but you didn't know how or if things were going to work out.

Just what kind of result did he want with Ms. O'Malley, he asked himself. As several very graphic pictures leaped into his mind, he fought to rein in his runaway imagination.

Slow down, he ordered himself. *There isn't any hurry.*

He and Ms. O'Malley were going to be spending a

good deal of time in each other's company over the next few weeks. There wasn't going to be any problem getting to know her.

He forced himself back to work, but after another forty-five minutes he realized it wasn't going to be a very productive Sunday morning.

Getting up from the computer, he pushed a button that dispensed the right amount of instant coffee, water, creamer and sugar into a mug. After a robotic arm stirred it all together, the finished product slid toward him.

He took a sip. Perfect. His department had done a great job of programming the machine, but marketing had never gotten it into mass production. It was one of those products that had fallen through the cracks a few years ago when Randolph Enterprises had been on the brink of disaster.

That was a time he'd promised himself he wasn't going to think about. Now his Adam's apple bobbed painfully as memories came flooding back. It had all started when Dad had hired a private detective to find out who was responsible for the industrial espionage robbing Randolph of its most promising designs. The espionage had stopped, although there had never been any definite proof of who was responsible. But the price had been too high. Cam still blamed the detective who had exceeded his instructions when he'd dug into the mess.

Cam found his hand was clenched around the coffee mug. With a sigh, he relaxed his fingers, set the mug down, and walked to the window where he stood staring out at the parking lot.

His mother had died when he was only seven, and for years the three males in the Randolph family had been a close-knit unit. At least until Collin had— He clenched his teeth together and willed away the painful memories of surprise and shock. He loved his brother and would have stood by him. But Collin hadn't given him the chance. Shock had followed shock. Within the month, Cam had lost what remained of his immediate family—both his father and his brother. Ultimately, the only way to deal with the grief had been to shove the whole pitiful mess into a locked compartment of his mind. But there were times when the locked door came bursting open, and he'd be so enraged that only climbing into the Lotus and taking the precision machine up to 120 miles an hour could wipe out the need for retribution.

Why was all this coming back now when he was usually so efficient at keeping his dark emotions under control? He sighed. One thing he did know, mental connections didn't pop up at random. They were triggered by data stored in the brain—even if you didn't understand the correlations. However, there might be a way to get at the information.

Sitting down at the keyboard, he accessed the industrial espionage file his father had carefully kept. All at once, the grim facts flashed to life on the high-resolution screen. Documentation on the stolen development plans. Financial loss estimates. Status reports on the investigation. A couple of letters of reference on the detective Dad had hired. His name was Skip O'Malley.

Cam's eyes narrowed. Skip O'Malley. His conscious memory had deliberately lost the name. But it had been buried in his subconscious like a corroding container of nuclear waste.

He'd even talked to the man a couple of times, he remembered now. He'd been tough, experienced and in his forties. Now additional details were coming back to him. Several months after being dismissed from the Randolph case, Skip O'Malley had been killed in a waterfront shoot-out. Was Jo a relative? Perhaps she was the daughter who had taken over his business.

Although he didn't have a copy of the obituary, it was easy enough to retrieve it from one of the on-line data bases Randolph subscribed to. Five minutes later he was scrolling through the relevant section of the *Baltimore Sun*.

Cam's fingers froze on the keyboard. It was worse than he'd suspected. The little redhead who'd been occupying his thoughts that morning wasn't Skip O'Malley's daughter. She'd been his partner. And his wife.

He pushed back his ergonomically designed chair and meshed his fingers behind his neck. Well, this certainly put a different perspective on things, he mused, picking up a pencil and tapping it against his lips. Fate had handed him an opportunity, and he was never one to turn down that kind of gift.

The pencil began to seesaw between his fingers as his formidable intellectual powers kicked into overdrive. There were exponential possibilities, but he'd better consider his strategy carefully.

He was just starting to explore a promising plan of action when there was a perfunctory knock. Almost immediately, the doors to the lab swung open. Cam's head jerked around, and he found himself staring at Phil Mercer. The trim, gray-haired executive had a thick sheaf of papers under his arm.

As he advanced toward Cam, the scientist quickly blanked out the data on the screen. Theoretically he and management should be entirely open with each other, but he knew damn well that Mercer had his quota of hidden agendas. So did he, for that matter. The digging he'd been doing this morning was private—not something he wanted to share with the CEO.

"Glad I caught you today," Mercer was saying. "I've got some questions about your expenditures for the next fiscal year."

"I don't think they're out of line."

"I have the feeling you're not taking the present economic slowdown into consideration."

Cam sighed. Now he was in for a two-hour lecture on the delicate balance of profits versus R&D. Just when he was itching to start digging into the background of one Ms. Josephine O'Malley.

CHAPTER THREE

JO STOPPED by Laura Roswell's office Monday morning before unlocking her own door.

"How are you doing?" Jo asked Laura's secretary as she pulled off her ivory knit hat and gave her red curls a little shake.

"Fine." Noel Emery cut off the personal conversation to answer a phone call, which was interrupted by the second line. As she smoothly handled both conversations, she held up two fingers indicating that she wouldn't be long.

Noel ran Laura's office with top-notch efficiency. But it hadn't always been that way. When she'd first come to 43 Light Street, her self-esteem had been at rock bottom.

Jo had wondered why Laura had hired a secretary who lost messages and misfiled important briefs. All Laura had said was that the young woman needed the job.

It had been months before Noel told Jo what had happened at her last place of employment. Her boss, a partner in one of the city's most prestigious law firms, had pressured her into dating him. Next he'd tried to get her into bed. When she'd refused, he asked her to work late one night and raped her on his office sofa.

Noel had threatened to call the police, but he'd laughed and asked who she thought they were going to believe. She'd quit her job without a reference, and Laura Roswell had hired her when she'd been at the end of her rope.

With the encouragement of the other women at 43 Light Street, Noel had pulled her life back together. She was going to night school, and by day she guarded Laura's waiting room with the loyalty and tenacity of a bulldog.

Jo listened to Noel reading the riot act to a father who'd called to say he had no intention of coughing up child support payments. As she hung up, she rolled her eyes. "Laura's not in this morning. She's in judge's chambers on a custody case."

"Too bad. I wanted some free legal advice on canine vandalism."

Noel consulted her boss's schedule. "It looks like she has an opening around two. I'll give you a call if she can see you."

"Thanks."

Jo took the elevator up to her office. For a moment she stood in front of the frosted glass door panel that still proclaimed the occupants "O'Malley and O'Malley." It wasn't just sentiment that kept her deceased husband's name on the door and in the Yellow Pages. There were clients who still wouldn't hire a female detective. If they didn't ask about the other member of the O'Malley team, she'd let them assume he was an active partner in the business.

She smiled as she remembered back to when she came to Baltimore years ago. Like Noel, she'd been looking for a better job than she could find in rural western Maryland. Skip O'Malley, who'd been in desperate need of of a secretary, had quickly discovered Jo didn't have much talent for office management. He'd fired her three or four times but always hired her back—because her insights often helped solve cases.

She'd become his de facto partner in six months and a real one in a year. A year after that, he'd given up fighting his attraction for a woman fifteen years his junior and married her.

Skip had taught her everything he'd learned in his twenty years of private investigation. More than a mentor, he'd been her best friend and lover as well. It would take a hell of a man to replace him. Certainly not Cameron Randolph, she told herself, and then wondered why she'd even entertained the idea.

Turning her attention to the blinking red light on the answering machine, she cleared a place on her desk, grabbed a yellow legal pad and a pencil and hit the button.

The first call was from Sid Flowers—but it predated their conversation of the night before. The second was from a prospective client who wanted to know if Jo worked on a contingency basis. "Sure," she muttered. "Plus up front expenses." She didn't take down the number. If the man wanted to call back, she'd explain her fee schedule.

The machine clicked again, and she raised her pencil to take notes.

"Hi there, Jo. Sorry I didn't catch you in." The words were friendly enough, but the voice was electronically distorted as if it might have been generated by a computer. Had those blasted direct marketing companies finally figured out a way to personalize their greeting, she wondered.

"You've got a gorgeous little body, angel face, you know that?"

Jo's head snapped around toward the machine. What kind of product were they selling, anyway?

"Just thinking about what I'd like to do to you makes me hot all over, baby. The problem is, I can't decide whether I want to give you a poke with my sugar stick or stick you with a hot poker." The observation was followed by a high-pitched laugh made shrill by the electronic distortion. The noise was like the buzz of malevolent insects. Jo felt them surrounding her, descending, crawling on her skin. Dropping her pad and pencil, she rubbed her arms as if that would rub away the invasion.

"Get the wordplay? But when you and me play, baby, it ain't just gonna be with words."

Jo continued to stare at the machine. Then she shook herself free of its spell. "Just who do you think you are, buster?" Still, her hand reached out and pushed the save button, a silent acknowledgment that the message had disturbed her more than she wanted to admit.

It was this damn Eddie Cahill business, she told herself vehemently. When she let her guard down, he had her feeling as if she were balanced on the edge of a razor knife.

Had he made the call?

She forced herself to think analytically. Whoever it was had used her first name, which wasn't in the agency's telephone listing or on the directory board in the lobby. It had to be someone who knew her—either personally or professionally.

That didn't mean it was necessarily Eddie. Over the years her job had put her in conflict with a fair number of people. But who would pick this method of getting even? If this was Eddie's little joke, maybe she'd lucked out. But she couldn't quite convince herself he'd be satisfied with long-distance vengeance. Not after the look he'd given her in court.

Was there some sort of clue to the caller's identity in the recording? Before she could change her mind, she replayed it, struggling to blot out the crawling feeling from the electronic distortion and listen dispassionately as she cataloged details. The caller sounded vaguely masculine, yet she knew that someone speaking into the right electronic equipment could make his voice sound like anything from Donald Duck to Darth Vader.

She ran through the tape one more time, listening for background noise. If the call had been made from a phone booth, there might be traffic sounds. She couldn't detect any. On the other hand, she thought she heard music in the background. Radio? Television? There was no way to tell. What would that prove, anyway?

Well, the last thing she was going to do, she told herself, was blow the whole thing out of proportion. There was no point in jumping out of her skin over a crank call. What she would do was get busy.

First she put in another call to Sid Flowers. He didn't have anything more to report—except that Jennifer Stark, the Assistant D.A. who'd prosecuted Cahill, was vacationing with her husband in the Virgin Islands.

"Lucky her," Jo muttered.

Flowers agreed.

Since the police weren't making much progress on the case, Jo decided to see if she could lend a hand.

Cahill. *C*. She opened the top file drawer and began shuffling through folders. Once she'd had the bright idea of color coding cases to make everything easy to find.

Red for active, blue for deep freeze, green for paid up. Except that she'd gotten tired of transferring materials. So most of the folders were still red.

Cahill should be between Cable and Callahan. But the file was missing. Had someone been riffling through her papers? Before she could investigate, the phone rang.

It was Sandy Peters at the *Baltimore Sun*.

"Jo, the Carpenter family you were telling me about. My editor's interested. If you can get me those pictures and documents this morning, I think I can swing a feature for you on Sunday."

"You've got it. I'll meet you in fifteen or twenty minutes."

The Carpenters had been a family of five siblings. When the parents had died thirty years ago, the kids had been separated. One of the younger brothers had hired her to try to locate the rest of the family. Jo had posed as a social worker to get access to adoption records and had found two sisters and another brother. Then she'd started calling Maryland newspapers to see if they'd run a picture taken of the children when they were little—along with a human interest story on the search.

When she reached the lobby, Lou was cleaning the glass on the directory. Purple-blue light from the transom above the door pooled around him like a soft spotlight. "Some party last night, huh?" he observed.

"Right."

"You shoulda seen the baked Alaska flamin'."

"I had a little indigestion and went home early."

He gave her a closer inspection. "You do look kind of peaked."

"Thanks." Jo hesitated for a moment. "You

haven't—uh—seen any strangers hanging around, have you?''

"Nobody any weirder than usual. Why?''

"There's this guy who escaped from prison last night.''

"The one whose picture was in the paper?''

"Yes. I'm not on his Christmas card list.''

"He's got a grudge against you or somethin'?''

Jo hated broadcasting her troubles. Yet in this case, she reasoned, the more people who knew about Cahill, the better. "I helped arrange for his state expense-paid vacation.''

Lou whistled through uneven teeth. "Want me to keep an eye on the hallway outside your office?''

"If you happen to be up there.''

Lou casually stopped his polishing and ambled to the door after Jo. She knew he was watching as she strode across the street to the garage where her blue Civic was parked. Beneath his crusty exterior, he was a real softy, she thought. He wasn't just someone who took care of an office building for a living. He cared about the tenants of 43 Light Street as if they were his children.

Lou watched Jo's back until she'd disappeared into the shadows of the parking garage. Perhaps if he'd waited until after her car pulled out, he would have noticed the gray van that drifted down the street in back of her.

The driver of the van wore workman's coveralls. A painter's cap partially hid his face. He looked like a handyman, but his talents were far more sophisticated. The interior of the van rivaled an FBI surveillance unit. There were directional mikes that could pick up a whispered conversation from across the street. And the computerized tracking system and racks of radio receivers, recording equipment and spectrum analyzers weren't found in any standard electronics catalogs.

He whistled an old Billy Joel song as he drove. His foot was light and easy on the accelerator as he kept the van several hundred feet behind Jo. He didn't have to keep her in sight. The directional finder he'd put on her car this morning was working perfectly.

He slowed down as Jo turned in at the fenced lot of the *Sun* complex and spoke to the guard at the gate. Instead of pulling in after her, he drove on by the red-brick building. No way was he going to explain his business to some rent-a-cop. But he did activate the directional mike and caught the second half of her conversation with the guard. She was dropping off material for a missing persons story. The coincidence made him laugh. The high-pitched sound echoed around him in the van, and he stopped abruptly. He hated it when his voice went all high and piercing like a dolphin in distress.

He checked his reflection in the rearview mirror. He looked like he was perfectly in control. And that's what he was. He swung around the corner and headed back toward the downtown area. He had time for a cup of coffee and a doughnut with cherry icing and sprinkles.

THE TWO-STORY LOBBY of the Sun Building with its black-and-white marble and stylized murals always impressed Jo, since the office of the weekly newspaper back in her hometown looked as if it hadn't been renovated since the Civil War. When you stepped through the glass-and-metal doors of the *Baltimore Sun*, you felt the power of the Fourth Estate. Which was just what she wanted, because the more people who saw the story on the Carpenters the greater the possibility of bringing the scattered siblings back together.

Sandy Peters thanked Jo warmly for bringing the file over so quickly. Getting out her notepad, she asked a few more questions about the case. "Can I quote you as the detective conducting the investigation? Or do you just want to be background?"

"Oh, what the heck. Go ahead and quote me. It can't hurt business."

There were so many aspects of detective work that churned up dirt and muck. It was nice to play fairy godmother for a change, Jo mused as she drove away from the newspaper building.

The sharp blast of half a dozen car horns made her body jump. With a sizzling bolt of awareness she realized she'd just turned the wrong way on a one-way street. Her car was facing four solid lanes of traffic—all coming toward her!

She did a quick U-turn on the wide avenue and sped back toward her office, pretending that the drivers in back of her weren't staring and that she didn't feel like an utter idiot. She'd sworn she wasn't shaking in her shoes over Eddie Cahill—and that she hadn't been rattled by the message on her answering machine. Obviously she was wrong.

Well, work was the best way to get back on track. Fifteen minutes later she was at her desk with the Cahill file, which she'd found stuck in the middle of another folder. She opened it just as the phone interrupted.

"O'Malley and O'Malley," she answered brusquely.

"Hello, Jo." The voice was thin and raspy and instantly flashed her back to the obscene call on the answering machine. In reaction, her scalp tingled.

"I called you, but—" the sandpaper voice continued. Jo cut him off before he could get any further.

"I will not tolerate being harassed," she spat into the phone. "If you try something like that again, buster, you're going to regret the day you ever messed with me." As she finished the warning, she slammed the receiver back into the cradle.

Fifteen seconds later, the phone rang again. Jo snatched it up ready to do battle again.

"Jo?" The same raspy voice inquired. This time she took a few seconds to make a rational judgment. It wasn't the electronic distortion she'd heard on the answering machine.

"Who is this?" she demanded.

The caller made an effort to clear his throat. "Cameron Randolph."

"Cam?" After she'd ducked out of the party, she hadn't expected him to call.

"I woke up with laryngitis."

"Oh, sheez. Cam, I'm sorry." A wave of relief mixed with chagrin washed over her. "I thought—"

"I take it you've been getting some—uh—offensive phone calls," he croaked.

"Just one. It's no big deal. How are you feeling?" She wasn't planning on talking about her problems to him.

"I'll live. This happens sometimes."

She pictured him in bed, alone, with no one to comfort him. "My mom used to give me honey and lemon when my throat was sore," she said softly.

"I've been using lozenges. Maybe I'll try your remedy."

"Do you need anything?"

He was silent for a moment. "I sound worse than I feel. Anyway, I should be all right by Thursday."

"Thursday?"

"You know, the party my aunt's giving for Steve and Abby. You didn't say whether you were coming."

Jo cringed. Maybe he thought she hadn't responded because of him. That wasn't the problem. She remembered getting the invitation weeks ago and sticking it somewhere safe. She'd simply forgotten to R.S.V.P.

For a moment she flirted with the idea of admitting her oversight and adding that she'd bought tickets to the Baltimore Blast indoor soccer game, for that night. The excuse never made it to her lips.

"I was planning to come. Unless it's too late." Maybe circumstances would decide for her.

"No, no. We're all looking forward to seeing you. Especially me."

The last part wasn't very loud but it sent a shiver up her arms. Had he really said it? She certainly couldn't ask for him to repeat it. "I guess I should get directions," she muttered.

He cleared his throat again. "Why don't I pick you up?"

"I don't want to put you to any trouble."

"No trouble. Tell me where you live," he requested as if he hadn't already checked out the location of her Roland Park house.

Jo gave him directions.

"Then I'll see you around six-thirty on Thursday."

"Fine."

Jo hung up, surprised that she was actually looking forward to the party but still feeling a bit uncertain.

Cam hung up feeling slightly guilty, slightly nervous, and more than a little excited about the prospects for Thursday night.

JO DIDN'T HAVE TO WAIT until the afternoon to talk to Laura. She ran into her friend at the deli in the office building across the alley. Jeff and Mutt's specialized in upscale sandwiches like turkey with avocado slices and chopped liver with bacon. But when Jeff saw Jo come through the door, he slapped her usual hamburger onto the grill and lowered a basket of onion rings into hot oil.

Laura was just paying for a shrimp salad sandwich on five-grain bread. "Noel said you stopped by," she told Jo. "I was going to call you as soon as I got back to my desk." She looked down at her sandwich. "But a conference in judge's chambers always makes me ravenous."

"How did you do?"

"We got custody. But we're still working out the child support. What did you want to discuss?"

"I need your advice about a neighborhood problem."

Laura looked out at the clear blue sky. "I was going to eat at my desk. But it's gotten so nice and warm this afternoon. There won't be many more days like this before winter sets in. Why don't we walk down to the harbor?"

"Sounds good."

As they strolled past the parking garage on their way to the refurbished inner harbor, neither woman was aware of the activity inside. The man who had been following Jo that morning was fine-tuning the modifications he'd made on her car. His tracking device was going to cause her some future problems. On the other hand, because he was otherwise engaged at the moment, he wasn't eavesdropping on the conversation between Jo and Laura.

Ten minutes later, the women arrived at the waterfront. Not so long ago the area had been littered with decaying factories and warehouses. Now luxury hotels, glass and steel pavilions, and plush office buildings proudly proclaimed the inner city's rebirth.

The pleasure craft that crowded the harbor in summer had departed, but the U.S. *Constellation*, the oldest ship in the U.S. Navy, still waited for the lines of children who came regularly on school field trips.

Half the downtown work force was taking advantage of the unseasonable weather. Jo and Laura were lucky to find a bench along the brick quay.

"What's on your mind?" Laura asked as she poked her straw through the top of her can of lemonade.

"Dogs. I'm thinking of strangling some," Jo quipped, aware that she was channeling her other anxieties into this particular problem.

"As your lawyer, I'd advise against it."

Jo laughed. "It was just a passing fantasy, but seriously, I do have a problem." Succinctly she explained about Sunday morning's backyard activities.

Laura commiserated. "But you can't accuse any dog owners unless you have proof."

"What do I have to do—stake out the area?" Before her friend could answer, her face lit up. "I've got it. I'll rig a camera with a motion detector."

Laura grinned. "I'm impressed. You really know how to do that kind of thing?"

"Piece of cake." She told Laura a bit about the technique.

"I could help you set it up this weekend."

Jo regarded her friend. They were closer than family but if Laura wasn't going to explain why she wasn't spending the weekend with her husband, she wasn't going to press, not when they only had a few minutes to talk.

"Great. At least that's one problem I can solve," she said instead.

"You have others?"

"Nothing I can't handle," Jo murmured.

"If you need help, you've got it."

"You, too."

Back at the office twenty minutes later, Jo finally reviewed the Cahill file. The notes brought back memories of the risky operation where she'd infiltrated the Baltimore drug culture to get the goods on him. If Eddie really was hanging around plotting to get someone, the person in the most danger was his ex-wife.

Karen was blond, beautiful, delicate, and not very independent. She'd been horrified at the chain of events that she'd set in motion by trying to prove that her husband was cheating on her. All she'd wanted to do was get out of the marriage with some of the money Eddie was throwing around like confetti at a New Year's Eve party. Instead she'd ended up testifying against him at a drug trial that had been page one news for weeks.

When Jo called Karen Cahill's home number, the phone just rang and rang. She was able to locate the woman on her next try—at her mother's Highlandtown row house.

"Jo, how did you figure out where I was?"

"I'm a detective, remember."

Karen clicked her teeth nervously. "If you can find me, Eddie can, too."

"You haven't heard from him? Or seen him?"

"No, thank God." Karen's voice quavered. "But he said he was going to get me. What am I going to do?"

Jo considered what advice to offer. Giving false assurances could be dangerous. On the other hand, she didn't want to make the woman panic. "It might not be a bad idea to get out of town until they recapture him."

"I just started dating this real classy guy. He's not going to like it if I disappear."

He won't like it if you get killed, either, Jo thought but didn't voice the sentiment.

"If you're going to stay in town, talk to the police about taking precautions."

"What precautions?"

"Don't go out alone. Check the locks on your doors and windows. Keep the curtains drawn at night. Let the police know if Eddie gets in touch with you." She went on to enumerate several other suggestions.

"I don't know whether I feel better or worse," Karen said. "I can't live my life like a prisoner. Tyler likes to go out at night. Dinner and dancing. You know."

Jo struggled with exasperation. This woman couldn't have it both ways. "Karen, just be careful," she advised.

"I wish I'd never met Eddie."

That was one point they agreed on, Jo observed silently. "Good luck," she offered instead.

"You, too."

After she hung up, Jo cupped her chin in her hands. Karen hadn't been much help. In fact, the woman had her priorities all screwed up. Talking to her had served an important purpose, however. It had made the danger more real.

Unlocking one of the bottom desk drawers, Jo brought out the snub-nosed .32 she rarely carried. After checking the action and loading the weapon, she put it into her purse.

CHAPTER FOUR

Jo KEPT several changes of clothes at the office for the various roles she needed to assume in her work. Over the years, she had played everything from a cocktail waitress to a nun to get information. Today after donning jeans, a plaid shirt and a bulky sweater, she inspected herself in the mirror. She'd do.

The solid weight of the gun felt reassuring as she left the office again. This time she was headed for Lucky's Cue Club, a pool hall just off Dundalk Avenue. Eddie Cahill had hung out there before he'd made it big, and from time to time he'd come back to hustle games and brag about his success.

Jo knew there had been a fair amount of jealousy among the old crowd in Eddie's former working-class neighborhood. In fact, a couple of his former buddies had testified against him. Probably they had a bet going on the time and hour he'd be picked up. If anyone at Lucky's had a lead on Eddie, perhaps they'd share the information. For a price.

In the garage across from 43 Light Street, Jo turned the key in the ignition and backed out of her parking space.

The moment her engine turned over, a warning signal sounded in a workshop ten miles away.

The man monitoring the alarm typed in a sequence of

commands on his keyboard, activating a satellite link. Almost instantly, the high-resolution computer screen transformed itself into a grid map of the downtown area. The garage was at the center of the grid. As Jo's car began to move, the map changed so that a red blinking dot could follow her progress through the city. She was heading up Eastern Avenue. Where was she going?

LUCKY HADN'T SPENT much on exterior frills since the last time Jo had been to the pool hall hustling information about Eddie. The *L* on the neon sign in the window was still out. It had been joined in death by the *Y*. Now the sign simply said "uck." Which was a passable description for the dimly lit interior.

At two in the afternoon, the large room was just beginning to fill. A group of kids hooking school were in the back at the game machines, and the bar was lined with men in leather jackets and work boots. A lot of them were on unpaid vacation from the local auto plant.

The only other women in the place looked as if they weren't there to hustle pool. Ignoring the speculative stares, Jo bellied up to the bar and asked for a Miller Lite.

Before she'd taken more than a couple of sips, she was joined by a slim, dark-haired fellow who had been hidden in the shadows at the far end of the bar. He had the wolfish look of a ladies' man, but the broken veins in his face made him unappealing. Jo remembered him. In addition to women, he also liked his booze.

"What brings you to downtown Dundalk, beautiful?"

"You tell me."

His eyes flicked over her petite figure. "You're looking for a little action."

Jo stared back. "Guess again."

He changed tactics. "You're tryin' to get a line on Eddie Cahill." Apparently he also remembered her.

"Bingo."

"Eddie's too smart to show his puss around here."

"Is he still in town?"

The wolf man shrugged elaborately.

Jo pulled out the twenty-dollar bill she'd tucked into the side pocket of her purse.

Her companion studied the bill. Jo was pretty sure he wasn't trying to get a make on Andrew Jackson.

"You heard anything?" she asked.

Before he could answer, a younger guy who'd been listening to the conversation joined the group. His hair was shaved on the sides, stuck up on top, and hung in a long lock down the back of his neck making him look like an Indian chief. She liked his looks even less than the wolf man's. But she only wanted to talk to him; she didn't have to date him.

"Heard something about Eddie from a buddy of mine," he ventured.

"Yeah, what?" the wolf man demanded.

"This is between me and her." The newcomer glanced at Jo.

She nodded, and he lifted the twenty from between her fingers. The wolf man gave them a sour look before sauntering off.

When he had disappeared back into the shadows, the informant leaned toward Jo. "This friend of mine, Dick Petty, gets cars for people at the auction out at the fairgrounds. And other ways."

Jo didn't inquire about what the other ways might be.

"Eddie got in touch with him. Said he wanted a car.

Nothing flashy or hot. But it has to be reliable. Said he'd pay cash."

"Did he give Petty a phone number?"

"No. He said he'd be back in touch."

"How can I get a hold of your buddy?"

"He's around, you know, but sometimes you can find him at Arnold's Gym up on Holabird."

"Appreciate it," Jo told him. If the information was true, it meant Eddie was still around town, and he had some cash. That was bad news.

At the door of the pool room, she turned and looked back at the man. He was drinking her beer.

Starting toward her car, she dug her keys out of her purse. At the corner of her vision, she saw a figure push away from one of the form-stone buildings and start toward her. She had a quick impression of spiked hair, black jeans and a black jacket with iridescent colors. Another punk.

She didn't want to stare; she didn't want to look intimidated. Yet something about the purposeful way he moved made her step briskly as she turned the corner and headed toward her car.

There was no one else on the side street, no one to help her, she realized as she bent to insert the key into the lock. A burst of movement and the instinctive knowledge that she had become a target made her turn and reach inside her purse. But she was a split second too late. Before her fingers could close around the butt of the gun, the leather strap over her arm fell away.

Cut, she thought, even before she saw the knife blade glint in the sun. Reflex took over.

The keys dropped from her hand. Fast as a whip, her foot lashed out with the technique she'd practiced in martial arts class. It caught her attacker in the thigh. He cursed. Then the knife was slashing down toward her arm. The blade sliced the knit of her sweater and pierced her forearm.

The slash sent a scream tearing from her throat. The stakes had escalated.

They were face-to-face: hers drained of blood, his covered with bumps and red splotches.

She was backed up against the car, and he had the knife. His fist grasped her purse. Why didn't he run? What else did he have in mind? Jo wasn't going to wait and find out.

"You slimebag," she shrieked as she launched her hundred-and-eight-pound frame toward him.

For a moment he seemed dumbfounded by the attack and her fighting skill. The two-second hesitation allowed her to kick the knife out of his hand. Now it was an even fight, she thought. Her brains and his strength.

She tried to wrestle her property out of his grasp, but she hadn't counted on his desperation. With one hand he clasped her purse against his neck.

Her fingers scrambled and clawed down his face. In the scuffle she vaguely heard her keys fall through the nearby storm drain.

With bone-jarring force, he slammed her back against the side of the car. As her knees buckled, he turned and ran.

Jo sat on the sidewalk, struggling to catch her breath. Now that the fight was over, she was aware of a burning pain in her arm. Looking down, she saw blood soaking into her sweater.

"Sheez!" No car keys. No purse. Cut and bleeding

and sitting like a drunk on the sidewalk. She needed help, but she'd rather die than go back into Lucky's bar.

"You want an ambulance? Or the police?" someone asked.

She looked up to see an old man squinting at her from the front stoop of a house a few doors down.

"Could I use your phone to call a friend?"

"Yeah."

Jo grimaced as she pushed herself to her feet. In his living room, she called Abby and quickly explained her problem.

"Can you pick me up?" She gave the address. "Honk and I'll come outside."

"Sit tight," Abby said. "Help is on the way."

THE PURSE LAY on the passenger seat begging him to drag it over and riffle through the contents. He couldn't give in to the siren call until he'd pulled the van onto a side road where he knew he wouldn't be disturbed. Even if a car happened to pass, there was no reason to connect him to the mugging. When he'd used the transmitter to lead himself to his quarry, he'd parked well away from the pool hall. And Detective O'Malley had been in no shape to follow him back to the van.

Yet, as he made a sharp turn, he could feel his thigh throb. She'd studied self-defense. That's why she'd been able to get in a few licks. He'd be ready for that next time.

He was glad the windows were smoked glass as he unwrapped a cleansing pad and began to wipe off the makeup. She'd smeared the stuff, but he was sure she wouldn't recognize him in a police lineup. Only after his face was back to normal did he reach across the console and spill the contents of the purse out on the seat.

The pistol captured his attention. He thought she'd reached for a can of mace but she'd been going for a gun. The bitch could have shot him.

The brush with danger sent a little thrill down his spine like the caress of a lover's fingers. He sucked in a sharp breath.

Instead of just taking her purse, he could have bundled her into the van and taken her then. But that would have cut out half the fun. He wanted her to know he was after her. He wanted the terror to build until he was ready to strike.

The more you knew about a person, the easier it was to freak them out. And there were so many ways to collect information. With stiff fingers, he set the gun aside and began to poke through the rest of her stuff. Not much makeup. Just a lipstick. In one of those dumb colors women liked. Warm melon. He caressed the tube, raised it to his nose, smelled the faint cosmetic scent— and the scent of her body clinging to the cold metal. It made him feel close to her, very close. Just like her comb did. Pulling a bouncy red strand from the teeth, he wound it around his finger like a wedding band.

Her wallet was the biggest treasure trove. Baltimore Shopping Plate, phone credit card, VISA, gasoline cards, insurance, AAA, professional organizations. There was also a snapshot of a man. For several seconds he stared at the smiling image. Then he crumpled the photo in his fist.

He was going to make her sweat. She deserved it. Then, when he was ready, he'd strike with the coiled speed of a rattlesnake. Only there wouldn't be any rattle to give her warning. The thought made him giggle.

OUTSIDE A CAR HORN honked. Jo struggled to her feet, thanked her host once more and opened the front door. Shock had enfolded her injured body as she huddled in a faded wing chair. Now she grasped the railing to keep from toppling down the marble steps of the old row house.

A car door opened and someone rushed toward her. Not Abby Franklin. Cameron Randolph.

"What are you doing here?"

"Abby couldn't get away. She called me."

He was staring at her, taking in her white face, her tangled hair, the blood soaked through the arm of her sweater. His own face drained of color.

"My God, Jo. What happened?" As his hand gripped her good arm to steady her, his voice was edged with more than the hoarseness she'd heard earlier.

"A mugger. I'm okay. I just need—"

Her knees belied her words. They gave way unexpectedly, and she pitched against him. His body absorbed the shock as if it had been designed for that purpose. When he caught her and held her upright, one arm at her waist, the other across her back, she had the odd sensation of having come home.

Jo's head fell against his chest, and her eyes fought a losing battle to stay open. Walking down the steps had been a bad idea. She was on the verge of blacking out.

"I'm taking you to the hospital." Cam left no room for protest. For a moment, she gave in to his care, shocked at how good it felt. Even as he spoke, he was carrying her to the sports car and settling her in the seat.

She leaned into the comfort of the sun-warmed leather, only peripherally aware of him climbing into the driver's seat. In the next moment, the car accelerated like a jet going through the sound barrier.

"Are you sure I'll live to make it to the hospital, Mr. Sulu?" she managed in a weak voice.

"Is there ever a situation when you can't come up with a smart remark?"

"A few."

She cast him a sidelong glance as he wove expertly in and out of traffic. She would never have imposed on him like this. Yet when Abby had called him, he had come charging down here to help her as naturally as if they'd been friends for years. No, more than friends.

"I thought you were sick," she muttered, still not quite acclimated to his presence or the situation or her reaction to him.

"I'm better."

He had her to Francis Scott Key Medical Center in record time.

"Can you stand up by yourself?"

"Of course I can stand up!"

But her steps were still none too steady as he escorted her in from the parking lot. When she reached the desk, she realized she had a big problem. "Damn."

"What?"

"No medical insurance card, no ID and no money."

"I'll take care of everything."

"Cam—"

"We'll settle up later."

The admitting nurse had called the police, so while Jo waited for treatment, she made a brief report. She and the officer agreed that there wasn't much hope of getting her personal property back.

Finally her name was called, and she was ushered into a curtained-off cubicle. It was still half an hour before a nurse practitioner came in to stitch and bandage her wound.

She had told Cam she didn't need him anymore. He was sitting in a hard-back chair watching the doorway. As she came back into the waiting room, he jumped up.

"How's the arm?"

"I'll live."

Wordlessly, he took off his jacket and draped it around her shoulders. Now that the emergency was over, they faced each other uncertainly.

"Thanks," she murmured.

"I'd better get you home."

When they stepped out the door, she was astonished to find that it was dark. She'd been here for hours.

As the car headed northwest, she found she was almost back to normal—except for the throbbing of her arm and the oddly tight feeling in her chest as she sat next to Cam Randolph. It was because she didn't like being helpless or dependent, especially with him, she told herself. Well, it was only for another fifteen minutes. Ignoring the pain and the man beside her, she started cataloging the things she'd have to do: call her insurance company about the credit cards, get some money from the bank, talk to the DMV, report the theft of the gun...

The car had pulled in at a shopping center on Cold Spring Lane. "What are you doing?" she asked in surprise.

"Getting dinner."

"Cam, really, you don't have to do that."

"I want to. Do you like Chinese food?"

"Yes, but you don't—"

He got out of the car before she could argue any further. She sat with her arms folded, less and less pleased with the way he had taken charge. It was one thing to come to her rescue. It was another to— She stopped herself. The least she could do was accept his offer graciously.

When he returned fifteen minutes later and she caught the scent wafting from the bag he carried, she felt her stomach rumble.

Minutes later, they pulled up at her door, and she hurried up the front walk. However, when she reached the door, she stopped abruptly. No key.

"You're going to have to get the locks changed."

"Not unless that son of a gun digs them out of the storm drain. That's where they landed in the scuffle."

"At least you don't have to worry about his breaking in. But *we* might have to."

"There's a spare key at my neighbor's. I'll be right back."

After Jo opened the door, Cam didn't immediately follow her inside. She turned and found him studying the control panel for the security system. It wasn't the kind of thing she'd expect from most guests. But then the man had designed the thing, she told herself.

"It's a B9N8-150. We don't make that model anymore."

"Doesn't it work right?"

"Of course it works right! Correctly. It's just that we've incorporated some new features."

"Like throwing unwanted visitors off the porch?"

He laughed. "You need the inventor around to do that for you." He looked at her disheveled appearance. "Want to clean up before we eat?"

"Yeah."

"Are you up to sitting at the table? I could bring you up a tray."

"No! I'll come down," she answered quickly.

"I'll put the stuff in the microwave."

Upstairs she stripped off her clothes and washed away the street grime as best she could without getting the bandaged arm wet. Anything she put on was going to hurt. She settled for one of Skip's old sweatshirts over a pair of jeans. It was too much effort to pull on shoes and socks so she stuffed her feet into her bunny slippers.

Cam was in the living room when she came back downstairs, looking through Skip's collection of twentieth-century fiction. Her husband had been into Faulkner and Hemingway. She read the detective stories.

When he heard her footsteps, he turned. "Are you all right?"

"Do I look all right?" The minute she'd said the words, she was sorry.

She'd invited his inquisitive eyes to make an inspection. He started with the hair she'd quickly combed and progressed to the oversize sweatshirt and worn jeans. It ended abruptly at the bunny slippers. She'd thought the outfit wasn't in the least bit sexy; somehow his look of male appreciation made her feel otherwise.

In the car, she'd deliberately turned her mind to practical matters. Now that they were alone in her house, she was conscious that he was her first male visitor in a long time and that her hands were trembling slightly. She shoved them into her pockets.

He cleared his throat.

Her gaze swept up to meet his gray eyes. Men in glasses weren't dangerous, she'd always said. Who was she kidding? She knew he was just as aware of the sudden intimacy of the moment as she.

She took a step back, then quickly turned and headed toward the scent of Chinese food drifting in from the kitchen.

He watched the back of the baggy sweatshirt disappear into the kitchen. The way it swallowed up her slender form was endearing. The effect shouldn't be sexy but it made his body tighten. Maybe stopping to buy dinner was a mistake, after all.

The shirt was probably her husband's, he realized, and felt an unexpected stab of something he didn't want to label as jealousy.

Uncertainly he followed Jo down the hall. When Abby had called him, he'd decided she was handing him a golden opportunity to check up on Ms. O'Malley. That was before he'd seen her as pale as death and soaked with blood. Or before she'd pitched into his arms and he'd caught her slender form against the length of his body.

Jo moved a new Dean Koontz novel and a stack of bills off the kitchen table and onto the radiator and then got plates and cutlery.

The clutter made her self-conscious. At the moment everything made her self-conscious.

The house and furnishings had been Skip's. They were both comfortable in a warm, unconventional way. When she'd first seen the place, she'd assumed he'd acquired furniture on a need-to-use basis. There wasn't any particular style and nothing much matched. Most women would have launched a reform movement, but she hadn't cared enough about home decor to make any major changes. Besides, it was luxurious compared to the rural poverty in which she'd grown up.

Cam had turned to study the old-fashioned chestnut cabinets she and Skip had kept when they'd put in new appliances.

"The furnishings don't look very—" He searched for the right word. "Coordinated."

She laughed. "My husband's special brand of decorating."

"Oh."

They both busied themselves pulling out cartons and inserting spoons.

Eating, that should keep them out of trouble, Jo thought.

"I hope you like it hot and spicy." Damn, he hadn't meant it to sound that way.

"Um. But Skip had ulcers so we could never share any Szechuan dishes." As she finished the sentence, she realized she'd just mentioned her husband two times in as many minutes. It didn't take a Freudian analyst to figure out that subconsciously she was trying to warn Cam off.

She looked up to find the man in question studying her again. Their eyes searched each other. She was the first to lower her gaze.

"He was a lot older than you were."

Somewhere in her mind, the remark registered with more than face value. She was too off balance to grapple with the implications. "Fifteen years," she clarified.

"Did he teach you a lot?"

There was more than one interpretation to the question. "Like what?"

He watched her bite into a piece of chicken and then couldn't tear his eyes away as she flicked out her tongue to remove a bit of sauce from her lip.

He needed to know how deeply she'd been involved with Skip's cases. He couldn't stop himself from wondering about the sexual side of their relationship. How had the difference in their ages affected that? "Detective stuff," he clarified, his voice a shade raspier than before.

"He taught me everything I know."

"You worked closely with him?"

"Usually. Sometimes we had our own cases." She could remember a couple of times when he'd told her it was best for her not to get involved in what he was doing. She didn't see any need to go into explanations with Cam.

They were both silent as they concentrated on the food. Jo chewed and swallowed a mouthful of crunchy meat. "This is good."

"Crispy beef. In Chinese cuisine, the beef dishes are usually the least rewarding. But if they make this one right, it's wonderful."

"Do you know a lot about Chinese cooking?"

"I didn't mean to sound pedantic. It's just that when I get interested in a subject, I tend to go a little overboard."

"It's okay. Skip was like that, too, sometimes."

Cam wasn't sure he liked being compared to her late husband. "He made a study of Chinese gastronomy?" he asked stiffly.

"No. He knew everything there was to know about firearms and baseball."

The man on the other side of the table didn't reply.

"What do you—uh—do for fun?" she asked.

"The same thing I did when I was a kid. Tinker with stuff. Only now I'm designing new products instead of taking apart the family appliances or fixing things that don't work."

"That doesn't sound too relaxing."

"Well, in the evening I've got a stack of mysteries beside the bed."

Her eyes lit up. "Me, too. I like the women detectives best."

"I'm more into police procedurals. The logic appeals to me."

It would, Jo thought. She considered telling him that she was thinking of writing a book herself. But he'd probably just laugh.

As they finished the meal, they continued the literary discussion, both relieved that they'd found a safe topic.

Jo was reaching for a little more crispy beef when she saw the carton was almost empty. They'd put away an awful big meal.

"I never thought of Chinese food as a substitute for chicken soup." She grinned.

"Chicken soup?"

"Didn't your mother bring you bowls of chicken soup when you were sick?"

"I hardly remember my mother. Dad and Collin weren't much into cooking."

"Your mother—"

"Died when I was seven. Dad and my older brother, Collin, raised me." As he delivered that last piece of information, his face was watchful.

"I guess I'm not the only one who had it rough," Jo

murmured. She didn't elaborate. Neither did he. Instead they both got up at the same time to start clearing the table. His hand brushed against her sleeve and she winced.

"Sorry."

"You should have told me it was still hurting."

"I'm okay."

"Did they give you anything to take?"

"I don't need anything."

He reached out and gently grasped her shoulders. She glanced down at his strong, lean fingers on her sweatshirt.

"If you need to take something so you can get to sleep, go ahead and do it. You don't have to tough out the pain."

She looked away, embarrassed that he'd read her so accurately.

"You're not used to having someone take care of you."

"I'm out of the habit."

"I never got into it."

She might have asked why. He hurried on. "You didn't like my showing up instead of Abby to take you to the hospital."

"She's already seen me at my worst. I guess you have, too—now."

"I like you at your worst as much as I liked you all spiffed up for Abby's party."

"Sure."

His hands dropped back to his sides. "Listen, I should probably let you rest."

"Well, thanks—for everything."

"See you Thursday."

"I'll be looking forward to it." As soon as she'd said the words, she knew they were true.

"I will, too."

They stood regarding each other for a moment. She saw his gaze drop to her lips. Seconds stretched or was it only her imagination that drew the moment taut. Then he turned abruptly.

She followed him down the hall and locked the door behind him.

The unexpected dinner with Cam had been edged with a man-woman awareness Jo didn't really want to examine too closely. They'd each been reluctant to reveal too much about themselves—except just before he'd left when she'd found herself admitting things she usually kept to herself. Jo was too worn out to ponder the implications.

Fifteen minutes later she had settled down in bed with the book she was reading. The phone rang, and she automatically picked up the receiver.

"Hello."

"Hi there, angel face. I'm glad I caught you. It's about time we got a little more up close and personal."

That voice! It was him again! Jo's spine tingled as if icy fingers were walking down her bones.

"Who—who is this?" she demanded.

The high-pitched laugh assaulted her again like swarming bees. This time, their stingers penetrated all the way to her marrow.

"Want to meet me at the Giant Food Store at the Rotunda Mall? We can see if the bananas are ripe."

"No!"

"You didn't tell me you liked M & M's. They're one of my favorites, too."

"Who are you?"

"Someone who's going to have his way with that gorgeous little body of yours," the caller continued. "It's going to be a lot of fun. We'll smear warm melon lipstick on your mouth, and you can leave love marks all over my skin. Unless you'd rather use those little white teeth of yours."

"No!"

Jo slammed down the phone. Her whole body had begun to shake. She felt physically assaulted. Invaded. Not just by the sexual threats, but by the mundane details of her life he'd tossed out at her. To keep her teeth from chattering, she clamped them together.

Ten seconds after she hung up, the phone jangled again. She let it ring. When the answering machine clicked, she shut that off too. Pressing her hands over her ears, she squeezed her eyes shut, drew up her knees under her nightgown, and huddled in a ball under the covers. Yet now she couldn't blot out the awful knowledge that the first call to the office hadn't been a fluke. This one was to her home number. Someone was stalking her. And he knew exactly where to find her at any minute of the day or night.

CHAPTER FIVE

BEFORE GOING to bed Jo unplugged the telephone jack in her room. But she wasn't able to sleep. Questions with no answers circled in her head like caged animals desperate for freedom.

Who was calling her? What did he want?

She tried to stop thinking about the threatening words. They were burned into her brain tissue. The caller had mentioned the Giant. Had he seen her buy M & M's? And he knew the color of her lipstick. Was he someone who had been watching her? Or was he talking about the lipstick that had been in her purse? Did he have her Giant check-cashing card?

Panic jerked her to a sitting position. As chill air hit her shoulders, she clutched the covers up to her chin. The sudden movement jarred her injured arm, and it began to throb.

She'd been mugged this afternoon. When she'd clawed his face, his splotchy complexion had come off on her fingers. He'd been wearing makeup. Could it be the same man who was calling her? Was it Eddie Cahill? Was that why he'd been disguised?

She'd certainly baited him by invading his territory. If he had her purse, now he knew a whole lot more about her. Driver's license. Credit cards. Medical ID. Insurance. Oh God, he had everything. Except her keys.

Suddenly it was impossible to sit there in the dark, and she switched on the light beside her bed. For a few moments she squinted in pain. Then her gaze shot to the curtains that were pulled across the window. He could be out there now. Did it give him a charge to know she'd turned on the light? Was he laughing at her?

Stop it, she told herself firmly. *You're making more out of this whole thing than it's worth. The calls and the mugging probably aren't connected. Nobody's out there in the night under the hydrangea bushes watching your house.*

The ludicrous image called forth a brittle laugh. At least she could still joke about it, Jo told herself. That was a good sign. Getting out of bed, she crossed to the bathroom on legs that weren't quite steady, turned on the water, and filled the glass that sat beside her toothbrush holder. A few swallows of cold water made her feel better. Compromising, she left the bathroom light on when she returned to bed. She didn't fall asleep until just before dawn.

The face that greeted her in the bathroom mirror showed the effects of the sleepless night. Grimacing, she vowed she was going to take control of the situation.

Jo dug out her spare set of car keys and called a cab to take her to the Department of Motor Vehicles for a duplicate driver's license and registration. With that taken care of, she tackled her next problem—getting her car, although the thought of going back to Dundalk was as appealing as a trip to the dentist for a root canal.

Marching to the phone, she called another cab. After she'd slid into the back seat and given the driver the address, she leaned back and closed her eyes.

"You okay, lady?"

"Fine." Jo sat up straighter and pretended interest in the business establishments along the highway. She was actually picturing faces. Eddie Cahill the way he'd looked at her before they'd dragged him off to jail. The mugger with his punk haircut and makeup. She couldn't make the two images match up.

"What address did you say?"

"In the next block. You can pull up in back of my Honda." As the cab drew abreast of the spot where she'd been assaulted, she felt a hundred fists clench in her stomach. She knew the fear was ridiculous. The mugger wasn't hiding around the corner.

"Would you mind waiting until I check my car?"

"I can't stay long."

She slapped another five-dollar bill into his hand. "Indulge me."

First she peered into the storm drain. As far as she could tell, the keys were probably in the Chesapeake Bay by now. Then she turned to her car, inspected the tires for slash marks and started the engine. When she was satisfied, she gave the driver the high sign and roared out of the parking space at Cameron Randolph velocity. It felt good to put distance between herself and the scene of the crime.

But she still hadn't regained her equilibrium. The closer she got to her office, the more she found herself picturing the answering machine crouched on the bookcase like an animal poised to spring. Relief flooded through her when she saw that there weren't any messages waiting.

Flipping through her Rolodex, Jo found the number of the employee at the Chesapeake and Potomac Telephone Company business office who'd been helpful when she'd handled harassment cases for clients.

"Haven't heard from you in a while," Sheila Douglas replied to her greeting. "I guess you're still in the detective business."

"Yes. But this time I'm not making inquiries for a client. I've gotten a couple of nasty calls myself."

The woman made sympathetic noises.

"I know you ask customers with harassment complaints to keep a log for a week. But assuming the calls continue, I want to understand my options."

"Are there any distinctive specs?"

"Yes, the voice was electronically distorted. I got one message on the answering machine and one in person."

"An answering machine. That's not typical. Usually telephone harassers want a live reaction on the other end of the line. Let me try a couple of searches of our new computer base."

In a surprisingly short time, Mrs. Douglas was back on the line. "I did find some incidents that might be related. But it's not procedure to give out that kind of information without written authorization. I'll need to check with my supervisor."

"I'd appreciate that."

"Meanwhile, we do have some new tools to fight telephone misuse. Maryland is one of the states where you can get a caller ID phone that displays the number from which a call is placed."

Mrs. Douglas launched into an enthusiastic sales pitch for the new equipment. "Or, if you think the problem is serious enough to bring in the police," she went on, "you can take advantage of the new tracing option in the system. After the call is completed, you dial a special number that initiates the trace. The results are sent directly to the police department.''

"I guess I'd like to start with a caller ID phone."

"We don't sell the equipment, but I'll give you the number of the company that does."

After thanking Mrs. Douglas, Jo phoned the supplier and found she could get the attachment on her business and home lines by early the next week. She hung up feeling optimistic.

There were several more things she should take care of. Yesterday she'd been ready to go over to Arnold's Gym and look for Mr. Petty. Now she reconsidered the idea. After a silent debate with herself, she admitted that Jo O'Malley, P.I., wasn't too enthusiastic about putting herself in danger again. Instead she called Sid Flowers, who promised the police would follow up on the lead.

Over the next couple of days, Jo felt steadily better. She'd planned to talk to Abby about the psychological profile of telephone harassers. But there weren't any additional phone calls, so she didn't bother her friend with the problem. There also hadn't been any more news about Eddie Cahill. Perhaps he'd decided to cut his losses and get out of town after all. Maybe he'd even left the country. Or the planet!

Wednesday night Jo crawled into bed early, determined to catch up on some of the sleep she'd missed lately. Her light was off by ten forty-five, and she was asleep by eleven.

She dreamed of Cam. They were at a dance, swaying together to the music, their bodies drawing closer and closer. Her arms circled his neck. She tipped her mouth up to his. Their lips met, and she felt a warm surge of pleasure. Then he and the dance floor were gone, and she was alone in an endless park.

She was hurrying among beds of bright columbine, searching for him, when the flowers caught her attention. She had thought they were real; now she saw they were made of tiny wires, little filaments, electronic parts. Bees flitted between the blooms. Jo gasped as she took a closer look. The bees weren't what they had seemed, either. They were miniature robots with tiny glowing electric eyes like digital displays. Their silicon wings were veined with printed circuits.

But it was their mechanical hum that made her scalp crawl. *Bzzzzzzzzz*. It was the sound of danger. The laugh from the answering machine. Slowly, afraid to run, lest she attract their attention, she began to back away.

It was no good. Her skin prickled as more and more of the bees stopped moving among the grotesque flowers and hovered like toy helicopters—their green eyes all locked on her.

Fear choked her throat now. The fear swelled as the tiny robots rose from the flowers, circling and buzzing in a huge swarm. They poised in the air, the sun reflecting off a thousand beating wings. The whirring grew louder.

Desperately she turned to run. But too late, too late. Giant metal spikes sprang up to block her way. The bees were swooping toward her.

For what seemed like an eternity, she fled for her life, dodging the spikes. Her feet pounded the ground. Her breath hissed in and out of her lungs. But it was no use. She couldn't outrun them.

They overtook her, buzzing, whirring, diving for her arms and face, stinging her flesh, choking off her breath.

Scream after scream tore from her lips. Then she was sitting bolt upright in bed, heart hammering, sweat pouring off her body.

It took several moments to convince herself she was safe in her own room. But the noise hadn't stopped. Then she realized what she was hearing. It was the buzz and whir of the automatic garage door opener. Opening and closing, opening and closing by itself. The sound must have triggered the awful dream.

It was a relief to focus on reality. The damn door was on the blink. Or maybe it had been activated by an airplane radio frequency. Unless—

No. It must be a plane, she assured herself. The problem had occurred once before, and Skip had had to change the frequency on the opener. Tonight she'd have to turn it off.

The clammy fabric of her nightgown clung to her body as she eased out of bed. Stripping it off, she tossed it on the chair and found another in the drawer. Then she donned her robe and slippers.

In days past she wouldn't have hesitated to investigate a weird noise in the middle of the night. Now she couldn't afford to take any chances. Before going downstairs, she slipped Skip's .357 Magnum into the pocket of her robe. Then she turned on every light she encountered as she moved through the house.

Her ears were tuned to any unusual noises. She almost expected to catch the sound of insects buzzing. But all she heard were her own footsteps creaking on the old floorboards. Even the malfunctioning door had stopped whirring.

When she reached the entrance to the garage, she hesitated, picturing an intruder crouched in the shadows.

First she turned on the garage light. Then she shouted a warning through the door. "The police are on their way. And you'd better get the hell out of there." No response came from the garage. Still, she was holding the gun in a police assault stance as she threw the door open.

It took only a few seconds to determine that the garage was empty—except for her car. Even after she'd turned off the door and gotten into bed, she lay awake staring into the darkness conjuring up an electronically distorted laugh. Or was it the buzzing of a thousand bees?

JO HAD PLANNED to come home early Thursday afternoon to get ready for the party, but a new client walked into her office at four-thirty. The woman was in tears because her husband of three months had cleaned out their joint bank accounts and skipped town. Jo spent an hour and a half calming her down and getting as many facts as possible. However, there was nothing she could do about starting to trace the man until Monday.

By the time Jo got home, she was running late. She was about to dash upstairs when she remembered the mail. Along with the usual assortment of letters and bills was a package wrapped in brown paper. A note from her neighbor Mac Lyman was attached.

"A catalog company was offering a special on these things. They're guaranteed to keep unwanted animals out of your yard. If it works, we won't be picking up any more trash."

Jo smiled. That was certainly sweet of Mac to have ordered one for her. She'd have to insist that he let her pay him. She wanted to open the package and take a look at the device. But right now she'd better get ready.

Or Cam was going to come over and find her still dressed for work.

After a quick shower, Jo used the blow dryer on her red curls and put on a little makeup. But she'd always been a sucker for gadgets, and the package downstairs kept tugging at her curiosity. Maybe she could spare a few minutes to open it. If it wasn't too hard to operate, she might even be able to get it set up outside before she left. But she'd better do it before she got into her dress.

After shrugging into Skip's robe, Jo padded downstairs in her bunny slippers. Bringing the package to the couch, she sat down and began to undo the wrapping. The unmarked cardboard carton inside was held together by two thick rubber bands.

Jo slipped the bands off, and the packing material fell away. She found herself sitting with a box about the size of a five-pound bag of sugar. Hefting it, she noted that the weight was about right, too.

Danger. Her intuition screamed a warning. She pictured herself hurling the box through the window. In her mind she saw it smashing against the sidewalk. But her body didn't carry out the command.

As far as her senses could detect, nothing happened. There was no noise from the box. No odor. No change in temperature. No flashing lights. No electrical discharge. No explosion.

But she felt as if an explosion had gone off inside her head. Somehow she *knew* that the box was the source of the sudden terrible pain.

Get away, her brain screamed. With a superhuman effort, Jo stood up. Her legs were no stronger than flower stems. Before she could take a step, her knees buckled, and she collapsed to the floor. As the box bounced beside her on the carpet, shock waves reverberated in her head. She tried to scream. No sound came out. The agony was locked inside her throat.

Get away. Arms and legs twitched. They wouldn't obey her commands. She lay on her side, helpless, disoriented, a prisoner in her own body—and more terrified than she'd ever been in her life.

TWENTY MINUTES later when Cameron Randolph rang the bell, there was no answer. He rang again and, to deny his own feeling of nervousness, waited with tuxedo-clad arms folded across his chest. When he still didn't get any response, he turned and looked back toward the street but didn't see Jo's car. It could be in the garage. Or maybe she had forgotten about the party. His stomach tightened with a mixture of disappointment and annoyance. He'd already told himself all the reasons why he shouldn't be attracted to Jo O'Malley. This was one time when his emotions didn't yield to logic.

He could see a light on in the living room. Cupping his hands against the glass, he peered inside. A figure lay crumpled on the rug in front of the couch. Through the window he saw a man's robe. Below it protruded the bunny slippers he remembered. Above it was flaming red hair. Jo. Her hand was stretched toward a black box that lay beside her. The box was sickeningly familiar.

"Jo," he called and banged on the glass. "Jo."

He couldn't see her face. She didn't stir, and he felt a knot of unexpected fear tie itself inside his chest as his eyes riveted on her limp body. My God, he hadn't anticipated anything like this! How long had she been lying there?

His first impulse was to smash through the window. He stopped himself. In his pocket was the new tool he'd been working on to test Randolph Electronics security systems. It wasn't designed as a lock picker, but he could use it that way.

It took less than ten seconds to electronically retract the bolt. As soon as he threw open the door, the dials on the instrument in his hand went haywire. Something inside the house was generating a powerful electromagnetic pulse.

He knew what it was. His eyes swung to the black box on the floor beside Jo. Guilt drove all shreds of common sense from his mind. When he took a step forward, readings on the meter doubled. At the same time, a wave of nausea swept over him, and he struggled to stay on his feet. It took all his remaining strength to struggle backward out of the field. When he reached the door, his head stopped spinning.

The box was small. It couldn't affect a very large area. From the door he calculated the distance to where Jo lay sprawled in the living room. Only eight feet, but it might as well have been eight miles. If he got any closer, he'd crumple before he reached her.

But he had to get her out of there. Before she— His brain wouldn't let him finish the thought.

Was there something he could use to shield his head? Wildly he looked around the porch and saw nothing that looked remotely useful. Then he spotted the garden hose still connected to the outside faucet. If his luck held, Jo hadn't gotten around to turning off the water for the winter.

When he opened the spigot, the hose stiffened and water spurted erratically from the nozzle. Tensely he waited to see if he was just getting leftover water from the pipes. Seconds later, he muttered silent thanks as the flow steadied.

Running back to the door, Cam adjusted the nozzle to produce a narrow stream and aimed at the box. When the force of the water struck the target, the box jumped as if it had been hit by a bullet. Water sprayed the room but the box was taking the brunt of the dousing. It sparked, crackled, and finally gave out a shuddering wheeze.

There was no other apparent change inside the room. But Cam checked the meter and saw that the room was now safe. Twisting the nozzle to shut off the water, he flung the hose onto the porch. Before it hit the wide boards, he was sprinting inside.

He knelt on the wet carpet beside Jo. *Not set to kill. Not set to kill.* The words were like a chant in his mind.

Gently he turned Jo over. For some reason, he was shocked to see that the rough fibers of the rug had pressed a pattern into the skin of her cheek. He was even more shocked by how deathly pale she looked.

With trembling fingers, he reached to find the pulse in her neck. Panic seized him when he couldn't find it. Finally he located the steady beat and breathed a sigh of relief.

At his touch, Jo stirred and moaned.

"It's all right. You're going to be all right," he murmured, praying that he spoke the truth. He didn't have much experience giving first aid. Or tending to unconscious females, for that matter, he thought, as he scooped her up and cradled her against the pleated front of his dress shirt. Even wearing a half-soaked robe, she was feather light in his arms. Under the bulky fabric her body felt fragile and very feminine.

Her color was returning.

"What?" she muttered, still not quite awake.

"You're all right," he repeated. This time he was pretty sure it was true.

He bent and pressed his cheek against hers. He was about to set her on the sofa when he saw that the cushions were wet.

Damn! Now that the immediate danger was passed, he could see that he'd made a mess of the place.

Still holding Jo in his arms, Cam turned toward the stairs. There was no problem figuring out which room was hers. The rest of the house leaned toward dark colors and sturdy furniture. The first bedroom on the right was an oasis of feminine warmth and country charm. The cabinet pieces were pine and oak including a carved armoire. Instead of a chest of drawers, there was a pie safe against the opposite wall. The curtains and chair cushions had been made from a matching blue and peach print.

Drawing back the antique quilt, he laid Jo on the four-poster bed. When he opened the front of the sopping robe, he forgot to breathe for a moment. She was wearing only a delicate bra and lacy panties that hid almost nothing.

He would have jerked the robe back in place except that his mission hadn't changed—he had to get her out of the soggy thing. When he tried to slip the garment from her arms, he didn't make much progress—probably because his fingers were now too clumsy to function properly.

Sitting down on the edge of the bed, he pulled her up

and forward. But her body was boneless. She collapsed against him, the air whooshing out of her lungs.

As her head drooped against his shoulder, the air rushed out of his lungs as well. For a moment he couldn't move. He'd been fantasizing about her. Now he was held captive by the pressure of her breasts against his chest, the silky feel of her skin, and the wildflower scent of her hair.

His arm came up to cradle her body protectively against his. At that moment, she was so sweetly vulnerable that he felt as if his heart would burst if he didn't kiss her. Turning his head, he pressed his lips against the soft skin where her cheek merged into her hairline.

He was confused by the strength of his emotions. But he wasn't the kind of man who took advantage of unconscious women, he told himself firmly. Letting out an unsteady breath, he forced his attention back to the job at hand. He'd just removed one of her arms from a sleeve, when he heard her murmur.

"Coming home..."

"Jo. Thank God."

Her body jerked as if she'd just realized what was happening.

"What in the hell are you doing this time?" she demanded. Her words were slurred but the message was clear.

"Your robe is soaked. I have to get it off."

"Soaked." She shifted and seemed to become aware of the sodden fabric—and also the proximity of her body to his.

When she pushed away from him, he didn't try to hold her. "From the hose," he mumbled.

"I was out in the yard?" As she spoke she shrugged

off the wet garment and pushed it onto the floor. For a moment she sat there as exposed as a butterfly newly emerged from its chrysalis, the scar on her arm still a vivid red. Then she snatched at the quilt and pulled it up to her chin.

"No." He managed.

"No, what?"

"You weren't in the yard."

"The box," she muttered, sinking back against the pillow.

Cam reached for her hand. "How do you feel?"

"Weak. Confused." Her fingers gripped his as if she could draw strength from him.

He fought the urge to take her in his arms again. "Do you think the box came from your escaped con?" he asked instead.

She shrugged. "I don't know. It was with the mail. There was a note from my neighbor saying he'd ordered it from a catalog. It's supposed to be an ultrasonic pest repeller."

"That thing's no pest repeller."

"What is it?"

He wished he hadn't been so emphatic. "I had to douse it with the hose to short the circuits."

"What is it?" she repeated.

He sighed. She wasn't going to be sidetracked so easily. "My guess is that it generates an electromagnetic pulse."

"Something like an electromagnetic field? I've heard of them."

"No. Something different."

"What?"

"A crowd control device, I think. I'll take it back to my lab and check it out."

Jo pressed her palm against her forehead as if the gesture would help her brain function. The box would be evidence if she decided to call the police. After what it had done to her, however, the thought of having it in the house made her cringe. What if it went off again?

"How did it make you feel?" he asked, as if he had read her mind.

"Sick. Shaky. Frightened. Gonzo headache."

"I'm sorry."

"It wasn't your fault."

She missed the culpable expression that flashed across his face and the way his gray eyes were squinted in momentary pain.

There were a lot of things he wanted to ask. But she was in no condition to come up with explanations. Besides, he couldn't start raising questions until he'd gotten some answers of his own. "I'm going to get you some aspirin."

"Okay. It's in the medicine cabinet. There's a glass on the sink."

As she watched his tuxedo-clad back disappear through the bedroom door, she remembered what he was doing here. They were supposed to be going to a party at his aunt's house.

Thank God he'd come to pick her up. If he hadn't, she'd still be lying in the living room with that thing microwaving her brain. The image sent a massive shudder through her body, and her mouth went as dry as chalk as she realized what a close call she'd had.

He was gone longer than it should have taken. Maybe he was giving her time to collect herself. When he handed her the glass, she took a gulp. Then, self-conscious, she swallowed the aspirin.

He sat down in the rocker by the window. "This room's nothing like the rest of the house. Did you redo it after your husband died?"

"We had our own bedrooms. I brought a lot of these things from western Maryland. My grandmother made the quilt. The pie safe was hers, too."

"You and Skip had separate bedrooms?"

"Yes. I—we—" She flushed.

"You don't have to explain anything to me."

"I don't want you to think we didn't—" God, she wondered, why was she fumbling around like this? It must be the aftereffects of the box. But that didn't explain why she cared what he thought. "He used to read until three or four in the morning. The light kept me awake." The explanation ended on a slightly defiant note. "Where are your glasses?" She changed the subject.

Now he was the one who looked slightly embarrassed. "I thought I'd wear contacts tonight."

"You didn't have to go to any special trouble on my account." She started to push herself out of bed, until she remembered she wasn't exactly dressed for company.

"The party. We're supposed to be at your aunt's house right now."

"I hardly think you're up to it."

"Yes, I am!" Even as she issued the protest, a wave of dizziness swept over her.

"I'll be downstairs. You get some sleep and we'll talk about it in a couple of hours."

Perhaps to forestall further argument, he got up, strode

to the door, and turned off the light. She heard his foot-steps on the stairs.

When she closed her eyes, she knew she didn't have a prayer of going to sleep. She'd been too confused to think straight. Now the implications of what had happened were starting to sink in. If the box wasn't a dog control device, then Mac hadn't sent it. Which meant it had come from someone else—someone who wanted to hurt her. Had they set the whole thing up? Had they scattered the trash in the first place? Was that why Mac hadn't heard any dogs barking?

Under the covers her body went rigid, and her heart began to thump. She could feel sweat beading on her upper lip.

She was in her own bed, but suddenly she felt like an animal in the forest—an animal being stalked by some unseen predator. Only it wasn't a beast coming after her through the underbrush. It was a person. Someone who was poking and prying into her life and using the knowledge to terrify her. He knew her neighbors. He knew where she shopped. What candy she liked. Did he also know what soap she used? What cold capsules? Was he going to empty them out and fill them with cyanide?

Stop it, she told herself. But she couldn't halt the awful speculations.

Who? The same person who'd been calling her on the phone? Eddie? Had he trashed her yard the night he'd escaped from prison? Or was it someone else?

If she kept on like this, she was going to unravel like the slashed sweater she'd thrown away earlier in the week. She wasn't going to let it happen.

Since childhood, Jo O'Malley had had more gumption than most full-grown men.

After her father had died in a logging accident, there hadn't been much money. Her mother had supported the family by clerking in the country store down the road. The five kids had pitched in to keep the garden going; her brothers had supplemented the family diet with small game they brought home from the surrounding countryside.

As a child Jo had learned to mend a pair of jeans or a pair of shoes on the old treadle machine in the dining room. At twelve, she had gotten a job after school working as a maid at one of the ski resorts that dotted the mountain area. In summer the operation switched to boating, fishing, riding and the like.

Jo had learned three things very quickly. She wasn't cut out to be a maid. There was more than money that separated her from the vacationers. And education was going to be the key to a better life.

Teachers at the local high school had admired her determination and her ability and had tried to curb her natural proclivity for getting into trouble. They'd helped her win a scholarship to the University of Maryland. But when Mom had been laid up after an automobile accident, the family had needed money. Jo had quit school and gone looking for a job.

She hadn't counted on falling under the spell of Skip O'Malley. Now she knew that part of the attraction had been his age—and his ability to take charge. He became the stable male influence she'd never had. And something in him had responded to this girl from the country who had needed taking in hand. The relationship had been good for both of them. She'd played Eliza Doolittle to his Henry Higgins. But like Eliza, she'd outgrown the student-mentor relationship and matured into her own woman.

Now she pushed herself to the side of the bed and swung her legs over the edge. For a moment she swayed and had to steady herself against the nightstand. Then the spasm passed.

Somehow she walked across the floor to the bathroom. Somehow she ran the shower and got under the hot water. It seemed to have a restorative effect. Or perhaps it was a combination of the hot water and her determination to feel normal.

By the time she dried her hair for the second time that evening she was feeling almost human. To compensate for her still-pale complexion, she put on a bit more makeup than usual. Then she donned fresh underwear and the dress she had planned to wear to the party.

When she came downstairs, Cam was stamping on the fifth towel that he'd used to blot the rug. It still wasn't dry, but it was a whole lot better.

Hearing a noise in the hall, he spun around in surprise. When he saw Jo standing in the doorway, his jaw dropped open.

"I guess you forgot your spot remover."

He smiled. "This is too big a job, anyway."

"Then let's go to the party," she suggested.

"But you can't—"

"You can take me home early if I give up the ghost. Come on. We're already late."

CHAPTER SIX

"MAYBE I should call a doctor. The aftereffects of that EMP may be worse than I assumed."

The woman who stood rebelliously in the entrance to the living room stiffened her spine. "Do I look like I need a doctor?"

Cam studied the pint-size figure of defiance. From the top of her red hair to the toes of her black leather pumps, she looked ready to take on Baltimore's best. And the parts in between were definitely worth a second look.

The aqua silk dress she was wearing did wonderful things for her eyes and skin. The soft folds of the material played hide-and-seek with the curves he'd become acquainted with upstairs.

If she realized how much she turned him on, she'd probably use it to her advantage, he told himself. Better to get out of here while the getting was good.

He sighed. "You win. Let's go."

She seemed surprised and perhaps a little disappointed that they weren't going to do battle over the issue. He turned away so she couldn't see his grin.

The women he had dated would have slipped a fur coat over the silk dress. Jo pulled a trench coat out of the closet. On her the belted style was flattering and gave her an air of mystery.

But after they'd gotten into the car, he knew she

wasn't quite as recovered as she pretended by the way she leaned back in the padded leather seat and closed her eyes.

"I hope you don't mind if we make a quick stop."

"Why?"

"Got to change my shirt. I was already dressed for the party when disaster struck."

"Oh—right."

The questions he wanted to ask about what had been happening to her hovered on the edge of his tongue. But he still didn't want Jo turning around with questions of her own, so he found a classical station and let the third Brandenburg Concerto fill the silence.

Cam pulled up in front of his Cross Keys town house.

"I'll be right back," he told her as he turned on a couple of lights and ushered her into the living room.

Jo melted into the comfortable cushions of an off-white couch and looked around with interest at the place where Cam lived. Even a girl from the mountains could see that the furnishings were very expensive. But the house certainly wasn't "decorated" in any high fashion sense, and it was a lot smaller than she would have expected. She didn't have much time to study the layout. As promised, Cam returned quickly. Then they were on their way to his aunt's nineteenth-century Mount Vernon residence.

As they ascended the steps, she fixed a smile on her face. When Abby Franklin greeted her inside the foyer with its fourteen-foot ceiling and carved mahogany woodwork, no one would have guessed that less than two hours before Jo had been flat out on her much more modest living room floor immobilized by EMP waves.

"I'm sorry we're late," she apologized to Cam's aunt.

"But I had to see a new client just as I was getting ready to leave the office."

Cam watched the performance, amused and impressed with how well Jo handled the situation. Her claim might be true but it didn't begin to explain what had happened a few hours ago.

Steve came into the hall, and he and Jo hugged each other warmly.

"Making progress setting up your stateside air cargo business?" she asked.

"Sure am. Some of those contacts you gave me look like they're going to pan out."

The three of them discussed Steve's business plans for a few minutes. Cam was glad to see his friend sounding enthusiastic. He'd been worried about how a modern adventurer was going to fit into a more conventional lifestyle. Apparently he was finessing the situation. Was Abby as delighted with the arrangements? Perhaps she had decided it was better to have her husband flying around on this side of the world.

Steve clapped Cam on the back. "You and Jo are two of my favorite people. I hope you're getting along."

"Oh, we are."

Cam took her arm and they moved into the drawing room. Now that he'd gotten to know Jo better, he would characterize her behavior as watchful. What was she looking for, he wondered. And would her state of alert make it more difficult for him to take care of an important piece of business? Was she watching him as well as everyone else?

Just after the sit-down dinner for fifty, he got his chance. One of his aunt's friends had gotten into a gar-

dening discussion with Jo, and they were exchanging
tips on dividing irises and the best compost mix.

Quickly he slipped away from the group and made his
way up the curved Georgian staircase. In the guest bedroom he quietly closed the heavy paneled door. Then he
picked up the phone and dialed the familiar number he'd
been waiting all evening to call.

BY TEN-THIRTY Jo knew that she couldn't keep up the
game much longer. She'd wanted to go to the party to
prove to herself and to Cam that she was functioning
normally despite her mishap earlier in the evening. She'd
also decided it would be foolish to give up the chance
to check out the guests.

A whole bunch of nasty things had started right after
the last party. If they weren't the work of Eddie Cahill,
then perhaps there was a connection with the circle of
Franklin-Claiborne-Randolph friends. Much as she hated
to entertain the possibility, she couldn't dismiss it. So
she spent the evening gliding through the authentically
decorated Georgian rooms getting to know people.

Last week she'd felt out of place in the society crowd.
Once she'd decided to employ her detective skills on her
own behalf, she found that she was no longer feeling at
a disadvantage.

However, as she chatted with Abby's cousin Glen
Porter, she found her attention wandering. He was about
her age and had worked as an extra in a couple of the
recent movie productions set in Baltimore. She must be
in bad shape, however, if she was having trouble focus-
ing on his stories about Tom Selleck on the job. The
aftereffects of the box were finally catching up with her,
she conceded.

As if Cam had tapped into her thoughts, he appeared at her side, her coat draped over his arm.

"I have an early day tomorrow. I hope you don't mind if we make our excuses."

"I can give her a ride if you want to go ahead and leave," Glen offered.

Cam's expression took on a look of male possessiveness.

"No, I'm ready to go home," Jo broke in, strangely pleased by her escort's sudden show of covetousness.

PRISON TAUGHT YOU patience, Eddie Cahill thought. If you planned a job down to the last detail and waited for the right moment before you struck, you were sure of success. He'd already had a busy evening. Now he was waiting in the shadows when the flashy Buick pulled up in front of his ex-mother-in-law's house. He'd staked out the place before—as well as most of Karen's other haunts. In a day or two, he'd be ready to grab her.

The car had pulled up under a streetlight, and the driver cut the engine. Eddie wanted to stride across the cracked pavement and wrench the door open. Instead he pressed farther back into the darkness of the narrow alley. His stomach twisted as he watched Karen say good-night to her new lover boy.

It hadn't taken sweet little Karen long to replace him, Eddie thought. While he'd been rotting in prison, she'd worked her way through a series of guys with flashy cars and money to burn. They all liked to walk into a restaurant or a club with a drop-dead, good-looking blonde on their arm.

The observation brought a mirthless laugh to his lips.

When he finished with her, she wasn't going to be beautiful anymore. But she was definitely going to be dead.

Then after he took care of her, he was going to switch his full attention to that other bitch—Jo O'Malley.

CAM DIDN'T SPEAK until they were settled in his luxury sports car once more. "Maybe I was out of line. Did you want Glen to take you home?"

"Of course not."

She saw his hands relax on the wheel.

"How are you feeling? I was sure you were going to fold before the main course. You must be Superwoman."

Jo mustered a laugh. "And I thought I was out with Superman."

Cam looked startled.

"Hasn't anyone ever mentioned you look like Christopher Reeve?"

"No one else would dare." He turned onto Charles Street. For several minutes they rode in silence. "One thing about you, Jo O'Malley, I never know what to expect."

"A detective has to keep the opposition off balance."

"Do you consider me the opposition?"

"I guess I did at first."

"Why?"

"Your family probably served wine with dinner. Mine was lucky if we had root beer."

"So?"

"It's funny about the upper class. They take things as simple as food on the table or indoor plumbing for granted." In the dark, Jo worried a thumbnail between her teeth. She hadn't planned to dump her insecurities in Cam's lap. Now her tongue was flapping like a hound's ears.

Up ahead a traffic light flashed red, and Cam downshifted to a halt. "It sounds like you had a rough childhood."

"Rural poverty builds character."

"I guess that's true—if you're an example."

"What do you mean?"

"Don't you know you're an extraordinary woman?"

"Extraordinary? I'm just a simple country girl trying to survive in the big city."

"In my experience, most women fish for compliments. I try to give you one, and you throw it back in my face."

"A sexist compliment. That's a new twist."

"I hadn't thought about it that way." There was the hint of a grin in his voice.

Jo slid him a sidewise glance. A few minutes ago she'd thought she was too exhausted to put together a coherent sentence. Now she realized the conversation with Cam was having a stimulating effect. She suspected the reaction wasn't one-sided.

When they pulled up in front of her house, Cam cut the engine.

"You know, most guys don't care whether you have a thought in your brain," Jo said, turning his observation around on him as he escorted her to the porch. "They're more interested in figuring out how to make a move on you."

There was a long silence. "I'm not going to pretend I haven't had some thoughts along those lines. Does that bother you?"

Jo had been inserting her key in the lock when his words sank in.

"Yes...no."

The air around them was suddenly crackling with tension as though someone was beaming an entirely different EMP charge in their direction.

Superman moved quickly when he set his mind to it. Cam turned the key, whisked them both inside, and entered the security code that turned off the alarm system before Jo could blink. Then he was pulling her into his arms.

He'd been spinning fantasies about Jo O'Malley all week. Now, as his lips slanted over hers, he tried to hang on to the tattered shreds of his reason. He told himself he was conducting a scientific experiment. She couldn't possibly be as exciting as the daydreams that had been interfering with his work, and he was going to prove it.

Cameron Randolph had never been all that aggressive with women. When he'd been a kid in high school, the football stars—not the science fair winners—had made it big with the girls. After a couple of major disappointments, he'd told himself there were more important things in life than scoring. The tables had turned in college. In the right circles, intellectual prowess was a sexual stimulus. Being a good catch didn't exactly hurt, either. Without much real effort on his part, he'd found himself in the enviable position of picking and choosing the women who spent a few weeks or a few months in his bed. None of them had lasted very long, because none of them had claimed as much of his interest as his current lab experiments.

Things hadn't changed a lot in adulthood—even during the six months when he'd been engaged.

But now he held a woman in his arms who didn't give
a damn about his money and who was a billion times
more exciting than anything his fevered brain had invented. At odd moments all evening, he'd been torturing
himself with mental pictures of the way she'd looked in
her lacy bra and panties. Each time he'd felt as if he'd
grabbed hold of a high voltage line.

His mouth moved over hers. Her lips parted on a bare
whisper of a sigh. She was as warm as biscuits fresh
from the oven. As sweet as homemade strawberry jam.
As rich as fresh churned butter. Suddenly he was starving for the unaccustomed luxury of downhome cooking.

Experiment be damned! He knew the moment his lips
touched hers that he had only been kidding himself.
There was nothing experimental about the urgency of
his need to feel her mouth open for him, nothing ana-
lytical about the shudder of excitement that raced
through his body when her tongue met his.

Jo had told herself right from the first that she and
Cam Randolph didn't have a damn thing in common.
They were worlds apart socially, philosophically, eco-
nomically. If she'd been capable of coherent thought at
this moment, she would have acknowledged that none
of it mattered.

They were male and female locked in the grip of a
force older than time. When she felt his body shudder,
she answered with an involuntary tremor of her own.

His lips moved over hers, changing the angle, changing the pressure, changing everything between them.

He muttered low, sexy words deep in his throat. The
syllables were almost obliterated by the primitive assault
of his lips on hers.

When his hands skimmed down her back and found

the curve of her hips, she automatically raised on tiptoes, her body seeking the masculine hardness that fit so perfectly with her feminine softness. It had been years since she'd felt this way. Perhaps she never had.

But she was seeking more than simply physical gratification. Warmth, closeness. All the things she'd told herself she didn't long for.

"Coming home," she murmured. That was how being in his arms felt.

He shifted her body so that his hands could cup her breasts. They were small—but firm and perfect. Earlier when he'd taken off her robe, he'd seen the shadows of her nipples drawn to taut peaks from the cold water. They were taut now—from the heat he and Jo were generating between them. Through silk and lace, his thumbs stroked across the swollen tips, drawing a little gasp from deep in her lungs.

He ached with the need to go on touching her, kissing her, making love to her.

Instead he dredged air into his own lungs. He hadn't meant to go this fast.

"Jo, I—"

"Cam—"

They stared at each other, dumbfounded that they had traveled so far and turbulently. It was just a kiss, wasn't it? No, it was much, much more. Suddenly neither of them knew how to cope with the implications.

Her fingers trailed across her own thoroughly kissed lips.

"I'd better leave. Are you going to be all right?" he asked.

She nodded.

"I'll call you tomorrow."

Fingers still pressed to her lips, she watched him close the front door behind him. Then she turned the lock. She stood there until long after he had driven away, her emotional equilibrium in tatters.

She'd known sexual satisfaction with Skip. She'd known love. She had never known this white-hot energy arcing between a man and a woman. The closest she'd come to this feeling, she thought with a little grin, was when Tommy Steel had slipped her some white lightning at a church social.

But she wasn't high on anything now except Cameron Randolph. Was it just the skill of his lovemaking? Even as she asked the question, she dismissed it. She'd dug a moat around herself after Skip had died. No one else had dared to stick his toe into the shark-infested waters. But Cam had waded right in and forged across the dangerous channel. He'd charged up the opposite bank and into the stronghold—sword drawn—ready to help her fight the dragons breathing fire down her neck.

She shook her head. She was doing it again, casting him in another super-hero role. Drifting down the hall, she was headed for the stairs when she noticed the answering machine light was on. Still slightly drunk from the aftereffects of the kiss, she pressed the button.

"Did you have a good time at Mrs. Randolph's party, angel face?" the frightening voice that had become so familiar asked.

Oh God, he'd been watching her again. Couldn't she make a move without his knowing?

Jo's euphoria metamorphosed into razor-sharp horror. She pressed her shoulders against the wall in an effort to remain on her feet.

"I'm surprised you went out this evening after your little taste of my power."

She fought to swallow her scream. But her knees gave up the struggle to hold her erect, and she slid down to the rug. It was still soggy. Instantly chilly water soaked through her silk dress. Her teeth began to chatter and her body started to shiver—as much from fear as from the cold.

"Now you know that when I turn the switch, you'll do anything I want you to." The observation was followed by the high-pitched laugh Jo had come to know and fear. Moments ago her skin had been soft and tingly from Cam's caresses. Now it crawled with the pressure of a thousand insect wings. Beating. Beating.

"I have a nice brass bed all ready for you. I'm looking at it now. I can picture your red hair against the white pillow, your silky skin waiting for my touch, your wrists and ankles strapped to the brass rails. You're going to get everything you deserve."

Jo gagged. Unable to take any more, she reached out and pushed the fast forward button on the machine. An electronic garble assaulted her ears. When it cut off, she saved the message.

Her fingers dug into the soggy fibers of the rug. It was something to grip, a fragile hold on reality. Helpless fear threatened to swamp her. She wouldn't let it.

"You bastard," she hissed through clenched teeth, breaking the spell. Ejecting the tape, she clenched the small plastic cassette in her hand.

"You've had your fun. But I'm going to get you. You're going to be damn sorry you ever messed with Jo O'Malley," she grated, thinking about the caller ID attachment that soon would guard her phone. Then she'd know who he was!

Pushing herself to her feet, she started for the stairs. Her foot was on the second tread when she stopped abruptly, all at once aware of exactly what Laughing Boy said. He'd told her he was the one who'd sent her the nasty little present this afternoon.

It could have killed her. Maybe that was what Eddie had in mind. If it was Eddie.

When he'd started with the phone calls, she'd doubted it was him because the revenge had seemed too tame. But he'd escalated from words to deeds. What was next?

Well, she wasn't going to wait around and find out. She was going to take control of the situation. First thing in the morning she'd call the police and tell them about the EMP attack. No. She'd better get the box back from Cam first or they'd never believe anything so farfetched. But there were other things she could do, too. Eddie—Laughing Boy—whoever he was—had given her a big clue about his identity. That box must have come from somewhere. Cam had said it produced an electromagnetic pulse. She needed to find out what the devil EMP really was. Then she'd see who manufactured the units.

The next morning she called Cam, but he wasn't in his office. Disappointment warred with other emotions as she acknowledged that she was having a morning-after reaction to their kiss. Last night she'd been so wound up with Cam that Skip O'Malley had been completely wiped from her mind. Now she couldn't help feeling a bit guilty and disloyal.

Jo had planned to go straight to her office. But as she dumped her soggy robe in the dryer, she remembered the clothes she'd dropped at the cleaners six weeks ago. She'd better pick the outfit up before they got pitched.

One was an apricot cocktail dress she'd planned to wear to a couple of the parties. Another was a tweed suit she often wore for initial interviews with clients when she wanted to look professional.

On her way downtown, she stopped at the cleaners. "My pocketbook was stolen, and I don't have the ticket," she explained to the woman behind the counter. "But my name is Jo O'Malley, and I brought the items in last month."

The woman behind the counter checked her records. "Our files show that those were claimed."

"Are you sure?"

"The ticket receipt is here."

How could that be? She hadn't picked them up. "Do you remember who collected them?"

The woman shrugged. "It was three days ago. There have been hundreds of people in here since then."

"Was it one of your regular customers?" Jo persisted, unable to squash the tight feeling building in her chest. It was happening again. Another invasion into her life. Or maybe the guy who'd gotten her purse was going to sell her clothes for ready cash. Maybe it wasn't related to the other stuff at all. "Can I talk to your manager?"

"Sure."

The most Jo could get was a promise that if someone realized they had the wrong laundry, she'd be called. If not, her homeowner's insurance would pay for the loss. She should have felt relieved that she wasn't going to be out the couple of hundred dollars, but she couldn't shake the foreboding hovering over her.

Still, there was nothing more she could do about the

missing clothes. And there were more pressing matters to take care of. Back at her office, she flipped through her Rolodex until she found the name of Harvey Cohen, Ph.D., past president of the Institute of Electronics and Electrical Engineers, former Princeton professor, and author of *The Electronic Warfare Game*, an exposé that had rocked the Pentagon a decade ago. Antiestablishment money had set him up in a Columbia, Maryland, think tank where he nipped at the heels of government agencies eager to spend public funds without regard for public health and safety.

Jo smiled as she conjured up a mental picture of Dr. Cohen. He'd been in the thick of the sixties radical movement. Thirty years later he still wore his curly hair in a halo around his face and favored cords and turtlenecks instead of suits. A suit would have hidden the little potbelly that spilled over his belt buckle.

Jo had met him a year ago when she'd done some undercover work aimed at stopping the Defense Department from filling in Eastern Shore wetland and building a weapons plant. They'd both been dressed as duck hunters that morning at dawn when she'd taken him out in a small boat to tour the area. He'd asked her to call him anytime she needed his help. She was still surprised when his secretary put her right through.

"Jo! Glad to hear from my favorite sneak boat pilot. I assume this isn't just a social call."

"Very astute, Professor. I'm wondering what you can tell me about EMP."

"As in Operation Sleeping Beauty?"

"If you say so."

"That's the code name for one of the government's

secret research projects. I assume you don't want technical jargon.''

''Right.''

''In a nutshell, the Defense Department is very interested in using EMP to disrupt the functioning of the body's central nervous system. Actually it could be a very effective weapon against terrorists who have hijacked an airplane. Once they're on the ground, you zap the plane with EMP waves and everybody inside starts throwing up or goes temporarily blind and deaf or keels over. Or if you want to turn up the juice, you could use focused beams of high-powdered radio-frequency waves to kill by literally frying brain cells.''

Jo shivered. She'd felt as if her brain cells were being fried when the box had switched on. Obviously it hadn't been set to kill. Or she wouldn't be talking to Dr. Cohen.

''So it's all still experimental. Who's doing research in the field?''

''The Navy has a contract out. U.C.L.A. had something going at their Brain Research Institute.''

Jo could hear papers being shuffled on the other end of the line.

''Hmm—let's see—there was a local contract that never panned out. With Randolph Enterprises. Wonder boy Cameron Randolph was supposed to be working on a prototype for the Army.''

CHAPTER SEVEN

"CAMERON RANDOLPH?" Jo repeated carefully, hoping she'd heard Harvey Cohen wrong.

"Do you know young Randolph? Hell of an inventor."

Jo's mind tried to process the new information. "We've met," she managed.

"I'm a little vague on what happened with the EMP deal, but as I understand it, he reneged on the government contract. He paid back what they'd already given him plus a penalty, but there was some talk of suing him, anyway. I don't think it came to anything."

"Why did he renege?" It was hard to speak around the wad of cement that had wedged itself in her throat.

"The rumor was, he declined to test his prototype device on prisoner volunteers—said there was no way of knowing whether there were any permanent effects."

Jo realized that the hand gripping the receiver had turned clammy. Permanent damage. Did she have any permanent damage from that session with the box last night? Transferring the phone, she wiped her palm on her skirt.

"I can send you a summary of the current literature. You might want to take a look at an article in the I.E.E.E. Journal."

"Uh, thanks."

When Jo hung up, her heart was thumping around in her chest like a tennis shoe in a clothes dryer.

"Get a grip on yourself," she hissed between clenched teeth. "You've still got all your marbles." But her body simply wouldn't respond to the command. She wasn't just worried about her brain cells. Cam had lied to her last night. No, that wasn't exactly true. He'd simply forgotten to mention that he'd invented the device that had mowed her down like a field of tobacco in a hurricane.

What else had the man lied about? The possibilities were so hideous that her whole body turned clammy. Scary things had been happening to her ever since the engagement party for Abby. Last night she'd wondered if someone at the Franklin mansion was responsible. What if that someone were Cameron Randolph? The man who'd conveniently come along and rescued her. The man who'd made her feel as if Fourth of July fireworks were exploding in her body when he'd held her in his arms last night.

The phone rang, and she snatched the receiver from the cradle.

"Hello!" she barked.

"I was calling to find out how you were feeling. If I had to answer the question myself—I'd say belligerent."

"Cam."

"Jo, what's the matter?"

"Do you think you could come down to my office? I need to talk to you."

There was a long pause on the other end of the line. "Right now?"

"Yes."

"I'll be there in twenty minutes."

As she hung up the phone, Jo could hardly believe the brief conversation. The gut-wrenching need to confront Cam with her knowledge had banished any other considerations. She had to know what was going on. Now she wondered if she were stupidly putting herself in even more danger.

Opening her desk drawer, she made sure that the revolver she'd brought from home to replace the stolen one was loaded. Then she methodically began to clear the piles of folders and mail off her desk. She didn't make any attempt to sort the material. She simply swept it into stacks and set them on the floor of the closet. When the surface was clear, she pulled the two answering machine tapes from the middle drawer and placed them on the blotter. Then she positioned a tape recorder in front of them.

She had barely finished when a loud knock made her jump. Less than twenty minutes, she thought as she glanced up to see the male silhouette filling the rectangle of frosted glass. Had the man driven or had he flown through the air with his red cape streaming behind him? She got up and hurried across the room but stopped with her hand on the knob—suddenly remembering an important detail that had failed to penetrate her fogged brain last night. Cam had gotten into her house without battering down the door or breaking any windows.

What was she dealing with? Well, it was too late to change her mind now. If he wanted to get in, she couldn't stop him. When she flung the door open, they stared at each other. Jo was struck with a feeling of unreality. Friends? Strangers? Enemies? She didn't know. She couldn't trust her judgment.

As she backed away, he followed her inside and closed the door.

"What's bothering you?"

Jo circled around so that the large bulk of the desk was between them. Deliberately she sat down and positioned her hand near the desk drawer. Taking his cue from her, Cam pulled up one of the sturdy wooden armchairs.

Now that he wasn't looming over her, she was able to study his appearance. He looked as if he'd gone home, changed out of his tuxedo and spent the night in a pair of gray slacks and a white cotton shirt. They were both rumpled. And his lean face was haggard and unshaven.

"You tell me what's bothering *you*." She turned his question into a demand.

"Last night at my aunt's I called Phil Mercer to get some stuff ready for me at the lab. I've been up all night running tests on that box that had you down for the count—and going through Randolph Enterprises records."

"And?" she prompted.

His Adam's apple bobbed. "That box. Jo, I'm the one who invented it."

She had pictured the way they'd play this scene. It wasn't following the script.

"I had the feeling you weren't being straight with me yesterday. Why didn't you tell me the truth?"

"I wasn't one hundred percent sure of the facts."

"How did your invention end up in my living room?"

"I've been asking myself that question for hours."

The look of anguish on his face made Jo's chest squeeze painfully, but she met his gaze squarely, studying his features. In her profession, she'd encountered her share of accomplished liars. All were natural performers, outgoing, charming people—not introverted research scientists. Liars betrayed themselves in all sorts of little ways. Flashes of emotion that revealed their real feelings. Lopsided expressions that were slightly stronger on one side of the face than the other. None of the signs were evident. She was willing to stake her reputation on the certainty that Cameron Randolph wasn't lying to her.

Jo clutched the knowledge to her breast like a child clutching a security blanket in the middle of the night. However, she needed to know more if she were ever going to trust him again. It wasn't a question of staking her reputation. It was more like staking her life.

"I think you'd better tell me about it," she prompted.

"Do you want to know why I took the government contract in the first place? Or the part about how the damn invention slipped out of my control?"

"Why don't you start from the beginning?"

He pounded his fists against the chair arms. "God knows I didn't need the money. In fact, the damn project ended up *costing* Randolph Enterprises a hell of a lot. When I first started investigating the concept, the intellectual aspects of EMP research excited me. That's why I put in a bid in the first place. When it came down to conducting tests on prison volunteers, I realized I didn't want to take that kind of responsibility."

Jo nodded. Without any prompting on her part, he was confirming what Harvey Cohen had said. He went on to tell her about canceling the contract and paying back the money. Then he stopped abruptly. His teeth were clenched together, and his hands gripped the arms of the wooden office chair. Jo felt her own tension leaping up to match his.

When he began to speak again, his voice was as brittle as a batch of semiconductors plunged into a vat of liquid nitrogen.

"I thought I'd closed that chapter of my life—until I found you lying unconscious on your living-room rug. When I got the box back to the lab last night, I took it apart and checked the circuitry. Then I checked my specs on the project. I hadn't realized it before, but the EMP files must have been some of the ones that were copied from us several years ago."

"Copied?"

"As in industrial espionage. All the original records are still there. But the box is a perfect replica of my design—down to the casing. The only difference is that someone added a pressure trigger so it would switch on when the cardboard wrapping was removed." His gray eyes were hard. "We had some other plans stolen before my father died. A couple of prototypes I developed ended up being marketed by other companies."

"Who was stealing the plans?"

"We never found out."

"But the problem stopped?"

"Yes," he clipped out. "Jo, this is strictly confidential information."

"I understand."

Before she could ask him another question, he cut in with one of his own. "You didn't get me down here because you knew anything about the espionage, did you?"

"No."

He nodded, as if the answer satisfied some need of his own. Then he gestured toward the machine in the middle of the blotter. "Are you recording our conversation? Or did you want to play a tape for me?"

The ghost of a smile flickered around her lips. It vanished almost at once. "To play a tape. Cam, a lot of disturbing things have been happening to me lately. Not just the EMP stuff last night." Picking up one of the cassettes she inserted it into the recorder and pressed the button.

"You've got a gorgeous little body, angel face, you know that?" the electronically distorted voice began. Jo had heard it before and thought she was prepared. Still, her palms dampened and her skin began to crawl. She shot Cam a glance. His expression was grim.

"*This* is the call you got the other day?"

"Shh. Just listen."

"...what I'd like to do to you makes me hot all over, baby. The problem is, I can't decide whether I want to give you a poke with my sugar stick or stick you with a hot poker."

Listening to that sort of smut in private was one thing. Now her cheeks heated as embarrassment overlaid her other reactions to the recording.

Cam muttered a curse. His expression had gone from grim to murderous.

"Get the wordplay? But when you and me play, baby, it ain't just gonna be with words."

"My God, Jo—" Cam began.

"There's more. Let me play the other one before I lose my nerve." Her hands were shaking now as she removed one tape and inserted the other one into the recorder.

"Did you have a good time at Mrs. Randolph's party, angel face?" the distorted electronic voice that had become a part of her life asked once again. Unconsciously Jo wedged her shoulders against the back of the chair the way she'd pressed them against the wall last night when she'd first heard the message, but she couldn't stop her whole body from trembling. Her hands were clenched. Her fingernails dug into the palms of her hands the way she'd dug into the fibers of the rug.

Cam was out of his seat and around the desk before the caller delivered his next line. Pulling Jo up, he took her in his arms. Then he lowered himself into the chair and cradled her in his lap.

"I'm surprised you went out this evening after your little taste of my power."

She felt Cam's body tense, heard him swear again.

"Now you know that when I turn the switch, you'll do anything I want you to. I have a nice brass bed all ready for you. I'm looking at it now. I can picture your red hair against the white pillow, your silky skin waiting for my touch, your wrists and ankles strapped to the brass rails. You're going to get everything you deserve."

She'd sworn listening to the tapes again with Cam wasn't going to knock the props out from under her. Somehow his arms around her shoulders and his chin pressed to the top of her head shattered her fragile hold on equanimity. She'd been dealing with this alone. Now her teeth began to chatter the way they had when she'd collapsed on the wet rug.

He rocked her gently, waiting for the attack of fear to pass. In his embrace, the trembling subsided.

"Cam, I tried to call you this morning. When I couldn't reach you, I did some checking on my own. I knew you had invented an EMP prototype."

His body jerked. "I can imagine what you must have

concluded. At least you picked up the phone instead of a gun.''

Perhaps because of the tension in the room, the observation made her a little giddy. Turning around, she pulled open the desk drawer. ''I wasn't taking any chances. The gun's right in here.''

He whistled through even white teeth. ''I'm glad we're on the same side.''

''Who are we fighting? Was Eddie Cahill ever in a position to get into Randolph Enterprises files?''

''Eddie Cahill. The escaped con you told me about at the party? Last night I was wondering if he might have sent you that box.''

''Me, too.''

''What does Cahill look like?''

''There's a picture in my file.'' Jo slid off Cam's lap, opened the closet door, and went down on her knees to go through the folders.

''You keep your files on the closet floor?''

''About every two weeks, I catch up with them.''

She brought a stack of folders back to the desk. A few minutes later she handed Cam several photographs of Eddie Cahill.

He studied the man. Slight build. Medium-length brown hair. Black eyes that were both defiant and watchful. A scar on the right side of his upper lip. ''He doesn't look familiar.''

''He was vain about his haircuts. He's probably making death threats against the prison barber, too.'' Jo closed the folder.

''Did he make a death threat against you?''

''Not those exact words.'' Jo sank back into the chair opposite the desk. Succinctly she filled Cam in on the

history of her association with the drug dealer—ending
with his courtroom curse.

"He could be the one making the calls. Even if he
didn't steal the EMP plans, he may know the person who
did," Cam conceded. "Maybe he bought the box.
Maybe they've become a new intimidation device
among Baltimore's criminal element."

"I think I would have heard about it. Unless I'm a
test case."

Cam worried his bottom lip between his teeth.
"You've only received those two calls?"

"Three. One was live."

"The guy on those tapes knows a hell of a lot about
you."

"Why do you think it's a guy?"

"Would a woman say those things?"

"I guess not." Now that they had begun to discuss
the problem, Jo found herself wanting to share some of
her insights. It was just like the old days, when she and
Skip had hashed over one of their cases. "I was wondering last night if someone at the party was responsible—since everything started right after the reception at
the Franklins'."

"So that's why you were playing social butterfly. You
were looking for leads."

"Yes. Cam, what if it's not Eddie at all? What if it's
somebody else?"

"But who?"

She shrugged. "Someone else with a grudge against
me. I don't know."

"Have you talked to the police?"

"About Eddie. And I reported the mugging. I was
going to tell them about the box—but you took it away."

He looked chagrined. "Have you told them about the calls?"

"I've talked to the phone company. I'm getting one of those new caller ID systems. That's going to solve the phone harassment problem. When I have the evidence, I'll take it to the police."

"Don't you think they ought to have the whole picture now?"

"What do you think they're going to do? Put a twenty-four-hour guard on me? They don't have the manpower, and even if they did, private detectives don't call the police every time they get an obscene phone call."

He swore vehemently. "Did Skip O'Malley teach you that claptrap?"

She sat up straighter in her chair. "Skip O'Malley was the best. He taught me everything I know."

"He got himself killed on a case, didn't he?"

"How do you know that?"

"I checked some back issues of the *Baltimore Sun*."

"Why?" she demanded.

"I wanted to know more about you," he pointed out reasonably.

"You could have asked."

"When I want facts, I go look them up. Isn't that what you did this morning when you checked up on me?"

She glared at him. "I didn't know that checking up on EMP was going to lead back to you."

"Why is it," he asked slowly, "that when the two of us seem to be getting closer, Skip O'Malley steps between us?"

"He was my husband."

"He's been dead for three years and you're still wearing his ring."

Her eyes went to the narrow gold band she'd transferred to her right hand. "What's wrong with that?"

"Jo, I understand why you're on edge. Anyone would be after getting those calls. I even understand why I represent some kind of threat to your loyalty to Skip. Last night when I kissed you, you weren't thinking about Skip O'Malley."

She'd admitted as much this morning. Somehow when he said it, her defensive shields went up. "Of all the colossal male arrogance."

"Okay. You're not ready to talk about it. I'll call you in a couple of days. Or if you need me—"

"What I need is for you to get out of my seat so I can get back to work."

He got up as if he'd just realized whose chair he had confiscated. Sheepishly he headed for the door. When he reached it, he hesitated.

Jo didn't call him back. Long after he'd left, she sat staring at the frosted glass of the door. Damn him, she thought. Damn him. He was right. He was the only man who'd made her insides melt in the three years since Skip had died.

But that didn't mean she hadn't made a big mistake.

OUT ON THE STREET, Cam folded his arms across his chest. When Jo had summoned him down here, she'd sounded so upset that he'd dashed out of the office without a coat. Earlier he hadn't even felt the November chill. Now he did.

He thought about surprising Jo by marching back into her office, taking her by the shoulders and shaking some sense into her. Then he was shocked by his caveman thoughts.

Instead of acting on the impulse, he walked briskly toward the garage where the Lotus was parked. When he'd reopened Skip O'Malley's investigation, he'd thought he'd understood his own motives. Now his stomach knotted as he grappled with confusion. He'd always prided himself on his rational, scientific powers. Well, his cool detachment had been shot to hell.

He cared about Jo. A lot. Unfortunately his new feelings were at war with his old loyalties. He still hadn't told her everything. Perhaps that wasn't fair. His stomach clenched tighter. What had happened in the past had hurt him. He couldn't just let go. If he did, he'd be letting go of part of his life. Somehow he had to make it all come out right.

JO DELIBERATELY kept her mind off Cam. Instead she called Mrs. Douglas at the phone company again. The woman had already talked to her supervisor. "It's highly irregular to give out information about harassing calls," she repeated, and Jo was afraid she wasn't going to get the names. "But under the circumstances," she continued, "I've obtained permission."

"I appreciate that," Jo told her sincerely.

When she came down to the office, Mrs. Douglas handed a sheet of paper across the desk. Jo scanned the names, addresses and now-unlisted home numbers— along with work numbers. There were also notations of when the calls had been received. Some were almost three years ago. "Thanks."

"If you get a lead on the caller, I assume you'll share the information with us."

"Of course," Jo agreed. "Is there an office I can use?"

Mrs. Douglas led her down the hall to a cubicle with a modular desk and set of phones.

"This will be fine."

The first woman she tried wasn't home. The second, Melody Naylor, worked at the Hairsport—a unisex salon on Route 40. She wasn't able to talk on the phone because she was giving a customer a perm. When Jo persisted, she said if the detective could stop by in the next hour she wouldn't mind answering a few questions.

Melody turned out to be a petite blonde in her late twenties who was wearing blue jeans and a fringed cowgirl shirt. Two pairs of dangling gold earrings hung from her small lobes.

"Yeah, I did get a couple o' calls about eighteen months ago," she told Jo as she expertly rolled and clipped sections of hair. "But, see, I figured it was my ex-boyfriend. We'd just broken up, and he wasn't taking it very well."

"Did you ever get him to admit it?" Jo asked.

She shrugged. "He just laughed when I asked him."

Laughed, Jo thought. That could fit.

"He left town about the same time the calls stopped," Melody continued.

"Why did you make a report to the phone company if you thought you knew who it was?"

"The jerk was calling me at work and tying up the line."

Jo was about to ask another question when the shop door opened. The women who entered fixed Melody with a sharp look. "My manager," the hairdresser whispered. "I thought she was gonna be out longer."

Jo followed her gaze. "I could get back to you later."

"No. There isn't much else I can tell you. The whole thing's been over for a long time, and I'd rather forget it, anyway."

Jo left wishing she'd gotten more information. Back at the office, she tried phoning several other names on the list. One of the women had moved. Another didn't want to talk about the incident.

With progress like this, she might have the case solved in a couple of hundred years, Jo thought on a discouraged sigh. She was about to go home for the day when the UPS man knocked on the door. To Jo's delight, he'd brought the caller ID attachments for the phone. Now she had a much more productive way of attacking the problem.

As soon as the delivery man left, she hooked up one box at her office. She'd plug the other one in at home. Then when that bastard called back, she'd nail him—and she wouldn't have to bother with a bunch of dead-end interviews.

All through dinner, she kept glancing at the phone. For the first time in days, she hoped it would ring. But it didn't.

After she washed the dishes, she called Laura.

"Do you still want to help me set up that special photo equipment?" she asked her friend. Initially Jo had thought she might get a shot of marauding dogs. Now she wondered if she were on the trail of bigger game.

"Why not."

"Is Sunday morning still okay?" she asked, noting that Laura's enthusiasm didn't match her own.

"Uh-hum."

"If you want to get out of it, I'll understand."

"Sorry. It's not you. I'm just kind of down."

"Want to tell me about it?"

"I'll bend your ear on Sunday."

Saturday Jo rented rug and upholstery cleaning equipment and spent the day putting the living room back in order.

Sunday she skipped her usual breakfast. Despite getting the house back in shape, she was feeling a little depressed, and she suspected her friend's visit wasn't going to elevate her mood—since Laura hadn't sounded very chipper, either.

But when the blond lawyer knocked on the door, she had an upbeat expression on her face. The People section of the *Baltimore Sun* was tucked under her arm. She pulled it out and waved it aloft.

"Hey, you're famous."

"Famous?" Then Jo remembered the article about the Carpenters. She hadn't even brought in the paper that morning.

They spread the section on the kitchen table. The Carpenter story was the lead feature article. On the top of the first page were two photographs—one of the Carpenters as children and one of Jo's client as he looked now.

Jo scanned the text.

"This sure is going to call attention to the family," she said with a note of satisfaction.

"Bet it'll bring in some business for you. The whole second half is full of words of wisdom from Detective O'Malley."

"Yeah. I didn't think Sandy Peters was going to quote me so much."

"You're quotable. And it's interesting to hear about your methods."

"I didn't tell her all my tricks." Jo gestured toward the motion detector and camera, which were also on the kitchen table—along with a wooden birdhouse. She picked up the house and removed the roof. "I thought we'd put the camera in here, to protect it from the weather and prying eyes."

"Clever."

"We'll run the connecting wire along the fence and attach the motion detector to the underside of one of the horizontal supports."

Although Jo could have done the work herself, she was glad to have the company and hoped that Laura would open up about what was bothering her. After they had set the equipment up, they tested it by taking turns entering the line of fire. They got a picture of Jo mugging as she lifted the lid of a trash can and one of Laura with her hands over her face like a murder suspect ducking the media.

"You didn't really need me," Laura commented as she washed her hands at the sink. "Nobody needs me."

"Oh, come on."

"Well, Dr. William Avery certainly doesn't."

Jo spun around. "What do you mean?"

"He told me he wants a divorce. Yesterday he moved all his stuff out of the house."

"Sheez, Laura, I'm sorry."

"Maybe it's for the bes—" The sentence finished on a little sob. Jo wrapped her arms around her friend, and they stood in the middle of the kitchen for several moments.

"I promised myself I wasn't going to break down," Laura sniffed.

"Just let it out," Jo said softly.

Laura couldn't stop the bottled-up tears from flowing. But in a few minutes she had control of herself again. Jo handed her a tissue, and she blew her nose.

"You definitely think it's over?" Jo questioned.

"I found out he's been seeing a physical therapist from the clinic. When he moved out of our house, he moved in with her."

Jo snorted. "I can imagine what kind of physical therapy she's giving him."

Laura laughed. "Yeah. Let's see how she likes keeping his dinner warm when he doesn't come home till nine. Or listening to fascinating gall bladder surgery details when she's dead tired and has to get up at six-thirty in the morning."

Jo chimed in with a couple of ridiculous suggestions, and they both started to laugh. Then the conversation turned serious again.

"The scary part is worrying about making it on your own," Laura admitted. "I don't mean financially. I guess I mean emotionally. Not thinking of myself as part of a couple."

"I felt that way when Skip died. I'd come home at night and there would be things I wanted to talk to him about. It was hard getting used to the empty house." She didn't mention the way she felt now. She and Cam could have become a couple. That wasn't very likely anymore.

"I've had months to get used to that. Bill's hardly been around." Once Laura opened up, she spent the next hour talking about the marriage. Finally she sighed. "I don't know what got into me. It's a wonder you're still awake."

"You can talk to me anytime. That's what friends are for." Jo cast around for a way to lift Laura's spirits—and her own. "Hey. I've got an idea. There's a great Sunday brunch at the Hunt Valley Inn. Omelettes, Belgium waffles, the best coffee in Baltimore. I don't know about you, but I didn't eat breakfast this morning. What do you say?"

It didn't take too much persuading to get Laura to agree. They spent a pleasant couple of hours avoiding references to the men who were the source of their anxiety.

"Thanks," Laura said as she dropped Jo back at her house. "That was just what I needed."

After unlocking her door, Jo stopped to check the answering machine. When she saw there were several messages, her body went rigid. Then she reminded herself that the caller ID service was in place. If he'd called her again, she'd know where to find him.

First she checked the phone numbers. None were familiar, so she wrote them all down. Then, almost eagerly she pressed the Play button. No electronically distorted voice. No threats. Did the perp know she was ready for him? No, he wasn't clairvoyant, she told herself firmly.

The messages were all from people who'd read the article in the *Sun.* Two wanted to hire her. One had information he thought might be helpful in the Carpenter case.

The day had gone well, and Jo was in a better mood than before Laura had arrived. For dinner she microwaved herself a baked potato, slathered it with butter, and heaped it full of vegetables and cheese.

While she ate, she checked the cable schedule. She hadn't turned the TV on all week. But HBO was showing *Tin Men* again. Since she got a kick out of both Danny DeVito and the Baltimore locale, she decided to watch.

Just before eight she fixed herself a bowl of popcorn, changed into her most comfortable flannel gown, and settled down in bed. When she used the remote control to switch to HBO, the wrong movie flashed on the screen.

The scene made Jo cringe. It looked like one of those horror flicks where a guy with eight-inch steel fingernails chased a bunch of half-naked teenage girls around a high-school locker room before he started ripping out their throats.

Ten seconds of the mayhem made her gag, and she pressed the button to change the channel. The screen jumped for a second. Then the same scene snapped into focus. She pressed again. More gore.

With a muttered curse, Jo tossed the malfunctioning remote control onto the bed and marched over to the set. Reaching out, she grasped the channel knob, and a jolt of electricity shot through her body.

A scream tore from her throat as she jumped back. Rubbing her hand, she felt the pain ebb. Her eyes were fixed on the television picture. It took a confused moment to realize what she was watching. Instead of a high-school locker room, the scene had switched to the deep woods. Now a group of teenage campers was being ripped apart by werewolves.

Squeezing her eyes shut, Jo gave her head a savage shake. That didn't shut out the screams of the victims. She was reaching for the volume control when she snatched her hand back. It tingled with remembered pain. She couldn't risk that again.

Her gaze dropped to the plug. Pulling on it could be just as dangerous as touching the controls.

Jo was backing away from the television set as if it were an alien when a flicker on the screen made her freeze in place. For a split second, the image had changed to something even more frightening.

Mouth dry and heart pounding, she held herself rigid watching the mayhem in the woods. Twenty seconds later, it happened again, and she gasped. A quick cut to another scene. She was left with the impression of a woman tied to a brass bed. A red-haired woman.

Jo's bare toes dug into the rag rug in front of the television set so hard that they started to cramp. But she couldn't tear her eyes away. The little insert flashed again and again on the screen—interspersed with a dismemberment in a sawmill. Hardly able to breathe, Jo viewed the next intrusion. Now she could see the back of a man as he advanced on the helpless woman. A knife was in his hand. Next time the image appeared, the knife arched down toward his victim.

Jo screamed and covered her eyes with her hands. Somehow that broke the spell. Snatching up the brass barrel-shaped piggy bank that sat on top of the pie safe, she flung it at the television. The screen exploded.

CHAPTER EIGHT

IT SHOULD be over. It wasn't. Although the picture was gone, the sound remained. It was as if a demon had taken possession of the set.

Turning, Jo fled the room. Sheer black fright nipped at her heels. She hadn't realized that the volume on the TV had been steadily escalating. Wails and screams followed her down the stairs. No. The sound was actually getting louder the farther away she ran.

When she reached the living room, she came to a screeching halt. The television. She hadn't turned that one on. But the horror she'd fled in the bedroom confronted her anew. Now it was on a twenty-five-inch picture tube. The sawmill. The helpless victims. And the woman on the bed. Only now her body was cut and bleeding.

On a choked sob, Jo sagged against the doorjamb. Terrifying calls. The EMP waves. Now this. Someone was trying to reduce her to a quivering mass of fear. Her hands balled into fists. She wasn't going to let it happen.

The circuit-breaker box was down in the basement. She could turn off the sets that way. The cellar stairs were rough. Slivers of wood dug into Jo's feet as she pounded down to the utility room. When she snatched open the electrical box, she thanked God Skip had been much more organized than she. Each circuit was labeled.

Furnace. Air conditioner. Refrigerator. Bathroom. Dining room. Living room. Bedroom.

Throat raw, breath hissing in and out of her lungs, she stood with her hand hovered above the last switch. A shock from the power box could kill. But if someone had wanted to electrocute her she'd be dead already, wouldn't she? Gritting her teeth, she threw back the circuit. Her hand throbbed, but only with the anticipation of pain. After the living-room switch, she flipped the one from the bedroom. The house was plunged into blessed silence.

Jo stood beside the circuit box, gasping. When she'd caught her breath she tiptoed back upstairs. The living room and the front hall were dark and silent. So was her bedroom.

Someone had gone to a lot of trouble to scare the stuffing out of her. Was it all Eddie Cahill's doing? Was this how he'd decided to punish her?

Had he rigged the television sets while she and Laura were at lunch? Was he in here now? Suddenly her scalp began to crawl, and she cringed into the shadows trying to make her body small and inconspicuous. Then she got a grip on herself.

She hadn't watched television since last Sunday. He could have done this anytime during the week. And if he'd wanted to spring out of the spare bedroom and attack her, why hadn't he already done it?

What if the phone and the EMP generator had been just the first and second acts of his private little melodrama starring Jo O'Malley. This was the third. What had he planned for the fourth? Tying her to the railroad tracks?

Or was it more like tying her to a brass bed and—

All at once she knew she couldn't stay in the house straining to hear a lock turn or a window rattle. By the time she reached her darkened bedroom, she was limping. There must be splinters all over the bottoms of her feet, she realized. She couldn't do anything about that now. From the pie safe she snatched a pair of sweatpants and a shirt. The orange pants and the turquoise top didn't match, but she wasn't going to stop and coordinate her outfit. Then she grimaced as she yanked on socks and thrust her feet into loafers. The shoes made the splinters hurt all the more.

Despite the pain, Jo made it across the garage and into her car in two seconds flat. After locking the doors, she activated the opener and started the engine. Roaring out into the driveway, she paused only long enough to close the door again. Halfway down the street she remembered that she'd forgotten to reset the security alarm. But what difference did it make if he'd already been in her house?

Taking a deep breath she put her foot to the accelerator and sped off into the night. For the first few blocks, she kept one eye on the rearview mirror just in case somebody was following. To her intense relief, no set of headlights tailed her around the twisted course of streets through which she drove. She didn't realize until she'd found herself on Jones Falls Expressway that she was heading for Cam's.

She didn't even consider his reaction to the unexpected visit until she'd rung the bell. Then it was too late. Before she could think of exactly what she was going to say, he'd thrown open the door.

His eyes widened when he took in her disheveled appearance. "My God, Jo, what's happened now?"

"Well, my television has a big hole where the picture tube used to be."

He seemed to know she was starting with the least important detail. "You'd better come in and sit down," he said gently.

She followed him into the living room and flopped onto the couch. He sat down beside her looking uncertain.

Jo squeezed her eyes shut and struggled to get a grip on her emotions. Now that she was in the warm, sheltered environment of Cam's town house, she was afraid she was going to come apart.

"Do you want a cup of—uh—tea, or something stronger?"

"Something stronger."

Cam poured brandy into two snifters. While he stood at the bar in the corner, Jo willed the strands of her self-control to knit themselves back together.

When her host turned around, she was feeling a bit more composed. Yet she couldn't stop herself from gulping a swallow of the brandy. The unaccustomed fire in her throat made her cough. Cam waited patiently until the spasm subsided.

"Better?"

"I think so."

"Jo, are you going to tell me what really happened to you tonight?"

"Someone's trying to drive me nuts," she repeated the conclusion she'd come to earlier. "Or maybe the neighborhood Halloween committee is getting a jump on next year. When I turned on the television set tonight, all I could get was horror movies. When I tried to turn one off, it gave me a hell of a shock."

"Oh, honey." Before she finished the account, he'd crossed the two feet of space that separated them and folded her into his embrace. She didn't resist. In fact, she went almost limp in his arms.

His hands smoothed across her back. Her body absorbed the comfort. When she'd seen him last, they'd both been on edge with each other. Now it was as if the angry words had never been spoken.

"Not just regular horror movies." She swallowed low and slowly. "Interspersed with the commercial stuff was another scene. I could only see it in flashes. This guy had a woman tied to a brass bed. She was small, and she had red hair. I guess she looked a lot like me. He came at her with a knife. And he—and he—" Jo wasn't able to continue.

Cam gave her a few minutes to collect herself. "Tell me everything, honey," he finally murmured. "Everything that's happened to you."

"You know a lot of it."

"I want to understand the whole picture."

Jo gulped. "All right."

It felt surprisingly good to say it all. The longer she went on, the more convinced she was that everything fit into a pattern. While she talked, Cam held her close and stroked her back and shoulders.

"What do you think he's going to do next?" Jo finally asked the question that had been preying on her mind since she'd fled her house.

"I don't know. But one thing's for sure," Cam muttered, "you're not spending the night at home."

She nodded.

"And you're going to call the police and have them meet you over there so they can check this out."

"I already decided that."

Fifteen minutes later, they were heading back to Jo's. When the Lotus turned the corner onto her block, neither she nor Cam paid any attention to the van parked under the branches of a maple tree. Instead Jo's eyes were focused on her home. It was a strange experience viewing her house from the curb. Although it was after midnight, most of the lights were on because she'd flipped every switch she could reach as she'd fled the shrieks and cries blaring from the upstairs television set.

Jo stared at the windows as she climbed out of the car. Something wasn't right. Something— Then it hit her. She'd thrown the circuit breakers that shut off the electricity in the living room and her bedroom. Now the lights of both rooms blazed as brightly as those in the rest of the house.

"Cam! The lights. In my bedroom and the living room."

He'd listened intently to her earlier narration of events. Now his mind quickly followed her train of thought. His feet were already pounding toward the porch. "Stay out here," he ordered.

Ignoring the shouted command, Jo followed him down the front walk and up the steps.

He had halted at the front door. This time he hadn't come prepared with his lock picker. Jo produced the key. As soon as the door was open, they rushed inside. The living room was empty. Upstairs, floorboards creaked in rapid succession.

Cam took the stairs two at a time. Despite the pain from the splinters in her feet, Jo charged right after him. As Cam reached the second floor, he was greeted by the sound of shattering glass.

Something heavy hit the porch roof. By the time Jo made it into her bedroom, Cam was out on the roof. Jo was about to climb out when he came back into the room.

"Damn! He was out of here before I got upstairs. I couldn't even see where he went. If he broke in, I wonder why the security alarm wasn't blaring when we pulled up."

Jo looked down at her toes. "I, uh, forgot to reset it when I left."

Outside a car engine started with a grinding noise. They couldn't see the vehicle. But they heard it speed away into the darkness.

"He was here. Now I know the bastard was right here!" Jo spat out. She stared around her bedroom. The armoire was open. So was the pie safe. Along with the broken glass from the television picture tube, clothes were strewn around the floor.

"But I think he wasn't here long—because he'd only gotten to the clothes." She hobbled across the room and sank onto the bed.

Cam noticed the limp she'd managed to hide when he was looking. "What's wrong with your feet?"

"Splinters. From when I ran down the basement stairs."

A heavy pounding on the front door sent her springing to her feet, and she winced.

"That must be the police," Cam told her. "Too bad they didn't get here five minutes ago."

He went down to answer the door. Jo hobbled after him.

The officer who took the report was Detective Evan Hamill. He was a big man with ebony skin, close-cropped hair and a face that sported a two-inch scar across his chin. Jo had never met him but she knew the type. A fifteen-year veteran who had grown up in the inner city. When she told him about the bizarre episode with the television set, he looked surprised. But he pulled out a pad and pen and took a report.

"I guess this guy wasn't from the customer service department of ComCast Cable," Hamill quipped.

Jo gave him a weak smile. At least the man had a sense of humor.

"Can either of you give me a description?"

"No. He was gone before we made it upstairs," Cam said. He had found a pan and filled it with hot water. During the interview, Jo sat with her sweatpants pushed up to her calves and her feet submerged. The wet heat felt good, and she shot Cam a grateful look. He smiled encouragingly at her.

"It's not just what happened tonight," he said. "Ms. O'Malley has had problems over the last several weeks—ever since a man who she helped send to prison escaped."

That got Hamill's attention. "What's his name?"

"Eddie Cahill."

"Yeah I saw the report. He's one mean dude. And cagey. It looks like he started planning his escape the minute they slammed the gate behind him."

Hamill fumbled in his pockets. Jo expected him to pull out a pack of cigarettes. Instead he removed a bag of smokehouse almonds.

"You mind? I missed dinner."

"Go ahead."

With Cam's moral support, Jo forced herself to go

through the story of Eddie Cahill, the phone calls, the mugging, the EMP, and the television sets again.

"It sounds like you're a target, all right," Hamill agreed, wiping his hand on his pants' leg.

"What kind of protection are you going to give her?" Cam asked, gesturing toward Jo.

"We don't have the manpower to keep someone with her twenty-four hours a day. About all we can do at this point is increase police visibility in the neighborhood and send more patrol cars past her house."

Jo shot Cam an "I told you so" look.

"I think it would be a good idea if she spent the night somewhere else," Hamill continued.

"That's already been arranged," Cam muttered.

"I want to have the lab dust for fingerprints in the morning. Why don't we make an appointment for ten."

"I'll have her back here by then," Cam told him.

When the detective had left, Jo closed her eyes. "Cam, I don't think I can face the mess in my room. But I need some stuff for tomorrow." She swallowed, wondering exactly what he thought she'd agreed to when she'd said she'd accepted his hospitality. "And a nightgown."

"Um-hum."

Their eyes locked for several heartbeats.

"I'll bring some stuff down."

"Thanks."

"Is there anything I can use to board up that window?"

"I think there's plywood in the basement. And my overnight bag should be in the top of my closet."

Half an hour later, for the second time that evening, Jo fled her own home. As she looked up at the plywood covering the bedroom window, she silently admitted to herself that she felt a whole lot better with Cameron Randolph next to her.

When they reached his Cross Keys town house, Cam opened the car door and swung Jo into his arms.

"I can walk," she protested.

"Your feet have taken enough punishment for one evening."

He set her down on the sofa where they'd first talked. "I'll be right back."

Jo nestled into the comfortable cushions.

When Cam returned, he was carrying a first-aid kit and a small lamp, which turned out to focus a narrow but powerful beam.

"We'd better get those splinters out before they get infected and you're really laid up."

"Yeah."

"Lie down."

When she'd complied, he sat down so that her feet were in his lap. Then he adjusted the beam of the lamp, swabbed her feet with a cotton ball soaked in antiseptic, and sterilized a needle and tweezers.

"That long soaking in hot water should help. But tell me if I hurt you." The tone was matter-of-fact, but the hand that grasped her ankle was amazingly gentle. So were the fingers that held the needle.

She peered up at Cam who was ministering to her as if they did this sort of thing all the time. A wave of warmth and gratitude swept over her. Out there in the night, someone had been stalking her. In here, she felt safe—and cherished.

Cam worked with precision, finding each splinter and

easing it from her flesh with no more than a bad twinge or two each.

Several times he grasped one of her toes so that he could move one or the other foot to a different angle. There was a strange intimacy having him work on a part of her body that was usually covered up.

"I think that's the last of them," he finally announced. His voice told her that he felt the intimacy as much as she did.

Jo leaned back and closed her eyes. They blinked open again as cold antiseptic made her wince.

"Sorry."

"I don't think it can be helped."

Cam turned off the high-intensity lamp and set the first-aid supplies on the coffee table. But he made no move to get up. His hands continued to stroke Jo's ankles and to wander over her toes.

Now that the medical procedure was finished, she was free to enjoy his attentions. With one finger, he traced the arch of her foot, sending little shivers up her legs.

"Feet never turned me on before." Cam's voice was rough. "Did anyone ever tell you yours are damn sexy?"

"No."

He lifted one of her ankles, bringing her toes to his mouth. When he brushed his lips back and forth against the soft pads, Jo closed her eyes. When he started to nibble on them, she sucked in a surprised breath.

"Sorry," he repeated his earlier apology, quickly lowering the foot.

"That wasn't exactly a complaint. I didn't know feet were a turn-on, either."

When he'd brought her inside, she'd been exhausted

and in pain. Now the air in the room had become erotically charged. They stared at each other for a long, breath-stopping moment. Then Jo held out her arms, and he came into them.

Stretching out beside her on the couch, he clasped her tightly. His lips skimmed along her jaw and over her cheeks before settling possessively over her mouth.

He kissed her for long, hungry minutes. She met each thrust of his tongue, each sensual movement of his lips with one of her own. When he finally lifted his head, they were both gasping for breath.

"Jo, honey. Oh Lord, Jo." He cradled her body against the length of his. "Friday when I left your office I told myself I wasn't going to call you again. I spent Saturday climbing the walls of my lab. Then tonight I called Steve because I needed to talk to someone who could give me a clue about how to handle you."

"How to handle me! What did he say?" She tried to pull away, but there wasn't much room to maneuver between his hard body and the sofa cushions.

"He told me to—uh—how can I put this politely— make love to you until you couldn't stand up."

"Sheez!"

Cam swallowed. "I'm not effectuating this very well."

"You and Steve Clairborne. I thought he was my friend."

"He is."

"He thinks sex is the quick fix for interpersonal relationships."

"No. If he did, he wouldn't have left Abby last spring and gone back to India."

Jo nodded slowly.

"He said he thinks you and I would be making a big mistake if we didn't give the relationship a chance. I think so, too."

Jo considered the words and the vulnerability she detected behind them. He had just offered her a chance to reject him.

She looked into his gray eyes, reading her own uncertainty but also an unspoken promise. Reaching out, she cupped Cam's face in her hands. "I think I keep littering the area with my emotional baggage. Then I get angry when you trip over it."

"Everybody has emotional baggage. If they've loved someone—and lost them. Or if they've been hurt by someone. Or if their childhood wasn't perfect."

"How do you know so much?"

"I'm smart."

"That's one of the things I like about you."

"What else?"

"I like the way you effectuate."

"Now you're making fun of me."

"I like the way you kiss, too."

"Gently or libidinously?"

"Every way." She relaxed in his arms once more.

Her words and the physical invitation drew him closer. He kissed her gently. He kissed her passionately. He kissed her tantalizingly. And while he kissed her, his hands began to move over her body.

His fingers slipped beneath her sweatshirt and inched upward. When his hand closed around her breast, the breath trickled out of her lungs.

They were lying on the couch facing each other. Ducking down, he caught the hem of the shirt with his teeth and edged it the rest of the way up. Then he began to caress her with his face and lips. "I could go mad from just tasting you."

When he began to tease one taut nipple with his tongue, a shaft of intense pleasure shot through her. She felt the madness, too, and her body arched into his.

Cam raised his head and looked into her eyes. "Could I interest you in a tour of the upstairs, starting with my bedroom?"

Jo grinned. "Yes, I think you could."

Pulling her shirt back into place, he helped her up.

Arm and arm they climbed the stairs. The light from the hall filtered into the master bedroom through the partly opened door. Cam folded down the covers on the king-size bed. Then he turned back to Jo. Between kisses and murmured endearments he stripped off her clothes. She did the same for him.

Naked in his bedroom. The reality was overwhelming. His body was lean and tough and very masculine. Tentatively she reached up to touch the dark mat of hair on his chest, feeling her fingers crinkle the curly hairs.

"Don't be shy with me, Jo. One of the things I like about you is that you're so direct."

She swallowed. "This is different."

"Jo O'Malley acting cautious. I never thought I'd see the day."

"Don't tease me."

"Honey, not holding you in my arms is teasing the hell out of myself." With a growl deep in his throat, he tugged her into his embrace, and they clung together.

When he lowered her to the mattress, it rocked gently.

"A water bed. I might get dizzy."

"Then you'll have to hold on tight."

She stared up at him as her arms circled his broad back, still half stunned just being here with him like this. "I've fantasized about you naked in my bed," he murmured, echoing her thoughts. "I thought I was going to go crazy if I didn't make love to you."

Despite his statement, he didn't seem to be in a hurry. He enticed her with soul-searing kisses and tantalizing caresses until she was half out of her mind with need. And always he kept release just out of her reach.

But his body wasn't out of her reach. When her hand closed around him and began its own tender assault, she knew she'd tipped the balance.

She felt him shudder. "Jo, you're going to—"

"—have you inside me."

The hand that held him captive guided him into her body. They gazed into each other's eyes, acknowledging the moment's potency.

Then his hips began to move. He'd made a turbulent assault on her senses. Now he overwhelmed her with the power of a primitive male claiming his mate.

Her response was just as elemental. She moved with him, against him, around him, her fingers digging into his back as she reached the peak of sensation.

The tempest seized them both, racking their bodies with sensual spasms, sweeping away all reality but the two of them locked together in passionate fulfillment.

Little aftershocks of pleasure rippled over her as she nestled in his embrace.

He held her fiercely. Since the angry confrontation in her office, he'd come to realize that she was more important to him than what had happened in the past. Now there were things he had to tell her about his run-ins with Skip O'Malley.

Or maybe it was already too late for confessions. Maybe no matter what he said or did from now on, she was going to end up hating him.

No. There must be a way to keep it from happening. If she just got to know him better—to trust him—before she found out the truth, everything might be all right.

OUT IN THE MORE, the man sitting in the driver's seat of the van bumped his fist against the steering wheel. She was in there with that know-it-all, swell-headed Cameron Randolph.

Goddamn Republican.

He'd make her hotter so he could get into her pants. A picture of the colonel and lovely, rolling on a bed with the little redhead tucked into his mind, and he spat out a stream of curses.

Once again, he got up and fell in with the entourage in the van. With anyone else, he'd be able to keep what they were saying. Although probably they weren't even anything more than tight and proper.

He started again, resolution must have simmered of his mood attending around his town house, then drove he had around his fan now.

The guy was a slow learner, but he'd finally caught on to the possibility that someone could be watching his precious inventions.

In the same times, he'd made a little study of Cam Randolph. The way he saw it, the inventor had been born with the two forward wars—money and family. Sure he'd done okay with some pretty good gizmos—the reports. That didn't prove anything. He'd gone to the best schools—gone to the best college.

CHAPTER NINE

OUT IN THE NIGHT, the man sitting in the driver's seat of the van banged his fists against the steering wheel. She was in there with that know-it-all, swell-headed Cameron Randolph.

Cam Randolph.

He'd taken her home so he could get into her pants.

A picture of the conceited inventor rolling on a bed with the little redhead leaped into his mind, and he spat out a stream of curses.

Once again, he got up and fiddled with the equipment in the van. With anyone else, he'd be able to hear what they were saying. Although probably they weren't communicating with anything more than sighs and groans.

He cursed again. Randolph must have some kind of electronic shielding around his town house. Just the way he had around his lab now.

The guy was a slow learner. But he'd finally caught on to the possibility that someone could be stealing his precious inventions.

In his spare time, he'd made a little study of Cam Randolph. The way he saw it, the lucky stiff had been born with the two big advantages in life—money and family. Sure he'd come up with some pretty good gadgets over the years. That didn't prove anything. Hadn't he gone to the best schools—gotten the best training money could buy. And he hadn't had to work for a living like everyone else. So he'd been able to shut himself up in his lab for as long as he wanted—until he'd gotten lucky a few times.

Everybody was always talking about how smart and how creative Cam Randolph was. Didn't they see the real reasons for his success? Didn't they understand what a cold-blooded bastard he was and that he never gave anyone else a chance?

FOR LONG MOMENTS Jo was content to just snuggle against Cam's chest, listening to his heart beat a strong, steady rhythm against her ear. "For years I told myself I didn't need this," she said softly. "You've changed my mind. But I never dreamed I'd get hooked up with anyone like you."

"You might say you have your hooks into me."

"That sounds painful."

"In a way it is. But then it's a new experience for me."

"You've never—"

"—cared enough about a woman to go after her like this."

Her eyebrows lifted.

"It's kind of nice to hold a woman in my arms who somewhere in the back of her mind isn't counting my money."

"Oh, come on. They've also got to be thinking that you're smart and good-looking and charming and a wonderful lover."

"Oh?"

The implications of her rash statement sank in. "You

also have a habit of spouting big words when you're tense or embarrassed.''

"I know. They're a kind of protective circumvallation.''

They both laughed.

Jo was suddenly feeling better than she had in weeks. She nestled her head against Cam's shoulder, and he clasped her to his side. "When I was a kid in that shack in the mountains, I kept a stack of library books beside my bed. I went through everything I could get my hands on. My favorites were the Oz books and the Narnia books because they were about a magic place where some lucky children had gone to get away from the real world. I dreamed about doing that.''

"I think I can understand why.''

"One thing I learned when I got older—there's no point in sitting around daydreaming. You make your life what you want it to be." She swallowed. "Except that from time to time, Fate throws you a wild card. Like your husband gets killed. Or a psychotic decides he's going to show you slasher movies—and then come slash you to pieces.''

His arms tightened around her. "He's not going to do that.''

"It would be a damn bad thing, just when I've gotten my hooks into this brainy, charming, sexy guy.''

"Jo." His mouth found hers again. And for a little while, they both shut out the danger waiting to envelop them.

WHEN THEY PULLED UP at Jo's front walk the next morning, a police car was already parked in the driveway. Detective Hamill had arrived in a separate car, which was parked across the street. As they got out of the Lotus, he ambled around the side of the house. His jaw was working. More almonds, Jo thought.

"It looks as if the special TV programming was rigged through your cable hookup," he said.

"That was my hypothesis last night," Cam agreed. "But I didn't get a chance to check it out."

"By the way, what's the fancy photo setup out by the trash for?" the detective added.

"Photo setup?" Cam asked.

Jo explained to both of them, "I thought I was going to get a picture of some dogs. Maybe we got lucky last night." She went around back and checked the camera. The film hadn't advanced.

"Too bad," Cam said.

They all tromped back to the front porch, where Jo let the fingerprint crew inside. As they went upstairs to start in her bedroom, Jo headed straight for the living room. When she saw the answering machine was blinking, her body went rigid.

Cam was right behind her. "Let's find out who's left a message," he suggested in an even voice.

First Jo activated the recall mechanism on the caller ID unit. The number she wrote down definitely wasn't familiar.

Then she took a deep breath and pressed the Play button on the answering machine.

"Well, miss newspaper celebrity, I guess you think you're too important to have anything to do with me. I'm afraid you don't have a choice. How did you like the little movie show I set up for your personal viewing enjoyment?"

"He saw the article in the paper," Jo whispered, her

skin growing clammy. God, she'd been a fool to put herself in the public eye like that. "I never should have let that reporter quote me."

Cam wrapped his arms around her and began to rub the goose bumps on her arms.

"That wasn't nice of you to bash in your television set like that. But I understand why you might have flipped out." The words were followed by one of his high-pitched laughs. Even the security of Cam's embrace couldn't stop the shudder from rippling over her skin.

"Easy, honey," he whispered.

She gave him a shaky little nod. This time she wasn't facing the voice and the threats alone.

"And it wasn't nice of you to go off with that slime-bag inventor," the voice continued on a harsher note. "Don't tell me you let him play bouncy bouncy with you. After that has-been Skip O'Malley, you need to develop better taste in men."

Jo's hands were balled into fists. With a look of helpless rage, she glanced around the room. "How dare he. How dare he," she gritted.

"He's just trying to get a rise out of you," Cam said. But he couldn't quite keep the anger out of his own voice.

When the message finished, Hamill pressed the Save button. "So that's the kind of trash you've been hearing," he muttered.

"I call him Laughing Boy," Jo told him.

"I can see why. Mind if I take the tape?"

She shook her head. "You can have the other ones, too. They're down at my office." Her fingers sought and found Cam's. His almost crushing grip was like a safety line.

Hamill was already dialing a special number at the phone company. In a brusque voice, he spoke into the receiver. A few minutes later, he swore. Slamming the phone back into the cradle, he turned to Jo and Cam. "It looks like we're not going to catch the bastard this morning."

"Why not?"

"He used a phone booth off Charles Street."

Solving the problem with something as simple as caller ID had been too much to hope for, Jo told herself. "He was here last night," she reminded the detective. "He must have seen the unit."

"Damn!" The exclamation came from Cam.

"If he called from a phone booth, how did he get that distortion in the transmission?" Hamill wondered aloud.

"Portable equipment?" Jo asked, her tone matter-of-fact now. She was going to think about this just like any other case. If she did that, the fear wouldn't swallow her up.

"I'd like to see what kind of setup he has," Cam mused. "EMP. Portable electronics equipment."

"Yeah." The police detective looked thoughtful.

"Do you think it's Eddie Cahill doing this?" Jo asked.

"I dug out the court records last night. You did some prime undercover work to nail Cahill. No wonder the mother said he was going to get you," Hamill answered. "But there's no hard evidence linking him to any of this."

"There's plenty of evidence that Ms. O'Malley's life is being torn apart." Cam looked toward the answering machine and back at Hamill. "Are you going to tell me you still can't commit yourself to protecting her?"

"I know you're worried—"

"Dammit, man."

"Cam, please," Jo whispered.

"I'll put everything I can into the investigation," Hamill promised. "And we've already increased patrols in the area. Basically Ms. O'Malley's doing the kinds of things I'd recommend. An alarm system. Good locks. Maybe she should put in some extra lighting in the yard," the police detective continued.

Then he turned to Jo. "Where can we reach you?"

"At my house," Cam answered.

She shot him a startled look. Helping her was one thing, making decisions for her was quite another. "Since when do you do the talking for me?"

"You sure can't stay here alone."

"I'm sure I'd be welcomed at my friend Laura's. She has a big house all to herself."

"Do you want to put your friend in danger?" Cam asked slowly.

"I—no."

Hamill cleared his throat. "I'd recommend taking Mr. Randolph up on his offer. He's likely to function as a deterrent. Whoever made the calls and rigged the TV stunt has been going after a woman living alone. He ran when Randolph discovered him in the house. He might give up if you had a protector."

Jo snorted.

Cam tried not to look victorious.

They waited until Hamill had left before continuing the personal discussion.

"I'm not going to spend the day hiding at your place," Jo informed Cam.

"What are you going to do?"

"I'm going to go back to those phone company records on other women who had similar calls and see if I can find out if they have anything in common with me."

"Would you mind if we stopped back at my place and had a look at your car? I'd like to check something out."

The question and his conciliatory tone of voice astonished her. "Cam, I'm not used to having a bodyguard."

"I know."

"I—things are moving so fast. I mean, with you and me."

"Honey, when this is over, I'll send you flowers and take you out to dinner at the Conservatory. Right now, I want to make sure you're going to be safe."

Jo nodded, unsure of how to act in this unfamiliar situation. "Okay," she agreed in a barely audible voice.

"Okay, we can go check out your car? Or you'll permit me to help you?"

"Okay to both."

Back at Cross Keys, Cam pulled into a parking place near Jo's Honda. She watched as he walked over to the car, stooped down and began to run his hands along the underside of the bumpers and under the chassis. When he reached a spot under the back bumper, he paused.

Seconds later he turned back to Jo. In the palm of his right hand lay a dull metal disk.

"What is it?"

"A directional transmitter. That's why he thought you were still at my house last night. He knew your car stayed."

Air wheezed out of Jo's lungs as the extent of her tormentor's scheme hit her. Her knees began to wobble and she sat down heavily on the curb. "He's been following me. Poking into my life. He's known where I was every second of the day and night because he's been tracking me.''

"Yes." Cam was beside her, holding her.

"My God. What else has he been doing? If he's got a bunch of electronics stuff—he—he could have been listening to us." She gulped. "Like in your house last night."

"Not in my house! The place is shielded. Nothing gets in or out of that house without my knowing about it."

"Why?"

"I told you about the industrial espionage. Sometimes I take work home—or make business calls from there."

She nodded slowly and then raised an eyebrow in surprise as Cam got up and put the transmitter back where he'd found it.

"What are you doing?"

"I think we can lay a trap for the bastard." He worried a knuckle between his teeth. "Just let me think about how I want to set it up."

"Do me a favor. Let me help you think about it."

"Sure."

They drove in separate cars to 43 Light Street. While Jo waited in the back alley, Cam went down to talk to Lou Rossini. The building superintendent agreed to drive Jo's car to the vicinity of the pool hall where she'd been mugged. He'd take a cab back. Cam would park in a nearby alley and see who showed up at the car.

Before he left, Cam pulled Jo into his arms and gave her a hard kiss. "Remember, you're not going anywhere without letting somebody know about it," he reminded her.

"Yes, Mother." She wrinkled her nose. She didn't

like having a bunch of constraints. On the other hand, the careful arrangements were comforting.

Sitting at her desk, she drummed her fingers against the wooden surface. She'd pinned her hopes on the caller ID equipment. It had done her as much good as a tissue paper dress in a rainstorm.

Now what? Maybe it was time to go back to the phone company list of women who'd been harassed.

Again she had to dial several numbers before getting anyone at home. The third woman she called answered the phone with the kind of cautious greeting that had crept into Jo's own voice recently.

"Is this Penny Wallace?"

"Who is this? How did you get this number?"

"My name is Jo O'Malley. I've been receiving some threatening phone calls. Since I'm a private detective, the phone company has given me permission to contact other women who might have been harassed by the same man."

"I really don't want to talk about it."

"Please. I'll only take a few minutes of your time."

"Are you the detective who was in that article in the paper Sunday?"

"Yes."

"What kind of calls have you been getting?"

"From someone with an electronically distorted voice." She kept her tone as steady as possible. "He seems to know a lot about me. And he's been leaving messages on my answering machines as well as speaking to me in person."

Penny made a choking sound. "That's what happened to me six months ago."

"Could I come over and talk to you?" Jo asked.

There was a long pause. "All right," the woman finally answered.

Jo got directions. When she hung up, she thought about the newspaper article again. The man stalking her had read it. So had Penny Wallace. On balance, the notoriety was probably more of an advantage than a disadvantage.

After locking the office, Jo went downstairs and started out the door toward the parking lot where she usually kept her car. Then she remembered the Honda was in Dundalk—and she'd promised Cam she'd stay at the office. Well, what Cam Randolph didn't know wasn't going to hurt him. Besides, this might be an important lead in the case. Going back inside, she called a cab and waited in the lobby until it arrived.

Penny Wallace lived in a redbrick row house in Catonsville. When she answered the door, the two women stared at each other in shock. They were both petite and both sported heads of short, curly red hair.

"You could be my sister," Penny said in amazement.

"That's just what I was thinking. Let's see if we can find out if we have anything else in common." Jo's voice brimmed with excitement. Finally she was getting somewhere.

Penny Wallace blew her nose and ushered her visitor into a small, neat living room decorated in a stark modern style. Well, taste in decor is something we don't share, Jo thought as she took off her coat and folded it beside her on the sofa.

"You're lucky you found me here. I've got a cold so I decided to stay home."

Jo sympathized before getting down to business.

"When did the calls start?" she asked as she took a seat in a low-slung leather chair.

Penny faced her on the chrome-and-leather sofa with a box of tissues at her side. "May 15. I remember exactly because I'd just come home from Alice's wedding shower."

"You were in a wedding?" Jo asked carefully.

"I was the maid of honor."

The words sent a strange chill sweeping over Jo's skin as if an icy finger had reached out and touched her shoulder. "My calls started a couple of weeks ago when I came back from an engagement party for one of my best friends. I'm the matron of honor in the wedding."

Penny leaned forward. "That's spooky."

"Yeah."

"I know what you're going through. He's making sexual threats, isn't he? And he knows a lot about you."

"He knows everything about me."

"It was creepy. Especially the way he laughed."

"Yeah." Invisible insects buzzed around Jo for a moment. She willed them away.

"If it's any consolation, the calls stopped after the wedding."

"That's definitely something to look forward to. But I'm not just dealing with this on a personal level anymore. I'd really like to nail the guy if I can."

"I just wanted him to leave me alone," Penny whispered. It was apparent that talking about the episode had brought the whole thing back to her.

"Is there anything else that might help me track him down?"

"The music in the background. It sounded like a band."

"Yes! What about the stuff he threatened?"

"My therapist said the best thing I could do was put this out of my mind."

"I understand." Jo could empathize with that. "Did he just call? Or did you have any physical contact with him?"

"Just calls."

"Are you sure?" Jo gave a brief account of the electronic devices that had been used at her house.

Penny's eyes grew round. "Thank God I didn't have anything like that. It was all over the phone."

They talked for about fifteen minutes longer but Jo didn't get any more facts. "I wonder where he got the names of the wedding attendants," Penny mused.

"He could be a wedding photographer. He could work for the caterer or the florist. Do you know who provided those services for your friend?"

"No. I'm sorry. I could ask Alice and get back to you."

Jo gave Penny one of her cards and then asked if she could call a cab.

"A private detective without a car?"

"It's a long story."

Back at her office, Jo tried some more numbers and got another one of the victims, Heather Van Dyke, who was at home because she ran a sewing business from her recreation room. Now Jo had a better idea about what to ask. This woman, too, was a redhead within an inch of her height who'd been the matron of honor in her sister's wedding.

As Jo put down the phone, she leaned back in her chair. Two redheads and a blonde. How did that add up?

Was Melody Naylor an unrelated case? She wished she'd asked the woman more questions.

Then a crucial fact flashed in her mind like the payoff light on a slot machine. Melody Naylor was a beautician. A lot of beauticians change their hair color the way other women change dresses. Maybe she had been a redhead when she'd gotten those calls.

When she phoned the shop, Melody was on a break.

Jo reintroduced herself and explained that she'd been talking to some other victims of phone harassment and might have discovered a common link. "Was your hair a different color when you were getting the calls?"

"Gee—let me think. I change it so much," the woman said, confirming Jo's speculation. "I was using Champagne Blond for a while. Then I decided to see if redheads have more fun, so I tried Fantastic Autumn."

"Your hair was red?" Jo clarified, her heart skipping a beat.

"Yeah. But I dyed it back just before Lucy's wedding because it didn't go with my pink dress."

"You were in a friend's wedding?" Jo asked, struggling to keep her voice steady.

"I was the maid of honor. And this real great-looking guy was one of the ushers. For a while I thought things were going t work out with us. Then he went back to his damn motorcycle racing."

Jo made appropriate responses as Melody prattled on about her love life. But her mind wasn't on the conversation. Redheads. Weddings. She touched her own red curls. She had the link between her and the other women. Could she find out why—and then who?

CHAPTER TEN

WITH RENEWED ENERGY, Jo picked up the phone again. The next name on the list was a Margaret Clement. An older woman answered.

"Who's calling my daughter?" she asked in a strained voice.

Jo went through her now-familiar explanation, adding that she'd already talked to several other victims.

For long moments there was a silence on the other end of the line. "Margaret was getting calls like that," the woman finally said.

"Is she a redhead?"

"Yes."

"Was she the maid or matron of honor in a wedding?"

"Yes. Her cousin's."

"Did the calls stop after the wedding?"

"No. They got worse. He was calling every day and saying such horrible things. And she started getting weird packages in the mail. One was a Christmas angel with red hair. Another was an electric bell that started buzzing when she opened it up." Jo's gasp was drowned out by the choked sob on the other end of the line. "Then Margaret disappeared."

Jo's fingers clenched the phone in a death grip.

"Back in August," Mrs. Clement continued. "She

left her office to come home one afternoon, but she never got here. We haven't heard anything from her since.''

"Could she have run away to escape the harassment?" Jo grasped at an explanation.

"She didn't take any of her clothes. And she didn't leave me a note or anything like that.'' Mrs. Clement's voice rose. "Margaret wouldn't have left me to worry like this. I just know she wouldn't. Besides, where would she have gone off to on her own?''

Jo had thought she understood the pattern that was developing. The new information and the anguish in the other woman's voice made her throat contract. "I'm sorry,'' she managed. "What did the police say?''

"They've been looking. So far nothing's turned up.'' The woman hesitated. "Did you say your name was Jo O'Malley? Didn't I read something about you in the Sunday paper?''

"Yes.''

"I couldn't afford to pay you very much. But maybe you could help me find Margaret. She's such a good girl. Do you think he kidnapped her the way he said he was going to?''

"He made specific kidnapping threats?''

"Yes.''

Jo shuddered. "I'm investigating the man, Mrs. Clement. I'll do what I can. Would it be all right if I came out and talked to you in the next few days?''

"Just call and let me know when you want to come.''

Jo put down the phone. Her mouth went dry as she considered the new evidence. She'd been operating under certain assumptions. What if— She was saved from further speculation by a knock on the door. Her head jerked up, and she recognized Abby through the frosted glass.

"What's new?" she asked as Jo unlocked the door.

"Did Cam send you down here to check up on me?"

"Yes. It sounds as if you had quite an evening."

"And Cam told you all about it."

"Of course he did. Sweetie, the man has fallen hard for you. He can't keep from worrying himself sick over what's happening. Do you really blame him for that?"

"No," Jo admitted.

"You're under a lot of stress right now." Abby switched the focus of the conversation. "I'd say it's partly from the harassment and partly because you told yourself no one could take Skip's place—but you're beginning to wonder what a long-term relationship with Cam would be like."

Jo hadn't planned to discuss Cam. Now a sort of confession came tumbling out. "Last night, when he took me home, we made love. It was good, Abby." Jo's voice softened. "Not just good, better than...anything I can remember." The end of the sentence was as revealing for what it didn't say as for the actual words.

Abby crossed the room and put her arms around Jo's shoulder. "You're feeling guilty because being with Cam was warm and satisfying and made you feel cherished."

"How do you know it was like that?"

"I've gotten to know Cam Randolph over the past few months. At first I was sad for him because I thought here's a great guy, with so much to give the right woman—only he'd never found her. Then I started wondering if the right woman might be you."

"So you set things up."

"Not exactly. Steve wanted Cam for his best man. I wanted you for my matron of honor. But let's not get sidetracked from the real issue—your feelings."

"We sure wouldn't want to do that, Dr. Franklin."

"If you were in therapy, I'd make you work through things. But you're not. Jo, I've known you for a long time. I understand how you felt about Skip and what you went through when he died. You don't have anything to feel guilty about now. It's not a question of Cam's taking anyone else's place. It's a question of opening yourself to the possibilities of a new relationship."

"What about all the questions of money and social class? That kind of stuff. I mean, we hardly—"

"If Cameron Randolph had wanted a society girl, believe me he'd have one."

Jo nodded slowly. "You've given me a lot to think about."

"Good."

"Can we talk about my other problem? Unfortunately it's just as pressing."

"Fire away."

"I need some insights into the psychological profile of a guy who goes after redheaded maids of honor."

"Cam didn't say anything about that."

"He doesn't know yet. I finally made a breakthrough with the list of women I got from the telephone company. One of them let me come over and interview her. Abby, it was spooky how much she looked like me. And she'd been the maid of honor in a wedding." Jo went on to summarize the rest of what she'd learned, including the conversation with Margaret Clement's mother.

Abby looked alarmed. "That doesn't fit the usual pattern of a phone harasser."

"Or of a guy that was in the state pen until a couple of weeks ago—not when the records I have from the phone company go back two or three years."

"How do you think the wedding angle figures in?" Abby asked.

"Well, I'm not the psychologist here. But if I had to make a quick guess off the top of my head, I'd say that a redheaded woman rejected the guy who's been calling and maybe married someone else, and now he's getting even."

"And the caller is the same one who hit you with the EMP box and rigged your television sets."

"He told me he was."

"Oh, Jo. I hate to think that being in my wedding is putting you in danger."

"We still don't know for sure what's going on. Maybe Eddie knows about the wedding guy and is imitating his M.O."

Abby looked doubtful.

"Do you have any thoughts on handling the creep if he shows up in person?"

"I could tell you more if I heard the tapes."

"Two of them are still in my desk drawer." Jo pulled them out and popped one into the recorder. As she played the messages for Abby, she gritted her teeth and tried to evaluate them in light of the conversations she'd had with the psychologist.

"That man is seriously disturbed. He's not just trying to get a rise out of you with the sexual content. He's trying to terrorize you," Abby whispered when the second message had run its course.

"He's doing a pretty good job. What do you—uh—think about that brass bed? Didn't he make it sound kind of like a sacrificial altar?"

"That's stretching things."

Before she lost her nerve, Jo forced herself to spell out the terrible thoughts that had been in the back of her mind since she'd talked to Mrs. Clements. "He didn't just tell me about it. You know, I'm pretty sure that's what was flashing on the TV screen last night. Quick glimpses of a woman who looked a lot like me. Strapped down and helpless. In the early scenes she was wearing a long, white dress, then she was naked. I—I keep thinking," Jo gulped and made herself continue. "Maybe it was Margaret Clement. Maybe he was actually going through some kind of ritual murder with her. And he filmed it."

Abby's face had drained of color. She stared at her friend. "Oh, Jo—"

"I could be right, couldn't I?"

Abby nodded slowly.

"So if I end up in his clutches, it would probably be a good idea to stay off that bed."

"You're not going to end up in his clutches."

"What if I do—"

"Yes. Stay away from the bed."

BY THE TIME Detective Hamill came to collect the tapes, Jo was in control of her emotions. As if she were talking about any old investigation, she filled him in on what she'd discovered.

He was impressed with her detective work. "We could use you downtown."

"Don't count on it."

"I'll go back and pull the files on those cases to see how it fits in with the Eddie Cahill stuff."

"I'll get the names of the caterers and other service people each of the wedding parties used. Maybe there will be a name or address from their employee lists that will be some kind of link."

"And we'll keep each other up-to-date on our progress," Hamill added.

By the time Cam called at four to say he was coming back, Jo was deep into information gathering. She hadn't found out anything startling. But doing the work gave her the feeling that she was accomplishing something.

When Cam explained in a disgusted voice that the stakeout hadn't turned up anything, she was quick to reassure him that the idea had been worth trying.

"I debugged your Honda," he said, when he came into the office. "Then I put the transmitter in the garage across the street and stashed your car at Abby's apartment building." He stopped abruptly before continuing in a less confident voice. "If you wanted, you could see how Laura feels about a houseguest. I mean, if we made sure you weren't being followed, there wouldn't be any way he'd know you were there."

Cam wasn't pressing. He was giving her choices. That and the conversation she'd had with Abby tipped the balance.

Jo closed the file she'd been trying to make some notes in. "I'd rather go home with you," she said.

"I was hoping you would. Do you want to stop at your house and get some more clothes?"

For tomorrow or the next couple of weeks, Jo wondered.

As they drove up Charles Street, she told him about

her new discoveries. His head snapped toward her when she came to the part about the redheads and the bridesmaids. "So maybe this isn't what we thought at all."

"I don't know how the new stuff fits in." Unconsciously she pulled her trench coat more tightly around her slender body, as if the fabric could protect her from more than the elements. "Do you think it's possible that two different people are involved?"

"God, Jo. I hope not."

"Then what?"

"We'll figure it out. Meanwhile, we'll keep you safe."

At her house she breathed silent thanks when she saw that the answering machine didn't have any messages. Then her mind reevaluated the implications. Laughing Boy knew everything else. Maybe he hadn't called because he knew she wasn't going to be home.

Wanting to spend as little time in the house as possible, she grabbed some clothes out of the closet and raided a few drawers. Then Cam was ushering her back out to the car.

He didn't drive straight to his place, and she knew he was making sure they weren't being followed. The way he handled the Lotus, only a stunt driver could have kept up with him.

Fifteen minutes later they pulled up in front of his door. Knowing that Cam's house was protected by every security device that was on the market or still in the development stages gave Jo a profound sense of well-being. Or maybe it was just being with Cam.

She wondered if he was feeling something similar. Once he'd closed the front door, he pulled her into his arms. At first it was enough to simply hold each other close. But as they stood in the hall, the feeling of comfort escalated quickly into sexual awareness.

They exchanged hot, hungry kisses. His hands were tracking up her back when they stopped abruptly. "When I get you in my arms, it's hard to remember about more mundane things."

"Like what?"

"Dinner, for instance."

"Oh, yeah. Dinner."

"I've got steaks, stuffed potatoes and green beans in the refrigerator," he told her. "So we don't have to go out to the store."

"Steak and potatoes," she said in a slightly dazed voice as she followed him down the hall to the kitchen.

Jo fixed the vegetables while Cam put the steaks on an indoor grill.

"We'll eat in the den," he said as he began to put plates and cutlery on a large tray.

He led the way into a comfortable room with sofas, a fireplace, and a thick shaggy rug. To her surprise, he set the food on a glass coffee table and pulled pillows off the couch. Then he used the built-in gas jets to start the wood in the fireplace. The dry logs were blazing in moments.

"Neat trick," Jo observed as he turned off the gas and let the wood take over. She wondered if she'd ever get used to that kind of casual luxury.

"I wish I had invented it," Cam remarked half seriously.

Jo, who had forgotten to eat lunch, tackled the food. "You grill a mean steak, Randolph. You're handier in the kitchen than you'd let on," she observed.

"It's just a basic bachelor skill."

"Before I married Skip he survived on meatball subs and frozen entrées. Then when we used to come home from work together, I was the one who had to get dinner on the table."

"Did you resent having to do all the cooking?"

"No. I grew up in a family that was pretty traditional. The women did the cooking and the cleaning. Of course, if Skip had offered to fix dinner once in a while, I wouldn't have turned him down."

She looked at Cam to judge his reaction. Apparently their relationship had progressed to the point where she could mention her late husband without the two of them automatically getting uptight.

"How about some dinner music?" Cam asked as he slid open a panel in the side of the table.

"Sure."

Jo expected Chopin or Mozart. Instead when the eight-speaker system sprang to life, it delivered a Kenny Rogers ballad about two teenagers whose love finally triumphed over the long arm of the law.

"I like Kenny Rogers."

"I thought you might."

"If you'd rather hear something else—"

"I've got eclectic musical tastes." Pressing some buttons, he adjusted the speakers. "The system can reproduce any size effects from a large concert hall to a small cabaret. What's your choice?"

She closed her eyes for a minute. "Let's pretend we've got lawn seating at Oregon Ridge."

He laughed. "You're a cheap date." When he held out his arms, she nestled against him as they listened to the rest of the song.

The smile curving her lips froze as the phone rang.

Jo's eyes riveted to the brass telephone on the end table. Cam followed her gaze. "It's all right. He's not going to call you here."

She nodded tightly.

Cam picked up the receiver. It was a business discussion, and her host was obviously uncomfortable talking in front of Jo.

"I'll clean up while you're busy," she mouthed.

He nodded. "Sorry."

Jo loaded the tray. In the kitchen, she put the trash in the compactor, rinsed the dishes and stacked them in the dishwasher. Cam didn't appear. To give him some more time, she made coffee. When she brought it in, he was just putting down the phone. There was a scowl on his face.

She set the coffee cups down. "Problems?"

"Nothing that can't be straightened out. I've got Phil Mercer working on it."

Instinct told her he was being evasive. "You didn't get to work at all today, did you?"

"No." He reached up and pulled her down beside him onto the thick rug.

"Is there anything I can do to help?"

"Yes."

His mouth slanted over hers with a kiss that should have driven every coherent thought out of her mind. When he lifted his head, she gave it one more try. "Don't get your priorities screwed up because of me."

"Honey, I'm not. I don't think I've ever had my priorities in better order."

He lowered her to her back, trapping her body between his hard length and the plush rug. The feelings that had been simmering between them during dinner came to a full, rolling boil.

She could come to no harm when she was in his arms. The knowledge was as liberating as it was arousing.

With primitive urgency they began to explore each other's bodies, twisting and arching together with the need to get closer and closer still. If there was a note of desperation in Cam's lovemaking, Jo didn't question its source.

SOMETIME during the evening they moved upstairs to Cam's bedroom. When Jo woke up at seven in the morning, she was naked with the covers down around her waist, and Cam was lying on his side, his gray gaze locked on her.

She reached down to drag up the sheet, but he pulled her back into a tight embrace.

"I thought guys slowed down after thirty."

"You do potent things to my hormones. Or maybe it's because I'm falling in love with you."

Her eyes flew open. "Are you teasing me?"

"I wouldn't tease you about something like that."

"Oh, Cam—I—don't know what to say."

"I'll let you get used to the idea."

He began to kiss her and touch her once more. Now there was a tenderness in his lovemaking that made her heart ache to be able to return his declaration. But it was too soon. She had to know that she wasn't just turning to him in a crisis. She had to know her feelings would stand the test of time, because if she ever got married again, it was going to be for keeps.

He seemed to sense her mood as she got dressed later and followed him downstairs. As they made breakfast, she saw his pragmatic, empirical persona slip back into place.

"I have to put in an appearance at Randolph Enterprises," he told her.

"You can't spend all your time chaperoning me."

"There's another car in the garage. A BMW. Why don't you drive that down to Light Street, and I'll meet you for lunch."

"If you can't get away, I'll understand."

"I'll get away."

"Do you mind if I make a few phone calls here? It's early enough so I might be able to catch some of the women who weren't home yesterday."

"Of course not."

Before Cam left, he gave her the keys to the car and the house and showed her how to set the security system—which was much more elaborate than hers. Then he gave her a bear hug. "Take care of yourself."

"I will," she promised.

Jo decided to use the phone in the den. As she sat down at Cam's desk, she was amused to note that all his mail was sorted into labeled cubbyholes. At least if she married him, he'd organize the clutter that swirled around her. Or would the disorganization drive him bananas?

She smiled, suddenly optimistic that they'd somehow work things out.

Just as she was reaching for the phone, it rang. Jo tensed. Until this was over, she was going to be suspicious of all incoming calls, she acknowledged. But it could be Cam with something he'd forgotten to tell her.

"Hello?"

"Angel face! Did you think you could hide from me?"

Her heart started to pound and she almost slammed the receiver back into the cradle. Then she realized Laughing Boy was handing her an opportunity. This was the first time she'd talked to him since she'd interviewed some of his other victims. "How did you get this number?" she asked, hoping her voice sounded calm.

"I have my ways."

"I've talked to some of the other women you've bothered."

He laughed. "So?"

"What have you got against redheads?"

"Wouldn't you like to know?"

His mood was different, Jo noted. He wasn't bombarding her with sexual innuendos. This time, even through the electronic filter, she detected a note of tension. Good. Maybe he was worried because she'd gotten somewhere with the phone company.

"I know something you don't," he taunted.

"What?"

"Something about Randolph."

Despite her resolve not to let him get to her, she clutched the receiver. "Cam?"

"There are some very interesting things your boyfriend would rather you not know."

"Are you going to tell me what they are?"

"No. I think it would be more fun for you to find out by yourself, miss hotshot detective. But I'll give you a hint to get you started. Go back to those old files of your husband's. The ones involving cases he didn't talk to you about."

"Which case?"

"Oh, I'm sure you'll figure it out." Before Jo could ask another question, the line went dead, and she was left with white knuckles clutched around the receiver. What possible connection could there be between Cam and one of Skip's cases?

Nothing! she told herself firmly. The jerk was just trying to rattle her. But now she had to crush the seed of doubt he'd planted—before it took root and started poisoning her mind. Instead of making phone calls to the other women on the list, she'd better go right to the office and check back through the files.

On her way to the garage, however, Jo hesitated for a moment. Laughing Boy had called and maneuvered her into checking her files. Was he outside somewhere waiting for her to leave Cam's house? Maybe this was just a ploy to get her out in the open where he could pounce. Cautiously she looked out both the downstairs and upstairs windows. As far as she could see, no one was lurking around. If he were around the corner, Cam's BMW could certainly outrun just about anything he had.

Her prediction about the car proved correct. It was fast and powerful and a joy to drive. After whipping around several blocks, Jo was sure no one was following her. But as she approached the garage on Light Street, she began to tense up again. Her tormentor knew where she was going. He didn't have to follow her to the office to scoop her up.

Jo circled the block, once more looking for suspicious cars or pedestrians. On a downtown street, it was difficult to determine whether the panhandler on the corner was collecting money for his next bottle of Wild Turkey or watching for her.

She hesitated at the entrance to the garage where she

usually parked. Then instead of driving inside, she pulled up in the loading zone in back of 43 Light Street. From there it was only a few steps inside the building. In the basement she found Lou and asked if he'd mind parking the car. He was quick to oblige.

"I wish they'd catch the guy who's botherin' you," he muttered.

"They will," Jo assured him. As she took the elevator up, she sagged back against the wall and closed her eyes. Over the years she'd worked for a number of women who were being harassed or threatened. She'd been sympathetic, but she'd never really understood the sense of defenselessness—the growing terror as you lost control of your life. Now she did.

As she walked down the hall to the office, a man stepped out of the shadows. Jo stopped short, her heart in her throat. She'd been so careful, and he was already in the building waiting for her! She was about to turn and dash for the stairs when he called her name.

"Ms. O'Malley. Wait. It's Detective Hamill."

"I'm sorry, I thought—"

"I didn't mean to startle you."

"I guess I'm just jumpy this morning."

"I called you, but you must have left Randolph's house. So I took a chance on intercepting you here."

The grim set of his mouth and the tone of his voice put her on guard. "Something's happened."

"Yes. Can we go inside your office?"

As Jo unlocked the door and flipped on the lights, she felt her stomach clench. Turning to face him, she steeled herself for something unpleasant.

"We found Eddie Cahill's ex-wife early this morning. There's no way to put a good face on this, so I'll just give it to you straight. She was beaten and murdered."

CHAPTER ELEVEN

WITH ALL THE FOCUS on redheads and weddings, Jo hadn't been thinking much about Eddie Cahill's wife. News of her death was the last thing Jo had been prepared to hear.

A gasp escaped her lips. "Oh, poor Karen." Suddenly she knew her legs wouldn't support her. Before she could embarrass herself by falling on her face, she dropped into one of the visitor's chairs opposite the desk. Hamill brought her a drink of water from the cooler, and she sipped gratefully.

"I know it's a shock."

"I suppose Eddie did it."

"There's no hard evidence yet."

"What about Jennifer Stark? Is she okay?"

"The prosecuting attorney? I understand she's taken an extended leave of absence."

"Yeah." Jo sat numbly clutching her paper cup while the officer told her what they knew about the murder. Karen had been reported missing by her mother the night before. Under the circumstances, the department had mounted an extensive search. Her partially clothed body had been found near Loch Raven reservoir by a man walking his doberman that morning. "The dog pulled the guy off the path and into the underbrush," Hamill said. "There wasn't much attempt to hide the body. It was almost as if the murderer wanted it to be found."

"Where does that leave me?" Jo asked.

"We can keep a tail on you for a few days, and we'll certainly increase the patrols near your home and office and Mr. Randolph's town house. I'd also like to suggest putting a decoy in your house—a policewoman with your general physical characteristics."

That wasn't Jo's usual style, but she agreed.

"You didn't think Cahill was going to make good on his threats, did you?" she asked.

Hamill looked embarrassed. "You know what kind of constraints we operate under. When he wasn't recaptured immediately, there was no way we could put you or his ex-wife under indefinite surveillance."

Jo nodded. That was what she'd told Cam.

"Do you have an extra key to your house?" Hamill asked.

Jo produced one from her desk drawer. "I'll get a few more things I need this afternoon. Then the place is all yours."

Hamill's visit left Jo feeling strangely lethargic—as if she hadn't slept in days and couldn't summon the energy to cross the room. Partly, she acknowledged, it was guilt. Last year she was the one who'd told Karen Cahill that she was going to have to go to the D.A. with the information about her husband's drug dealing. Now he'd killed her.

On the other hand, it was Karen who had come to her with the request for some ammunition she could use in a divorce case. At the moment, the circular reasoning was too much for Jo. Finally she forced herself to get out of the chair and go over to the large storage closet where she'd stuffed Skip's out-of-date records.

They were stacked in cardboard boxes, and the thought of shuffling through all of them made her even more weary. But she forced herself to start the task.

It was too much trouble to carry the boxes to her desk. Instead she heaped them in a semicircle on the floor, sat down in the middle, and began to dig through them.

It didn't take long before she began to get interested in the project—particularly after she came across the first case she and Skip had worked on together. They'd both posed as street people and staked out Fells Point to catch the runaway daughter of an old Baltimore family.

There were other cases, many of which she'd worked on. Finally she came across a box that contained folders Skip had kept to himself. Some of the assignments had been before she'd come to work for him. Despite her protests, others had been jobs he'd considered too dangerous to involve his wife. And a few had been situations where clients had insisted on strict confidentiality.

As Jo thumbed through the last two categories, her eyes bounced off one of the names, and she stopped dead. Where her fingers touched the manila folder, they seemed to burn. The tab read Randolph Enterprises. Cam certainly hadn't mentioned anything about that.

With a feeling of dread, she pulled the file from the box and began to read Skip's carefully penned notes.

Morgan Randolph, Cam's father, had hired Skip to find out who was responsible for a series of disturbing incidents. Randolph products still in development were showing up in the commercial lines of competitors. That must be the industrial espionage episode Cam had told her about, Jo thought, with a little sigh of relief. He hadn't tried to hide that from her when she'd asked.

Yet he hadn't said a word about Skip being on the case. Hadn't he known?

She got her answer several pages down, when she found a carbon of a letter from Skip to Cam requesting a list of compromised projects. His detailed reply was clipped to the carbon. Jo leaned back against the wall.

So Cam *had* dealt with Skip. But most of her husband's contacts had probably been with the father. Perhaps Cam hadn't remembered the detective's name.

With shaky fingers, she turned more pages. There was also a memo from Cam's older brother Collin Randolph. Since he was in charge of personnel, he had listed employees he thought Skip ought to check. From Skip's subsequent reports, it appeared that none of those investigations had panned out.

Reading between the lines, Jo gathered that the elder Randolph had started pressing for results. Skip's next tack had been a background check on the members of the Randolph family. Jo breathed a sigh of relief when she saw that there was nothing questionable in Cam's background. About his only indiscretion had been to get drunk at a couple of parties in his freshman year at Dartmouth.

The next report was on Collin. He'd also been a model college student. Interestingly, he'd had hardly any social life when he'd lived in the dorm at Brown. Former classmates had spoken of him as not being particularly friendly. Things had changed when he'd come back to Baltimore to work in the family company. Sporadically at first and then on a regular basis, he'd begun frequenting gay bars. Jo paused as she digested that bit of information. According to Skip, Collin had hidden his homosexuality from his family, even when he'd developed relationships with several men who became more than casual lovers.

Skip had handled the revelations discreetly. He'd quietly gone to the older Randolph brother with the information and asked if there was anybody who might be taking advantage of him because they knew about his secret life. Collin had responded in a very flat, emotionless manner and had assured Skip that his private life would not put the company in jeopardy. Two days later, he had stuck a pistol in his mouth and pulled the trigger.

Jo's hands clenched the edge of the paper. How tragic. No wonder Cam hadn't wanted to talk about the case. It had inadvertently led to his brother's death.

She almost put the file away. But there were a few sheets of paper left. Under an obituary in the *Baltimore Sun* was an official letter from Morgan dismissing Skip from the case along with payment of $2,000 to cover his expenses to date.

The final entry in the file was the summary of a conversation Skip had had with Cameron Randolph a month later. Morgan Randolph had just died of a heart attack. An angry Cam had called to accuse Skip of destroying the family. According to Cam, Skip hadn't been asked to investigate family members. Furthermore, the dirt he'd dug up had driven Collin to suicide, and their father had never recovered from the shock of his son's death. Which meant that he was responsible for not just one but two deaths. Skip's notes added that Cam had threatened to put him out of business.

Jo closed the file and let her head flop back against the wall, fighting the sick feeling that had begun to churn in her stomach. Cam had never mentioned that he'd known Skip. But they'd certainly been acquainted. More to the point, he'd worked himself up into an irrational hatred for her husband. Now she thought back over all the subtle and not so subtle signals Cam had given off when Skip's name had entered the conversation. She'd assumed Cam was just jealous because she'd been married before. Viewed in this new light, Cam's behavior suggested open hostility to Skip. Just where did that leave her?

With fingers that felt as if they'd been numbed in an ice storm, she shuffled through the papers again, scanning disjointed paragraphs and sentences, somehow hoping that things would look different on a second reading. As she was skimming the paragraph on Collin's college career, a knock at the door made her jump. Her head jerked up. Through the glass she recognized a familiar silhouette.

When she got up and unlocked the door, there was a smile on Cam's lips. It quickly faded when he saw the grim expression on her face.

"What happened?"

She considered the question for several heartbeats. "Well, for starters, it looks like Eddie Cahill made good his threats against Karen. She was beaten and murdered."

"Oh, Jo— Honey, I'm sorry." He moved to fold her into his arms but she evaded his embrace. "What else is wrong?"

"I have the feeling you can figure it out if you really try."

He looked from her to the stacks of boxes and open folder on the floor. "You were going back through

Skip's old files.'' On the surface his voice was flat but Jo could hear the edge of tension he was trying to control.

"And I've been reading his notes on the industrial espionage at Randolph Enterprises. Why didn't you tell me the whole story when we had our frank little discussion about the EMP?''

"It wasn't relevant.''

"Not relevant! Sheez!'' Jo stamped her foot, paced to the window and then whirled back toward him. "What wasn't relevant? That you blamed my husband for your brother's death—and your father's? Or that you were just getting close to me so you could figure out a way to put me out of business—the way you threatened to do with Skip?''

He winced as he faced her across the room. "I'd decided you didn't have anything to do with that.''

"From your investigations of me, you mean?''

"Yes. And personal observation.''

"How magnanimous of you.''

"Okay, I admit it. Meeting you brought it all back.'' He swallowed convulsively. "All the sorrow and all the anger. Right after I realized who you were, I decided to see what I could find out about you—with some vague idea of settling the score.''

She muttered something unladylike under her breath and folded her arms across her chest.

"Jo, I swear,'' he continued, "as I started getting to know you, I felt horrible about our relationship not being honest. Then when I realized that you were more important to me than anything that had happened in the past, I just wanted to keep from destroying what was developing between us.''

"Did you think I wasn't going to find out about your letter to Skip?"

"I was going to tell you—later."

"Sheez!"

"I'm not very good at this sort of thing."

"You're right about that."

"Jo, please—"

She shook her head before he could finish the sentence. "It's pretty hard for me to operate on an open, honest level with someone who isn't being open and honest with me." Her eyes drilled into him.

The accusing look on her face would have made a lesser man drop his gaze. Cam held his ground. After several silent moments, it was Jo who felt too uncomfortable to continue the standoff. She looked away.

"Dishonesty isn't my strong suit," Cam said. "I knew I'd made a mistake. I was trying to work my way out of it—without losing you."

"Do you still think Skip was responsible for your brother's death? And your father's?"

"Jo, I—"

"Do you?"

"He wasn't authorized to go digging into our family."

"What do you mean he wasn't authorized? Your father hired him to find out who was stealing Randolph product designs, and he was conducting the investigation according to his best judgment. He was authorized to do anything he needed to do to get the job done. He hadn't turned up anything on the employees. The next logical step was to see if someone in the family was responsible."

"He should have cleared that with my father."

"What if your father was the one involved?"

"My father hired him, for God sakes."

"Weirder things have happened in this business. People torching their own warehouses to get the insurance money. Clients hiring a private investigator and laying a trail of clues leading to someone else."

"My father wouldn't have done that."

"Then let's go back to the facts and try to figure out what did happen. I gather from our previous conversation that the espionage stopped after your brother's death. That suggests that it did have something to do with him. Maybe one of his gay friends had threatened to go to your father if Collin didn't cooperate. Collin knew the revelation would crush your father, so he complied."

"That's preposterous. I won't have you besmirching my brother's memory."

"I'm drawing logical conclusions from the information in that file. You ought to understand that. You're big on logic, aren't you?"

He glared at her.

"Your father didn't let Skip continue the investigation after Collin died. Perhaps if he had, we wouldn't be standing here making guesses about what caused the information leak at Randolph Enterprises."

"You're a lot like Skip, aren't you?"

"If you mean logical, dependable, persistent, fair-minded, yes."

"Fair-minded!"

"A private investigator has to put personal biases aside when he takes on a case."

"And he or she doesn't care about who gets hurt as a result of the investigation," Cam grated.

"Of course we do. But facts are facts."

"Facts are facts," he repeated sarcastically.

"And while we're on that subject, what was it that you were trying to hide from me last night when Phil Mercer called? Or were you even talking to Mr. Mercer?"

"Certainly I was talking to Mercer. He was following up on an assignment I gave him. I was trying to find out how someone could have gotten into your house to screw around with your television set when your Randolph Enterprises security system was on."

"And?"

"I'm still working on it," he clipped out.

"Why didn't you want to tell me about it?"

"I was upset about the system failure and wanted to wait until I had some answers."

"But you didn't trust me enough to get my input."

"Trust wasn't the issue."

"Don't you think I have a right to be angry with you? And I'm not talking about the damn security system. It's the business with Skip."

"Yes. You have the right to be angry," he admitted in a low voice.

"At least we've reached a point of agreement."

Cam sighed. "Jo, I think we're both too upset to be having a rational discussion." He waited for some sign that might contradict the statement. When it wasn't forthcoming, he walked slowly toward the door.

Anger and Jo's need to defend Skip had kept her going during the argument. Now her throat was too raw with unshed tears to call him back. As he carefully closed the door, they welled up in her eyes. But the emotional release gave her no comfort. Deep inside she ached from a mixture of outrage, hurt and sadness.

THE MAN panhandling on the street corner across from 43 Light Street glanced up with interest as Cameron Randolph stalked out of the building. The defeated look on the inventor's face brought him an immense surge of pleasure. Jo had checked her late husband's files and discovered that mister rich-and-powerful Randolph wasn't such a nice guy after all.

He turned his head toward the rough brick wall and hunched his shoulder as if he were shielding his body from the wind. He was really hiding the smirk that had plastered itself across his features. He'd won a major victory this afternoon. He'd pried Jo O'Malley away from that smart bastard. It was only a matter of time before he got the rest of what he wanted.

He spotted a plainclothes policeman also dressed like a panhandler working the other end of the block across from Ms. O'Malley's building. The irony didn't escape him and he couldn't hold back a little giggle.

He wasn't stupid enough to try to scoop Denise up now when the heat was on.

He blinked and felt a momentary wave of confusion. Denise. No, this one was named Jo O'Malley. Or was she Denise? She looked like angelic little Denise. But she wasn't going to get the chance to hurt him the way Denise had. This time he was the one who was going to call the shots.

He wanted her to know how much power he had over her. Then he'd show her his brass bed in the wedding chapel.

OVER THE NEXT FEW WEEKS, Jo's life evolved into a strange motif. She felt as if she were simply going through the motions of living—without any rhyme or reason to her existence. Her further attempts to find out who had made the phone calls to the other women turned up nothing. Since she was barely capable of functioning, she wasn't surprised.

If the period before Abby's wedding was marked by anything for her, it was chiefly the lack of any regular routine. Jo varied the time at which she left for the office and when she came home. She wore a changing array of disguises that would have done central casting proud. She used the back entrance to 43 Light Street as often as the front. She rented a series of cars—never driving one for more than a couple of days. Some afternoons she gathered up a handful of the files she'd need and tried to work from one of her temporary homes. Devising and carrying out the precautions became a game on which she could focus. It was better than dwelling on the disappointment of discovering that the future she'd dared to imagine with Cameron Randolph was just a stupid fantasy.

As soon as Laura heard about what had happened, she quickly invited Jo to stay with her. Jo gratefully accepted—on condition that she minimize any danger to her friend by making arrangements at the last minute and never over the phone. She also found she could count on a warm support group ready to help her in any way they could. Noel Emery, Laura's secretary, and Abby's mother also volunteered to put her up. So Jo bounced between the extremes of a lumpy sofa bed in Noel's tiny living room and a plush suite in the Franklin mansion.

There were still wedding activities at which her presence would have been expected. But everybody understood that Jo could be in danger, which turned out to be the perfect excuse for ducking out. She skipped the mixed groups where Cam would be on the scene and only attended a couple of the showers and luncheons that were just for the female contingent. And she avoided getting into any serious discussions with Abby.

But the Wednesday before the wedding, Abby showed up at Jo's office with a bag from the deli.

"I brought us some lunch," she announced. "A hamburger and French fries for you and chicken salad with sprouts for me."

"Thanks."

"I need the company. Every time I'm alone, I start getting the jitters," the bride-to-be admitted.

"You?"

Abby unwrapped a straw and twirled it between her fingers. "No matter how much you think you love someone, getting married is a big step."

"Yeah."

"I missed you at the Stacys' reception last night."

Jo slowly chewed a bite of hamburger. "You know why I wasn't there."

"For two reasons. One of them is certainly valid. But you can't keep avoiding Cam."

"Sure I can."

"What about the rehearsal dinner Friday?"

"I can skip the dinner and just come to the walkthrough."

"Jo, please."

The detective wadded her hamburger wrapper into a ball and pitched it at the trash can. It bounced off the edge and landed on the floor. "I don't think you have the jitters. I think you came up here with lunch so we could talk about how stupid I've been acting."

"Do you think you've been acting stupid?"

"No, Dr. Franklin. I think I'm being perfectly realistic about my nonrelationship with Cameron Randolph. It's over."

The psychologist sighed. "It's kind of a conflict of interest counseling both you and Cam. That's why I haven't brought up the heated conversation that ended with you ordering him out of your office."

"Is that what he told you? Well, I didn't order him out of the office. He was the one who said he was going to leave."

"Just seeing if I could get a rise out of you. Your emotions have been as flat as a loaf of pita bread lately."

Jo sat up straighter in her chair. "Just what the hell did Cameron Randolph say to you?"

"Do I detect a tiny spark of interest in your question?"

"No. All right, yes."

"If Cam were a patient, I'd have to consider the things he told me confidential."

"He's a friend."

"A good friend," Abby agreed. "He's also a man whose mother died when he was a little boy. His father and his older brother raised him. How do you think it made him feel when one of them committed suicide and the other had a fatal heart attack within a matter of weeks?"

Jo dragged a cold French fry through the catsup and laid it back on the paper plate. "Bad," she murmured without raising her head.

"Devastated is more like it. The loss of his brother

and his father one right after the other was the worst thing that ever happened to him—and that was coupled with the shock of finding out that the brother he loved had been hiding a secret life from his family.''

Jo's whole body was charged with tension, but the only sign was in the bloodless caps of her knuckles where she'd clenched her fingers.

''He had to find a way to deal with it,'' Abby continued. ''Unfortunately part of his coping mechanism was looking for someone to blame.''

''Too bad it was Skip. And me.'' Jo didn't allow her voice to reflect her churning emotions.

''Over the past few weeks he's had time to think about his own motivations—and about how his behavior affected your relationship.''

''He hasn't called to share his insights with me.''

''He's terrified to face you.''

Jo laughed mirthlessly.

In contrast, her friend continued in a calm voice. ''One thing about a man like Cam, when he chooses a course of action, it's hard to see things any differently. As he got to know you, the relationship cast a whole bunch of earlier assumptions he'd made in doubt. He had a terrible time dealing with that.''

''If he'd come clean with me up-front, it would have been a lot better.''

''Would it? Can you honestly picture him calling you up the morning after my parents' party and telling you he blamed Skip for the major tragedy in his life?''

Put that way, the suggestion was ludicrous, Jo admitted.

''Even if he'd waited until he knew you a little better,

with your hot temper and your sense of loyalty to Skip, you would have given him the heave-ho.''

Jo nodded slowly. "You're probably right. But there had to be some better way than what he did."

"Hindsight is wonderful, isn't it?"

Jo flushed.

"There's no point in speculating on what might have happened," Abby continued. "Now that you've both had a chance to cool down, why don't you talk about it? A lot of major misunderstandings between people could be cleared up if they'd just sit down and have a sensible conversation."

"I said some things he didn't want to hear."

"He said things you didn't want to hear."

"Yeah. Like about Skip."

"Perhaps you made him realize that his feelings toward Skip were a defense mechanism," Abby said gently.

"I did?"

"The only way you'll find out for sure is to talk to him about it," Abby reiterated.

Jo was silent for a moment. Finally, she took a deep breath. "You think he—uh—that he still—?"

"Yes." Abby's voice was full of encouragement.

"He hurt me—with the stuff he said about Skip."

"But how does he make you feel otherwise?"

"What if it was all wishful thinking on my part?"

"Do you really believe that?"

"Abby, I know it doesn't make perfect sense, but in a way, after Skip died, I felt like he'd let me down. I mean, I'd opened up and let myself lean on him. Then he pulled the rug out from under me." She looked pleadingly at her friend.

"A lot of people feel that way when a loved one dies."

Jo sighed. "I felt guilty about that for a long time. And then, you know, I was just getting to the point where I thought I could take a chance on Cam..."

"Sometimes you have to take a chance to get what you want."

The two women ate in silence for several minutes, neither one of them making much progress with the meal. Finally Abby wrapped up her half-eaten sandwich and stood up. "I'd better get back to my office. I've got a patient coming at one o'clock."

"Thanks for lunch. And for...provoking me."

Abby grinned. "No charge."

After her friend left, Jo sat staring out the window at the office building across the alley. For the first time in weeks, she felt the dark cloud that had been hovering over her begin to lift. She had only thought about certain parts of that last angry conversation with Cam. Now she allowed herself to remember the look on his face and some of the things he'd said. He'd talked about sorrow and anger, but she hadn't let herself react to the pain in his voice. When he'd said he'd been afraid of losing her, she'd been thinking that he already had.

Now she couldn't help wondering what it would be like to see him again. The more she wondered, the more she felt something tender and protective inside her chest swell with hope.

Abby had said you had to take risks to get what you wanted. Wasn't everything in life a risk?

What was the worst thing that could happen, she asked herself. That she and Cam couldn't work things out. Well, Abby had made her see one thing pretty clearly: they didn't have a chance the way things stood.

The wedding rehearsal would be neutral territory. Maybe if he didn't make the first move, she would.

THE NEXT EVENING as she stood before the ornately carved cheval glass in Laura's guest room, Jo surveyed her appearance with more interest than she'd shown in weeks. The strain of hiding and of being estranged from Cam had both taken their toll. She'd lost weight, and her face was pale. She'd compensated with a bit more makeup than she usually used. Earlier that afternoon she'd driven her rental car out to Columbia and found a silk shift at Woodies that helped camouflage her thin figure.

Dinner was in a private room upstairs at the Brass Elephant, an elegant restaurant in a restored town house on Charles Street. Its unusual name came from the brass fixtures throughout the building that were shaped like elephant heads. Steve had been pleased with the choice of location because he knew Abby was providing a little reminder of his years in India. The meal would be followed by a walk-through at the Greenspring Valley Church where Abby and Steve were getting married.

To minimize the risks to Jo, Abby had waited until the last minute to make firm arrangements for the party. It was understood that Jo and Laura would arrive a bit after the stated dinner hour and slip in a back door of the restaurant. Jo wasn't thinking about security as she and Laura drove down to Charles Street. In fact, she could hardly contain the keen feeling of anticipation that had been building ever since she'd talked to Abby that afternoon.

Her steps were quick as she hurried toward the little dining room several steps ahead of Laura. When she walked through the archway, she noticed two things almost simultaneously. The bride-to-be was looking anxiously toward the door. And Cameron Randolph was conspicuously absent from among the assembled members of the wedding party.

CHAPTER TWELVE

THE MINUTE ABBY spotted the maid of honor, she came rushing forward. "Oh, Jo, I'm so sorry. He called a few minutes ago to say he wouldn't be here." There was no need to name the man they were talking about.

Jo tried to keep the disappointment off her face.

Abby squeezed her hand. "I don't know what to say. I shouldn't have gotten your hopes up."

"It's not your fault." Jo turned quickly away toward the bar that had been set up in the corner. She didn't really want anything to drink. Still, she needed a few minutes to pull herself together before she faced the happy throng assembled to honor Steve and Abby.

Cam didn't show up for the actual rehearsal, either. Jo found herself playing her matron of honor role opposite an empty spot on the stone floor.

It was no less empty than the hollow that had opened up inside her chest. She'd gotten her hopes up, and they'd been dashed.

She went through the rehearsal in a daze, unaware that her friends had thrown a sort of protective net around her—both physically and emotionally.

But the man standing in the shadows at the back of the church with neck rigid and jaw clenched was very aware of what was happening.

Denise...

Jo O'Malley...

Denise...

They were together in church again.

The first time he'd seen her standing under the stained-glass windows, it was like a light from heaven had streamed in on both of them.

Watching her now, the feeling came back, strong and sure the way it had been in the beginning. He needed her again.

The craving to have her with him once more almost choked him, almost choked off all rational thought. Sudden energy surged through his body, and he almost started up the aisle. Then at the last minute, he caught himself. Not now when everybody was watching. But soon. He had the power. And when he chose to use it, no one could stand in his way.

IT WAS STRANGE, Jo thought as she stood in front of the inexpensive door mirror in Noel's hallway, how different she felt this morning. The dime-store looking glass reflected back a slightly distorted image, elongating the middle of her body as if to accent her recently acquired gauntness.

She tugged at her skirt. But that didn't make it hang any better over her bony hips. Two months ago when Abby had selected the elaborate blue velvet gown, Jo had simply felt overdressed in the rich creation. Now she was going to feel like an out-and-out fool walking down the aisle.

Except that no one was going to be looking at her, she told herself. They'd all be focused on Steve and Abby. Maybe she could even slip away right after the receiving line and come back here to lick her wounds.

She hadn't slept much. She hadn't been able to choke down more than a cup of weak tea for breakfast. And she hadn't been able to get her mind off Cameron Randolph.

After that talk with Abby, she'd been stupid enough to be optimistic. Well, Abby had made a mistake in her analysis of Cam. Because she was in love and getting married, she'd blithely assumed that the rest of the couples in the world would work out their problems.

She made an effort to bring her mind back to the wedding. At least there was one thing to look forward to. Whoever was making calls to redheaded maids of honor almost always stopped as soon as the big event was over. After today, she'd only have to worry about Eddie Cahill, she thought with a grim little laugh.

All her cynicism evaporated, however, when she walked into the room at the back of the church where Abby and her attendants were waiting for the service to begin.

The bride looked radiant and excited and nervous in her taffeta gown studded with tiny pearls. When she smiled uncertainly at her, Jo crossed the room and embraced her friend.

"I'm so sorry about last night," Abby apologized again.

"It's all right. Really. Don't let anything spoil today." Jo took a step back. "You look beautiful."

"Thank you. So do you."

Jo stifled the automatic denial that sprang to her lips. If the bride wanted to entertain that kind of fantasy, why put up a protest?

Laura and two friends who'd gone to school with Abby fluttered around trying to make conversation. They were all a bit teary as they listened to the organ music drifting in from the chapel.

Finally one of the deacons and Abby's father appeared at the door and told them it was show time. He didn't look any too calm himself, Jo thought as his daughter took his arm and they started for the back of the church. Probably they were both glad they didn't have to walk down the aisle alone.

Which was not the case with Jo. The bouquet of rose-buds and baby's breath trembled in her hands as she followed them out. She glanced at the private security guard stationed by the door. He was there for her, she thought and squeezed her eyes shut for a minute. *Don't let anything mess up Abby's wedding,* she prayed silently as she took her place at the central portal.

In front of her, the church was filled to capacity, the crowd waiting in hushed expectation.

Then, as the organ music reached a crescendo, Jo was marching down the aisle, her eyes fixed on the stained-glass window above the altar so that she saw the assemblage on either side of her only in her peripheral vision. The bridesmaids and ushers had already taken their places amid the red roses perfuming the chancel. Then the organist began to play Wagner's traditional wedding march. A minute later, Abby and her father joined the group in front of the altar.

The music stopped, and a door to the right of the choir opened. The groom and his best man stepped out. Jo knew she had been waiting for this moment. She was sure all other eyes were focused on Steve, but she couldn't take hers off Cam. Her breath caught in her throat as once more she was struck by how incredibly handsome he looked in a tuxedo. Except that now his face was pale and his features were drawn. Only his eyes held the energy she remembered. They seemed to glitter in the warm light of the chapel as they locked with hers. For a dizzying moment, some wordless communication passed between them.

"This is the day the Lord has made. Let us rejoice and be glad in it," the minister said.

Cam continued to watch her intently. She gave him an uncertain smile, and he nodded almost imperceptibly.

"God created us male and female, and gave us marriage so that husband and wife may help and comfort each other, living faithfully together in plenty and in want, in joy and sorrow…"

The words took on a special meaning as she and Cam stared at each other. In front of her, she heard Steve and Abby exchanging vows.

"Abby, do you take Steve to be your husband and promise before God and these witnesses to be his loving and faithful wife…?"

"I do."

Jo saw Cam's expression soften. Her hand reached out toward him. When she realized they were standing five feet apart, she dropped her arm back to her side. A current seemed to flow between them. Or was it just because she wanted to believe in the power of love?

When the service was over, the organ music swelled up as Steve and Abby kissed. At the same time, Jo felt emotion swell in her chest.

With radiant smiles on their faces, the newly married couple hurried back down the aisle. Cam's eyes were not on the bride and groom. He was staring at Jo. He caught her hand and simply held it for a moment as if he'd forgotten where they were. Then they fell into place

behind Steve and Abby. As they reached the back of the
church, the rest of the party automatically headed for the
limousines waiting to take them to the reception. Cam
looked around, and Jo had the feeling he was about to
pull her out of the line. Then one of the deacons appeared and ushered them out to the waiting cars. They
piled in beside Laura and another bridesmaid.

"We have to talk," Cam whispered.

"Yes."

But there was no opportunity for a private conversation as the car sped toward the exclusive Greenspring
Valley country club where the reception was being held.
And there was no chance to talk as they stood in the
endless receiving line making polite conversation with
friends and family.

Jo felt a thousand butterflies clamoring for attention
in her stomach. Beside her, she could feel Cam's tension
building. Her own nerves were drawing as tight as an
overwound clock spring. She shifted from one foot to
the other as she gave Cam little sideways glances.

Finally he muttered something under his breath,
grabbed her hand, and yanked her out of the line. "I
think they can finish without us," he commented as he
looked around for a place where they could be alone.
The lobby was crowded with elegantly dressed guests,
and heads turned in their direction as they made their
way through the throng.

Cam didn't waver. His face set in determined lines,
he pulled Jo through double doors and they found themselves in the serving pantry off the kitchen, surrounded
by rolling carts of food destined for the buffet tables.

"I thought you knew where you were going," Jo observed.

Cam shrugged. "I'm through hiding from you. We have to talk. Now."

As they stood facing each other, words seemed to freeze in Jo's throat. And Cam wasn't doing much better.

Suddenly the ice jam broke and apologies came tumbling out.

"I didn't mean to hurt you."

"I should have called you."

"I don't know what I was thinking about."

"I—"

Before the sentence could be completed, the door flew open, and a man bolted into the room.

Startled, they both whirled to face him. Suddenly details registered in Jo's mind: the brown hair. The scar on the right side of his upper lip. The malevolent look in those dark eyes she remembered from that day in court.

Eddie Cahill.

From under his coat, he pulled a sawed-off shotgun.

"You thought you were so clever switching cars and houses. But I've been watching you and I've got you now, Ms. Super Detective," he gloated, his voice seething with hate. "When you play hardball with Eddie Cahill, you'd better watch your back."

Time seemed to slow as Jo shrank away from the man who had been stalking her for weeks. He had killed Karen. He had said he was going to kill her, too. He was going to do it. Now. Just when she and Cam had found each other again. In his face, she saw how much he was enjoying her agony and his triumph.

Out of the corner of her eye, she detected a slight movement. Cam was edging toward Eddie.

No! The warning was frozen in her throat.

The gun wavered as if Eddie had suddenly become aware that he and Jo weren't the only people in the room. At that moment, her hip bumped against one of the serving carts. Another, heaped with shrimp and cocktail sauce, was immediately to her left. Acting on desperate reflex, she reached out and shoved it with all her might toward the man who had sworn to kill her. It plowed into his waist, and Eddie grunted just as the gun went off. The shot went wild. Plump shrimp and red cocktail sauce flew into the air—some of it landing on Jo's dress and the rest splattering to the floor.

Cam dived toward Eddie and wrestled him to the tile. There was another shot as they fought for the gun.

"Cam, Cam," Jo screamed, her voice at last unfrozen.

The shots had attracted attention, and moments later, the door flew open. Steve Claiborne bounded into the room, his face grim, his body primed for action. Behind him, moving more slowly, was one of the Franklins' security guards. He was staggering and holding his chin.

Jo barely noticed the intrusion. Her eyes were glued to the men at her feet. One of them had been shot. But who?

They stopped struggling, and a groan issued from the tangled pile of arms and legs. Jo's whole body went rigid with tension. For several seconds, nothing happened. Then Cam slowly sat up. He was holding the gun. And Eddie Cahill was holding his side. Blood oozed from between his clenched fingers.

As Steve swiftly assessed the damage, Jo dropped down beside Cam. "Are you all right?"

"Yes."

"Thank God." She was reaching for him when his eyes riveted to the red splotch spread across her dress.

"Jo—what—are you—?"

She followed his gaze and noticed the stain for the first time. "Cocktail sauce."

Cam sagged with relief.

"Where were you?" Steve was looking pointedly at the security guard.

"He hit me. Afraid I was down for the count, but I'm all right now." All business, he knelt over the gunman. "Cahill's going to make it. But he's through harassing you."

"Good." Jo stared at the man sprawled on the floor. The attack had happened so fast. Her brain was just starting to catch up with the action. After Eddie Cahill had killed his wife, he'd been waiting for his opportunity to ambush her. The excitement of the wedding reception had given him the perfect chance.

The wedding! This was happening in the middle of Steve and Abby's wedding reception. Jo felt her face heat as she shot the tuxedo-clad groom a mortified glance. "I'm making a shambles of your big day," she muttered.

"Don't be ridiculous." Steve didn't miss a beat. "You've just livened up the occasion. The important thing is that the two of you are all right."

Jo looked at Cam. "You know, I was really looking forward to the shrimp. Too bad, I'm wearing them and the sauce."

"Damn! Another missed opportunity to field test my spot remover," he struggled to match her ironic tone.

A blond waiter pushed his way through to the front of the crowd that had gathered around them. Jo remembered him from the reception Abby's mother had given. "Let me give you a hand," he offered kindly. "I think I've got something that will take that stain out."

"Thanks."

She was about to follow him out of the room when Cam reached toward her. They clenched hands, and for several heartbeats she was caught up in the sensation of his strong fingers gripping hers.

Oh, Cam, don't ever let me go again.

"Come on. You want to get back to the party," the waiter urged.

"Yes. Right." Jo allowed herself to be led away, conscious of the tight hold on her arm. The man was gripping her as forcefully as Cam had. At the door, she hesitated.

"I'll meet you back here," Cam told her, and she knew that before they returned to the reception they were going to settle their own unfinished business.

"Yes."

The waiter gave her a little tug. "Hurry. Before the stain sets."

She nodded, vaguely confused and uneasy. Something was wrong. Something— But the experience she'd just been through had robbed her of the ability to think clearly.

They headed down the hall toward the employees' washroom.

"What's your name?" She tried to start a conversation.

"Art."

"I guess the staff has to be equipped for anything."

"That's right. I'm equipped for anything."

In the next moment she felt cold metal against her ribs.

"This time it's not your friend Rossini playing jokes. I've got a gun. Bring your hands together behind your back."

Jo briefly considered bolting—or screaming. The menacing jab of the gun against her side convinced her it was safer to play along. Seconds after she'd complied with the order, she felt metal cuffs clamp around her wrists. They were hidden from view by the man in back of her.

Panic welled up in her throat as she tried to shift her hands. Her chances of escape had just dwindled to near zero.

"Move it." Then he was shoving her through a door and into the parking lot.

Jo's mind scrambled for sanity—for rational explanations. Was this an accomplice of Eddie?

She stumbled. The man with the gun cursed as he jostled her down the sidewalk.

They were almost to a gray van. Panic and little flashes of mental clarity pinged through her mind with lightning speed. He was going to shove her inside and drive away. When he did, no one would know what had happened to her.

Was there anything she could drop? Some clue she could leave? Not with her hands manacled behind her back.

What about her shoe? No, he'd see it. Then she remembered the gold band that was still on her right hand. With her thumb, she worked it down her finger. As it dropped she held her breath. It didn't hit the concrete and give her away. It was on the grass.

The door of the van slid open. Once Jo was inside, her kidnapper's tense expression changed to one of confidence. As he secured the manacle to a ring riveted into the wall, a little giggle escaped from his lips. Her heart froze. She recognized the sound. The man on the phone! The man who had told her exactly what he was going to do to her.

A scream tore from her lips as the van pulled out of the parking lot.

ABBY, WHO HAD GONE searching for her new husband, joined the group in the kitchen.

"What happened?" she asked, aghast as she spotted the wounded man still lying on the floor.

"Eddie Cahill, the escaped drug dealer who was after Jo," Steve explained. "He's gonna live to serve out the rest of his term. On top of ones for murder and attempted murder."

"Where's Jo?" The bride's voice was still anxious.

"Cleaning up." Cam gestured toward the mess on the floor. "I'm afraid Cahill turned the kitchen into a giant shrimp cocktail."

Abby lifted her white dress away from the ruined party food, and Steve slung his arm around her shoulder.

As the groom recounted the action for the bride, more and more employees gathered to listen. But Cam hardly paid any attention to the narrative as he kept glancing at the door.

The police came to cart away Eddie Cahill, and he had to answer some questions.

"We'll need to talk to Ms. O'Malley, too."

"She'll be right back."

The minutes stretched.

"Where is she?"

"I'll get her."

Cam went out in the hall and glanced around, fighting the tension knotting his stomach. There was no sign of Jo or the waiter who had hustled her out of the room so quickly.

"Excuse me," he asked one of the passing busboys. "Did you see the maid of honor and one of the waiters?"

"The lady with the big red stain on her dress?"

"Yes."

"They went through there." The boy gestured toward a door and hurried off.

The knot tightened into a strangle-hold as Cam jogged down the hall and pushed open the door. He was only half surprised to find that it led to the parking lot behind the kitchen.

Nothing moved as he walked toward the catering trucks and employee vehicles. Maybe the busboy had been mistaken.

If his head hadn't been bowed in concentration, he would have missed a small piece of metal in the grass. It winked in the sunlight.

Cam stooped to pick it up. Jo's ring. The one she'd never taken off.

Oh, my God! What had happened to her? Clasping the ring in his fist, he dashed back toward the building.

WITH HER HANDS angled in back of her and secured to the wall, every sway of the van sent a painful jolt through Jo's arms and shoulders. And every jolt was like a stab of fear piercing her breast.

Get away. Escape, her mind screamed. *Before he—Before he—*

Physically flight was impossible. The temptation to shut down her mind, to withdraw to a deep, guarded place within herself where she'd be safe was overwhelming.

The vehicle jounced over a bump and a wrenching jolt of pain ricocheted down Jo's arms. It brought her back to reality.

She lifted her head. For the first time since she'd been shoved into the van, she took in her surroundings. The interior was filled with boxes and cartons of wires and circuit boards and tools—along with a small workbench. Racks of electronic equipment lined the walls.

The implications suddenly hit her in the gut like a street fighter's punch. The transmitter Cam had found on her car. The mystery of the malfunctioning garage door opener. The electromagnetic pulse. The television gone haywire. Eddie Cahill hadn't done any of that.

Her eyes shot to the man in the driver's seat. He didn't look back at her. But she could hear him muttering in a low, urgent voice.

The sound was no longer electronically distorted, yet the speech rhythms were the same ones she knew so well from the phone calls.

Now he had her. Just like—just like—Margaret Clement.

No. Oh, God no.

Desperately she wrenched at the ring that bound her to the wall. She was no match for the thick metal.

Instead she forced herself to listen to the words spewing forth from the man driving the van. He was talking to himself. No, he was really talking to her. The same phrases over and over.

"Wedding party... Denise... Maid of honor... Like an angel... Redheaded bitch."

"Denise?" she gasped. "You have the wrong person. Let me go. Please, let me go."

He swiveled around and fixed her with an angry look. "I liked you, you know that? With your short hair and your slim little body, you reminded me of a boy. And I thought I could—I could..." His voice trailed off for a moment, and she saw his features tighten. "I could have done it!" he insisted, but there was an undercurrent of uncertainty in the assertion. "I asked you to marry me, and you laughed at me. You shouldn't have laughed, Denise. You shouldn't have laughed because I needed you. You could have saved me. You could have changed my life."

Even as she caught a note of desperation in his tone, Jo cringed away from his piercing stare. "Please, I—I—don't know you," she stammered.

"Sure you do, Denise."

"Please—"

"Don't play games with me, angel face. You'll make me angry."

He turned back to the road.

CAM YANKED at the door that led back into the hallway. It was locked from the inside. He might have gone around to the front of the building, but he wasn't exactly thinking clearly. Raising his fists he began to pound against the metal barrier.

"Okay, keep your pants on," somebody shouted from

the other side. Then a man in a white apron threw the door open.

Cam didn't stop to explain. Instead he pushed past him and sprinted down the hall to the employees' washroom. A startled salad girl looked up from the sink and then shrank away as he advanced on her.

"The woman with the stained dress?" he demanded sharply.

"Haven't seen her since she left the kitchen. And I came in here right after that."

She had hardly finished the last sentence before Cam was on his way back to the pantry area. Steve and the security guard were still talking to Abby. He'd been gone for less than five minutes. It just seemed like five hundred. The policeman who'd taken his statement had given up waiting for Jo and started interviewing some of the kitchen help.

"Cam, what's wrong?" Abby gasped when she saw the wild look on his face.

"Jo and that waiter have both disappeared."

"Maybe they're still in the washroom," Abby suggested.

"I checked. They're not there." Cam held up the ring. "I found this outside in the grass beside the parking lot. It's Jo's. It couldn't have slipped off her finger. She had to have taken it off deliberately."

Abby stared at Cam. "But why? The danger's over. You got Eddie."

"Then where's Jo? I think the waiter hustled her down the hall and outside into a car."

Abby gulped. "The phone caller. Jo just about proved it wasn't Eddie."

"The waiter was at the Franklins' house. I remember

him because I was thinking he didn't exactly fit in,'' Steve entered the conversation.

"The maids of honor…the ones Jo talked to…'' Abby rambled. "One of them was kidnapped. And she hasn't been heard from again.''

Hoping against hope, they dispersed to separate areas of the building to search for Jo. They were joined by the security guard and police officer still on the scene. By the time they'd finished, everyone at the reception had heard about the incident.

The grim news ended the party. The guests departed, leaving the bar fully stocked and buffet table loaded with food. The bride and groom and the best man hardly noticed.

Laura, Lou Rossini, and Noel joined the circle of anxious friends in the kitchen where Cam was drilling the staff. He found out quickly that the waiter's name was Arthur Thorp.

"What do you know about him?'' Cam demanded.

Various staff members contributed bits of information, Thorp looked to be in his early thirties. He was a temporary employee of Perfection Catering Service who only worked at peak periods.

Another one of the waiters remembered that he hadn't known the business very well at the beginning. But he'd sure been a handy guy to have around. Several times he'd pulled Perfection's chestnuts out of the fire by stepping in to fix malfunctioning kitchen equipment.

Cam looked up from the middle of the interrogation to find Abby ushering Evan Hamill into the kitchen.

"I decided we need the detective who's been in on the case from the beginning,'' she explained.

"Yeah," he agreed, his voice grim.

Hamill's arrival put the situation into bleak perspective. Finding Jo wasn't going to be easy. And every second she was missing put her life in greater jeopardy.

CHAPTER THIRTEEN

ART OPENED THE DOOR of the van and unfastened the handcuffs from the ring on the wall. Lowering her arms brought a sting of pain to Jo's numb limbs.

She shrank away from his touch as he forced her out of the van. But he kept a firm hold on her biceps as he hurried her through a large garage.

They were parked next to a silver Toyota. He caught her glancing at it.

"Alternative transportation in case anyone's looking for my van," he explained. Then his voice changed as he hustled her past a workbench and machine tools. "We're going outside for a minute. If you scream, you're dead. Got it?" The gun barrel in her back emphasized the order.

"Yes," Jo whispered.

The air outside was cold and raw. It was a tantalizing hint of freedom that was quickly squelched as Jo's captor bustled her into a backyard full of weeds and screened with unclipped privet hedges. Jaunty music floated toward her on the wind. Something strident and jarring would have been more appropriate.

The upbeat tune persisted. It was being played by a band. The same one that she'd heard in the background on several of the phone calls.

She was ushered quickly up rickety steps that led to

a back porch. Her kidnapper paused to turn off a sophisticated security system that looked out of place in
its seedy surroundings. A Randolph deluxe model, Jo
thought.

The house was about the same vintage as her own
Roland Park home, but no one had kept up the interior.
In the dim light, she could see that the wood floors were
unpolished and uneven, old wallpaper hung down in yel-
lowing strips in several places, and cobwebs festooned
every corner. The air of mustiness made it hard to take
a deep breath.

The whole effect made Jo feel closed-in and queasy.
She fought back her revulsion and ordered her detective's mind to store as many details as possible.

When she lingered, her captor gave her a shove down
the hall. It was lined with several closed doors. He directed her toward the second one on the right. She
breathed a sigh of relief when she saw he wasn't taking
her upstairs where she'd have to climb down a drainpipe
or something to get away. She stopped short when she
saw the door was guarded by a separate security monitor.

Taking her arm, Art jostled her inside where she
squinted in the bright light that contrasted so sharply
with the rest of the interior.

He pushed her toward a narrow bed lined up against
one wall. At least it wasn't *the* bed, the brass one in the
video. But a ring and a chain dangled from the wall.

"Please…" Jo didn't try to keep the quaver out of
her voice. Maybe if she played on his sympathy.
"Please, my arms hurt so much. Don't chain me."

Art laughed. "You expect me to trust you? The day
I snatched your purse, you kicked me."

"You—" The revelation numbed her to the bone.

"Sit down," he ordered.

Jo's glance flitted to the bed, which was covered with a homespun quilt, and then back to the gun trained on her chest.

Her captor followed her gaze. "I don't want to shoot you, but I will if I have to," he growled.

She sat gingerly on the very edge of the bed while he secured one hand to a cuff that dangled from a chain attached to the wall.

When he was finished, he stood over her for endless moments contemplating her slender frame. Jo steeled herself to keep from quaking like a sapling in a windstorm. She didn't raise her gaze to meet his. She didn't want him to see the horror in her eyes.

Now that he was completely in control, his voice took on a subtle note of satisfaction. "I worked hard to get things ready for you."

Crossing to the closet, he opened the door. Like a mouse dropped into a cage with a snake, Jo fought paralysis as she followed his movements.

When he brought out several garments on hangers, she gasped in surprise. Two of them were the suit and apricot cocktail dress that had disappeared from the cleaners. The others were slacks and blouses he'd stolen from her closet the night he'd rigged the television set.

There were other personal things, too, she saw, as she looked around the room. Novels that she'd read were on the bedside table. The lipstick from her purse was on the dresser, along with a number of the toilet articles she used. And then there was the quilt, so much like the one on her own bed at home.

Such simple, everyday objects. Yet because they were

here in this room, terror threatened to carry her away in its undertow.

The room was like a carefully constructed stage setting. Unreal, yet with the appearance of reality. What drama was going to be enacted? She was pretty sure she knew what the director had in mind for the finale. Her only chance was to change the script.

"For dinner, I'll fix you some of your favorite foods. I looked in your trash and found out the kind of stuff you like to cook."

He'd been spying on her for weeks, collecting her things, dogging her every move. He'd even pawed through her trash! Nausea warred with terror.

Then she realized he might have made a fatal mistake. Her trash. If it was after the camera— No, she was grasping at straws. But if he had— If he had— Jo tried to keep any hint of hope out of her voice. "You know so much about me," she whispered instead. "You must know who I am. I'm Jo O'Malley. I'm not the woman who hurt you. I'm not Denise."

"Shut up!"

Jo nodded. *Careful*, she warned herself. *You just made a mistake*.

"Denise," he repeated, staring at her, his eyes slightly out of focus. "Denise. You were going to make an honest man of me. And then you slapped me. You shouldn't have done that. Do you understand?"

"Yes," Jo whispered. She fought to keep her teeth from chattering and her body from trembling. The man who had her in his clutches was stark-raving mad. Anything could set him off.

His eyes seemed to snap back into focus. "You're Jo O'Malley. But you look like Denise. You're playing her role in the wedding. You'll do fine as her stand-in. Only this time, things are going to come out differently.

Her control cracked. "You can't get away with this. The police will catch you."

"No they won't. The police can't trace the phone calls. And they don't know who I am." He giggled and reached up to his full head of blond hair. "You thought you were so clever with your costumes. Mine are better." With a deft motion, he tugged at the covering. It was a wig, and it came away in his hand to reveal stringy brown hair.

Jo couldn't stifle a tiny exclamation. He grinned at her as he tossed the wig into the trash can. "The punk hairdo was another one of my disguises," he boasted. Crossing to the mirror he pulled a layer of rubber makeup away from one cheek and then from the other. More rubber came off his nose. "Good stuff," he commented. "I should have used it that day in Dundalk. But I didn't think you were going to claw my face."

Jo watched the skinlike appliances follow the wig into the trash. She hadn't spotted the camouflage.

"No more Art Thorp," he said airily. "After this, I'll have to build up another persona. Get a job at another catering company."

"Art Thorp?"

"That's who they think I am." He giggled again. "They don't know anything about the real me. Art Nugent." He was still speaking into the mirror, suddenly he turned and faced Jo again. "I've been waiting for weeks to tell you all this," he crowed.

"You know so much. Like the stuff you told me on the phone. About Cam."

"I just pointed you toward the files."

"That wasn't a lucky guess. You have inside information."

"Yes!"

The way he said the word brought a choking feeling to Jo's chest. But she kept up the game.

"I was impressed."

He took a step forward, and she thought again about all the sexual references he'd made in those tapes. She backed up on the narrow bed and found her shoulders pressed against the wall.

He smiled. But only with his lips, not his eyes. "You don't like me any more than Denise did. She was just pretending to be nice. Until the wedding was over."

"That's not true. I do like you."

"I know what you're trying to do with your clever little conversation. You're trying to feed my ego—and get information. It won't make any difference what you do. I have you, and Cameron Randolph doesn't. I keep wondering, was it chance or fate that paired you with Randolph that night of the Franklin party?"

"Why do you care so much about Cam?"

"Your boyfriend is that inventor bastard who thinks he's the king of Randolph Enterprises. The man who wouldn't let me into the design department, even after Collin recommended me. His majesty Cameron Randolph still thought I wasn't good enough. Well, I was. And I paid him back." He couldn't repress one of the giggles that had made her skin crawl when he'd talked to her on the phone. Only now they were in the same room. "Too bad Skip O'Malley isn't around to sweat out where you are. I beat him once, but I can't touch him now. I can only make sure Randolph pays."

At that moment, Jo was too stunned to reply. Later

she thought about good and bad luck—and what it meant to her that Art Nugent chose that moment to turn and bolt from the room.

GOOD AND BAD LUCK. Was this all going to hinge on good and bad luck, Cam wondered as he sat before his computer, which was swiftly running through number and letter combinations.

As the digits flashed on the screen, he took off his glasses and rubbed the bridge of his nose. He looked like a man who had gone ten rounds with Mike Tyson. Then he shook his head and roused himself from the dark mood.

You're going to make it, Jo. We'll find you. It's going to be all right, he prayed. He had to believe that. Because if they didn't, there was no more meaning to his life.

The door opened behind him, and he looked around expectantly. It was Abby. Silently she shook her head, and he turned quickly back to the screen so that she wouldn't see the raw disappointment on his face.

He, Laura, Abby, Steve and Noel had established a command post at his town house. Most of them were still out checking various leads and looking for clues they might have missed at Jo's house or office. He was manning the computer link to the police department and doing his own checking of data bases.

"You and Steve should be off on your honeymoon," he said in a low voice.

"You don't really think we could leave now, do you?"

"I wasn't suggesting that you go. I'm just trying to tell you I feel guilty."

"Don't."

"If I'd been straight with her, this wouldn't have happened."

"The man who grabbed her had every detail planned. He would have gotten to her anyway."

Cam had been over all the arguments with himself. Why punish Abby by continuing the discussion with her? He glanced at the screen. The program didn't need any help from him at this point, so that his mind was free to rehash the events of the past few hours.

There had been no problem convincing Hamill or the Baltimore County police that Jo's life was in jeopardy. Cam had been amazed at the way the detective had cut through red tape that would have tied another man's hands for days. Because the Social Security Administration was in Baltimore, Hamill had worked personally with a number of executives in the government agency. One of them agreed to go down to the office and check out Art Thorp, even though it was Saturday afternoon. He called back with the news that an area man named Art Thorp had applied for a social security number three years ago. Regular deposits had been made into his account since then by employers.

The recent vintage of the account almost certainly meant the kidnapper was using an assumed name. And the address on file was a town house in Camden occupied by a young couple who knew nothing about a man named Art Thorp.

The information from the Social Security Administration led nowhere. Also, Thorp's personnel file had disappeared from the catering office, and his phone number had been pulled from the office Rolodex. On the other hand, a number of the employees at the catering service remembered Art Thorp's gray van—which had been parked near the entrance through which Jo had been hustled out of the building. Thorp had been very secretive about what was inside. When another waiter had recently asked him for a ride to the bus stop because his car was in the shop, Thorp had made what sounded like a flimsy excuse not to grant the small favor.

The incident in itself wouldn't have been significant, except that the waiter remembered looking at the license plate on the van. Although he didn't recall the whole number-letter combination, he was sure that the last two digits were 64—because that was the year he'd been born.

Hamill had arranged for the Randolph Enterprise computer system to access the records at the Motor Vehicles Administration. Cam was now laboriously searching the data base, looking for vehicles with that particular combination in the last two positions. There were thousands. Which meant they needed to eliminate most of the tags from the list.

Abby came up behind Cam again and stood watching the numbers moving across the screen. "You must be tired."

"I'm all right."

"Want some dinner? I brought some food back from the reception. I figured we might as well eat it."

"Maybe later."

Abby reached out and began to knead the tense muscles of his shoulders.

Cam sighed. "That feels good. But what would your fiancé think if he came in right now?"

"Her husband, buddy. He's her husband." Steve regarded them from the doorway. He'd come in quietly and chosen to wait for the right moment to make his presence known.

"Luckily he knows you're just good friends," Steve continued. "Otherwise, he'd break a few important bones in your body. Besides, you've got a girl of your own. As soon as we get her back, she can take over the R and R duties."

JO SAT STARING at the closed door, feeling Art's presence on the other side. Her ears detected tiny clicks as he set the security alarm.

She raised her hand and looked at the metal chain and cuff. Medieval technology. But the security system was state-of-the-art. Her captor was covering all the bases. At least she hadn't given him another advantage by blurting the first thing that had sprung to her tongue when he'd mentioned Cam and Skip.

But how did you act with a lunatic? How did you keep from setting him off? His grip on reality was so fragile. Sometimes he didn't even know who she was.

Denise. Margaret. Jo.

The depth of Nugent's insanity brought a wave of cold sweat sweeping across her body. Then, by brute force, she pulled her mind back from the brink of its own destruction. Maybe his previous victims had simply given up. She wasn't going to do that.

She had too much to live for. *Cam. Oh, Cam,* she thought. *I'm coming back to you.*

For precious moments she let her lids flutter closed and allowed herself to think about him. How it had been in his arms. How it would be again. Warm. Loved. Cherished. Everything she'd secretly longed for but hadn't dared seek.

At first in the fantasy, he simply held her and told her over and over that everything was going to be all right. But as she clung to him, he began to talk to her in a low, urgent voice.

"Use what he said to you. He's given you some clues. Some important information."

"Yes!"

Deliberately she focused on Art Nugent's mad babblings.

He'd worked for Randolph Electronics, gotten angry and paid Cam back for not letting him into the design department. He talked as if he hated Cam. Could she use that? How? She had to think of a plan.

Jo glanced at the closed door again. How long did she have before he came back? And what could she accomplish in his absence?

Methodically, as if she were going over a crime scene for clues, Jo began to inspect her surroundings. The first thing she determined was that the security system covered the window as well as the door.

Next she began to inspect the bed. It was made of iron and bolted to the floor. The ring that attached her chain to the wall seemed solidly mounted. Perhaps she could find some tool to pry it loose.

The length of the chain was also of considerable interest. It allowed her to move a few feet away from the bed. She could reach the dresser. Hopefully there was something in one of the drawers that would be useful.

She had gotten up when a noise in the hall stopped her in her tracks. The realization that her captor was coming back was like a blast of frigid air against her skin, and she wrapped her arms around her shoulders.

What was his timetable? How fast did he plan to move? What she needed was to buy herself some time.

Buy some time! The phrase triggered an idea—the plan she'd been searching for began to jell.

Do it right, she warned herself. *Don't let him catch on to what you're trying to pull.*

THERE WAS STILL no way to narrow down the thousands of license numbers flagged by Cam's computer program. The police didn't have a clue about the real identity of the man holding Jo. And Cam felt as if the seconds of her life were ticking by.

Abby had gone off to interview some of the other women from the phone company list.

Laura still hadn't come back from Jo's office.

Cam wandered into the den, sat down on the sofa and began to fiddle with the stereo system. The last time Jo had been here, they'd listened to Kenny Rogers.

He found the compact disc and began to play it again, unable to hold back the wave of longing for Jo that would have knocked him off his feet if he'd been standing up.

You'll be here with me again, he promised silently. *Safe and sound. Then I'll tell you all the things I was going to say when Cahill burst into the kitchen.*

He'd thought the music would make him feel closer to her. It only made things worse.

Getting up again, he went back to his home office. Hamill had dropped off the tapes from Jo's answering machine. Maybe if he played them, he'd get some clue.

There was nothing useful, but because he'd just been listening to music, the faint tune in the background caught his attention. The police had told them the notes were too distorted to recapture. But his equipment was probably better than theirs. If he ran the recording through his computer, he could bring the tune into sharper focus. Picking up the tapes, he started for his electronics workshop.

It took several hours of fiddling, but Cam finally got an acceptable rendition of the music. It sounded like a college football song, but sports had never been one of his big interests.

Had Art Thorp, or whatever his name was, been watching the game of the week when he'd made the call? That seemed unlikely.

People had come in and out of the house while he'd been working but no one had disturbed him. But when Laura wandered back to see what he was doing, the music made her linger in the doorway.

"Why are you playing that?" she asked.

He turned bloodshot eyes toward her. "You don't recognize it, do you?"

"Of course I recognize it. It's 'Stand up Towson.'"

"What?"

She sang a few bars. "'Stand up Towson, Stand up Towson, Strike that note of fame.' It's my old high-school song. Why are you playing it?"

"You never heard the tapes?"

"Tapes?" She looked puzzled for a moment. "You mean the ones Jo got."

There was a note of excitement in his voice. "Yes. The song was in the background, but until I enhanced it, it was too faint to identify." He rewound the cassette and played it again. At one point the music stopped, backed up several bars, and started again. Later the drum was definitely out of synch with the rest of the instruments.

"It sounds like the band practicing," Laura mused.

"Which means that the place he was calling from must be within hailing range of the high-school football field."

Cam pointed to the computer terminal, which was networked to the one in his office. "I've been racking my brain trying to figure out a way to narrow down the set of license numbers from the DMV. And you've just handed it to me. Where is Towson High School?"

"Off York Road. Near the Towson State University."

Cam brought up a gridded map of Baltimore County on the screen and zoomed in on the area around the school. "Right here." He pointed at the screen. "The bastard was right around here when he made two of those calls. Let's hope he still is."

AS THE DOORKNOB turned, Jo schooled her features to match the role she needed to play.

Art was carrying a tray. The pinched look on his face, the spacey expression in his eyes told her that his hold on reality was slipping.

"Macaroni and cheese," he announced in a cheery voice that didn't sound as if it were coming from his lips. He set the tray down on the stand beside the bed. "One of your favorites."

Jo peered at the goopy, overcooked mess and pictured it sticking to the roof of her mouth. But she dutifully sat down on the edge of the bed and picked up the fork in her unbound hand. *Better follow directions. Better act as if you're eager to do what he says.*

A glass of Coke and a brownie completed the menu.

As soon as she got home, she'd have to start eating better, Jo told herself. And she would get home, she added.

"So how long have you lived here?" she asked in a conversational tone.

"I grew up here. I kept the house after my parents died."

"Oh."

"Don't you like your dinner?" He sat down in the overstuffed chair across from the bed.

"Oh, yes, it's very good. I just can't eat very fast," she murmured.

"You need to keep your strength up. We're going to have a very special time together, Denise. It's going to be the way it should have been all along." He was looking at her again in that strange, unfocused way. The tone of his voice was suddenly leaden with grief. "I killed a man, you know. He was my best friend."

"What?"

"It was an accident. Please. You have to believe me. I didn't mean for it to happen."

"I believe you."

"He just got caught in—in—the investigation. And he didn't know what else to do." Art buried his head in his hands for long seconds.

Jo hardly dared breath, wondering what this erratic madman would do next.

When he looked back up at her, his eyes were bright. "I was a lost soul. Damned to hell for everything I'd done. Then I met you. That day when I saw you standing there in church, I thought you were my salvation. You were an angel come to save me, Denise. Angel face, I called you. You were going to change my destiny. Make everything different. Make me pure and whole again."

"I will make you whole again. Just tell me what to do," she whispered.

"You had your chance. Now it's too late for you to do it on your own. I'm the one in charge."

Oh, God. He was so mixed up. Angels. Salvation. Destiny. Could she get him to remember who she really was—to think about her and Cam, again.

"You're such a good engineer," she said softly. "Cameron Randolph should have let you work in the design department."

"Yes!" His face reformed into a mask of anger.

"And now you're going to get even with him," Jo continued. "You're going to use me to get money out of Cam, aren't you?" she asked in a small, trembly voice.

The room grew very still. Jo didn't dare glance up. Instead she pushed a clump of macaroni and cheese around the plate.

"Yeah, that's right," Art finally said. "Your boyfriend is worth millions, and I'm going to get some of that undeserved cash away from him."

Jo was positive he hadn't thought of the idea until now. He'd been too focused on Denise being his salvation and how she'd betrayed him. "You're going to trade me for the money," Jo stated as if the assumption were fact.

He looked at her consideringly. "That depends on how you treat me, angel face. Maybe I'm going to get the money and keep you."

"The money is the important thing."

"No. The important thing is our relationship."

Jo held her breath.

"Denise wouldn't marry me. She wouldn't save me.

Denise—'' He stopped abruptly and stared at her face.
''But you will.''

The words and the way he was looking at her made
a tide of nausea rise in her throat. What did she have to
do to save him? She wanted to scream out her denial. It
was all a mistake. He had the wrong woman. She was
mixed up in his madness—and some fantasy he'd conjured up about salvation for his sins.

She hadn't really expected him to jump at the idea of
letting her go. But collecting a ransom took time.

He got slowly out of the chair, and she stopped
breathing.

''I'm going out for a while. When I come back, you
can practice being nice to me,'' he said in a chatty voice
as though the whole previous conversation had never
existed.

Jo felt a mixture of elation and revulsion.

Time. He'd just given her some time. But then what?

CHAPTER FOURTEEN

CAM LOOKED at the salmon pâté from the reception and thought that if he tried to swallow a bite, it would stick to the roof of his mouth. None of the food on the kitchen table held much appeal—to him or anyone else. Even Hamill had given up his smokehouse almonds.

Everyone except the detective from Baltimore County who'd recently joined the task force looked dead tired. But no one seemed inclined to go to bed—except Laura who'd excused herself an hour ago.

When the phone rang, Cam listlessly crossed the room and picked up the receiver.

"Hello?"

"I have your girlfriend." It was the same electronically distorted voice he'd come to know so well.

Fatigue rolled off him like water after a rainstorm. He stood up straighter. He'd never handled a call like this, but he'd better get it right. "Who's calling? Where's Jo? Is she all right?"

The voice on the other end of the line ignored all but the middle question. "It's going to cost you a million bucks to find out."

"That's a lot of money."

Cam glanced toward the table. Everybody was watching him, their tension mirroring his own.

"Don't you think little Ms. O'Malley's worth it?" the caller prodded. "She sure is hot in bed."

"You bastard."

"Now now. You have to learn to share. I expect to have the money in small bills tomorrow."

"Nobody can raise a million dollars that fast."

"You'd better try."

"You'd better prove to me that Jo is alive before I pay out anything. I want to talk to her."

"That's impossible."

"I'll pay the money, but only if I can be sure of what I'm getting."

"I'll think about it," the voice rasped.

The line went dead.

"I'll tell you where the call was made in a minute," Hamill said.

"Oh God, he said he raped her."

Abby got up and put her arm around Cam's shoulder. "He could be lying to get a rise out of you."

He tried to comfort himself with that.

"I wasn't sure what to say. I didn't expect him to contact me."

"The most important thing is that he's changed his pattern. He's never asked for a ransom before—which means it was probably Jo's idea."

"She's manipulating him?"

"Yes."

"Then she must be…okay."

"Yes."

He felt the two-ton weight pressing against his chest ease up an inch or two.

Hamill joined the conversation again. "Another phone booth. In a shopping center north of the city."

"Not far from Towson?"

"Right. I've got every patrol car in the area looking for a van with those last two numbers on the license plate."

"We'll catch him," Abby cut in.

Cam didn't answer. Instead he reached for the phone again.

"Who are you calling?" Steve asked.

"My bank. I'll have to cash in some securities."

"You can't call the bank. It's closed."

Cam blinked. He hadn't been thinking about the time or the day of the week. All he'd been thinking about was Jo.

"He's not going to exchange Ms. O'Malley for the money," Hamill said in a quiet voice.

"I'm going to have to operate under the assumption that he will."

ART HAD BEEN GONE for over an hour. Jo hadn't wasted a moment of the reprieve. As soon as he'd closed the door and set the security lock, she'd pushed away the food and taken a good look at the arrangement that held her chain to the wall. A round metal ring similar to the type used to cover a plumbing pipe hid the attachment. Jo couldn't remove it with her hands so she went looking for a tool. It wasn't too difficult to pry off a metal corner brace from the bottom of the bed. With it she carefully pulled up the ring. Underneath she could see that a bolt had been cemented into the wall.

Experimentally she began to work at the cement with the corner brace. It yielded to her efforts, but it was going to be slow work. What if her captor discovered what she was doing? The speculation made her go momentarily numb. What would he do if she didn't get away?

Slipping the ring back against the wall, she saw that it would hide her handiwork as effectively as it had hidden the connection. If Art didn't lift up the covering, she'd be all right. Except that chipping away at cement was going to create dust and other debris. A dead giveaway. She'd have to contain the mess.

In the middle dresser drawer, she found one of her T-shirts. Spreading it out along the edge of the bed, she began to chisel at the cement. It was slow going. She forced herself to get up periodically, empty the dust into the bottom dresser drawer, and cover the evidence with the remaining pieces of clothing.

While she worked, she imagined Cam there beside her. Encouraging her. Telling her that she could get away.

Conjuring up his image again helped more than she would have believed possible.

She kept her ears tuned for outside sounds. But in her mind, as her hands worked, she was continuing the silent dialogue she'd started with Cam.

"In the van, he said I reminded him of a boy. But that he couldn't—"

"That makes it sound like he's gay."

"Yes!" Her heart began to thump. "All those sexual threats—he just wants to talk about sex with women. He won't actually follow through." She prayed it was true.

Her hand chipped away at the cement. Her mind kept up the internal dialogue.

"He said he worked at Randolph Enterprises and you wouldn't let him in the design department. He said he killed his best friend—but it was an accident."

"Collin?"

"Maybe Collin tried to get him the job because the two of them were involved. Maybe that's how he got the designs, too. It fits what we know. Your brother killed himself after he found out someone he trusted was responsible for the industrial espionage.

"Cam, I'm scared. He's so crazy." Jo had been fighting to keep her thoughts on a logical, rational level. Now she stopped chipping at the cement and let out the little whimper she'd been holding in.

"Honey, I know you're afraid. But we're going to get through this," Cam whispered reassuringly in her mind. Jo swallowed and went on with the silent speculation. "Probably he was pretty unstable—but he managed to hide it. Collin's suicide tipped the balance. It drove him insane because he couldn't cope with what he'd done."

"Yes. Suppose he's one of those gay men who never came to terms with his sexual identity? Maybe he'd sworn to himself that he was going to turn over a new leaf after his lover died. He told me Denise looked like an angel come to save him. In his crazed mind, he pinned all his hopes on her. Then she rejected him."

"I'll bet she was afraid of the madness in him as much as anything else. Maybe he was already so far gone that he started babbling to her about angels and lost souls and damnation."

"Maybe."

"The important thing is that when she turned him away, she confirmed his worst feelings about himself."

"He punished her for that. And he's kept on punishing her—through women who looked like her and who were playing the same role."

It all made a kind of terrible sense. Jo went over it

again, refining the theory and thinking about how to use what she'd figured out as she worked on freeing herself. What if she could convince Art she was really his savior? Would he let his guard down? Unchain her? Or was he too far gone for that?

When she heard the back door to the house open, every muscle in her body tensed. Fearfully she looked down at the pile of cement dust. Not much!

With rapid, jerky motions, Jo pushed the ring back into place, folded the mess into the T-shirt, and shoved it under the edge of the mattress. Her improvised tool followed.

As she looked wildly around, she saw that a few flakes of cement remained. She was just sweeping them away as heavy footsteps came down the hall. The security alarm gave her a few extra seconds.

Heart pounding, Jo smoothed out the quilt, flopped back against the wall, and struck an attitude with head bowed as if she'd been sitting in defeat the whole time Art had been gone. Silently she prayed that he wouldn't figure out what she'd been doing.

He opened the door and stood studying her for several moments.

"Your boyfriend isn't sure he wants to pay to get you back," he finally said, his voice rising on a taunting note.

She kept her expression blank.

"I told him you were great in bed."

She couldn't hold back a choked little sound.

Her captor stared at her for endless seconds, his tongue sweeping across his lips. "Maybe we'll find out about that later. Right now Randolph wants me to prove that you're still breathing before he coughs up the cash. How did you meet him, Denise?" He looked puzzled.

"I—uh—"

His expression brightened. "At that party. It was my lucky day when you met at the party."

"Yes. Please, let me talk to him," she begged.

"Not a chance. You might give something away."

"You could make a recording and play it."

She could see he was considering the idea.

"I'll write the message and you can read it over before I make the tape. It will be a lot more persuasive if it's in my own words like the interview in the paper. Remember, you read it?"

He nodded slowly.

"We're going to get married so I can be your savior. But we need to start off with a nest egg," she tossed out casually. She sat as still as a nun in prayer while he considered the proposal.

"All right," he finally agreed.

Did he believe her? Or was he playing his own game?

"If you try any tricks, I'll slit your throat. And I won't wait for the ceremony."

Jo tried to swallow. Her throat felt scorched. "No tricks," she managed.

"I'll get you a pencil and paper."

For once, she was glad that her captor came back so quickly.

"Here." He handed her the writing materials.

"Thank you," she whispered, almost overwhelmed by the chance to communicate with Cam. But she couldn't let Nugent realize how much it meant to her.

Oh, Cam, she thought, blinking back the moisture that filmed her eyes. *When I'm alone, I can pretend you're*

*here. But there's so much I want to say—need to say—
to you in person. He's letting me send you a short message, but it won't really be personal. I want to tell you
I love you. I can't do that. What I say has to be just the
right words. It has to say what Nugent wants—and give
you a clue to help you find me.*

"I'M SORRY to bother you. Phil Mercer says he wants to
talk to you," Abby interrupted Cam's reveries. He'd
been sitting at the computer pretending he was having a
conversation with Jo.

Without turning, Cam snapped out an answer. "I told
him he was in complete charge at Randolph for the time
being. I don't want to be bothered with any details."

"He says it's important."

Sighing, the inventor got up, stretched cramped muscles, and reached for the phone.

"He's not calling. He's in the living room."

Cam didn't bother to mask his surprise as he started
for the door.

The Randolph CEO stood by the window. The thin-
ning hair on his round head was mussed, as if he'd run
his fingers through it repeatedly. His normally ruddy
complexion was tinged with gray. A manila folder that
hadn't been there before lay in the middle of the coffee
table.

"What brings you out here?" Cam asked.

"The two of us haven't always seen eye to eye on
policy at Randolph."

Cam acknowledged the observation with a slight inclination of his head.

"I've tried to keep things running smoothly. Then this
terrible business with Ms. O'Malley made me—" He

stopped and started again. "Remember a couple of weeks ago when someone used that EMP generator against her, and you had me checking our records?"

Cam nodded.

"When Collin and your father died, you were pretty upset. I decided you wouldn't want to rake all that up again—"

"For God sakes, man, stop stuttering and spit it out."

"Your brother Collin requested copies of the EMP files. He had them for several weeks before they went into inactive storage."

"Collin?"

"It was his signature on the request." Mercer gestured toward the folder on the table.

Cam snatched it up and flipped through the contents. "This request form?" he asked, shoving a piece of paper toward Mercer.

"Yes."

"I know my brother's signature," Cam said in a deceptively quiet voice. "This isn't it."

"But—"

"Someone forged his name."

"Cam, are you sure?" Abby interjected from where she stood in the doorway.

He whipped around to face her. "You think I'm still not able to deal with it, don't you?"

"I just want you to admit the possibility your brother was involved."

He snapped the folder closed and stalked past Abby out of the room with the papers clutched in stiff fingers.

"Cam—wait."

"I'm not going off to sulk," he said in a strained voice. "I'm going off to think."

It wasn't exactly the truth. But it was as close as he could come at the moment.

Like a man walking some grim last mile, Cam climbed the stairs to the attic. With the same solemn determination, he brought down the boxes of Collin's papers that he hadn't looked at in three years.

He hadn't been capable of sorting through them after his brother's death. Now he knew he had to face the truths he wanted to deny.

Was the man who had kidnapped Jo linked to the stolen designs, the EMP generator, Collin's secret relationships? Cam was afraid he already knew the answer. But he'd been too stubborn to listen when Jo had waved the evidence in his face.

With his lips pressed together in a tight line, he tackled the contents of the boxes. The first one contained greeting cards Collin had saved over the years. As he looked through them, he remembered some of their good times—birthdays and Easters and Valentine's Days.

Another box held old school papers. He didn't bother with those.

The next was full of work Collin had brought from Randolph Enterprises to his home office from time to time. It was all pretty predictable, until he got to a sealed manila envelope buried underneath a stack of interoffice memos.

Inside were photocopies of requests for various project specs—including a duplicate of the EMP request Mercer had showed him. Why would Collin have that? Or applications for other designs that had turned up in rival product lines? If he'd been stealing from his own company, wouldn't he have wanted to destroy the evidence?

For long moments Cam sat like a man in a trance. Then he flipped to the back of the first request. It bore the same forged signature that he had seen downstairs.

But Collin had known about it. He'd gone to the trouble of collecting the requests. Had someone else and Collin been in on the industrial espionage plot together? Was Collin protecting himself with proof of the forged signatures? Or had his brother finally realized his secret relationships had made him vulnerable?

Cam raised his eyes and stared off into the distance, trying to imagine his brother's sick panic after his conversation with Skip O'Malley. Maybe it had triggered his own investigation. He wanted to believe that. He wasn't sure he could.

Cam's breath was shallow as he sat sifting through the evidence of what had happened at Randolph Enterprises. He hadn't believed Skip. He hadn't listened to what Jo was trying to tell him about his brother because he still hadn't wanted to know the truth.

The guilt was terrible. If he hadn't tried to block out what Jo was saying, maybe she wouldn't be in the clutches of some madman now. With a curse, he flung the papers across the room and buried his head in his hands.

After a long while he stood up and wiped his eyes. Then he gathered up the scattered papers and went down to do everything in his power to repair the damage. He didn't allow himself to wonder if it might be too late. That possibility was too great a threat to his sanity.

He needed hard copy data from the personnel office. He was halfway out the front door when he remembered he couldn't leave the house. He had to stay here in case the kidnapper called.

Jogging back to the living room, he was surprised to see Phil Mercer still there talking in a low voice to Abby. Maybe the man wasn't as emotionless as he'd thought. "Phil, I want you to go to the office and bring me the Randolph personnel files. Everybody who was working for us three years ago."

"You're talking about a lot of files."

"I expect to see a batch of them on my desk in an hour. Then you can go back for more."

TIME HAD BLURRED into a strange distortion of reality. It was the middle of the night. Jo's nerves were raw as she watched Art read the message she had composed for Cam.

I guess you're wondering what's happened to me. Unfortunately, I'm not free to tell you what's going on. Give the man the money. Everything will be all right. Not to worry, Superman. Trust me.

When her captor's eyes narrowed, her heart leaped into her throat. Had he figured out what she was doing? Please, God, don't let him get it, she prayed.

"Why does it say not to worry, Superman?" he demanded.

It's the only personal thing I could say. "That's what I call him. That way he'll know it's really me. It's important for him to believe he's hearing my own words."

She held her breath as Art mulled over her logic.

"Yeah. All right. It's just like that bozo to think of himself as Superman."

Jo bit back any comment.

"What about the last sentence?" Art continued. "Superman's supposed to trust me—not you."

"We can make it trust *him*. You're the one with the power."

"Yeah. Right. That's a lot better."

Jo watched him pull a small recorder out of the canvas bag he'd brought with him. He was in a hurry. Would that make him careless?

Was he going to kill her as soon as he'd proved to Cam that she was alive? Was he going to stop her if she made a small but critical change in the first sentence?

She gripped the edge of the bed with numb fingers as she waited for him to press the button.

Holding the recorder in his lap, he reached into the canvas bag again and pulled out something that looked like a portable microphone. The wire was attached to some device still hidden by the bag.

First he turned on the recorder. Then he lifted the microphone to his lips and spoke.

"Your girlfriend made you a tape."

The words had the familiar high-pitched electronic distortion. Jo gasped and literally jumped several inches off the bed. Over the past few weeks he'd sensitized her to that unnatural voice like a lover stroking her skin. Again, she felt a cloud of mechanical insects skittering over her body. Frantically her hands tried to brush them away.

When Art saw her reaction, he laughed into the microphone. It was all she could do to keep from screaming.

She had to get a grip on herself. Wrapping her arms around her shoulders, she hugged herself tightly and rocked back and forth.

He thrust the microphone toward her. Your turn, he mouthed.

"Now—now—I guess you're wondering what's happened to me..."

Her voice was unsteady when she began to talk. It gained strength as she read the message she'd composed for Cam.

IT WAS FIVE in the morning. Cam's compulsively neat work area was littered with hundreds of haphazardly scattered personnel files. He was looking through the record of every engineer who had worked for the company eight to three years ago—looking for some link to Collin.

We'll find him, Jo, he muttered under his breath. *We'll find him. Just hang on until we find him.*

So far he'd turned up nothing.

Laura Roswell burst into the room. Her eyes were bright with excitement. Cam's gaze fixed on the photograph she was waving in her hand.

"Look at this. Look at this," she shouted, shoving the picture at him.

He held it under the light. It showed a man with stringy hair and an intense face bent over a trash can.

"What the hell—"

"It's him. The guy who has Jo. Don't you see, it's got to be him. He's been following her around—learning about her. He must have gone back some time in the last couple of weeks and looked through Jo's trash." The words tumbled out one after the other. "I didn't want to get your hopes up, so I didn't say anything when I left. A couple of hours ago, I remembered the camera Jo set up to get a picture of those dogs."

Cam studied the face in the photograph. It didn't look familiar. Not even much like the waiter who had abducted Jo. But maybe—

Quickly he began to shuffle files together.

"You take that stack," he directed Laura. "I'll take this one. They've each got a photograph. One of them may be the guy."

Forty-five minutes later, he acknowledged that none of the men looked like the creep at the trash can. He cursed under his breath.

Another desperate lead that hadn't panned out. Like the van. It wasn't registered in the Towson area.

Cam was sitting with his palms pressed against his burning eyelids when the phone rang.

"Your girlfriend made you a tape."

There was no need to explain who was calling. His hand jerked as he activated the ultrasensitive recorder that he'd hooked up to the phone.

There was a pause of several seconds. Then Jo's voice came on the line. It quavered and he pictured her alone with this madman and terrified.

"Now—now—I guess you're wondering what's happened to me."

Her voice grew in strength and confidence. *That's it, Jo,* he silently encouraged.

"Unfortunately, I'm not free to tell you what's going on. Give the man the money. Everything will be all right. Not to worry, Superman. Trust him."

The sound of her voice sent little prickles of electricity along his nerve endings.

"Jo!"

"Just a recording, stupid."

"How do I know—"

"You don't. But if you want to see her again, you'll put the money in your car and drive to the big boulders near the science building at Goucher College. Monday evening at five. You'll find further instructions there. If the police are following you, your girlfriend is dead."

Cam tried to imagine the further instructions. They probably included disabling his car phone.

"Wait. What if I can't get the money together that fast?"

"Too bad for Ms. O'Malley."

JO WORKED STEADILY—chipping and gouging and hiding the cement dust. Every few minutes she gave a harsh tug on the chain. It didn't budge. The bolt was deeper in the wall than she'd imagined. There wasn't a chance that she could dig it out in time. But she had to try.

Again she tried to keep her spirits up by thinking of Cam. Of getting back to him. Of how happy they'd both be when he held her in his arms again. Now it was hard to make the fantasy work, and she realized she was losing hope.

Denise. Margaret. Jo.

No, she wasn't going to end up like the other two.

When she heard the outside door open, her hand froze, and she looked down at the pile of cement dust and chips on the T-shirt. More cement dust clung to the front of her ruined dress. She'd forgotten to keep things cleaned up.

Eager footsteps hurried down the hall.

Jo swiped her hand across the front of the dress. Then, as the doorknob turned, she swept the metal brace, T-shirt and cement under the covers.

Arthur Nugent's eyes were bright as he opened the

door and stood looking at her with strange possessiveness.

"It's time for the wedding ceremony, Denise."

She didn't bother to tell him she was Jo. What difference would that make now?

"We haven't had our rehearsal dinner yet," she murmured instead.

"Dinner! It's almost morning."

"Please. I'm hungry now. Fix me something special."

He considered the request and then grinned as if pleased with one more opportunity to show his knowledge of her habits. "Biscuits. You like biscuits for breakfast."

"Yes."

"All right. I guess that's fair. It will have to be the kind from the refrigerator."

"That's fine."

"I'll be back in a few minutes. Then Denise and I— I mean you and…" He let the sentence trail off, his eyes looking at her meaningfully.

The second the door closed, Jo pulled out the piece of metal and turned back to the wall. Desperately she began to gouge away at the cement around the bolt. She didn't try to work neatly now. This was her last chance. Either she got it loose, or he came to take her away for the ceremony.

THEY HAD ALL GATHERED around the tape recorder. Cam played the message for the fifth time while he stared at the transcription he'd made.

She'd called him Superman so there was a good chance the message was in her own words. Had she used the recording to send him some information?

Cam tried to focus on the message. He'd always been good at word games—at seeing patterns. Now when Jo's life depended on him, his brain was almost too numb to function.

Doggedly he repeated the words.

"Now I guess you're wondering..." That was a strange way to start off, and not at all like Jo's usual speech patterns. "Unfortunately... Give the man... Everything..."

He looked around the room and knew that everybody else was engaged in the same life or death struggle. Steve was hunched forward with his fists clenched. Laura's eyes were shut in concentration. His friends. Jo's friends. And he'd been riding them unmercifully. When this was over...

He realized his mind was wandering and forced it back to the word puzzle.

For endless minutes there was complete silence.

"Nuget," Abby murmured.

Cam's head swiveled toward her. "What?"

"No. N-U-G-E-N-T. If you look at the first letter of each sentence's first word, they spell out "nugent." I thought it was "nuget"—that maybe it meant something."

"Nugent." Cam's mind was racing. He'd seen that word. It was a name. A familiar name. Because—because he'd just read it on one of the Randolph Enterprises personnel files.

Leaping up, he began to scramble through the stacks of folders.

"Nugent. It's a name. There's a guy named Nugent here somewhere," he practically shouted.

The others joined him in the hunt. Steve was the one who pulled out the file.

The guy's picture looked as if it had come from a high-school yearbook. He appeared twenty years younger than the man who'd been caught by the trash can. Which was why Cam had passed right over him without reading the contents of the file. Now he could see a resemblance.

COLD SWEAT broke out on Jo's forehead as she hewed away at the cement. When she stopped to tug at the chain, it moved. It moved! With renewed will, she doubled her efforts.

She could wiggle it back and forth now. If she just had a few more minutes—

She'd been so intent on her task that she hadn't heard the door open.

"You bitch! You lied to me again."

With every ounce of strength she possessed, Jo yanked on the chain. The superhuman effort paid off. The bolt came free of the wall. But she hadn't really expected it to give way. In the next second, she tumbled backward onto the hard wooden floor.

Art tossed away the tray he was holding. As biscuits, jelly and hot coffee crashed against the wall, he was sprinting toward Jo.

He was on her in seconds. With more instinct than finesse, she flailed at him with the chain still attached to her left wrist. He grunted as the end careened into his shoulder.

She didn't have time to draw her arm back for another whack. Cursing, face contorted with rage, he went crazy. His hands came up around her neck, shaking and choking. In blind panic, she struggled and gasped for breath. But her air supply was completely blocked. Blackness rose up to meet her.

ARTHUR NUGENT. Skimming his performance appraisals, Cam understood why he didn't remember the man. As an engineer he'd been mediocre. Yet buried in the middle of the material were several recommendations from Collin. He'd hired Nugent above the objections of a senior manager. Later he'd tried to get him transferred to the design department.

Nugent had quit the company three years ago. Just before Collin had died.

Cam felt a mixture of old sadness and new excitement constrict his chest. He'd been looking for someone like this. Someone with a personal connection to his brother. And Jo had sent him the name.

He flipped to the back for the personal data.

"Six years ago he lived in a town house in Randallstown. He listed his father as the person he wanted notified in case of emergency. His father lives in Towson," he told the circle of waiting faces.

"What's the address?" Abby demanded.

Cam read it aloud.

"That's right in back of Towson High School," Laura confirmed.

JO WAS CONSCIOUS of several sensations. Her neck hurt. Drawing in a breath was like sucking in fire. Firm hands grasped her ankles. The handcuff was gone. She was no longer dressed in the ruined maid of honor dress. Cold stone scraped against her hips.

Cautiously she looked down at her body. She was

wearing a white dress now. A thin white dress that would have been more appropriate for June than December. The flimsy fabric had ridden up around her waist as Arthur Nugent dragged her across a stone floor.

She held back the scream of black terror that bubbled in her chest. Instead she willed her body to remain limp and peered at the maniac through a screen of lashes. Let him think she was still unconscious. Above her was a vaulted church ceiling. He'd dragged her to a church? How was that possible?

The ceiling looked like granite. No, it was painted plywood. On either side were stained-glass windows made from heavy panes of plastic. Spotlights behind them made the colors glow.

Around her, recorded organ music floated. The wedding march. She could hear Art muttering the words of the ceremony, his voice high and cracking now, weirdly distorted without the need of the electronic device.

"We have gathered here to give thanks for the gift of marriage and to witness the joining together of Arthur and Denise."

He'd brought Denise here. And Margaret, too.

The scream hovered in her throat now. She refused to give it life.

The chapel was tiny—only two rows of pews and then the altar flanked by white flowers. On a low table covered with white linen, a long knife had been laid out. Behind it loomed the brass bed. The one from the home movie. Jo lost the battle to remain limp. Her body jerked, and a scream tore from her lips.

Arthur turned and cuffed the side of her head, momentarily stunning her again. "Shut up! You're spoiling everything. You tried to trick me," he shrieked. "Now we don't have time to do things right."

As he spoke, he hoisted her onto the bed and dragged her arm toward one of the handcuffs that dangled from the headboard.

When she began to struggle, he climbed on top of her, straddling her writhing body with his legs, pressing her down with his weight. She fought him with every remaining ounce of strength. It wasn't enough. Closer, closer. Her right hand drew inexorably closer to the cuff. If he chained her to the bed, the game was over.

Instead of concentrating on Arthur, she switched her attention to the band of metal. Her fingers scrabbled and slid against the smooth surface. Then, miraculously, she had the thing in her hand. With a little gasp of triumph, she squeezed. The cuff snapped shut around empty air. Her hand was still free.

Arthur howled with rage.

Another cuff dangled from the other side of the headboard. He grasped her left hand and folded the fingers closed in a painful grip. Then he began to repeat the process that had just failed.

Somewhere above the music she thought she heard a shout and then an alarm bell clanging. The security alarm. No. It was probably a fantasy. A last desperate rescue fantasy. Her mind had finally provided her with the only escape route possible.

In the next second she was slammed back to reality. Her world had narrowed to the man on top of her dragging her fist toward the handcuff. This time she couldn't close the metal band. This time he had her.

Just as the metal touched her flesh, the door burst open.

"Hold it right there, Nugent," a deep voice barked.

She saw the dazed look on her captor's features. He whirled as if to face the police officers spilling into the room. Then he was lunging for the knife.

It was swinging down toward her chest when shots rang out and he fell backward onto the stone floor.

CHAPTER FIFTEEN

HAMILL HAD TRIED to keep him from joining the rescue operation. But Cam hadn't taken no for an answer. The detective had given in, but when they'd arrived at the house, Cam had been held back behind the police vans while a special unit armed with automatic weapons had surrounded the house and broken in.

It was the longest fifteen minutes of his life. Each hammer beat of his heart was an accusation. The more he thought about it, the more he felt his own culpability. *If you'd had the guts to face up to your brother's role in the industrial espionage, this wouldn't have happened to Jo.*

Now he was finally in the house. But he wore his guilt like a coat of nails with the points gouging into his skin. Jo had to be all right. She had to be! Determinedly he pushed his way through the dozen armed men who separated him from the woman he loved.

He could see her now, huddled on the bed in a torn white dress. She was alive. Thank God she was alive! But she was crying quietly.

Everything else faded into the background. The wedding march that was still playing at full volume. The pews that must have been salvaged from an old church, the garish windows, the cloying smell of the gardenias flanking the altar.

He had to step around a pool of blood on the floor where Nugent's body had lain moments earlier. For an instant he was struck with a strange sense of déjà vu. Another killer. Another threat to Jo's life had ended in a very similar fashion. Only this time the man was dead.

He knelt beside the figure huddled on the bed. She looked so young and defenseless. Against the white sheets, her skin was as pale as marble.

"Jo, honey. It's all over."

Even after the torture of the EMP and the television set, she'd held on to some shreds of self-control. Now somehow his words brought a fresh torrent of tears. What had that bastard done to her?

Or was she crying because she didn't want to face him?

"Oh, God, Jo, are you all right?" *Please be all right.*

He reached out and pulled her into his arms. She hid her face against his chest and clutched his arms as she continued to sob into his shirt.

His fingers soothed over her back and shoulders. It was so damn good just to hold her again. "Oh, Jo, Jo. You're safe. Thank God you're safe."

He could sense her struggling for control. "You got here...I'm sorry...I just..." But she couldn't finish the sentence.

"Jo, forgive me."

She didn't answer. Maybe he didn't deserve her forgiveness.

He felt the sobs ebb. She was still trembling. "Cam— please—"

"Anything, honey. Anything."

"Where is he?"

"Dead. He won't hurt you anymore."

He heard her sigh, felt her relax against him. As she began to speak, he knew she'd gotten back some measure of control. "He was so crazy. I never knew what he was going to do. I couldn't be sure he remembered who I was, even."

It was hard to imagine the horror of it.

"Cam, you saved me."

"We got your message."

"Not just the message. I would have cracked up without you. Well—maybe I did. I kept imagining you there with me, encouraging me, telling me I was going to make it."

"Oh, Jo, honey. I kept thinking those things. Maybe you read my mind."

But as he held her and stroked her and talked softly to her, they both silently admitted that they hadn't been sure they would see each other again.

"I'd like to examine her," a police doctor broke into their reunion.

Cam reluctantly relinquished the contact and moved aside.

"How is she?" he asked anxiously.

"She needs rest. I'm going to give her a sedative. And I want to keep her in the hospital for observation."

After the man had administered the drug, Jo stretched out her hand to Cam. "Don't leave me."

"I won't."

He was still holding her fingers tightly as he felt them relax and saw her eyelids flutter.

"I'm riding in the ambulance with her," he told the doctor.

"She won't know you're there."

"I think she will."

JO AWOKE to ribbons of sunlight filtering through half-closed venetian blinds. She didn't know where she was. For one terrible moment of confusion, the fear was back.

Dig the bolt out of the wall. Get away. Before he takes you to the chapel. She struggled to push herself up. A hand pressed against her shoulder, and she gasped.

"Jo. It's all over. The nightmare is over."

"Cam."

Safety. Freedom. She looked up at him in wonder, still not quite able to believe that they were here together.

"You've been sitting there beside my bed," she said softly.

"Yes."

Eons passed as they stared at each other—taking in details that only lovers see. Transmitting silent messages that only lovers hear.

She was still so pale.

A two-day growth of beard darkened his jaw.

Her eyes were so large and blue.

A lock of dark hair had fallen across his forehead. She reached up to push it back.

"Jo, I've been sitting here, wondering how you were going to feel about me when you woke up."

"Why?"

His voice was raw. "Because if I'd only believed what you were trying to tell me about Collin, none of this would have happened."

"Oh, Cam, that's not true."

He swallowed. "My brother and Art Nugent, the man who kidnapped you, had a—a—relationship. Art was the one who stole the designs from Randolph Electronics."

"I figured that out—from things he said, hints he dropped."

"Did you figure out why he picked you for his next victim? He wanted to get back at me—for not giving him a job in the design department at Randolph."

She found his hand and squeezed it. "No, Cam. Getting back at you was just a dividend. An accident, really. He told me it was a piece of luck for him."

She saw some of the tension go out of Cam's expression and continued, "He kidnapped me because I was the maid of honor in a wedding—like Denise. He was doing the same thing over and over again—repeating his experience with her."

"Denise?"

"He talked a lot about her—about what she meant to him. It's all pretty crazy. But it made some kind of twisted sense to him. It goes back to Collin. I think he really cared for your brother, and he cracked up after he died. He blamed himself for the suicide. It made him want to change his life—to go straight. Right after that, he saw Denise in church and in his disturbed mind, she reminded him of an angel. He thought she could save him—turn his life around. He tried to convince himself he was attracted to her. But she rejected him, and he killed her."

"Oh, my God. He told you all that?"

"Some of it. In bits and pieces. Some I figured out. After that, he kept repeating the experience because he hated her so much and blamed her for his failures."

Cam's voice struggled for even timbre. "Jo, the tapes. The things he said he was going to do to you—"

"Just threats. To make it sound like he wanted a woman. I don't think he could function with a female."

"Jo—I—"

"Cam, stop punishing yourself. It's over. Just hold me, please."

There was no way he could refuse that request. But there were still things he had to say. "Jo, I need you so damn much. I didn't realize how much pain was locked up inside me until I started loving you. But I was still afraid to trust my feelings. It was as if I had to choose either you or Collin. Then when I started to suspect what he'd done to his own company, to my father, I really couldn't handle it."

Jo tightened her arms around him, knowing that it would take time for him to get over the sorrow. But she would be there to help him. "What Collin did doesn't wipe out all the good years when you were growing up. I know it's hard for you now, but you'll see that eventually."

"But he—"

"Probably he was being used—not doing the actual stealing. I think he realized that and couldn't find a way out."

"Yes."

"It's hard to let go of the past—to let yourself see things differently."

"Yes."

"I'm not just talking about you. I'm talking about myself, too." She raised her head so she could meet his eyes. "I was attracted to you the moment we met."

"Attracted to a nutty inventor?"

"Not nutty. Intense. But I was afraid to trust my feelings, too. Abby helped me understand what I was doing. I kept telling myself no one could replace Skip. I was really afraid to take another chance on happiness."

"Jo, I swear I'll make you happy."

"I know you will."

They smiled at each other. Then his lips found hers again for a long, deep kiss, rich with promise for the future.

It was incredible to be held by him again. She felt sheltered. Cherished. Everything she'd been terrified to let herself want.

It was incredible to hold her again. His joy soared. She wanted him. She wasn't blaming him for all the things he'd failed to see and all the things he'd failed to do. Instead she was clinging to him with the same desperation he felt.

"Jo, I love you."

"Oh, Cam, I love you, too. I wanted to tell you that when I made the recording. I knew he wouldn't let me."

"Hearing your voice—knowing he had you..." He couldn't say the rest of it. But he didn't have to. She understood.

All the forces of nature couldn't have separated them as they clung together.

After long moments, she looked up into his eyes, her own twinkling. "I guess this means you've gotten over your aversion to detectives."

"You do have a smart remark for every occasion."

"Yup."

"How would you feel about my putting a certain sassy redheaded private eye on a lifetime retainer?"

For once, Jo O'Malley was speechless.

"Does that mean she'll take the job?"

"You've got a deal."

LOVERBOY
by Vicki Lewis Thompson

Loverboy originally appeared as a
Harlequin Temptation® novel.
Each month there are four new sexy,
sassy and seductive Temptation® books
by your favorite authors.

LOVERBOY
by Vicki Lewis Thompson

Loverboy originally appeared as a
Harlequin Temptation novel.
Each month there are four new sexy,
sassy and seductive Temptation books
by your favorite authors.

CHAPTER ONE

A CHANDELIER SPRINKLED with rainbows dominated the elegant room where Sheila stood waiting, her eyes wide, her breathing rapid. Luke's glance settled hungrily on the rise and fall of her creamy breasts barely contained by the plunging neckline of her black silk dress.

He crossed the room in three strides and pulled her into his arms. The silk rustled against the stiff denim of his jeans. "Now, we'll settle this." He gazed into her upturned face. He didn't love her, but that didn't matter. As he had so many times before, he'd pretend she was Meg. His voice was low, urgent. "You know what I want."

"I can't give you that anymore!"

A muscle twitched in his jaw as desire pounded through his body. "Then I'll just have to take it." Ignoring her protests, he crushed his mouth against hers.

"Cut!"

MEG TOOK A DEEP BREATH and reached for the phone, her hands shaking as she punched in Didi's number. While she waited for her friend to answer, she glanced at the stack of posters propped against the desk of her home office. A cartoon version of a long-lashed ostrich advertised the Chandler Ostrich Festival only two weeks away.

Her gaze traveled to a box of silk-screened ostrich festival T-shirts in one corner of the room before roaming over the festival paperwork littering every available surface. Festival brochures and advance news clips covered the bulletin board over her desk, along with a lapel pin announcing Meg O'Brian as Board Member, Chandler Chamber Of Commerce.

Didi answered on the fourth ring. Meg and Didi had been friends since third grade, so there was no need for Meg to identify herself. "The TV network just called." Meg's stomach was churning. "They've chosen our parade grand marshal."

"And?"

"Luke Bannister."

"I'll be damned. The return of Chandler's favorite son."

"Right. The drag-race king of Arizona Avenue. The guy who appeared on stage smashed out of his mind for the school musical and turned a skunk loose during graduation."

"I doubt those things are in his press release. But don't panic. It'll be okay. Would you believe he has a local fan club?"

"What?"

"I'm only slightly embarrassed to tell you I'm in it."

"Didi, you're not!"

"I know you don't watch the soaps, but you really should tune in to *Connections*. Trust me, one episode with Luke as Dirk Kennedy and you'd be hooked."

"I don't *want* to be hooked. I—"

"For goodness' sake, Meg. It's only harmless fantasy."

Maybe for you, Meg thought. *Luke didn't break your heart.*

"When's he coming in?" Didi asked. "As parade chairperson I should confirm the presidential suite at the San Marcos and arrange for a limo at the airport."

"You can cancel the suite. He's staying with his brother."

"I guess he and Clint must've patched up their feud. When should I schedule the limo?"

"Well—" Meg's pulse raced as the full impact of Luke's visit hit her "—for some reason, he sent word that I'm supposed to pick him up."

"You're kidding!"

"He probably just wants to brag about his accomplishments."

"That would fit the Luke we all knew and loved. Be careful, toots. If he tries to stir the embers, you'd be in deep—"

"I'm not that stupid. Besides, I can't believe he's interested in me, after years of dating starlets."

"Maybe not, but be careful, anyway."

"I will. And as long as I have you on the phone, I have a couple of questions about the parade." As they talked, Meg forced her attention away from Luke, but every so often her heart repeated a reminder that he was coming back, like a news bulletin along the bottom of a television screen. They hadn't spoken in ten years, and their last words had been bitter. The ride from the airport to the Bannister cotton farm could be a long trip if Luke spent the time boasting about his success.

"Listen, Meg, *Connections* is almost on," Didi said. "Maybe you should take a look and familiarize yourself with Luke's character, in case the media ask you questions about the show.''

''Uh...okay.'' Meg's stomach pitched. She'd avoided the show on purpose, figuring there was no use in summoning the ghost of old passions.

''You're probably the only person in Chandler who hasn't seen it at least once. You'd better watch it, if only to make sure you recognize Luke at the airport.''

''Right. Bye, Didi.'' There wasn't a chance in hell she'd mistake Luke at the airport. Sometimes, in her dreams, she still saw his eyes. Like a sailor walking the plank, she left her office, strode into the living room and turned on the television.

The episode opened with a scene between two women named Sheila and Daphne, who had an argument Meg couldn't follow. During the commercial break Meg drew a deep breath and lounged back on her green plaid sofa. Luke probably wasn't even on today's show.

Suddenly, there he was. She leaned forward as the blood sang in her ears and her skin prickled. There he was.

He paused in the doorway of an ornate room lit by a crystal chandelier. His hair was a little shorter than he'd worn it in high school, but it still fell dark and untamed over his forehead. The extravagant set made his worn jeans and denim shirt look roguish by contrast. He gazed purposefully at Sheila. Meg's pulse quickened. She remembered that look, the blatant sexuality in those blue eyes. Oh, God, how she remembered.

Then he crossed the room. His walk brought a familiar pang of longing. He moved with a loose-hipped stride that seemed to announce he knew exactly where he was going. When he reached for Sheila, Meg almost stopped breathing.

As they kissed, Meg spun back through time. She'd written an ode to Luke's kiss and then burned it in a teacup; her tears had helped put out the tiny fire. It made no sense that she could feel the anguish still, but the pain of her first heartbreak had seared deep, creating a scar she would carry forever.

The scene ended and a commercial flashed on. Meg sat in a daze, not looking at the TV. All she could see was the image of the first man she'd ever loved. And he was coming home.

TWO WEEKS LATER on Wednesday afternoon, Meg stood in the terminal of Phoenix's Sky Harbor Airport and tried to keep her cool. Luke's plane had just landed. Any minute now he'd walk through the dark passageway and she'd be face-to-face with the man who'd haunted her dreams for the past two weeks. She'd come alone as he'd requested, although back in Chandler preparations were under way for an elaborate welcoming celebration.

She'd been in an ornery mood since early morning, when she'd rejected the business suit she'd planned to wear in favor of worn jeans and a forest green knit pullover. Luke would probably arrive in some Hollywood glitz outfit, but she wouldn't play the game of one-upmanship with him. As her rebellious mood had blossomed, she'd decided to drive her twenty-year-old green truck to the airport instead of the silver BMW she and Dan had bought two years ago. Let Luke parade his success before her and appear gauche for doing so. Let him be embarrassed for a change.

The door to the jetway opened and passengers filed

out. Meg scanned the group, comparing each person who appeared with the man who'd been on her television screen for the past two weeks. She'd secretly watched every episode of *Connections*, searching for things to hate about Luke. Her search had produced mixed results. His character on the show was arrogant and ruthless, traits she could despise, but Dirk Kennedy was also as sexy as hell. Of course, on the show he'd had the benefit of makeup artists and wardrobe consultants. He couldn't possibly look as magnetic in person as he did on screen.

She hadn't counted on him looking better.

When he walked into the terminal wearing formfitting jeans and a tight blue T-shirt, Meg gripped the back of a waiting-area chair to steady herself. If he'd been handsome in high school, he was magnificent now. Dammit.

He had a garment bag slung over one shoulder and a small duffel bag in his other hand. The harsh fluorescent lights of the terminal couldn't destroy the impact of his square jaw, his sculpted mouth, his prominent cheekbones. His walk, his gaze, even his grip on the duffel bag projected sexual power. Meg saw several women stare at him. Two women glanced his way and talked excitedly to each other. Meg decided she'd better get him out of the terminal before somebody recognized him. Or perhaps that was what he wanted.

She waved. He spotted her and smiled, but before either of them could move, a camera flashed. Meg glanced at the photographer, a scruffy young woman in baggy shorts and tank top, with a Dodgers baseball cap on backward. She had a second camera slung across her chest like a bandolier, and she snapped off shots as if firing a weapon. Meg had never seen paparazzi before, but the commando tactics of the young woman suggested she was one of that tenacious breed. Her flurry of activity drew more people, and Luke was quickly surrounded.

As Meg wondered what to do next, the knot of people began edging in her direction. She backed up a step before realizing that the group was moving toward her simply because Luke was.

"You'll have to excuse me, but I'm due in Chandler and I wouldn't want to disappoint the people waiting for me," he said, lifting his voice over the crowd.

He must relish announcing he had a whole town at his beck and call, she thought. His tone had deepened in ten years, but Meg recognized the same voice that had spoken words of love in the back of a pickup truck. The same voice that later had told her to get lost.

He'd put his duffel bag on the floor and was scribbling autographs on ticket envelopes and napkins. The young woman with the camera contorted her body to get shot after shot. "Dirk, aren't you afraid Sheila's husband is going to find out about you?" a woman on the fringe of the crowd called out.

Meg was startled by the question until she figured out that the woman thought Luke really *was* Dirk Kennedy and that he was actually carrying on an affair with Sheila behind her husband's back.

Luke didn't seem confused at all. He smiled at the woman who'd asked the question. "Sheila and I are very discreet. Besides, her husband keeps his nose in the *Wall Street Journal* all the time. The man has tons of money and no imagination. He'll never guess." The crowd laughed, but Meg's jaw tightened at the arrogance he displayed. "Well, gotta go." Luke flashed the same naughty-little-boy smile he'd used to such effect on the show. "Got another beautiful woman waiting for me."

Meg recoiled. How dare he lump her in with his bevy of conquests? The patronizing so-and-so! The crowd and the photographer immediately turned their attention on her and she shrank back in dismay.

"Sheila will be jealous!" someone shouted. *Flash, flash* went the camera.

"Sheila doesn't ever have to know, does she?" Luke picked up his bag, transferred it to the same hand that held his garment bag and winking, put his free arm around Meg. "Let's go," he urged in an undertone. "Hustle that little butt of yours."

"You mean run?" She was seeing spots from the camera's flash and she flinched from his invasion of her space. His touch was the same. Even his scent was the same. Her memory had lost nothing in ten years.

"Yes, run. Pretend we just stole oranges from old man Peterson's tree."

"If you say so." Meg took a deep breath and grasped her purse firmly.

"Now." Luke squeezed her shoulder and released his grip. They sprinted forward, catching the group surrounding them by surprise. They reached the elevators leading to the parking garage, and by a stroke of luck, the doors of one slid open in front of them. They dashed in.

Panting, Meg turned to him. "Any more luggage?"

"This is it." He grinned at her. "Out of shape, are we?"

She noticed he wasn't even breathing hard. "Some of us don't have personal trainers," she snapped.

"There was a day when you could run a mile without

even getting winded, and with a load of oranges tied in the hem of your T-shirt besides.''

"Then apparently I haven't aged as well as you.''

His smile faded and his gaze traveled over her. "I wouldn't say that. You look great, Meg.''

She flushed, and hated herself for doing it. She had a master's degree in political science and a responsible position in the community. Why was she reacting to his compliment like a love-struck teenager? "Thank you,'' she said, regarding him with what she hoped was calm indifference. When the elevator doors opened she led the way into the tiered parking garage and hoped to hell she could remember where she'd parked.

"What'd you bring?''

"My truck.'' She waited for his snort of derision. None came.

"You don't mean Kermit?''

She nodded. *Now all I have to do is figure out where I put him.*

"That's great. Is he still green?''

"New paint job, but he's still green.'' She squinted down the row of vehicles in one direction. Then, trying to appear nonchalant, she gazed in the other.

Luke began to laugh. "Same old Meg. I can remember roaming the parking lot at school, looking for your truck.''

"I've gotten much better.'' *Except today.*

"Are we on the right level?''

"Yes.''

"Then let's start walking.''

Feeling like a dope, she fell into step beside him. "You must wonder how I'm running an entire community festival if I can't even remember where my truck is parked.''

"I don't wonder at all. You were always a whiz at organizing things. Usually you had so much on your mind you'd be thinking of details while you robotted your way through the ordinary stuff, like parking. Of course you'd forget where you put your truck.''

"That's a very nice rationalization,'' she said primly.

"Isn't this it, right here?''

She looked where he pointed and felt warmth rising in her cheeks once more. She'd almost walked right past the darn thing. "Yes, that's it.''

"Boy, does this bring back memories." Luke put his hand on the tailgate. "Remember when I made that romantic remark that your truck matched your eyes?''

The comment jolted her and she glanced away. "Not really." He had a lot of nerve bringing that up, as if he thought they could laugh about it together. Their first real date, and she'd had to drive because his license was still suspended from his latest drag-racing incident. He'd told her that her truck matched her eyes, and then he'd kissed her. A transforming kiss, one that awakened needs she'd never known existed until his lips caressed hers.

He heaved his luggage into the back of the truck. "It was on our first date." He glanced back at her, as if prompting her to remember.

She shook her head and forced a gay laugh. "Goodness, that was *so* long ago." She avoided meeting his eyes as she hurried to unlock the passenger door. "We'd better get going. The welcoming committee is waiting for you.''

After navigating the concrete ramps of the garage, Meg paid the parking fee while batting away Luke's offer of money. He wasn't going to pull the big spender routine on *her*.

"This ostrich festival sure was news to me," Luke said as they drove away from the airport. "Do you really draw a crowd of two hundred thousand?"

"Last year we did. It's the chamber's biggest fundraiser. We got the idea because they used to raise ostriches here, back when there was a market for ostrich plumes."

"Yeah, I read that in the publicity package they sent me. But I've been having a lot of trouble picturing an ostrich race."

"They're trained to run, after a fashion, anyway. The company who brings them in has camel and llama races, too. And we arrange for the other stuff you'd expect, like a carnival, food booths, entertainment."

"Carnival?" His tone was teasing. "Do you personally check out the rides?" When she shook her head, he laughed. "Didn't think so. You always were a chicken about heights." His constant references to their shared history were unnerving. She wouldn't have thought he'd want to dredge up the past this way, because if he kept it up, eventually they'd come to the unpleasant parts. "I was surprised at the band you got for Saturday night," he said. "Real headliners. There was a time I would've given anything to play with those guys."

"But now you wouldn't?"

"Actually I still would give a lot. I haven't touched my guitar in a long time, and I miss playing. But my schedule's so tight—"

"I'm sure it is," she cut in, trying to forestall a recitation of his important, busy schedule.

He shifted his gaze away. Then he rolled down the

window and stuck out his head. "Hey! Look at that sky. And the air doesn't smell like smelly socks, either. Good, clean air."

"Except when they're ginning cotton." She really was in a perverse mood.

"Oh, yeah. That is pretty gross. You know, in some ways I feel as if a century has gone by since I lived in Chandler. But then in other ways, like tooling along the road with you in this old truck, it seems as if I never left."

"The scene at the airport should have convinced you that everything's changed."

Luke grimaced. "It's that photographer. She must have been on the plane. I think she's just a kid working on her first celebrity, and I'm it. She's looking for a compromising shot, so she'll be hanging around a lot, unfortunately."

"Are you going to give her one?"

"I don't plan to." Looking back, he breathed a sigh of relief. "Thank God, she's not following us yet. She probably had to rent a car. She obviously hasn't learned all the tricks yet." He glanced at the dashboard. "Does your radio still work?"

"Yes."

"Got it on KNIX?"

"Yes." So some things hadn't changed. Luke still liked country music. When he switched on the radio, Garth Brooks was crooning an old favorite about being glad he didn't know how it all would go, how it all would end. Meg figured that would be a good philosophy for the next five days. She didn't want to know the outcome.

"So it's Meg O'Brian now."

"That's right." She tensed. Now the questions would begin.

"I guess you found yourself an Irishman. That must have pleased your folks."

She glanced at him. "Yes."

"But you're not wearing a ring. Is that some sort of feminist statement?"

He'd certainly been observant in the short time he'd been with her. She delivered her explanation with a certain grim satisfaction, glad to take him down a peg. "I don't wear a wedding ring because Dan was killed in a car accident two years ago."

"Oh, God." He looked away, staring at the freeway traffic. "Meg, I'm sorry."

"So am I."

"I feel like such a jerk. All I heard from the network was that Meg Hennessy O'Brian was running the festival. I thought you'd have a husband, maybe some kids.... I'm sorry. Me and my big mouth."

She felt a stab of pity for his obvious distress. "It's been two years now. The pain's not as bad." She paused and the music from the radio filled the silence. "Clint must not be a very good source of information."

"No. But that's not all his fault. I ticked him off pretty good when I didn't come home for Dad's funeral last summer."

"A lot of people didn't understand that."

"Did you?"

She hesitated. She didn't want to be his friend. After all, he hadn't been hers at the end of their relationship. But she couldn't forget the bruises Orville Bannister had left on him. She might be the only one who had known. "I understood," she said.

"That's good." He sighed and settled back against the seat. "I wanted to be there for Clint, but I didn't think I could stomach the funeral, with everybody making pious statements about Dad. Clint and I never did agree about our old man."

"But you're staying with Clint this weekend. Things must be better between you two now."

"I guess. The network notified him I'd be coming."

"You didn't call him?"

"I tried, but I never seemed to catch him at home. Probably out with some woman."

"Debbie Fry."

Luke chuckled. "I see Chandler's still a small town, even if the population figures say different."

"It's a good town, Luke."

"You're happy here, then."

"Yes, I am."

"Makes sense. You always belonged. Chandler and I never were a good fit. After being away, I can see it more clearly than ever. I can appreciate the good things about the place, but I could never live here again. Never."

Meg fell silent. His complete rejection of the town she loved, the town she planned to live in forever, felt like a slap. But what had she expected from a big important star like Luke Bannister? Some announcement that he planned to make Chandler his weekend home? Apparently she'd been watching too many soap operas.

CHAPTER TWO

A WIDOW. As he'd fantasized about this meeting he'd often dreamed that she was divorced, or unhappily married, and he'd rush to the rescue. But he'd never imagined this, wouldn't have wanted it for her. Poor Meg. The thought of her grief tore at him. But underneath his shock lurked a thought he was almost ashamed of…she was free. And frosty as hell. Undoubtedly she still nursed a grudge, which wasn't all bad. Anger was better than indifference.

Now that they were on Chandler Boulevard, she drove with her window down, the breeze blowing her long hair back from her face. He remembered her hair had been nearly white when she was little, but now it had deepened to the color of the Cracker Jack popcorn they used to eat.

In preparation for this trip, he'd told himself she might be fat; she might be pregnant; she might be oblivious to him. She was none of these. Her awareness of him was a palpable thing—just as it had been ten years ago, when he'd figured out what love was all about. Then, as now, it was all about Meg.

Surreptitiously he studied her as they drove. She still had that open, fresh-scrubbed face that reminded him of the models in an Eddie Bauer catalog. But an element of mystery had been added through her marriage, her widowhood. Ten years ago he'd imagined he knew everything about her. Now he was missing the most elemental knowledge of all, and he felt illogically cheated.

"Everything sure has changed," he said, breaking the silence between them.

She nodded. "The population's about five times bigger than when you left. You can see the evidence along this road."

He hadn't really been talking about Chandler, but he'd allow her to misunderstand him for the time being. In keeping with that, he looked obediently out the window at the fast-food restaurants, shopping centers and high-tech business plazas lining the street that had once bisected open fields. At least the familiar San Tan Mountains east of town hadn't changed. At four thousand feet, they weren't the "purple mountain majesties" he'd sung about in school, but he liked them, anyway. They had a coziness about them, as if a giant had spilled a huge box of brown sugar across the desert floor.

They passed what he was sure had been his and Meg's old make-out road. Once a dirt lane bordering an irrigation ditch, it was now a paved drive skirting a warehouse. A half mile or so down the road a cottonwood tree had towered forty feet in the air. On summer nights bits of fluff from the tree had floated down and drifted over their half-clothed bodies like snow. The tree was gone, but the memory made him ache with the same ferocity as when he'd been eighteen.

How he'd suffered on those nights when they'd spread a blanket in the back of his pickup and made out, doing just about everything except intercourse. He'd even brought condoms along one night, but hadn't used them. At the last moment he'd decided he and Meg should wait until they were married—one of the few decisions he could be proud of in his youth.

"I guess I ought to warn you about something," Meg said.

"What?"

"Instead of the keys to the city, the chamber is presenting you with a male ostrich."

"Excuse me?"

"A young male ostrich. Still pretty much a baby. He's the mascot for this year's festival."

"Ho, boy. Just what I've always wanted."

"He's named Dirk Kennedy, after your character in *Connections*."

Luke groaned. "Here it comes. I suppose because he struts around."

"That, and the fact that male ostriches keep at least three females at one time. This one hasn't gone through puberty yet, so you don't have to worry that he'll start chasing the chicks, so to speak."

Luke had to smile at the tartness with which she delivered that speech. "An ostrich. What am I supposed to do with it?"

"Pose. And watch out for its beak. They love to peck at anything shiny."

"Well, I don't have on anything shi—" He glanced down at his button fly where metal fasteners winked up at him. "Uh-oh."

"Maybe the welcoming ceremony will be short."

"I can guarantee it." As they approached the center of town, Luke's eyes widened. "My God, look at all this."

"That's the Rocky Mountain Bank Center. Most of the storefronts on the square have been remodeled to blend in with it and the exterior of the San Marcos Hotel."

Arizona Avenue had been widened, and a grassy mall added. He gazed at the lush greenery and fountains, the turquoise metal canopy arching over the street. But mostly he noticed the crowd of about one hundred people gathered in front of the peach-colored building on their left, the new bank building. "Everyone's here because of me?"

"That's right."

Then he saw the ostrich. Dirk Kennedy stood about five feet tall from feet to beak. As they drew closer, he could see the black-feathered body and stubby white feathers that would eventually be plumes. It had to weigh at least two hundred pounds. A man was holding it on a leash, but Luke didn't believe for a moment that the man could control that bird if it decided to bolt. "Good Lord."

"The ostrich is pretty tame. It was hand-raised," Meg said.

"I'll bet that took a lot of hands. Meg, who are all these people? Is that the pep band?"

"The pep band, which is delighted to get out of school to welcome you, plus the members of the Luke Bannister Fan Club, some of whom asked for time off work to be here, the mayor and his wife, the chamber president and his wife and most of my committee heads for the festival, many of whom are also members of your fan club, I discovered recently."

"I expected the network to send a crew for publicity purposes, but this is amazing."

"Nobody wanted to miss your arrival. By the way, a rental car's been following us for the past three miles. I expect your eager photographer's in it." She pulled the truck over to the curb and the pep band struck up the Chandler High School Wolves' fight song.

Luke took a deep breath. Whoever said you can't go home again? he thought. You can go anytime you want, but you have to be prepared. They might be waiting for you with a five-foot ostrich. "Okay, Meg. Let's do it."

MEG WATCHED HIM go into action. He climbed down from the truck with a brilliant smile and a big wave befitting his star status. The old Luke, the one she'd fallen in love with, would have begged her to get him out of here. The new sophisticated Luke had learned to face the music, which had now become a jazzed-up version of the theme song from *Connections*.

But, even the pep band couldn't drown out the cries and squeals of the fan club. Meg rolled her eyes at the crowd of women waving signs that said We Love You, Luke, and Dirk Kennedy For President. Some people had no shame, she thought.

She spotted Didi standing with her husband, Chuck, and watched as they sidled up to Luke like long-lost friends. During the months Meg had dated Luke, he'd been accepted by her crowd, which had included Chuck and Didi. After he'd dumped her, they had given him the cold shoulder, but she could hardly expect her friends to snub him now, ten years later. She couldn't expect it, but she did wish Didi had been a little less enthusiastic, for loyalty's sake.

Gradually Luke made the rounds of well-wishers, shaking hands with the men and accepting single red roses from the women. At last he came to Joe Randolph, who was holding the ostrich. The mayor, Keith Garvey, stood beside Joe. When Luke reached them, Keith signaled to the pep band for silence.

"Luke Bannister, you have made your hometown proud of you," he announced, "and we appreciate your presence at our annual ostrich festival more than we can say." The TV cameraman moved in. The mayor smiled. "Perhaps this will be some indication of our gratitude. We've named the festival mascot after your character in *Connections*. We've got him on a leash, because if he lives up to his namesake, he's liable to go after every female ostrich within a hundred miles."

The crowd laughed and the women from the fan club whooped in approval. "May I present," the mayor continued, "Dirk Kennedy." He handed the leash to Luke as the crowd whistled and cheered.

"I don't know when I've ever been so moved," Luke said, warily accepting the leash.

Meg couldn't help noticing he held his bouquet of flowers over his crotch. Cameras whirred as Luke made a little speech about the honor of being the festival's grand marshal. The scruffy young woman had alighted from her rented blue Honda sedan and was taking more pictures.

"Chandler holds a special place in my heart," Luke continued. "I hope that—" The ostrich's head snaked forward and Luke leaped back, but not before the bird got a beakful of roses. He began placidly chewing, the red petals sticking out of the side of his beak, his long-lashed eyelids drifting half-closed.

Luke looked from the bird to his mangled bouquet. Then he smiled at the crowd. "I've always wondered what it was like to be deflowered by Dirk Kennedy."

Meg grimaced at the bad joke but the crowd loved it.

Amid laughter and applause, Luke handed the leash back to Joe Randolph and glanced at Meg with a can-we-go-now look. She nodded, and with a wave Luke headed back toward the truck as the pep band struck up the school fight song again.

"How'd I do?" Luke asked as Meg drove the truck carefully past waving onlookers and headed for the Bannister farm.

"Just fine." She chose not to elaborate. Maybe he was used to a constant stream of praise, but she didn't plan to provide that.

A cavalcade of cars and the TV van followed. He glanced in the rearview mirror. "This is incredible."

"You're a big hit around here."

"To tell you the truth, once I'm over the embarrassment of it all, I'll probably think it's funny as hell. I've dreaded coming back. Apparently I've been worried about the wrong things."

The hint of vulnerability piqued her curiosity. "What were you worried about?"

"I was considered nothing but a two-bit punk when I left. I was afraid the people around here would make me feel that way again."

She digested the comment, which didn't quite square with her image of him as an arrogant egomaniac. "Not likely, judging from this cavalcade."

Luke glanced around at the string of cars, trucks and vans. "Your parents weren't in that crowd, were they?"

"No."

He settled back in the seat. "Didn't think they would be. They still live down the road from Clint?"

"Yes. But I don't think they see him much."

"Didn't think they would."

They passed the house where Meg had grown up, and Luke glanced at it. "Kept the place up nice, didn't they?"

"You know Dad. Fresh coat of paint every five years, whether the place needs it or not. And Mom has a personal vendetta against weeds."

"Yeah, I remember."

Meg recalled the last discussion she'd had with her mother and father on the subject of Luke Bannister coming to town. "Don't spend too much time with him," her mother had warned. "You know those Hollywood types."

Her father had been more direct. "If you want to be the chamber's next president you'll guard your reputation. You've got enough strikes against you being young and a woman. If people see you hanging all over somebody like Luke Bannister, you won't have a chance."

Meg had assured them she had no intention of "hanging all over" Luke Bannister and adding to his overblown idea of his own importance.

They reached the Bannister farm, which stood in stark contrast to the Hennessy place. Luke's mother had died when he was eleven and Clint was nine. Meg remembered that Luke had tried to keep up his mother's flower beds after her death but one night his father, in a drunken rage fueled by grief, had plowed them under. Luke had given up on beautifying.

The weathered house, surrounded by a spring crop of new weeds, had a covered porch that ran the length of the front and a swing suspended from the rafters. Clint Bannister levered his lanky frame out of the swing as they climbed out of the truck and walked toward him. While Luke had taken after their dark-haired father,

Clint resembled their mother, with light brown hair and gray eyes. Meg had always thought Clint had been spared the beatings Luke got because Clint reminded Orville of his late wife.

Clint took a swig of his beer and tipped his straw cowboy hat back with his thumb. "Looks like some famous person has come to call."

"Yeah." Luke held out his hand. "How are you, Clint?"

"Okay." Clint kept his hand at his side.

The insult stunned Meg. She didn't want Luke's opinion of himself to be unduly inflated, but she wouldn't wish this sort of public rejection on anyone. From the corner of her eye Meg saw the photographer closing in.

Luke lowered his hand and his gaze became wary. "Hope you don't mind my bunking in with you for a few days."

"Matter of fact, I do."

Meg squeezed her eyes shut. Clint was denying Luke access to his own home?

Luke nodded and backed up a step. "I see."

"I got work to do," Clint said. "About time to plant the fields." The camera flashed. "See that?" Clint gestured toward the young woman. "People taking pictures, the whole town gawking. I won't be able to get a damn thing done with you staying here. I suggest you find someplace else."

"All right." Luke turned toward Meg. "Let's go."

She stood there stupified. "Where?"

"Chandler has hotels and motels. I'll stay in one."

"Uh, okay." She doubted it. The town was already packed with visitors. This promised to be the biggest festival yet, and all the hotels in the area had been

booked for weeks. "Let me talk to the TV folks a minute. I know they wanted footage of you here at home."

As she walked toward the television van she worried
that the carefully stitched fabric of the festival she'd
planned was starting to unravel. She'd seen the look in
Clint's eyes. It was a familiar Bannister expression—she
knew there was no point in arguing. There would only
be a scene, and she didn't want news of a family feud
showing up in some tabloid and besmirching the festival's good name.

She explained to the television crew that shots of the
two brothers at home would be delayed. After repacking
their equipment in the van, the crew drove away. The
townspeople, too, turned their cars back down the road.
Only the young photographer remained.

Clint went into the house and Luke headed for the
truck. Meg followed him and climbed in behind the
wheel. "We'll find a pay phone and make some calls."

His jaw tightened. "Right."

Forty minutes later, Meg had confirmed what she'd
suspected earlier. Not a room anywhere. Even her parents weren't a possibility after what they'd said about
Luke. And all her friends had out-of-town guests here
for the festival. It was some sort of a record population
swell, she knew, a record she should be proud of because
her efforts had helped create this situation. It looked as
if there was only one logical place for Luke to sleep that
night. And it was not a very appropriate solution.

"Come on," she said, starting the truck. "We're going to my house."

"Sounds like a last resort."

She glanced at him as the truck idled in neutral.
"Somebody might want to make something out of it.

I'm in line to be the chamber's next president, and I'd rather not start any gossip.''

"Chamber of commerce? Don't you have to own a business or something to be in that?"

"Dan and Chuck were partners in a computer consulting firm. I'm still part owner, and I help with bookkeeping. Since I want to go into politics, it's a perfect setup for me.''

"So your mother was right.''

"What do you mean?''

His gaze was steady. "I guess she didn't mention my call.''

"What call? When?''

He shrugged and turned away. "It doesn't matter.''

"Luke Bannister, stop that!'' She felt an ancient frustration stirring her blood. He'd pulled a protective cloak around himself, just as he used to do when he was eighteen. At sixteen she'd never mustered the courage to challenge him when he shut her out. "Tell me about the call,'' she said.

As he stared silently out the window, she thought he wasn't going to answer her. Finally he said, "When I got the role in *Connections* I...wanted to tell you. I didn't really expect you to be home, but...'' He shrugged again.

Her pulse quickened. So he had tried to contact her again. She made some mental calculations. "I must have been away at graduate school.''

"Yeah. Political science major, your mother said. You and your fiancé were moving back to Chandler after graduation so you could get into local politics.''

Her heart twisted. Of course her mother would have mentioned Dan, to underline that Meg was spoken for.

And her mother would have also conveniently forgotten to tell Meg about Luke's call. Meg wondered if her life would be different today if Luke had called when she was home on break. "Did you leave a number or anything?"

"Yeah. When you didn't call back, I figured...well, I could understand."

"I never got the message."

Slowly his gaze swung to hers. "And if you had?"

"I...I don't know."

He took a deep breath and let it out. "Look, let's find another place for me to stay. I don't want to be responsible for ending a promising political career."

"That's noble of you, but there is no other place. You're our guest of honor, Luke. I can't have you sleeping on a park bench, and I happen to have a spare room."

Luke angled his head toward the blue Honda still parked and waiting. "Then if you don't want gossip, I think you'd better ditch her before you take me home with you."

Meg glanced at the car and swore under her breath.

"You still got three hundred and fifty-two horses under this hood?" Luke asked.

"Yes. But if you blow my engine..."

"I won't. Trade places with me. If I could outrun Chandler's finest, I sure as hell can take that Honda."

CHAPTER THREE

MEG TRADED PLACES reluctantly, mentally calculating her options. Keeping Luke's visit impersonal was getting tougher by the minute. The knowledge that he'd tried to reach her before she'd married Dan had shaken her. He'd called after a triumph in his life. He wouldn't have done that without plans to reestablish contact between them. What would she have done if he'd wanted to see her again, if he'd invited her to L.A.?

Luke peeled away from the phone booth in a shower of gravel, throwing her against her seat belt. She grabbed the door handle with one hand and the edge of the seat with the other. "Watch for cops," he commanded, and sped around a corner. "And that damned blue Honda, of course. Where do you live?"

She told him.

"Okay. We'll take the long way home."

A fresh set of memories assaulted her. That had been their code phrase in high school when they'd decided to park. Luke would say softly, "Let's take the long way home tonight," and her heartbeat would thunder in her ears because she knew she'd soon be in his arms. She wondered if he remembered that's what he used to say. Probably not. He was a Hollywood star now, and he'd had torrid encounters by the dozen.

She checked for police cars as Luke veered off onto

a side street. The blue Honda followed them. "Still back there," she said.

"I'll lose her." He passed a sedan and stepped down hard on the gas. "Kermit still has what it takes."

Wind from the open window buffeted Meg's face and tangled her hair. She glanced over at Luke. "I don't think you ever drove like this when I was around."

"Nope." He kept his eyes on the road. The wind had tousled his dark hair, making him look more like the renegade she'd known in high school.

Meg battled her volatile emotions. Watching Luke court danger inspired a feeling that she'd never had with anyone else. He'd always been able to make her feel this way—wild and ready to take risks. She'd almost forgotten the sensation. At sixteen her yearnings had been vague but powerful. They were still powerful…and no longer vague.

"See the Honda?"

Meg checked in the rearview mirror. "Nope."

"Keep watching. I'll slip down a few more side streets before we head for your house. Good thing she doesn't know the town. It's amazing I can still find my way around, the way things have changed. But the basic grid's still the same." The tires screeched as he rounded another curve.

"I'll probably hear about this tomorrow. Everybody recognizes this truck."

"Tell them I was practicing for a new episode of *Connections*."

"Do you usually use your celebrity status to get out of a jam?"

His eyes narrowed. "Only when it gets me into one."

CLINT STAYED INSIDE the house until the last car pulled away. Then he popped the top of another beer and returned to the porch swing. So his hotshot brother thought he could move in and take over the place after ten years. Probably envisioned some sappy homecoming scene like when Dolly Parton did her Christmas television special back in the hills of Tennessee. Hah.

Clint took a long swallow of his beer and thought about his brother—how Luke had made his bed ten years ago, taking off and leaving Clint to deal with their boozed-up old man and a neglected cotton farm. Luke probably thought he'd made up for that by deeding over his share of the farm to Clint when the old man died. Clint didn't think so. He'd trade his life around here for a cushy job like Luke's in a minute.

The next few days would be sickening, with everybody gushing over Luke, the TV star. Once upon a time Clint thought Luke was pretty special, too. Then Luke cut out for fun in the sun, and before too long somebody came offering Luke a job making commercials. The old man had been so friggin' proud of that it had made Clint want to throw up. He never appreciated Clint's working in the fields until he was tanned darker than the foreman, Juan Soledad. Just kept carrying on about Luke in some stupid jock-itch commercial.

Then, when the old man died, Luke couldn't even be bothered to come home for the funeral. So Clint got the farm. Big deal. He gazed out at the weed-choked front yard and across the plowed fields to his right. In point of fact he had a little spare time right now. He planned to hold off another week before planting, let the ground dry out a little more. But he didn't want to spend that week with his older brother.

Down the road he saw a car approaching from town, a blue sedan. When it turned into the drive he thought about going inside and not answering the door, but he hated the thought of being chased from his own front porch while he was enjoying a beer.

The person who got out looked familiar. Where had he seen somebody wearing a Dodgers baseball cap on backward? Oh, yeah. That crazy fan who had stayed behind to take pictures. She had sunglasses on now, and no cameras strapped around her body. She had a decent figure, although she obviously didn't much care if anybody noticed. Her tank top and baggy shorts looked as if they belonged to somebody three sizes larger. Spiky sections of her brown hair stuck out from her baseball cap. She was chewing gum.

"He's not here," Clint said as she approached the porch. "So if you're looking for a scoop, you'll have to go someplace else."

She shoved her hands into her pockets and braced her legs. "You could just be saying that." Pop went the gum.

"I could be, but I'm not."

"I lost him on the back roads. There was always the chance you two staged that little disagreement and he doubled back here."

"Didn't happen."

She hesitated and chewed her gum as if weighing the possibilities.

"Hell, go on and look through the house if you don't believe me. I don't want you lurking in the bushes all night hoping he'll show up. I might accidentally shoot you or something." She stiffened, and he smiled. So she wasn't quite as tough as she tried to look. He took a swig of his beer. "How old are you?"

"Never mind that."

"You're supposed to say old enough, and stick out your chin. If you're going to look like some kind of mean kid, you'll have to learn to talk back like one."

Her shoulders slumped a little and she started to turn around.

"Want a beer?" She glanced back at him. "I'm going to assume you're old enough to drink." She nodded. "Then come on and have a seat." He got out of the swing and went in for another can. He had no idea why he was doing this, except he was a sucker for people when they were down and out, when everything they tried seemed to blow up in their faces. She looked that way.

When he returned she was sitting on the porch steps. He handed her the beer, and she popped the top with a murmured thanks. After sticking her wad of gum on the edge of the can, she practically chugalugged the whole thing. When she came up for air, she gave him a tentative smile. "Thanks. I was so excited I didn't eat or drink anything on the plane. After that there was no time."

Clint leaned against the porch railing and sipped his beer. "You got a name?"

"Ansel Wiggins. I was named after Ansel Adams, the photographer."

"And you're following in his footsteps?"

She laughed. "Hardly. He was an artist. I just chase celebrities and try to make a buck."

"You like it?"

"Yeah." Her face became more animated. "It's like

a game, trying to figure out how to trap them when they least expect it. In L.A. I'm pretty good at that, but out here I don't know the territory.''

''How long have you been doing this?''

She ducked her head and mumbled something.

''What?''

''Six months, okay? I'm new. I haven't actually sold any pictures yet, but I got a lead that Luke Bannister might have a motion picture contract coming up, and the part sounds decent. It could make him a superstar, and if I get some hot shots of him, I'll make a bundle.''

Clint stared down the road. ''I don't understand why he tried to ditch you, then. I thought the whole idea was to get his damned picture in the papers.''

''Not *my* kind of pictures. His agent only wants the publicity photos his office releases. Mine aren't always so flattering.''

''Ah.''

''How come you didn't want Luke staying here?''

He glanced down at her. Nice skin. And she wasn't as naive as he might have thought, either. That wasn't an idle question. ''No comment.''

''Does he visit here much?''

''Look, Ansel, I may be a farm boy, but I'm not stupid. Back off.''

''I never thought you were stupid.'' She stood up and stretched. He noticed the nice muscle definition in her calves. Then she handed him the beer can. ''You recycle these?''

He didn't, but he took it, anyway. He should start, just like he should mow the weeds in the front yard and get the house painted. When Luke had arrived today, Clint had seen the place through Luke's eyes and hadn't much liked the view. Damn Luke for coming back and stirring things up.

"Thanks for the beer," Ansel said. "Guess I'll go buy a map and learn the country before I start the chase again."

For one crazy moment he thought about helping her. It would be kind of fun, and it would have the added benefit of irritating the hell out of Luke. But no, there were some things even he wouldn't stoop to. "Good hunting," he called after her as she walked back to her rental car.

"Don't worry. I'll leave here with something good."

He wondered if she'd succeed. It would serve his brother right.

LUKE PULLED INTO the gravel drive of the house Meg directed him to and parked behind a silver BMW. When Meg didn't say anything about having company, he reasoned that the silver car was hers. Yet she'd brought the old truck to the airport. He liked her spunk. "Wasn't this the Whitley place?"

"They sold out and moved to Oregon. Dan and I contacted the developer before he tore the house down, but we couldn't afford to buy all the land, too. Since we didn't want to farm, the developer subdivided the rest."

He turned off the motor. "It's a nice house."

"Thanks."

And not so different from the one Clint had booted him out of this afternoon, he thought, climbing out of the truck. Except that this one was in good repair. Maybe he should have guessed Clint would turn him away, but he hadn't thought Clint was bitter enough to deny him a roof over his head. Tomorrow he'd have to go over and straighten things out with his little brother.

For tonight, though, he'd have the bittersweet experience of sleeping in Meg's house, the one she'd once shared with her husband. How many times in the past ten years had he tried to imagine the house she lived in? Too many to count. He glanced at the frame construction, double-hung windows and front porch. A couple of pink geranium plants sat in pots on either side of the screen door. The yard was neat, but not fussy, with a mulberry tree for shade. It was a family kind of house. Meg had probably planned to hang a swing from the tree, like the one he remembered at the back of her house twenty years ago.

He heard the clang of the tailgate and turned to find Meg wrestling his stuff out of the truck bed. "Here, I'll do that."

"I just thought we'd better go inside before the woman in the blue Honda gets lucky and drives past here. In fact, why don't I take this inside while you pull the truck around behind the house? I'll let you in through the kitchen."

He grinned. "So this is going to be a backdoor affair?" When her eyes narrowed and her cheeks turned pink, he regretted his impulsive wisecrack. "Sorry. I'll move the truck."

As he drove around the side of the house he cursed himself for making the remark. It had been a bad joke, implying all the wrong things—that he found the idea of a secret affair with her intriguing and wouldn't want anything more solid than that.

He parked the truck in front of a battered garage that looked as if it hadn't been used since the Whitleys moved away. As he got out of the truck a golden retriever bounded toward him. He scratched the dog's ears. Of course she'd have a dog, a big fluffy one like this. Glancing up, he saw Meg standing in the open kitchen doorway smiling at him, her corn-silk hair loose around her shoulders the way he'd always loved it best. His heart turned over. Backdoor affair, indeed. He wanted the same thing he'd dreamed about since he was six years old—to marry Meg Hennessy.

THE MINUTE HE STEPPED into her house, Meg knew she'd been unwise to think this would work. But she could come up with nothing else on such short notice. Maybe tomorrow she could find him a room. She'd have to— he was too powerful a force to deal with at such close range. "I see you've met Dog-breath."

"Yep." He let the dog inside and closed the kitchen door with a soft click. "I'm really sorry about what I said a minute ago."

"Don't be silly. It was just a joke." Meg opened up a cabinet and scooped out some dry food for Dog-breath. She poured it into his bowl and spilled some in the process. He started munching noisily as she bent down to retrieve the stray pieces. Her hands were shaking.

"Bad joke. Here, let me help." He crouched down next to her.

She waved him away. "I've got it." Her heart pounded as if she'd been running. "Let me show you your room. You can pick up your things on the way through the living room. I left them on the couch."

"Okay."

She led him through the house and took several steadying breaths as she walked. Maybe having him here would get easier once her nervousness wore off. After all, they'd known each other since they were children. She paused before the guest bedroom with its brass double bed. "Here you are. The bath is across the hall. After I put some sheets on the bed you'll be all set."

He walked into the room and laid his garment bag and duffel on the fringed white spread. "Isn't this the same bed you had in your room when we were kids?"

"Same headboard and footboard, different mattress. You have quite a memory."

"For some things. Listen, if you'll go get the sheets, I'll make the bed myself. I don't want you to go to any extra trouble."

"It's no trouble." But making up his bed might be far too erotic for her strained nervous system.

"Come on, Meg. Get the darned sheets. We'll do it together."

Protesting again would make more of it than was already there. She retreated to the linen closet and returned with a set of blue-and-white striped sheets. He'd already hung his garment bag in the closet and put his duffel on the closet floor. He stripped back the spread and draped it over a pine rocker in the corner. Then he walked to the other side of the bed and held out his hand. "Throw me a corner."

She did, and they began making the bed as if they'd been doing it together for years. Except Meg couldn't shake off the feeling they were assembling the equivalent of a nuclear bomb. "The sheets smell great. I bet you hung them on the line."

"I did." She'd forgotten the high level of Luke's sensory awareness. When they were dating, he'd made her try out at least twenty perfumes in the drugstore and finally decided he liked her natural scent best. She'd never worn perfume after that, although that had been really stupid, she thought now. He'd had way too much influence on her life.

"I haven't slept on sun-dried sheets since I left Arizona." He tucked in the top sheet and reached for the bedspread. As he handed a section of it to Meg, their eyes met. "It's great of you to let me stay here," he said in a low voice. "I won't abuse the privilege."

She dropped the section of bedspread as if it were on fire. "You certainly won't!" His announcement sounded as if it were all up to him!

He chuckled and shook his head. "Right. Toss me a pillowcase, Meg."

She did, and wondered how the act of catching a pillowcase in midair could be so sensuous. Or why she was so fascinated with watching him tuck the pillow under his chin and work the case up one end of the pillow. He shook the pillow into place and plumped it before laying it on the bed. Meg followed suit and set hers beside it. So inviting, those two pillows. An unwanted ache settled between her thighs, an ache she hadn't felt in a long time. She busied herself smoothing the spread and adjusting the fringe. She could never acknowledge her attraction to him, mainly because he seemed to expect she would be attracted, the egotistical lout.

"I think the network said something about a dinner tonight."

She looked up in dismay, belatedly remembering the scheduled affair. "You're right." She glanced at her watch. "We have exactly an hour before we have to be out of here. I told them we'd be at the San Marcos for cocktails by five-thirty, and I haven't even checked my messages yet.''

"Then you'd better get going. Don't let me interfere with what you have to do in the next few days.''

She gazed across the bed at him. He was doing it again, assuming his presence would unsettle and distract her. He must be used to having that effect on women. She'd be damned if she'd let him know he bothered her at all. "I won't let you interfere.'' She spun on her heel and nearly walked into the wall. Correcting course, she managed to make it through the door without tripping. She didn't look back, afraid she'd discover him laughing at her. "See you in an hour.''

She hurried down the hall to her office. The message light was blinking on her answering machine. One of the exhibitors wanted their booth placement changed to a corner space, and someone wanted to know if they could still get a raffle ticket for a date with Luke Bannister. The last message was from Didi, who hoped Meg had been able to find Luke a place to stay.

"I found him one all right,'' Meg muttered to herself as she walked into her bedroom and closed the door. "Let's hope it's not my downfall.''

As she showered and dressed for dinner, she replayed every moment of being with Luke since he'd arrived. No question that he had her blood racing as it hadn't in years. Even the mundane job of making a bed took on new significance when Luke was around.

She hadn't been in a bedroom with him since they were nine and eleven years old. That was the time Clint had had the flu and had to stay home. She and Luke had been playing Parcheesi in her room, but had become bored with it. After they'd goofed around some, Luke

had suggested kissing with tongues. He'd kissed her before, just lips, but this was different. She hadn't liked
the tongue part at nine. At sixteen she'd liked it far too
much.

As a nine-year-old with no secrets, she'd made the
mistake of telling her mother about Luke putting his
tongue in her mouth, and her mother had forbidden them
to be alone again. She'd branded Luke as "too sexually
advanced for his age."

Her mother's description hadn't meant much to Meg
then, but when puberty hit she recalled with new interest
that Luke was supposed to be "sexually advanced," and
he became the focus of her erotic fantasies. When he
finally asked her out during her sophomore year in high
school, she thought she'd died and gone to heaven. Her
parents had had a somewhat different reaction.

But they allowed her to go out with him as long as
she kept strict curfews and double-dated. The dates always started out as a foursome, but sometime during the
evening Meg and Luke would usually end up alone, a
move probably engineered by Luke, she realized now.

During those precious moments alone with him, she
learned that "sexually advanced" meant that he kissed
like no other boy she'd ever known. His kisses softened
parts of her and set others on fire. It was she who unbuttoned her blouse the first time, because her breasts
ached for his touch, it was she who guided his hand
beneath the elastic of her panties. She would have let
him make love to her, and she knew he'd wanted to. But
each night he'd gently close up her blouse with shaking
fingers, kiss her softly on the mouth, and take her home
still a virgin. She fell hopelessly in love.

Then came the day he'd swaggered up to her locker

and told her he wouldn't be asking her out again. She was too young for him, he'd said, too inexperienced. He needed to date women his own age.

Meg still remembered the pain that had engulfed her for weeks. She'd lost fifteen pounds and almost failed geometry. Each time she'd seen Luke with one of the senior girls she'd wanted to scream. But eventually the hurt had turned to anger, and by the time Luke had left town, she'd sworn to everyone that she didn't care if a California earthquake swallowed him whole.

And now he was sleeping under her roof, this "sexually advanced" man of twenty-eight, who no longer was just her fantasy, but the fantasy of thousands of women. And if he could kiss that well at eighteen, what must he be like now? Meg shoved the thought away with a feeling of panic. She could not afford to find out.

LUKE BUTTONED a paisley vest over his white silk turtleneck and pulled on a gray jacket. He already missed his jeans and T-shirt, but his agent, who had supervised the packing for this trip, had reminded him about his image. The people at this dinner expected Hollywood glamour, so Luke would give it to them.

He smoothed his hair with his palms, pocketed his wallet and wandered out into Meg's living room to commune with her dog. He liked Dog-breath. Once he'd had a dog, a mutt, but his father had kicked it around so unmercifully that Luke had given it away to save its life.

Dog-breath clambered to his feet from his position on a rag rug in front of the green-and-white plaid couch. The dog was the perfect finishing touch to the country setting of the room. An antique pine cupboard, rattan chairs with dark green cushions and a brick fireplace still holding ashes from a recent fire gave Luke a picture that contrasted sharply with his sterile L.A. apartment decorated mostly in silver and gray.

Dog-breath pushed his damp muzzle against Luke's hand. Lowering himself to the couch, Luke rubbed the silky head and scratched down the dog's backbone until he wriggled with pleasure. When Luke leaned back against the cushions, Dog-breath put his head on Luke's knee for more attention.

"We all love to be petted, don't we, Dog-breath?" Luke thought about how long it had been since someone had touched him with honest affection. The simulated kind on the set didn't count. But even his real-life love affairs had been more about sex than love. Once he became well-known as Dirk Kennedy, he suspected his last two partners had imagined themselves going to bed with Dirk, not Luke. Heck, maybe they had. There was only one woman he'd trusted enough to be himself with, and she was just down the hall, dressing to go out to dinner with him.

But somebody had scripted this wrong. They'd given Meg political ambitions in a small town and stymied what might have been a wonderful weekend of rekindling an old flame. Cozying up to the parade grand marshal while she was supposed to be running the festival wouldn't do much for her image. He could be a real liability to her future if he acted on his impulses this weekend. And beyond this weekend, what did he have to offer? He was tied to L.A., and he couldn't ask her to give up everything she'd worked for in exchange for a life-style she'd probably hate. Had he found her again, only to be forced to give her up, just as he had ten years ago?

Then she came down the hall and he felt as if someone had punched him in the gut. He was no longer an unsophisticated farm boy. He'd escorted women who shopped on Rodeo Drive, beautiful women whose entire lives revolved around dressing well. Yet when Meg appeared, he rose from the couch in homage.

"It's okay?" Her prickly behavior had given way to feminine uncertainty about her appearance.

Maybe his own flashy outfit had prompted her insecurity, he thought, but whatever had, her tentative question tugged at his heartstrings. "Yeah," he said softly. "More than okay." The dress was the color of new leaves, and had the delicate look of fresh growth. Sleeveless, it crossed over her breasts and stayed in place somehow without buttons, reminding him of the robes of a Greek goddess. A wide belt the same color green emphasized her waist and the swell of her hips beneath the gently flowing skirt. She'd piled her hair on top of her head in a way he'd never seen, exposing her tender nape and the curve of her earlobes. Pearls dangled from her ears and circled her throat.

"You're sure?" She peered at him, as if his scrutiny made her doubt her choice. "You can tell me the truth."

"You wouldn't believe me if I told you the truth."

"Yes, I would. You've been out in the world more than I have, so I trust your judgment. If there's something wrong with this, I can change."

She really didn't know the effect she had on him. His arms ached to hold her. "The truth is, you are the most beautiful woman I've ever seen."

She blushed and looked away. "Now *that's* ridiculous. I'm no fool, Luke. I'll get my coat and we can go."

He followed her as she walked to the living room closet and pulled out a soft beige coat. "I said you wouldn't believe me."

"You're right. I don't." She sounded angry again, as if she suspected his motives for complimenting her. "I watch the Academy Awards, too, you know. I know what movie stars look like."

"So do I." He took the coat and held it for her. "You've got them beat."

"Luke, don't try to flatter me. Please."

He couldn't win, so he said nothing while nestling the coat over her shoulders. He breathed deep, savoring the scent of her clean, fresh skin, and for a moment he gripped her shoulders and longed to nuzzle the spot where a tendril of hair had escaped to curl across her nape. Then he released her.

He never remembered curbing an urge like that before. He'd never had to. In many ways his life had been tough, and he'd taken his share of knocks, but when it came to women, he'd always found a welcome smile, eager arms. But here with Meg, he feared rejection for the first time.

MEG LET OUT HER BREATH as Luke moved away from her. The moment he'd taken her coat, she'd wanted to snatch it back. But that would have looked stupid, as if she weren't lady enough to accept a man's gesture of helping her on with her coat. The problem was that the action brought him so close she could smell the mint of his shaving cream and feel his breath on her neck. When he briefly gripped her shoulders after putting on the coat, her knees grew weak.

She half feared he might turn her around and kiss her. Then she remembered why. That had been a little ritual from their dating days. When they left a dance or a movie, he'd help her on with her coat, turn her around and give her a soft kiss, as if his lips would protect her from the cold as much as her coat would. Back then, she believed they had.

"We'll take the BMW," she said, pulling out a small evening bag from the coat closet. She transferred keys and wallet from her shoulder bag hanging just inside the closet door. "That way maybe your friend in the Honda won't find you right away."

Luke followed her out the front door. "We'll probably be free of her until opening ceremonies tomorrow. After that she won't let me out of her sight."

A cool breeze ruffled the tendrils that had escaped from Meg's upswept hair. She slipped on her sunglasses to protect against the glare of a sun that wouldn't set for another hour. "Dodging people like that sounds like a grim way to live."

He put on his pair of designer sunglasses. "For her or me?"

"Both of you, actually." As she unlocked the passenger side of the BMW, she glanced at him. With his paisley vest, his dark hair combed into place and sunglasses concealing his blue eyes, he looked like a movie star. The emotional distance between them seemed to increase each time she was reminded that he no longer lived in her world. She slid into the driver's seat and started the car.

"I guess I take this paparazzi thing in stride because I'm used to being watched."

She glanced at him. "Oh, really?"

"Yeah. So are you."

"No, I'm not, and I wouldn't like—"

"Then why do we have to worry about me staying at your house? What's all this about guarding your reputation so you can move into the political scene?"

She fell silent. He had a point. She didn't have a photographer following her, but she might as well have. Chandler folks took lots of mental pictures and reproduced them on cue to interested parties. It was the small-town way of keeping track of everyone, a habit that continued despite Chandler's growing size.

"You're no more free than I am, Meg."

"You're right."

"For the heck of it, let's pretend that we could do anything we wanted right now. What would you do?"

"I...I don't know." And she didn't dare let her imagination work on the idea, either.

"I know what I'd do. I'd get in the truck, drive out to the desert, build a fire, roast hot dogs and drink beer."

"Hmm."

"Then I'd turn on the truck radio to KNIX and dance."

She arched a brow. "By yourself?"

"Not if I could convince you to come along."

As her heartbeat speeded up, Meg remembered Didi's warning. Apparently the time had come to take some defensive action. She took a long, shaky breath. "Okay, we need to get something straight. Neither of us is a teenager anymore." Her heartbeat pounded in her ears, but she pushed on. "You're a rising star in Hollywood and I have my eye on a political career in Arizona. If I stay in Chandler and keep my nose clean, I have a good chance of being in the state legislature one day. And I don't plan to stop there. I want to run for Congress eventually."

He grinned. "And the White House?"

"Go ahead and laugh, but you never know. I might, if everything falls into place for me."

"I'm not laughing. I think you'd be great. You've always had the ability to inspire people."

"And you're a natural on screen. I think we've both found what we were meant to do and we can go as high as we choose. We...shouldn't let some pleasant memories get us off track.''

''Nice speech. You'll make a good politician.''

She glanced at him and saw his smile. ''Luke, I'm only trying to—''

''I know.'' His expression became serious. ''And I understand what you're trying to say.''

''I hope so.''

''Believe it or not, I came to the same conclusion not long ago.''

''Good.'' Her sigh contained both relief and disappointment.

''Are we telling anyone where I'm staying?''

She hesitated. ''I hate lying, but the fewer people who know about it the better.''

''Then leave it to me. Don't forget that I act for a living.''

I won't, she thought. It was a good thing he'd reminded her. Maybe all his apparent interest in her, which she'd felt honor-bound to turn aside, had been an act. Luke Bannister had been put on this earth to charm women, and he did so effortlessly, without thinking. What she interpreted as interest might simply be his normal behavior with any woman.

Embarrassment heated her cheeks. She might have just made a colossal fool of herself with her prim little speech. Luke probably had no intentions toward her except those he had toward any woman: to bring her under his spell for the time he was with her. After that, she'd be forgotten as he wove his magic for the next willing victim.

THROUGHOUT DINNER in the San Marcos's Nineteen-Twelve restaurant, named for the year the hotel was built, Meg watched Luke in action. As a boy he had once scrambled under barbed-wire fences with her. Now the man looked perfectly at ease in the subdued atmosphere of the candlelit room, where guests nestled into cushioned rattan chairs and dined from gold-rimmed plates.

Luke entertained the large table of city council members and festival organizers with insider stories about the entertainment industry. He took their teasing about his steamy character with good-natured laughter. His performance was flawless, and Meg was sure that a performance was exactly what he was giving.

Back when they were dating, Luke had taken her out for a special dinner at Serranos, a cozy Mexican restaurant that still reminded Meg of Luke every time she went in. He'd been much quieter in those days, much less sure of himself. But she still remembered the way he'd gazed at her across the table, the candle flame dancing in his eyes, as if he were memorizing how she looked. Her little speech tonight notwithstanding, she caught him gazing at her that way again. Her hand shook as she reached for her water goblet and took a long, calming drink.

Over dessert, Didi asked about Clint, and Luke chuckled as he described his little brother's understandable behavior. Meg would have bet good money that Clint's rejection had hurt Luke, but no one would ever know it to see him brush the incident aside now. True to his word, he explained that he and Meg had worked out a place for him to stay, but they weren't going to reveal the location because Luke preferred not to have the press camped outside his door. The story wasn't even a lie,

Meg thought in admiration. Luke wouldn't make such a bad politician himself.

The talk turned to last-minute festival preparations, and Meg felt Luke's gaze rest on her as she handled the questions and problems. No doubt about it, she liked being in charge and leaving her fingerprints on various enterprises. She enjoyed a certain amount of the lime-light.

By nine o'clock napkins were laid beside plates and chairs moved back. There were handshakes and last parting jokes all around. Didi edged over to Meg and murmured under the flow of goodbyes, "See? This will be great, having him here for the festival."

"He does seem to be a good choice."

"People will remember the success of the event for a long time, and that's good PR for you."

Meg nodded. "By the way, nice outfit." Didi tended toward plumpness, but she knew how to dress in flowing material and brilliant colors that accentuated her dark hair and eyes, so people seldom noticed her extra weight.

Didi smiled, showing her dimples. "Thanks. You look great, too. And what was all that double-talk about where Luke's staying? Who's the paranoid person who's putting him up?"

Meg gazed at her meaningfully without answering.

"Uh-oh."

"It was that or a bench in the park."

"Well, be careful, sweetie. He's a charmer."

Meg glanced across the table. Luke was standing there, his head bent forward as he listened to something Mayor Garvey was saying to him. Then he smiled and winked at the mayor's wife. "That he is," she murmured.

As they walked out through the hotel lobby to the hotel entrance and the valet-parking stand, Meg silently rehearsed her excuses for turning in early. She didn't dare sit around making small talk with Luke after they got home.

Once they were in the car and driving down the road he leaned back against the headrest. "Well, that's over."

"You sound glad."

"I am."

"You looked as if you were having a ball."

"Never let them see you sweat."

"You were nervous? Come on."

"Some of those people wanted my head on a pole when I was back in high school. I was waiting for somebody to bring up the old days."

"So you kept them rolling in the aisles with Hollywood stories, so they wouldn't have time."

"Something like that."

"Well, I can testify from personal experience now. You're a terrific actor."

"And you're a born organizer. I was impressed, Meg."

She laughed. "Quite a mutual admiration society we have here." She wished she had some of his acting skills right now. She wanted to feign exhaustion but she was strung tighter than a guitar string.

"Let's not go straight back," he said.

Good. A distraction. "Where do you want to go?"

"I'd like to see the high school again, for one thing. If we take a tour at night, I can get away with it. By tomorrow I won't be able to do that in peace."

"Okay. The high school it is." She turned back toward town and headed down Arizona Avenue. "The main building is the same, but a lot's been added on since you left. The Chandler Center for the Arts was built right next to the school, so the city and the school district have joint use. It's an amazing performance center, Luke."

"I can see I chose the right tour guide."

She bridled at his indulgent tone. "Maybe it's not Hollywood, but I think even you will be impressed. Chandler has an exciting future, whether you realize it or not. We project growth in the next ten years of—"

"There's that chip on your shoulder again."

"Well, your comment sounded like a patronizing pat on the head."

"If it did, I'm sorry. I just get a kick out of your chamber of commerce plugs. It takes me right back to high school, when you were running for president of the sophomore class and making speeches about school pride. You were so...so—"

"Cute?" Meg smacked the steering wheel. "Don't you dare call me that."

"Well, if it makes you feel any better, you're not cute anymore."

"Good!"

"The fact is, you're damned beautiful."

She almost missed the turn down the side street where she'd planned to park the car. As she veered into it, the tires squealed. "I thought we could get out and walk." She turned off the motor and headlights in a flash and whipped out of the car. Once on the pavement she took a deep breath of the cool night air. Twice in one night he'd called her beautiful. It was enough to turn a girl's head. But she wasn't a girl anymore, and her head must stay firmly facing in the direction of her goals.

As they started down the sidewalk together, she shoved her hands into her coat pockets. Her heels made a hollow click, click, click on the concrete as they approached the Center for the Arts. The rhythm of her steps mingled with the splash of water as they neared the fountain in front of the building's curved facade. Soaring glass panels revealed sparkling chandeliers illuminating the lobby.

Luke paused to gaze up at the building. "First class, Meg."

"You should see the performance area. Red velvet seats, and sections revolve to face different stages. We can have three events going on at once in there."

"I remember playing on that old high school stage."

"I remember you staggering on that old high school stage."

"Drunk was the only way I could handle being there. I had the worst case of stage fright you can imagine."

Meg stared at him in surprise. Luke had won the lead in the school musical after he'd broken up with her. At that point, she'd no longer been privy to his thoughts. He'd had a fling with his co-star and Meg hadn't been able to like her ever since. "I never guessed that you were scared."

"Fortunately the booze wore off before the thing was over, and I had a chance to find out you can hide behind your character when you're acting. If I hadn't discovered that, I'd probably still be a California beach bum waiting tables by night and surfing by day."

"You actually planned to get into acting when you went to L.A.?"

"It was in the back of my mind, but I didn't know the first thing about breaking in. Then the second luck-

iest thing in my life happened. One of my surfing buddies heard about a job doing a commercial. He had some
contacts, got us a test, and I landed the role.''

''Selling what?''

''Stuff for jock itch.''

Meg laughed in spite of herself. ''And then?''

''The third luckiest thing in my life. One of the writers
for *Connections* saw the commercial and I fitted his image of a character he was creating.''

''Dirk Kennedy.''

''Yeah.''

''You said those were the second and third luckiest
things to happen in your life. What was the first?''

He hesitated and glanced down at her. ''Growing up
on a farm next to yours.''

She had to ask. His statement had been made with a
simplicity that convinced her it wasn't a line. Their
childhood memories meant as much to him as they had
to her. Her resolve to keep her distance slipped down
another notch.

He angled his head toward the historic old high school
farther down the block. ''Let's keep walking.''

A soft breeze carried the scent of freshly cut grass to
Meg as she matched her stride to Luke's. Her arm
brushed his and she mumbled an apology while clenching her hands in her pockets to keep from reaching out
to him. Above them, palm fronds waved in the night
sky, and aleppo pines stood sentinel on either side of the
main entrance to the school.

''It hasn't changed,'' Luke said, facing the two-story
tan building with its massive Greek columns and broad
front steps. ''Still looks like a Norman Rockwell version
of what a high school should be.''

"I guess you weren't very happy here."

"No, but I brought a lot of my problems on myself. If I ever had a kid, I'd like him to go to a school like this."

"It's a long commute from L.A."

"Yeah." He laughed dryly. "You have a point."

She could sense the tug-of-war in him, good memories fighting bad. But even if the good memories won, he'd already made his life elsewhere. She might have been important in his life once, but he'd moved beyond her reach. "Want to see the rest?"

"Sure. Is the oak tree still around back?"

"Still there."

"I'd like to see that."

Meg led the way around the side of the building to the back courtyard, where the gnarled oak grew. Security lights brightened the grounds, except for a shadowed area beneath the oak's dark branches. Luke walked over and propped one foot on the brick planter box surrounding the tree. "I spent some good times here, waiting by this tree."

Meg moved into the shadows with him. "Me, too," she answered truthfully. The tree had been their meeting place between classes and at lunch. Every day, she'd raced to get to that tree, but somehow he'd always arrived ahead of her. She could still see him lounging there wearing opaque sunglasses, jeans and a white T-shirt with the sleeves rolled, his books carelessly tossed at his feet. He'd be talking with one of his buddies, but the minute she arrived, he'd turn all his attention on her.

School officials and local police might have considered Luke a menace to the community, but every girl at Chandler High had a crush on him. Because he'd chosen

Meg, she'd felt like royalty. Ten years later he was making her feel that way again, acting as if he hadn't dumped her unceremoniously all those years ago. It was almost as if she'd been the one to discard him.

She gazed up through the tree branches and saw a glowing half moon that made her think of a quarter stuck in a jukebox. Her and Luke's song had turned out to be so heartbreakingly appropriate—Willie Nelson's "You Were Always on My Mind," a song about a neglected love affair.

Meg swallowed the lump in her throat. Maybe she was asking to be hurt again, but she had to know. "What happened, Luke? Back then."

He pushed away from the planter box and walked toward her. "I was asked not to talk about it, and I promised I wouldn't. But things look a little different to me now. I decided before I came to Chandler that if you asked me, I'd break that promise."

Her heart thudded in her chest. "About what? Who made you promise?"

"Your father."

She had a sick feeling she wasn't going to like what he was about to say, but she'd brought up the painful subject and couldn't back away now. "Tell me."

"It seems he got a report that we'd been seen out parking. Several times."

Heat coursed through her veins. Once she would have been thoroughly embarrassed by that knowledge, but now all she could think of was the passion of those nights.

"He got me alone one afternoon when he knew you weren't around. I think you had to work on the posters for your election campaign or something. He explained how different you and I were, how you were going to be somebody someday, and I obviously wasn't. He was giving me a clear message to stay away from you.''

"You broke up with me because my father told you to?'' The Luke she'd known would have stormed away from such a lecture.

"Not exactly. I knew your parents didn't like me. His opinion wasn't hot news. But he had an extra little persuader. He'd seen Clint coming out of the back of old man Baker's hardware store late one night, his arms full of merchandise. That was before Baker put in the alarm system. You know the trouble Clint was in. One more arrest and he'd have been locked up. I promised to straighten Clint out...and break up with you...if your father wouldn't tell what he saw.''

She stood there, her head reeling. "My father *blackmailed* you?''

"I guess that's one way of putting it. Looking back on it, I don't much blame him. I wasn't any good for you, but I was too selfish to see that at the time.''

"But he meddled in my life, in both our lives!''

"Parents figure they have a right to do that sometimes, especially if they think their kid is in danger.''

"I can't believe he did that to me. As if I had no sense. I wasn't in danger. I was—''

"You were in danger,'' Luke countered softly.

At his tone, the memories pushed away her anger— and she acknowledged that in the splendor of his arms she would have denied him nothing.

"I tell myself I wouldn't have lost my head with you, but who knows? And even if we'd used protection, nothing's foolproof. Your father's nightmare was that his beautiful, intelligent sixteen-year-old daughter would come to him and confess the town punk had made her pregnant.''

She stared at him, her heart pounding, her whole body at flash point. His confession had changed everything. If he touched her now, all her repressed longings would burst into flame.

He sighed and ran his fingers through his hair, mussing the careful styling job and making him look more like the boy she used to know. "I feel as if we're right back where we started.''

She swallowed, unable to speak.

"Here you are, working toward a career in politics, and here I am, the potential scandal-maker who could ruin your chances. I'm only here for the weekend. We both know I'm not right for you, any more than I was ten years ago.'' He looked straight at her and lowered his voice to a murmur. "But you see, I still want you, Meg.''

His words flowed over her like hot lava. A familiar ache began deep within her and spread quickly. This feeling hadn't been the product of teenage hormones ten years ago, as she'd tried to rationalize since then. The catalyst had been Luke.

"The trouble is, I'm not as selfish as I was at eighteen. I'm no longer willing to risk your reputation to get what I want. If your father showed up and told me you didn't need some Hollywood type screwing up your life for a weekend of fun, I'd have to agree with him.''

She stepped closer, drawn to him as if pulled by an invisible tether. "Is that what you are? Some Hollywood type?''

"Yes.'' He took a deep breath and gazed down at her. "I love the excitement, the challenge of fighting for the spotlight. I won't kid you about that. I'm hooked on this star thing, which means I'd never settle down in Chandler. You need a tractor salesman, a cotton farmer, somebody who'd be there for you."

The urge to touch him became irresistible. She slid her fingers up the silk of his paisley vest and felt the rapid beating of his heart. "I've been watching *Connections.* You're a natural on screen." His arms crept beneath her open coat and around her waist, cradling her gently. At the contact, she trembled and looked up into his face.

His half smile was barely visible in the dim light. "I thought you weren't a fan of the show."

"I decided to watch it recently, to familiarize myself with the characters in case the media asked me—"

"Save the speeches for the voters, Hennessy." He started rubbing her back with light, teasing strokes.

It took so little for him to arouse her. She was almost angry with him for doing it so easily. "What do you want me to say? That I never miss an episode, that I'm driven to watch you day after day?"

"Are you?"

Somehow her arms were around his neck and she was on tiptoe. Her mouth hovered inches from his. "Now I am. Are you satisfied?"

His embrace tightened a fraction, bringing her breasts into contact with his chest. "When it comes to you, I've never been satisfied."

She could feel his breath on her face. Her eyes drifted closed as she savored the increasing pressure of his body against hers. "Maybe that's the problem," she murmured. "I've been forbidden fruit for so long you think I'm something more than I really am."

"Maybe." He brushed his lips over hers once, twice. She moaned.

"And maybe you have the same problem with me. Maybe you'd be disappointed."

"Maybe." Her breath came in shallow gasps.

He touched his tongue to her bottom lip. "We shouldn't be doing this."

"No."

His lips hovered, his breath warm and sweet. "Push me away."

"In a minute."

"Too late." He settled his mouth firmly over hers.

It was as good as she remembered. He'd taught her how to kiss years ago, and the master had only improved with age. His lips played, coaxed, drew responses from her she'd thought gone forever. She tunneled her fingers through his dark hair and opened her mouth to invite the thrust of his tongue, that wicked tongue that promised things she now understood. She grew damp with a woman's need many times more powerful than the vague longings she knew as a girl.

He pushed her coat from her shoulders and it slid into a crumpled semicircle around her. "I need to hold you," he murmured against her mouth.

Her reply came between kisses. "I need you, too." She pressed against the firm wall of his chest, her nipples tightening into buds aching for his touch.

"Oh, Meg." He cupped her breast and stroked her through the thin material of her dress.

"I've missed you, Luke," she whispered, arching into his caress.

He kissed her throat as his hand slipped inside the folds of the dress and found her breast. She gasped in

response. He covered her mouth with his own and her
world began to spin as it always had when Luke loved
her. The musical whisper of the nearby fountain blended
with the soft sounds of the night. And Luke was touching her again, as only he could. She pressed closer to
his warmth. She needed this so much. She—

A car braked. Meg froze. A searchlight swept the area
and her stomach clenched. *The police.*

CHAPTER FIVE

LUKE SHIELDED MEG from the searchlight with his body. "Grab your coat," he muttered. Then he turned, keeping himself between Meg and the light, and shaded his eyes with one hand. "Good God, is that Bobby Joe I see before me?"

"Luke? Hell, I thought you were a couple of kids. Let me call off my backup." The tall policeman walked back to the squad car, switched off the searchlight and spoke into his walkie-talkie. When he returned he was smiling. "Sorry about that, but we patrol this area just to make sure nobody's pulling the kind of pranks you and I used to."

Meg had buttoned her coat and adjusted her hair by the time he arrived. She hoped the dim light would disguise her just-been-kissed look. "Hi, Bobby Joe," she said. "Luke and I were just touring the old spots. Didn't mean to startle you."

"Likewise." Bobby Joe shook hands with Luke. "It's been a long time."

"Too long, apparently." Luke grinned. "I come home after ten years and find Bobby Joe Harris decked out in a fuzz suit."

"Look who's talking!" Bobby Joe laughed and tapped Luke's vest. "The old Luke Bannister wouldn't have been caught dead in paisley."

"Yeah, well. Things have changed since the days we drag raced through town, buddy."

"Yeah." Bobby Joe hooked his thumbs in his belt. "I got two kids of my own already."

"I hope they give you just as much trouble as you gave your old man."

"They've already started." Static crackled from the squad-car radio and he glanced back toward the parking lot. "Hey, I gotta go," he said, holding out his hand to Luke. "Good seeing you. I'll be working a pop booth at the festival, so I'm sure we'll bump into each other again."

"Sure. See you." When Bobby Joe was out of earshot, Luke spoke in a low tone. "I'm sorry, Meg. What an idiot move on my part."

"Don't take all the blame on yourself. I'm responsible, too. God, I hope he didn't see anything." She touched her hair again. It was definitely coming loose from her careful arrangement. She groaned. "Even if he didn't, he could probably take one look at us and make an educated guess about what had been going on."

"Maybe. But he used to be the kind of guy who could keep his mouth shut."

"I hope you're right."

"Listen, if someone brings it up to you, tell them I lured you out here for my own devious plans. Tell them you were fighting me off when Bobby Joe showed up."

"Luke! I most certainly won't make up a story like that. It wouldn't work, anyway. I'm a terrible liar."

He looked into her eyes for a long moment. "In that case, you've just settled the question of what will happen, or rather, what *won't* happen when we get back to your house," he said quietly.

"What do you mean?"

"I saw you talking to Didi tonight. She knows I'm staying with you, doesn't she?"

"She guessed."

He tilted up her chin with his finger. "And if I know Didi, she'll ask a few leading questions tomorrow."

The banked fires of passion stirred to life. "She might."

His smile was both tender and sad. "I can't make love all night to a terrible liar, now can I?"

LUKE'S LOGIC was impeccable. Meg had to agree that whatever happened between them would be written all over her face for the whole town to see. She reminded herself of that over and over through the long, frustrating hours as Luke spent the night in the guest room and she stayed behind her own closed bedroom door. She lectured herself about the pitfalls of short-term happiness that sacrificed long-term goals.

She could walk down that hall and spend the rest of the night in Luke's arms. If she went, he wouldn't turn her away; she could only expect so much restraint from a mortal man. The hours would be filled with ecstasy, and in the morning she would emerge a changed woman. She might become a woman who dropped all responsibility in exchange for time with her lover. Luke had a powerful effect on her. She could easily blunder her duties for the ostrich festival, ruin all the months of preparation, and along with them her hopes of becoming chamber president.

So what? argued her passionate side. She could forget about her political ambitions and run off to Los Angeles with Luke. And be happy for a few weeks, maybe a few months, before her need to make a real difference in the world reasserted itself.

Her best, perhaps her only chance to realize that goal was to start here in Chandler, among the people who knew her. They held her ticket to the future, and it was the luck of the draw that they also held the keys to her imprisonment tonight. *Grow up*, she whispered into the darkness. *You need your rest*. But sleep wouldn't come, and the ache for Luke wouldn't leave.

DAWN SEEMED A LONG TIME arriving in the guest bedroom. When the dark sky turned the color of pearls, Luke dressed quickly in jeans, T-shirt and denim jacket. In the kitchen, Dog-breath wagged his tail and looked expectant.

"Sorry, boy. I can't take you. Wish I could." He left a note for Meg and headed off at a jog toward the Bannister farm. He had to straighten things out with Clint and convince his little brother to let him stay there. Luke couldn't spend another night under Meg's roof and keep away from her. Not after the way she'd responded at the high school last night. Some things were beyond a man's endurance, and keeping his hands off Meg after that brief taste of her passion was one of them.

A rooster crowed. He couldn't remember the last time he'd heard one. White-winged doves gathered on the telephone lines to watch his solitary passage down the deserted blacktop, and a cottontail scampered under a creosote bush by the side of the road. Luke slowed his pace and began to enjoy the cool morning air and the pale pink clouds at the horizon. Rural living had its moments.

Although he couldn't call the surrounding countryside

strictly rural anymore. Some farms remained, and now and then a field contained a flock of sheep or a small herd of grazing dairy cattle. But now housing developments, some rising two stories, with bright red-tiled roofs, wedged themselves between the fields and changed the shape of the horizon. The way of life Luke remembered was slipping away.

The Bannister farmhouse hadn't changed much, just weathered to a lighter shade of gray. If Luke blocked out the cluster of houses about a mile down the road, the house looked almost picturesque in the pink light of dawn. The rising sun winked off the chrome bumper of Clint's candy-apple red truck. It was brand-new, as out of place on the run-down farm as a rose in a Dumpster. Luke could imagine what the payments were on a machine like that, but he understood why Clint had bought it. Clint's favorite toy when he was a kid had been a bright red truck.

Luke felt a tug of homesickness remembering the good times before his mother had died. He'd gather eggs from the henhouse first thing in the morning while his mother started bacon sizzling in a pan on the stove. In those days his father had helped with breakfast and had sung along with country and western songs playing on the kitchen radio while Clint set the table. His father had been musical. Luke had almost forgotten that. His guitar had been a birthday present when he was ten, and his dad had taught Luke his first chords.

Luke hadn't realized it was all so special, until the day his mother told him she had cancer. They'd all tried to keep the routine the same, but it proved impossible, and finally, when his mother had been too sick to stand, they'd given up the pretense. Luke wished his father had been stronger, but Orville Bannister had depended on his wife to keep him steady. When she died, he couldn't hold to the course. "We just aren't lucky, son," he'd told Luke as he slugged back another beer on the day of her funeral.

When Luke was forced to give up his relationship with Meg, he wasn't really surprised to have lost her. His father had lost the only woman he'd ever loved, and now Luke had, too. Bannister men were unlucky that way.

Apparently Clint wasn't faring any better. Debbie Fry might be a good-looking redhead, sweet in her way, but she was a party girl, not a potential wife for Clint. She'd been at least seven years behind Luke in school and five behind Clint, which made her barely twenty-one. Clint needed someone with more maturity if he ever expected to grow up himself.

Luke shook his head. Here he was passing judgment on his younger brother as if he had some right to do it. That kind of attitude wouldn't get him very far with Clint.

He walked past the truck through a weed-choked side yard containing a split garden hose and a rusty wheel-barrow. Birds twittered and chirped in the feathery-leaved tamarisk trees that served as a windbreak for the house. The wooden steps leading to the kitchen door creaked when he mounted them. Several boards were warped and needed to be replaced. Luke tried the kitchen door. It was unlocked.

He poked his head inside. "Clint?" No answer. He stepped into the kitchen and grimaced at the pile of dirty dishes in the sink. His mother had kept the white Formica counters spotless. "Clint! It's me, Luke."

"Hold on." Clint came into the kitchen, barefoot and bare-chested, buttoning the fly of his jeans. He peered at Luke. "What you want?"

"To talk to you."

Clint glanced out the kitchen window. "You bring the whole town this time?"

"No, and I'm sorry about yesterday. I should have known there'd be some sort of—"

"Oh, but it just caught you by surprise, is that it? How modest of you."

"Clint, can we cut the crap and just talk? How about some coffee? I'll make it." He started toward the coffeepot.

"This isn't a good time. I got company."

Luke glanced back at Clint. "Debbie?"

"You been checking up on me or something?"

"I didn't think it was a secret."

"Clint?" Debbie appeared in the doorway, rubbing her eyes. She had on one of Clint's old western shirts and precious little else, it looked like. "How're you doin', Luke? I thought I heard somebody out here."

"Hi, Debbie." Luke couldn't fault his brother's taste. Debbie's long, shapely legs and cloud of red hair would excite most men. His first inclination was to ask if her mother knew where she was, but he restrained himself. A twenty-one-year-old was capable of making her own decisions about spending the night with a man.

Clint turned to her with a frown. "I think you'd better put some clothes on."

"I *have* clothes on." Debbie walked past him into the kitchen. "Have you offered Luke a cup of coffee or anything?"

"Luke can't stay. I'm sure he has all kinds of big-star things to do today, don't you, Luke?"

Luke sighed. "Later on I have to be at opening ceremonies, but right now I was hoping that we could—"

"Clint Bannister, you can at least give your brother a cup of coffee!" Debbie stood in the middle of the kitchen, her hands on her hips in such a way that the western shirt revealed a fair amount of bosom. "How do you like it, Luke? Black or with cream and sugar?"

Luke glanced at her and saw the spark of interest in her eyes. Damn. She was making a play for him in front of Clint. "Actually I don't feel much like coffee. Bad stomach this morning. I wanted to discuss some family matters with Clint, so if you'll excuse us..." He raised one eyebrow.

"Well, uh, okay." Debbie looked disappointed. "I'll just go take a shower, then, and get ready for work. I'm a teller at Valley National, down on the square, so if you should need any cash, just drop by and I'm sure we can—"

"Debbie." Clint scowled at her.

"Just trying to be neighborly, Clint." She flounced out of the room.

"Yeah, right." Clint gazed after her, and when he turned back to Luke, his gray eyes were hostile. "I suppose you get tired of that, women throwing themselves at you all the time."

"It's meaningless. They mix me up with my character and imagine I'm somebody I'm not."

"Don't give me that. This is your brother you're talking to, the one who got the leftovers, remember? I think they only dated me because they thought somehow, by hanging around me, they'd get a better chance at you."

"Clint, I don't want to fight with you. I'm not after Debbie, for God's sake."

"Doesn't matter. She's after you. I should have known last night when she asked where you were staying that she was hoping there'd be some brotherly get-togethers." He walked over to the sink, rinsed out a glass and filled it with tap water. "Nothing ever changes."

"A lot changes. You never used to hate me."

Clint took his time drinking the water. Then he put the glass down and wiped his mouth with the back of his hand. "You never used to be a jerk."

"Look, I know this celebrity stuff gets to you. I'm not crazy about it, either, but—"

"Are you kidding? You eat that garbage up. Just watching you makes me want to throw up."

Luke's jaw tightened. "Publicity's part of the job, but I can control it. I was hoping you'd let me stay here after all, Clint. The arrangement I have now isn't working, and besides, this thing between us is ridiculous. We're the only family either one of us has left, and we ought to be able to get along."

"Get along?" He gave a harsh laugh. "I'm not the one who waltzed off to California to lie on the beach, leaving my brother to cope with a drunken old man. I'm not the one who lives the life-style of the rich and famous, while my brother struggles to keep the friggin' cotton fields producing and the machinery working. It's not you who has to dicker with the cotton-gin people and pray that the price of cotton doesn't slip another notch."

"I *gave* you my share. Isn't that enough?"

"No, big brother, it's not half enough. But it does give

me the right to tell you to get the hell out of *my* kitchen.''

Luke clenched his fists, sorely tempted to take a swing at Clint. But that wouldn't solve anything. His brother saw only one side of the picture—his side. And right now, with his girlfriend singing in the shower down the hall, probably for Luke's benefit, Clint wouldn't be in the mood to see the other side. Without another word, Luke turned and walked out the kitchen door.

MEG WOKE UP FROM a light sleep when the back door closed. Luke had gone out, and she couldn't blame him. This was an impossible situation.

When Dog-breath scratched at her door, she threw on her robe and slippers and padded into the kitchen to feed him. She found Luke's note on the kitchen table, saying he'd gone to his brother's and would be back that afternoon in time for the opening ceremonies.

So Luke had gone to patch things up with Clint. He'd left on foot, too, considering the truck and car were still here. It wasn't far, maybe a little over two miles. She hoped they'd be able to work out some kind of truce, both for Luke's sake and for hers. If he and Clint could come to an understanding, then Luke could stay there as originally planned.

After putting Dog-breath in his run in the backyard, she showered and dressed in black jeans and an ostrich festival T-shirt. Her interview on the morning television news show wasn't until eleven, but if Luke came back early she wanted to be dressed, although she doubted that clothes would offer her protection against the sensual urges he inspired.

She wasn't hungry, but she forced down juice and

toast to give her at least some fuel for the day. By eight the calls started coming in—last minute details that had to be settled. At ten she left for the station.

The interview started out well. Meg mentioned the names of the entertainers scheduled during the festival and the hours of the ostrich races. "And what about our grand marshal this year?" the show's host asked. "I've heard the women of Chandler are pretty excited to have Luke Bannister back in town."

Meg felt heat rise to her cheeks. Damn! "It's great to have a celebrity who grew up in Chandler as our grand marshal," she said.

"I understand you grew up here, too." The interviewer lifted an eyebrow. "Tell me, did Luke have a reputation with the ladies back then?"

Meg searched for a noncommittal answer while trying to calm her racing heart. "Luke's quite a guy," she said at last.

"And we'll look forward to seeing him in the parade on Saturday," the man said. The interview was over.

Meg escaped from the station and breathed in big gulps of fresh air to steady her nerves. Would people notice how flustered she'd become when the subject of Luke came up? She didn't doubt that a lot of people remembered she used to date him. She'd have to be careful when they next appeared in public together.

On her way home from the station Meg stopped by the neat clapboard house where she'd spent the first eighteen years of her life. She had to drop off two T-shirts for her parents, who had volunteered to help out during the festival. Meg needed all the bodies she could get, so she put aside her instincts to avoid her mother and father until after the weekend. She was furious about the way they'd interfered in her relationship with Luke, but didn't feel ready to discuss the matter while she was so preoccupied with the festival.

She went around to the back door as she had always done, and rapped once before entering the kitchen. "Mom?"

Nora Hennessy sat at the kitchen table eating a bowl of soup and watching a television program on the small under-cabinet model Meg's father had installed for her last Christmas. She was a small, trim woman with short, honey-colored hair, which had just started graying at the temples. She glanced at Meg with a startled expression. "Goodness! I didn't expect to see you on a busy day like this."

"Well, I just…" Meg paused as she became aware of the show her mother was watching. She glanced at the screen and back at her mother, who had the grace to blush. "*Connections*?" Meg asked, incredulous.

"It has a good story line."

"I didn't think you watched *any* soaps, let alone this one."

"Well, um, this is the only one I watch."

Meg stared at her mother. "I wasn't going to get into this, but it keeps hitting me in the face. Apparently you're one of Luke's secret fans, too."

Her mother's cheeks turned a deeper shade of pink. "I didn't say that."

"But you are, aren't you? I've heard how people talk about that show. Luke is the primary draw. People, or should I say *women*, don't watch it unless they're crazy about Dirk Kennedy." In the background she could hear Luke's voice. No wonder. He was on camera much of the time. And her mother watched him, just like a million other swooning women.

Nora picked up the remote beside her soup bowl and shut off the television. "There's nothing wrong with fantasy, Meg. The problem comes when you mix it up with real life."

"Is that what you thought I'd do? Is that why you didn't tell me Luke called here after he got the role in *Connections*?"

Nora seemed to have regained her composure. She rose from the table and started toward the pantry. "Sit down. I'll fix you some soup."

Meg tossed the T-shirts onto the kitchen table. "Actually I don't have time, but I'd love to have an answer to my question before I go."

"All right." Nora turned and faced her daughter. "Yes, I thought you'd leave Dan and run off to Hollywood if I gave you that message. Luke Bannister has always had that kind of influence on you, and your father and I have fought it every step of the way."

"I'm aware of your personal war against Luke," Meg said tightly. "I just found out Dad blackmailed him into breaking up with me in high school."

Tension lines bracketed her mother's mouth. "Obviously Luke's been telling you a few things. I hope that doesn't mean he's trying to work his way back into your life."

"Has it ever occurred to you that I might have been happy with Luke?"

"No." Her mother's voice remained steady. "If you thought about it logically, you'd agree. Luke's turned out better than your father and I expected, but his lifestyle is not for you. That big-city, glitzy style doesn't fit you at all. Besides that, you've wanted to be in politics for as long as I can remember, and this is the place to begin—the place where you grew up and have an established reputation. He's not going to leave California, and if you went there with him you'd be starting from scratch.''

Meg took a deep breath. She couldn't bring herself to admit that her mother was right. ''I just wish I'd been given the chance to make my own decisions about that.''

''From the way you're talking, it sounds as if you still have a chance to make that decision.''

Meg decided she'd rather not get into that with her mother. ''I'd better go.''

''Don't be foolish, Meg. He's an exciting man, but if he stood between you and your dream, the excitement would fade.'' Meg looked into her mother's eyes. ''We love you, Meg. The Lord saw fit to bless us with only one child, so you're all we have. Your welfare has been our only concern since the day you were born.''

''See you, Mom.'' Meg hurried out the door before she said something she'd regret and got herself into even more trouble.

From the frying pan into the fire, she thought as she drove to her house. Luke would surely be home by now, with opening ceremonies about two hours away. When she pulled the truck in the drive behind the BMW, she glanced into the side yard and noticed that her dog wasn't in his run. Evidently Luke was back. Taking a deep breath, she opened the front door. The sound of the shower and Luke singing confirmed that her nemesis had returned. Dog-breath glanced up from his position on the living-room rug and thumped his tail.

''You're enjoying this, aren't you?'' she said, walking

over to scratch behind the dog's ears. The trouble was, so was she. Driving home, knowing Luke would probably be there waiting for her, had been nerve-racking, but exciting, too. For the first time in nearly two years, she felt like a desirable woman, and it was a heady experience. She'd grown so accustomed to thinking of herself in nonsexual terms, as a widow, part owner of a business, a public servant. Luke had changed all that when he kissed her.

He obviously hadn't heard her come in. He was singing an old Rolling Stones tune about not getting any satisfaction. She sighed. That made two of them. Tossing her briefcase full of festival information on the couch, she walked into the kitchen for a glass of water. On the counter sat a bag of oranges, freshly picked, judging from the glossy stems and leaves still attached to some.

Surely he hadn't stolen them? She hoped not. This reliving the past stuff could get them both in hot water. But the oranges smelled good, and she hadn't eaten much all day. She took one from the bag and started peeling it over the sink.

"I thought I heard somebody rustling around in here."

She turned, the half-peeled orange in her hand. He stood in the doorway, toweling his hair. He had on a pair of the tightest jeans she'd ever seen on any human, and nothing else.

CHAPTER SIX

"DO YOU CARRY a permit for those?"

Luke draped the towel around his neck and glanced down at his skintight jeans. "My agent advised me to wear them."

Meg nodded. "Did he provide a bodyguard, too?"

"Shoot, this is the age of MTV. Nobody will blink an eye."

"I wouldn't bet on it." Her mother's words came back to her. *He's an exciting man.* Her mother didn't know the half of it. But apparently Luke took his sex appeal in stride, which might be the secret of his success. He was completely unself-conscious about his looks.

"I see you found the oranges."

She wrenched her gaze away from his well-developed chest and the curly dark hair she used to run her fingers through ten years ago. "Uh, yeah," she said, rediscovering the orange in her hand. "Where did they come from?"

He walked over to the table and rummaged through the bag. "Old man Peterson's tree."

"Luke, you didn't."

He picked out an orange and smiled at her. "Nah. I went over, knocked on the front door and talked to Mrs. Peterson. Mr. Peterson died a few years back—I guess you knew that."

She nodded. How could she manage to stand in the same kitchen with this sexy man and not throw herself into his arms? She felt sticky juice running between her fingers. Glancing down at the orange she was unconsciously squeezing, she relaxed her grip. "Mrs. Peterson gave you these?"

"Traded is more like it. She needed her tree wells dug out a little, and we swapped my labor for a bag of oranges." Luke came over to the counter, tore off a paper towel from the holder, and began peeling the orange into it as he stood beside her. His clean skin gave off the vanilla scent of the soap he'd used, and his biceps bulged with each movement. "I went over there in the first place to apologize for stealing fruit when I was a kid."

"Did you apologize for me, too?"

"Not exactly. I told her I'd led you astray."

"I see." And he was threatening to do it again. She watched as he plucked the rind from the orange. Last night, he'd cupped her breasts in those same hands. She wanted him to touch her again.

"She acted like she didn't even know I'd gone away." He glanced at Meg. "That took me down a notch or two, in case I was getting above my raising, as they say."

"You're not cocky, Luke."

"Tell that to my brother." He poked a section of orange into his mouth and chewed. "Great. Just like I remember."

"What happened with your brother?"

"Well, he—" Luke glanced at the orange in her hand. "You gonna eat that or hold it?"

"I'm going to eat it." She dutifully peeled the rest of the orange and put a slightly crushed section into her mouth. She ate the orange without tasting it, her heart pounding as fantasies of loving him swirled through her mind.

"Clint has a real chip on his shoulder, Meg. He pictures me as living the good life in California while he slaves away on the farm. I guess he's forgotten I had to learn how to survive on my own while he stayed here in familiar territory and was handed a farm. All he sees is that he has it tough and I have a glamorous career."

"That's too bad." Meg's orange got messier, and she had to lean over the sink to keep the juice from dripping onto her shirt. Still, some splattered. "Darn it."

"Here." Luke grabbed the dishrag draped over the faucet and dabbed at the spot just above her left breast. "I didn't mean for you to get—"

"Luke." She caught his hand, her heart racing. "For God's sake."

He went very still and his blue eyes turned smoky. He didn't move his hand, and the dampness of the dishrag chilled her heated skin. "I thought about you every minute of today," he said softly. "Walking along the roads we used to walk along, seeing the old places where we used to play hide-and-seek, the mesquite grove where we built the fort, the irrigation ditch where we went swimming. You were everywhere."

She couldn't move, couldn't speak.

He opened his hand, and the dishrag fell to the floor. He stroked the side of her neck before sliding his hand beneath her hair and cradling her head. "I've missed you so much. I need you, Meg," he whispered, and lowered his lips to hers.

She rested her trembling hands against his chest and he shuddered. He was so warm. She breathed in his familiar scent mingled with the sharp sweetness of oranges. The taste of oranges flavored their kiss as he took possession of her mouth.

She spread her fingers and combed them up though the luxurious pelt covering his chest. *Luke.* His name eddied through her consciousness. When she wound her arms around his neck, he pulled her close. She pressed against the firm mound beneath the tight denim of his jeans and her body responded with an aching rush of moisture. He thrust his tongue deep into her mouth. She yielded to him, mindless of anything but the melding of their bodies.

Then with a groan he released her. "I wasn't going to do this!"

Dazed and breathless, she opened her eyes and steadied herself with one hand against the counter. He was breathing hard, and his gaze was filled with agony. She struggled to speak and finally got the words out. "But you see, I'm as much to blame. I want you, too."

"No, you don't. Maybe now, at this very moment, but later you'd be sorry. I don't want to louse things up for you this weekend, Meg. I really don't. I tried to get Clint to let me sleep there, but he won't listen to reason. And if I stay here with you another night we'll make love. I can guarantee it."

She glanced away and took a deep breath. "You won't be staying here. I checked with the San Marcos this morning and they were able to make some adjustments and book you into a suite. We can move your things over as soon as you're ready."

"Good. That's good."

She glanced back at him. "I wish I hadn't done it, Luke."

Desire blazed in his eyes for a moment, and then he seemed to deliberately snuff it out. "It's the right decision. Let's get me packed up and out of your life while I still have some self-control."

THEY TOOK THE BMW into town, although Luke said he was resigned to the paparazzi picking up his trail again once the opening ceremonies took place.

"The San Marcos will keep your room number confidential," Meg said as she took a back road around the hotel's golf course to avoid the crowded square. "As long as you can keep that photographer from following you to your room, and I'm sure the staff will help you with that, you should be able to have some privacy at the hotel."

He glanced at her. "It doesn't really matter. I'm public property from now until Sunday, anyway."

"I guess so." She felt irritable and possessive. He'd added boots and a blue satin Western shirt to his tight jeans, and she didn't want him to be public property looking like that. She swung the BMW into the circular drive in front of the hotel.

"Come to think of it, you're public property now, too," he added.

But no one would be pawing her, she thought. "Luke, I wish—"

"Hey." He touched her arm. "You have a job to do. I understand that."

"Do you?"

His smile was rueful. "As long as there's a safe distance between us," he said, looking into her eyes. "But when you're in my arms, I turn into this selfish guy who only wants—"

A valet opened the passenger door. "May I take your luggage, Mr. Bannister?"

Luke turned to the valet. "Sure." Then he glanced back at Meg and winked. "Showtime," he said softly and got out of the car.

She watched him walk into the lobby and draw the attention of every woman along the way. If only she could turn the clock back. For twenty-four hours she'd had him all to herself. She hadn't cherished those moments nearly enough.

THE NEXT HOUR WAS A BLUR. Meg picked up the walkie-talkie that would be her constant companion for the next few days and the green John Deere utility cart she'd use to drive around the festival grounds. She checked to make sure the streets surrounding the festival area had been roped off before heading back to the San Marcos to pick up Luke.

When she found him in the lobby, he was surrounded by autograph seekers. As she maneuvered into the crowd and signaled to him that it was time to leave, she wished his agent had sent bodyguards. Getting him to the utility cart took skill, diplomacy and some deft moves. She waved him into the seat beside her and slid in behind the wheel. Snapping on her walkie-talkie, she lifted it to her mouth. "This is Meg. We're on our way."

Luke glanced at her and grinned. "Reminds me of the dune buggy Bobby Joe used to have. Don't pretend this isn't fun, driving this puppy around."

Meg grinned back as she steered a course between food booths and arts and crafts displays. "Okay, it's fun."

The festival grounds hummed with anticipation. Food

vendors stoked up popcorn poppers and electric grills while carts delivering bags of ice zipped past. Craft booths were crowded with wind chimes and bola ties, jewelry and original art. The candy colors and serpentine loops of the carnival stood silent and poised for action after the opening ostrich race at five, and a legion of stuffed animals hung ready to be claimed by anyone who could accurately pitch a quarter, a softball or a dart.

Meg pulled in next to the yellow-and-white-striped VIP tent set up at one end of the oval racetrack where the ostriches, llamas and camels would run. Parked next to the tent were the livestock tractor trailers that had brought the animals to Chandler. Bleachers at the opposite end and along one side were already filled, and the overflow crowd sat on a grassy hill opposite the bleachers. Service-club members hawked beer and soft drinks to the crowd while country music blared from loudspeakers.

"This is quite an operation," Luke said as he climbed out of the cart and followed Meg into the tent, where chamber of commerce members and city officials were sampling a colorful buffet.

"It has to be. If the festival doesn't go well, we'll struggle all year to fund our community programs."

"They've entrusted you with a big responsibility."

Meg laughed. "If I screw this up, I'll have to leave town. Come on, let's get something to eat before it's too late."

After they moved through the buffet she quickly lost track of Luke as people jockeyed for his time and attention. The tent area was off-limits to general spectators, but Meg noticed the paparazzi hanging around. She still wore her Dodgers cap on backward, but she'd changed into a long-sleeved shirt and bib overalls.

Meg worried that the young woman might try to sneak into the gathering. When Bobby Joe drove up in a utility cart just like hers, she walked over to talk with him. He was out of uniform, helping the service club with beer and soft-drink sales, but Meg had never known him to be truly off duty.

Meg glanced back at the photographer. Then, turning to Bobby Joe, she said, "I'd like to make sure that woman with all the cameras stays out of here."

"Sure thing." Bobby Joe adjusted his sunglasses. "How's it going?"

"Everything seems to be fine." She gazed at him, but couldn't see his eyes through the sunglasses. "About Wednesday night, Bobby Joe, I—"

"Hey." He held up one large hand. "That's your business, Meg."

The knot of anxiety loosened. "Then you didn't make a report or anything?"

"Why should I? You and Luke are both my friends. Consider it forgotten."

Meg sighed with relief. "Thanks, Bobby Joe."

"No problem."

Meg returned to the crowd of city officials. The air seemed more balmy now, the mood more festive. She'd made a mistake, but fortunately the mistake had been discovered by someone with loyalty and consideration. Her reputation was still intact.

The owner of the racing ostriches took the center of the arena, and called for attention over the loudspeakers. Meg tensed, knowing what was coming next. The man ran through his usual speech of being happy to be back with the fine folks of Chandler. Then he paused. "This year we have a new wrinkle in the program. The Chandler Chamber of Commerce is auctioning off a date with the parade grand marshal, who is none other than local celebrity and star of *Connections*, Luke Bannister!"

The crowd cheered and Luke went to the front of the tent and waved.

"The winner will be picked up in a limo, driven to the San Marcos to have dinner with Luke in the Nineteen-Twelve restaurant, presented with a dozen roses and given unlimited rides at the carnival. So, if I can have one of my assistants draw from this bowl of names, we'll find out who the lucky lady is."

Meg held her breath. She didn't want anybody going on a date with Luke. No matter that the raffle had raised a sizable amount of money for the chamber or that it would generate some good publicity for Luke. She hated the idea.

"And the winner is..." The announcer paused for dramatic effect. "Debbie Fry!"

A shriek went up from the bleachers and Debbie bounded down waving her arms. "Yes!" she cried, "yes, yes, yes!"

"I think she's happy about it," the announcer said. "Now, Miss Fry, if you'll go over to the VIP tent and identify yourself, Luke Bannister will know who he's taking out Friday night. I would say he's a lucky man."

Meg forced herself to meet Debbie and congratulate her. Luke stepped forward with a smile and said he was delighted to be her escort the following night. Meg suspected he was acting again, but still, her insides twisted with jealousy. She wasn't proud of the emotion, but it had her firmly in its grip.

Flash! Meg was temporarily blinded by the flare of light. Through the black spots dancing in front of her eyes she saw the paparazzi moving away. Meg felt certain she'd been in the shot. She hoped her emotions hadn't shown on her face. She could imagine the tabloid gossip now: "Former girlfriend watches jealously as Luke charms new woman." No, she was becoming paranoid. The photographer had no interest in her. Meg had just been in the way.

The first ostrich race began, with three ostriches pulling small chariots in red, white and blue. The drivers wore Roman helmets and sweeping capes in matching colors. The crowd laughed and cheered as the ostriches nearly ran into each other circling the track with their prancing, long-legged gait. Meg faked some enthusiasm; in the past she'd been fascinated by the huge, swift-footed birds with their long plumes and backward-folding knees. But from the corner of her eye she could see Debbie smiling up at Luke and Luke smiling back. Meg gritted her teeth.

Thankfully a call came in on her walkie-talkie. Something had gone wrong with the giant bubble-gum machine set up by the crafts booths. Meg went over and told Luke he was on his own for a while, and sped off in her utility cart.

CLINT DROVE his newly washed truck over to Debbie's house at six-thirty that night. They had a date for the carnival, although after the scene that morning with Luke, he didn't relish taking Debbie anywhere his brother might happen to be. But all Clint's buddies were taking their wives and girlfriends to the carnival tonight, and Clint didn't want to miss the fun. Luke just better stay the hell away from Debbie, and vice versa.

Debbie rented a little guest house behind her parents'

place, which was why he and Debbie always ended up at his house. The guest house was too close to her mom and dad for Clint's comfort when he was enjoying the charms of their daughter.

Debbie came out the front door as soon as he drove up. He liked that about her—she watched for him and was always on time. His gaze flicked appreciatively over her tight lavender jeans and pink blouse. She wore the collar of the blouse turned up and the shirttails tied at her waist. Clint thought she looked sexy as hell. The guys would sure envy him tonight.

He leaned over and opened the passenger door. When she climbed in, he took a deep breath of her perfume. "You smell great, sugar."

"Thanks." She didn't look at him.

"Got a kiss for me?"

"Sure." She leaned over and kissed him quickly, without putting much feeling into it.

"Hey." He grabbed her and pulled her close for a good long soul kiss. Then he let her go and put the truck in gear. "That's better."

Usually she talked a mile a minute when she got in the truck, but tonight she was quiet, letting the country music from the radio fill the silence.

His curiosity grew. "Something wrong, sugar?"

She glanced at him nervously. "I guess I'd better tell you. You'll find out pretty quick, anyway."

His stomach churned. This had something to do with Luke; he just knew it. "So tell me."

"I won the raffle."

"What raffle?" He had no idea what she was talking about.

"The one for a date with your brother."

"What?" Clint veered to the side of the road and

slammed on the brakes. He felt sick. "You actually bought a ticket?"

"Twenty."

His shoulders sagged. Of course she'd bought twenty tickets. Who was he kidding? All along she'd gone out with him because he was Luke Bannister's brother. And now that Luke was around, who needed him?

"It's just for one night," she said, her voice softer, less defiant. "Friday."

He straightened and gazed out the windshield as he assessed the damage. To be honest, he wasn't in love with Debbie. But he liked her a lot, and she was known around town as his steady girl. She might not break his heart if she ran off with Luke, but she'd sure knock a hole in his pride. Damn Luke. Why couldn't he have stayed where he belonged?

Debbie's question was barely audible. "Are we still going to the carnival tonight?"

Clint shoved the truck into gear. "You're damn right."

"You're mad, aren't you?"

The tires squealed as Clint turned a corner. "Nah. Not old Clint."

LACK OF SLEEP was beginning to catch up with Meg, but she couldn't go home just yet. People still needed to consult with her, and Didi said there was a problem with one of the entries in the parade. Meg drove her cart toward the command tent the festival committee used.

Since the opening ceremonies she hadn't seen much of Luke, at least not in the flesh. A giant-screen television had been set up near the row of arts and crafts booths, and it featured continuous footage of *Connections*. Occasionally Meg would walk past and catch a glimpse of Luke, twice his normal size, bending over whatever woman he was bedding during that particular episode. She always had to turn away, just as someone on a diet might have to ignore the dessert menu.

She'd almost reached the tent when Luke suddenly stepped in front of the cart. She had to brake quickly to avoid hitting him.

"Park that thing and come with me."

"What's wrong?"

"I need to talk to you. Come on."

She wheeled the cart into an empty space between two booths and climbed out. "Is it that photographer? The baby ostrich? What?"

"I'll tell you on the Ferris wheel. It's the only spot in this crazy place where we can be alone."

"Luke, I don't like the Ferris wheel."

"I'll protect you."

He'd never forced her on a carnival ride back in high school, but tonight he seemed desperate enough to drag her there. "I could get sick all over you."

"Trust me. You won't get sick." They reached the ride and Luke motioned to the ticket taker, who waved them to the head of the line.

"Guess it helps to be Dirk Kennedy, huh?" someone called out.

"Always," Luke said, and flashed a smile. Several people asked for autographs. "When I get back," he promised, and handed Meg into one of the swinging cars.

Her stomach lurched. "This is not a good idea."

"It's a great idea."

The car started forward as the wheel began its slow grinding upward motion, lifting them higher off the ground. "Oh, Luke." Meg's stomach felt as if someone had dropped a stone into it. She gripped the handrail.

"You'll be fine." He took her hands between both of his. "Look at me."

She did, and immediately began to relax. Who could think of anything terrible looking into eyes the color of the Arizona sky? And such gentle eyes. The wheel carried them upward, but she kept gazing into his eyes and didn't feel the least bit sick.

He smiled. "That's better. I knew you could do it."

Then she made the mistake of looking down at the kaleidoscope of lights below her and almost passed out. "Oh, my God."

"Look at me."

She held on to his gaze like a talisman and her stomach stopped quivering.

"Just keep looking at me, then. I like that better, anyway."

"This is almost like being hypnotized, Luke."

"Hey, I never thought of trying that."

She chuckled. "It would be overkill."

"Oh, Meg, what I wouldn't give..." He sighed. "Time to change the subject. I brought you up here to see if we can do anything about this date with Debbie Fry."

"Do? Do what? What's wrong?"

"She's Clint's girl."

"I know, but she won the raffle legitimately, and you saw how excited she was. I can't imagine trying to talk her out of it."

"You're sure? Because I thought maybe, if you offered her the roses and the limo ride and the dinner, to be used with Clint instead of me, then we could choose somebody else for the date. I'd cover the extra expense.''

''I can try, but I saw her face, Luke. She may be Clint's girl, but she wants that date with you.''

''Damn.'' He smiled sadly. ''I was even fantasizing that you could rig it so that you could go on the date with me.''

''Wouldn't work. I'd be run out of town on a rail.''

''No, you wouldn't, because I'd ride in and save you, like Lancelot did with Guinevere when they were going to burn her at the stake.''

''You always were a romantic.''

''Yeah. Did you know we've made three complete circles and you haven't been sick yet?''

Meg chuckled. ''Now *that's* romantic.''

''And now we've stopped on the very top, my favorite spot.''

She kept her gaze fastened on his, but her stomach still gave a little flip. ''Don't tell me where we are. I don't want to know.''

''There's a tradition about stopping at the top of the wheel. Of course you wouldn't know about it, because you won't ride in one.''

''If it has something to do with rocking the car like crazy, we can forget tradition.''

''That's one tradition. This is the other one.'' He took her face between his hands and kissed her. It was a soft kiss, undemanding and sweet. He pulled back and gazed into her eyes. ''Do you like that tradition?''

She felt as if she were floating. ''You're crazy.''

''Let's kiss until we start moving. Nobody can see us up here.''

''This is dangerous, Luke.''

"Only if you attack me and start ripping my clothes off. If you can control yourself, we'll be fine."

She laughed, and he kissed her while her mouth was slightly open. His tongue slipped inside, and her heart hammered in her chest. What was she doing, recklessly kissing him like this? But she couldn't stop. He tasted so good, and she needed the pressure of his lips, the clever thrust of his tongue.

The car started with a jolt, and he drew back to gaze at her. "Maybe you'd better try frowning or something."

"Why?"

"Because right now you look like a woman who wants to make love."

"It's your fault."

"Frown at me."

She frowned, and then started laughing again. She was still laughing when they stepped out of the car and the camera flashed in her face.

CHAPTER SEVEN

"I HAVE TO GO," Meg said, releasing Luke's hand and hurrying away. She glanced over her shoulder to see fans surrounding Luke and the paparazzi taking more shots. Meg shrugged away her concern. What could someone do with a picture like that? It was hardly incriminating. All the incriminating action had taken place off camera.

She hastened back to her cart and drove to the festival command tent. After finishing her business there, she thought about trying to find Debbie in the crowd, but her walkie-talkie crackled again and she was off to find a replacement light for one of the soft-drink booths. One chore led to another until finally the rides and booths started closing down for the night. Meg figured Debbie had gone home. She'd have to catch her at the bank in the morning. Meg doubted she'd give up her date with Luke, anyway.

For a moment, Meg allowed herself to imagine a double date with Clint and Debbie, Luke and her. Just like old times, except Debbie hadn't been the girl on Clint's arm back then. She'd been far too young, still in grade school. She wasn't too young now, and Meg hated the thought of Luke's hand in hers, his arm draped around her shoulders. Would Luke kiss her good-night? Would he do more than that? Of course not. The thought was unworthy. And yet, he was a hot-blooded man, and he had no strings....

THE NEXT MORNING she found Luke over by the petting zoo, where Dirk Kennedy, the baby ostrich, was the main attraction. People wanted pictures of Luke with his character's namesake. Luke's jeans weren't as tight as yesterday's, but he made up for that with a wide-sleeved, collarless white shirt unbuttoned almost to the waist, and knee-high leather moccasins that accentuated the curve of his calves. Dark glasses made him look like a mysterious and dangerous pirate. Somebody sure knew how to dress him to advantage.

Meg caught his attention and signaled to him. In a few minutes he excused himself and walked over to where she stood in the shade of the auto-show tent. He pulled off his sunglasses and smiled when he reached her. "You look terrific. And you smell a lot better than the petting zoo."

"You're an old farm boy. You should be used to a little manure."

"Actually I'm having a good time. In fact, seeing you here makes my day complete."

"Thanks." She looked into those blue, blue eyes and her concentration disappeared.

"Did you need me for something?"

Yes. She forced herself back to reality. "I drove over to the bank just now and talked to Debbie. She wants to go through with the date tonight."

He squinted off into the distance and twirled the sunglasses. "That's too bad."

"I suggested she use the whole package with Clint instead of you." Meg's gaze wandered to the open shirt and the dark chest hair it revealed. "Debbie said going out with Clint instead of you would be stupid."

"I don't know what she expects. I plan to treat her the way I'd treat a little sister if I had one."

"I doubt she expects that."

He gazed down at Meg. "As they say in the old songs, if I can't have you, I don't want nobody else."

Her pulse raced. She loved hearing words like that, even if she didn't quite believe them. On Sunday he'd go back to L.A., and she couldn't picture Luke staying celibate for long. "Well, let's hope Debbie has a nice time with someone who acts like her older brother."

"She won a date, not a seduction."

Meg smiled. "You sound a little testy."

"Frustration can do that to a man." Then he gave her a quick grin. "But I can handle it, and Debbie, and my little brother, if it comes to that. I see how important all of this is to you. I don't want to mess it up." He watched a couple of kids walk by with sticky pink goo all over their mouths and two empty cardboard tubes. "Say, can I buy you some cotton candy for old times' sake?"

"It's a nice thought, but I have a million things to do. Incidentally, a TV crew is coming tonight to film you and Debbie enjoying the carnival."

"Okay. And thanks for trying to change her mind about the date."

"Sure." She watched him walk away and gather people like filings to a magnet. She understood. He pulled at her that way every time she come near him.

THAT EVENING THERE WERE no major problems erupting at the festival, so Meg decided to work at the chamber of commerce beer concession near the entertainment pa-

vilion. Traditionally it had been the busiest, most boisterous place at the festival, so Meg hoped she wouldn't
have time to think about Luke and his date with Debbie.

She managed to keep them at the back of her mind
until the moment they arrived at the festival and walked
right past the beer truck. Luke sported a dark Western
suit that emphasized his broad shoulders, while Debbie
wore a slinky silver number that glistened with each sinuous step. She carried her bouquet of roses in one arm
and looped the other one firmly though Luke's. As they
walked she kept bumping into him and leaning her cheek
against his shoulder.

The paparazzi was energetically getting the couple on
film. Debbie posed and pouted for the camera as if she
were a budding starlet. Meg remembered vaguely that
acting was Debbie's ambition, so of course she'd make
the most of tonight. Still, the sight of Debbie draped all
over Luke gave Meg a headache. The only thing that
helped was Luke's unguarded expressions. For the most
part he smiled and looked pleasant, but Meg noticed one
moment when he projected total boredom.

Luke and Debbie walked in the direction of the entertainment pavilion where a well-known Southern rock
group was playing. They were nearly out of Meg's line
of vision when Clint stepped into their path. He was
weaving. Meg yelled at one of the other workers to take
over her station and ran out the back of the booth.

As she raced toward the cluster of people gathering
around Luke, Debbie and Clint, she imagined disaster.
The televison crew was due any minute. Luke in the
midst of a brawl would embarrass everyone.

Clint stood, feet apart, in front of Luke and Debbie.

"I see you got yourself a sweet young thing, brother," he drawled.

"Back off, Clint. Debbie and I are just doing our part for charity."

"Yeah. That little gal can be real charitable."

"How dare you?" Debbie started forward, hand raised.

Luke pulled her back. "Let me handle him." Debbie looked adoringly at Luke and moved back to give the brothers room. Luke stepped toward Clint and lowered his voice. "Watch your step, little brother. Debbie's a terrific woman, but she's a friend, and that's all. Don't make this into something ugly."

Clint jabbed a finger at Luke. "Don't pull that high and mighty act on me. This is your brother, Lukey-boy. I was around when Dad tanned your bare butt with a willow switch because you were getting too friendly with the girls in the neighborhood. You've never met a woman you didn't want. I know you. But Debbie's my girl. Stay away from her."

"I'm not anybody's girl," Debbie called out from the sidelines.

Meg saw the television crew approaching from the right. For a moment she stood rooted to the spot, unsure of what to do and dreading Luke's reaction to his brother's defiant confrontation.

Luke's eyes narrowed. "Go home and sleep it off, Clint."

"Make me, pinup boy."

Luke's hands clenched and a muscle in his jaw twitched. Meg, reacting instinctively, pushed through the crowd and grabbed Luke's arm. She felt as if she'd latched on to a corded steel cable. ''Don't,'' she whispered. ''Please.''

A shudder coursed through him. He gazed down at her, and she had trouble believing eyes so filled with anger could have looked at her so lovingly the night before.

''You could ruin the festival. Don't fight,'' she pleaded. Slowly the fire faded and the gentleness returned. The muscles in his arms relaxed. ''Thank you, Luke,'' she murmured.

''Is loverboy backing down?'' Clint taunted.

''I won't fight you,'' Luke said. ''Let's go, Debbie.'' He held out his hand and started back the way they'd come.

''Chicken-livered son of a bitch!'' Clint yelled. ''I know why you won't fight. You're afraid of messing up that pretty-boy face of yours!''

Meg held her breath as Luke paused and his shoulders tensed. He glanced over at her, took a deep breath and grinned. Then he mouthed the word ''showtime'' and guided Debbie off toward the carnival.

Clint tried to run after him, but a couple of his friends held him back. Shaking, Meg leaned against the nearest booth for support. That was all she needed—to have a parade grand marshal with a black eye and broken nose.

The television reporter approached her. ''Are you Meg O'Brian?''

She nodded.

''Wasn't Luke Bannister the guy arguing with somebody?''

''Luke's on his way over to the carnival,'' Meg said. ''If you hurry you should be able to catch him.''

''Well, what was that argument all about?''

Meg forced a smile. "Absolutely nothing."

The reporter stared doubtfully at her for a moment and finally shrugged. "If you say so. Come on, guys, we have a midway to film."

LUKE STOOD WITH DEBBIE on the outskirts of the crowd listening to a slow, sexy song the band had pushed to number one on the charts a few months ago. Some couples were dancing in the soft grass. Debbie had suggested they do the same, but he'd made an excuse about not being a good dancer. He turned his wrist just a fraction to look at the time. Another half hour and he could reasonably call this date over. He could hardly wait.

When he'd agreed to go along with this idea of a "Date with Dirk," he'd thought it would be no big deal. He'd taken out his share of women for promotional purposes, and this would be the same thing. Except that yesterday he'd held Meg in his arms, and now the touch of any other woman grated against his skin. Debbie's perfume assaulted him with its stridency, and her voice was pitched in the wrong key. He wanted Meg.

He was beginning to understand the spot he'd put himself in by coming back here. Over the years Meg had evolved into a fantasy figure, still desirable, but not an obstacle in his pursuit of pleasure with other women. Now she'd moved into the forefront again, and no other woman could be an acceptable substitute after holding her. Since he couldn't have Meg, his love life was going to be in big trouble. Maybe in another ten years he'd forget her sufficiently to enjoy other women. Then again, maybe not.

Debbie linked her arm through his and snuggled closer. "You're wonderful, Luke."

He eased away from her blatant attempt at intimacy. "I'm just a guy."

"I'm beginning to wonder about that." There was an edge to her voice. "I usually don't have any trouble encouraging a man to make a move. And I've heard you have a reputation with women. So what's wrong, Luke? Don't you find me attractive?"

He looked into her pale blue eyes. "You're very attractive, Debbie." He wondered how much he dared say. Even a suggestion that there was someone else might cast suspicion on Meg. They had been seen together a lot, and no telling if Bobbie Joe would keep his mouth shut.

"You haven't even kissed me once."

He smiled. "I don't think that was part of the raffle."

"We could make it part of the raffle. If you want."

A week ago he would have accepted the invitation in those half-closed eyes, those parted lips. But last night he'd kissed Meg at the top of the Ferris wheel, and he could still feel what that was like. He didn't want other lips messing with his recollection. "I'm sorry, Debbie."

"You're sure nothing like your brother."

"You'd probably have been better off with him tonight."

"Clint's okay, but he's not going anywhere with his life. He's a dead-end street. If I stay with him, I'll be stuck here, too."

"Ah." He should have figured out her motivation sooner. It could have saved them both a lot of time. "I guess you want to know if I can help you with contacts in Hollywood."

"Of course not!" Her expression turned sulky. "I just want to get to know you better, but you won't let me."

"Debbie, you don't have to be coy. I'd be glad to help you if I can. You look like you'd be photogenic. I can't promise anything, but I could talk to some people, see about an audition for *Connections*."

"You could? That would be *great*."

"In return, I want you to tell Clint that nothing happened between us tonight. In fact, I'd appreciate your spreading the word that I was a perfect gentleman."

She frowned and cocked her head to one side. "I don't know. That kind of makes me look bad, you know, that you didn't try anything."

"Then say I was coming down with a head cold or something, and you didn't want to catch it." He sighed. "I'd just like to get Clint off my case on at least this one issue."

"So you'll do this for me, and I don't have to sleep with you or anything?"

"Surprise, surprise."

"Not that it would have been so *horrible* if I had. My girlfriends would all have been jealous if I'd gone to bed with Luke Bannister."

"Just remember that stuff on-screen isn't real. Like I said, I'm just a guy."

"Then all the stories I heard about you in high school aren't true?"

"Gross exaggerations. Come on, let's go find that kid we paid to hold your flowers."

A half hour later, Luke put Debbie in the limo and walked back to the San Marcos. Thank God that was over. Debbie was happy, but Clint was still one screwed-up guy. He hoped Debbie's description of her night out with him would make a difference. Luke didn't want the difficulties between him and his brother to get any worse. In fact, before he left Chandler he'd like to iron out a few of them.

When he got back to his suite the message light was blinking. He called the front desk and retrieved the message from his agent Henry Davis. The message said "Screen test on Monday."

Screen test. He finally had a shot at a movie part, the one he and Henry had hoped would come through. This could be the biggest career break he'd had since landing the part in *Connections*.

He wanted to tell somebody, to rejoice with somebody, but who? He could call some of his friends back in L.A., but most of them were sitting around waiting for the same break. It would be like rubbing salt in their wounds. Clint wouldn't care. But Meg—Meg would be happy for him, even though his career was one of the reasons they were being forced apart.

Luke remembered the time he'd won a new bike by entering a contest on the back of a cereal box. Clint had been jealous, but Meg had whooped with joy. Then she'd managed to bring Clint around, convincing him that he'd benefit because he'd get Luke's old bike, and she'd help him paint it to look brand-new. Even back then Meg had been a little politician, Luke thought with a smile.

Maybe, just maybe, she was the key to this trouble with Clint. She might even be able to act as a go-between, get them back on track. He picked up the phone by the bed and dialed her number. He got her machine and put a message on it for her to call. He left his extension.

WHEN SHE GOT HOME, Meg played her messages from the answering machine in her bedroom. When Luke's

voice came on, she automatically took down the number
and the extension. Then she stared at the pad of paper
as the machine beeped and whirred back to its starting
position. Whether he'd meant to or not, Luke had just
given her his room number.

She hadn't wanted the information and had deliberately not listened when the clerk at the San Marcos had
told her. Luke hadn't mentioned it, either. But now here
it was, as if written in neon, flashing at her from the
page. And he wanted her to call. Or so he said. Was this
really an invitation?

She paced the bedroom floor and wrestled with longings that threatened to hurl her out the door and into
Luke's arms. Then she thought of an explanation for his
leaving the extension number for her. If she'd called and
asked for Luke, the desk had instructions not to put people through. If she didn't have the extension number,
she wouldn't be able to call him back. He'd had no
hidden agenda. He just wanted to talk to her.

More disappointed than relieved, she dialed the number. He picked it up on the second ring. "Hi, it's me,"
she said, in the same way they'd indentified themselves
to each other ten years ago.

"Hi, me." He fell into the same pattern.

"What's going on?"

"Well, for one thing, my agent called and I have a
screen test on Monday for the movie part I've been trying to get."

"Luke, that's wonderful!" The news was bittersweet.
Now he'd really be lost to her. But she could imagine
how much he'd wanted this break. "By the way, thanks
for keeping cool tonight with Clint. I guess it's just as

well you didn't fight and risk bruising your face right
before this screen test."

"Yeah, I guess so. Listen, it's Clint I really called
about. I need to talk to him—someplace where nobody
else can butt in. When I first arrived, the whole damn
town was there, and when I went over to the house the
next morning, Debbie was hanging around. I think if he
and I could sit down with no distractions, we might be
able to get some things talked out."

"Could be." Meg wasn't so sure. She'd seen the look
on Clint's face tonight.

"You've always been good at being our go-between.
Could you get a message to him tomorrow that I'll be
alone in my room after the festival, and that I'd like him
to come over for a beer or something? Do you think
he'd come?"

"He might." Meg heard the hope in Luke's voice and
her heart ached for him. Clint probably missed Luke,
too, but he was so pigheaded he'd never admit it.

"Debbie promised to tell Clint nothing happened between us tonight. I'm hoping that will help."

"Uh, yeah, it could." She felt her own personal victory at his announcement. "Did you…have a good time,
at least?"

"No."

"I'm sorry…no, I take that back. I'm not sorry at all.
I hated the idea of you and Debbie out together."

"Maybe almost as much as I did."

Meg closed her eyes and pictured him in the dark
Western suit over a crisp white shirt, and underneath
that—just Luke. She wanted him so much.

"Meg?"

"I'm here. I'm just…"

"I know."

"It's stupid of me, Luke. We can't be together, and that's that."

He hesitated. "Yeah," he said at last.

"So let's hang up and go to sleep."

"I miss you, Meg."

"I miss you, too." Slowly she placed the receiver in its cradle and stood by the phone, willing it to ring, hoping he'd need her too much for caution.

CHAPTER EIGHT

AT NINE-THIRTY SATURDAY morning Meg wound her way through the floats, convertibles and horseback riders gathered on Arizona Avenue two miles from the center of town. She wanted to make sure Didi wasn't having any problems with other entries.

She passed the Chandler High School Band, resplendent in blue and white. The horn section gleamed in the sun as band members ran through scales. Drummers marched in place practicing their staccato parade rhythm, and the pep squad rustled blue-and-white pom-pons in time to the beat. Meg caught the sense of excitement as she moved past prancing horses and crepe paper-covered floats. The air smelled of farm animals, gasoline fumes and the freshly cut wood used to build the floats.

Before she found Didi, she spotted her parents' decorated buckboard. They'd driven the buckboard in each of the ostrich festival parades, with her mother dressed in a long gingham dress and bonnet for added effect. Her mother stood watching as her father struggled with a harness on one of the horses.

Meg glanced down at her white slacks and blazer. She was wearing an ostrich festival T-shirt underneath, but she'd dressed up a little more today in honor of the parade. If she helped her father, she'd probably get dirt all over her outfit. Meg's mother caught sight of her and waved. Meg waved back and walked over to say hello. "Trouble with the harness?"

"Oh, you know how old the thing is. Your father can't make up his mind whether or not to sell this buckboard, so he keeps putting off buying a new harness. Right now the last patch job isn't holding."

The sun warmed Meg's back as she glanced at her father. "Parade starts in about twenty minutes, Dad."

"We'll make it." He didn't look up from his repair work. "Nora, can you hold those horses still?"

"If I do, they'll soil this dress, and after all the time I spent making it, I—" Her eyes widened as she looked past Meg. "Why, hello, Luke."

Meg turned, her pulse automatically accelerating. She'd known he was here somewhere but hadn't seen him yet. For the parade he'd chosen a black silk Western shirt tucked into tight black jeans. A black Stetson was pulled low over his eyes. He looked like a devil, and only a devilish urge would have brought him over here to taunt her parents with his presence.

"Hello, Mrs. Hennessy. I'll hold the horses."

Meg's father looked up, his manner painstakingly formal. "Thanks, Luke, but I'm sure you have more important things to do. And you might ruin that fancy outfit."

"Don't worry about it. I have a few minutes. Besides, the parade marshal should be marshaling the parade, don't you think?" He cast a quick smile in Meg's direction and grasped a bridle in each hand. Meg sneaked a peek at her mother. Nora Hennessy's cheeks were bright with color, but Meg couldn't decide if it was from excitement or embarrassment.

The horses, a matched pair of black geldings that were

one of her father's few impractical possessions, tossed their heads and shifted restlessly. The harness jingled and Jack Hennessy swore softly under his breath. Luke murmured to the horses and held the bridles firmly. "Nice team," he said to her father.

"Thanks. I should either get them a decent harness or give them up, but I can't seem to do either."

"It's easy to get stuck in your thinking sometimes."

Meg sucked in her breath. Had Luke really said something so pointed? Her father didn't respond, just worked faster. Luke was obviously making him very uncomfortable. He pricked his finger twice. After what seemed like a century to Meg, but was probably only a couple of minutes, her father straightened. "There, that should do it. Appreciate your help." He held out his hand to Luke.

Luke smiled and started to release the bridles, but before he did a camera flashed several times in succession. Meg knew without looking it was that photographer again.

Meg's father let his arm sink to his side. "Guess I should have known it was a photo op, or whatever they call it in Hollywood. In Chandler, we're used to people doing things to be neighborly."

Watching Luke's expression harden, Meg felt her heart break. "Dad! Luke didn't hold those horses for you because he hoped somebody would take a picture. He's been trying to avoid that woman ever since he got here."

"Never mind, Meg," Luke said gently. "I'd better be going." He pulled fringed black gloves out of his hip pocket. "The parade's about to start."

As he walked away, Meg rounded on her father. "You're being unfair."

"I'm being realistic, Meg. Avoiding cameras? The man's paid to stand in front of one. He offered to hold the horses because he knew the fans would love a picture of him in his black outfit next to those black horses. Even I can see it'll be a great shot."

"You're misjudging him, just like you always have."

Her mother stepped forward. "Now, Meg, this isn't the time to drag all that up."

"I didn't. He did, by being rude to Luke." She glared at her father. "I found out about what happened back in high school, Dad. About how you made Luke break up with me."

Her father met her angry gaze. "I won't apologize for that. Look where you are now. If I hadn't stepped in, no telling what would have happened to you. I guess he told you, huh?"

"Yes. And I was shocked that you'd stoop to blackmail."

"Be shocked, then. Someday if you're a parent, you'll understand what I did. What's he telling you now, for? Does he want to worm his way back into your life?"

"For your information, he told me he understood why you acted the way you did. He's forgiven you, Dad, but you haven't changed, have you?"

"Not when it comes to you. And he's still bad news in my book. I don't care if he ends up with an Academy Award. He's wrong for you. And you know it."

"Your father's right, dear."

Meg turned to her mother. "You're a fine one to talk, considering that you—" She stopped when she saw the anxious expression on her mother's face. Her father didn't know his wife had defected and started watching *Connections*. It was a small thing, but a defection, nevertheless. Meg decided to let the subject drop. ''You were right in the first place, Mom. Now isn't the time to be dragging this out.'' Relief softened her mother's face.

Meg hadn't ever thought much about her parents' relationship, but it seemed strange to her that they would have this sort of secret, no matter how harmless, between them. It made them seem more flawed, less capable of passing judgment on her life. She was both saddened and unburdened by the insight.

''Listen, I have to go. I need to check some last-minute details with Didi.'' She hurried away.

She found Didi at the registration table set up in a shopping-center parking lot. ''Everything looks great,'' Meg said and gave her a hug.

Didi smiled with pleasure. ''Especially our grand marshal. Have you seen the horse they found for him?''

''Horse? I thought a grand marshal rode in the back of a convertible.''

''Luke asked for a horse. Somebody arranged to have an Arabian brought in from a farm in Scottsdale. Luke's right over there. He just mounted up.''

Meg looked in the direction Didi was pointing and almost stopped breathing. The horse was black as midnight, with a shimmering mane and a tail that swept the pavement. Sunlight winked on the silver-studded saddle and bridle as Luke guided the prancing animal through the crowd. The yoke of his Western shirt emphasized the breadth of his shoulders, while the black silk revealed the play of muscles beneath it. His black-clad thighs gripped the saddle with practiced ease while his

gloved hands firmly controlled the powerful horse. The
hat pulled low over his eyes cast his face into mysterious
shadow.

"Have you ever seen anything sexier in your life?"
Didi whispered.

Meg slowly shook her head. Years ago she'd thought
herself a fool to have fallen under Luke Bannister's
spell. Maybe now she was a fool for fighting it.

THE REST OF THE DAY passed quickly. Saturday always
brought the biggest attendance, and Meg drove her utility cart from one end of the festival grounds to the other,
taking care of emergencies. She kept busy until the sun
settled below the horizon and the lights of the carnival
sparkled against the cinnamon glow of the sunset.

She'd kept her eye out for Clint but hadn't seen him
all day. That wasn't surprising. Clint was a party animal
who preferred to carouse after dark. But she hoped to
find him before he started drinking.

At seven-fifteen she checked backstage at the entertainment pavilion to make sure the country and western
group she'd booked was ready to go on at seven-thirty.
She was surprised to find Luke there talking with the
band members. He excused himself and came over to
her. "Can you believe it? They're going to let me play
a couple of songs with them. It's a chance of a lifetime,
Meg."

She smiled. "What fun. The crowd will love it."

"Come and give me moral support, okay? About eight
o'clock."

"I'll try. I haven't found Clint yet."

"He'll show up for this concert, I'll bet. This is one
of his favorite groups."

Meg nodded. Clint probably would appear, and he'd see his older brother up on stage, claiming the limelight again. But she couldn't say that to Luke, who looked so excited to have a chance to play with the band. "Good luck with your gig," she said with a grin. "What are you going to play?"

"A couple of easy songs. I told them I was rusty, so they're giving me the simple stuff. I shouldn't screw it up too much."

"You'll be great." Meg knew that all he had to do was stand there with a guitar and the women in the audience would go crazy. "I'll try to be back here by eight."

She kept close track of the time after that. Barring a catastrophe, she'd watch Luke fulfill his dream of playing guitar with a well-known country band. At eight, she arrived at the fringes of the crowd and sat in her utility cart facing the stage.

The crowd was already warmed up by a half hour of their favorite songs before the lead singer announced Luke Bannister as a guest artist on steel guitar. Wild cheering followed as Luke walked out on stage in his black shirt, tight jeans, cowboy hat and a guitar strapped over his shoulder. When he smiled, the women shrieked, just as Meg had expected they would.

During each number Luke stayed in the background, but for Meg, there was no one else on the stage. She forgot the crowds around her and her responsibilities as festival chairperson. For eight minutes, as the group played two songs and kidded with Luke in between, Meg gave herself up to being a woman in love.

After the second song, amid deafening applause and cries of "More, Luke!" he lifted the guitar strap over his head and leaned the guitar in a corner of the stage. Then he slipped behind the back curtain. Meg watched hopefully in case he came back for an encore, but he didn't. The lead singer started talking about the band's new album, and Meg knew Luke wouldn't return to the stage. She sighed and wished she'd borrowed a video camera for his performance. He was slipping away. Soon he'd be completely gone, and all she'd have would be a well-rehearsed performance on a television screen.

"Did you like it?"

She turned to find him standing beside the utility cart. "I loved it."

"Good. Come down here a sec."

She left her seat and stood beside him. "What?"

"I saw something you should have." He took her hand and led her over to a vendor waving phosphorescent light wands in the air. He bought a multicolored one and fitted the glowing purple, pink and blue rod into a circle. "Hold still." He nestled it on her head like a halo. "There. Perfect."

She gazed up at him with a bemused smile.

He touched her cheek. "You are so beautiful. Dance with me."

"Dance? But—"

"Listen."

She focused on the music coming from the stage, and her hand went to her mouth.

"Just one dance." He slipped his arm beneath her jacket and pressed his palm against the small of her back.

She went into his arms without protest, as the lead singer crooned "You Were Always On My Mind." Ten years slipped away and they were dancing as they had in high school, nestled together, swaying in time to the music, the silk of his shirt making soft shushing sounds whenever she moved.

"Remember?" he whispered into her hair.

"Mmm." She closed her eyes. "We shouldn't be doing this."

"It's our last chance."

"I know." She spoke the words, but they were just words to her. She hadn't allowed herself to focus on his leaving. She hadn't allowed herself to focus on much of anything today. The frantic pace of the festival had kept her occupied, relieving her of the burden of thinking.

Luke brushed her ear with his lips. "I always loved dancing with you. Doing this makes me feel eighteen again."

She sighed and relaxed in his arms. "I'm sorry my father was so rude this morning."

"Don't be. You're not responsible for what he does, Meg."

"If only that photographer hadn't shown up."

"I talked to her today. She's just a kid, really inexperienced. She's got a heck of a name, Ansel Wiggins."

"What did you say to her?"

"She did most of the talking. Wanted to know about you. I said we were old friends, that we'd been brought up like brother and sister."

"Did she buy it?"

"If she didn't, I can't call myself much of an actor, can I?"

Meg knew she should push away from him, but she couldn't force herself to do it. "This isn't exactly the way you'd dance with a sister."

"We're safe for a while. Turns out she loves carnival

rides, so I treated her to some tickets earlier tonight, and I didn't tell her about playing with the band. As I said, she's just a kid. She can be handled.''

''You asked them to play this song, didn't you?''

''What do you think?''

''I think you're a devil.''

He held her tight. ''Dancing with an angel. But don't worry. This is just a dance. I'm in control.''

That was fortunate, she thought, because she didn't have any when he was holding her like this. She rested her head on his shoulder and wished the song would never end.

Luke's breath fanned her ear and sent shivers down her spine. With each breath she drew in the musky, inviting scent of him. The words of the song tore at her. So what if she was always on Luke's mind, and he on hers? What damn good was that?

The song ended, and Luke slowly released her. ''Thank you,'' he murmured.

She gazed up at him, her eyes filling with tears. ''I hate this.''

He smiled. ''Maybe someday when I'm too old to get good parts and you've served your stint in the White House, we can ignore the world and run away together.''

''That's so blasted practical!''

''Want to change your mind about everything?''

She stood there in anguish, wanting to do just that, yet knowing it would be a mistake. ''No,'' she choked out, and whirled away. She ran back to the cart before she started to cry right in the middle of her own festival. She wanted him to follow her, but of course he didn't. She'd made her decision and he was holding back for her sake. There was one thing she could do in return, and she'd do it now. She would find Clint.

Eventually she did, at the shooting gallery with a couple of his drinking buddies. Debbie was nowhere in sight. Apparently Clint was punishing her for Friday night. Meg left her cart and waited while he fired off his allowed shots, missing every one. His friends jeered and clapped him on the back. Clint was reputed to be a good marksman, so obviously she hadn't caught him before he'd started drinking.

As the trio turned away from the booth, Meg called out Clint's name. He squinted in her direction, waved his buddies on toward the beer truck, and swaggered over. "Hi there, Meg. What's up?" He smelled of beer.

"I need a favor."

"Sure."

When he grinned at her, she caught a glimpse of the fun-loving boy he'd been when they were kids. She held on to that memory and tried to forget the beer fumes assaulting her now. "We don't see much of each other these days, Clint."

"Nope." He swayed a little and kept smiling.

"Remember all the good times we had—you, me and Luke?"

His smile faded. "I don't want to talk about him. Can't even watch my favorite group without Luke showing up on the damned stage."

So he had been at the concert. Meg wondered if he'd seen Luke dancing with her. "Luke cares about you, Clint. And he misses you."

"Give me a break. It's all a big publicity stunt. Like everything he does." He started to walk away.

She stepped in front of him. "Wait. Please."

He glanced down at her. "Come on, Meg. Leave me be, okay?"

"Talk to him, Clint. His life hasn't been a bed of roses, either, going out to California alone, making a whole new life for himself."

"I'm crying crocodile tears. Are you through now?"

"No. I promised to deliver a message." She stepped closer and pressed a piece of paper into his hand. "Here's Luke's room number. He wants you to come over to the San Marcos after the festival tonight, so you two can talk."

"And pose for some nifty publicity pictures? No, thanks."

"Nobody else will be there. You're the only one who will know where he is. It's a chance for the two of you to talk after all these years. Come on, Clint. Luke's the only family you have. Maybe you'll never get along perfectly, but at least give it a try."

"Why should I?"

"Because you need each other, you and Luke."

"He doesn't need anything from me. And I don't want anything from him."

"Go anyway. Please."

Clint looked away from her at the gyrating carnival rides. Then he glanced back at Meg. The drunken haze had left his gray eyes and they'd become brittle. "Sorry, but I don't think I can do that." He turned on his heel and strode off.

Meg's shoulders slumped. There was a slim chance Clint would change his mind. She'd hold on to that hope and not tell Luke just yet that Clint had thrown his offer of friendship back in his face.

THE MORE CLINT THOUGHT about it, the madder he got. He'd been *summoned*, by God. Like some hired hand. Clint pictured Luke relaxing in his suite at the San Marcos, probably with some goddamn silk bathrobe on and a room-service tray at his elbow.

Clint was supposed to go over there and apologize for trying to pick a fight, probably. And then, after Clint begged forgiveness from his majesty, Luke would call in the photographers for a few shots of the two brothers with their arms around each other's shoulders. Fans ate that stuff up.

Clint rode the wildest rides at the carnival with his friends, but he couldn't get rid of the hard knot in his gut. Luke had some nerve. Some damned nerve.

While they were all standing in line for the Whip, he saw that photographer, what was her name? Ansel. How could he forget a name like that? He told his buddies he'd catch up with them later and trotted after her. "Hey, Ansel!"

She turned, took a second to recognize him, and smiled. "Hi, Clint."

"How's it going?"

She shrugged and readjusted her Dodgers cap.

"I take it that means you're striking out."

"I've got lots of pictures, but nothing anybody will pay for, if you know what I mean."

"So you haven't caught him swimming naked in an irrigation ditch or boffing somebody in the back seat of a car?" From what Debbie said, and Clint was inclined to believe her even if he pretended not to, Luke hadn't gotten any sexual exercise on Friday night, at least.

"That's what's so frustrating! My instincts tell me

he's involved with the woman who's running the festival, but I can't catch them *doing* anything.''

Clint stuck his hands in the back pockets of his jeans. ''You think Luke and Meg are getting it on?''

''If they haven't yet, I think they want to. And tonight's the last night he'll be here.'' She sighed. ''So tonight's my last chance to get a worthwhile shot, too. I've spent a lot of money on this trip. I don't think the pictures I have will be good enough to pay my expenses, let alone give me some extra.''

Clint turned her theory over in his mind. He'd seen the way Meg had convinced Luke not to fight. He'd seen them dancing after Luke did his sickening bit on stage. Then she'd brought the messsage about Luke wanting to see him. There could be something going on between Meg and Luke. But if Ansel caught them, it wouldn't go so good for Meg. Clint had always liked her.

Except she'd sided with Luke, which come to think of it, she usually had when they were kids. And if she was stupid enough to get mixed up with his brother, then maybe she deserved whatever happened to her.

He dug into his jeans pocket, fished out a crumpled piece of paper and handed it to Ansel. ''I don't know if you're right about Luke and Meg, but if you are, this might help you get something juicy.''

She held the paper up to the light coming from a concession stand. ''What's this?''

''Meg gave it to me. It's Luke's room number at the San Marcos.''

CHAPTER NINE

MEG STAYED UNTIL everything had shut down that night to make sure the trash pickup service had done its job, and the arts and crafts booths and concession stands had been closed and locked up tight.

As she walked to the parking garage where she'd left her car that morning, she thought about Luke and hoped Clint was with him. That hope died when she saw Clint gunning his candy-apple red truck through the exit of the parking garage. She dashed out to the street to see where he was going, but as she feared, he turned left on Arizona and headed away from town. If he'd already gone over to see Luke, the talk hadn't gone well.

But what if he hadn't gone at all? Meg pictured Luke waiting patiently, hoping that, at last, he could forge a link with his troublesome brother. He was counting on Meg to come through for him, and she hadn't done it.

She glanced around the deserted streets. No one would see what she did. She started to head toward the San Marcos. If she met anyone along the way, she could make some excuse about checking a booth or looking for something she'd lost. She wasn't committed to a course of action. Yet.

She passed the dark shapes of carnival rides and the closed flaps of food and crafts booths. A breeze stirred a cardboard cone, which still had bits of cotton candy clinging to it. She picked it up and tossed it into a nearby trash can. No one saw her. No one called out "Still here working, I see."

She crossed Arizona Avenue and glanced to her right at the darkened stage where Luke had performed a few hours ago. The grass had been trampled by thousands of feet, but no one lingered now that the show was over. The beer truck had served its last drink. She turned right, toward the San Marcos.

She'd go in the side entrance, past Cibola, the resort's lounge. If anyone asked, she'd pretend she was going in to have a drink and relax. No one asked. Finding no familiar faces, she kept on walking past Nineteen-Twelve into the patio area.

The pool glowed turquoise in the still night air, and she remembered her halo. She'd kept it on all night, as a private reminder of the dance shared with Luke. She took it off and tucked it into the pocket of her slacks. If she was going to try this crazy stunt, no sense glowing in the dark while attempting it.

She walked under a trellis covered with wisteria vines just beginning to trail their fragrant purple blossoms over the latticework. Pots of petunias hung from the timbers supporting the trellis, and the honeysuckle beside the walkway perfumed the air.

She would only see Luke for a minute, to tell him that Clint hadn't cooperated. Then she'd turn around and go home. Simple as that. The alternative was to leave him waiting for hours for a brother who would never show up.

Meg's heart pounded as she glanced around and crossed to the outside stairway. Who was she kidding? She wanted another chance to be alone with Luke. She could cloak this move on her part with all sorts of noble motives, but the truth was, she couldn't resist the chance of being with him when no one would know.

She climbed to the fourth floor, pausing on each landing to look for observers. There were none. Her mouth grew dry. What was she doing here, risking everything? No, there was nothing to fear, really. Everyone was asleep now. Of course, she knew some of the staff here, but they were all home in bed, not lurking in the halls trying to catch her in some clandestine activity.

She'd stay five minutes, no more. More would be dangerous. She wouldn't let him kiss her, or she'd be lost. Ah, but to be lost with Luke...

She approached his room, out of breath from excitement and nervousness. She reached up to rap on the door, put her hand down, took a deep breath, and finally tapped softly. There was no response. She knocked a little louder and looked around, sure someone would appear and ask her what she was doing. No one did. Then the door opened.

Luke gazed at her for a long moment. Then he opened the door wider, and she stepped inside without saying a word. He quickly closed the door and turned the lock.

Her apprehensive gaze took in a cherry dining table, a gray sectional, a round brass coffee table mounded with flowers. And through another door, a bed with a pink comforter and mauve sheets. The bed was turned down.

She faced him and realized she was quivering. He was still wearing his black shirt and jeans, but he'd taken off his boots and unbuttoned his shirt halfway down. She licked her dry lips. "Clint's not—"

"To hell with him." Luke stepped forward and

cupped her face in both hands. "Did anyone see you come up here?"

"No."

The lines of concern around his eyes lessened. "Then nobody knows you're here?"

Her heart thundered in her chest. "That's right."

"Oh, Meg." He sighed and caressed her cheeks with his thumbs.

"I just wanted you to know about Clint."

"Thank you."

"I should be going now."

"I don't think so." He leaned toward her, his lips slightly parted.

If I let him kiss me, I'm done for. He held her gently but firmly. One kiss, and then she'd go. This would be the last time she'd ever kiss Luke Bannister. Surely she deserved... Her thoughts ceased as his lips touched hers with a restrained passion that left her shaking.

He lifted his head. "Don't go," he murmured, and kissed her again.

She'd never meant to leave. She knew that now, as she returned his kiss with a fierce joy, opening her mouth to accept what he had to offer, wrapping her arms around his neck and holding on, matching him breath for breath.

He moved from her lips to behind her ear, to her throat. "No one has to know," he murmured. "Surely we deserve this much."

"All I know is how much I need you."

"You have me, Meg." He lifted his head and gazed into her eyes. "You always have. God, but you're beautiful." And with a low groan from deep in his throat, he scooped her up and carried her through the bedroom door and deposited her on her feet next to the bed.

Combing his fingers through her hair, he kissed her gently. "But before anything more happens tonight, I want to get something straight."

She could barely think, let alone imagine what he was talking about. "Okay."

He dropped another kiss on her lips before turning and walking into the bathroom. He came back with a fistful of condoms and tossed them onto the bed.

Meg gasped. "You *planned* this?"

"No, I didn't, but I knew that's the conclusion you might make. At my agent's insistence, I bring these along on every trip."

Jealousy surged through her. "Do you...ever use them?"

"Sometimes. When I'm very lonely, and some woman is hooked on Dirk Kennedy. I won't tell you I've never had a one-night stand, because I'd be lying. But it's a joke, really. They go to bed with Dirk Kennedy, and I go to bed with..."

She stepped closer, needing to claim her place with him. "Who, Luke?"

He gazed into her eyes. "It's not easy sometimes. Most women wear perfume, and the fantasy keeps slipping away when I smell their skin." He brushed a strand of hair back over her shoulder. "And no one has your exact shade of hair color, or eyes the same vibrant green." He ran his knuckles softly down her throat. "No one else feels quite the same."

"But you make do."

"I'm only human." He pushed her jacket from her shoulders and let it slip to the floor. "Do you know I remember the exact angle of your collarbone? And if someone gave me a piece of clay I could mold the shape of your breast.''

"You never should have left!''

"I thought I had to.'' He tugged her T-shirt out from her slacks, pulled it over her head and let it drop. "Do you know I've never seen you in full light? But I imagine I have.'' He unhooked her bra and tossed it onto the floor. He was silent for a while as he drank in the sight of her.

Meg lifted her chin. "But you've seen dozens of women like this.''

He looked into her eyes. "They weren't you.''

"I hate them all.''

He stepped forward and drew her into his arms. "Forget them. I'm going to make love to you all night, every minute. We won't sleep. I want to spend every second until dawn holding you, kissing you, moving inside you. Maybe a lifetime isn't in the cards, but we won't think about that, either.'' He brushed her lips with his. "Let me love you, Meg. I've wanted you for so long.''

"And I've wanted you, Luke.'' She reached for the snaps of his Western shirt and popped them open, the sound as much a celebration as champagne corks bursting from the bottle. "I've dreamed of making love to you from the day I first understood what men and women did behind closed doors. You were the only man I ever wanted.''

"That's not true.'' He unfastened her slacks and pushed them over her hips. "You were married.''

"Lord help me, I thought of you every time we made love.''

He kissed her hard, so hard she felt the impression of

his teeth against her lips. "I hate it that you've been with another man."

"How can you say that?" She ripped at his belt, fumbled with the buttons of his fly. "You've slept with countless women. How do you think I feel when I see you in living color, in bed with somebody else? *That's* why I didn't watch your show, dammit!"

He shucked his jeans, pushed her back onto the bed. "I want to wipe out the memory of anybody else you've been with." He pulled her panties down and threw them to the floor. "I want to love you so hard and so long that you'll never make love again without thinking of me."

She tore at his briefs. "And I want to claim you as no other woman can. They'll never have what I have from you!"

"And no man will know you as I will." He sheathed himself quickly.

"You do that so easily. I hate your having so much practice with other women."

He braced his hands on either side of her head. "There were no other women. Just substitutes for you. Substitutes for this." He pushed forward and gasped. "Oh, God, Meg."

She gazed up at him, his name a sigh on her lips.

His voice was hoarse. "I love you. I've always loved you."

"I've always loved you." She moaned as he thrust again, deeper this time.

"That's it. Cry out. Burn me into your soul. We only have one night."

"No." She dug her nails into his back as he rotated his hips and pressed against the throbbing center of her arousal. "We've had a lifetime. Oh…ohhh!" He moved again, finding the exact spot, honing in on her cries of pleasure, capturing her open mouth with his and mimicking his movements with his tongue.

She'd never been loved like this. Luke knew the flash points of a woman's body the way some men knew the secrets of the internal combustion engine. When she'd nearly reached the point of no return, he withdrew, leaving her gasping. He whispered in her ear, "Not yet." Then he roamed over her breasts with warm, moist kisses and sucked on each nipple until she thought that alone would bring her to climax.

At last he reentered with a rhythm that carried her to the edge. At the crucial moment he slowed his movements. She called out his name in desperate need for fulfillment.

"Easy," he murmured, slowing even more. "Take your time, my love. Now that you're there, make it last." She panted and arched her slick body against his. "Easy." He lowered his head and licked her damp breasts. "You taste like the rim of a margarita glass. Mmm. Like good Russian caviar."

"I'm melting, Luke…melting into you." She felt balanced on a knife-edge, ready to fall at any moment.

"That's what I want. If you wait, if you hold off as long as you can, the end will blow you away."

"It's not fair," she gasped. "You know so much, and I—"

"I've always yearned for you. Wishing someday I could make you feel like this." He eased in and out with the exquisite control of a master.

"Now, Luke, please." Her head thrashed from side to side. "Please."

"Yes." He increased the pace just enough, no more.

She cried out as her body bucked and clenched in a response more powerful than she'd ever known. Wave upon wave of sensation swept over her as he murmured soft encouragement in her ear. The throbbing grew fainter, but before it disappeared he began stroking again. The sensations returned, and she whimpered as he impelled her up, up, back to the pinnacle she'd just left. She clutched his shoulders. "Luke!"

"I love you." He plunged deeper, with an urgency that told her he'd climb the summit with her this time. She lifted her hips to meet each thrust. Her body was a paradox, fluid, yet coiled tight in preparation for the next moment of release.

When that moment arrived, bringing with it a shuddering sweetness that left her trembling, he groaned and buried himself deep within her. She held him fast as convulsions racked him. They lay bathed in moisture and gasping for breath. She caressed his nape, his sweaty back, the firm mound of his buttocks.

He nuzzled her neck and sighed. "Keep touching me, Meg. Don't stop."

"I love touching you. I always have."

"I used to dream about your hands…every-where…all the places you were too shy to touch when we were dating."

"I used to dream about this…you inside me, filling the hollowness, the ache."

"I was so afraid you'd be disappointed."

Her soft laughter shook their joined bodies. "I've never been so undisappointed in my life. I don't even want to think about how you learned to please a woman like that."

"Then don't think about it. Just know that I didn't love them. I love you."

She sighed. "This is so complicated."

"Hush." He nibbled her ear. "Tonight isn't complicated. Don't think beyond tonight. You know what I have in this suite?"

"Lots of condoms."

"Besides that. I have a Roman tub. With jets."

"That sounds interesting."

"It could be. Want some champagne?"

Meg began to feel giddy. "Why not? If this is going to be a night of decadence, we might as well do it right."

"My thoughts exactly. Stay here and fantasize while I find a robe." He disentangled himself from her and levered himself off the bed.

"For me?" she called out after him as he went into the bathroom.

"No, you don't get one. You're not allowed to wear clothes for the next few hours, but somebody has to sign for the champagne."

"Ask for one glass in case they get suspicious."

"I will, but they won't. I'm a crazy actor from Hollywood, right? Did you know they've had people like Clark Gable staying at the San Marcos?"

"Yes. And Errol Flynn and Gloria Swanson. And now you." She heard the squeak of a tap opening and the soft rumble of a tub being filled.

Then he reappeared wearing a terry robe. "I'm not in their league, but all my publicity paints me as a playboy. I could easily have an orgy going on here and no one would be surprised."

"Are you a playboy?"

"No." He walked over and picked up the bedside

phone. As he punched in the room-service number, she rolled toward him and loosened the belt on the robe. He glanced down at her, and as she reached beneath the robe to touch him, his lips parted and his eyes closed. He ordered the champagne in a husky voice and slammed the phone into its cradle as he tumbled onto the bed over her. "You witch," he breathed, capturing her hands and holding them over her head. "You wonderful, sexy witch. Don't you realize I have to answer the door in a few minutes?"

"I couldn't help myself."

"And I can't help myself, either." Holding her wrists with one hand, he kneaded her breast and raked her nipple with his teeth.

She writhed against him, unable to believe so much passion existed. He sucked on her breast and stroked his way down across her belly, through the damp hair to the nub of sensation already aching for his touch. She moaned as he rubbed her there. "The tub will overflow."

His breath was hot against her breast. "I don't care." A rap on the door stilled his movements. "But I do want the champagne." He scooped her up. "Kiss me, Meg."

She did, opening her mouth to the hungry thrust of his tongue as he carried her into the bathroom and lowered her into the warm, rushing water. At last he drew back, released her gently and turned off the faucet.

"You've soaked your sleeves."

He shrugged. "I keep telling you, they expect anything from people like me. They're used to wild and crazy celebrities."

"I'm beginning to get used to them, too. At least one of them."

"Be right back."

She slid down, her head propped against the edge of the tub, her body nearly submerged in the jetting water. Every nerve ending was alive and singing. She felt as if she could make love to Luke for days on end and never grow tired of it. He was the only man she'd ever known who could inspire such insatiable desire. No wonder women followed him everywhere. No wonder she'd ended up here tonight, pulled into his arms, into his bed, even into his tub by an irresistible force.

He returned with the bottle of champagne, froth dripping from the neck, and one glass. He poured it full and handed it to her. She raised it in salute and sipped the sparkling gold liquid while her gaze held his. The bubbles coursed through her system, the perfect counterpart to the passions zinging through her body.

Slowly he set the bottle on the edge of the tub and untied his robe. He let it fall to the floor and stood before her, fully aroused. She set the glass beside the champagne bottle and held out her arms. "Come here."

CHAPTER TEN

LUKE'S GAZE TRAVELED from Meg's flushed face to her rosy breasts cradled by the swirling water. Her nipples beckoned like wine-colored rose petals waiting to be plucked. Her green eyes sparkled with anticipation, and her mouth curved in a smile of welcome. Desire pounded through him.

But he couldn't take her there in the tub. He had to protect her. Already he wanted more than he could have with her. He wanted to throw away the condoms and experience the joy of sliding into her without barriers, the excitement of knowing he could make her pregnant. She was the only woman who made him long for children and permanence.

Foolish thoughts. She wouldn't want children now, maybe not ever, and what kind of father would he make, jetting around the country making appearances?

He wouldn't risk pregnancy tonight. But he could make her cry and moan with pleasure, and that would bring its own kind of satisfaction. He stepped into the frothy water and slid down beside her. She brought the glass of champagne to his lips and he drank. The tart liquid seemed the perfect way to celebrate the realization of a dream. He took another drink, draining the glass.

"More?" she asked.

"Later." He took the glass from her hand and set it

on the edge of the tub. Then he drew her forward so her legs rested on top of his and her thighs were open, maddenly close yet not touching his turgid flesh. He positioned her to allow a stream of water from the jets to sluice between her legs. He knew the pulsing water had struck its mark when her breathing quickened and her eyes grew wide.

He smiled. "Nice?" She nodded. With one hand splayed across the small of her back, he reached down and massaged her sensitive spot, adding his touch to the rush of the water. "And that?"

"Yes." She clutched his shoulders and her eyes fluttered closed. He increased the pressure slightly, and she shuddered in reaction, making her breasts quiver. She threw her head back, arched her hips.

He could watch her forever like this, even with the demanding ache in his groin. He would ease that soon. There was still plenty of time. But for now, he concentrated on Meg, his Meg—lost in sensation, immersed in the pleasure he gave her.

She was almost there—he could tell from her quick little gasps, the rocking motion of her hips. He kept on until her gasps became cries and her fingers dug into his shoulders. "Let go," he murmured, pressing harder.

"Luke!" She shook from the force of her release. Then she sucked in great gulps of air. Her face and shoulders were dewy with moisture and the ends of her hair were damp where she'd arched back into the water. Slowly she straightened and focused her gaze on him. "You...are a devil."

He smiled.

"I can't believe how you make me feel."

"Tell me."

"Like a courtesan, like someone whose whole life is devoted to physical pleasure."

"That's the way I want you to feel."

"I keep thinking I should be embarrassed because I'm so eager for this. But I'm not."

"Good. Don't be."

Her gaze became dreamy. "And what about you?"

"What about me?"

Beneath the water her hand closed around him. "How do I make you feel?"

His answer was thickened by a fresh onslaught of desire. "As if I could make love to you forever."

"Here in the water?" Her hand glided up and down, and she gazed at him with knowing eyes.

"No." He clenched his teeth as she fondled the sensitive tip.

"Why not?"

"I can't protect you here."

"Surely you know there are ways that don't require protection."

Her hand and the swirling jets were destroying his control. He wasn't sure what she had in mind, but he loved the feral look in her green eyes. She wasn't naive any longer, and he really didn't want her to be. They had no time for games. "I suppose."

She patted the edge of the tub. "Sit here."

"I—"

"Just do it, Luke. Let me make you happy, too." He raised himself to the edge and braced his feet against the bottom. "Perfect." Reaching for the bottle of champagne, she poured more bubbly liquid in the glass. Instead of drinking it, she dipped her finger in and painted a streak of champagne down his throbbing erection.

Then, rising to her knees, she licked it away. His senses reeled, and he gripped the edge of the tub. "Nice?"

He nodded. He wanted her to do it again. She did. And again. He trembled.

She took a small sip of the spakling wine without swallowing. Then gently she took him in her mouth. He'd never known such an erotic shock. Cool liquid, fizzing against his skin, and her warm tongue teasing him, coaxing him, driving him closer, ever closer...he couldn't hang on much longer. She took another sip and continued her sweet assault. He groaned. "Meg, I can't..."

She didn't seem to hear him, or didn't care. She was taking control, and he was losing it. Her tongue, her marvelous tongue... He gasped once, and surrendered, the blood roaring in his ears as she took what he could no longer hold back.

When it was over, he sank into the tub and cradled her in his arms. He leaned his forehead against hers and struggled to breath normally. "That...was fantastic."

"I hoped it would be."

"For someone who complained about having no experience, you're very creative. Have you ever—"

"With champagne? Never. But it seemed like a fun idea."

"Oh, it was that." He tilted up her chin and kissed her smiling lips. "And now I think it's time to go back to bed."

"To sleep?"

"Not likely."

He dried her lovingly, and she him. She'd satisfied him completely, yet as he moved the thick beige towel over her body, he felt his craving return. Ten years of

wanting had built up a powerful need. He led her to the
bed and threw back the comforter. She lay down on the
mauve sheets with the sensuous languor of a well-loved
woman. God, he treasured seeing her like that.

"The mirrors are a nice touch."

He glanced in the direction of her gaze. She was looking at an entertainment center opposite the bed. He'd
paid scant attention to it before, but now he realized that
the cabinet's mirrored doors reflected her alabaster body
against the dusky mauve sheets. Apparently he'd loved
every ounce of bashfulness out of her, because she
stretched enticingly and smiled. "This suite seems made
for everything we might have in mind."

"It certainly does." He put his knee on the bed and
leaned toward her. "Although I'd rather look at you than
your reflection." He kissed her mouth, her collarbone,
the tip of each breast. She made a soft, feline sound of
delight, and when he looked into her eyes, he saw that
she was watching him love her. The sight brought a fresh
glint of passion to her gaze. "I think I understand the
concept of the mirror, now." He trailed kisses over every
inch of her smooth skin, careful to pay close attention
to the sensitive areas at the crook of her elbows and the
back of her knees. She trembled and sighed…and
watched all his moves. He grew hard knowing she
watched.

With any other woman he would have been self-
conscious, but his trust in Meg only heightened his
arousal. As she fastened her gaze on him, putting on the
condom became an erotic act. When at last he lowered
himself deep inside her and they began their special
rhythm, she whispered detailed praise of his body in a
language that inflamed him even more.

And he realized he wanted the same privilege. Securing her hips tight against his, he rolled onto his back. He looked into her eyes and saw her willingness. Then he gazed past her shoulder and caught his breath at the beauty of her body entwined with his, his hands spread over the seductive curve of her backside.

He touched a small scar there. "Remember?"

She gazed down at him and nodded. "Crawling under the barbed-wire fence trying to get away from a bull."

"I would have fought that bull to keep you safe."

"I know," she said softly. Slowly she began to move, and he was enchanted at the view. Between ragged breaths he told her how much he loved watching her, told her with the same exquisite detail she'd lavished on him. Then passion blurred his vision as together they catapulted over the brink.

Later, as they lay side by side stroking and touching each other as if they'd never have enough, he asked what had happened to the light wand he'd given her before they danced.

"It's in the pocket of my slacks. I took it off when I decided to come up here."

"I want it now." He reached over the side of the bed and searched through their tumbled pile of clothes until he found the glowing circle of light. Then he snapped off the bedside light and unfastened the halo, which became a sinuous strip of color. "I'll never forget dancing with you when you wore this," he murmured, drawing it gently over her body, dappling her skin in pink, blue and violet. "I wanted you so much."

She trembled as he trailed the light wand over her thigh. "And now?"

"I want you even more."

"You're insatiable."

"Do you object?"

"No." She writhed under his touch. "You see, I'm insatiable, too."

With a groan he gathered her close. Tossing the rainbow light to the floor, he began loving her again.

THE CLOCK WAS HER ENEMY. Meg grew angry every time she glanced at its luminous face taunting her from the bedside table. Its bright green hands seemed to spin with breathtaking speed.

She'd never been loved this way, but her precious time with Luke meant more than just enjoying physical passion. They shared quiet times when they talked of their moments together in the past, boisterous times when they laughed and finished the bottle of champagne. She wondered why she wasn't tired at all and gradually realized that love was a far stronger stimulant than caffeine. Love and desperation. She couldn't waste a second in sleep, because these hours might be all she'd ever have. She had to store up enough of Luke to last a lifetime.

She'd decided to leave at four, but as the hour approached she stalled for extra minutes. Reluctantly she began to dress, pausing for kisses, one more caress, his lips on her breasts before she covered them. She had to accept the fact they wouldn't make love one last time, no matter how much she wanted to. Luke pulled on his jeans as if to help her resolution to resist the lure of passion.

She wanted him to ask her to come away with him, yet knew he wouldn't. And deep down, she knew it wouldn't work. She had to stay and he had to go. At last she stood by the door of the suite. "I don't know if I can do this."

"Yes, you can." He gathered her close and kissed her on the forehead. She'd already tucked her halo back into her pocket, although the glow had nearly disappeared.

"I don't know how I can bear seeing you today. I'm afraid I'll give everything away."

"I'll make myself scarce." He cradled her head against his shoulder.

"And the airport." She felt panic rise in her chest. "I was supposed to take you back there tonight."

"I'll get somebody else. Chuck or Didi. Somebody."

"That's good." She was shaking. "I couldn't do it, Luke."

"I know. I probably couldn't get on that plane if you were standing in the terminal."

"Oh, Luke. Why did life have to turn out this way?"

He rubbed the small of her back. "Don't think like that. We had tonight. Some people go their whole lives without a tenth as much."

"That doesn't make me feel any better." She sniffed and wiped her eyes.

"Meg." He held her face in both hands. "Be honest. You may want me, but you don't want my life-style. I'm an actor, not a cotton farmer."

"Maybe...maybe I'll give up politics. Maybe—"

"Don't talk like that!" He gripped her more tightly.

"But I love you."

He relaxed his hold and stroked her cheek. "You have a lot more to do in life than love me," he said more tenderly. "So go out and do those things. Be president some day. I'll vote for you."

She gave a watery laugh. "That's a start."

"It's late, Meg." She nodded. "When you leave, go fast. I don't expect anybody will be stirring yet, but if you wait much longer, you might run into an early riser."

"Okay." She lifted a trembling hand to his cheek. "I love you, Luke Bannister."

"And I love you, Meg Hennessy. Now I'm opening this door." He reached for the knob.

She took a deep breath. "Ready." She squeezed his hand and let go as the door opened. Then she hurried through the opening and nearly fell as she tripped over something...someone? There was a cry and Meg stared in horror as a familiar young woman raised her camera. As if in slow motion the camera lens focused on her like the barrel of a gun. *Flash, flash, flash.*

"Meg?"

Numb, she barely heard Luke call out.

The woman scrambled to her feet and backed away, now aiming the camera at Luke, wearing only his black jeans, as he charged forward. *Flash, flash.* Luke swore and grabbed for the camera.

The woman dodged his arm. "Touch me and I'll sue the pants off you!"

"I don't give a damn! Give me that camera." He started forward again.

Meg grabbed his arm and spoke in an urgent whisper. "No. Let her go. Someone will hear us if we don't stop yelling. This could get worse, Luke. Much worse."

A muscle twitched in his jaw. "I'll sue the hotel. They must have told her my room number."

The paparazzo laughed. "That's what you think. I got the number from your brother. Guess he doesn't much care what happens to you."

"My brother?" Luke turned, his expression bleak as he gazed at Meg. "I did this to you. I asked you to give him the room number, and he betrayed me."

She shook her head. "I chose to come up here, Luke. Nobody's responsible but me. If I leave quietly now, maybe this young woman will let me go. She has what she needs, but if we can persuade her to keep her mouth shut, if only for today, the rest of the festival won't be ruined."

"I'm not talking to anybody," the woman said. "In fact, I'm going straight back to L.A. to peddle these pictures. If you get that part you're up for, they'll be worth a lot more."

"You bitch. I'll cancel the screen test."

Meg faced him. "Don't you dare. Maybe I can ride this out. Maybe nobody will want her pictures. They weren't very juicy, anyway. But if you cancel that screen test, Luke Bannister, I will never forgive you. Never."

His chest heaved and his eyes burned with repressed rage. "I guess you'd better get out of here, Meg." He glanced at the photographer. "And that goes double for you."

Meg gave him one last look and started for the stairs. Her heart was pounding and her chest was tight. Okay, maybe it wasn't a complete disaster. Maybe the pictures would never appear in any publication, or if they did, maybe nobody would see them, at least not until after the chamber of commerce election. Maybe, in her haste, the paparazzo had made the wrong settings on her camera.

Meg kept repeating these reassurances to herself as she hurried down the dimly lit stairway. Once she left the hotel she started running. She reached the parking garage out of breath and had trouble putting her key in the lock because she was shaking so much. Not until she was safely home and in her bedroom did she allow the tears to fall.

LUKE WATCHED UNTIL he was certain the photographer hadn't followed Meg. Then he went back inside the room and stood with clenched fists, staring sightlessly at the floor. He'd jeopardized Meg's future. He could never forgive himself for that. He'd give up the screen test in a second if he thought it would do any good, but it would be an empty gesture. Ansel Wiggins would sell her pictures, regardless of whether he became a film star or remained with *Connections*. The only difference would be the price.

He paced the room trying to figure out what had gone wrong. He'd never thought his brother would go this far to hurt him. Obviously he'd misjudged the depth of Clint's anger and jealousy—and immaturity. Giving Wiggins Luke's room number had been vicious and cowardly, but more to the point, childish.

And that in fact was the problem. Clint had never really grown up. What was worse, nobody had ever forced him to. Luke had covered for him back in high school, and the old man had taken over doing it after Luke left. Now, without either of them around, Clint was letting the farm go to hell while he spent a good part of his time soused and joyriding in that shiny red truck.

Luke headed for the bedroom where he grabbed a T-shirt and some boots. This time Clint had gone too far. The joyride was over.

CHAPTER ELEVEN

LUKE HITCHED A RIDE with a hay-truck driver making an early-morning delivery to a farm near Clint's. He still had to walk about a half mile, and the hike didn't improve his disposition.

The sun had just rimmed the horizon when he reached the Bannister drive. He surveyed the neglect with far less generosity than he had on his earlier visits. The shabby farmhouse surrounded by weeds had ceased being picturesque and now looked shameful. Clint didn't deserve the farm if he couldn't care for it better than this.

Luke went in the kitchen door out of habit. He couldn't remember the last time he'd used the front. The door was unlocked as usual. Luke banged it back on its hinges. "Clint!"

He didn't wait for a response. Maybe Clint was in bed with Debbie Fry. Luke no longer cared. He stormed into the bedroom that had once belonged to his parents.

Clint was alone in the double four-poster. He'd apparently passed out still wearing his T-shirt and jeans. He sat up and rubbed his eyes. "God, my head."

"More than your head is gonna hurt, little brother. Get out of that bed."

Clint peered blearily at Luke. "What in hell —" He paused and then a slow grin spread over his beard-roughened face. "She caught you and Meg, didn't she? I say it serves—"

"Are you going to get out of there, or do I have to drag you out?"

With surprising swiftness, Clint rolled off the bed and landed in a crouch. "Want to get it on, big brother? Or are you still protecting that pretty face of yours?"

Luke faced him, breathing heavily. "I want some answers. What goddamn right did you have to put Meg's career on the line like that?"

Clint moved to the side, positioning himself. "If she went to your room, she did it to herself."

Luke circled in the same direction. They'd choreographed this years ago, in dozens of fights. "Nobody would have known except for you."

"All right." Clint bared his teeth in a sneer. "So I set that up. Small payment, I'd say, for the way you've been setting me up all along."

"Setting you up?" Luke watched Clint's hands, waiting for his first move. "Who took the beatings when something went wrong around here? Who covered for you in that hardware-store deal? Who left without a dime and gave you a clear shot at owning the farm some day?"

"Maybe I don't want the farm!"

"Since the place looks like hell, that's obvious. I'm buying it back."

Clint's bloodshot eyes narrowed. "Like hell you are."

"Why not? Isn't that what you want, a ton of money and no responsibilities? Isn't that what you think I have?"

"I don't think. I know. Prancing around in front of the cameras all day, while I'm breaking my ass—"

"Then give it up, you miserable punk. I could run the place better from L.A. than you can run it living here."

"What a joke. You're a city boy, now. You wouldn't know a boll weevil from a white fly."

Luke flexed his hands. Any minute now Clint would take a swing. He hadn't wanted this fight, but Clint apparently needed it. "I know a son of a bitch when I see one."

The muscles worked in Clint's jaw. "You planning to back that up, or are you gonna refuse to fight, like before? Can't mess up that pretty face, now can we?"

"Try me." Luke licked his lips as they circled.

"Oh, maybe we're serious?" The light of battle gleamed in Clint's eyes. "Well, that's good news. I can hardly wait to beat the shit out of you."

"Same here. You're a sorry excuse for a Bannister." Luke watched the taunts hit the target. "You're a disgrace to the family name. You can't even——"

Clint swung and Luke blocked it neatly. His uppercut caught Clint a glancing blow on the jaw and he staggered. But Clint had been in enough brawls the last few years to have built up his stamina. He came roaring back with a right to the stomach, which Luke dodged, but his left to Luke's chin landed with a solid crack. Luke bit his tongue and tasted blood.

"Better give up," Clint rasped, dancing in front of him. "The next one will break your nose."

Luke swallowed the blood and heaved himself at Clint. They went down, the rag rug by the bed twisting beneath them as they pummeled each other and rolled on the floor. Luke cracked his head on a chair leg, but not before he bloodied Clint's nose. He felt a fierce triumph that he'd drawn blood, even though, in the next second, Clint landed a punch that split his lip.

They grunted and groaned, punched and wrestled, neither getting a clear advantage, neither willing to give up. Luke staggered to his feet and Clint scrambled sideways. Warily he stood and the two began circling again.

"You're weaving," Luke said, steadying himself against a chair. "Give up."

"Not on your life. You're wobbling more than I am." Clint launched another punch and Luke barely sidestepped it. Thrown off balance, Clint slammed into the wall with a solid thud, sending a picture crashing to the floor. He stood still for a moment looking dazed.

Luke shook the sweat from his eyes and tried to catch his breath. "Watch what you're doing."

"*You* watch," Clint panted, "I'm too busy." He lumbered forward, catching Luke in the midsection and sending both of them to the floor again.

Luke tried to push him off but gave up. His arms wouldn't work right. "Get off me, dammit."

"Not now." Clint sprawled over him. "I got the advantage."

With a mighty effort Luke rolled, taking Clint with him. They'd both given up trying to punch each other. Luke now lay on top of Clint, his head spinning.

"Damn," Clint swore, struggling to work his way out from under Luke. "This is hard work."

Luke chuckled. He couldn't help it.

"You laughing or coughing up blood?"

"Both."

"Wanna quit?"

"Do you?"

"Maybe."

Luke rolled over on his back and gazed up at the ceiling. Then he turned his head and looked at Clint. "You're a mess."

Clint returned the look. "You're not too gorgeous yourself. What in hell did you go and do this for? You're gonna be a mass of bruises pretty soon."

"I didn't know any other way to get your attention."

Clint stared at him, and then he looked back up at the ceiling. "You screwed up God knows how many days of shooting that damned soap opera, probably get fined or some such thing, just to get my attention?"

"Worse than that. I have a screen test tomorrow for a movie."

Clint looked at him sharply, and a new emotion flickered in his eyes. "You're an idiot," he said softly. "I'm not worth it."

"I happen to think you are."

Clint closed his eyes. "Damn," he whispered. "Was it...bad...when Ansel showed up?"

"Wasn't great, but it could have been worse. At least we had most of our clothes on."

"I'll talk to Ansel. Maybe I can buy the pictures from her."

"Too late. She's already on her way back to L.A. She probably had some idea I was a threat to her and that film. Which I was."

Clint's Adam's apple moved. "Well, I sure screwed this up good."

"Yeah. But maybe the damage can be controlled."

"Just tell me what to do."

Luke sat up slowly and winced as he touched his bleeding lip. "Sounds as if maybe you do give a damn."

Clint eased himself up and leaned against the side of the bed. "You, Meg and me go back a long way."

"I got the impression you'd dismissed all that. What changed your mind?"

Clint grinned, but the smile became a grimace when it reached a puffy place on his cheek. "The fact that you were more interested in knocking some sense into me than protecting your face for the cameras. That's the old Luke, the one I remember."

"I've never changed."

"That's not the way I saw it. Ten years ago you washed your hands of me."

"Not you. It was the old man. I got sick of him taking out his frustrations on me, and coddling you."

"Coddling? I worked like a dog around here!"

"All right. Maybe coddling's the wrong word. But he didn't hit you. Maybe to me, at eighteen, that felt like coddling. I hated him and resented you. I got over resenting you, but my stomach still turns over when I think of him."

Clint sighed and leaned his head back against the mattress. "I guess I knew that. I wasn't really surprised when you didn't come to the funeral. I wish you had, though."

"I wish I had, too." He raked back the hair that had fallen over his forehead. "Funny, but I think I could handle that funeral now."

Clint squinted at him. "How come?"

Luke touched his tongue to the cut on his lip. He should probably get some ice, but hell, ice wouldn't fix his face enough for the screen test. So what? "I just think I could, that's all."

Clint studied him for a long while. "It's Meg, isn't it? Getting together with her, I mean."

Luke met his gaze and slowly nodded.

"What now? You moving back here or something?"

"No. I like my job. And I don't want to get in the way of her political ambitions, either."

Clint heaved himself to his feet. "If this is going to be some noble speech about self-sacrifice, I can't face it without a cup of coffee."

Luke laughed and followed him into the kitchen. The back of his head hurt like hell. He felt it gingerly and discovered a nice lump growing there. "Got any ice?"

"Maybe." Clint waved a hand toward the old refrigerator. "Damn thing doesn't always work."

Luke rummaged around in the freezer compartment and found a half-full tray of cubes along with a hoary container of ice cream and a pound of hamburger with freezer burn where the wrapping was torn. He took out the ice tray and ran it under warm water. "This place is a disaster, Clint."

"I know."

"Are times really that tight?" He wrapped some cubes in a dish towel and handed it to his brother. Clint's cheek needed attention as much as Luke's mouth.

Clint plugged in the coffeepot and took the dish towel full of ice. "Yeah, times are tight." He placed the towel against his cheek. "Ow. That smarts."

"You could sell."

"To you?"

"No." Luke pressed his own towel full of cubes to his lip. "I wasn't really serious about that."

"Too bad. What I'd really like is for you to take your half back."

"Why?"

Clint gazed out the grimy kitchen window. "So there'd be somebody else who cared about the place, somebody to talk things over with, help me make decisions."

Luke stood there listening to the coffee perk. He'd thought Clint would be happy to own the farm all by himself. Apparently Luke's gift had been taken as a rejection, a sign that Luke didn't want anything more to do with the farm or Clint.

Clint turned to face Luke. "Okay, lousy suggestion. You don't want to screw around with a farm anymore, and I—"

"No, it's a good suggestion. I'd like my half back. I'd like it a lot."

"Really? You're serious?" Clint's eagerness made him look about seven years old.

"Sure I'm serious. Except we'd have to do most of our business over the phone. I know how you hate all the people I seem to attract these days."

Clint shrugged. "It's no big deal."

"Yeah, but we'd never get anything done."

"I know what." Clint's eyes lit with mischief. "You can come over in disguise. You're an actor, right? Glue on a fake mustache, stick a pillow under your shirt, stuff like that."

"It could work." Luke was miles ahead of him. If he could visit Clint that way, maybe he'd be able to sneak over and see Meg... But no, another backfired plan could wreck her hopes for good. He shouldn't even consider it. And yet... But for now, he had to concentrate on straightening out the problems he and Clint had already made for Meg.

"Then it's settled." Clint stuck out his hand. "You're now the proud co-owner of the Bannister cotton farm."

They shook hands. For a moment their eyes met and they grinned. Then Luke dropped the handshake before either of them got too embarrassed. He glanced around the kitchen. The sink was filled with dirty dishes and beer cans overflowed from the trash. "And the first thing we're going to do as partners is clean this place up. Did you really drink all that beer?"

"I think so."

Luke held his brother's gaze. "Gonna end up like the old man?"

Clint looked away. Then he sighed and ran his fingers through his hair. "I've been thinking about that. Especially after what I said to Debbie Friday night. I never would have insulted her like that if I hadn't been tanked."

"That was my conclusion."

Clint glanced at Luke. "If it's worth anything, I apologized to her yesterday."

"Good."

"But then I got drunk again last night, and hurt you and Meg."

Luke couldn't let him off the hook. "That's right."

"So I guess it's time to lay off the booze for a while."

"Yep."

Clint nodded. "It was losing its appeal, anyway." He was quiet for a few moments, and then he tossed his dish towel full of ice in the sink. "How about some breakfast? I'm a damned good cook."

"I'm glad one of us is," Luke said. He felt as if a weight had been lifted from his shoulders. Underneath his party-boy exterior, Clint had a strong will. If he'd decided to give up drinking, he'd do it, and probably without a lot of fanfare. "I'll pour us some coffee," Luke offered. "And while we're eating and cleaning up the kitchen we'll figure out how to help Meg."

"Yeah. We got her into this, so it's up to us to get her out."

"Just like in the old days."

Clint smiled. "Just like in the old days."

AFTER DRIPPING SOME Murine in her eyes, downing two cups of coffee and putting Dog-breath in his run, Meg headed for the ostrich festival at nine. The festival opened at ten, and the chairperson needed to be there early. She didn't want to go—in fact, she would rather clean the floors of the livestock trucks with a toothbrush, but she had to see the day through and somehow pretend everything was fine. If she kept away from Didi, she might succeed in fooling everyone else.

Sure enough, Didi's was the first call that came from Meg's walkie-talkie after she arrived. The box of extra festival programs had disappeared. Meg had no choice but to drive her utility cart over to the information booth and find out what had happened to the blasted programs. On the way over she decided to keep her sunglasses on at all costs.

She drove up to the information booth where she found Didi rummaging through boxes looking for the brochures. "Good morning," she called, hopping down from the cart and giving Didi a big smile.

Didi glanced up, stared at Meg and got up from the box she'd been searching through. "Okay. What's wrong?"

"Why, nothing." Meg held onto her smile with great

effort. "Have you tried that green box over there? I think the last time I saw the brochures, they were in—"

"You look like hell."

Meg glanced down at her T-shirt and jeans. "It's the same outfit you have on."

"Not your outfit, your face. Your posture. You look like somebody died."

Meg glanced away and swallowed. "I was hoping nobody could tell."

"Tell what?" Didi frowned. "Oh, God." She pushed through an opening between two tables and hopped into the driver's seat of Meg's utility cart. "Get in." Meg obeyed and Didi drove the cart to a secluded area behind the entertainment pavilion. "Okay. What happened?"

Meg took off her sunglasses and wiped her eyes. "The worst." She told Didi the whole story, only omitting the intimate details of her passionate night with Luke, but leaving no doubt as to what had happened between them. When she finished describing the disastrous ending, Didi put her arms around her while she cried.

"Don't blame yourself," Didi murmured. "I doubt any normal woman in your circumstances would have done any different. And no one would ever know, except for that snake in the grass Clint Bannister. I could wring his neck, not to mention performing a few other alterations to his anatomy."

Meg sniffed and blew her nose on the tissue Didi gave her. "If this gets out, I can kiss that chamber presidency goodbye. And my plans to run for the legislature."

"Maybe it won't get out."

Meg shook her head. "You know how these things go, Didi. They *always* come out, and usually at the worst possible time. I have no doubt that woman will sell her pictures to someone. If Luke gets the part he wants, the pictures will get more play than ever. My only hope is that they don't appear where Chandler people can see them until after the chamber election.'' She sniffed again. ''Of course I could be thrown out after I'm elected. That would be even worse. Maybe I should just drop out of the running.''

''You most certainly should not. We need you in that job and we can't let one little thing—''

''One big thing, Didi.''

''All right, one *big* thing stop you. Now, my first bit of advice is to announce you're plagued by allergies, so people will have an explanation for your appearance.''

''But I've never had allergies.''

''You do now. Came on just like that.'' Didi snapped her fingers. ''It can happen. Second thing is, talk to Luke before he leaves and find out if he can do anything to supress those pictures. I'm sure he has some contacts in L.A. and even in New York. Maybe if he agrees to do an exclusive interview, or pose as a centerfold for somebody—''

''Didi! I couldn't ask him to do that.''

''Then I will.''

''No! I'll talk to him. I promise.'' Meg's pulse raced in alarm at the thought of dealing with Luke again, but Didi was right. Maybe Luke could do something, something honorable of course, in exchange for the pictures.

''Okay. And number three, except for that brief conversation, and I emphasize brief, keep away from Luke Bannister. Unless, of course, you want to change the whole course of your life?'' She glanced at Meg with eyebrows raised.

Meg stared down at her hands twisted together in her lap. "No."

"I wouldn't blame you if you did."

"I've thought about it a hundred times since I left him this morning, and always come to the same conclusion. I've been fascinated with politics ever since I was president of our Girl Scout troop. This is my shot, Didi, and I'd never forgive myself if I threw it away."

"Then you can't."

"Besides, Luke would lose respect for me if I ran away with him. One of the things he loves about me is my commitment to causes I believe in. He admires me for going into politics." Meg gazed at Didi. "I wouldn't be the person he loves if I gave all that up."

"What about him? Would he come back here?"

Meg shook her head. "And I wouldn't want him to. He's so exciting the way he is, Didi. It would be a crime to try to turn him back into a Chandler farm boy."

"I agree." Didi sighed. "Well, ready, kid?"

"Sure."

Didi started the utility cart. "You can help me find those damned brochures, and I think Luke's making one last appearance with the festival mascot at ten. You can go over to the petting zoo then."

"Right."

CHAPTER TWELVE

AT A LITTLE PAST TEN Meg drove the cart over to the petting zoo. For the past few minutes, she'd taken deep breaths and tried to stay calm, but nothing seemed to work. How could she stay calm when she was about to come face-to-face with a man she'd loved intimately hours before and would probably never see again after today?

As she neared the petting zoo, Luke was signing autographs. His back was to her, so she slowed the vehicle and allowed herself to adjust to seeing him again. He wore a tan cowboy hat, a white Western shirt and a pair of tight blue jeans. Her eyes burned with unshed tears as she watched him lean toward a little girl and return her stuffed autograph hound. Luke had always been good with kids. She'd forgotten that. Once, a long time ago, she'd dreamed of having Luke's children.

The little girl pointed toward Luke's face and asked a question Meg couldn't hear. Luke laughed and said something that made the girl smile. She left with her parents, and Meg decided to grab her opportunity. She hopped out of the cart and walked quickly over to him.

When he turned in her direction, she gasped. His lower lip was swollen and cracked. His right eye was half-closed and puffy, with bruises underneath, and there was a long scratch across his cheek. "Luke! What on earth—''

He smiled as best he could. ''You should see the other guy.''

''You had a fight with Clint, didn't you?''

Just then, Clint walked up, a cup of cola in each hand. ''The truth is, *I* fought him. And I won.'' He handed one cola to Luke and offered the second to Meg. ''Want this?''

''No...thanks.'' She stared at the two brothers. They acted as if they were the best of friends.

''Then I'll drink it. Or hold it against my cheek for a while. That feels good, too.''

''I don't know which of you looks worse.''

They both spoke at once. ''He does,'' they said, pointing at each other. Then they began to laugh, but the laughs soon turned to groans of pain.

Meg was totally bewildered. she'd never understand men. ''Well, I hope you're both really proud of yourselves. Especially you, Luke. What about your screen test tomorrow?''

''Maybe they'll let me read the fight scene, or I should say, the scene after the fight scene.''

''You don't seem very upset about it.'' She was impatient with his attitude. Didn't he understand what he'd done to himself?

''I'm not upset.''

''He's not upset,'' Clint said, jerking his thumb at Luke. ''By the way, you should be nicer to him, Meg. He busted his face for you.'' Clint chuckled until the laughter hurt too much and he stopped.

Meg glared at them. ''I hope that's not true.''

"Nah, it's not." Luke sipped his cola and winked with his one good eye. "It just made me feel better."

"That's great. Just great. And I thought you two had grown up. What sort of example are you setting?"

Luke glanced at Clint. "Does this sound like a familiar speech to you?"

"Seems I've heard those words a few times. And she always tilts her chin up that way when she's giving us a lecture about our behavior."

"It's kind of cute, don't you think?" Luke's good eye twinkled.

Meg clenched her fists. "Luke Bannister, you are the most maddening—"

"It'll be okay, Meg. Don't worry. They can reschedule the screen test if they really want me, and makeup can do wonders."

The underlying softness in his voice was nearly her undoing. She swallowed. "I hope you're right."

"I'll be fine."

She stood there trying to remember what message she'd been sent to deliver. Oh, yes. The photographer. "Listen, I, uh, talked to Didi."

He raised an eyebrow.

"She made me promise to ask. Is there any chance you can talk the photographer out of publishing those pictures?"

"I plan to try."

Clint stepped closer and lowered his voice. "And if that doesn't work, and they come out, I've got a friend who distributes those magazines and tabloids around to the stores. I think I can delay the pictures hitting the stands until after the election."

"And then they'll throw me out of office."

Luke shook his head. "I don't think so, Meg. You have a lot of support in town."

"Hey." Clint put his arm around her shoulders and shook her gently. "Don't worry. Luke and I will come through. Remember the bull? Didn't we save you from that stampeding bull?"

Meg glanced at Luke and blushed. "I guess so." His gaze was steady, and she knew he wasn't remembering the day they'd run from the bull, but the passion of their early-morning lovemaking, when he'd rediscovered her scar.

"The only problem you had was sticking your fanny in the air when you crawled under the barbed wire," Clint said. "Any idiot knows not to do that."

"I wouldn't call her an idiot," Luke said. "What about that day you tried to build a fire with cow chips, pretending they were buffalo chips?"

"How would I know they'd stink like that?"

Meg smiled. "And then we couldn't put it out. The water made it steam like crazy, remember?"

Clint held his bruised cheek while he laughed. "Like a hundred cows passing gas."

"Yeah," Luke said. "Then we had to cart the whole mess off in our wagons. Never did get those wagons to smell good again."

"I tried to paint mine," Meg said. "Ugh."

"And remember the time we found that half-dead chicken, and—" Luke paused as two teenagers came up to him for autographs.

Meg edged away. "Maybe I'd better go."

"Wait a sec." He signed the autographs and posed for pictures, kneeling down with a girl on each side and the baby ostrich in the background. Clint offered to operate the girls' camera.

"What happened to your faces?" one of the girls asked.

"One of those revolving doors," Luke said. "He was coming in and I was going out."

"Yeah," Clint added, "a killer revolving door. Watch out for them. They just keep coming at you."

The girls looked at each other, giggled and ran away.

"You two are a pair," Meg said. And they were a pair, she thought. Whatever else would come of this, Luke and Clint were back to being brothers again. In a twisted sort of way, she'd brought it about, just like when they were all kids together. From the corner of her eye she saw another group of autograph seekers approaching. And she couldn't stand here forever. People might talk. "I really have to go."

Luke grew very quiet. "I'll call."

Her heart wrenched. "Maybe...that's not such a good idea. I don't think talking on the telephone would...I mean, it's not..."

Clint turned his back on them and professed great interest in the baby ostrich.

"You're right," Luke said softly. "Bad idea."

"But I would like to know if you get the part."

"I'll let you know through Clint. He'll tell you if I get it."

"Okay."

"Say goodbye to Dog-breath for me."

"I will."

"Take care."

"You, too." She gazed at him until tears blurred her

vision. She turned quickly and hurried away without looking back.

ENDURING THE DAY until four, when Luke was scheduled to leave, was an experience Meg hoped never to repeat. His presence dangled temptingly in front of her and several times during the day she had to remind herself of the reasons why she couldn't get on the plane with him. Whenever the tears came, she used Didi's allergy story as an excuse if anyone caught her with red eyes and a sniffly nose.

Then, at last, he was gone. The festival continued with ostriches racing, music blaring and vendors aggressively marketing their wares for the last two hours available to them, but for Meg the grounds seemed empty and lifeless. A wave of fatigue overcame her now that Luke was gone. Fortunately everyone expected her to be exhausted, and they made jokes and patted her on the back. Congratulations came from all sides on the success of the festival. The best ever, many said. Even the Bannister boys fighting and making up again added to the fun, some commented. She began to wonder if she'd imagined her night with Luke.

Then, as if to confirm she hadn't, Didi came along, looked deep into her eyes and gave her a big hug. "You'll survive this," she murmured.

Meg wasn't so certain.

WITH DIDI'S HELP, Meg got through the next two weeks. Didi was taking over as festival chairperson the following year, so Meg spent long hours with her making the transition. Meg was glad to have the work, and especially grateful to be doing it with Didi, who understood her mental lapses and emotional outbursts. Meg used much of her spare time helping get the books in order for her computer consulting firm.

Evenings were tough. She took Dog-breath for long walks to tire herself out so she'd sleep at night. The walks helped, and she savored the scent of citrus blooms that filled the air, the gentle warmth of the air and the rising moon. Nevertheless, her unhappiness persisted. Sometimes Meg would sit down in a grassy field sprinkled with wildflowers, hold Dog-breath close and cry into his soft coat. He'd endure stoically and lick her face before they made the long trek back home.

Although it was like flaying herself, she still tuned in *Connections* every weekday. Watching Luke on screen made her ache with longing. She'd tried to break herself of the habit, but with no success so far. Apparently Luke hadn't gotten the part in the movie. Clint hadn't called with any news, and she wasn't about to call him. At least not yet. She should have asked him to let her know one way or the other, but it was a wonder she'd had any coherent thoughts the day Luke left.

She hadn't spoken to her parents since the festival. When her mother called and invited her to dinner, Meg reluctantly accepted, and suffered through the meal making small talk about the cotton crop while worrying about what would happen if the paparazzi's photos appeared on the newsstands in Chandler. Unfortunately her parents would share in her disgrace. And they'd warned her to stay away from Luke.

Over cherry cobbler dessert, her father cleared his throat, usually the signal that a pronouncement was coming. Meg waited, her heart pounding in her ears. Maybe he'd heard about the incident already.

"Talked to Clint the other day," her father said. "It seems Luke's taken back half ownership of the farm."

Meg blinked. She was unprepared for the rush of hope the news brought. "You mean he might be spending time here?"

Jack Hennessy glanced sharply at his daughter. "That isn't Clint's understanding. The idea is that now Clint will have somebody to talk over plans and problems with. Luke will be more of a silent partner. I think Clint needs that. He's pretty young to have sole responsibility for that farm."

"I suppose." Meg tried to hide her disappointment. Of course Luke wouldn't be reestablishing himself in Chandler. He'd made that clear before.

"Anyway, after hearing that, I think I might have misjudged Luke, and I wanted to tell you so. He behaved himself while he was here. Even that fight with Clint turned out to be a good thing. Clint mowed the weeds and the painters are out there now. I figure that's Luke's influence."

Meg gazed at her father. He didn't know the half of Luke's influence, or whether Luke had "behaved himself," but she wasn't about to snatch defeat from the jaws of victory. "Too bad you can't say that to Luke himself."

"Well, I will, if I ever get a chance, although I probably won't. When would I ever have reason to be around a big Hollywood star?" He rested his arm on the table. "Now don't get me wrong. I maintain my position about you and Luke. He's wrong for you. Always was, always will be. I...uh...understand you know about the deal in high school."

"I know, and I don't like it." Meg was still angry

about what her father had done ten years ago, but her worry about the revealing photos of her and Luke took precedence over her anger.

"You don't have to like what I did. I didn't do it to win a popularity contest."

"Jack, now let's not spoil the mood with this kind of talk. You wanted Meg to come over so you could tell her about Luke taking back half of the farm. Let's not get into that other business. It's over with, anyway."

Jack Hennessy frowned and rustled his napkin as he shoved it under the edge of his plate. "I didn't want her here just to talk about Luke, Nora. It was time we had Meg over to catch up on how she's coming along."

"That's true." Her mother smiled nervously. "We're so proud of how you handled the festival. Everyone is raving about how good it was this year. And now you'll certainly be elected president of the chamber. Just think."

"She's achieving her goals, that's what she's doing," her father said, his voice gruff. "She's not allowing herself to be sidetracked. With an attitude like that, you can have anything you want, Meg."

Meg fought the urge to tell them about Luke and about the pictures, just to get the agony over with. But her parents had always counseled her not to buy trouble. Maybe Luke could convince the photographer not to sell them. Maybe he already had.

HENRY DAVIS RANTED and raved about Luke's bruises, but eventually he got on the phone, called in some favors and had the screen test postponed. The shooting of *Connections* for the next week was no big deal—the writers enjoyed the challenge of explaining his battered face as part of the story line.

And finally Luke asked Henry to help him track down Ansel Wiggins. Fortunately Henry knew almost everyone in town, and within twenty-four hours he had a phone number for Ansel Wiggins, photojournalist. Luke called the number during a break on the set.

The answering-machine message began with the screeches and trumpeting of jungle animals. Then Ansel said, "Ansel Wiggins is covering an African safari with Prince Charles. Her assistant will forward your message. Please leave your name, number and position on the food chain after the beep."

Luke grimaced. He wasn't crazy about leaving his home number. She might sell that, too. But he did it, anyway.

When she hadn't returned his call two days later, he tried her number again. The message had changed. This one began with flute music and the howl of a wolf. "Ansel Wiggins is covering ancient Native American ceremonials with Shirley MacLaine. Please leave your name, number and astrological sign after the beep."

Luke left both his studio and home numbers and told Ansel that the call was urgent. He decided to give her another day before he tracked her down in person. She called at midnight, waking him up. "I'm sorry. I'm a night person and I didn't think about the time," she explained.

Luke shook off the fog of sleep. "Can we meet for coffee?"

"Sure. How about now?"

He groaned and glanced at the clock. He was due on

the set in seven hours, but this elusive woman had to be dealt with, and fast. "Okay. Now."

Half an hour later he walked into the all-night coffee shop she'd agreed upon. She was tucked into a booth, chewing gum and studying the menu, still wearing the backward baseball cap, sloppy T-shirt and oversize shorts. The only difference in her appearance was the lack of cameras. Luke sighed and headed over.

She glanced up. "I'm having a triple hot-fudge sundae. How about you?"

"Just coffee." He sat opposite her. "I want to apologize if I was rough on you the other morning, but that woman is a close friend of mine."

She folded her arms and leaned on the table. "So I gathered."

She had a smart mouth. He steeled himself to ignore her or they'd be shouting at each other before long. He took a deep breath. "I'll make this short—" he paused as the waitress arrived and took their order "—I want the pictures, negatives, too. I'm prepared to pay for them."

"I'll bet you are." She popped her gum. "What happened to your face?"

"Never mind that. Name your price."

"Can't."

"Why not?"

She gazed at him. "Because somebody else already bought them. I got the money up front, and if you land the movie contract you're trying for, I get a bonus."

"Dammit! Don't you realize you could ruin a potential political career? You look like a feminist. Don't you want a woman in a position of power?"

"Yeah, I do. Me. And I finally made it." Her order

arrived. She parked her gum on a napkin and ate the cherry off the top of her sundae.

"But you made it at the expense of someone else."

"Now just a minute, Luke Bannister. If you get that movie part, won't that be at the expense of someone else?" She waved her spoon at him. "I'm sure you're not the only actor in town who'd like to star in that film."

"But it's not the end of a career to lose one part."

"How do you know that? How do you know if this is not the last chance before that person packs up and leaves town? How do you know whether the guys trying for this part are down to their last nickel and another rejection means going home to sell used cars in Topeka? You know as well as I do what the world is like. Your friend might as well know it, too." She dug into her sundae and rolled her eyes at the first gooey bite.

Luke's stomach knotted as he realized how helpless he was to stop the publication of her photographs. No matter how right Ansel was about the ways of the world, he didn't want Meg buffeted by the same winds that had pounded at him for most of his life. But he could take it, was used to it. She wasn't. "Where did you sell the photos?"

She was proud enough of her sale to tell him, with her mouth full of ice cream. He winced. The New York-based tabloid had a wide circulation. Tossing some money on the table, he left his coffee sitting there and walked out of the restaurant. He had some thinking to do. The tabloid wouldn't squelch the photos. They'd run them, even if he didn't get the part. Meg was in trouble.

CHAPTER THIRTEEN

ON THE EVENING OF April first someone knocked at Meg's front door. She glanced down at her cotton blouse, the shirttails hanging out over a worn pair of plaid shorts, and her bare feet. If this was chamber business, she wasn't dressed for it.

Dog-breath ran ahead of her as she went to answer the door. She looked through the peephole and saw an overweight man with a beard, thick glasses and a feed-store cap. He was dressed in a flannel shirt and baggy jeans, and carried a thick catalog under one arm. A blue Geo sedan was parked in the drive.

"He's selling something," she muttered to Dog-breath. Taking a firm grip of the dog's collar, she opened the door a crack. "Yes?"

"Your neighbor Clint Bannister sent me, ma'am." His voice was reedy and rather unpleasant. "Said you might be interested in looking at some seed catalogs."

Meg sighed. "I'm sorry, but I don't have time to put in a garden this year. Besides, it's a little late in the spring for seeds."

"I can have bedding plants shipped, too."

"I—hush, Dog-breath." She glanced down in surprise at the retriever, who was whining and wagging his tail. She'd always considered him a good watchdog, but now she was having her doubts.

"Then maybe I could trouble you for a glass of water, ma'am."

"Excuse me a minute." Leaving Dog-breath to guard the door, she walked back to the kitchen to call Clint and verify that this guy was legit. Clint confirmed that he was and suggested she order something from him.

Meg returned to the door, still debating whether to do that or not. She knew the old glass-of-water ploy. Once inside the door the guy would convince her to look at his stupid catalogs. Then again, maybe she should plant a few vegetables. At any rate she was glad Clint had ordered some; it was a sign that he was getting his life back together.

The man looked kind of pathetic standing there, and Meg relented. "All right. I'll get you a drink." She opened the door. "If you'll sit down, I'll be right back with the water." She closed the door and started toward the kitchen. Looking back over her shoulder, she noticed Dog-breath licking the man's hand. What had gotten into that mutt?

When she returned with the water, the man was leaning back against the cushions of her sofa and making himself at home, although he still hadn't taken off his cap. Meg regretted her softheartedness already. The guy would probably stay forever. Apparently Dog-breath had taken leave of his senses, because he'd laid his head on this stranger's knee. "Your water."

He took the glass and set it on her coffee table without drinking it. Then he gazed at her.

"I'm really not interested in a garden this year," she said. "So if you'll drink your water, I have some other things to do this evening."

"Then maybe I can interest you in a new product that takes care of jock itch."

She stepped back, startled. Her heart began to pound as she looked more closely at the man. The lenses of his glasses were very thick, and his eyes were brown. He reached out to stroke Dog-breath's head and she looked at his hand, then back at his face. She gasped.

He took off his glasses, then his cap. He popped out the brown contacts and put them on the table. Last of all he peeled off the beard and tossed it onto the coffee table next to the untouched glass of water.

"My God!"

He stood and grinned in triumph. "April Fools! I thought if you didn't know me, no one would."

"Luke!" She hurled herself at him and he caught her in his arms.

His lips found hers, but he groaned in frustration as the padding under his shirt wedged them apart. "I've put on a little weight and I can tell it's going to come between us."

"What about your movie deal? What about your screen test? Did you—"

He cradled her face in his hands. "Dirk Kennedy is dead. Shooting starts next week for *The Unvanquished*. The only problem is—"

"Then you got the part?"

"Yes, but I'm afraid it will—"

"Luke, that's wonderful." She gave him a long, lingering kiss. "Tell me about the movie."

"It's a historical romance set in the eighteen hundreds, based on a book by Helen Goodwin. I get a young girl pregnant and then I'm captured by Indians before I can make an honest woman of her. I escape from the

Indians just in time to save her and the baby from a raid.''

''Sounds steamy.'' She began unfastening the buttons of his shirt. ''Speaking of which, isn't this flannel hot?''

His eyes darkened with passion. ''Oh, Meg, I hope you know what you're doing.''

''Inviting a door-to-door salesman into my bed. And don't tell me you don't want to be there.''

''More than you know.''

''Then come with me.'' Without another word, she led him to her bedroom and closed the door.

Leaning against it, she held his gaze as he finished unbuttoning his shirt. She remembered the last time he'd undressed in her presence. And all that had followed. An insistent ache invaded her loins.

Maybe she was just setting herself up for more heartbreak. But he was here, and in the bedroom where she'd fantasized about him every night for two weeks. She couldn't send him away. Not yet.

He pulled the padding out of his shirt and tossed it aside. The jeans, way too large now, rode low on his hips. She walked toward him and caressed his bare chest, stroking her fingers through the thick mat of hair.

''Oh, Meg. I've missed you so much.'' He undid the buttons of her shirt.

''I've missed you.'' She kissed the hollow of his throat as he pushed the blouse off her shoulders. ''I never thought I'd be able to touch you like this again.'' She felt his heart pounding rapidly against her palm. She leaned down and flicked her tongue over his nipple until it hardened in response.

He fumbled with the back hook of her bra before he

finally got it undone. "I want you too much. I'm shaking."

She stood on tiptoe. "Kiss me, Luke. Kiss me hard." His mouth ground against hers with a sweet pain that she welcomed because it made his being there with her real. She kissed him back, teasing his tongue with hers, plowing furrows through his hair with her fingers.

With one hand he stripped away her shorts and panties before carrying her to the bed. He tumbled with her onto the comforter, kicking off his shoes as he kissed her shoulders, her throat, her breasts. "I've missed you, missed you, missed you," he chanted, running his hands over her body until she writhed against him and tugged at the waistband of his jeans.

He unfastened them quickly and shucked his briefs. She filled her hand with him and he groaned with pleasure as she squeezed and stroked. At last he stilled her hand and reached over the side of the bed, searching in his jeans pocket. In a moment he was back, and she helped him ease the condom on, placing kisses along the way.

"I wanted to take this slower," he gasped, moving between her legs. "But I can't, Meg."

"Love me," she begged, pulling him down, pulling him into the center of her being.

His movements were basic, elemental. She rose to meet each powerful thrust with a deep need of her own. Now was not the time for flourishes. They strove to reconnect, to drive their love into each other's body with a force that would never shake it loose. Their climaxes came quickly, and they clung together through the ebbing waves of passion.

Finally they lay quiet, breathing in the same rhythm,

listening to each other's heartbeat. Luke propped himself up on one elbow and gazed into her face. He smiled, but his eyes were shadowed.

"What is it, Luke? You were trying to tell me something before, but all I could think about was your movie."

"And this?"

"Oh, yes."

He kissed her gently and drew back. "It's not right that something as wonderful as this can end up hurting you."

Then she knew. "You can't stop the publication of the pictures."

He shook his head. "I've talked to some people in New York, and it doesn't look good. When they learn I've signed to do this film, they'll give the pictures even bigger play."

Meg swallowed. "I guess that's show biz."

"When's the chamber meeting where you'll be elected?"

"The third Wednesday of this month."

"I'll think of something to stall them."

"Remember, there's Clint's friend, the one who knows when the tabloids are delivered to the stores."

"Clint's already talked to him. He's an old drinking buddy, so he'll do what he can, as long as we don't ask him to put his job on the line." He caressed her cheek with his thumb. "I hate how the whole thing has turned out for you."

"I don't. I'll weather it. And I don't regret a minute we've spent together, Luke."

"I can't regret it, either. I probably should, considering how it's affected you, but I can't. Even coming here tonight was a silly risk, but I had to see you."

"I'm glad you did. How long can you stay?"

"I'm leaving tomorrow. I spent the afternoon at the house with Clint."

She refused to let sadness overwhelm her at the thought of him leaving so soon. "And the night belongs to me."

"I belong to you."

Meg circled his ear with the tip of her finger. "So Dirk is really gone?"

"Yep. Piloted a plane over the Bermuda Triangle to prove it was no big deal. He was never heard from again."

"Sheila will miss him."

"Mmm."

"You sure look convincing in bed with her." Meg didn't tell him of the jealousy that knifed through her every time he touched the actress. "You're all sweaty and flushed, just—"

"Like this?" He nuzzled the side of her neck.

"Yes."

"It isn't anything like this."

"You could have fooled me."

Luke chuckled and pushed himself away from her. "I'll be right back, and then I'll show you just how it's done—on the set." He returned from the bathroom and put on his French-cut briefs. "First of all, I wear something like this."

"That's a relief." She viewed the bulge of masculinity revealed by the skimpy navy briefs. "Sort of. And what does Sheila wear?"

"A bodysuit. It looks like she has nothing on, but

she's covered everywhere important. It's all camera angles.''

"If you say so."

"Okay, we'll imagine you're in the bodysuit. I lie down and arrange myself so I'm partially covering you, and the comforter hides the rest, but we reveal just a little skin here, and here." He lay across her with his weight on his elbows. "Push your breasts up a little. That's it. Very nice."

"How do you feel when you're on top of Sheila like this?"

"I'm thinking about my lines."

"Sure you are."

He grinned at her. "Okay, most guys aren't going to gripe about holding a woman with a nice body, but let me tell you the downside. If you were Sheila, you'd have on a ton of makeup."

"Want me to put some on?" She started to get up.

"No." He held her close. "We're simulating here. Also, you'd have your hair in a certain arrangement, with hair spray and stuff on it. It wouldn't feel like yours does." He ran his fingers through her hair. "I love your hair."

"You're digressing."

"Okay, so here we are, makeup and hair spray, and people all around us. Hot lights. Cameras moving in. This is not an intimate experience. Then somebody mists us with a spray bottle."

Meg laughed. "They spray you with water?"

"That's how we look all sweaty and flushed, like we're really worked up." He ran a finger down the side of her cheek. "Fortunately you have the genuine thing, so we'll skip the spray bottle."

"What happens next?"

"I look into your eyes, and I say my line."

"Say one. Be Dirk Kennedy."

"Okay." He cleared his throat, and glanced away from her for a moment.

She watched in fascination as his features hardened just a little. When his gaze returned to hers, it glittered with a quality she'd never seen in Luke, and she was reminded that Dirk Kennedy wasn't a very nice guy. His voice was tight, almost ferocious. "You lured me to your bed, Sheila. Don't think you can tell me to stop now."

A shiver slid down Meg's spine. "I don't want you to stop."

Luke's mouth came closer; his breath fanned warm air across her face. "I think you want your husband to find out about us."

"No! I swear!"

"I've heard you taunt him." He hovered over her lips. "Just as you taunt me."

"No," she whispered, wanting his kiss, no matter who he was pretending to be.

"Yes, and you'll pay for your taunts, my love." He kissed her almost brutally while he reached for her uncovered thigh and raked his spread fingers down it.

Meg responded to his kiss, opening her mouth and arching her back, crushing her breasts against his chest. Luke plunged his tongue into her mouth and rotated his hips against hers. She pressed upward against his arousal and whimpered at the barrier of cotton between them.

He lifted his mouth from hers a fraction. "Do you want me?"

"Yes!"

"Then beg me, you witch."

"Please, Dirk...oh, please."

He chuckled low in his throat and continued to caress her thigh. "And what will you do for me if I satisfy you now?"

"Anything!" Playacting or not, his teasing was driving her crazy. She wanted his lips on hers, his hard maleness deep inside her.

"Then you'll use your influence to get me that piece of property?"

Her laugh was breathless. "That's what you want? Property?"

His hot gaze traveled over her so suggestively she grew moist just from his insolent perusal. "Among other things."

"Take what you want," she whispered. "All of it."

"With pleasure." His lips covered hers and he thrust forward, but his briefs prevented the joining she craved. His kiss deepened, and she moaned in frustration. He lifted his lips. "You want more?"

"You know what I want."

"It's not in the script."

"Then ad-lib."

"You're a demanding lover, Sheila." He reached beneath the comforter and tunneled his fingers through the curls at the apex of her thighs. "But I want that property," he murmured, stroking her until she gasped. "Is it mine?"

"I'll...try," she said, panting.

"That's not good enough." He stroked and teased. "Is it mine?"

She twisted beneath him. "Yes!"

"That's good, Sheila. Very good. Now enjoy."

She did. When the glorious spasms subsided, she gazed up at him. "Tell me it's not like that with Sheila. Not really."

He laughed softly. "Not even close. We don't have climaxes on the set."

"But sometimes...I bet you get aroused."

"Sometimes."

"Oh, Luke, I shouldn't have asked you to demonstrate a love scene. This isn't easy for me, thinking of you pretending to—"

"Hush, now." He reached for a cellophane package on the nightstand and quickly sheathed himself. "It's only pretend," he murmured, moving between her thighs. "This is for real." Then he drove into her, and his powerful rhythm blotted out her fears. "I love you," he whispered as she moved toward another shattering release. "I love only you."

JUST BEFORE DAWN Luke left Meg's bed and began to dress. She started to get up, but he urged her back under the comforter. "Stay there. Let me think of you lying there, dreaming of me."

"I always do. Luke, what's going to happen to us?"

"I don't know." He pulled on his briefs and reached for the flannel shirt. "I thought I could stay away from you, but two weeks later here I am, disguising myself to be with you again."

"My dad said you'd taken back your half of the farm."

"Yeah. In fact, Clint's the one who suggested I disguise myself so I could come back and check on things without stirring up the whole town. Of course, once I was here, I couldn't stay away from you."

"Well, if the disguise worked…"

"This time it did. And if anyone noticed the car parked in your drive, you can always make up something about an old college friend. But we can't keep that sort of thing up for too long, Meg." He pulled on the baggy jeans. "You can only have so many visiting college friends before someone thinks you're running a house of prostitution or a drug ring."

"Then I'll make trips to L.A."

"That would look suspicious, too."

Meg groaned in frustration. "I can't imagine my life without you. When you left before, I tried to resign myself to it, but I never did."

"Obviously neither did I."

"We're two intelligent people. Can't we figure out a way for this to work?"

He sat on the edge of the bed and trailed his finger down her arm. "We probably could, but how would it work in Chandler?"

"To hell with—"

"Don't say it. You don't mean it."

"When the papers reach the newsstands, my decision may be made for me. If they throw me out of Chandler, would you take me in?"

He smoothed her hair away from her face and gazed down at her. "As if you have to ask."

She laced her fingers through his. "I don't want you to go. I want to fix you breakfast. I've never done that."

He brought their joined hands to his lips and kissed her fingers one by one. "And breakfast would become lunch, and lunch would become dinner, and in between we'd make love, and I'd never go back."

Meg sighed. Slowly she relaxed her grip. "Go quickly," she said, "while I can still stand it."

On Tuesday, and after the chamber board meeting

CHAPTER FOURTEEN

FOR THE NEXT FEW DAYS Meg studied every strange man
she saw on the street or driving down the road. One of
them might be Luke, in disguise. If he did it once, he
could do it again. But she knew he was back in L.A.
preparing for the first week of shooting for *The Unvanquished*. He had lines to learn, costumes to be fitted. And
a co-star to meet. Meg tried not to think about that. He'd
convinced her that love scenes in soap operas weren't
filmed in the nude. But as for love scenes in the movies,
she knew better.

She had no right to be jealous. She had no right to
anything involving Luke Bannister. She believed that
she would see him again. They might even make love
again. But their future, which neither of them wanted to
face, would be a few stolen moments between long ab-
sences. Meg didn't like that idea. Once, she might have
spurned it as not enough. But now she was willing to
take whatever crumbs might fall her way. She couldn't
renounce Luke completely. She simply wasn't that
strong.

The day of the chamber meeting to elect a new president grew closer. Everyone on the chamber board talked
as if she'd have no opposition, especially after the re-
sounding success of the festival. But Meg knew that,
before the vote was taken, anyone could be nominated

for the position from the floor. If a scandal broke, a new nominee was sure to be put up against her. The humiliation of losing under those circumstances would be public and complete.

On Tuesday, one day before the noon board meeting on Wednesday, Clint called. "The story's been published."

Meg clutched her stomach. She'd been expecting it, but still her insides curdled. "Are you sure?"

"My buddy called me from the warehouse."

"I can't believe the timing. Tomorrow's the board meeting."

"I know, but it could be worse. My buddy's got a tight group there, and the paper won't go on the stands until Thursday. He couldn't stall much longer than that, so in a way, we're lucky it didn't show up last week."

"I guess you're right, although if it had, the suspense would be over. Did your friend say what the article looked like?"

"Just that it's on the front page. He was rushed and couldn't talk long, but he promised to hang in there for us."

"Clint, I appreciate your help."

"It's the least I can do, considering most of this mess is my fault."

"And mine."

"Hey, women never could stay away from Luke."

"And that's one of the crosses I have to bear."

"Well, I'll tell you something, Meg. He's never been serious about anybody else. Never. I quizzed him about the women he's known in L.A., and he could barely remember them. You seem to have made him forget all about them."

"That's encouraging."

"Yeah, when he showed up here the last time, all he could talk about was you. When I threatened him with bodily harm, he finally got down to business and helped me decide whether to repair one of the old harvesters or buy a new one, but his heart wasn't in it."

Meg smiled. "Thanks, Clint."

"I just wish there was some way you two could get together."

She met his comment with silence. What could she say?

"Well, I'd better get back to work. Call if you need anything. A shoulder, a beer, whatever."

"I'll do that." She hung up and stared at the phone. Everything was proceeding as planned. She'd helped manipulate things so she'd be voted in before the story came out. Except the more she thought about it, the more wrong that manipulation felt. She stared at the phone a moment longer, and before she lost her nerve, she punched in Clint's number.

He answered sounding out of breath. "Meg? I was on my way out the door. What's up?"

"I know this sounds crazy, but I'd like you to call your friend and tell him to deliver all the papers tomorrow."

"What?"

"I know you've gone to a lot of trouble to arrange this, and probably bought a few rounds of drinks for the guys after work, but I don't feel right about getting into office under false pretenses."

"Don't be an idiot, Meg! Having those papers on the stands tomorrow is like crawling under barbed wire with your fanny in the air. Don't you learn, woman?"

She sighed. "Apparently not. I told you you'd think I was out of my mind, but it has to be this way, Clint. If you want to tell me how to contact him, I'll talk to the guy."

"No, no. I'll do it. But I don't like this. And neither will Luke."

"I appreciate how hard both of you have worked to keep this quiet, but I honestly wish it had come out during the festival. At least now I'd know where I stand. Keeping secrets isn't my style. I should have realized it earlier, but I didn't."

"Boy, when Luke said you were an idealist, he wasn't kidding. I was prepared to buy all the papers we could find and put them through the shredder, but Luke said you'd never go for that."

"That's right. I wouldn't."

"Listen, you'll probably need that beer and a shoulder to cry on after the board meeting tomorrow. I've given up on the stuff for myself, but I'd be glad to pour one for you."

"Thanks, Clint. Sounds like a good offer. I'll see you then." She hung up the phone and gripped the edge of the desk. Public and complete humiliation. After tomorrow, nobody in Chandler would look at her the same way again.

She called Didi, who had known about the plan to delay the papers. She tried to talk Meg back into doing that, but Meg held firm. "Want to come over tonight?" Didi persisted. "I can throw together some pasta and break out a jug of wine. I'm not sure you should be alone to contemplate this."

"I won't be alone. I've decided to go over and tell my parents."

"Oh, my God."

"It's only fair, Didi."

"You and fair! I think the word will be inscribed on your tombstone. I wonder if the chamber deserves somebody as good as you."

Meg laughed humorlessly. "After tomorrow, I don't think people will think of me as good, Didi."

MEG TIMED HER VISIT to her parents so dinner would be finished, the dishes washed. She didn't want to have to choke down a meal during this discussion. She knocked on the kitchen door and opened it. "Mom, Dad?"

"In here, Meg," her mother called from the living room. Televised laughter indicated they were watching a sitcom.

Her father chuckled as Meg walked in. "You should watch this show, Meggie."

He hadn't called her Meggie in a long time. She wondered if it was his way of reestablishing the affectionate relationship that had eroded during the festival. Her heart ached for the camaraderie that might never exist again. Her father leaned back in his leather recliner, his face relaxed. Her mother sat on the couch with a pile of shirts that needed buttons, her new reading glasses perched on her nose.

Her mother glanced up from her sewing. "What a nice surprise, Meg." She moved the shirts aside and patted the seat next to her. "Sit down and enjoy the show."

Meg sat, feeling like the grim reaper arriving to shatter their contentment. "I'm sorry to interrupt," she said, "But I have something important to tell you."

"Oh?" Her father glanced over, a smile on his broad

face from the latest joke on the screen. His smile faded as he gazed at his daughter. "What's wrong?"

"Could we turn off the TV?"

"Sure." He fumbled with the remote and the set clicked into darkness.

Meg looked at her mother, who had taken off her glasses and held them tightly in her lap. The jovial atmosphere of the room was gone, and it was Meg's fault. If only she'd had brothers and sisters, maybe this wouldn't be so hard. Maybe she wouldn't feel so responsible for their happiness.

She took a deep breath. "I need to warn you about something that will happen tomorrow. There's a tabloid that's coming out—I know you don't usually read them, but somebody will tell you about it, I'm sure—and my name and picture will be in it."

Her mother frowned. "You mean something to do with the festival?"

"No. Something to do with Luke."

Jack Hennessy snapped his recliner forward. "I saw that damned photographer running around. What did she do—rig something by superimposing your head on somebody else's body? We'll sue them, that's what we'll do. Don't worry, Meg. Nobody will believe—"

"The pictures are legitimate, Dad. I was caught coming out of Luke's hotel room at four in the morning."

Her mother gasped and her father stared at her in slack-jawed amazement.

"The photographer was waiting by the door. She took pictures of me, and then pictures of Luke coming out wearing only his jeans. Luke has just signed a contract to do a major motion picture, and his name's bigger than ever. I'm sure the story will be something about his one-night stand with the festival organizer in Chandler. And it's true.''

Her father tried to speak, cleared his throat and tried again. "Couldn't...couldn't Luke have put a stop to it?''

"He tried. This was the photographer's first big break, apparently, and she wasn't about to give up her chance to advance her career.''

Nora Hennessy touched her daughter's arm. "You mean everyone, not just in Chandler, but all over the country, will see this?''

"I'm afraid so, Mom. I'm sorry. I'm truly sorry. You've both tried so hard to raise a daughter who would be a credit to you, and you warned me about Luke. Now you'll have to go through the humiliation this story will bring. Neither of you deserve it.''

Her father ran a shaky hand over his face. "What about you becoming president of the chamber?''

"I doubt they'll vote me in. By noon, when the board convenes, the story will probably be all over town.''

He stood up and started pacing across the room. "Did the damned paper time it this way, just to ruin you?''

"No. Luke's been trying to stall them, but I guess he couldn't hold them off any longer. Clint had a link with the people who distribute the paper in Chandler, and he was going to have them hold it for a day, but I told him not to.''

Her father whirled. "Well, call him back! That sounds like a reasonable plan. Get yourself into office and then deal with the story.''

"No, Jack.'' Her mother glanced at Meg. "She wouldn't want to be voted in under those circumstances. Better to have it come out beforehand.''

He continued to pace. "I'd love to get my hands on

that Luke Bannister. He seduced you into going over to that hotel. Here I thought he'd changed, and it turns out he hasn't changed at all!"

"Dad, that's not what happened. Luke didn't ask me to come to his room. I sneaked over there Saturday night after the festival was over. He didn't even expect me. This is my fault, not his."

"You're always trying to protect him!"

She stood. "That's because you never understood him! Did you know his father beat him all those years after his mother died? No, I'm sure you didn't, because he never told anybody. I'm probably the only one who guessed. Luke may have seemed like a swaggering punk to you, but inside he was hurting more than any of us will ever know. It's a miracle what he's done with his life. And I...I love him very much."

Her father stopped pacing. Slowly he turned and faced her. "What did you say?"

"I said I love him. I was sorely tempted to leave Chandler and go back with him to L.A., but he convinced me not to. He believes in my future as a public servant and doesn't want to interfere with that."

"So instead he ruins your future?"

"That wasn't his doing! It was mine! Why can't you be angry with me?"

Slowly her father crossed the room to her. "I could never be angry with you. Don't you understand?"

"But I'm the one who's hurt you. Hurt you and Mom."

"Never mind about us."

"Your father's right." Nora came over and put her arms around Meg. "Whatever happens tomorrow, we can take it just fine. Whatever you do won't affect the price of cotton, or the sunshine in my flower garden. If some false friends snub us, we were better off without them, anyway.''

Meg's eyes brimmed. ''I thought you'd be devastated.''

''Then I guess you don't know us as well as you thought,'' her mother said, hugging her.

''It's you we're worried about, Meggie.'' Her father patted her shoulder. ''We know how much you wanted the chamber office. And if this story comes out the way you describe it, you may be out of the running.''

Meg sniffed and glanced at him. ''Well, then I'm out. I'll hold up my head and try again another time. After all, I come from strong stock.''

''Damn right,'' her father said, squeezing her shoulder. ''Meg Hennessy's no quitter.''

''And neither are you guys,'' she said, her voice choked with emotion.

MEG DECIDED THE ONLY WAY she could handle the board meeting at noon the next day was if she hadn't seen the article and hadn't discussed it with anyone. She unplugged her phone before she went to bed and didn't answer her door. At eleven-thirty, dressed in a crisp, mint green linen suit, she drove to Chops Restaurant, where the chamber held its monthly board meetings in a conference room behind the main dining area.

She looked straight ahead as she walked through the restaurant and pretended not to see heads turning and comments exchanged. Whispered snippets of conversation pelted her like hailstones. ''...looks upset...wouldn't have guessed...amazing...sexy...''

Perspiration dampened her forehead and the small of

her back. No doubt about it, the word was out. The board members would know. But wasn't that what she wanted? She fought the urge to turn and run. She didn't have to go through with this. She could take her car and drive away from here, away from Chandler. Luke had said he'd take her in.

Except they hadn't thrown her out yet. If she left now, she'd be running away, quitting. If she ever expected to contribute something to the world, she needed to prove to herself that she had the backbone to take what the world dished out. She had to find out what she was made of.

She walked into the back room. Nearly every one of the eighteen board members was there, plus the ex officio members who included two people from the press and representatives from the city and the county. They'd probably gathered early to pick another nominee for president of the chamber. The procedure was simple. Her name would be presented and then nominations would be taken from the floor. No one had ever been nominated from the floor in the history of the chamber, but today would undoubtedly make history.

Conversation stopped as she walked in. She forced a smile and glanced at the one friendly face she could count on—Didi's. Didi gave her a discreet thumbs-up. Tables were arranged in a U-shape, with the current president and executive director at the bottom of the U. Meg took her seat at a chair along the side. She crossed her legs and folded her hands together to control her shaking.

Ralph Handley called the meeting to order. Meg tried to concentrate on the preliminary business—approval of the minutes, executive committee business, policy matters. She couldn't focus on any of it. She glanced around the table and noticed the edges of what must be the tabloid sticking out of briefcases and hiding under yellow legal pads. Her heart pounded as the meeting's agenda moved with maddening slowness toward the confirmation procedure.

French doors opposite her led to an area of grass and trees, both verdant with the lush green of springtime. Meg fantasized about getting up and going outdoors into the fresh air, feeling the sun on her back. A gardener was working out there, using hand clippers on a small hedge. She remembered what her mother had said— what happened today wouldn't affect the price of cotton or the sunshine on her flowers.

Meg thought about people all over the world who wouldn't give a damn what happened in this room today. Business would go forward, babies would be born, vacations would be enjoyed. And Luke. No matter what happened today, he would star in a wonderful movie and become known all over the world. She loved thinking about that, even if the idea was bittersweet, because he would inevitably move away from her.

The sound of a lawn mower startled her out of her reverie. A board member excused himself and went out to ask the gardener to move his operation away from the French doors until the meeting was over. Meg realized with a start that they were about to vote on her. Without the noise from the lawn mower, she might have been caught daydreaming at the crucial moment.

As Ralph proposed her name and asked for nominations from the floor, a sense of calm came over her. At last it would be over. Someone else would be named; someone else would be the president.

Except that no one else was nominated.

Meg glanced around the room in surprise. Her fellow

board members gazed at her with interest, not condemnation. Ralph cleared his throat. "No other nominations being offered, I call for a voice vote for Meg Hennessy O'Brian as president of the chamber. All in favor, signify by saying aye."

A chorus of ayes followed.

"Nays?"

No one spoke.

"Abstentions?"

Meg struggled to find her voice. "I abstain," she croaked.

"Congratulations," Ralph said, smiling at her. "You're our new president-elect."

Meg's head buzzed. This couldn't be happening. "I don't get it." Her gaze traveled from face to face. Didi was grinning from ear to ear. "What about the story?"

"What about it?" Ralph said. "I think most of us found it charming. Good publicity for the festival, as a matter of fact."

CHAPTER FIFTEEN

CHARMING? GOOD PUBLICITY for the festival?

Meg wondered if she could be dreaming this scene. Had all the Chandler Chamber of Commerce board members read about her torrid night at the San Marcos and decided the account was "charming"? She glanced at Didi for some clue as to what was going on.

Didi met her gaze and mouthed the words "Did you read it?"

Meg shook her head.

Didi pushed back her chair. "Could we have a short recess before we finish the agenda? Five minutes?"

Ralph looked puzzled, but he nodded. Chairs scraped back and Anna Cruz, who was sitting next to Meg, leaned toward her. "Frankly, I think you missed a golden opportunity," she said with a wink.

"I'm not sure what you—"

Didi grabbed her arm and pulled her out of her chair. "Come with me, sweetie."

Meg followed Didi, who glanced around and ducked through the kitchen door with Meg in tow. She had a copy of the tabloid in her hand. When the kitchen door closed behind them, Didi shoved the paper at Meg.

There was the picture of Meg, looking disheveled and guilty, right next to the picture of Luke flying out the door wearing only his jeans. Meg steeled herself for the

torrid headline, and as she read it she gasped. Lover Boy
Strikes Out! Meg glanced at Didi. "Keep going."

Meg read aloud.

"'Luke Bannister, heartthrob of the hit soap *Connections* and star of the upcoming feature film *The
Unvanquished*, admits he couldn't get to first base
with lovely childhood sweetheart Meg O'Brian
when Luke came home last month for Chandler,
Arizona's annual ostrich festival. "I tried to stir up
an old flame, but she wasn't impressed," Luke said.
"Guess I'm not such a hot lover after all."

"'O'Brian was the organizer of the festival. Bannister says he asked for special "star" treatment,
but O'Brian told him to get lost. "She came to my
hotel room to discuss business and refused to let it
become pleasure," Bannister said. "If this keeps
happening, my reputation's going to be shot."'"

Meg folded the paper with shaking hands. "But Didi,
that's not the way—"

"I was afraid that's how you'd react. Luke made himself look like a fool for you. Are you going to make his
efforts wasted by calling him a liar? What sort of gratitude is that?"

"But this story isn't true!"

"It's all he could think of to help you. Let him do it,
Meg."

"Do people really believe that nothing happened between us?"

"Some do, some don't. But even the ones who don't
are impressed that Luke would go to such lengths to save

your reputation. They're willing to let the whole thing ride.''

"Didi, I don't know what to say.''

"Don't say anything. Don't blow this, gal. Think of the future. Do you honestly believe that your sneaking over to the San Marcos that night is a big enough deal that it should stand in the way of your whole political career?''

"I guess not.''

Didi snatched her newspaper back. "Then don't let it. Time to get back to the meeting, Madam President.''

Meg followed her in a daze. True to his word, Luke had saved her. And he knew her so well that he hadn't told her his plan. He knew she would have vetoed it.

As she sat through the rest of the meeting, Meg slowly realized the enormity of what Luke had done for her. He'd sacrificed his pride. All his life he'd guarded that pride and now he'd made himself the laughingstock of the entertainment world for her. She pictured the taunts and ribbing he'd get, the comments on talk shows, the sly innuendos that Luke on screen was a far cry from Luke in person.

Even if she denied his story, she probably wouldn't be believed. His was the more believable, because it was the most outrageous. Men bragged about their conquests, not their failures. Most men. But not Luke. Not the man she loved.

After the meeting she drove to a convenience store and bought the tabloid. She didn't think her mother or father had seen it yet. They'd indicated the night before that they wouldn't dirty their hands on it, nor would they discuss the story with anyone who called. They'd be as ignorant as she had been.

Her mother was on her hands and knees in the flower garden when Meg arrived. Meg tossed the paper onto the ground next to her. Nora Hennessy stared at the large headline in silence. Then she shielded her eyes and glanced up at her daughter. "What does this mean?"

"Luke lied to save me."

Her mother picked up the paper and scrambled to her feet. Then she hurried into the kitchen to find her reading glasses. It was the first time Meg ever remembered her mother walking in from the garden without brushing off her slacks or wiping her feet. Meg followed her into the kitchen and leaned against the counter while her mother read the article, and then reread it.

At last she put the paper down on the table and took off her glasses. "So what happened at the meeting?"

"They voted me in as president."

"Did you tell them this article is wrong?"

Meg gazed at her mother. "No."

"Thank the Lord." Her mother walked over and gave Meg a hug. "You are so honest that sometimes it's ridiculous. I was afraid you'd throw what Luke did for you back in his face."

"I almost did. Didi talked me out of it."

"Let me call your father. He's out on the tractor, but he has that new cellular phone I got him for Christmas." Meg waited while she relayed the news. Her mother turned off the phone and pushed down the antenna. "He says to tell you that's wonderful, and he's so glad you showed some good sense in not spilling all the beans."

"Now I have to go find Clint." Meg picked up the paper. "He invited me over for a beer after the meeting to drown my sorrows, so I don't think he knew about this, either."

"Before you go, I have something to say." Meg paused in the door. "Once I warned you to keep straight what was fantasy and what was reality." Her mother took a deep breath. "The truth is, I don't have a lot of experience with men. Your father's been about it. I didn't realize before that some men...can make fantasies come true."

Meg swallowed the lump in her throat. "Yes, Mom, they sure can."

WHEN SHE WAS WITHIN a hundred yards of the Bannister drive, Meg noticed the rental sedan parked next to Clint's red truck. Probably just a friend, she thought, trying to stay calm. Luke wouldn't have time to flit over to Chandler today.

Still, when she parked her car behind the sedan, her heart was hammering louder than the woodpecker banging away on one of the nearby tamarisk trees. The afternoon was warm, so she left the jacket of her green suit in the car. She picked up the paper and walked around to the kitchen door, her heels crunching in the newly spread gravel. The weeds were gone.

She heard their voices through the screen door. He was here. The man she wanted to spend her life with. The man she couldn't have. She had to be upbeat, send him back to L.A. with her gratitude, but send him back, nonetheless. Perhaps they'd meet again, perhaps not. She had to accept that. She had to be strong.

The back steps smelled of new lumber and paint. She knocked on the door. Clint appeared on the other side holding a soft drink. "Took you long enough." He glanced over his shoulder. "When did you say that meeting was over? An hour ago?"

Luke's voice carried outside. "Something like that. I had enough time to get back here and shower off all the grass clippings. Lord knows what she's been doing."

Meg pushed through the door and stared at Luke sitting at the kitchen table dressed in an old T-shirt and faded jeans, with a can of cola in front of him. "You were the gardener?"

"And it's a good thing, too. I glanced through the door once and you were staring off into space just when they were about to vote on you. I started up the lawn mower, just to wake you up."

"I can't believe it. You listened in?"

"Yep." He sipped his drink. "I was driving around the restaurant wondering how to spy on the meeting, when I saw these two guys working on the landscaping. I slipped them a twenty and borrowed their equipment for an hour. That was long enough for me to hear you get elected." He paused. "Congratulations."

"But...but don't you have to be on the set or something?"

Luke nodded. "First thing in the morning. I begged and pleaded for the day off, and the director took pity on me. Tomorrow it's back to the salt mines."

Meg glanced at Clint and then down at the paper in her hand. "So I guess you know about this."

Clint nodded. "I do now. I didn't until this morning. I tried to call you, but no one answered."

"I unplugged the phone." She returned her attention to Luke and held up the paper. "You know I almost contradicted this at the meeting."

"I figured you might. It was worth the risk."

"Luke, you allowed everyone to think you're some sort of lecherous guy, and a dud in bed, too!"

He grinned. "Nobody's perfect."

"You shouldn't have done that, you big, crazy, foolish, lovable—"

Clint put a hand on her shoulder. "It's been a blast, but I'm outta here. The south forty needs plowing, or something. Don't expect to see me for at least three hours."

Meg turned her head in time to catch Clint's wink as he went out the kitchen door. She glanced at Luke. "I owe you a lot."

He pushed away from the table and stood. "I was hoping you'd feel that way. Real grateful."

"I am grateful."

He approached her slowly and took the paper from her hand. "Grateful women usually agree to all kinds of things."

"Anything you want."

His blue eyes sparkled as he drew her close. "This is starting to sound like one of my soap-opera scenes. Are you sure you mean 'anything'?"

"Yes." She didn't think he'd ask her to, but she would resign her office if necessary, follow him around the world, and take whatever moments of passion he had to give.

"Marry me."

"What?" She blinked in surprise. He *had* asked her to give up everything for him!

He caressed the small of her back. "Come on. You said 'anything.'"

She swallowed. Of course she wanted to marry him, no matter what the cost. "I'll tell them tomorrow that I can't serve. I'm sure there's plenty of time to—"

"Wait a minute. Who's talking about that?"

"But I can't be president of the chamber and live in L.A."

"I don't expect you to live in L.A."

"But—"

"Listen to me." He combed her hair back with his fingers. "You said once that two intelligent people should be able to work this out. I think we can. I've learned that making feature films is a lot different from the soaps. I earn more money. I can have more time off between movies. And sometimes I'll be working nearby. They're shooting part of *The Unvanquished* on location in Tubac. That's less than a three-hour drive from here."

She gazed up at him, hardly daring to believe what he was suggesting.

"And another thing. We didn't want people thinking we were shacking up during the festival, but if we got married, I can't imagine it would hurt you politically. Especially now that everyone thinks I'm a dud in the bedroom."

She laughed, unable to contain the joy bursting within her. "And I don't intend to change anybody's mind, either."

He leaned down and nipped at her earlobe. "Oh, yeah? I thought you were the one who couldn't keep secrets?"

She wrapped her arms around his neck and settled her body against his. "I'm learning that a few well-kept secrets are part of surviving in this world. I'm the only one who needs to know what a sexy guy you really are."

"What timing I have." He cupped her behind and urged her closer. "Just when you're capable of handling a secret affair, I propose marriage."

"Want to take it back?"

He tensed. "Come to think of it, you haven't officially said yes."

She savored the moment, knowing she'd remember it for the rest of her life. "Yes."

His sigh of relief was warm against her neck. He leaned back to gaze into her eyes, and his own were moist. "It'll be a crazy life."

She reached up and cradled his face in her hands. "I'm counting on that. Kiss me, loverboy."

And just like in the movies, he did.

THE KEEPER
by Margot Early

The Keeper originally appeared as a
Harlequin Superromance® novel.
Four new provocative, involving stories that
celebrate life and love appear each month in the
Superromance® series.

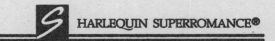 HARLEQUIN SUPERROMANCE®

CHAPTER ONE

Moab, Utah
Suddenly last winter
Separated…

HER FATHER WAS DEAD, her marriage was over, and she'd left a career she loved for *this?* Standing in gravel and sand just yards from the red-brown flow of the Colorado River, Grace Sutter clutched a bottle of Drambuie and gazed, stupefied, at the sign.

It read:

RAPID RIGG RS RIVER AND JEEP EXPE ITIONS
EXCITI G WHITE WATER RAFTIN .
SCEN C 4WD TOURS.

Watching the "T" in "EXPEDITIONS" rock back and forth on a single nail as though ready to cartwheel away in the blowing dust, Grace tried to suppress the disloyal thoughts penetrating her grief. She could not. Who would venture into the wilderness with an outfit that couldn't maintain even a billboard, let alone serviceable rafts and vehicles?

Beside her, Day was balancing on a patch of gravel in a pair of white high-heeled sandals, lighting a cigarette. Grace asked her, "Would it have been too much trouble to fix the sign?"

Day drew on her cigarette, expelled the smoke and tossed fluffy flaxen bangs out of her eyes. Gesturing at her aqua mohair dress and black tights, she answered, "Do I look like a woman who repairs billboards?"

Grace eyed her sister. Day was twenty-five, only ten months younger than Grace. For the past decade Day had worked nearly full-time as girl Friday of the Rapid Riggers outfit, but she would never look like a woman who fixed billboards. At the moment she didn't look like someone who had just come from a funeral, either, but neither did Grace. Anyhow, she loved Day, and right now she needed her.

Still, she couldn't help murmuring, "You look like a woman who could persuade one of the boatmen to fix a billboard." Grace lifted the bottle of Drambuie to her lips and took a drink, liking the smooth heat, not wanting to quit. She hurt like hell—and not just about her father.

God, make it stop, she thought. Make it stop.

Day glanced at her, and the cigarette floated to her mouth again. Stepping away from Grace to exhale the smoke, she answered, "Persuading boatmen is one thing. Persuading Dad to cough up money for paint or even a rusty nail is another." She paused. "Was another."

Grace nearly snapped back that Day could have taken some initiative, that *she* would have done something. This place mattered to her. The Sutters had been in Moab since the turn of the century, and Rapid Riggers was the oldest river outfit in town. Her great-grandfather had built the old River Inn, seven miles downstream, back when dreamers were running riverboats with paddle wheels on the Colorado and the Green, fighting sandbars and shallow water at every bend.

But Grace said nothing. After all, she could have stayed in Moab and helped her father. Before she'd gone to New York to become a chef, she'd been one of his best river and Jeep guides—and more. He'd treated her as both partner and apprentice.... But she'd left. And now Rapid Riggers was in the red, and the Sutter properties, which had once dotted both sides of the river, had winnowed to two parcels. Grace and Day stood on one— the river outfit on the north bank, just below the Moab Bridge, at a place where the fault severing the river gorge had created the expanse of the Moab Valley. The other was their father's house, which had once been the River Inn. Grace knew the inn would become her refuge now. Home.

She frowned, disentangling a wisp of light brown hair from one of the three earrings in her left ear. Her short French braid was coming loose, and though it was February, she felt hot and dusty in the fitted denim dress and cowboy boots she'd worn to the funeral. At the moment she wasn't going to climb up onto any billboards, either.

She took another drink, and her gaze panned the surrounding area. Across the highway to the north lay Courthouse Wash and the boundary of Arches National Park, where rocks rose in strange and myriad formations, their colors ranging from beige to deepest burgundy and black. To the east were the high walls of the river gorge upstream of the Moab Bridge. The Colorado swept beneath the bridge, broadening as it flowed past Rapid Riggers. There were no rapids here, and the flow meandered first to the west, then back to the east, disappearing in a forest of salt cedar and tamarisk. Come spring, the tamarisk would be a mosquito haven. Now dead branches folded into the river's current, catching other debris flowing seaward toward the portal, where the gorge began again. Beyond lay miles of wilderness—an undammed river.

Seeing it all, Grace knew she was home and she was glad, but also chagrined. When she'd left for New York, reaction in Moab had been mixed. Some thought that any river-running daughter of Sam Sutter's could show New York a thing or two. Others thought that city people were untrustworthy and Grace Sutter would find out.

Grace had.

So why this sense of deprivation? She longed to be back on that lumpy futon with Zac. How could she still want him so much?

With no answer, Grace focused on her new existence—Rapid Riggers. Glancing around the gravel-and-dirt lot beside the office, she noted that the sign wasn't the only aesthetic problem. Trailworn Chevy Suburbans—two with the hoods lifted—sat beside the office. The logos had worn off the doors and their bright blue paint had faded to a dull gray.

Studiously ignoring another vehicle in the lot—the U-Haul—Grace thought of the events that had brought her home.

Her father's heart attack had come on Valentine's Day, and her sister had called her, worried. Sam Sutter needed surgery, but Day was afraid he wouldn't slow down afterward. Rapid Riggers was in trouble. Their best guide was on an expedition in South America, and… Grace had wanted to come home. Who else would cook nutritious meals for the crusty outfitter? Or take care of the defunct River Inn, which Day had forsaken years ago in favor of a home of her own in town? But Grace's place was in New York....

Not anymore.

She took another drink.

"You're going to get sick," said Day.

Day was a lightweight. Grace was a river guide. Grace said, "Good. If you'd been through what I have, you'd want to throw up, too."

From the corner of her eye, she saw Day stare thoughtfully at the U-Haul. They'd never had secrets between them. Even when Grace was in New York and Day in Moab, they'd remained close. Bad moments could be erased with a phone call from city to desert town. Instant laughter, instant love.

But she hadn't told Day everything this time, and now Day gave her a look that meant, *Since you brought it up...* "So what's going on with your husband?" She gestured at the U-Haul. "You've brought more than a suitcase."

Grace had brought everything. What was "going on" should be obvious. But Day, always fascinated by human drama, would want the blow-by-blow, the way Grace always wanted every detail of a recipe.

Okay, thought Grace. *How to make a Zachary Key. Take one seven-year-old younger son of a peer, dress him in an uncomfortable uniform and send him away to school to learn to be a perfect English gentleman. Then...*

She tried out the words. "Zachary married me for a green card."

Day made a choking sound.

A burst of wind lifted dust from the other side of the

road and from the ground beneath them and swirled it up through the air. Both women turned their backs to the devil and started up the bank toward the two-story gray building that housed the Rapid Riggers office. As Day's sandals navigated a maze of yellow-blossomed goatheads growing among the gravel, she said, "Isn't that, like, against the law?"

Grace rolled her eyes. She capped the Drambuie and tightened the lid. Despite what she'd told Day, she didn't want to be sick. She said, "Well, in any case, it's a slimy thing to do to one's lover."

For a moment she saw Zac sitting on the bed that last day—Valentine's Day. They'd both been naked, because they'd been making love when Day called. It had made it so much worse somehow—their first fight right there on the sacred space of their bed. Zac had grabbed her by the shoulders...

Don't do this, Grace. I need that green card.

Green card.

It just slipped out, didn't it, Zac?

After four months of marriage.

Closing her mind to the rest of the argument—the careening emotions, everything—Grace climbed the steps and paused on the porch. She told Day, "You cannot imagine how it feels to know that a person I loved used me that way. Zachary asked me to marry him *the same day* he got a part in an off-Broadway play. He never mentioned that he needed equity and a green card. And I didn't think twice when on the day we were married—on the way home from the courthouse, no less— he wanted to stop at the INS office."

"INS?"

"The Immigration and Naturalization Service. You

don't want to meet these people. Zac had to take a medical exam where they checked for everything from tuberculosis to insanity. Then we had this interview that was like a cross between "The Newlywed Game" and a Senate investigation hearing. They put us in separate rooms and asked us incredibly personal questions. 'What side of the bed does your husband sleep on?' 'What color is his toothbrush?' 'Does he wear boxer or jockey shorts?'"

Day blinked. "Which does he wear?" As Grace unscrewed the lid of the bottle again, she said, "Sorry. Just kidding."

Both sisters were silent while the wind beat at the international flags flying along the porch eaves.

At last Day said, "Well, no one could blame *you*. I mean, you sent me a picture. The guy's sexy."

Grace thought it was kind of her sister not to mention the words "whirlwind courtship." But Zac *was* sexy. Skin the color of honey, and beautiful lips and jaw and chin and the straight aristocratic nose that wasn't quite aquiline. Painfully Grace remembered her lover's body. Zac's washboard-hard abs and pecs and the swell of sinew in his thighs and calves—and her legs tangled with his. He'd been a rower at Eton and at Oxford....

Lost in thought, Grace remembered the intimacy of daily routine. Mornings they'd gone running together in the East Village before that world recovered from its nightly bacchanal. Zac loping ahead of her beside the river, then circling back to be with her, urging her on to their destination, the Brooklyn Bridge. On the way home, they'd always stopped for cappuccinos to go at a coffeehouse on Avenue B. From there it was five blocks to the turn-of-the-century hotel-gone-apartment building whose lobby smelled like cabbage. They would climb the four flights of stairs to their studio, strip off their clothes, and make love under the spray of the shower.

Grace shut her eyes as another gust of wind came, spreading red sand through the air, scattering it against her body and the never-clean windows of the river office.

Day said, "Grace, are you sure it was just the green card? I mean, I talked to him on the phone. He was so sweet and cute about that wedding gift I sent you."

The red leather teddy with peekaboo cups. He'd been sweet and cute, all right. A hundred and eighty-five pounds of excited male.

Day said, "I think he loves you, Grace."

Once Grace had thought so, too. Now one suspicion bedeviled her, and the green-card revelation told her she was right. Zac had been acting.

The possibility appalled her, but she knew he possessed the skill. On stage he had a cool riveting presence noticed by all the critics who'd seen him in *Leaving Hong Kong*. That play. The play that meant enough to lie for.

"He loves his career, Day. He's only twenty-six, but you can tell he's going to *be* someone. Nothing matters more to him."

But as she spoke, a wave of homesickness rushed over her, and she thought not of Zac the actor, the Zac who was so very good and got a wild look in his eye at the thought of being deported and losing this role. Instead, she thought of Zac in waiter's black and white at Jean-Michel's, slipping her notes between orders. Zac beside her on the subway and walking her home from the First Avenue station—past darkened doors of clubs that wouldn't open till three, past people shooting up on the sidewalks, past the homeless and the strange and the scary. They'd fallen in love hard, Grace had thought. Discovering each other, unable to get enough of each other. Together every minute. Zac had made the squalor and crime fade away. He'd introduced her to opera and to smoky jazz clubs and to Greek plays that made her soul ache, and he'd brought her not flowers but wheels of fine cheese and specialized cooking utensils, a chef's dream. In their walk-up, he'd dispatched colonies of cockroaches, replaced old baseboards, painted, constantly fixed things to make it better—for her. He'd unearthed the old hardwood floor so that they could dance in their bare feet to scratchy music from the ghetto blaster, Ella Fitzgerald crooning their song, George and Ira Gershwin's "Love Is Here to Stay." He'd risked eviction over a stray cat.

He was easy to love.

When Grace had told him about her family's tradition of making "coupons" for gifts, Zac had seized the idea and taken it to new heights, creating beautiful, elaborate IOUs that could be redeemed for housework or breakfast in bed or...anything. Grace still had three she hadn't used. With Zac, she'd seldom had to ask for what she wanted.

On his nights off, he'd ridden the subway to Tribeca to meet her when she got off work. In faded Levi's and patterned thrift-shop shirts no one else could wear so well, he was no longer the immaculate waiter with the Oxford polish but just her lover—comfortable and familiar. When she came outside he was always there, and he hugged her tight under the streetlights, hugged her until they were both desperate to be home in bed....

For a moment, remembering, Grace imagined he *must*

be missing her, needing her. But she knew she was drunk.

She told Day, "He won't return my calls. I've left about six messages on his machine." *Their* machine. "He doesn't even know about Dad. What am I supposed to do? Tell the answering machine my father died in surgery?"

Day looked at her thoughtfully. "If you do, he might call you back."

New York

WHEN THE PHONE RANG it sounded inordinately loud, and Zachary jumped as though someone had slammed a door. He stared at it for a long time. It was a red rotary instrument. Grace had called it the Bat Phone.

He waited for it to ring again, and after what seemed like a long time it did. He watched it some more. The click of the answering machine was like a gunshot in his ears, and he could hear the tape revolving on its spindles as his own voice boomed into the room. "You have reached the Key residence. Please leave a message."

The beep sounded more like a screech. Fingernails on a chalkboard.

"Zac, this is Grace. I guess you're not there.... Look, I apologize for leaving this kind of message, but you haven't returned my calls, and I want you to know— I've wanted to tell you in person...my dad died after his surgery. There were complications.... I want you to call me. Please." The sudden disconnection was harsh, amplified.

Swallowing hard, Zac stood in the middle of the room

as he had for a long time. Had Grace spoken to him? Had the phone rung?

My dad died...

Had he imagined that? He stared at the blinking light on the answering machine. It seemed profound, a symbol of something he couldn't grasp. A message? The fan whirred in the window, and he heard it as he heard all the other sounds on the street. Sounds had never been so keen before.

Keen. Keening.

The words popped into his mind, uninvited and disconnected. They echoed. Keen. Keening. Keen. Keening.

He turned his head and looked at the picture on the milk crate beside the bed—the nightstand. The photo was of the two of them, a snapshot taken outside the courthouse the day they were married.

Zac tried to focus on her features, tried to see her mouth, tried to think what it was about her mouth that had been interesting to him, that he had always liked. But he couldn't concentrate on anything smaller than her whole image. A tall pretty stranger with mouse-colored hair and black eyebrows. *Hot,* he thought. In the photo, tights covered her long legs, but for a moment he remembered a bare thigh against his lips and his face.

Then the feeling and the flash of emotion went away.

He looked at the man in the picture. It was him, kissing her cheek, but he thought, *Is that me?* The photograph seemed fluid, as though the surface was liquid, a subtly moving liquid that made edges sharp. Alive.

Why was everything so noisy?

The noise made it hard to think, except for one clear wish. *Grace, come back.*

He almost reached for the phone. Had it rung? If he knew, then he could call her.

My dad died...

The sounds assaulted him, a cacophony. The fan, the cars, a child crying in number four, the refrigerator humming. Why had he never noticed that the electricity in the building was so loud? He could hear the bulbs in the light fixtures.

He remembered that he had a performance that night, but then the thought slipped away. It didn't seem important. There was something else important to do. Something he had to do. Something monumental.

He didn't know what it was.

He felt disoriented, frightened, confused. Everything had changed without Grace. Everything had new significance.

Everything seemed so...strange.

GRACE SET DOWN the phone, uncapped the Drambuie and wondered why her heart was pounding. *Because you're in love with him, stupid.* At least for four months you thought you were.

But her heart wasn't pounding the same way it did when she saw him or when she actually heard his voice, really him and not the machine. This was a different kind of pounding, almost as though she was afraid for him, which was ridiculous.

Afraid he'd be mugged or shot or...

Grace lifted the bottle from the reception desk and took a drink, thinking. Her address book was in the U-Haul. She could call a neighbor. *Excuse me, have you seen my husband lately?*

The plan was humiliating but sensible. What if something *had* happened to Zac?

Something *should* happen to him, she thought with a touch of venom.

The worst would not be learning Zac had been knifed in the subway or struck by a taxi. What she dreaded more was hearing that he'd been coming and going as usual—and ignoring her calls.

Why didn't he call her back? Was he hurt because she'd left? Did he really love her?

Had she made a terrible mistake?

At her elbow, the phone jangled, startling her. Grace blinked at it, then, barely breathing, lifted the receiver. "Rapid Riggers River and Jeep Expeditions. This is Grace."

There was a long pause.

Zac said, "Hi. It's me."

Grace shook. "Zachary."

The cultured English voice she loved said, "I'm sorry about your father, Grace."

She waited for him to say more—that it was a pity he'd never had a chance to meet Sam Sutter. But he was quiet.

At last she said, "Thanks. It was horrible, finding out." She brushed her hand across her eyes. Dammit, she was crying. She didn't want to start now, when he was on the phone and she was drunk. Things would get out of control in a hurry. She screwed the lid on the bottle.

The pause seemed endless, and Grace wondered what he was doing, what he was thinking. About her father's death? Or about her? Should she try to bridge the gap between them? No. Zac was the only one who could do that. He could say, *I fell in love with you. I wasn't even thinking about a green card when I met you.* He could say, *It was you I wanted.*

Instead, he said, "Do you hear that?"

"What?"

"That noise on the line—in the background. It's very loud."

"I don't hear anything," said Grace.

He made a noncommittal sound. Then in a rush he said, "Everything seems so different with you gone. It's all more *intense*. Even the textures. Every sound is sharper. Every color is brighter. Like Wordsworth's Margaret— '...I dread the rustling of the grass; The very shadows of the clouds have power to shake me as they pass....' I never liked Wordsworth." He stopped. "I wish you were here, Grace, so I could make love to you and feel what *that's* like now that everything's changed."

Grace's brow furrowed, and she clutched the phone more tightly. "What do you mean? What's changed?"

He said nothing for a moment, as though registering her words, as though pondering them. Finally he said, "I just miss you. Grace, have you ever thought this phone might be tapped?"

Grace lifted her hand to her forehead, taking a small breath. *All he can think of is the INS!* She said, "I don't believe this. My father just died, and you're worried the immigration authorities have tapped the phone."

He said, "Don't yell."

"I'm not yelling." She wasn't.

"I find you deafening. Maybe it's the phone. Look— I'd like to come and see you if I can find a way."

Zachary? Miss a performance? Grace tried not to be

cynical. "I'd like that." Together. Being held. Zac in her bed. Zac, with her.

"Good. We'll talk later. I love you."

He hung up, and Grace slowly lowered the receiver, wondering if he would really come, feeling how badly she wanted him, whispering his name in her mind. *Zac,* she thought, *don't break my heart.*

But for a time she stood at the counter, frowning, thinking how odd he'd sounded. Idly she wondered who Wordsworth's Margaret was.

ZAC UNPLUGGED the answering machine and waited alone in the apartment until dusk. Several times the phone rang, but he never answered it. Once, someone knocked on the door.

At seven he went out into the hall, leaving the door unlocked and his key behind, and walked down the four flights of stairs to the funky lobby that might have been elegant in another era. Then he slipped outside onto Avenue B.

He was assaulted by sound and sight. He squinted to block out the neon light from the gay bar across the street, and he almost put his hands over his ears to quiet the sounds of passing cars, their tires spinning through the residual slush left over from an early-spring snow. He had no reason to be outside, just a longing to be somewhere besides the apartment. Though he'd brought no coat and his breath rose in steam puffs from his nose and mouth, he didn't feel the cold.

Hours passed like minutes as he walked down toward Fourteenth Street, making his way through the Avenues—D and E, F and G. The area became increasingly seedy as he moved farther east, yet he felt invincible.

People tried to sell him crack, men offered him money for sex, and he ignored them. When someone stood in his path with a knife, he said, "Leave me alone," and the body moved. Clearly his power was more than physical, more than human.

He was chosen.

He was special.

Nothing could hurt him at all.

CHAPTER TWO

Moab, Utah
Fourteen months later
Reunited....

THE DAY the Ben Rogan jeans "I like to be close to my clothes" advertisements appeared, they were banned in Salt Lake City, in Phoenix and in Raleigh, North Carolina. In other cities where the brouhaha made the news, magazines flew off the stands, and women gaped at their television screens, asking, "Who is that *guy?*"

One woman who could have answered the question had never seen the ads, though she'd heard about the censorship. She gave it little thought. She was too busy running her deceased father's river outfit—and trying to find the husband who had vanished from her life after one strange phone call more than a year before....

AT FIVE O'CLOCK on the day Zachary reappeared in her life, Grace stood in the kitchen of the Rapid Riggers office, her hands caked with grease from changing the oil in Suburban number two. Through the dirty kitchen window, she could see three first-year boatmen, fresh off the river, engaged in a water fight. Hoses, buckets and the mud rapidly accumulating in the yard were all employed in the fray, and as a sloshing bucket of muddy water hit the window, Grace thought, *That's enough!*

She grabbed two paper towels in each grimy hand and used them to protect the frame as she unlatched the window and raised the sash. Seeing a boatman douse a nubile female guide with two gallons of filthy water, Grace yelled out the window, "You're making a mess! Cool it."

She slammed the window as a pair of high heels clicked on the linoleum behind her. Grace spun to see Day peering past her shoulder out the wet window. In a broomstick skirt and appliquéd vest, she looked as fresh and beautiful as she had that morning, and there was a copy of *W* under her arm. She said, "Lighten up on the boatmen, Grace. They're paid by the day, and they put in a long one. It's April. They've just got spring fever."

Grace used the two paper towels to wipe ineffectually at the grease on her hands, and Day helpfully snatched a bottle of heavy-duty liquid soap from the windowsill and squirted it on her sister's palms. Then she turned on the sink water.

Grace said, "Thank you." Day was right about the boatmen. Nonetheless, as she soaped her hands at the sink, Grace looked over her shoulder to say, "Well, if they have so much energy, one of them can wash the windows in this place tomorrow." As she spoke, she saw her sister's mouth tighten. Wheeling from the sink, she demanded, "Well, what's wrong with that?"

Day's blue eyes were sympathetic, and that alone sent the emotion crawling up Grace's throat. She didn't want sympathy. She just wanted— She didn't know what she wanted.

Day said, "Grace, this is a happy place. It has to be.

We're serving the public, and we've got to be cheerful to make them feel good.''

"I'm cheerful," Grace said. "As cheerful as I can be when my partner's been gone all afternoon working on the spring musical while I've been changing oil in two vehicles, painting a raft and waiting for that sinfully overpaid Nick Colter to get his handsome rear end back from Cataract Canyon. Where is he?''

Day restrained a sigh. "He's not that late, Grace. Anyhow, I just passed him downtown. He had a flat tire on the way back from Hite Marina, and now he's dropping two passengers at their hotels. As for his salary, you and I both agreed it was worth it to hang on to him. He's our best guide, and he doesn't need this job. He does it because he likes it. He's got money in the bank, and if we don't watch it, someday he'll walk out of here and start a river outfit of his own.''

"Good riddance," Grace murmured, not meaning it. They couldn't get along without Nick.

Day said, "And I'm sorry about the rehearsal. They're usually at night. How about cutting everyone some slack, Grace? Ever since you've come back from New York, you've been a full-time killjoy.''

It was more than Grace could stand. She snatched at the roll of paper towels and pulled it off the holder. Catching it as it threatened to tumble to the floor, she exclaimed, "You mean, ever since I've been in business with you?''

"I mean, ever since you left that jerk who hurt you!''

Grace gasped, and the paper towels slipped from her hands and rolled across the floor, unraveling sheet after sheet as she clutched the end tightly in her fingers. It came out then, though she'd intended to keep it a secret until it was over. "I'm getting a divorce."

Day's face changed. She stared for a moment, and then she said, "Oh, Grace, why didn't you say something?" She grabbed her, and Grace was enfolded in the only embrace she knew these days, the comforting arms of her sister.

Her brow creased in deep lines as W dug into her back. Remembering her greasy hands, she pulled away. "I'm sorry." She retrieved the paper towels, then pulled several off the roll to dab at the spots on her sister's vest. "It's just water, I think." She couldn't meet Day's eyes. "You're a great business partner and a great sister. I didn't mean anything."

"Maybe you meant you'd rather be a chef," said Day comfortingly. She changed the subject. "Since you brought up the unmentionable, I have some news. Maybe you already know. Guess who likes to be 'close to his clothes'?"

Close to his clothes? Grace recognized the infamous slogan for Ben Rogan jeans only because the designer's racy advertisements had recently been banned in Salt Lake. But before she could make sense of Day's words, a horn sounded outside the office, and a blue Suburban hauling a twenty-foot raft pulled around the side of the building and into the yard.

Grace glanced at the clock. "That's Nick."

The river guide was hours late returning from the outfit's first white-water trip of the season, a four-day float down Cataract Canyon. Even though she'd grown up in the business and was an experienced guide herself, Grace had imagined the worst. A flip in Satan's Gut, a boat wrapped on a rock or the most serious—orange life vests laid out in a giant X on the beach, signaling air traffic to send a chopper with a medical team.

Day was right. She needed to get used to things not running like clockwork. This was a wilderness-tour outfit, not a restaurant kitchen.

Day said, "Anyhow, about Zachary—"

"I don't want to talk about him." The last thing Grace wanted now was to entertain questions about her missing husband. They plagued her without Day's help, but she tried not to brood about Zac while she was at the office. A Colorado River outfitter couldn't afford to be that preoccupied.

Hearing tramping feet on the scarred wood floor of the reception area, Grace hurried out of the kitchen, following the sound. In the front office, Nick Colter—shirtless, suntanned and silty from four days on the Colorado—was accepting tips from three dirty passengers who told Grace how much they'd enjoyed the trip. Grace returned the pleasantries, but as she helped them separate their belongings from the Rapid Riggers sleeping bags and tents, her mind was on the river.

Two weeks earlier the snowmelt had begun to trickle down from the mountains and into the Colorado River. Precipitation in the eastern Rockies had been high that winter, and throughout Moab river guides were rubbing their palms in anticipation of big rapids.

Like them, Grace knew the thrill of navigating massive waves and guiding rafts around treacherous "keeper" holes, whose hydraulic turbulence could capture boats and bodies alike, sucking them under the surface and churning them like the agitation cycle on a washing machine. But she also knew what high water meant to a river outfit—danger, bad press and canceled trips. Each day as she drove along the Colorado from her home at the old River Inn to the Rapid Riggers office, Grace watched the swelling river with apprehension. Fortunately, both buildings were on rises of land high up the banks. Neither had ever flooded. That left only the white water to worry about.

When the passengers were gone, she asked Nick, "How's Cataract?"

Long black hair swinging below his shoulders, Nick made a face of mock terror, then sobered. Unlike the outfit's less experienced boatmen, he understood the impact of water level on business. "The waves were bigger than the boat. There's a mammoth whirlpool in Capsize and a boat-eating keeper in Satan's Gut. And I think we can look forward to, what, four more weeks of runoff?"

In other words, the rapids were big—and getting bigger. Grace tossed the sleeping bags in a corner to be taken to the cleaners and began pulling tents from their stuff sacks to check and repack them for the next trip. "How are we going to manage that movie?"

Since the days of John Wayne, the red rocks of Moab had attracted filmmakers hunting for showy scenery. Grace had been thrilled when Rapid Riggers landed a contract to provide technical support on *Kah-Puh-Rats*, a feature film about the nineteenth-century exploration of the Colorado River by Major John Wesley Powell. But could she ask her boatmen to guide historically accurate wooden dories through Cataract in extreme high water?

Nick grinned. "Don't worry, Grace. Rapid Riggers has the best. *Me*." He blew a kiss to each sister as he disappeared into the kitchen with a cooler.

Day rolled her eyes. "Let's just hope we don't have

to cancel on the movie. Saga Entertainment is big time. And speaking of big time..." With the air of a woman who would not be pushed aside again, she turned to her sister and proffered a tabloid-size ad supplement from her copy of *W*. "Have you seen this?"

Grace abandoned the tents and came over to look at the insert. On the cover was a black-and-white ad for Ben Rogan jeans. At least, judging from the words on the ad—"I like to be close to my clothes"—Grace assumed it was for the jeans. But the model wasn't really *wearing* them.

His body had more ripples than a rapid, each as familiar as a river she'd run a hundred times. But what got to her were his hands—though only one, his left, showed in the photo. A long-fingered, strong, masculine hand—hanging on to those jeans that were sliding either up or down his thighs, it wasn't clear which. She would know his hands anywhere.

Drawing her eyes away from his fingers, Grace stared at the long dark hair pushed off his forehead. As always, a stray lock angled forward toward one corner of that generous, sensuous mouth. Her eyes froze on those of the model, and she wavered on her feet. *Zac*. She had found him. "I've got to call my lawyer." Moving toward the phone, only half-aware she was shaking, she told Day, "I haven't been able to trace him. We haven't been able to serve him—"

Trailing after her, Day said, "Boy, you really meant it when you said you were getting a divorce. I didn't realize you'd actually filed."

Grace couldn't look at his picture again. *He was fine*. Dammit, he was okay. "Do you think I want to spend the rest of my life married to an illegal alien who doesn't call, write or answer the phone? Especially when we don't even live together?''

Day studied the ad at arm's length, as though considering.

Rolling her eyes, Grace moved toward the telephone, just as it rang. She lifted the receiver. ''Rapid Riggers River and Jeep Expeditions. Grace speaking.''

It was her lawyer, and the conversation was short. He, too, had found Zac.

And Zac had been served.

As Grace hung up the phone, the pain came. It was a surprise. She'd known this was happening; she'd set it in motion herself. But she hadn't expected it to hurt so much. Divorce. This was what it was like.

What hurt most was that Zac, alive and well in Santa Monica, had never bothered even to call or write. It was a cruel end to fourteen months of waiting. Empty nights, empty bed, aching and scared...for him. Embroidering fantasies in which he returned—with an explanation for his absence. And proof he really hadn't married her for a green card.

But prosaic life had just handed her the facts. Zac did not love her.

Grace resisted taking home the Ben Rogan ad at the end of the day, but when she reached work the next morning, after a long night, she saw it lying discarded on the couch in the inner office, and temptation was too much. She picked it up and took it to her desk.

I like to be close to my clothes.

Zac looked sexy and his half smile was inviting. His body was smooth and hard and indecent. But when all was said and done, this was an advertisement.

Grace set aside the ad, opened her center desk drawer

and wriggled her hand into the back. Her fingers touched a snapshot, and she pulled it out. Casual and handsome in a peacoat and muffler, snow floating down on his hair, Zac smiled at her from the steps of the Metropolitan Opera House. They'd just seen *Aida*. Grace had never been to the opera before, and she'd cried while Zac sat beside her with a quiet, still expression that had made her want to own his heart. That evening, they'd made love for the first time.

The photograph hurt, like the memory. She put it away.

Hearing a vehicle in the lot, Grace glanced outside to see a Federal Express van arriving. She went into the reception area and saw that Day had already come in with the package.

Reading the shipping label on the square box, Day lifted her eyebrows slightly. "It's for you."

Grace's stomach rolled with foreboding as she took the package from her sister. It was from Zachary Key, on Ocean Street in Santa Monica.

"Obviously, he's a man of action," said Day.

He'd been served only yesterday. Trembling, Grace set the box on the reception counter and opened the pocket knife on her key chain. As Day perched on a stool and watched her take a gift box from the carton, Grace's heart thudded hard. The box was wrapped in paper made from a grocery bag, on which Zac had painted peace signs and hearts and pictures of himself and her together, pictures to be explored later. Along with the card.

Day said, "It's hard to hate a man who makes his own wrapping paper."

Grace said nothing. This box was her first communication from her husband in fourteen months. Later she would explore motives. Now she just wanted to absorb what he was trying to say. Now, for one moment, she wanted to believe. Carefully she opened the paper, her eyes catching an image he'd painted of the two of them on a subway seat, hugging. Not great art, but Grace could feel that bear hug.

Lifting the lid of the plain white box, she saw an object wrapped in tissue paper and carefully pulled it out. A music box. Custom-made.

"Oh, look," said Day. "It's you two."

Indeed, the music-box figurines were Grace and Zac, dressed for their first date. Recognizing her retro mini-dress and black tights, his black shirt with large red polka dots, Grace remembered the occasion and how badly she'd wanted to go out with him, like she'd die if he didn't ask. They'd stayed out all night—dancing, talking, never running out of things to say, and they'd watched the sun rise from the roof of an old theater. Outside her apartment, they'd kissed like two people who'd been waiting their whole lives to kiss. To find each other.

The figures on top of the music box were dancing cheek to cheek against a stage set made to resemble the East Village apartment she and Zac had shared.

Day said, "Wind it up, and see what it plays."

"I know what it plays." Grace's emotions boiled in her throat, volatile, threatening to erupt. Torn between hope and distrust, she gathered up paper and card, leaving the music box where it sat. Avoiding her sister's eyes, she said, "You can wind it, if you like," and went into the inner office.

At her desk chair, she tore open the card, which

showed movie-star footprints at Mann's Chinese Theater. Inside was Zac's writing, still familiar, and Grace felt anger and pain and hope and excitement as she read.

Dear Grace,
I am coming to Moab to work on a film. Your river outfit is a technical consultant on the picture. I would like to spend time with you and discuss what happened between us. I'm sorry it's taken so long. You are never far from my mind.

Love,
Zachary

Grace was stunned. Zac was coming to Moab? He had a role in *Kah-Puh-Rats?* And he knew Rapid Riggers was involved with the filming.

She read the card twice, then pored over the wrapping paper, the pictures he'd painted. One showed her and Zachary in a dory on the river.

Zac. He was coming to see her.

Because of the movie.

Of course. Acting had always mattered more to him than she did. *As a matter of fact, Sutter,* Grace reminded herself, *it's why he married you.* And he was coming back for the same reason. To save his green card, now that a movie role was on the line. He'd sent the music box by overnight courier, undoubtedly after being served with divorce papers.

But Grace disbelieved her own explanation. The music box had been specially made. The time and care the artist had taken showed in the workmanship. This wasn't a dozen roses ordered on the spur of the moment.

You are never far from my mind.

Her hope scared her, because the pain of the night was still fresh. Raw. Grace tried to harden her heart, to be as strong and insensible as steel.

But from the reception area came the tinkling sound of the music box playing, "Love Is Here to Stay."

ZACHARY KEY stood at the window of his room in Moab's Anasazi Palace and stared out at the dusk. The gaudy new Santa Fe-style motel was one block off Main Street, close to a restaurant and a bicycle shop with an espresso stand in front. The stand was closed now, and Zac considered walking somewhere to find a cup of tea.

He'd left Santa Monica at six the night before, just hours after the process server had appeared at his door. After sending the music box, he'd packed in a hurry and gone, driving straight through, possessed. Twelve hours in darkness, then six more as the day began, the lights rising on a wonderland of rock like he'd never seen. Miles and miles of desert landscape so strange and exquisite it seemed unreal. When he'd reached the hotel, he'd fallen on the bed and slept for four hours. Now he was up, showered and shaved. Ready to see Grace.

But the urgency of his cross-country chase had died.

Zac stared bleakly at the gutter below. Letting the curtain fall against the glass, he turned from the window and his eyes caught the manila packet lying on his bed, the envelope containing the divorce papers.

A familiar fear settled upon him, and he lay down on the bed, overcome by an agony of indecision.

He shouldn't be trying to do this. He'd never even seen a doctor after that episode in New York. How could he go back to Grace not knowing what had happened or why?

But he was fine now.

Fine, and working as an actor again. Deliberately he focused on that. His career. He'd virtually destroyed it during that month after Grace left. Reflecting on the details, Zac closed his eyes. *I just lost control.* Things were hard after a breakup. Everyone knew that.

But it had taken a year to repair the damage. If Grace divorced him now, if the immigration authorities began investigating him...

He tried to think rationally. Even in the worst-case scenario, he was unlikely to lose his green card. He made too much money, paid too much tax, for anyone to want to deport him now. That wasn't why he was here. Nor was the role in *Kah-Puh-Rats*—his *only* role in more than a year—the reason he'd come.

He was here to see Grace. Grace, who thought he'd married her to legalize his resident status.

Hadn't he?

He hadn't denied it fourteen months earlier, the day her sister had called, the day she'd asked, *Is that why you married me, Zac? For a green card?*

To say no would have been at least partly a lie, and lies had a way of sticking in his throat. So he had said, *I love you.*

That's not what I asked.

If she'd believed he loved her, she hadn't cared. And now she wouldn't believe. He'd waited too long. He'd had to wait.

Zac envisioned an unpleasant scene—explaining to Grace. He wasn't ready for that. *She'd* left *him.* And even their both working on the movie was no guarantee she'd have anything to do with him. Zac held no illusions about what the music box might have accomplished. He'd had it made for love of her, but it wouldn't make her love him back.

Lying on the bed, Zac stared at the smoke alarm on the ceiling and tried to construct a plan. If only he had some leverage, some means of persuasion. A promise. A contract. A——

He sat up and grabbed his wallet from the nightstand. Flipping it open, he fished in the slot behind his driver's license.

Oh, God. There were *three* of them, scrawled on the backs of register receipts from Jean-Michel's. Not works of art like the coupon book Grace had given him on Valentine's Day, which had been full of pictures from magazines and sprinkled with glitter. Just quick coupons, dashed off generously, like kisses, one night at the restaurant when they were both so hungry for the shift to end, so hungry to be alone.

Coupons. Those promises they'd made as gifts, words on paper that meant, *I love you. Let me help you. Let me make your life better.*

Aside from their marriage, which Grace wanted to dissolve, the coupons were the closest thing to a contract Zac could wish for. With anticipation, he unfolded each slip of paper to see what she'd promised him.

1 Five-Course Dinner by Grace.
1 Anything of Zachary's Choice.

And one clearly defined sexual favor, the thought of which made him hard. Seeing that coupon, Zac thought of a half dozen like it in his sock drawer at home in

L.A. He'd never had to cash even one with Grace, nor she with him. A cynical friend had told him he should hang on to them until they'd been married longer.

Redeeming that coupon now sounded like food to a starving man, but Zac knew it wasn't the place to start—nor, speaking of starving, was asking her to cook for him.

But the other...

An *Anything* coupon.

He lay back on the bed, dizzy with relief. He had found a way.

SOAKING UP to her shoulders in lemongrass bubble bath, Grace leafed through a chef's magazine, watching for recipes that could be prepared in advance and kept chilled in ice chests to be eaten on the river. Or recipes that could be cooked in a Dutch oven or fried over an open fire. When she was attending the Culinary Institute, she'd never anticipated such uses for her skills, but since she'd returned to Rapid Riggers the outfit had become famous for its gourmet river meals.

As Grace dog-eared a page showing an unusual orzo salad and a recipe for black walnut bread, the doorbell tolled through the house. There was a clock on the edge of the sink and she squinted at it. Nine-thirty. Who could be at the door? Day sometimes dropped in late, but she never used the doorbell.

Trying not to slosh water onto the floor, Grace stood up and reached for a towel, then climbed out of the tub as the bell rang again.

She toweled herself swiftly and slipped into her brown sand-washed silk lounging pajamas. Grace had ordered them by mail the day she filed for divorce. It wasn't that she anticipated finding a lover. She still couldn't imagine even kissing anyone else after Zac. But his charade had violated her femininity, and she'd wanted it back.

She hurried downstairs and into the foyer. Filmy, slightly yellowed curtains covered the glass panes of the front door, and all that showed through was a tall, dark shape. Undoubtedly it was some boatman low on cash, asking if there were any late-scheduled trips going out the next day.

She twisted the handle and opened the door.

At the sight of the man on her screened porch, illuminated only by the dim table lamp in the foyer and the moonlight flickering on the river behind him, Grace felt the world sway. Zachary.

He said, "Hi."

Her response to the sight of him, a desire to hurl herself at him, was leashed by doubt. Zac... Here. Despite the music-box gift, she hadn't expected to see him so soon. Filming wouldn't start for two weeks, but here he was on her doorstep, ready to save...his immigration status.

Zac didn't wait for her to speak, either to ask him in or order him gone. Brushing his hand at a mosquito whining near his ear, he stepped into the foyer and asked, "Do you open your door at night to just anyone?"

His voice hit her like a fist. It was low, striking, the voice of a man who'd grown up in a manor house in Kent and been educated at one of England's oldest public schools. A voice meant to ring through a theater, to linger in people's souls after they left a performance.

Was he questioning her living alone by the river, in a

grand old house that had once been an inn? *Did she open her door at night to just anyone?*

She said, "Obviously so."

Fighting a smile, Zac shut the door behind him.

Grace backed against the arch that led into the living room. Then she turned and began snapping on lights. The living room sprang into sharp relief. The chandelier in the foyer blazed. Everything was bright.

She felt no safer. Instead, she could see him better, and that was worse. He towered over her five-foot-nine-inch frame, and old reactions shuddered through her. Here was the man who had walked beside her down so many streets. Her handsome defender. Her lover.

Grace searched for something to say. "Do you want a drink?"

Zac didn't answer at once. He was looking at her. The brown silk pajamas clung to every contour of her body. She was as hot as he remembered, with an earthy sexiness that reminded anyone who saw her that she was female. And an exterior toughness that hid a vulnerability he loved.

Her damp hair hung loose about her shoulders, its fairness a contrast to her dark lashes and flushed cheeks, and her brown eyes were serious. Seeing her mouth, Zac knew what had eluded him about it for so long. When she spoke or smiled or laughed, the left side moved more than the right. It had made him want her the first time she'd spoken to him at Jean-Michel's, before he even knew her.

As he studied her now, Grace returned his scrutiny and said, "That's an ugly shirt, but it looks good on you." It was red, with a ghastly floral print. Silk, worn with faded Levi's. *Only Zac,* she thought, glancing at his face. He must have just shaved, but she knew where his beard grew, the sexy line of mustache that looked like it belonged to a bandit chieftain, the brush of stubble on his chin and jaw. His dark hair—longer than when she'd seen it last, longer than in the ad—was damp, pushed back from his forehead and eyes, but a few strands still crept forward. Sexy. Everything about him was.

Creep, Grace thought, trying to forget the music box on her armoire upstairs, the box that had so charmed her when she heard the song—their song—and saw the figures dancing. The box she hadn't been able to keep from playing again and again. It made up for nothing.

Finally she asked again, "Would you like a drink?" When he didn't reply, she suggested, "Water? Brandy? A cup of hemlock?"

Zac's dark-lashed green eyes crinkled to crescents. "You've missed me."

Grace's mouth twitched. She'd forgotten that Zac could dish it back—and it tasted good. She had missed him.

Lost for a response, she turned and moved toward the dining room. He followed more slowly, examining her home, eyeing furniture and pictures on the wall, the black-and-white photo of her parents on the credenza. Her mother had been dead since Grace was a baby.

As she crouched beside an antique liquor cabinet and opened the doors, Zac admired the house, noting the French doors, the molding along the edges of the ceiling. Outside he'd seen the silhouettes of ornately carved balustrades rimming wide semicircular verandas, dormers with steep gables, and several chimneys stretching toward the sky. Now, as he surveyed the interior, the contrast between Grace's house and the flat on Avenue B made him ashamed. Yes, they had lived in New York, and the walk-up had been the best they could afford. But still...

He thought of Oakhurst, his family's home in Kent, which he and his brother, Pip, and his father had worked to convert to a hotel, to pay the upkeep.

Grace interrupted his reflections. "Well, if I can't talk you into Socrates' last drink, how about..." She faltered, staring at his left hand. His ring. He was wearing it. She had put hers away when she filed for divorce. A memory shot at her. *We have to go to Tiffany's, Grace. It's romantic.*

Grace peered into the liquor cabinet again, so that she wouldn't have to look at him. "Well, I have brandy."

"Thank you."

The words were laced with subtle humor, and Grace vowed to say nothing else caustic. In a battle of words, Zac could cut her to the ground if he chose, but she'd never seen his dry wit descend to sarcasm. He was too basically kind.

Grace removed the brandy bottle from the cabinet, shut the door and went into the darkened kitchen. Using only the light above the stove, she took two snifters from a cupboard and poured the brandy. She turned to offer him a glass.

Their fingers brushed as he took it, and Grace tried to avoid meeting his eyes. But then she saw there was no need; his were focused on her stove, the restaurant range she had brought with her to their apartment when she moved in with him. Zac had installed a special exhaust system to let the extreme heat escape... Uncomfortable with the recollection—not to mention the memory of their loading the stove into the U-Haul together just a few months later—she said, "Shall we go back in the other room?"

He didn't reply but followed her through the house to the brightly lit living room, where they sat at opposite ends of the velvet sleigh-back sofa.

Zac's eyes swept the room, taking in everything. The closed double doors opposite the foyer with a plaque overhead reading Princess Room; the paneled walnut bookcase; the baby grand piano; a print over the hearth—John Waterhouse's *Ophelia*. Lines of Shakespeare invited themselves into his mind: *Is't possible a young maid's wits Should be as mortal as an old man's life?* Bothered, he looked away from the picture.

The room was nice, the decor vastly different from that of their New York apartment. In fact, he didn't recognize a single piece. Had Grace put everything in storage—or sold it?

And where was the music box? Did she like it?

At last he turned to her and lifted his glass. "To potable beverages."

Grace returned the salute, telling herself he wasn't funny. He deserved to be poisoned.

They drank, and the liquor burned her mouth. It sloshed against her lips as she drew it away. She could feel his eyes on her, that steady gaze, his sable eyebrows drawn toward the bridge of his nose as he watched her.

Glancing out the translucent curtains at the river, he said, "You're isolated out here."

Was he implying that it wasn't safe? Sipping her drink, Grace remarked, "Don't start worrying now. You've been gone a year. I could be dead, and you wouldn't know."

Zac thought he would have to step outside. *I could be dead...*

He could read the questions in her eyes: What had he been doing for the past year? What had been more important than getting back to her?

He knew the answer and didn't want to explain. It wasn't just his pride, though he couldn't have faced Grace the way things were. There were other reasons. Time, for instance. Time to make sure it wouldn't happen again. And now he had money, and he was putting it away. Just in case...

Just in case it did.

He told Grace, "I'm glad you're not dead. I'd never have gotten over it."

Grace heard him soberly. Was he sincere? Once she'd discovered he'd lied to her, every action had become suspect. And Zac had never been easy to read. He didn't show his emotions like other people she knew. Granted, in bed...well, things had been intense. Good. But he'd stayed away a long time.

Grace put her glass on the table. "What do you want, Zac? The music box is lovely. Thank you for the thought." And the warning about *Kah-Puh-Rats*. The hint that he might appear at her door. "You said you want to discuss what's happened. Does that mean you have some explanation for why in fourteen months you've never tried to see me?"

Zac looked pale. Silently she begged him to speak, to say something, anything, that would make it all right. That he'd been in jail. That he'd been in an accident. That he'd been in a coma.

That he'd wanted to see her and couldn't.

But he said nothing, and at last she exclaimed, "You

know, Zachary Key, I deserve a life—not to be used by you. Has it never occurred to you that I might want to marry and have children? That I might want a real marriage?''

A real marriage?

Zac's reaction was visceral. In a breath he was back in New York City, back in time. Running beside her before dawn, stopping for coffee, getting quarters for laundry—*he* had washed the clothes and shopped for groceries and changed light bulbs and fixed things they knew the landlord never would. He remembered long subway rides to meet Grace after work, to see her home, to keep her safe, just to *be* with her. They'd kissed on the platform while they waited for the train; and when they came home to their walk-up, they'd hardly thought to close the door or lock it before they began tearing at each other's clothes. Her hands parting his fly...

He set down his glass. ''We *had* a real marriage, until you left me for your father's business.''

''I left because our marriage was a lie.''

He wanted to shake her. *''I loved you.''*

''And that's why you've called and written so faithfully?''

He tensed. Silence fell, and they both heard the rustling leaves of the cottonwood trees outside and the tick of the grandfather clock in the foyer.

Grace waited. *Please,* she thought. *Say something that will make it all right. I'll forgive you if you just have a reason.*

When she realized he had no answer, her heart fell. Sitting back from him, she said, ''Fourteen months, Zac. That's how long it's been since we spoke. When we talked on the phone after my father died, you said you might come out to see me. I would have loved that. I needed you.''

Zac listened, afraid. What she was describing was something he couldn't recall, and a familiar question needled him. *What had happened to him after Grace left?* That period of his life, a month or more, was a blur of fragmented memories, all strange. Afterward, everyone treated him differently. People said he'd done things he couldn't recall doing, things he *wouldn't* do. But his few vivid recollections also involved things he wouldn't ordinarily do.

Grace said, ''You told me we'd talk again, but you never called, and when I phoned you the machine was disconnected. You never answered my letters—''

She stopped speaking, as though recollecting something strange, and Zac thought, *What did I do?* If he was responsible for the behavior other people had ascribed to him, what might he have done to Grace? What might he have said during this phone conversation he couldn't remember?

''I even called your parents, and—'' Stopping, she reddened.

''And what?''

''A servant answered. Your father wasn't there, and your mother wouldn't talk to me.''

Zac drew a breath. He knew why his mother hadn't come to the phone, and he should explain. But how? Grace had probably never seen anyone too depressed to get out of bed.

But she was still talking. ''I've faced some facts about our so-called marriage, Zachary. A man who loves his wife does not lose touch with her for a year. He does not virtually ignore the death of her father. He doesn't marry her for a green card, and..."

Leaning forward, Zac put his hands over his face. He had done those things.

Grace exclaimed, "Stop acting! I'm a real person. I really loved you! Stop doing this to me."

Zac sat up and grasped her shoulders, feeling her slender woman's bones through the thin shirt she wore with no bra. The silk clung to his fingers, and the feel of her made his throat swell with emotion, so that he could hardly speak. "It's not an act, Grace." He caught his breath. "I was a good husband."

Grace stared at him, her eyes connecting with his. Zac's hands were warm on her shoulders. She put hers on his chest and shoved.

He moved his hands.

Grace wrapped both arms around herself. "I want you to leave."

"I'm not going anywhere. I want to hear you say it. 'Zac, you were good to me. Zac, I know you loved me.' *Say it.*"

No, thought Grace. He was pretending. Zac always said the right things—like an actor who knew his lines. "A loving husband would understand when his wife's father is ill and needs her."

"You didn't leave me for your father."

"I left because you married me for a green card."

Zac's hand slid over hers and closed around her fingers. As she shuddered under the touch she'd cried for, as both his hand and hers suddenly clung more tightly, he said, "Grace, I was twenty-six. I'd known you two months, and we'd been sleeping together for two weeks. You want me to say I would have married you even if

I hadn't needed a green card, but it's not true. I loved you. But no, I wouldn't have married you so quickly in other circumstances.'' Then, as though realizing what he'd just admitted, he dropped her hand and put his own over his face again.

Grace felt ill. ''Would you ever have married me?''

Zac jerked his head up. ''I did marry you. I loved you. I promised to spend my life with you, and you promised to spend yours with me.''

''You didn't answer my question.''

''*I don't know.* It doesn't matter, Grace. We were in love.''

''You deceived me!''

''That wasn't my intention.''

''Oh, please,'' she said with disgust.

They fell quiet.

After a long time he broke out, ''I loved you, Grace. I lived with you, I worked with you, and I played with you. We made love together.'' There was vulnerability in his eyes. ''You're my wife and I want you back.''

Grace's heart raced wildly. Panic filled her. He seemed sincere—but she was sure he was lying. ''Get out of my house.''

''Will you have dinner with me tomorrow night?''

Grace gave him a look of disbelief. ''No.''

He felt a thrumming in his chest. He had one chance. It had to work. Carefully he reached into his pocket, pulled out a piece of paper and pressed it into her hand. ''Please.''

Grace looked down. She recognized the narrow strip of paper at once.

Her eyes watered.

She resisted reaching for her brandy glass and gulping

the rest of it; instead, she unfolded the coupon and read what she'd promised:

1 Anything of Zachary's Choice.

She stared at it for a long time, then lifted her gaze. "Do you have any more of these?"

Zac glanced at the coupon. "I have two more with me. Not just like that," he added, wondering why she'd asked.

She sat up very straight. "I have three, as well. Let's just...trade."

Incredulous, Zac snatched the coupon from her hand. "I think not!"

Grace sat back. "It's sensible, Zachary. I mean, we're getting divorced. I'm not going to owe you all kinds of...coupon things."

Was it his imagination, or had her color heightened? Zac said, "Well, whatever coupons I gave you are still valid, and—" he considered the register receipt "—I don't see any expiration on this, either." He withdrew two more pieces of paper from his shirt pocket, examined them and held them up for her inspection. "Nor on these."

Seeing what one of the coupons was for, Grace opened her mouth, then shut it. Surely he couldn't imagine she would— Blotting out memories of when she *had*—lovingly, eagerly—Grace disciplined her eyes not to drop to his lap. She said, "I'll buy them back from you."

"*Buy them?*" Zac lifted his eyebrows, then bent his head for a moment to inspect the coupons. "Hmm..." His eyes narrowed, and he lifted his chin, as though calculating. "Let me see. The value of a five-course dinner from a woman who attended the Culinary Institute and worked under the great French chef Gilles Guignant..." He tossed the coupon in her lap. "I'll let it go for two hundred dollars."

"Two hundred—"

"Ah, this, though—" he held up another "—very dear. The street value of this particular service...well, it's probably only about fifty dollars, but it's priceless to me."

"You swine." Grace grabbed the receipt from his hand, crumpled it in a ball and threw it into the cold fireplace. "That's what I think of you and your—"

"Well, we both think a great deal of you." As Grace glared at him, cheeks scarlet, he eyed the wad of paper in the hearth. "Just for the record, I don't consider that coupon void, but in any case, I have another. And it says—" he studied the slip in his hand, then her body "—anything."

Grace leaned against the back of the couch, crossing her arms under her breasts. "You're living in a dream-world if you think I'd even kiss you."

"That's academic, since I don't plan to try at the moment. Don't look so disappointed, Grace. Actually I'll forgive you the sexual favors you owe me—and by the way, I have a stack of those coupons in Los Angeles—"

"I do not owe you—"

"—if you'll just honor this one." He held up the Anything coupon.

"Oh, anything you want!" said Grace. "I suppose you're going to ask me to rip up those divorce papers and let you go on your way."

He shook his head, moving nearer. Suddenly his scent was in her nostrils, and Grace remembered how strong desire could be. She didn't breathe.

"I want you to let me court you."

CHAPTER THREE

I WANT YOU to let me court you.

He was too close. Grace stood up. "You're good, but you're not that good."

Zac leaned back on the couch with a groan. "I'm not trying to be *good*. I'm just trying to..." He looked profoundly frustrated. "I'm trying to save our marriage."

"You're trying to save your green card. Believe me, I've had time to think this through. You've got a movie role, and you're afraid of the INS."

Zac was on his feet in a second, diminishing the space between them until she was crowded between an end table and the baby grand.

Grace didn't breathe. Their bodies were so close....

He said, "You're calling me something worse than a whore. I don't need to be married to keep my green card, Grace."

That stopped her. Her thoughts were wayward. Making love, Zac holding her so tight she could feel his heartbeat and his breath. This man holding her. She said, "What do you mean?"

"Well...my employment. I have a job that pays very well, and I could make a strong case to the INS that it's a job no one else—American or otherwise—could do."

Realizing he must mean being "close to his

clothes''—in other words, barely wearing them—Grace burst out laughing.

"It's true."

Humor gone, Grace shook her head. His argument was nice, but it wasn't the whole picture. "Maybe. Maybe not. Still, I doubt you want to deal with the INS again, and I don't think you want them looking at our marriage.

"Remember, Zac, I was there. I brought you hot tea in Federal Plaza at three in the morning while you waited in lines just to get the forms you needed. I was the woman who sat in the next room and told the men with the crewcuts that you prefer cappuccinos to lattes and that you shave the right side of your face before the left. And I know those same men would have loved an excuse to snap a pair of handcuffs on you and put you on the next paddy wagon to wherever they take people like you.''

Stepping around him, Grace escaped to the center of the room. "You know, I have this picture in my mind of what happened after I left. First you spent a few days worrying if you were going to be deported and lose the greatest role of all time in *Leaving Hong Kong*. Then you probably decided the INS might go years without noticing we no longer lived together. So you went on with your life." She shrugged. "Just like that."

From his place beside the piano, Zac stared at her, his features forming those sober, almost too-perfect lines. Grace could detect little emotion in his expression, but his gaze was unnervingly still.

"Grace, if you never hear anything else I say, hear this. When you left me, I was devastated."

Grace watched him distantly, wondering why she was shaking so hard, listening so hard....

"I lost my job. I lost the role you just mentioned so glibly. I lost my agent. I lost our apartment." He stepped toward her and looked down into her eyes, his own showing a familiar detachment. Grace had once suspected it hid his deepest feelings. Before she'd found out he'd lied.

"I loved you as much as a man can love a woman. I loved you. I needed you." His eyes searched her face, and she watched the pulse in his throat, the constriction of muscles, the apparent stifling of emotion. He whispered, "And I begged you not to leave."

Then he left, and the sound of the front door closing behind him was final and empty and lonely.

LYING AWAKE, Grace watched the shadows from a cottonwood tree outside her window play over the ceiling. She wished she could sleep. But she kept thinking of Zac and five words he had spoken, words that had carried the desperation of truth ignored.

I was a good husband.

No, you weren't, Grace thought. You were a great husband.

With a moan, she rolled onto her stomach and buried her face in the pillow, remembering the things he'd said, the expressions she'd seen on his face. Remembering the past. Real feelings. Separation had blurred her perception. Seeing Zac, touching him, brought it back into focus. What they'd had was complicated. Many layers deep.

When you left me, I was devastated.

Devastated.

Zac said he'd lost his job at Jean-Michel's. He had

lost the part in *Leaving Hong Kong*. He had lost his agent and lost their apartment.

Grace couldn't see it, couldn't believe it. Zac never failed.

But obviously he hadn't made this up.

She should have been there for him after he'd lost that role. But Grace recalled the larger crisis *she* had faced alone—her father's death. The memory of Zac's response killed any sympathy she felt.

Still...how had he lost the part? How had he lost his job? He never used drugs, and he drank little. He'd barely touched his brandy tonight.

I was devastated.

What did he mean?

Grace lay in bed, frightened, remembering the times she'd called him in New York and listened to the phone ring and ring. Once she had called in the middle of the night, and no one had answered....

Let me court you....

I loved you.

If that was true, why had he waited so long?

And how could she trust him now?

ZAC LAY BACK on the bed, trying to forget what had happened at Grace's. Why had he told her those things? She wasn't going to be impressed that he couldn't hold a job.

Things were better now, thanks to Ben Rogan—and to a casting agent who'd seen Zac at a photo shoot and said, *If that man can talk, he's got the part.*

It was a good part—Seneca Howland, one of the nine men who had joined Major John Wesley Powell in his 1869 exploration of the Colorado River. Zac had never wanted to be in films; he loved the stage. But the role of Howland in *Kah-Puh-Rats* was a godsend, and the film's being shot in Moab had seemed like fate. A chance to reconcile with Grace.

Her divorce suit had changed everything. He'd hoped the film would bring them together; Grace saw it as one more reason he couldn't afford trouble with the INS.

After *Leaving Hong Kong*, Zac had other troubles. His agent had said, *No one will touch you, Zac. Look, maybe you need to get some help. I'm hearing some pretty wild stories.*

Stories more bizarre than the one Grace had told him tonight—that they'd talked on the phone after her father's death. He'd known her father was dead. But how had he found out?

Nothing. No recollection. Of that. In a flash that came and went like a falling star, he saw the shadows of an alley and the overly bright red eyes of wrinkled, sunbaked men whose faces had looked so...wrong.

He swallowed.

The chaos of that period of his life was undeniable.

His agent. His career. His wife. In the space of a month they were gone. It had taken a whole year to even begin to undo the damage. Now, after a year, he once again had the first. And a chance at the second.

But what he wanted most was the third.

He wanted Grace.

THE NEXT MORNING, Grace awoke with feelings that reminded her of when she'd first fallen in love with Zac. As she dressed for work at the river outfit, her mind was full—with him. When will I see him again? Where is he now? What is he thinking? Is he serious about "court-ing" me?

They would be seeing each other on the movie set. So far, Grace had resisted trying to get a cast list to see what role he played. But she couldn't help imagining their being together on the river during filming. What would happen?

While she dressed, she played the music box, watch-ing the figures dancing in front of the stage set; and as she drove to the Rapid Riggers office, she found herself humming "Love Is Here to Stay." *Our love,* she thought.

Zac.

When Grace arrived at work, her sister was in the reception area opening a box of new brochures. Day was turned out in a powder blue linen shift and angora sweater. She was the only outfitter in Moab who wore stockings and heels to work, and she hadn't been on a river trip in more than a decade, but first-year boatmen soon learned that Day knew an oar from a paddle. She *was* a good partner.

After she and Grace checked the new brochure for pricing errors, Day lit a cigarette and began putting the pamphlets in a rack on the counter.

Grace examined her nails, found a trace of automotive grease. She and Zac had held hands.... Checking the adjacent doors to make sure she and Day were alone, Grace announced, "Zac's in town. He came to see me last night."

Turning, Day put down her cigarette. "That was fast." Her expression reminded Grace of the past four-teen months. It was a loyal sisterly look that meant, *You spit in his face, didn't you?* But even Day had liked the gesture of the music box.

Grace told her, "He said he wants to get back together." It didn't sound too good when she said it out loud. It sounded like Zac was scurrying to hang on to his green card. "I don't know. It's just interesting." Interesting? She had fantasized all night.

Looking like someone who hated to burst a bubble, Day asked, "Did he happen to say why he never called or anything? Was he abducted by aliens? Living with Elvis?"

Grace laughed hollowly and shook her head. That was what Zac hadn't said. What she needed to know. Concealing her hurt, she shrugged. "He just wanted to have dinner. And I nixed it. It probably won't amount to anything." Coupons. Courting. She glanced toward the kitchen. "Coffee time."

As she stepped around the reception counter and started to push through the swinging bar-style doors to the kitchen, Day's voice stopped her. "Grace?"

She looked back.

"I shouldn't have joked. It's okay to still care about him. You were married. It's a big deal."

Grace met her gaze. The words came without thought, but she knew they were true. "We *are* married. That's a bigger deal."

ZAC SHOWED UP later that morning when Grace was on the phone. Nort Stills, a coproducer for the Powell movie, had called to say the film crew had arrived in town; the call had come at a bad time, while Grace was preparing lunch for a women's club. The ladies would dine in the picnic area at Hittle Bottom, then set off on a half-day raft trip down a stretch of the Colorado known as the Daily. *If* the meal was ready.

While Day typed reservation confirmations into the company computer and Nick lurked in the doorway waiting for instructions on preparing the custard for asparagus tarts, Stills asked Grace the dozen or so questions no river guide can accurately answer. How deep is the river? How cold is the water? How big are the rapids?

"What kind of nightlife do you have out there?"

That was a new one. Grace echoed, "Nightlife?"

"Yeah. On the river. I mean, we've checked out the bars in town. This place is pretty up-and-coming, kind of like Taos or Telluride. What's there to do on the river? Where are the best spots? Any good bands?"

Struggling to contain herself, Grace resisted answering that the Doll's House was a beautiful section of sandstone monoliths and that sometimes, after a day on the river, the boatmen started mud fights for entertainment. Clearly Stills did not realize the vastness of Utah wilderness, and that was unsettling. How many hours had she spent on the phone with the studio coordinating the logistics of this venture?

In a level tone she said, "Mr. Stills, I think you have misperceptions about the terrain. Let me clarify some things so you won't be shocked by, well, the rather rustic conditions on the river."

As she spoke she heard tires on gravel outside, and Day rolled her chair backward from her desk so that she could see out the window.

"What a pile of junk!" Day said. "The car, not the man." She looked at Grace. "Guess who."

Zac? Grace peered out the dusty pane but saw only

the tail of an old sports car painted with primer. The front of the vehicle was hidden by a banner hanging along the porch railing.

Quaking inside, she tried to focus on her phone conversation. The studio knew they were going into wilderness. Hal Markley, the producer, had told her he'd applied for a filming permit from the park service.

Grace told Nort Stills, "For example, Cataract Canyon, where you plan to film part of your movie, is 120 miles from here. It's a three- to seven-day trip by river—"

Nick walked over to look out the window, blocking the glass. As footsteps sounded on the porch, he told Day, "That's not junk. It's an Austin-Healey."

Into the receiver, Grace said, "Accessibility by land is two hundred miles and strictly by four-wheel drive or helicopter. There are no hotels or gift shops—"

The bell sounded as someone entered the front office, and Nick and Day tripped over each other and several river bags as they tangled their way out the door.

"—no bars and no bathrooms," continued Grace, unrelieved by their departure. Obviously they wanted to gawk at Zac. "We sleep in tents and cook in Dutch ovens we bring with us. Our river permits require that we operate under strict conditions, carting out all waste—"

"Oh, my God!" Stills exclaimed.

Grace put her hand over her face. When she could speak, she said, "Mr. Stills, I'm sorry if anything I've said has fostered a false impression. Given the film's topic, I just assumed that everyone had some idea what it's like on the Colorado and the Green."

"No, no, that's all right," said Stills. "Just let me

recover from the shock. I mean, my idea of camping out is, like, the Holiday Inn. Y'know? But I'm sure Hal must know... Yes, I'm sitting in the office, and apparently everyone here knew we were going into no-man's-land. Everyone but me."

Grace would've smiled but she wanted to get off the phone and see Zac. Stills said, "Miss Sutter?"

"Grace, please." *Mrs. Key,* she thought. Stills must know Zachary....

"Grace, then, and it's Nort on this end. Grace, we've set up offices down here on, ah, what is this—Mill Creek Drive. Used to be a uranium company or something. The Uratomic Building, Hal says. Is there any chance you could come down here and talk to the director about what to expect in the white water?"

Grace agreed to come to the Uratomic Building in an hour. Hanging up, she listened for sounds from the front office.

Day was saying, "Um...I think she just got off the phone. Grace?" She stuck her head in the door. "Zac's here."

He appeared behind her sister. The room felt ten degrees warmer.

Standing, Grace glanced from Day to Zac. "Did you two meet? In person, I mean."

"Your sister introduced herself," said Zac. It had been awkward. All he could think about was how Grace looked in that wedding gift Day had sent. He could like any woman who sent his bride a red leather teddy with naughty cups, but he didn't think Day liked him now. He'd hurt Grace.

Day said, "Grace, I'm driving Dirty Bob downtown to pick up his new boatman's license." Seeing Zac's puzzled look, Day explained, "All our guides have special names. Dirty Bob. Fast Susan. Cute Nick." She paused. "Amazing Grace."

The jab was hard to miss. Zac said, "I've always thought so myself."

The moment Day left, he stepped into the office with Grace and shut the door. They were alone.

Grace forgot her sister's skepticism—and her own. Zac stood before her in blue jeans and her favorite of his shirts, red polyester with grizzly bears on it. Grace felt as if she was scouting the Big Drop in Cataract Canyon. Nervous enough to babble.

While he surveyed the office, she said, "You never knew I liked squalid surroundings, but I do. We invite the boatmen to come in here after trips and shake out their dirty socks. The sand rises off them in clouds, and we get this ambience of filth. The tourists really go for it. It's cowboy stuff."

Zac laughed, his eyes sweeping over her. Her worn-out Rapid Riggers T-shirt gave him ideas about her breasts. *Want you,* he thought. *I miss you.*

He looked elsewhere. At the computer, the fax machine, the life vests piled in a corner beside the filing cabinets, the old brown couch with the springs popping through, the waterproof "dry" bags on the floor and an oar hanging on the wall. The last made him think of another river, the Thames, and another kind of rowing. He'd never seen white water. He'd never seen a desert like this.

Grace said, "I guess you'll be spending some time on the river with the movie."

"Yes." Zac looked at her. "Will you?" Or would she stay behind in the office to avoid him?

"Oh, yes. I'll be rowing." The movie required too many boatmen for her to skip out.

Zac studied her. *One more time.* "Grace, please say you'll have dinner with me tonight."

It felt like a long time since she'd said no, although it was only last night. A long night. She'd met too many of those. "Okay."

One moment Zac was looking hard at her eyes, and she was looking at his. The next they were in each other's arms, holding tight. His head pressed against her hair as he drew her closer. The embrace felt much deeper and more serious than what Grace had held in her mind for a year, than the travesty she joked about with Day so she wouldn't cry about it, instead. Wouldn't cry the way she had those first few weeks she'd spent alone. This felt good.

Grace was afraid to feel.

Zac tilted back her head, made her look at him.

His eyes probed hers. Watching his gaze move just slightly, Grace knew he was exploring her face. As she was his. His hair grazed her cheek, and she felt his fingers near her temples and on her jaw, and his thumb touching a side of her mouth.

She whispered, "Don't kiss me."

"All right." His cheek brushed her hair, her skin. Grace's eyes burned with memory and longing.

A rustling near Zac's foot startled him. It was a piece of paper sliding under the door.

Grace moved out of his arms to pick it up, and Zac read the words from over her shoulder: *How do I make the custard?*

The tarts. Telling herself the interruption was timely, Grace grasped the doorknob. "Nick and I have to make tarts. And then I have an appointment at the other end of town.''

Nick? *Cute* Nick undoubtedly. Day had introduced them, and Nick Colter had not taken his hand—only looked at him coldly.

Zac stared down at Grace. "You're making tarts with another man?''

Was he joking? "It's not quite adultery.''

"It's practically foreplay. You're very exciting in the kitchen. You were cooking the first time I saw you. At Jean-Michel's," he added, as though she might have forgotten.

She hadn't. She never would. Grace had turned at the stove, and across the kitchen, dressed in black and white, was the most beautiful man she'd ever seen. She'd known he was the new waiter everyone said was so gorgeous, but she hadn't counted on that immediate meeting of eyes or on the jolt that had gone through her, straight to her toes. She hadn't counted on his looking at her so long. Seconds. While nothing else happened. Just eyes.

She had thought, *I want that man.*

That man was now saying, in a low, private voice, "You're very sexy when you cook. It makes me hard to think about it.''

Grace bit her lip, trying to figure how her hip had come to be situated against his. Yes, he was hard, and he was easing her back against the door, easing himself against her. It felt familiar and warm and intimate. So did his breath as he asked, "Have you changed your mind about being kissed?''

Grace tried not to look at the dark places where his beard grew, nor at his lips. She said, "Um...yes, as a matter of fact.''

Zac smiled.

His eyes were on her face, and then his hands were, too. His mouth touched hers. Grace's lips trembled, and he tried to soothe her as he tipped her head to the angle he wanted. But he was shaking, too.

Grace tasted him and felt his beard stubble, and her breasts remembered warm, tight embraces inside his wool coat in the winter. She could feel his heart beating as fast as hers. She moved her lips against his, with his, and then she opened her mouth and his tongue came in, stroking hers. Grace pressed against his erection because she couldn't help it, and in her mind she saw a picture too much like that jeans ad. But it was her hands unbuttoning, and she could hear his low moan, hear him saying, "Gracie…"

He was hers.

Because he'd needed a green card.

He'd never been hers.

Grace dragged her mouth away, but his followed. He nuzzled her cheek, traced her jaw with his lips, and she dodged kisses she wanted and whispered, "We have to stop. Stop, okay?"

He did, about as fast as a freight train stops.

Then he was hugging her tight, one of those bear hugs, a never-let-go hug. His voice came through her hair. "Let me help you in the kitchen, all right?"

Grace remembered other kitchens. Jean-Michel's. Their own. She said, "Sure."

SHE SENT NICK outside to finish rigging for the afternoon's trip and to supervise two first-year boatmen patching rafts. While Zac finished the asparagus tarts, she put the chilled parsley-and-tarragon soup and the spring artichokes into containers for transport to the river and began assembling everything else to go in the coolers.

As Zac poured the custard over the tarts, he asked her, "Do all the river outfits in town offer meals like this?"

"No." She put silverware and napkins in a paper bag on one side of the cooler. "But seeing that I went to cooking school..." Drawing Zac's attention to her restaurant range and the salamander or overhead broiler above it, she said, "I had a friend ship them to me last summer. Serving gourmet meals on the river is challenging. There are some interesting limitations."

Zac recalled her frustration cooking in their old apartment before he'd installed the exhaust system for her stove. Grace was a chef; he couldn't imagine that the limitations she'd mentioned were any pleasure to her. But she talked as though they were. Was Grace really committed to this place? Zac hoped not. He couldn't work as an actor in Moab, Utah. *Kah-Puh-Rats* was an exception.

He asked, "Business is good?"

Grace shrugged. "Moab has changed a lot in the last few years. More people are visiting and moving here, which is good for the economy. But a lot of our competitors have rich, out-of-town backers, which gives them an edge. When our equipment breaks down, we have to rely on ourselves—and any help we can get from the bank." She admitted, "Day wants to sell the house I'm living in—my father's house—and put the money into this place, but I don't want to. It might not have looked like much to you, but it's actually sort of historic. It used to be an inn."

Zac lifted his eyebrows, interested.

"My great-grandfather had a riverboat business, taking people from Moab to Green River and back. Some of them stayed at the inn. The steamboats back then were too big and unstable for these rivers, so that business went under. But my grandparents kept the inn going. So did my folks for a while. They even served meals. There's a big dining hall off the living room." Grace removed four loaves of bread from the racks where they were cooling and wrapped them in foil to take to the river. "But I guess the inn was too far off the beaten track. Finally my dad decided white water was the way to go."

Despite himself, Zac was fascinated. He knew what it was to belong to a place, to know that one's ancestors had lived and breathed and walked and loved within its walls. To know that someone before you had worked to keep it because they felt it was worth having—and worth your having.... Zac had been born five years too late to have Oakhurst. When his father died, it would be Pip's.

He asked, "You haven't thought of selling this place?"

"No way. That would be like...like selling my father." Hoping to make Zac understand, Grace crossed the kitchen and removed a framed photo from a nail on the wall beside the back door.

Zac came to her side and looked down at the faded eight-by-ten. It showed a man in a life jacket and Rapid Riggers hat rowing a six-foot inflatable boat through a torrent of white water. The waves were fifteen feet or more.

"That's my dad in Lava Falls, in the Grand Canyon. He was fearless. He was a world-class boater, and he'd run anything. He made three first descents."

Zac heard the pride in her voice. Curious, he pointed to the lower right corner of the photo. There, the white water became brown and scooped out a smooth, deep depression in the river flow. "What's happening here?"

"A hole. There's a huge lava block right there." Grace pointed to a spot just outside the photo. "The water pouring off it collides with the flow from river left. You can see the big wave starting to rise and break back on itself. Anything that big isn't really a keeper— not for people, anyhow. It's the kind of thing that sucks you under and spits you out fifty feet downstream."

No big deal. Zac stared at the massive hole. "A keeper?"

Grace explained. "Some holes will trap a person or a boat for a long time. You get churned around a lot—or Maytagged, as the boatmen call it."

Like a washing machine. Zac would have smiled at the expression if not for a disturbing vision of Grace in a keeper. Eyeing the Grand Canyon photo, he asked, "Have you run that rapid?"

"Yes, in a dory—more than twice the size of that boat."

This was a side of her Zac didn't know—the river runner. He wanted to know that side; without it he'd never know her. He should have suggested a trip to Utah a long time ago, after he and Grace had gotten married. But he'd been too busy with his career. And when Grace's father had died...

I should have come out for the funeral, Zac thought. Disturbed, he again tried to recall the phone conversation Grace had mentioned the night before. After she'd left him and come to Utah and learned of her father's death in surgery, she had called to tell him. And he had talked to her. *Why couldn't he remember?*

But he knew why—basically. He just didn't want to think about it.

As Grace stepped away and hung the photo back on the wall, Zac returned to the oven. He checked the temperature and glanced at the tarts. "Shall I put these in?"

"Sure. They look great." She went back to the counter and stared through the grimy window over the kitchen sink at the river beyond. Somehow Zac's presence stirred old dreams she had thought she'd put to rest...of being a chef again.

Thinking of *his* dreams, she turned and asked Zac, "What about you? What's your role in this movie?"

Zac slid the tarts into the oven and closed the door. "Cast member four. His name is Seneca Howland."

That was good billing. Grace thought for a minute. "Wasn't it the Howland brothers and William Dunn who left the expedition early and climbed out of the Grand Canyon?"

"Yes. I'm to be killed by Indians."

Grace smiled. "Where did they get the title?"

"It's what the Utes called Powell. It means 'rat missing an arm.' He lost an arm in the Civil War."

Grace remembered. As a Colorado River outfitter and guide, she knew Powell's history well. "Who's playing him?"

"Martin Place."

Grace was surprised. The fortyish actor had won two Academy Awards. *Kah-Puh-Rats* was a big-budget film.

The phone rang in the next room, and a moment later Day appeared in the doorway. "Grace? It's Bill."

Her lawyer. Grace had tried to reach him that morning, hoping to tell him Zac was in town and to get some advice. What would her lawyer say when he learned she'd agreed to have dinner with Zac.

Excusing herself to take the call, Grace tried to think it through again. Had the marriage really mattered to him? He'd said the green card had been the deciding factor in his marrying her. But he'd also said that he'd loved her. So why did he want her back? His green card? Love for her? Or both?

Grace thought the last might be hardest to accept.

WHILE SHE TOOK her phone call, Zac sat on the porch steps studying the rocks across the road, trying to identify the strata. Campers and four-wheel drives sped past on the highway, some headed north out of town, others across the bridge to Moab. The traffic was steady, but even the roar of the vehicles as they passed seemed quiet compared to New York or L.A. Overhead, the international flags waving from the eaves made a gentle flapping sound, the sort of sound one never noticed in the city because of the constant noise. Here Zac heard the distant drone of a lawn mower and the nearby buzz of a fly till it paused on the leg of his jeans. Quiet.

A semitrailer on the highway rumbled past, wheezing as it slowed to go into town, but Zac didn't amend his perception. Although there were many tourists here, Moab's small-town feeling reminded him of Belden, the village near Oakhurst. The thought made him feel rootless. And restless. Where was Grace, anyway? Still on the phone?

The screen door slammed behind him, and Zac glanced up. As Grace crossed the porch and sat down beside him, he said, "Who's Bill?"

"My attorney."

Divorce attorney. Another eighteen-wheeler roared
past. Zac asked, "What's this costing you?"

"Between the detective and my attorney, almost fifteen thousand dollars. So far."

A detective? thought Zac. He hadn't intended to hide
from her. He'd just wanted to get his life back together
and figure out what had happened to him during that
month after she'd left. The lost month. It had never occurred to him that she was looking for him—and that it
was costing her money. A lot of money.

He said, "I'll pay it."

Grace stared at his profile, partly hidden by his long
hair. "I'm not ready to drop the suit, Zac."

"More's the pity." He looked at her. "But it's my
fault this has gone so far. I'll take care of it."

Grace was stunned. He was being...chivalrous. Actually, when she thought about, he had always been chiv-
alrous. Except about his green card—and her dying father. "I'll have to ask my attorney."

"Fine." He paused. "Tell me where to book a table
for tonight. Is there a good restaurant?"

Grace thought of the advice she'd received from her
lawyer on the phone. *Sure. Find out what he has to say.
But don't let him pull the wool over your eyes.* The warning didn't seem to cover the melting feeling deep inside
her. She said, "The Moenkopi Café has a good chef."

"Wonderful. Shall I pick you up at seven?"

She should keep some distance. Letting him bring her
home was risky. If he kissed her like he had in the office,
she'd be touching him in inappropriate places and suggesting unbright schemes. *Let's go to bed....*

"I'll meet you there." Standing, she said, "I need to

go. I have an appointment at the production office." And she needed to see that everything was set for the half-day excursion. Mentally she was already making a list of things to tell Nick. *Don't forget to take the tarts from the oven. Send someone to nab picnic tables at the beach....*

Zac leaned back on his hands and looked up at her. "Want a ride?"

Distance, Grace thought. She said, "Sure. Thanks."

A few minutes later they left in the Austin-Healey with its sheepskin seat covers and gray-primer paint job. As Zac headed the car across the bridge and south into town, Grace asked, "Where are you staying?"

"The Anasazi Palace." He raised his voice over the wind and the rumble of the engine. "I drove out to your house this morning, but you'd gone to work. I was going to talk you into running with me."

Running.

Memory attacked, and Grace remembered running with him in New York. Showers afterward. *Sex.* She said, "Oh."

"Do you run anymore?" he shouted.

"Sometimes." Alone. Alone on the River Inn Road, on the northwest side of the river. The Colorado, instead of the East River.

Zac decelerated as they drove into town. Businesses crowded both sides of the road. River outfits, realtors, hotels, trading posts, T-shirt shops, restaurants, pubs. All were in gear for the tourist season. Pedestrians with cameras strolled the sidewalks, while cyclists in spandex shorts sped up and down the roadsides, the fat tires of their bikes caked with red desert mud.

Slowing to stop at a light, Zac said, "I like your house."

Grace stared at him. She'd seen pictures of Oakhurst, Zac's family home, with its leaded-glass windows and Elizabethan chimneys and manicured gardens. But he liked the River Inn? Grace loved the place, but the condition of the property made her blush. Thinking of the weeds choking the yard, the porches that needed paint and new screens, the peeling plaster and water-damaged floors upstairs, she said, "It's a wreck right now. Dad never had much time for it. He was busy with Rapid Riggers."

The light changed, and Zac eased the car forward. "I have some time. Tell me what to do." He winked at her. "You're good at that."

Grace ignored the allusion to past domesticity. A man was offering to work on her house without bidding on the job first. Zac had always done that kind of thing around their apartment, but... "Are you sure you want to?"

"Yes." *I'm your husband,* he wanted to say. *That's something I do for you. I fix things. And you make wonderful meals, and we make love together....*

His willingness to help touched her. He'd even offered to pay her legal bills. Thousands of dollars.... *I was a good husband.* Had she been a good wife? Was what Zac had done bad enough to justify leaving him?

And had Zac really been so upset by her leaving that he'd lost his job and a role and—well, everything? If things were that bad... It wasn't like her husband, the son of an earl, to show up on her doorstep when he was down on his luck. He wouldn't want her to see him unemployed, wouldn't want to risk being a burden to her in any way. He would get himself together first.

Grace was still thinking of that minutes later when they reached the Uratomic Building. The parking lot was busy, and through the opened door of a warehouse, Grace saw people constructing sets. There were vehicles everywhere, and a row of expensive automobiles with California plates stood near the front door.

Zac parked the Austin-Healey between a Porsche and a Jeep Grand Cherokee, got out and came around to open her door.

Surprised, Grace said, "You're coming in?"

"I have business here."

The sunlight caught his wedding ring. His hand. The sight seemed sexual to Grace, a reminder of all they'd shared. The ring had always been a nuisance for him. He'd had to remove it for performances. But he was wearing it now, though they were separated.

Which didn't mean she had to wear hers. Not when she wasn't sure what it signified. She asked, "Does anyone ever ask who you're married to?"

"I don't talk about it. If you're worried about our working on the film together, don't be. In this business, everyone's related to everyone else."

As Zac opened the glass front door of the Uratomic Building and they went in, Grace heard voices from rooms up ahead. Near the door, the craft service had set up a refreshment stand, with an espresso machine and other drinks and snacks. Zac asked, "Would you like something?"

Grace shook her head and looked down the corridor at the clock.

Pausing at the stand to get some tea, Zac told her,

"Go ahead, if you need to make your appointment. I'll find you."

Grace nodded and wandered down the hall, seeking Nort Stills.

Like the parking lot, the production office was busy. A woman stepped out of a door on the right and hurried past Grace with a smile, and a trio of technicians carrying lights and cables emerged from a double door at the end of the hall. They interrupted their talking to say, "Hi," as they passed Grace. Looking back toward the front door, Grace saw Zac had disappeared, probably into one of the rooms she'd already passed.

As she continued down the hall, voices reached her ears. The conversation was coming through an opened door on the left, and Grace recognized one of the speakers as Nort Stills. "I'm telling you, Hal, people are talking about him. Let's take advantage of it."

A woman's voice cut in. "Enhance his role?"

"Why not?"

A third voice—probably Hal Markley's—sounded dubious. "He's new."

Grace lingered in the hallway wondering how to interrupt. There was a sound of riffling pages, and a phone rang in another part of the building.

"Here, scene twenty-five," said the woman in the room. "He's saying goodbye to his wife. Let's make it hot. Does he do nudity?"

"I guess you've never seen those Ben Rogan ads," answered Stills. "Does Zachary Key do nudity? I should say so."

They all laughed.

Grace felt faint.

CHAPTER FOUR

WHEN HAL MARKLEY first offered her a seat, it had been all Grace could do not to say, *Wow, this is a really great chair.* The studio's temporary digs and hastily purchased office furniture would have been a face lift for Rapid Riggers, and the executives matched their surroundings.

Though dressed casually in slacks and polo shirts, Nort Stills and Hal Markley had the sleek, well-groomed look Grace associated with wealthy people from the city; coproducer Carrie Dorchester wore a tailored suit, stockings and heels. Only the director, Meshach Stoker, seemed different. He wore rumpled khaki trousers, a pile cardigan that looked as though it had actually seen some camping trips, wire-rimmed glasses and a full beard. Nonetheless, he seemed less relaxed than his clothes— running on creative energy, obsessed with making the film.

Grace and Meshach had been poring over a river guidebook together for twenty minutes, reviewing campsites and possible shooting locations, when Hal Markley removed his black horn-rimmed glasses and polished them as he said to Grace, "Maybe you have an answer to this. We've found a restaurant to cater for us through most of production, but no one will do the job down in Cataract Canyon."

Grace wasn't surprised. Leaning forward in the awesome chair, she explained, "It has to do with cooking equipment. Everything we eat hot on the river is prepared in a Dutch oven or over an open fire. It's tricky to turn out interesting meals."

In the past weeks she'd learned enough about moviemaking to be relieved when Hal Markley had said he'd hire a caterer to feed his crew of a hundred and fifty. Grace had cooked for big church groups on Rapid Riggers river trips in the past; but whoever provided meals for the movie crew would have to meet the demands of the filming schedule—which could change without notice. So why was she opening her big mouth? "If you'd like, we could do the meals in Cataract Canyon."

Carrie Dorchester, who half-leaned, half-sat against a stout table near the windows, exchanged a skeptical look with the others. The coproducer was the woman Grace had overheard asking if Zac did *nudity.*

Forget about it, Grace told herself for the twentieth time. *You can find out later what she meant.*

Hal Markley was shaking his head. "The cast and crew expect a lot of variety from the caterer. Anyhow, you'll be busy on the river."

Grace knew what he feared—a week of cowboy coffee and chili seasoned with river silt. "Mr. Markley, I am a graduate of the Culinary Institute, and we routinely serve gourmet fare on our river trips. If you're interested, I'd be happy to work up a menu for you."

Carrie's lined lips curved into a smile of surprise. "You're a chef?"

"I was sous-chef at a four-star restaurant in New York." For a moment Grace thought of Zac—and the simplicity of those days.

Nort Stills, a wiry man whose hair stood up around his head like the white seed tuft on a dandelion, shrugged at Hal. *Why not?*

The producer looked dubious. Replacing his glasses on his nose, he asked Grace, "But can you feed eighty people?"

That was the size of the "skeleton" crew they would be taking down Cat—half the regular crew. Grace said, "I've done it before."

Hearing a sound behind her, she glanced up to see Zac in the doorway.

Carrie Dorchester saw him, too, and pointed a finger in his direction. "We need to talk."

Nudity, Grace thought. What did they have in mind?

In the doorway Zac answered, "Fine." With a quick glance at Grace, he told the others, "By the way, this is my wife."

The sudden silence in the office was made more pronounced by the sound of hammering from the warehouse across the lot. The three producers exchanged uneasy glances, and Meshach, the director, stared at Zac. "You're married?"

Hal Markley burst into a wide, politic smile. "I had no idea."

Carrie Dorchester glanced at Grace, gave her a small smile, then continued smiling strangely as she stared at some distant spot on the floor.

Obviously they were all shocked that Zac had a wife in Moab, Utah.

He asked Grace, "Do you know how long you'll be?"

Hal looked at his Rolex. "Give us a half hour. And Carrie's right. We should talk."

Grace's appointment finished on schedule. Leaving

Zac with Hal and Carrie and Meshach, she followed Nort Stills across the parking lot to the warehouse to inspect a new fleet of custom-built wooden dories. Though Powell's expedition had used only three, Saga had built a dozen to interchange during the filming.

Grace and Stills spent thirty minutes in the warehouse, and then the producer suggested that Zac would probably be free. He wasn't, so Grace waited outside the closed door of Hal Markley's office, thinking about the weeks ahead. This Cataract Canyon expedition would not be the usual river trip. She had seen the producers' reactions to the prospect of sleeping in tents and using the rustic, mobile bathroom facilities. And Hal Markley had assured her that *his* cellular phone would work in the desolate Cataract Canyon section of the Colorado River gorge.

Not a chance, Grace thought. Cataract was a long way from anywhere.

How would Zac behave on the river? Part of her wanted to believe the worst—that he would hop off the raft at the end of the day, grab a beer and try to coax a female guide to set up a tent for him...then share it. But honesty intervened. When they'd lived together, he'd more than pulled his weight, in every way.

Finally the office door opened. Someone inside was still talking, and Grace heard Zac say, "I will," before he stepped out. Seeing her, he smiled tensely. "I'm sorry. Were you waiting long?"

Difficult meeting? Grace wondered. "No, just a few minutes."

Together they walked out to the parking lot where the midday sun had warmed the sheepskin seat covers in the Austin-Healey.

As Zac opened the door for her, Grace sensed the fine strain in him, just under the surface. "Is something wrong?"

"No." But it would be—as soon as he told her. The producers' offer was the worst thing that could have happened. And the best. Stills had said, *You're an actor. She'd better get used to it.*

Zac knew he was right.

As he started the car, Grace remarked, "You know, I'm a little surprised you're in a movie. You've always done stage."

Zac put the car in gear and turned to look over his shoulder as he backed out of the space. "Acting is acting." And a role was a role—especially when he hadn't had one for a year. Grace wasn't going to see it that way "The Ben Rogan ads have helped me, actually. I've been asked for several media interviews, even a television appearance." He braked at the parking-lot exit and checked for traffic. "It's a chance to promote the film, so the producers want to expand my part. A new contract, everything."

Grace tried to feel happy for him. But as he turned the convertible out onto Mill Creek Drive, she recalled the producers' conversation she'd overheard. *Nudity. That* was why he'd looked tense. "How are they going to expand your part, Zac?"

He glanced at her. "Several ways." He looked back at the road and tried to sound like he was talking about something as uncontroversial as the weather. "For instance, there's a scene in which I say goodbye to my wife before leaving with Powell. It's supposed to be poignant because I'm going to die."

Grace knew what he was going to say. *Yes,* she thought. You're going to die....

"They're going to turn it into a lovemaking scene."

Dazed, Grace pictured Zac in bed with some beautiful starlet, maybe one of those European actresses with no cellulite and with poreless white skin, instead of tan lines from working on the river in a bikini top and shorts.

She felt a craving for Drambuie.

Holding her blowing hair back from her face, she asked, "Who is she? Anyone well-known?"

"No." They reached a stop sign; Zac slowed the car and looked over at her. Vulnerable brown eyes. *Gracie,* he thought. I want *you.*

Grace stared out the windshield. Zac didn't blame her for being upset. He was sure she'd be more upset when she saw Ingrid Dolk, the nineteen-year-old Swedish girl who would be playing Seneca Howland's wife. But Nort Stills was right. Grace had to understand that a bed scene was just acting. Not the easiest kind, but part of his job.

Still, it rankled that the producers wanted to expand his role not because they liked his acting but because the Ben Rogan jeans ads had been banned, and suddenly everyone from Hal Markley to his own agent thought he was going to become...a sex symbol.

The irony was that he'd been celibate for more than a year. The love scene he wanted was a private one— with his wife.

He forced his thoughts back to the film, to what he had to do. "What they're offering is significant. More money. More exposure."

"I'll say. Not that you're shy."

He would have smiled, but he knew what underlined her words. She'd never liked it that he was an actor. The light changed, and he put the car into gear. "They're taking a risk, Grace. I've never worked in film, and it's my first role in more than a year."

A year? Grace thought. Zac had always had plenty of roles. All but *Leaving Hong Kong* had been off-off-off-Broadway—no pay—but what had been important to Zac was the acting.

As they passed the Moab visitor center, she asked, "Zac, what happened with *Leaving Hong Kong?* How did you lose that role?"

One hard heartbeat struck the wall of his chest. "I was upset about you. I told you that."

Upset enough to lose a role? "What do you mean? Were you drinking?"

The light ahead turned yellow. Zac slowed the car. *Drinking,* he thought. *That* sounded normal. "I did some of that, but it wasn't the problem." He needed to tell her. If she was going to remain his wife, she should know. But for now... He glanced her way. "I've been thinking about your house. What would you like done?"

Grace blinked at him. "We were talking about *Leaving Hong Kong.*"

Zac's eyes were on hers, and she sensed he was trying to communicate something he couldn't say. His lips were parted as though he *wanted* to say it...but the words that came out were "What would you like me to do on your house?"

For a moment they just looked each other. Again Grace sensed things unspoken. Something had happened.

Reminding herself that losing the role must have been humiliating for him—knowing he wasn't ready to tell her in any case—she let it go and thought about his question. What she'd like done on her house.

She didn't want to make requests. That would seem as though they were...married. Confused, she said, "Zac, it would take a year to get that place in shape."

Zac had thought the same thing. Slowing the car to stop at another light, he stared out the windshield.

He couldn't be in Moab for a year.

Pushing the thought from his mind, he looked at Grace. "Shall I start with the screened porch? And the yard?"

Grace smiled at him, the left side of her mouth twisting a little higher than the right, and for a moment Zac saw a look he remembered in her eyes. A look that was like the words *I love you*.

She said, "Thanks. Want to borrow a truck?"

THEY SWITCHED VEHICLES for the afternoon. Leaving the Austin-Healey at the Rapid Riggers office for Grace, Zac borrowed one of the Suburbans and drove out to her house to assess what materials and tools he'd need.

As he nosed the truck down the drive, a small gray shape darted from the tamarisk and into the road. A dog. It trotted clumsily, weakly, holding its right rear paw slightly aloft. Slowing the Suburban, Zac watched the dog limp back into the tamarisk.

Easing the car forward until he could see the animal again, Zac braked and stared out the opened driver's window. "What are you doing out here? You're just a puppy." He hadn't realized at first. The dog looked about half-grown, but was so malnourished its ribs showed under its muddy gray fur. Quivering in the brush, tail between its legs, it stared at Zac through one brown eye and one blue, then escaped through the tamarisk.

Zac whistled softly, but the dog didn't look back. At last Zachary put the car in gear and went on, but he was disturbed. The puppy must be lost, and it had to be hungry.

He was still thinking about it when he parked under the cottonwoods and got out to inspect the porch and the yard. As he made mental notes of what to buy in town, his mind kept returning to the dog he'd seen. Limping.

Starving.

Zac turned away from the house and started back up the sandy drive, peering into the tamarisk, whistling for the dog.

BACK AT HER OFFICE, Grace called her attorney and reached his paralegal, to whom she explained Zac's offer to pay her bills. The paralegal said it sounded like no problem, but she would check. Someone from the office would call Grace in the morning.

All afternoon, Zac was on her mind. He was relieving her of a huge debt. He was working on her house.

But that love scene. Unwillingly Grace envisioned him in a bed with another woman, cameras and technicians all around. Fake lovemaking, but Zac would be sensitive to the actress, thinking of her vulnerability in front of the camera. They would be naked together....

It reminded Grace of his marrying her for a green card. No compromise was too great for his career. Granted, she couldn't think of a serious film actor who didn't do love scenes—but could she live with it?

If she remained married to Zac, she must.

At four-thirty Grace headed home. The sun was lingering in the sky, resting against the tops of the red cliffs, as she drove the Austin-Healey along the River Inn Road. The car seemed like a toy compared to the Rapid Riggers Suburbans. As the dry spring wind whipped her hair about her head, she glanced a few times toward the river, checking the water level. High.

The road meandered past sheer rock faces where rock climbers with ropes and harnesses were ascending difficult cracks, just feet from where others had climbed centuries earlier to carve petroglyphs, rock art, in the desert varnish. She passed a sign pointing out dinosaur tracks, another designating a trail to a natural arch, and eventually she reached her sandy driveway.

Zac had been busy. The tamarisk encroaching on the drive had been cut back; the area under the cottonwoods beside the house had been cleared; and the path leading down the long grassy bank toward the concrete boat ramp was visible for the first time since Grace had returned from New York. Zac had accomplished more in an afternoon than she could have in a month.

She parked his car under the trees beside the Suburban and got out to look for him. He'd mentioned repairing the porch, but there were two—a spacious deck curving from the southern, river side of the house all the way around the east wall and another more intimate, enclosed area on the northwest corner. A sprawling stone patio with a low wall traversed the west side of the house, linking the two porches.

Wading through sagebrush and wild desert grasses, Grace walked around the outside of the house. In her father's old room hung a faded photo of guests at the inn sipping cocktails on the front screened porch, and

Grace enjoyed imagining those days. But now the porches were cluttered with junk—retired river gear, rotting furniture. Circling the house, she tripped over a boat trailer rusting in the grass at the foot of the patio steps.

Zac was down by the river, looking like something any woman would want to take home. Shirtless, he crouched in the weeds near the old boiler and rotting paddle wheel from the *Moab Princess,* her great-grandfather's riverboat, petting a strange dog. As he scratched the animal behind its pointed triangular ears and pulled sticks and leaves from its matted gray-and-white coat, Zac asked, "Do you know this dog?"

Crouching beside them, Grace shook her head. She didn't know the dog, but she could guess its story. Abandoned by tourists. "Looks hungry."

"Yes."

Something about the way he said it, his eyes avoiding hers, sent Grace's gaze sweeping toward the house. At the foot of the steps were two bowls and a twenty-pound bag of dog food. Grace bit her lip, uncertain whether to smile or frown. Zac and strays. That tabby, Chloe, for instance. It might explain how Zac had lost their apartment. Another cat.

I was upset about you…

Grace laid aside the recollection of their conversation in the car.

Now Zac had found a dog.

Determined not to become as smitten with the sickly mutt as he obviously was, Grace stood up and cleared her throat. "So…going to take it back to your hotel?"

Zac was gazing down at the dog, his face hidden, but Grace knew the expression he was wearing. The figuring-out-how-to-persuade-Grace look. It felt like old times. Good times. Standing, he bent over to give the dog a last stroke and waded out from the weeds to join her. The animal followed him, and Grace saw how skinny it was and how its tail drooped. The poor thing was starving.

Beside her, Zac smelled wild, like dirt and sweat. Grace tried to keep her eyes off his chest and corrugated stomach. Beard shadowed his cheeks and jaw and upper lip, and his skin looked smooth and brown as honey.

"I thought I'd call the pound. Put an ad in the paper. Try to find the owners." His green eyes searched Grace's face. "If I could keep her here for a few days…"

"What if you don't find them?"

Zac looked down at the dog. Mismatched eyes gazed up at him. Part Siberian husky. He thought he could detect faint markings in the puppy's muddy coat. "Someone will be looking for this dog. If no one turns up, I'll find a home for her." He'd done it before, with Chloe. She was still living happily with friends on Long Island. Of course, he'd love to keep this animal, but he wasn't home enough. Dogs needed attention. Besides, his apartment didn't allow pets.

He told Grace, "I'll come by and take her for exercise. Feed her." The dog had devoured the food he'd put in her bowl. Starving. He'd used Grace's phone to make an appointment with the vet for the next morning. "Really, she won't be any trouble to you."

The dog wouldn't, thought Grace. But what about Zac? He'd be around every day.

He was crouching again, rubbing the dog behind the ears. Those hands. His wedding ring… A little breathless, she said, "Okay." As Zac stood up, she told him,

"You're working on my house. It's the least I can do. And by the way, I'll reimburse you for materials."

He shook his head.

Grace opened her mouth to argue, but his eyes said the subject was not open for debate.

I was a good husband.

Avoiding his gaze, Grace looked about the property, scanning the shoreline and the house. He'd replaced several of the porch screens, and there was so much more he could do here. She remembered his penchant for fixing things in their apartment. Good handyman. Good carpenter.

Good husband.

Zac told her, "I'll have more time tomorrow. I have a one-o'clock call, but I can come here early. Now, I should go back to town, though." He needed to call his agent about Hal Markley's offer. The afternoon working had given him time to think about everything that was happening...and everything that had happened before.

Tonight he'd spend with Grace.

Would she ask again how he'd lost the role in *Leaving Hong Kong*? At some point he would have to answer. Tell her.

God. What would she think?

He squatted beside the puppy, petting her.

Grace stared at his fingers—and his wedding ring. At Tiffany's, she'd told him she didn't want a diamond because she didn't want anything to get in the way when she cooked. Zac had said she could wear it on a necklace. But in the end, he had bought her an earring with a heart and a diamond on it. *Engagement earring,* he'd said, kissing her neck beneath it. As affectionate with her as he was with that dog.

His hands— A terrifying realization swept over her. She still loved him.

BEFORE HE LEFT, Zac made a bed for the dog from a cardboard box, and Grace lined it with an old blanket. They put it on the screened porch, and when Zac had gone, Grace brought the puppy food and bowls up there, as well. She held the door open, and at last the dog came limping in, tail down.

Observing, Grace felt indignant. She was sure some tourist had brought the puppy along on vacation and lost her. It happened all the time. Occasionally, Rapid Riggers passengers embarking on the Daily asked her and Day to look after their pets at the office. Grace didn't mind that. But there were too many people who left dogs in hot cars or tied up at camp in the sun or set them loose in the unfamiliar desert.

As Grace poured herself a glass of wine in the kitchen, Zac's waif sat down beside the table and watched her. When she took a seat, the dog flopped down on the floor, tail limp, as though she'd never learned how to wag it.

Grace said, "I'll feed you again before I go out." Was the puppy housebroken? She would shut her in the porch when she left for dinner with Zac.

Zac...

Seeing him with the stray had been a graphic reminder that he was not the two-dimensional villain she'd painted in her mind for fourteen months. He was a complicated man she'd never fully understood. A man she'd adored anyhow, for the four happiest months of her life.

What if the things he'd told her were true? What if she'd really hurt him when she'd left? Today he'd said,

I was upset about you. That was why he'd been sacked from two jobs and lost his agent and—

Upset how? wondered Grace. She'd been upset, too, but she'd stayed in control. Burying her dad. Running his business. *What did Zac mean?*

She had to find out, and it might as well happen tonight.

Eyes on the dozing dog, Grace drank down her wine. It might as well happen now.

ZAC HAD ALMOST FINISHED shaving when he heard a knock at the door of his hotel room. He gave his jaw two last swipes before he wrapped one towel around his waist, grabbed another to wipe his face and walked out of the bathroom to open the door.

He expected to see someone from the studio, maybe Nort Stills. But it wasn't Stills at the door. It was Grace.

Her hair was in a loose braid, and she was wearing a dress he'd bought her in New York, a sheer powder blue silk with a small point collar and nineteen-inch skirt. The thin straps of the lining gave it a sexy, gossamer look, and the way it clung to her breasts made him remember her naked. Remember how deeply in love they'd been.

The towel about his waist stirred, like a snake charmer's bag containing a cobra, and he grabbed the white terry cloth and released a breath between his teeth. "Come in."

"Thanks."

Grace stepped inside. He pushed the door shut and stared down at her. "Let me dress. I didn't expect you."

As he moved toward the suitcase lying open on the hotel luggage rack, Grace glanced about his room. The clothes he'd been wearing earlier lay heaped in a corner, and his script was on the bed.

He went into the bathroom to pull on a pair of black Ben Rogan jeans. He didn't close the door, and Grace remembered what she'd said to him earlier about being shy. He wasn't. Somehow his going into the bathroom to dress emphasized both the intimacy they'd once shared and the fact that they no longer shared it.

But when he emerged from the bathroom, he came over, took her chin in his hand and kissed her mouth.

Grace swallowed hard. Electrified.

Dropping his hand, he gazed down at her. "You're sweet to come early." He went to the closet for a shirt. Indicating his pants, he asked, "Will I be all right for this place?"

"Yes." She watched him pull a shirt from a hanger and slide it on. It was red silk and patterned with black silhouettes of Mickey Mouse in various guises. The Sorcerer's Apprentice. A film director. She wondered if the shirt had come from a thrift shop or Rodeo Drive.

She sat on the edge of one of the two queen-size beds and thought of the reason she'd come. "So, Zac..."

Tucking in his shirt, he glanced at her.

"What happened to you in New York after I left?"

She knew he'd heard, but he showed no reaction. He continued to dress without answering. Grace watched him take some black socks from his suitcase and sit down on the edge of the other bed to pull them on. Then he got up and retrieved his black walking shoes from the closet. Returning, he sat down beside Grace. She could smell the hotel shampoo in his wet hair and the soap on his skin.

Zac could smell her, too. Lemongrass. Grace. The scent resurrected old feelings. Closeness. Love. Betrayal.

They had to forgive each other. They had to trust.

He had to answer her question.

"Do you even have a green card? I left before you got it."

Seizing the brief reprieve, Zac got up and grabbed his wallet from the desk under the mirror. Sitting beside her, he showed her the card.

The photo was a three-quarter profile of his face, with the right ear exposed, his long hair tucked behind it. The address was that of their New York apartment.

Grace stared up at him. His mouth was an immobile line, his face just as still. She didn't know why she felt afraid. "How did you get the card?"

"The INS mailed it to our apartment."

"When?" said Grace. "I sent a letter to our apartment six weeks after I left you, and it was returned to me. They said you weren't at that address."

She felt Zac's slight start beside her. He looked at her. "You wrote to me?"

"Of course I wrote to you! I was married to you and I loved you, and then you dropped off the face of the earth. I called you and we talked that once, and after that you didn't answer the phone, so I wrote to you. I told you that last night."

"I'm sorry. I didn't catch it." He said, "The card came a short time after you left. I lost the apartment sometime later."

"How?"

He'd dreaded this moment for a year. *Talk,* he thought. *If you just start talking, you'll get it out. Then it'll be over.*

But he didn't believe it.

He knew Grace. She wouldn't let this go. She would wonder and she would ask questions. Grace always asked questions.

But doesn't it bother you that your brother will get Oakhurst?... What does that mean, your parents "put you down" for Eton before you were born?... They sent you away to boarding school when you were seven?

She always sounded horrified, which was ridiculous. It wasn't fun to be separated from one's parents at that age, but there were worse things in life. Anyhow, all the men in his family had gone away to prep school when they were seven, then to grammar school and then to Eton, which was a great privilege. But the tradition offended Grace's maternal instincts. She *would* make a good mother.

Immediately Zac jerked away from the thought, trying to forget that she'd mentioned children the night before. Trying to forget everything that meant.

Grace stood up, impatient.

He looked into her eyes. "All right. I'll tell you what happened. I've wanted to tell you, but it's a very private matter."

Grace stared at him, astonished. "I'm your wife."

"I know. And you're trying to divorce me."

She felt the implication. He didn't trust her.

But he was talking.

"The day you left, I began feeling...strange. I don't know precisely what was going on, and my memories are unclear. It's like a dream, a very bad dream." Remembering, Zac searched for words to describe what had happened to him. He knew the right words. Precise words. But they would frighten her.

They frightened him.

He used layman's terms, instead. "I had all sorts of wild feelings, and my senses were overacute. I could hear things going on three blocks away, and there were...there were voices in my head to drive anyone mad." Rushing past it, he said, "Initially I was very confused. I missed a performance, but they accepted me back with a warning. About that time, I began to entertain the most florid delusions imaginable of persecution by the INS. I was afraid to go to work at Jean-Michel's. I was afraid to go to the theater.

"During a performance about a week after you'd left, I became convinced that there were INS agents in the theater, that they had wired my clothing with microscopic recording equipment to monitor my most private conversations, and that they planned to arrest and execute me. So during intermission I went upstairs, removed my clothing and left the theater by a fire escape."

He glanced at Grace. Her eyes were unblinking, her brow drawn into faint lines. Concerned? Perplexed? Aghast? He went on, aware how rehearsed his speech sounded, though he never had rehearsed, never had quite believed this moment would come. "There were people outside looking at me—theatergoers—and finally the director came out and— Anyhow, I didn't finish the performance, and everything got worse from there. I went home and cut a hole in the wall of our apartment and disassembled the plumbing, looking for wiretaps. I know it makes no sense. I was not in my right mind." He realized it felt good to be telling her, to be telling someone, anyone, but especially her. Not to bear it alone. "These kinds of things went on for a month. I was rude to everyone I knew, accusing friends and acquaintances of plotting against me, and I took up associations with homeless people of unhappily like mind with whom I lived in condemned buildings.

"When I awoke one morning in such a place, groggy but more myself, I remembered enough of what had happened to know what kind of hell I was in, and I hurried home to learn I'd been evicted. Surprise, surprise." Numbly he thought of the following days and weeks and months. Coming back to himself. Trying to put his life in order. *Trying to find out what in hell had happened.*

Not wanting to go into that, he said, "Perhaps all this can make you understand why I was reluctant to approach a woman I loved and admired. A woman who had already rejected me once." The last sounded bitter, and he laid his hand across his face. "I'm sorry."

Grace didn't move. She didn't want to think about the things he said he'd done or what it meant. All her reactions seemed wrong. Because, in a way, Zac's story was an answer to her long prayers, that he would have an innocent excuse for his long absence. Innocent, but...

She thought of what she'd been doing while he was imagining plots involving the INS. While he'd been having this...breakdown.

She'd been burying her father.

Wanting space of her own and knowing he must need some, too, she said, "Thank you for telling me. I'm going to have a glass of water."

Zac nodded, eyes remote.

Going to the desk, Grace selected one of the hotel glasses, then went into the bathroom and shut the door. She turned on the tap and filled the glass. As she drank, she stared down at the vanity and Zac's shaving kit, the same one he'd had when they lived together. His razor was still out, lying on a crumpled towel, as though he'd set it down in a hurry when she came to the door.

The details of his story came crashing down on her. Delusions of persecution. Zac standing on a fire escape naked.

It was beyond reason. Sure, he'd always been a little obsessed about the INS. What alien waiting for a green card wasn't?

But microscopic recording equipment...

A chill swept over her.

It sounded—well, sick. But it also made a painful kind of sense. She, the person closest to him, had walked out of his life. And it had hurt him enough that he'd unconsciously created an alternative reality.

Or, rather...unreality.

But I didn't react that way, thought Grace. *He hurt me, too. And I went on with life. I buried my father and comforted my sister and revived a failing business.*

Zac couldn't have been wounded more deeply than she was.

Could he?

The night before she'd left him, they'd slept together because there was no second bed but the floor, and Zac had held her tight in the night, saying, *Grace, don't do this. I love you. Please...*

A horrible realization swept over her. Her doubts...the decision she'd made to leave Zachary. He really had loved her. *I promised to spend my life with you, and you promised to spend yours with me.* Even their song had promised lasting love. Staying love. Though the Rockies could tumble and Gibraltar crumble...

But she hadn't stayed. Zac had loved her.

And she had left.

IN THE OTHER ROOM Zachary put on his shoes, then sat on the edge of the bed with his forearms on his knees and his head in his hands.

He'd told her.

Feelings bombarded him. Relief. Exposure. Doubt. What was Grace thinking? This wasn't over. He'd been right as rain for more than a year, but what if it happened again?

He'd been right to tell her. He should tell her more.

When she emerged from the bathroom, Zac stood up and met her eyes, half expecting to see revulsion in her gaze. But she was only frowning slightly, watching him as though she didn't know what to say.

Zac spared her the trouble. There was only one balm for times like this. He said, "Shall we go find a cup of tea?"

CHAPTER FIVE

WHEN THEY STEPPED outside, it was dusk and cooling off slightly. The whine of mosquitoes in the air was a reminder of the rising water in the river and the onset of spring. The Anasazi Palace had switched on its No Vacancy sign, and Grace saw many California license plates in the lot. The movie crew.

As they walked down an outdoor staircase to the street, Zac asked, "Do we need a car or can we walk?"

"It's four or five blocks to the restaurant."

They walked slowly, admiring the fading colors of the slickrock skyline to the east. Because their dinner reservation wasn't for an hour, they stopped at a deli on Main Street, got two cups of tea to go, then continued down the sidewalk, walking and window-shopping. Everything was open late, for the tourists.

Everywhere, women stared at Zac, and people who knew Grace looked curious. She was embarrassed, wondering if anyone noticed his ring and thought she was running around with someone else's husband. Her own ring was home in the bottom of her jewelry box with the coupons Zachary had given her last year on Valentine's Day. The day that had changed their lives.

As they walked, Grace pondered what Zac had told her in his hotel room. She'd never known anyone who'd done the kinds of things he had described. But Zachary wasn't like anyone else she knew. Sent to boarding school when he was seven, obsessed with acting...

Together, they perused the art and jewelry and pottery in the windows. Nearly all the merchandise reflected the locale. T-shirt designs depicted rafting, mountain biking, natural landmarks and figures copied from petroglyphs—the rock art of the Anasazi, the Old Ones who had built homes in the canyon cliffs centuries before, then mysteriously left the area.

Seeing Zac studying the primitive images, Grace volunteered, "If you'd like to see some rock art, there's a great pictograph panel across the highway from Rapid Riggers."

Zachary glanced down at her in the light from the shop window. "I'd like that." He put his arm around her and Grace hugged him, and they walked to the restaurant that way. Grace realized she was happier than she'd been in fourteen months.

Despite the disturbing things Zac had said.

At the Moenkopi Café, they sat at an intimate corner table lit by a candle in a Southwestern-style metal lantern. Over a bottle of chianti and food to satisfy any chef at the Culinary Institute, she and Zac talked about the puppy at her house, then about Rapid Riggers and *Kah-Puh-Rats* and his career. Zac told her how a modeling agent had approached him at a New York coffeehouse where he was waiting tables. He'd been in Europe several times in the past year doing Ben Rogan ads, and he'd spent Christmas at Oakhurst with his family.

Grace asked, "What do your folks think of your modeling? Have they seen any pictures?"

"One of the Rogan ads. My father didn't speak for several hours afterward, but my mother said she was glad I had a job." Zac thought of what he'd wanted to tell Grace the other night at her house. He said, "When you phoned Oakhurst looking for me, and my mother wouldn't pick up..."

Grace raised her head. "Yes?"

"She has spells of depression. It's bad sometimes."

Grace listened, hoping he'd say more. Zac seldom opened up like this.

Eyes on hers, he said, "You must have called during one of her spells. I'm sorry." And angry. But it was his fault, for not giving his wife a way to find him. For giving her a reason to leave him.

"She didn't answer the phone because she was depressed?"

"I'm sure of it. It keeps her in bed for days at a time. She won't answer the phone or the door." *Or her family.* How many holidays had he spent alone at school? *Your mum's going through a rough patch, Zachary. Try to understand.* He'd understood enough to be terrified.

He told Grace, "I think it's beyond her control." That was something he'd discovered only recently. Only since he'd begun looking into what had happened to him.

Of course, the two were unrelated. He'd never behaved like his mother.

Watching him closely, Grace asked, "Zac, did you tell them what happened to you?"

"I haven't told anyone. Just you." Biting his bottom lip lightly, he wanted to say more—to share the things on his mind. But why worry Grace when there was no need? He was all right now.

Grace sat lost in thought. *He'd told only her.* Even though she'd left him. But any guilt she felt was lessened by her reason for leaving. Nothing had changed that.

How could a man who lacked the integrity to tell a woman he was marrying her for a green card resist the temptations Zac would face in Hollywood? Their marriage was doomed.

Grace thought of the love scene, but she didn't want to bring it up. Instead, she asked, "Did the producers say anything about your announcement this morning? That we're married?" She doubted Zac would want the studio—or the public—to know why he wasn't living with his wife.

"Yes." His eyes made a quick pan of the room. "They fished, and I told them we've been estranged and are working on getting back together." Again he looked about the restaurant, assessing their privacy. Deciding they could talk, he asked, "Grace, would you like to discuss that scene?"

The love scene.

Grace watched a couple at a nearby table. They were laughing as people do when they've known each other for years and are having a wonderful time together. Looking back at Zac, she asked quietly, "How would you like it if I took off my clothes and got in bed with another man?"

Zac's abdominal muscles tightened. "I've pictured that scenario." He'd been picturing it for fourteen months; he'd also thought about it in relation to the film. How would he like it if Grace were in his shoes? He wouldn't. He didn't want her to share her body with anyone else—in any way.

He leaned closer to her over the table. "Men and women are different. Men are visually aroused, and any man would get an erection in a second seeing you naked."

It was gratifying he thought so, but... "And you're not going to get hard over Miss Whoever?"

"It's not an exciting situation."

"You just said it was."

"I said that *you* are exciting. I'm an actor, Grace, and a model. My body is public. Not sexually, of course. But visually."

"Zac, I don't mind your being 'close to your clothes.' I mind you being close to someone else's skin."

Zac wanted to be close to *her* skin—not just her cheeks and throat and arms but the paler skin that never saw the sun. He remembered her breasts against him and how it felt to run his hands over the backs of her thighs. How it felt to kiss her there. Everywhere.

Grace said, "I could name a dozen celebrity couples who met working on films together. Who, when they met, were married to other people."

Zac spoke quietly but with great intensity. "I have always been faithful to you, Grace. Even this past year. We covered this ground before we were married. Infidelity is anathema, and marriage is for life. You're the one who's trying to divorce me—not the other way round."

Her heart thudded as though nothing else mattered, nothing but commitment. Maybe her heart was right.

But she said, "If you want to be faithful, why tempt yourself?"

"Any temptation I feel is the result of sleeping alone for a year."

Grace's chest constricted. "You could have come to me."

"I told you why I couldn't."

How had the conversation begun to feel so sexy? Under the table, one of his long legs nestled against one of hers. As his hand found hers on the tabletop, his ring shone dull gold in the candlelight. Slender ring, ring from the time when they'd gotten by on two paychecks from Jean-Michel's.

"Grace, I'm telling you that what I have to do is just acting. Acting. It's not real. If you'd like to watch, I'm sure you can be on the set."

It was all Grace could do not to exclaim, *Thanks, I always wanted to watch you with another woman.* She remembered the feel of his body, the crushing weight of him on her, his hard thigh muscles straining between hers.

She didn't want to be on the set.

His ankle rubbed against hers, an under-the-table caress. Her heartbeat wouldn't slow down and she knew why. She was in love with him. She looked down at the marinated artichoke hearts and mushrooms on her plate. "Let's try and enjoy our food." *Let's forget about that damned scene.*

THE REST OF THE MEAL passed pleasantly. Afterward they were too full, so they walked for a while on Main Street, then down a side street to the Robber's Roost Tavern, Moab's most authentic cowboy bar. A band was playing, and Zac paid the cover and they went in. They each had a watery Utah beer—3.2 percent alcohol, because the state's Mormon heritage was still felt in its liquor laws—and they danced on a dance floor hazy with smoke and played two games of pool. When Grace looked at the clock, it was midnight.

She excused herself to go to the ladies' room, and when she came out Zac was reading flyers stapled to the wall near the phones. They advertised coming events—a concert, the spring musical, evening slide shows. When Grace joined him, he nodded at the poster for *Oklahoma!* and said, "That's coming up next weekend. Would you like to go?"

Another date. Grace felt absurdly thrilled. "I wouldn't miss it. The spring musical is an event around here. Anyhow, Day's in the chorus. We've got a good theater group. This fall, they're doing *Suddenly Last Summer*."

Tennessee Williams. Zac was impressed. It was a great play. Wistfully he remembered working with small theater groups on projects like that. It would be fun to see the musical with Grace.

They left the bar. As they walked back toward his hotel holding hands, Zac asked, "Are you all right to drive?"

"Yes." After a moment she added, "Thanks for dinner. I had a nice time."

"Good. That must mean you're going to let me court you."

Grace smiled, heart shaking. "I have an Anything coupon, too, you know."

Zac remembered when he'd given it to her.

Valentine's Day.

He'd made her a card with three heart-shaped promises inside.

That fast, the pall of the day, the bleakness of her leaving, slipped over him. He saw himself in the weeks that followed, and there was a feeling like a ball of snakes in his chest—the things he hadn't told her.

I told her the facts.

When they reached the Suburban in the hotel parking lot, he opened her door, planning as platonic a good-night kiss as he could get away with. Memory had made him cautious.

But Grace didn't get in the car. She stood in front of him, her breasts almost touching him, and asked, "When are you coming over tomorrow?"

Thinking of the obligations he'd made—to the dog and the house—he met Grace's brown eyes. Their expression made his chest tighten and blood rush to his groin. He said, "I'll come at six-thirty. We can go for a run." Then his hand went to her waist, and he pulled her against him, aware of her body beneath the blue silk dress dress he'd given her.

It wasn't platonic at all. Couldn't be.

Grace felt the demand of his arms, of his whole body. They stood just inside the open door of the vehicle, in the shadows away from the hotel lights. The spot was secluded, and the things happening between their bodies seemed deeply private. The fact that the warm hard bulge at the front of his jeans was not a mystery but familiar and dear to her intensified Grace's response. It would be so easy to go up to his room with him.

Zac's hands explored her shoulder blades, all the small places on her back, as he kissed her, tasting her with his tongue. He pressed closer, wanting to be inside her, to feel like her husband again.

The sound of laughter and clicking heels penetrated the stillness of the parking lot, and he blinked alert, then untangled himself from her. Some of the film crew walked by, returning from night revelry. Instinctively shielding Grace's body with his, Zac smoothed the back of her dress and tucked her into the driver's seat.

Making a sound of deprivation, Grace clung to his arms, then to his hand, then to the steering wheel as he pulled away. He leaned into the car, and they kissed some more before he said "Good night," and moved away and shut the door.

Grace caught her breath, then put the key in the ignition and started the car. The V-8 roared. As she backed out of the space, her headlights caught Zachary, watching her. His eyes were sober. With a jolt of awakening, as though she'd just rammed into a post, Grace remembered what he'd told her that night. What had happened to him in New York.

Her heart raced in another way. Scared.

Taking a last glance at him as she turned the car, Grace wondered if he, too, was thinking of what had happened to him. Because it *was* strange. It was troubling. And Zachary was a highly educated man, someone who thought deeply about things.

Oh, God, Grace thought. *How have you stood it alone?*

THAT NIGHT IN HIS BED in the Anasazi Palace, Zac's own cry awakened him, and he lay rigid in the dark, breaths shallow, the sheets damp and cold around him. The images that had recently filled his mind—the paneled Tudor-style door, the Karastan carpet, the bed—faded away, and he saw the hotel drapes, the light from a street lamp shining around them.

He knew where he was.

Hotel. Anasazi Palace. Moab.

Moab.

Grace.

She seemed far away now. Irrelevant. The nightmare had locked onto him, making everything dark. As the sheets clung to the light sweat on his skin, the dream images were replaced by memory. A blackened ceiling overhead. His shoes filthy. His body stinking.

Zac got up, resigned to the routine. Shower. Read a book. *That* book. *DSM-IV,* the book in his suitcase. The diagnostic manual accompanied him everywhere. He read it as though it was a religious tome, as though if he studied it long enough answers would emerge—and he would know if there was something wrong with his mind. Of course a doctor would have answers—but Zac didn't need a doctor. The problem had been stress. Grace.

Zac got up to look in the bathroom mirror. His skin was wet and clammy, his hair damp and limp with sweat. Seeing his reflection, he felt emotions so powerful and negative he couldn't examine them, and he dealt with them the only way he'd ever learned.

He ceased to feel.

GRACE MOVED the dog's bed into the kitchen for the night and encouraged her to lie in it. No dice. The puppy would not be left alone. She slept on the floor of Grace's room, and Grace found her presence comforting. Even more than the music box, the stray was a reminder of Zac. Almost as though he was there.

In the morning when the alarm went off, the first thing Grace saw was the gray dog, looking at her. Tail limp on the floor.

Grace took her downstairs and filled her bowl. The dog didn't let the food land before she snapped at it hungrily. Glad Zac had found the animal before it starved to death, Grace set the door of the porch ajar so the puppy could get out, then ran back upstairs to dress.

When Grace had moved back into the inn after her

father's death, she'd begun sleeping in the spacious front room that had been her parents' before her mother died. Now the plaster walls were peeling and the floor was scuffed and in need of refinishing. But an antique fan hung from the ceiling, and an enormous hearth warmed the eastern wall. To the south, French doors led to a wide patio balcony. It curved out over the screened porch downstairs, offering a view of the river and the mesa called the Amasa Back on the other side.

Grace opened the doors, and stepped out onto the terrace. It was still the charcoal light before dawn. But overhead, the sky was heavy with clouds, and already the river flowing past hinted at dusky red. She knew it would rain.

Returning indoors, she played the music box and dressed in a sports bra, tank top and shorts, then went downstairs to stretch. She heard Zac's car; heart racing, she hurried through the kitchen and out the side door to meet him.

It was raining. Zac had raised the top on the Austin-Healey, and when he got out she saw that he hadn't shaved. He was wearing black running shorts and an old blue T-shirt, and he seemed sleepy as he smiled at the dog limping up to greet him. He stooped to stroke the animal, but the smile didn't reach his eyes. When he straightened, he didn't quite look at Grace.

She remembered the night before, the way he'd kissed her, everything. *Maybe he was drunk,* she thought. They'd just had one bottle of wine, but he looked as though a hangover might be the problem. She said, "I fed the dog."

"Thanks." Again his eyes skirted hers. He felt disconnected—flat. Not enough sleep. He had come to

Grace's only because of his obligations there. The dog. The promises he'd made.

And because running helped.

After he'd stretched, they set out in the rain. The dog followed, hobbling, and Zac led her back to the house and shut her in the porch, saying, "When your leg's better, you can come." Then he joined Grace.

The rain was falling hard, sending russet water cascading off the canyon walls, cutting paths in the rocks, staining the river the color of blood, filling the air with the smells of wet plants and ozone and evaporation.

Grace was tour guide. She told Zac how the river was coming up, showed him where the water had swallowed familiar boulders. After a detour to show him dinosaur tracks beside the road, she headed up a footpath in a rocky talus slope.

Following cairns, she led him on a narrow trail high over a canyon. Sage, juniper and scrub oak poked between rock outcroppings. They ran until the trail merged with sandstone, which seemed to roll endlessly in all directions as the canyon widened. There, Grace stopped.

Turning in the rain, she said, "We shouldn't go any farther. When it's dry, you'd never know why they call the stuff slickrock, but on a day like this it's like walking on banana peels." She shrugged at Zac. Wet strands of hair, loosened from her ponytail, stuck to her cheek. "I just wanted you to see this. It's called Sutter Canyon."

It was spectacular. The rocks sprawled out in the distance, all the way to the mesa top. They stood before a wide natural bowl. Above it, on the opposite cliff wall, was an alcove, and Zac could make out toeholds worn in the rock leading up to it—and the ruin of a structure built of sand-colored rocks.

He asked, "Is that an Anasazi ruin?"

"Yes. You can climb up there, but it's too wet now. Let's go back to the road a different way, and I'll show you the spring and my grandfather's still."

"A bootlegger?"

"Oh, yes. He used to ferry moonshine on the river."

Grace's family history was here, Zac realized, as his was at Oakhurst. It was an unsettling thought. He shouldn't take her away.

As they returned to the Potash Road and finally slowed to walk down Grace's drive, Zac felt better than he had earlier. Tired, rain-soaked, breathing hard. Alive. He noticed the small round indentations the rain had made in the sand and the shades of green in the dripping tamarisk corridor around them. As they neared the house, Zac studied the lines of the gables and the chimneys and balconies. It was a graceful structure. Four thousand square feet, he guessed—too large to be practical for anything but what it had been, a hotel.

He climbed the stone steps a pace ahead of Grace and held open the battered side door that led onto the screened porch. The dog met them, and Zac immediately crouched down to pet her, to examine her matted puppy fur and let her lick his face. He said, "What kind of dog are you anyhow?"

"A mutt," said Grace with a smile. "She's a nice dog. She slept in my room last night." Opening the door that led into the kitchen from the porch, she told Zac, "You can use the downstairs shower, and I'll find you a towel and something dry to put on."

"Thanks."

The answer was painfully casual. Grace remembered other morning runs and other showers. As she left him with the dog and went upstairs, she considered Zac's apathy and wondered if he was uncomfortable about what he'd told her at the hotel. That would be natural.

Up in her room, she found clothes for him. They were some of his that she'd taken when she'd moved out—a pair of cotton gym shorts and an Oxford sweatshirt.

Coming downstairs, she heard a sound she hadn't heard in the house for years. The piano. But Day had never played like that. Grace didn't recognize the piece, only that it was classical. And even though the instrument was out of tune, Zac made it sound like something from nature. A bird. A human voice.

She followed the music to the living room and found him sitting there playing, in wet clothes and wet hair, the skinny gray dog lying at his feet. When he stopped to check a sticky key, he saw Grace. His eyes froze on hers; then he stood up and closed the lid over the keys. The dog sat up, too, watching him.

Grace said, "I forgot you could do that." Sometimes after work he had played the piano at Jean-Michel's. Classical pieces. Blues. "Love Is Here to Stay."

Joining her now, he indicated the baby grand. "It's a good instrument."

Grace nodded toward the double doors to the Princess Room. "There's an old player piano in there." She handed him his clothes.

Zac recognized them. When he was evicted, he had noticed them missing and wondered if she'd taken them—or if he'd done something with them that he couldn't recall. Now he lifted the garments to his face, breathing in. He smiled at her. "They smell like you. Lemongrass."

Grace was eased by his smile. Maybe the Zac she'd

seen the night before wasn't just something she'd dreamed up on heady Italian wine.

Once she'd gone upstairs, Zac did not go immediately to the shower. Instead, he went to the double doors. Princess Room. It must be the inn's dining room Grace had told him about. Carefully he released the bolts at the top and tried the doors. They opened.

Beyond lay a spacious room of almost a thousand square feet. It was cluttered with bicycles, a deflated raft, old tables and bed frames, rolls of tar paper and other sundry items. But Zac still noticed the big windows, which would admit the afternoon sunlight, and the French doors opening onto the screened porch and the patio. He could see where chandeliers or ceiling fans must have hung.

Making his way through the junk and around the player piano to the French doors, he looked out the dirty glass at the river. He could see the boiler from the riverboat, and he imagined the *Moab Princess* steaming down the Colorado, her paddle wheel turning.

Again it occurred to him that if he and Grace were to live together again, it couldn't be here. He needed to live where he could work. But how could he ask Grace to leave this place for him?

Of course, that wouldn't happen for a while. Reconciling with Grace had never promised to be easy. But now, new barriers had arisen between them. His sexier role in *Kah-Puh-Rats*. Her entrenchment in her father's business. And most of all, what had happened to him after she'd left.

He turned to leave the room and almost tripped over the dog. Sweet animal. Zac stooped to pet her. He'd grown up surrounded by dogs at Oakhurst, but he'd never seen one this starved—for food or companionship. As the dog looked up at him, waiting to see where he was going next, Zac reflected that he'd better find the owners soon—before he began to wish he couldn't.

Slipping out of the Princess Room with the puppy, he carefully secured the doors behind him, then started from the living room. His eyes caught the image over the mantel. Ophelia by the lily pond. Immediately he looked away. But as he headed for the downstairs bath Grace had said he could use, lines from *Hamlet* swarmed his brain: "They say the owl was a baker's daughter. Lord, we know what we are but know not what we may be...."

Ophelia. Mad, mad Ophelia.

When Zac emerged from the bathroom ten minutes later, showered and dressed in dry clothes, he was greeted by the dog and a burst of aromas from the kitchen. Coffee. *Huevos rancheros.*

His wife was making breakfast.

Feeling as though he was finding his way home, Zac walked slowly to the kitchen and discovered Grace standing at the stove in a pair of blue jeans and a cropped, wine-colored cable-knit sweater that showed a glimpse of her slender waist. Her hair was twisted up from her long neck, and she seemed tall and sexy and... Graceful.

As the puppy lay down in its bed, Zac joined Grace at the counter.

She glanced up at him. His expression reminded her of what he'd said the day before about kitchens. Eyes playful, he said, "You're trying to seduce me again."

Remembering his recent remoteness, Grace chose not to be charmed. She indicated a basket of fruit on the counter. "Why don't you squeeze the oranges for juice?"

Grace heard him laughing and turned around. He was eyeing her breasts affectionately. "I'd rather fondle a couple of grapefruit."

Obviously he'd recovered from his hangover or whatever it was. Grace shoved her fist against the board of his stomach, and he grinned at her. Shaking her head, she said, "And to think I ever thought you had manners. At least pour the coffee."

Obediently Zac opened cabinets until he found the mugs. As he took down two and filled them, he asked, "Grace, would you mind if I looked at the upstairs today? I won't go in your room."

Grace knew his plans were to work on her house until the dog's appointment with the vet. *I won't go in your room.* Thinking of when they'd had no private zones, no rooms or beds of their own, she said, "That's fine. You can go anywhere. You're...welcome." *You're my husband.*

AFTER SHE GOT into the Suburban and left for Rapid Riggers in the rain, Zac cleaned the kitchen, then toured the house and grounds, accompanied by the dog. Though he kept his word and didn't step foot in Grace's upstairs bedroom, he stood in the open doorway for a long time and looked at everything.

He found out what had happened to the things she'd had in their East Village apartment. She kept most of the items close to her, all but their quilt, which covered a bed downstairs. The heart crystal that had hung in their window now cast its rainbows from the French doors in Grace's room. A tapestry he'd given her of Echo and

Narcissus hung beside her mirror, and an aluminum pagoda wind chime they'd bought together in Chinatown dangled from a hook near the window. Her pink jewelry box sat on top of the Victorian armoire, the music box he'd sent her beside it; and on the bulletin board over a small writing desk, he saw a snapshot of himself.

The discovery was unsettling. Comforting. Strange. Grace had been thinking about him. She had cared about him.

She had left.

Finally turning away from her room, Zac continued exploring the upstairs. The hardwood floors and plaster walls showed old water damage, probably from roof leaks. Nonetheless, the house was wonderful—close to five thousand square feet, including wide verandas with elegantly molded balustrades, and spacious rooms with individual hearths and private baths.

His inspection concluded, Zac went out to the porch. Casually he explored the junk collected there. He recognized a few small metal tables from photos he'd seen inside, showing the house when it was an inn. A broken ceiling fan lay beneath several damaged oars. But there were other things that could be salvaged.

Wondering what else was about, he ventured out into the rain and climbed the grassy slope to the stone carriage house, the dog padding behind him. The road to the building was choked with weeds, and Zac could barely distinguish two ruts made by tire tracks years before. The carriage house had been remodeled into a four-car garage, but now the glass in the windows was cracked, and the roof needed repair.

He entered by a heavy wooden door at the side of the building, and as his eyes adjusted to the shadows, he saw the boat. It sat on a trailer against the far wall, a two-headed beast covered by a tarp. Both bow and stern were high and pointed, the gunwales arcing downward to the center of each side. Dodging spiderwebs, Zac waded around stacks of boxes and paint cans and life vests and oars to reach the boat. Even before he untied two of the lines and raised the dusty tarp, he knew it was Grace's dory.

It was painted royal blue, with a yellow stripe against the gunwales, and the name was lettered on the prow he had uncovered. *Persephone.*

As he covered the boat again, he found himself thinking of the morning more than a year earlier when Day had called them in New York. Deliberately he bypassed what had been going on before the phone call—great sex. Instead, he recalled Grace's determination to return to Utah and run her father's business. Zac had admired her readiness to help her father. But not at the price of leaving her spouse.

While rain pattered on the roof, he stared at her boat in the shadows, remembering the argument—and his fateful mention of the green card.

She'd reacted instantaneously, interrogating him. And when he hadn't denied her accusations but simply told her that he loved her, everything had fallen apart. *I knew there was something wrong with this picture. I thought it was just that you couldn't handle emotion. But the fact is, you're just a bad actor....*

He'd cooled toward her then—till late that night in bed. Then, those emotions she said he couldn't handle had come out. He'd begged her to stay. She'd told him not to touch her.

In the morning he'd helped her pack.

It had been very ugly. And the recollection made him wonder what he was doing here now.

DISASTER AWAITED Grace at the office.

"This is my last season at Rapid Riggers."

Grace and Day stood in the reception area, staring at Nick Colter, listening to the incredible words that were like the sound of money flowing away from their father's river outfit.

Belatedly Grace remembered Day's forecast, that Nick would quit someday. She'd never dreamed someday would arrive so soon. Judging from her sister's expression, Day hadn't, either.

Well aware of what they were losing—one of the best guides in town, who was also an emergency medical technician trained in river rescue—Grace stared into Nick's dark brown eyes, searching for some clue that he wanted something he wasn't getting. More money?

Then she remembered the rest of what Day had projected, and her bad feeling got worse. She asked Nick, "What are you going to do?"

He looked slightly embarrassed, and she knew what was coming. "Start an outfit. A guy in Green River is selling permits for Deso and Labyrinth."

Desolation and Labyrinth canyons on the Green River. Permits were the backbone of any river outfit; it was illegal to carry passengers for hire without them. There was only a limited number of permits in existence, controlled by government agencies, and new ones were rarely issued, so anyone hoping to start a river outfit had to buy permits from another outfitter.

Grace's heart felt like concrete. Nick might start with a few permits, but in time he would rise to be a formidable competitor. He was a popular guide. Without trying, he might take a lot of Rapid Riggers' business.

She said sincerely if coolly, "I wish you luck."

Day lit a cigarette and leaned back against the reception counter in her red-and-white checkered straight skirt and white cashmere sweater. "I don't." Grace and Nick both looked at her, and she said, "Well, good grief. Why be gracious?" She glared at Nick in disgust. "You rat fink."

Grace began laughing, and a minute later Nick was teasing Day, and the tension was broken. But as they went into the kitchen and she studied the logbook to see how many trips were out, she couldn't stop thinking about the reality of losing Nick and what it would mean to Rapid Riggers. She and Day could manage of course, but...

She put her arms on the counter and her head in her hands.

Day might end up managing alone.

Zac had come to claim her, and the path he'd charted for them to follow was a walk to the stars, chasing his dreams.

It was a place Grace wasn't sure she wanted to go. Because what if he left her along the way?

What if he didn't love her enough?

CHAPTER SIX

IT WAS STILL RAINING when Zac drove into the Rapid
Riggers lot later that morning. He needed to return to
his hotel to call his agent and clean up before reporting
to the production office, but he wanted to see Grace first.

As he ducked under the dripping porch eaves and
dried his feet on the mat, he peered through the front
window and saw her talking on the phone at the reception counter. When he pushed open the door, she was
saying, "Unfortunately, Nort, there are no dams upstream from here, and we can't control the water level."

Nort Stills, Zac thought. He glanced through the
streaming windows at the river. Today the Colorado was
living up to the name the Spaniards had given it, the
water an unearthly red. It was flowing fast, eating up the
banks. Would high water present a problem for filming
the movie?

Catching Zac's gaze, Grace said into the phone,
"That's a novel idea. I never thought of diverting the
water to run down the other side of the Rockies. But
unfortunately that's totally out of our hands. We're in
the state of Utah."

Zac was embarrassed. Who but someone from Hollywood would conceive of such a scheme? Nort's suggestion was absurd, and he felt ridiculous by association.

Hanging up the phone minutes later, Grace came

around the counter to greet him. "You're a nice surprise. Where's the dog?"

"Back home on your porch, enjoying a treat from the vet. I thought if you had a minute, you could show me the rock art you said was across the street."

"Sure. Let me tell Day."

When she returned to the reception area moments later, Grace took a jacket from the coatrack and pulled the hood over her head. As they stepped out onto the porch, where the pouring rain made a deafening drumbeat on the awning and metal gutters, she asked, "What did the vet say? Anything interesting?"

"Yes. The dog's a Siberian husky. Probably five months old."

"Purebred?" Starting down the porch steps to the soaking mix of gravel and red mud in the lot, Grace said, "I'd think she'd have more fur."

"Malnourished. But when you pet her, you can feel that downy undercoat. Her leg is just sprained. By the way, the vet agreed with your theory—lost on vacation. So I put an ad in the paper. In a town this size, the owners should turn up soon. If they're about."

Grace was sure they weren't. And she suspected Zac would like to keep the husky.

Changing the subject, she told him about her morning. "Nick's quitting at the end of the season." As she and Zac climbed the embankment to cross the highway, she said, "It's bad for us. He's our best guide, but he's more than that. He trains new boatmen and takes care of equipment. And he's leaving to start an outfit of his own."

Zac's conscience pricked him. Grace was trying to run her father's business, and she needed help—not someone trying to lure her away from it. If she left, Day would be abandoned. Zachary considered another option. He'd helped his parents with the hotel at Oakhurst, and he doubted there was anything he couldn't learn about the river business, given time.

But he wouldn't do it. Couldn't. He was an actor.

Grace said, "I knew we'd lose Nick someday. River guiding is great if you're young and single and don't want to be tied down. But Nick has a lot of drive—and some money."

Zac asked, "What does a river outfit go for?"

"Rapid Riggers? Maybe half a million dollars. Maybe more, the way tourism is hitting Moab. But Nick won't be starting that big." Grace nodded at a slickrock outcropping rising to a mesa on the far side of the road. "The pictograph panel is up there."

As they crossed the highway and hiked up a trail into the rocks, Zac noticed the geology. Some of the exposed layers were as old as the dinosaurs; in the rain it was easy to see how, over the millennia, the wind and water and minerals and the shifting of the earth had formed a landscape of such riotous colors and shapes.

Grace paused to point to the slope beside them. The ground was covered with a knobby black crust. "That's cryptogamic soil. It helps prevent erosion. It's held together by microscopic plant life, and it takes hundreds of thousands of years to form, so you shouldn't step on it."

Zac studied the cryptogam. The dark layer was composed of what looked like hundreds of tiny sand castles, some only half an inch high. He said, "It's beautiful." Hearing a low rumble behind them, he turned to see a sliver of lightning split the smoke-colored sky above the Moab Rim.

"It's far away," Grace said over the rain. "But we're pretty exposed up here. Let's hurry."

The path was steep, muddy sand and loose rock alternating with patches of sandstone as slick as its name. When they reached the base of a sheer vertical wall, Grace said, "There," and pointed at the panels. Zac saw them—russet figures as big as people, painted on pale beige stone.

Thunder boomed again, growing closer, and Grace peered through the downpour at the lightning, but it was still far off. She told Zac, "These pictographs were done by the Fremont Indians maybe a thousand years ago. They used pigments made from mineral deposits." The sky strobed gray-white, and a great crack made them both jump. Grace said, "That's our cue to go back." Cold mud and rain spattered their legs as they hurried down the trail, past sodden clusters of sagebrush.

As they crossed the highway and began their return to Rapid Riggers, Zac asked, "Grace, do you ever think about being a chef again?"

She shrugged. "My mom was a cook, you know. She was from New Orleans. She did all the cooking at the inn."

Zac hadn't known. Thinking of the Princess Room, the tables stacked against one wall, he said, "Perhaps your talent is inherited."

Grace gave him a smile like sunshine, reminding him that she'd never really known her mom.

Avoiding thoughts of his own mother, Zac focused on the inn. "That place has real possibilities." *Possibilities for what?* But he knew. Moab was a visitor town. Had Grace never considered—

As they walked, she tugged her hood more securely over her head. The rain was falling harder now. "It's still zoned commercial."

She *had* considered it.

"But bringing the building up to code would be expensive. Also labor intensive. Really...impossible," she murmured as they reached the Rapid Riggers lot.

Zac was glad she perceived it that way. To him, restoring the inn on the Colorado to what it used to be— and more—didn't seem impossible at all.

He followed Grace up the porch steps but grabbed her arm before she could go inside.

She turned under the dripping awning. "What?"

Zachary eased her back against the siding near the door, out of view of the window. His mouth bent down toward hers. "I didn't *really* stop by to see the rock art...."

THE RAIN STOPPED after lunch, and Grace drove out to the production office to present her proposed menu for the Cataract Canyon trip to Hal Markley. After much thought, she had suggested a week's worth of meals, with three different entrées per night, including dishes for the many vegetarians among the cast and crew. The producers had offered to fly in fresh ingredients daily from as far away as California. And with the studio's generators, Grace could actually run some restaurant equipment. A blender, for instance. She should be able to prepare almost any meal that she could at home.

Visiting the production office would serve a dual purpose. Perhaps she could get a look at the actress who would play Seneca Howland's wife—and lover.

Grace found the Uratomic Building busy, with people in the corridors and talking on phones in the various rooms. The door to Hal Markley's office was shut, so she continued down the hall. In a large meeting room on the right, Martin Place and Kip Hetherington, who would play George Y. Bradley, Powell's second in command, were rehearsing a scene under Meshach Stoker's direction. Carrie Dorchester stood at one side of the room watching. Grace considered giving the coproducer the menu, but instead, she kept wandering, peeping in other open doors. Where was Zac?

Snatches of conversation came to her as she made her way toward the front door, but Grace paid little attention until she heard voices from a room on her left. A man and a woman. One of them sounded like—

Grace stopped at the door and looked in. Zac was leaning against a counter at the far end of the room talking to a pretty blonde in a black schoolgirl-style jumper and white blouse. They were the only people in the room, and their scripts lay on a folding table nearby.

It took little to start that warm longing in Grace's stomach. Just seeing the naturally sexy posture of his tall body. And the way his long hair swept back from his eyes, then forward at the ends, begging to be touched.

He saw her, and his face brightened. His smile was for her alone. "Grace. Come in. There's someone I want you to meet."

Grace crossed the room, trying not to feel anything about Zac's companion. The girl looked maybe eighteen. She was only five foot four or five, and her figure was lithe and elegant. Prettily she exclaimed, "Ah! Zachary's wife?" Beaming at Grace, she held out her hand. "I am Ingrid. I'm very pleased to meet you." She had a Scandinavian accent.

Taking Ingrid's hand, Grace felt as though she was reaching into a black widow's nest.

Ingrid said, "Your husband—he is so kind to me." She gave Zac a look of affection and asked Grace, "You and I will be friends?"

Grace wondered how she could think so but said, "It's nice to meet you."

Ingrid smiled again, then looked at the clock. Gathering up her script from the table, she told Zac, "Ten minutes till we show Meshach how good we are. I'll see you later, Grace." She waved and left the room.

Grace said, "I'm glad you're kind to her, Zac."

Zachary lifted his eyebrows mildly, and Grace regretted the sarcasm. She sounded jealous. And she was.

Zac knew. Obviously the notion of the bedroom scene bothered her. But it was going to happen. "Grace, I'm accepting Hal's offer."

Grace held herself straight, tried to be as indifferent as the river. "I know that." At least, she'd guessed, which wasn't the same as hearing him say it. She restrained her emotions, composing herself. She couldn't control Zac. She couldn't make him do what she wanted. She had to trust him.

Grace glanced down at the menu, then toward the door. "I'd better go."

Zac knew she was angry. In a perverse way, it made him respect her. It also gave him hope. She cared what he did. He said, "I want to see you tonight. I should be done by eight. Is there a good movie in town?"

"Just the usual Hollywood pabulum."

It was a phrase of his own, from the days when he'd turned up his nose at feature films. And Zac knew the dig extended to *Kah-Puh-Rats*. "All right. What else is going on? When does Day's musical open?"

"Next Thursday."

"What about the canyonlands slide show?"

"It's playing tonight." Grace could hardly see straight. "So what position are you going to use?"

Zac expelled a breath and went to the door and shut it. Then he returned to where she stood by the table. He said coldly, "As the scene reads, I'm going to be sitting against the headboard of the bed, and she's going to straddle me and—"

Grace didn't know she was moving. She only felt the hard, slapping contact of her palm against his face.

"*Grace.*" He grabbed her wrist—then both wrists.

Grace's eyes were burning. She could see the red mark on his face, the hurt in his eyes, and she was ashamed of herself, but she couldn't stop. "You know why you're doing this? Because you want to. You're an exhibitionist." She tried to jerk her hands from his grasp.

He held her, and she felt the roughness of his skin, a roughness that came from working with his hands on her house. Those hands made her wild. Those hands should touch only her.

Zac was angry now. "Don't say things you'll regret, and don't provoke me to say things I'll regret."

Grace knew he spoke wisely. She said, "They can put together a love scene without making money from your naked body."

That was true enough to sting. Zac believed any competent actor should be able to handle nudity with professionalism and without a blush, but he also knew his anatomy was what the producers of *Kah-Puh-Rats* wanted. What Grace said struck so hard, at such a core place, that for a moment he hated her for saying it. She'd called him cheap.

He felt cheap.

He thought of how desperate he'd become to make up for what had happened in New York. Desperate to succeed. But he also thought of who he was and what he'd chosen to do with his life and the obvious fact that the woman he'd married hated it.

Enough to hit him.

Releasing her hands, he turned and collected his script, a sheaf of white and blue pages, from the table. He spoke sharply. "Grace, if you're remotely interested in saving our marriage, I suggest you get one thing through your head. You married an actor. And that isn't going to change."

Grace felt like crying—not because he was an actor but because she had revealed how she felt about it and because a patch of red still stained the honey skin of his left cheekbone. Her gaze swept over him. The hair she had stroked as they lay in bed at night. His face. His rangy limbs.

He had been hers. She couldn't stand the thought of another woman's legs around him.

Quietly, as though they had not argued or exchanged some of the harshest words of their marriage, as though his wife had not struck him, Zac said, "I think the slide show starts at nine. I'll pick you up at eight-thirty."

Grace nodded. He did not touch her again, nor she

him, and as they left the room together, she felt they were worlds apart.

SHE DIDN'T RETURN to Rapid Riggers immediately. Instead, she drove up the river road to a beach near the mouth of Negro Bill Canyon. Walking down a sand footpath to the river, Grace found that a mountain biker had claimed the spot for a camp site; so she followed the silty shoreline around the bend until she was alone.

On a low flat rock beside the river, she sat in the sun and watched the water. She had hit Zac. It was the ugliest thing she'd ever done, the ugliest thing that had ever passed between them. Even furious about the green card, she had not descended to that.

She was ashamed. Zac was an actor. What he was going to do wasn't adultery. She'd read a half-dozen times that filming love scenes was not remotely erotic for the actors.

But it made Grace crazy with fear. What if he became attracted to Ingrid?

Any temptation I feel is the result of sleeping alone for a year.

I can't sleep with him, Grace thought. *He hurt me too badly. He's hurting me now.*

But when she considered Zac taking off his clothes and pretending to make love with that beautiful girl, with her sitting on top and in front of him, where he would see her breasts and feel... And then going back to his hotel room, the same hotel where that actress was staying...

There was only one thing to do.

She had to get him back under her roof.

WHEN SHE RETURNED to Rapid Riggers, Grace put on her bikini and some cutoffs and went outdoors to repair a D-ring on a raft. She wanted to avoid Day. Grace had told her about Zac's role in the movie, but she wasn't ready to hear what her sister would say about the love scene.

Day had been around for the past fourteen months. And Grace couldn't break Zac's confidence and explain why he hadn't been. Naturally her sister was suspicious of him.

While she was working, Nick returned from rowing the Daily and came to see how the repair was progressing. Crouching beside her in the sand near the overturned raft, he said, "So, how are things going with your husband? Fast Susan said you went out with him last night."

News traveled fast at Rapid Riggers. Susan must have seen her with Zac. Grace longed to confide in Nick—ask him if *he* could lie in a movie-set bed with Ingrid Dolk without getting a hard-on. But what was between her and Zac was too personal to discuss with anyone.

When she didn't answer, Nick said, "I didn't mean to pry. I've just got a bug in my brain I can't shake. I wondered if you might be moving away from Moab with him."

Grace felt a little start go through her. She knew what Nick was working around to, and it felt threatening. "Day and I aren't selling this outfit, Nick."

As soon as she spoke, she wished she'd said it differently. Nick was more than an employee. She'd known him since he was fourteen and living a wild Huck Finn existence in caves along the river. No one knew where he'd come from or much about him, and her dad had looked after him as much as Nick would allow, just to keep social services away from the boy who was too much animal to sleep indoors, to answer to the orders of strict foster parents who didn't understand him.

It made her heart twist in a funny way to know that while he was thinking of starting an outfit of his own, he really wanted Rapid Riggers.

He couldn't have it.

Now he said, "Just checking." Smiling good-naturedly, he stood up and stretched. "I'd better go de-rig and carry out the trash for Her Royal Highness."

Grace squinted up at him. "We'll miss you."

Nick looked around the boat yard at the equipment— the buses, the Jeeps, the trailers, the rafts, all of which Grace knew he had somehow made his own through the work of his hands. He said, "I'll miss this place, too."

As he went inside, Grace thought of Zac and her marriage and what she'd told Nick. *Day and I aren't selling this outfit.*

What if they must?

What if she had to choose between her husband—a man who loved his career more than anything—and the business her father had built from scratch, one of the oldest river outfits in Moab, Utah?

Who am I kidding?

That was exactly the choice she faced.

SHE WANTED HIM home. She knew how much when she reached the house that evening, saw the work he'd done on the screens, saw the stray he'd taken in. The puppy was waiting for her on the porch, her coat clean and fluffy. Grace found the dog brush on a table near the kitchen door, with a box of dog biscuits. Zac had left the kitchen immaculate, and there was a vase of wild-flowers on the maple trestle table.

Seeing a note beside the vase, Grace snapped on the overhead, went to the table and found two pieces of paper from a Paris hotel. The words on the top sheet were written in French, but she grasped what they were—a recipe from a chef named Claude Renault at the Maison de Something-or-other. On the second page, Zac had translated the recipe for a cream sauce.

He had thought of her this past year. Gifts. The music box. The recipe.

The phone rang, and Grace jumped. Turning from the table, she lifted the receiver from the old-fashioned wall unit. "Hello?"

In the transportation office at the Uratomic Building, Zac tried to relax. Their earlier battle had been a draw and the war was still on; but he would make peace how-ever he could. Unfortunately what he had to say now wouldn't help. Glancing over his shoulder as a produc-tion assistant wandered in, he said into the phone, "It's me."

Zac heard her little intake of breath. Was she still angry, too?

She didn't sound like it as she answered, "Hi, Zach-ary."

It was only his name, but the way she said it made him feel as if he'd had the wind knocked out of him. The production assistant left the room, and Zac was glad. He had the transportation office to himself.

Grace said, "I'm sorry I hit you."

Zac was sorry he'd incited it. He had things to tell her, things he'd been thinking about, but he wasn't going to say them on the phone. Gently he replied, "Don't worry. I'll get my licks in sometime when we're alone."

Grace knew he wasn't talking about hitting. Heat seeped through her. And relief. He wasn't angry. He didn't think less of her. He was saying tender things on the telephone. She hugged herself.

Eyeing the flowers he'd left on the table, she said, "Thanks for the recipe. How did you get it?"

"It wasn't easy." Not wanting to think of the months he'd been without her or his habit of buying gifts for her, as though she was still his, he came to the reason for his call. "Grace, I can't make our date. It's going to be a late night here."

"Oh." Grace was crushed. She'd been looking forward to the date, to mending their rift. To making him forget how she felt about his job—and that she'd hit him.

This conversation was all she had. She asked, "Zac, would you like to stay here, instead of at the hotel? I could make up a room for you."

Zac clenched the phone receiver, his emotions see-sawing. He didn't ask if she was sure. He didn't want her to change her mind. "Thank you. I'd like that."

Grace's heart eased. Shaky-hot inside, she said, "Since you'll be late, I'll leave the kitchen door unlocked. Your room is the one off the parlor. You shouldn't have trouble finding it. It's the only one with a bed."

"I know which it is." He'd seen it that morning—the butter-colored walls and French doors, the antique writing desk and the rocking chair, the full-size bed with captain's drawers beneath. The mattress was covered with the purple satin-and-velvet quilt he and Grace had used in New York.

Needless to say, it was not Grace's room.

He said, "I want to sleep with you."

Grace trembled, visualizing him climbing into her bed late that night as he used to when he came home from the theater. She checked the fantasy. "First let's make sure we're not going to hurt each other again."

Zac couldn't argue. Hardly realizing he was holding one arm hard against his stomach, straining to hold in his feelings, he said, "I'll be there about one. And I'll look forward to seeing you in the morning. We'll run again, all right?"

Hanging up the phone moments later, Grace impulsively embraced the dog. Zac was coming home. As the husky licked her nose, Grace remembered their old routine in New York, things she'd done for Zac when she knew he'd be late after rehearsal or a performance.

While the puppy dozed in its box bed, Grace set a bread dough to rise. Next she sliced onions and leeks to sauté, peeled and chopped yams and carrots, and grated ginger and lemon and lime peels for a sweet-potato-and-carrot soup. While the ingredients simmered in the stock, she sliced nuts for a brandy walnut tart. The occupation was satisfying. This was not Rapid Riggers. This was not Jean-Michel's. She had someone coming home. Zac was coming home.

Between tasks in the kitchen, she cleaned the downstairs bathroom and changed the sheets on the bed in her father's old room. She and Day had cleaned out the room after his death, and Nick had taken his bed to the carriage house and brought down another from upstairs. The room received afternoon sunlight through French doors on the west wall, and often when she came home from work Grace had lain reading on the bed, on the quilt that had been hers and Zac's.

Now she felt bittersweet anticipation because he would be sleeping in this room. While she emptied the bureau drawers and lined them, she avoided thoughts of their long separation and strange tales of madness she couldn't comprehend. Nor did she ponder the distant future—Hollywood looming on the horizon, a lifetime of tabloids and sexy love scenes. She thought only of the present, of the man she loved coming into her house that night, eating food she'd prepared, sleeping between sheets she'd washed.

Sleeping apart. It was for the best. She wouldn't allow it to dampen her spirits.

When the soup and bread were done, Grace wrote Zac a note and then went through the house closing up for the night. Leaving the kitchen door unlocked, the soup warming and the light burning over the stove, she climbed the stairs to her bedroom with the husky behind her.

But after she'd gotten ready for bed, she didn't immediately turn down the covers. Instead, she went to her mother's armoire. Beside Zac's music box sat the pink jewelry case her father had given her when she was seven.

Opening the lid, Grace removed trays loaded with baubles and reached into the bottom. The band of gold and that small hoop earring with the diamond and heart winked at her seductively in the glow from her lamp, but she touched neither. Instead, she pulled out a handmade card with a picture Zac had sketched of himself in his waiter's clothing. He'd written the words "Love is…" There was another picture inside the card. On the right, her in a chef's hat. On the left, Zac the waiter brought her a heart on a platter. Or, rather, three removable heart coupons secured to the card through a slot in the paper. The words inside concluded the message on the front: "...you and me."

Love is you and me. Yours truly, Zachary.

The card would never lose its power for her. Whenever she looked at it, she believed he had loved her. She believed until she put it away and could think, instead of only feel.

She pulled out the three coupons. Penned across the topmost heart was the inscription, "This coupon is good for 1 Romeo and Juliet Bed."

A handmade bed, like the one in Franco Zeffirelli's version of the Shakespearean tragedy. She and Zachary had watched the movie on video, and she had said, *What a great bed.* They'd rewound the film several times to look at it. Zac had said, *I could make a bed like that.*

Grace knew he could. He was a good carpenter, a good craftsman. He'd made them a cherry coffee table once, a replica of one they'd seen at the Metropolitan Museum of Art.

He'd cut a hole through the wall of their apartment.

Grace couldn't imagine it. The image seemed unreal, and swiftly she replaced it with thoughts of the romantic gift Zac had given her on Valentine's Day. A promise to build a bed for them.

She couldn't use the coupon now, so she slid it behind the others and examined the next heart, which read, "This coupon is good for Anything." And the third: "This coupon is good for Doing the Income Tax."

Angel, Grace thought. Almost any man who would offer to do the income tax was a keeper in her book.

But what Zac had done to her was so grave, so unforgivable...

Grace peered out the French doors at the water moving through the moon's reflection on the surface of the river. The sight reminded her of Br'er Rabbit tricking his friends into retrieving the moon from the millpond. Grace knew how Br'er Fox and the others must have felt when they discovered the treachery. It was how she'd felt learning Zac had married her for a green card.

Their love was the moon fallen in the water, suddenly within reach. It was only illusion, though. Couldn't be anything else. But Zac had made her believe it was real.

Then stolen it away.

WHEN HE PARKED the Austin-Healey under the cottonwoods, the only light Zac saw was a small glow from the kitchen, and he knew Grace had gone to bed. In the dark he carried his suitcase and garment bag across the muddy yard to the house. Leaving his shoes on the porch, he opened the kitchen door and let himself in.

At once the smell of food filled his nostrils. Zac spotted the bread cooling on a rack in the oven and the soup pot simmering on the stove, but before he could investigate, the husky pressed against his legs. She rubbed the sides of his jeans, then sat in front of him, looking up expectantly. Zac set down his luggage, then spent some time with the dog, rubbing the fluffy fur he'd brushed that morning. The husky licked his face, showing more energy than she had the day before. Knowing he and the dog were alone, Zac murmured ridiculous endearments to her, petted her and generally made much of her before he stood and went to the stove.

Under the light he admired the loaves Grace had

baked and lifted the lid on the pot, inhaling. On the table
was a note tucked beneath the edge of a pie pan holding
a walnut tart—his favorite.

Leaning over the table, Zac read what she'd written.

> You can cut the bread and the tart and help yourself
> to some soup. When you're finished, please put ev-
> erything away. Also, there are tea leaves in the
> pot—no caffeine. Sweet dreams.
>
> —Grace

Zac braced his hands on the table and stood there
quietly for a long time. Then, picking up the pen she'd
left lying on the table, he wrote at the base of the note,
"Thank you, my sweet chef." He scrawled an X and an
O and signed his name, then filled the kettle and put it
on the stove and took out the cutting board to slice the
bread.

Perhaps it was because of exhaustion after twelve
hours at the production office, but as he worked under
her stove light Zac couldn't control his thoughts,
couldn't stop the unproductive ones. Unwillingly he remembered month after month of coming home at night
to an empty apartment that was like a shell and fixing
quick solitary meals that always left him hungry. For
Grace.

Now he was in her home. She'd made him a wonderful meal. They were coming back together.

But it felt neither complete nor secure. This glimpse
of the heaven that had once been his was only his now
by a tenuous thread. He wanted to keep it. He wanted
more. Things he'd once taken for granted that now he
might never possess. Grace. A family.

The teakettle began to spurt steam. Lifting the whistle before it could scream and bother Grace upstairs, Zac held the kettle until it really boiled, then turned off the burner and fixed some tea. Half an hour later, after he'd eaten, put away the food and straightened the kitchen, he collected his suitcase and garment bag and took them through the parlor into the room where Grace had told him to sleep.

The husky padded after him, and Zac smiled at the dog, liking her pointed ears and different-colored eyes. The vet had predicted the dog's adult coat would be black with white markings, and Zac could see the white mask already delineated on her face. Trying to forget that he'd always wanted a husky and trying to remember that this one could not be his, Zac asked, "Spending the night with me?"

The puppy collapsed on the braided rug.

Grace had left on a small tiffany lamp that stood on the Victorian bureau. In its mellow light, Zac walked about the room, examining everything. A rocking chair in the corner that looked a hundred years old. A wedding portrait on the chest—Grace's parents. On the wall, faded photographs of the inn in its heyday.

Zac studied the pictures with interest. The random-width planks on the floor of the screened porch were buffed to a high polish, and the painted pillars were truly white. Seeing a photo of Grace's father and mother standing on the porch, arms about each other, Zac wondered how the owner of such a showplace could have let it go to ruin.

But then his eyes caught those of Grace's mother, and though the photo was black and white, he knew they were brown eyes. Brown eyes with arched black eyebrows.

He saw the way Sam Sutter was looking at his wife, and Zachary knew exactly how the house had fallen apart.

The man had fallen first, when he lost the woman he loved.

CHAPTER SEVEN

AT SIX-FIFTEEN, as Grace filled the French press with
coffee grounds in the dawn light from the eastern window, she heard the alarm clock beep in her father's old
room, then water running in the bathroom. The husky
wandered into the kitchen, and Grace said, "Hello,
there." A few minutes later, Zac whistled from the front
porch, and the puppy trotted off through the dining
room, answering the call to breakfast.

Soon after, Zac joined Grace in the kitchen. He was
wearing threadbare gray sweatpants and looked sleepy
and unshaven, like the person she used to wake up with
every morning. Like her husband.

Grace had found the note he'd written beneath hers
and had taken it upstairs to keep. Now, however, she
thought of what had happened at the film office. It was
the last time she'd seen him, and she still felt embarrassed over her loss of control.

Zachary ended her anxiety. Meeting her at the
counter, he reached for her shoulders and hauled her to
his bare chest, and Grace felt his heart knocking through
her T-shirt as he hugged her close. As she held him, too.

"Good morning." His jaw scraped her silky skin, and
his nose burrowed into her neck, feeding on her scent.
Stepping back, he lifted her face with his hands, tipping
her chin up. Touching. "Grace. Yesterday—" She

opened her mouth, and he shook his head. "Let me talk. Obviously the idea of my filming a love scene distresses you." He remembered the shocking contact of her hand with his face. "I think you're overreacting. But I would never hurt you intentionally. If you don't want me to accept the expanded role, I won't." The words almost made him choke, but there was no alternative. When she'd struck him, he'd seen the pain he was causing. Self-assured Grace—hitting. He was sorry it had come to that.

Grace stared up at him, feeling both the tightness in his body and the tenderness of his hands on her face. She knew what he was sacrificing. Zac had worked long for this chance. *Kah-Puh-Rats* wasn't great cinema, but it might mean a step to better roles. And it was a matter of timing that the producers wanted to expand Zac's part. He was this season's hot male model. Someone else might be hotter next month.

Grace felt the gift he'd offered—choice.

She gave it back to him. She'd been without him, and now, like a miracle, he was in her arms. "It's okay. I want you to do what you think is best for your career."

Zac's heart pressed closer to hers. She had handed him her trust. She wouldn't be sorry. "Thank you."

He was crushing her fiercely, and Grace adored it. But it reminded her how deep things had been, how far down they'd gone, exploring together till they ran out of air. Then—there—where they'd needed each other, they'd separated. And Zac, her love... Suppressing panic, Grace said, "Let's go running. Then I'll make buttermilk, wild-rice, pecan pancakes for breakfast."

Zac didn't let go. He hid his face in her hair, trammeling his thoughts, but they broke loose and filled his mind. Recollections of empty nights and solitary mornings, of strange days and nights in New York, of the bleak world he'd seen around him as he took out a saw and began cutting through the wall of their fourth-floor walk-up, looking for hidden wires, wires to explain the voices he was hearing. Warding off those images and others—the frightening days he'd spent among library stacks in New York and California, trying to learn what had happened to him—he thought of the photo on the wall of the room where he'd just awakened, the picture of Grace's father and the woman with the brown eyes.

His heart whispered the words he knew his mouth wouldn't say again, not after he'd said them and been ignored.

Gracie, don't ever leave me. Don't go....

HE HAD REHEARSAL all day. Grace came home for lunch, but Zac wasn't there, and she ate alone with the dog for company. Nor was he home when she returned that evening. He'd been there, however. Grace saw he'd made more progress on the porch, and she found a note on the kitchen table saying he hoped to be back by nine—but not to fix a meal because he wasn't sure.

During the evening, three people called in answer to his ad in the paper—'"Found: Husky puppy. Call..."' As she and Zac had agreed, Grace asked each caller the sex of the lost pet, color, and so on. None of the owners belonged to the animal sitting at her feet.

It was ten when the Austin-Healey bumped down the sand road that night. As Zac climbed out of the convertible, script in hand, the husky pushed open the screen door and came down the steps to greet him. Zac petted the dog, then went up to the house, and Grace met him on the porch.

Barefoot, wearing a pair of old gym shorts and a man's sleeveless undershirt, she looked voluptuous and sexy and womanly. Familiar. His. He grabbed her and held on.

Hugging back, she said, "There's soup on the stove." White bean and mushroom. "Also some *perciatelli* and *biscotti*."

Homecoming. The feeling was so powerful Zac couldn't answer. He listened to leaves rustling and insects humming and the river kissing the shore. He felt the woman in his arms. The Anasazi Palace had nothing on the River Inn. The River Inn had Grace.

She finally pulled away. "Hey, Zac, don't knock yourself out fixing the house. You're working long days on the film."

Staring through a torn screen at the moonlight on the river, Zac wondered if she thought he was going to crack again, the way he had in New York. He didn't answer. He would refinish the floors upstairs and repair the walls, but it was wasted labor. His time in Grace's house by the Colorado was short. He had to return to California— or if not there, New York.

Nonetheless, he liked the work. He always had, even at Oakhurst, when he knew he was putting love and sweat into what would never be his.

The two situations seemed similar.

Grace said, "Come inside and eat."

Zac eyed her with pleasure and whistled a familiar melody as he followed her inside. "Love Is Here to Stay."

Grace glanced over her shoulder at him and smiled.

She'd laid a single place at the table. As the dog settled in its bed and Grace went to the stove to heat water for tea, Zac said, "You're not eating?"

"I ate earlier." Setting a bowl of soup at his place, she eyed the script in his hand and asked, "Why are some of the pages white and some blue and some pink?"

"Changes. The original is white. The first changes were blue. And I got the pink pages before I left tonight."

Wondering if the love scene was pink, Grace started to go back to the stove to get him more food. But Zac grabbed her hand.

"Don't wait on me, Grace. I can help myself."

She looked at him, at his tall body and the way his paisley flannel shirt clung loosely to his broad shoulders. Aware of his hand holding her fingers, touching her palm, she said, "I want to."

And he wanted to take her to bed. "Leave the dishes. I'll wash up."

"Okay."

Zac sat down and watched her return to the stove to get him a plate of pasta. When she set it in front of him, he said, "Do you have a calendar, Grace? Let's make some plans."

It sounded good to her. Turning away, she took a hardware-store calendar off the wall by the phone. Then she pulled out a chair beside him. When the calendar lay before them, Zac held her hand under the table and let their linked fingers rest on top of his thigh as he scanned her schedule. Production on the film would begin a week from Saturday. On the calendar, Grace had noted certain days with names of places. Desolation Canyon. Labyrinth Canyon. Cataract Canyon.

She told Zac, "That's when you'll be filming on the river."

Zac pointed to the week after the start of production. "I'm going to New York on Tuesday. I have an interview on 'JoAnn.'"

"The JoAnn Carroll Show"? Grace thought. "JoAnn" was big, one of the most popular of the afternoon talk shows.

"I'll be back late Thursday. They're filming around me."

Grace reached across the table for a pen and handed it to him so that he could write on the calendar. Still holding her hand beneath the table, he smiled at her and marked the dates, and Grace felt the intimacy of coordinating schedules, of planning together. Of sitting in her house at ten at night holding hands with him. Of his hard thigh, warm beneath denim... He pressed her hand to his leg and moved his own so that he could eat. After a moment, Grace withdrew. She felt melting hot. Aroused.

Between bites of soup and *perciatelli* and *biscotti*, Zac asked, "Would you like to come to New York?"

Grace's heart rushed, and she stared at the calendar, trying to think if she could.

"I won't have much free time," Zac said. "But we can be together at night. Go out for dinner. Do some things." His eyes suggested what things.

"I'd like that a lot."

"So would I." Zac returned his attention to his food, but Grace saw he was still thinking about plans, and at last he asked, "Did you talk to your lawyer about the money?"

"They faxed me something this afternoon. You can

pay them." She should drop the divorce suit now. They were really working things out.

But it had been only a few days.

Zac didn't seem interested in pursuing the topic. He said, "I want to give you some money for groceries and household expenses."

Grace felt strange feelings stirring inside her. He *had* been a good husband. Always. Until she'd left him and things had gotten so bad for him that he couldn't face her until he made his own life right again....

After a few minutes—after they'd set a date to see the musical and another for a picnic in Arches National Park—Grace got up from the table and hung up the calendar. While he sat at the table reading his script, she went upstairs and dressed for bed, putting on a long, white cotton nightgown that Zac used to like. Slipping a thick French terry robe over it, she went back downstairs. He had finished eating and cleaned up, and now he was in the bathroom with the water running. Remembering nights they'd shared a cup of tea before bed, Grace put the kettle on the stove. She was just filling the pot when Zac came into the kitchen.

He wore the faded jeans he'd had on earlier, and his flannel shirt was unbuttoned, as though he was ready to slide everything off and get into bed. Seeing that he could barely keep his eyes open, she set down the kettle and said, "Go to bed."

He smiled drowsily. "Not without a snack." He stood looking at her like a kid contemplating which end of a cookie to bite first. Grace stared back at him, studying all the bones in his face, his handsome features, the lips made for kissing her.

At last Zac took her face in his hands. She trembled,

feeling the rough pads of his fingers brushing hair from her brow. Grace knew he saw her shaking. There was a tenderness in his expression that meant he was aware of her vulnerability. Eyes smiling down into hers, he moved half a step closer, saying, "It's all right, Gracie. It doesn't have to end in bed."

Her breath felt dry as the desert, and her voice sounded like tissue paper. "I know."

Zac's mouth came closer, and then it was on hers. Her knees threatened to fold against his. He was untying her robe, and she pulled her head away and choked out, "No."

He didn't pause. He slid his hands inside, wrapped his arms around her between her nightgown and robe. "This is all right, isn't it?" It was all right with him. It was making him hard.

It was heaven. Grace nodded, and then they were kissing again, and she was touching his chest. The words came out although she didn't intend them. "I love you."

Afraid of what he might say, Zac covered her lips before either of them could talk anymore. Some things were easier to communicate without words. And some things shouldn't be said.

Don't leave....

THE NEXT MORNING Zac was up before she was. When Grace went downstairs, the French doors in the parlor were open, and she looked through the screen to see him crouched in the grass beyond the stone patio, studying the ground. He was shirtless, his hair mussed as though he'd just awakened, and the dog hovered near him, wagging its tail. New behavior.

Smiling, Grace pushed open the screen door and went out.

The sky was foggy gray, the air damp, and right away she noticed the mosquitoes were out. She slapped one on her arm as Zac crossed to meet her on the stone steps.

Grace remembered their long kiss the night before, his tongue in her mouth, his hands holding her head and then her shoulders. And she remembered how she had felt when they'd said good-night and he had gone through the house locking up. He was just one person, but suddenly her home was full.

And this morning he was still here.

Zac glanced at the weeds behind him. He wanted to share his idea—a croquet pitch. But he was just dreaming, just having fun imagining...the inn. This was Grace's home, a place dear to her. He shouldn't make her hope they could stay. So all he asked was "Did anyone answer my ad last night?"

Grace nodded. "But not the owners." She told him about the calls.

Zac smiled at the dog, reminding himself not to become attached. "If no one claims her first, we'll have to do something with her when we go to New York. And down the river, of course."

"I'll ask Day if she'll watch her." As Zac threw a stick and the dog bounded after it, Grace said, "She's a nice dog, isn't she? We should call her something."

"She's not ours to name," Zac answered, telling himself as much as Grace.

"Hungry?" she asked after a moment.

"Yes." Zac came up the last two steps and put his arms around her. She wasn't wearing a bra, and the worn cotton of her shirt was little shield between her breasts and his skin. He thought of sex and of food. She sharpened all his appetites. For a man who'd grown up on meals prepared by servants more efficient than friendly, in a world that had been perilously uncertain in the most primal way, Grace's strength and talents were aphrodisiac and nourishment. He would never get enough of her. He said, "I'm always hungry. Tell me where to find a gym, though. I miss my weight machine."

Grace smiled. Zac was lean and rangy and possessed of a bottomless stomach. Putting weight on him was a lifetime task.

And they could have a lifetime....

IT WAS DIFFICULT to explain to Day.

"He's *living* with you?" Day looked at her watch. She looked at the calendar on her desk. She looked at Grace.

Grace knew what she was thinking. Zac had shown up only days ago. Four days. She said, a little defensively, "Well, he has his own room."

Day burst out laughing. "We know how long *that's* going to last."

Grace shut the office door and dropped a life vest on the couch to protect herself from the springs popping through. Sitting down, she faced the sister who had been with her through the hardest times, who'd seen her missing Zac while he'd ignored her existence—while he'd ignored her father's death. Now Day was sitting in her stenographer's chair, the computer humming and a cigarette burning in the ashtray beside her, waiting to know how he'd earned forgiveness.

Grace said, "Day, he had a good reason why he

wasn't in touch with me, but it's nothing I can share." She added, "We're working things out."

Day's face betrayed a mix of reactions. Skepticism. Reflection. Acceptance. At last she said, "All right, if you like him, I can like him. Zac has his good points. Looks. Brains. Money. Sexy voice."

Kind to animals. Fixes things, thought Grace. Day would be less complimentary if she knew about the love scene Zac was going to do. Omitting that detail, Grace told her Zachary's movie role had been expanded and she was going to New York with him.

"Zac's going to be on 'JoAnn'?" Day exclaimed. "Is it because of those Ben Rogan ads?"

"I think so."

Day grinned. "You'll probably get to stay at some fabulous hotel and go to Twenty-One." Reaching for her cigarette with a mischievous expression, she asked, "Did you find out how much money he makes? Those Ben Rogan models rake it in. Some of those guys make three thousand dollars an hour."

Grace was stunned. No wonder he could afford to pay her legal bills.

No wonder he wasn't worried about the INS.

Day asked, "Are you bringing the movie star to the musical?"

"Opening night." Thursday, two days before shooting began. And on some unknown date after that, her husband would get into bed naked with Ingrid Dolk.

ON THURSDAY NIGHT Grace was home before Zac. The musical would start at eight, and he had promised he'd be finished with rehearsal by seven-thirty.

At six-thirty, Grace hurried downstairs in her bathrobe, wet-haired from a shower, to throw in a load of laundry. Remembering she'd told Zac she would wash some of his clothes, she went into his room to collect them. The puppy followed her.

She felt strange entering the room. It was Zac's space. It even had a masculine smell that was exclusively his. And all Grace's senses responded to the sight of clothes and books in one corner on the floor and of his shirts hanging in the closet. Once their clothes had been bunched together on the same rod.

Over the past week, they'd established a routine. After they took a morning run with the dog, Zac played the piano while Grace made breakfast. Then he left for the production office and she for Rapid Riggers, sometimes taking the husky along. If Zac had breaks during the day, he went home and worked on her house. And every night they spent a long time kissing…caressing. The night before, his hand had slid inside her gown, to her breasts. It had been hard to part and go to separate rooms. Separate beds. Grace had tossed restlessly, remembering what they'd had in New York.

But nothing would ever be that simple again.

Three times during the week she had found reasons to visit the production office. Meshach Stoker, the director, wanted the actors to practice rowing the Powell dories under the guidance of Rapid Riggers boatmen, so Grace had gone down to the film office to set up a time. On another occasion she'd given Cute Nick and Dirty Bob a ride to the Uratomic Building; they would be doing white-water stunts for the film and needed to be seen by wardrobe and makeup. And a third time Grace had gone to take another look at the dories. *Talk about a lame excuse….*

She'd watched Zac rehearse with Ingrid. Grace didn't think he was attracted to the actress—though he could make anyone believe it when he was acting. But Grace couldn't help wondering if he'd prefer to be married to someone who shared his work. A man who looked like Zac could have his pick of women. What if he became bored with her and picked someone else?

Grace hid her worry. She never again wanted to reveal the insecurity that had made her hit him. That had made her leave him.

As she stood in his bedroom, she thought of her doubts and wondered if she'd ever be sure. The green card...well, she'd never forget it. But at some point she would have to choose whether to divorce Zac or trust him.

Grace looked at his neatly made bed, and the decision was easy. *I'll tell him tonight.*

They would make love and sleep in each other's arms. Feeling light, both nervous and excited, Grace went to the corner of the room and gathered up a pair of Ben Rogan jeans, a polka-dot shirt, socks and the shorts he wore running. His Oxford sweatshirt was on the bottom, and she picked that up, too, and smelled it. Clean.

As she moved to set it back down, her eyes fell on the books and papers lying against the baseboard. The papers were articles about huskies photocopied from the periodicals on CD-ROM at the Moab library. Zac hadn't been able to find a book about the breed, and he'd said most of the available articles were about sled-dog racing.

Crouching with Zac's laundry in her arms, Grace picked up one of those articles and read a few paragraphs. Though sprint races were popular in the early 1900s, the first long-distance races were run in the seventies. In recent years, the latter had lost much of their sponsorship and been condemned by animal-protection groups because of the number of dogs who died, usually from heart failure. But even the race conditions sounded harsh. Temperatures sometimes fifty degrees below zero, surprise blizzards, the dogs' paws bleeding through their booties.... Nonetheless, huskies were born for that climate. Instinctively they dug holes in the snow for warmth at night. And the mushers used only voice commands to direct their dogs, no whips or reins.

Glancing down at the puppy Zac had found, Grace reflected that once dog sleds had been the only cross-tundra transport. That was the heritage of the Siberian husky. Now the dog at her feet was living in the desert.

But where was her home? Would her owners ever turn up?

Grace set down the article and straightened, then scanned the titles of Zachary's books. A battered paperback collection of Tennessee Williams plays. A novel by Julio Cortázar. And *An Actor's Handbook* by Constantin Stanislavski. Beneath that lay a large paperback volume with a crimson cover. Grace couldn't see the front, so she glanced at the binding.

DSM-IV. Strange name. Probably another book about acting. As she dropped Zac's sweatshirt on the books, Grace heard the kitchen door, and the puppy raced out of the room. Zac was home. Still holding the dirty clothes, Grace went out to meet him.

He was greeting the dog, rubbing her head and scratching her ears. He had a treat in his hand, and when he saw Grace, he told the puppy, "Sit. Sit. Good girl." He gave her the dog biscuit, then carried the laundry to the utility room for Grace. As he lifted the lid on the washing machine, he looked down at the clothes and froze.

He'd thrown them in the corner of his room.

On top of the books.

Heart pounding, he stuffed the laundry into the machine and hurried back into the kitchen, his eyes immediately searching Grace's. She smiled at him.

She didn't see it.

He fought down the tense, panicky feeling binding his chest. It wasn't as though he needed to hide the book from her. After all, he'd told her the facts.

But he couldn't lose Grace again. She was his stability. In the world of acting, anything could and did change without notice. The script was five different colors now, and new decisions faced him daily. An invitation to model for his own calendar. Offers for interviews. His life was hurtling forward faster than he could control it.

Coming home to the River Inn at night, waking up there in the morning to the dog licking his hand, eating the meals Grace made, running, hammering nails...made him feel strong, like a different person than he'd been for the past year, when he was alone, haunted by what had happened in New York.

Here, he slept without nightmares.

Grace was still smiling at him. She was in her bathrobe, not yet dressed for the play, and Zac briefly placed his hands on her shoulders. "Wait here," he said. "Don't move."

He hurried down the hall and through the parlor to his room, where he went to the closet and dragged out his suitcase. He found the shopping bag and took out the dress. It was a Ben Rogan design, a glove-soft leather sheath in four colors—red, yellow, blue and black. He'd bought it on Rodeo Drive for Grace, when he wasn't sure if he'd ever see her wear it.

Leaving his suitcase, Zac turned to go back out to the kitchen, but his eyes caught his sweatshirt in the corner of the room.

Pulse tripping, he went over and picked it up, looking beneath. Tennessee Williams, Stanislavski and *Hopscotch* on top. Breathing hard, he grabbed the book under them and looked around the room for a place to put it. The shopping bag caught his eye. Battling guilt, he wrapped *DSM-IV* in the bag and closed it in his empty suitcase.

Then he went out to Grace.

THEY REACHED the Moab Community Theater at twenty to eight and found places in the fifth row with a crowd of boatmen from Rapid Riggers. Zac sat between Grace and Fast Susan, a six-foot thirty-eight-year-old guide with a blond mohawk. Susan had just returned from a Cataract Canyon trip. While the accompanist played songs from *Oklahoma!* on the piano and while they waited for the lights to dim, Susan talked about the river. To Zac it was a foreign language, but he got her gist. The river was high; the rapids were big; Cataract Canyon was scary.

"A Current Adventures guide hit a lateral and flipped a mini J-rig in Mile Long Rapid. One of the passengers got Maytagged in a keeper for a *long* time...."

Zac glanced over at Grace. She looked beautiful in the Ben Rogan dress. She'd exclaimed over it—then, with Graceful candor, asked him how much money he made. Now he could see that her mind was on the river.

Turning to Zac in the seat beside her, she asked, "You're going to row in the movie, aren't you?" She couldn't imagine he wouldn't. Zac had won his blue—the equivalent of earning a letter—in crew at Oxford and rowed in the Oxford-Cambridge Boat Race. When he nodded she said, "You need to put in some time at the oars. Why weren't you at the white-water clinics we set up for the actors?"

He'd had to rehearse. The producers had said, *You'll be fine. Don't worry about rowing.* He hadn't—simply because he'd had bigger worries. But his daily training at the Moab Athletic Club was no substitute for practice in white water. He asked Grace, "Will you take me out in your boat? I have tomorrow afternoon free."

Grace knew how rare that was. "I'd love to. We'll have a picnic." As the lights dimmed in the theater, she looked over at his profile in the dark and remembered the decision she'd made about their marriage. Her hand smoothed the exquisite soft leather of her dress. It was a lovely gift. But what mattered was that he'd thought about her when they were apart. Enough to wangle a recipe from a French chef. Enough to buy a Ben Rogan dress in her size. Enough to order a custom-made music box to remind her of the sweet early days of their courtship.

Enough. More than enough.

THE MUSICAL was delightful, and the pleasure of the audience was tangible. In a town as small as Moab, the opportunity to see a play came only a few times a year, and Zac could see that the community appreciated its actors.

At intermission, while he studied the program, Grace told him about the players. "Conrad owns the ice-cream parlor. He's always in the musicals. Great dancer. And I think Bart is going to be in *Suddenly Last Summer*. He was really great when they did *One Flew over the Cuckoo's Nest*."

Listening to her, Zac envied the actors in the show—and in future Moab productions. Good plays. No twelve-hour days. No incessant script changes.

No money.

Zac knew he was lucky to be able to earn a living doing what he loved. He shouldn't think about how much more he loved the stage. But what attracted him about the theater had less to do with scripts or working conditions than with the interchange between actor and audience that occurred with a play. He missed it.

However, inevitably, watching the musical reminded him of the last time he'd been on stage and of the performance he hadn't finished.

Leaving Hong Kong.

As the lights dropped again and the curtain rose, he slid his hand into Grace's and held on, thinking of solitary nightmares and private things he'd never shared, even with her. And of New York.

He was still brooding when he became aware of Grace rustling in the seat beside him. She was making a note on her program. A note to herself, Zac thought.

But she passed it to him, and as the piano tinkled out the introduction to "Surrey with the Fringe on Top," Zachary peered down and read her writing in the dark.

COUPON. 1 Lifetime Married to You.

Zac felt a loose heat inside him at the top of his chest. He pressed back in the theater seat, his breath shallow. Eyes sliding over to hers, he placed the program back in her lap, and his hand closed on her bare thigh.

She looked at him with big dark eyes.

Moving his hand, Zac put his arm around her and pulled her against him. His head beside hers, his mouth touching her ear, he whispered, "I'll cash that right now."

CHAPTER EIGHT

ZAC WAS HARD for the rest of the play, thinking of sex, of getting home and removing Grace's clothes. After the final curtain call, he felt barely present as they congratulated Day and he gave her the flowers he'd bought.

Helping Grace into the Austin-Healey, he bent to kiss her, his tongue promising every conjugal pleasure. He wanted to be inside her, but he wanted other things, too. To hold her in his arms, her bottom nestled against his groin and his thigh, her back warming his chest as he drifted off to sleep. To awaken in the dark…with her.

They drove home with her hand over his on the stick shift, enough contact to call up the past, the way it had always been. The heat and affection and deep closeness. Impossible to take it slow.

When they reached the River Inn, Zac kept his arm around her and felt hers around him as they went inside. And when he turned to lock the door, Grace put her hands on the back of his jeans, feeling him. He ducked into his room to get condoms from his suitcase. Then, followed by the husky, he and Grace walked upstairs together.

On the way he unzipped her dress, and once they were in her room, standing in the moonlight coming through the French doors, she turned to him and began trying to unbutton his black paisley silk shirt.

The buttons were tight in the holes. Feeling his hands on her back where he'd opened her dress, Grace grew frustrated. "Take off your shirt, Zac." From the floor the puppy observed them curiously for a moment, then let her eyes flutter shut, as though content that all was well.

Zac kept his eyes on Grace's as he unbuttoned his shirt. She watched.

"Take off your dress, Gracie."

Her face felt hot. Loosening the leather sheath, she pulled it down. Off her shoulders. Over her breasts.

Zac stood looking at her underwear, the white cotton panties and bra with apples on them. They were his favorites, and Grace knew it. He said, "I think you planned this."

Grace met his eyes. "Yeah. The first time I saw you."

In the moonlight, Zac gazed at her long, strong limbs, her mix of tan lines from working outdoors in different clothes. Her high, beautiful breasts. She was the sexiest, most interesting woman he'd ever known. He wanted her hand on him, and he put it there, on his fly.

Grace's heartbeat quickened. Patience expired. She opened the buttons on his jeans. He unhooked her bra and drew it off. Greedy and eager, they came together, her nipples against his chest, all hands below deck. Sliding her panties down...

Grace felt old emotions shivering through her. She remembered this. Long subway rides, get home, rip off clothes. Make love for a long time. All night.

She jerked back from him, holding his arms lightly, savoring the feel of him as she said, "Wait." Naked she turned toward the armoire.

Immediately Zac noticed the music box. He stepped

up behind her, slid his arms around her and began to sing softly, his mouth pausing to caress her jaw. Trembling, loving it, Grace opened her pink jewelry chest.

Zac knew what she was doing, and the song died on his lips. *Our love,* he thought. Here to stay.

Grace turned in his arms. In the dark Zac couldn't see the objects she held, but he knew what they were. He lifted his palm beneath her hand, between their bodies.

The cool metal fell against his skin, and his fingers closed on the two tiny trinkets. He looked into her eyes, then reached up and smoothed her hair behind her right ear. He carefully placed the hoop in the little hole in her lobe, then secured the back. Touching the heart and the diamond that dangled from the hoop, he put his mouth on the underside of her jaw, drinking her skin. As he kissed her, he groped for her left hand, pausing to stroke the wet place between her legs. Her right hand closed around his erection, applying pressure, and her other hand spread on his chest. In the midst of that marital intimacy, he put her wedding ring back on her finger.

They were in bed in a second. Zac lay on his back and gazed up at her as she moved over him, her long hair sweeping his face. He pressed up against her, unable to help it, and slid his hands beneath her, touching her while she touched him. While they looked into each other's eyes in the moon's glow.

She moved against him, made him feel her wetness, and his head went back. He said, "Grace, wait." Birth control. No babies now.

He shuttered up dark thoughts. New York…

Grace, knowing why he'd stopped her, was tearing open a packet, touching him, her eyes on his. Banishing worry, Zac concentrated on her, stroking her the way she liked. He was so hard.... She slid down on him, taking him inside.

"Gracie." Pressing deeper inside her, he grabbed her and pulled her tight against him.

She was already shuddering over him, saying his name, lying down on him, her heart on his. It was a ritual they'd performed countless times, as many ways as they knew, and now she was moaning, calling to him. And as she ran the waves, as they jarred her, shook through her, she heard Zachary answering in the same language, with inarticulate cries that were the most articulate words of love.

It seemed to last a long time, and then she lay against him, her body nerveless, her face against his skin. His arms enveloped her. His kisses covered her face. Tender emotion and whispered words. "I love you." Rolling onto his side with her, Zac tucked the covers around her. Moving her hair, he kissed her mouth again, touching his tongue to hers. Grace watched his face in the night. The face beside her on the pillow. Her best friend. Her husband. She would never leave him again. She would follow him to the ends of the earth.

Or somewhere darker and deeper.

Thoughts came to her. They pecked their way out of the dark corners of her mind. She imagined things she didn't want to imagine. Things that seemed unimaginable.

Zachary, standing naked on a fire escape. Zachary, sawing a hole in a wall. Zachary, her lover, her *husband,* sleeping in condemned buildings with homeless people.

Zachary.

Mad.

Rejecting the word as soon as it came to her, she

brought her face to his chest, to his heart, smelling him, feeling the life in him. The strength. *He's all right now,* she thought. *He's all right.*

THE ALARM CHIRPED at six, and Zac felt Grace moving beside him, leaning across him to shut it off. As he rolled over and silenced the noise himself, the dog licked his hand. Grace relaxed against him, snuggling up to his back, her slim arm stretching around him, and Zac remembered the night before. Promises and love. Like it used to be but more. He found her hand, and his fingers wove into a knot with hers.

Grace felt the cords of muscles in his stomach as they held hands so tightly. After a while, he sat up sleepily and looked down at her from under sexy, bed-mussed hair. Her breasts were exposed above the sheet, and she saw him smiling at her body. He took her left hand and fingered her ring as he met her eyes, his own mossy green under a forest of black lashes. His five-o'clock shadow formed a rogue's mustache on his upper lip, a bandit's beard on his jaw, and Grace thought of the Ben Rogan ads. *If they photographed you like this, sales would really take off.*

He lay down beside her, the heavy weight of his arm falling across her, and drew her to him. Masculine insistence, powerful body, beckoning husband.

Grace moved closer. One of her legs slid between his, and their eyes met again, heads on the pillows. He was smiling, and she smiled, too.

He said, "Good morning, my wife."

They made love, coming hard enough to shake the floor, and afterward Grace begged off their run. While she showered, Zac went outside with the dog to stretch.

Against the gray day, the Colorado had assumed a hue like rust, and mosquitoes and gnats, spawn of the water, whined around him. Part of the bank had disappeared overnight. There was a lot of water flowing by. A lot of river.

Zac was glad the inn was out of reach.

As he headed up the driveway with the husky, Zac tried to prolong the good feelings of the night. Grace was his again.

But it felt impermanent. What had happened before could happen again. She could leave. And even if she didn't... *She doesn't know how bad it was,* Zac thought. She couldn't know. Telling wasn't the same.

He distracted himself with plans. They'd stay in his apartment until they could find a new place in California, maybe in the hills or beside the ocean.

But what about the River Inn? Would Grace sell it? In his mind, Zac saw the faded photos in the room off the parlor. He imagined the floor of the screened porch polished and glossy, a ceiling fan turning lazily overhead, European tourists and cyclists in spandex sipping drinks at small tables while a couple of scrubbed and adorable children brought them appetizers from inside. *Family.* A dog, too. He eyed the homeless husky, running ahead of him. He thought of Grace in the kitchen kneading bread, chopping, stirring...

No, he thought. *I'm an actor. I'll always be an actor. And as for children...* His stomach wrenched. *We've got to talk about it,* he thought.

Soon.

When he returned to the inn, Grace was cooking breakfast. She didn't want help, so he went into the living room to play the piano. He should have it tuned—

We're not going to stay here.

His fingers touched the keys, and he lost himself in one of Chopin's polonaises, then a slow, somnolent nocturne. But he couldn't stop the thoughts that had come over him on his run. Kids.

Numbly he thought of his mother, and a memory shivered through him. The sound of sobbing behind the door. Voices. At least he hadn't inherited his mother's problems. But what was wrong with him?

Nothing.

His eyes slid to the mantel.

Dear maid, kind sister, sweet Ophelia!

He stopped playing, covered the keys, and got up and left the room, the dog scrambling to her feet to follow.

Despite the rain, Zac and Grace decided to take the afternoon raft trip they'd discussed at the play. Before leaving for the production office, Zac backed the Suburban up to the carriage house and hitched the boat trailer to the vehicle for Grace. She would take the dory to work, and he would meet her when he was finished with rehearsal.

That morning at the office, between chores for Rapid Riggers, Grace packed a picnic dinner for the river trip, then put together some things she wanted to give Zac. One was a watertight ammunition can. The cans were the catchall container of outfitters, good for keeping small personal items dry on the river. Each passenger was issued an ammo can at the beginning of a trip, and each boatman had his own.

Zac would be spending days on the river filming, so Grace searched out an old gray can in the upstairs loft. Locating some brown paint, she decorated it with primitive petroglyphlike figures and wrote his name on the lid. Then she collected a new Rapid Riggers plastic coffee cup and a black baseball cap with the outfit's crossed-oars logo on the front.

She was unearthing another item from the back of her desk drawer when Day came in. Turning to her sister, Grace held up the object. "Do you want this?"

Day shook her head. "No. Really, it doesn't mean anything to me."

"Can I give it away? I offered it to Nick when Dad died, but he has a much better one."

Day smiled, rolling her eyes a little. "Yeah. Nick always has the best toys. New kayak. New climbing harness." She sighed. "New river outfit."

Grace regarded the item in her hand. It wasn't a toy. But then, Day wasn't a river guide.

For the first time in her life, Grace found that worrisome. Granted, Day understood the river business—the permit system, taxes, marketing, dealing with tour operators and so on. And she participated in a wilderness medicine course every two years and kept her Red Cross certifications current.

But she was not a river guide. In fact, she was removed enough from the actual reality of what occurred on a river trip that she'd referred to a boatman's knife as a "toy."

Grace knew she had to think about it. She had promised herself to Zac, and that meant she would be leaving Rapid Riggers.

Could Day run the outfit alone?

Her sister distracted her from the question. Freshly lit cigarette in hand, she tossed something on Grace's desk. It was a new issue of a popular film magazine, and Day said, "I saw that in the grocery store today. Thought you might like to have it."

The cover showed a picture of a cartoon character from the latest Disney animated feature. But farther down were the words Sexy And Close To His Clothes: Is Zachary Key Close To Stardom, Too?

Day flipped open the magazine to the one-page article in the middle and the picture of Zac with his shirt open, tails out, plenty of five-o'clock shadow, sexy green eyes—too much like the way Grace had seen him in bed that morning when he was supposed to be just hers.

Grace pulled up her desk chair and sat down, staring at the photo. He was a sight to arouse any woman's fantasies, and she imagined there were already fans out there who felt too keenly the impact of that body, that face, that sun-singed long hair. Fans who might obsess over him. Who might even become dangerous.

Fame was no one's master. It had a life of its own.

Tearing her eyes from Zac's image, Grace read the interview while her sister leaned against the edge of the desk, smoking. She was shocked. The introductory paragraph described women gazing slack-jawed at a man on their television screens whose fingers were unbuttoning the fly of his Ben Rogan jeans. The ad was so popular that women taped it on their VCRs to replay whenever they liked. They bombarded networks and modeling agencies with letters—to Zachary Key.

Grace had never even seen the television ad. It was banned on all the stations out of Salt Lake City, and she didn't watch that much TV anyhow. Clearly she'd been missing a big part of the...well, picture.

According to the article, Zachary Key was the stuff of women's fantasies, and he was on his way up. The writer mentioned the voice with which he spoke "the Queen's English" and the fact that he wore loud shirts and had a smile that immediately made a woman think of bedrooms. And of course his role in *Kah-Puh-Rats*. She left the rest to the questions, and Zac's sense of humor and intelligence came through in spades. But the journalist's final question set the tone for the piece.

"Are you presently wearing underwear?"

His answer was "a sexy and inconclusive smile." Grace knew that smile.

Nowhere did the article say he was married.

Day grinned as she drew on her cigarette. "What do you think?"

Grace closed the magazine and shrugged, more shaken than she cared to admit. Before she could answer, Day's gasp drew her glance upward.

Her sister was staring at her left hand. "Your ring!"

Grace nodded. She'd called her attorney that morning. It was over.

And it had just begun.

Day asked, "Will you move to California?"

Grace stared at the glossy film magazine. "Yes."

She heard footsteps on the porch outside, and the bell on the door chimed. Grace glanced out the window and saw the Austin-Healey. Standing up, eyes blinking past Day's, she stepped over Zac's ammo can and hurried out the doorway to the reception area.

Zac was leaning his head and shoulders over the swinging doors to the kitchen, looking for her. He wore blue jeans and a polyester shirt in a black-and-white checkerboard print—a Salvation Army special they'd chosen together. The pattern would have looked grotesque on another man. It epitomized Zac. *Don't change,* she thought. *Don't let them change you.*

As she slipped behind the reception counter, Zac turned. When she saw his face, Grace thought of the article and everything it meant. He moved toward her, and Grace couldn't stop. She hurled herself against his body and held on to him like a person trying to hold a planet and keep it from its orbit.

She knew holding back Zachary would be just as impossible—and just as wrong.

THE RAIN HAD STOPPED, so they changed into bathing suits, shorts and T-shirts for the river trip. Zac carried the cooler and dry bags filled with extra clothing out to the boat. Then he followed in the Austin-Healey as Grace drove the Suburban hauling the boat trailer across the bridge and left on the river road, heading upstream to the Daily. They stopped at the takeout to leave Zac's car for a shuttle vehicle; after that, he rode with Grace in the Suburban to a little-used put-in just above Onion Creek Rapid.

High water had submerged the boat ramp, but Zac got the dory in the water while Grace kept both car and trailer from being stuck in the silt. It took them twenty minutes to finish rigging. Everything had to be tied down, so that nothing would be lost if they flipped in a rapid. As they worked Grace told Zac the most important safety rules for the river.

When the boat was rigged, she locked the Suburban and joined him at the water's edge. Nodding at the name on the bow, Zac asked, "Why did you call her *Persephone?*"

"For Demeter's daughter in the Greek myth. You

know. Each year when she comes up from the underworld to visit her mother, spring returns—river-running season.''

Now the dory was riding high in the water, her blue paint immaculate, her form shapely. Grace hadn't used the boat since she'd returned from New York. She'd believed it would be a painful reminder of her father, but it was a good reminder, instead. And it would be a good boat for Zac to handle in his first white water.

Eyeing the water sweeping past the opposite bank, Grace shivered. The Daily should be a blast with this much water. But Cataract?

The morning clouds had disappeared and the sun was heating the beach, so she stripped down to her bikini and Zac pulled off his T-shirt. They were alone on the shore lined with tamarisk, isolated from eyes—rubbing sunscreen on each other's bodies became a lingering pleasure. As he massaged cream over her breastbone, his fingers sliding under the edges of her crocheted bikini top, Zac asked, ''Are there any side canyons on this trip? Private beaches?''

Grace lowered her eyes, already wanting him. ''Did you bring the condoms?''

''Of course. They're in my new ammo can. I'm glad we're going to make love, instead of war. At first I thought we needed ammo cans because you were expecting a shoot-out with a rival outfitter.''

Grace laughed. Remembering the other thing she wanted to give him, she turned away, inviting caresses to her exposed backside as she bent over her own ammo can and found her father's river knife in its sheath. Sweeping up a life vest from the beach, she tossed it to Zac. ''Here. Put this on.''

He did, and Grace zipped the front and adjusted the straps. Then she showed him the river knife. "This was my dad's. You can have it now. There's a thumb release on the sheath. See?"

Touched, Zac took it from her. He tried the thumb release and pulled the blade from the sheath.

"I sharpened it this morning. You can put it on your life vest here—" Grace touched the loop "—and you'll have it if you ever get caught on a line or something. They're good for cutting out the floors of pinned rafts, too. But you won't be on a raft."

Zac ducked his head and kissed her mouth. Eyes on hers, he said, "Thank you. I'll treasure it."

Grace was sober. "Just remember you have it. The Daily's nothing, but Cataract Canyon can be scary. The river report today said it's running at seventy thousand cfs."

Cubic feet per second, Zac thought.

"The usual for this time of year is about twenty-five. And I think it'll go up some more before you film there."

Zac wasn't concerned. If Grace could handle it, so could he. Clipping the sheathed knife to the loop on his vest, he nodded at the other life jacket on the beach. As Grace scooped it up and put it on, he saw that her knife was already attached—and he was glad of it.

He asked, "Shall I shove off?"

"I will. You row."

Zac moved agilely from a flat rock on the shore and into the dory. Grace handed him her ammo can, and he tied it down for her. She untied the bowline and shoved the boat away from the shore, accepting his hand as she climbed aboard.

While she settled herself against the cooler and dry bags, and Zac rowed them out into the river, Grace said, "Ship the oars and let us drift. The river's moving fast. We'll hit Onion Creek Rapid in a minute. Listen. You can hear it."

The low, roaring sound of the white water grew louder, and as Grace located a bail bucket just in case, she told Zac about rafting techniques and reading the river.

After listening to a long stream of suggestions, Zac grinned at her, adding, "And I should stay out of holes."

"Well," said Grace, "some holes you can actually run. You have to look at the shape of them, what the water's doing. If the surface current kicks outward and the hole looks like a smile as you approach it, then you can run it. The frowning holes, where the current flows inward, are the keepers."

As the sound of the water became almost deafening, Zac looked downstream and saw the churning foam. Grace stood up and stepped over one oar to get behind him. Taking a seat, she peered around him at the rapid. Onion Creek was not the bed of ripples she remembered, and the route of choice was no longer the way she'd described it to Zac.

But he found the tongue amidst the swirling white and dug in with the oars, guiding the dory down the smooth V at the top of the rapid. Grace could barely tear her eyes from his body to watch the river.

There was a hole on the left, formed by a rock that in most years was above water. Zac slid past it, seeming to know instinctively when to let the river make the choices. As the first in a row of six-foot standing waves washed over the bow, dousing them with cold water, Grace began bailing.

When they were through the rapid, Zac pulled up the oars and helped her. Grace said, "You're a good boatman. Want a job?"

Zac knew she was joking. But it hit him the same way it had when she'd given him her father's river knife. She had a life here, and he almost wished he could be part of it, rather than insisting she follow him. But he was an actor, and they needed the money.

In case...

He turned to her. She'd braided her hair and put on a wide-brimmed leather Indiana Jones hat that looked as though it had seen a hundred rivers. Finding her mouth beneath the dripping brim, Zac kissed her and said, "I love you."

In Professor Creek Rapid, they met a wave that swamped the boat. Spotting new rapids ahead, they eddied out and stopped at a beach on river right to empty the water. They'd started late in the day, and now theirs was the only boat on that stretch of the river. After Zac had tied the bowline around a bush growing beside the shore, he collected what he wanted from his ammo can and took Grace's hand.

Beyond the beach was an inviting side canyon. Holding hands, they followed a narrow path through scrub oak and over and around large red and black boulders, tall rock walls squeezing them from each side. Only because the sun was still high did patches of light reach the canyon floor, and the shape of the cliff walls hinted that they'd held walls of ice on cold winter days, year after year, for centuries.

As they walked he dropped her hand and slid his arm

around her. They'd left life jackets and sun hats with the dory. Feeling his skin, Grace thought, *This is real. We love each other, and it has nothing to do with sexy ads or love scenes or fans who write him letters....* But the other side of Zachary was real, too. She asked him, "When are you going to film that scene?"

Zac bent his head so that he could see her face. Her lush black eyebrows were drawn together almost imperceptibly. Wondering what she was thinking, he answered, "I don't know. I'll find out the day before we film it. By the way, it's scene twenty-five."

And it would be nothing like what he did with Grace. He would not be making love to Ingrid. He would not, he hoped, get an erection. It would all be...acting.

Grace, on the other hand...

They made love at the end of the box canyon, where water falling from the clifftop had created a deep pool, a sinkhole in the rock and sand. They sat on a warm boulder, kissing and undressing each other, and then he slid down to stand on a ledge below. From there, he could press his lips to the insides of her thighs and caress her in the most loving and private way he knew. Grace lay against the warm rock, shuddering from the feel of his mouth. Trembling, she clung to him as he lifted her down onto the ledge.

Zac unfastened her hands from him. Gently turning her, he placed her palms on the hot sandstone, and Grace let her breasts and her thighs touch the sun-warmed boulder. It felt dryer and more healing than a sauna or a bath. She'd spent much of her life lying on such rocks, never wanting to move. Now the hot sandstone kissed her on one side as Zac hugged her on the other. He was cradling her, protecting her, holding her tight, shielding her with his body.

His words poured in her ears, rained down on her neck as he pulled her closer, pressed deeper into her, made her ache with love. There was a crying sound coming from her throat, and his hands reached in front of her to rub the heart spot above her breasts, to touch her breasts themselves, to keep her close. His face against her hair, he whispered soothing words that made her forget everything but the healing warmth of the sun and Zachary, guiding her through a maelstrom of feeling to a sea of love.

Afterward they sat down on the rock ledge together, nuzzling, kissing, touching. They were closed away from the world, away from all eyes but those of a golden eagle soaring on thermals overhead, and Grace felt Zac's love for her as much as her own for him. She wanted him to know the promises she'd made him were true. As Zac settled against the boulder, she laid her head in his lap and asked, "Where are we going to live in California?"

Fingers stroking her hair, Zac closed his eyes and put his head back, letting the sun warm his face. "I have an apartment in Santa Monica. I thought we'd find something else." He wanted a place that was theirs, a permanent place. Like Oakhurst.

Or the River Inn.

"I spend a lot of time in hotels. Will you hate that?"

Her eyes fluttered open. "'Wherever you go, I will go. Wherever you lodge, I will lodge, your people shall be my people, and your God my God.'"

Zac smiled. "You know who said that, don't you?"

Her eyes were closed again. "No."

"Ruth—to her mother-in-law. They were leaving Moab."

Grace laughed, and he felt her moving her head, brushing her lips against his stomach. The part of him he'd thought she'd sated began to stir. Her tongue licked sweat off his skin.

"Grace, remember that coupon you threw in the hearth?"

Her lips teased him, began to take him. "When have I ever made you use a coupon?"

CHAPTER NINE

FOUR DAYS LATER they left for New York for Zac's appearance on ''The JoAnn Carroll Show.''

Before they left they took the husky's bowls and food and brush over to Day's house and delivered the dog to Rapid Riggers. Zac hated to leave the puppy, but at least she'd spent enough time at the river outfit to know Day. She shouldn't be too unhappy.

Sitting on the dirty office couch in a powder blue linen suit, stockings and heels, Day petted the dog as she asked, ''Does she have a name?''

Grace looked at Zac, but he was staring at the husky. He scraped his teeth lightly over his bottom lip. At last he said, ''Ninochka.''

After he'd said an extended goodbye to the puppy and he and Grace were in the Austin-Healey headed ten miles north to the airfield, she said, ''Ninochka.''

Zac's eyes remained on the road as he drove past the entrance to Arches National Park. ''Between you and me she'll have plenty of attention.''

Grace smothered a smile.

''We'll have her spayed when we get back.'' The vet had suggested it be done before the dog was six months old. Shots, too. Collar. Tags. Again Zac wondered where he and Grace would live when they returned to California. The husky would need room to run, as she had at the River Inn.

Grace asked, "Why Ninochka?"

He shrugged. "It's a Russian name. I heard it when I was young, and I've always liked it. It means 'girl.'" The husky had been Ninochka in his mind for a week, but he'd kept it to himself, never calling the dog anything. But now, like Grace, he doubted the original owners would return to find her. She'd been abandoned.

And she was his.

HE AND GRACE took a small propeller plane to Salt Lake City and flew first class to New York. Zac had no appointments till the following morning, when he would appear on "JoAnn," so they would have the evening to themselves in the city where they'd met and fallen in love.

On the plane they ordered Courvoisier and worked crossword puzzles and talked. As they flew over the Rockies Grace said, "This is kind of like a honeymoon."

They'd never had one. *Leaving Hong Kong* hadn't allowed it. Thinking of who he'd been when he married her—of why he'd married her—Zac looked down at Grace, in her denim bustier and jacket, jeans skirt and cowboy boots. He remembered her question that first night he'd come to the River Inn. Would he have married her if he hadn't needed a green card? He still didn't know. From the first their relationship had been like…white water. Faster and stronger than either of them.

Love that had made him lose his mind when she left. Zac borrowed her pen and scrawled on a cocktail napkin, "Coupon good for one honeymoon." Handing it to her, he said, "This trip won't be a honeymoon. But we'll have one." And in the meantime he'd give her everything he could. He wanted to remind her of what they'd been together, what they'd had. But he knew that nothing could restore the innocence of the early days of their marriage.

Grace's leaving had changed him. Before, always, things had come easily to him. Scholastically. Athletically. Socially. At Eton, he'd been Keeper of the Oppidan Wall, captain of his team for the traditional Wall Game, a rare honor in context. Rowing in the Oxford-Cambridge Boat Race, the same. Acting was as natural to him as other skills—carpentry, music. Women liked him. There'd been little he'd wanted that he hadn't been able to get, by wit or finesse or tenacity. Until he'd met the INS. And when he'd had to choose between his honor and what he wanted, a green card, he'd chosen the latter. He did love Grace. But he'd never counted on loving her so much. Or on her leaving. And what happened afterward had shown him he was as vulnerable as anyone.

He thought of the book he'd left at home in one of the bureau drawers. Nothing in the *DSM-IV* had pointed conclusively to a genetic problem. Nonetheless, as soon as he had a chance, another break in filming, he would make himself see a doctor—for Grace and their future. No need to worry her till he had some answers.

God. What those might be.

A LIMO TOOK THEM from the airport to one of the finest hotels in the city. Their room was on the top floor and furnished in elegant dark woods with an old feel. Sheer curtains played over the windows, and there was just one king-size bed. They tried it out first thing.

Grace went into the bathroom to put on the red leather teddy Day had given her for a wedding gift so long ago. When she came out, Zac's smile was tender and affectionate. As they slid between the sheets together, he gathered her against him like treasure.

Later, when the scrap of red lay in the far corner of the room where he'd tossed it, he leaned back against the fluffy white pillows with Grace in his arms. The red teddy had made him think of Day, and Day made him think of Rapid Riggers—and taking Grace to California. He asked, "What are you going to do about that river outfit?"

Grace knew what he meant. "How much time do I have?"

He shrugged, sliding down on the bed beside her. Grace saw honey-brown skin, broad shoulders over her, muscular arms reaching around her, mink-colored hair in her face. "You don't have to sell. But I've wondered—why don't you and Day swap? Your half of the river outfit for her half of the house. Or whatever's fair."

Grace barely breathed. "Are you thinking we could keep the house?"

"It's your family place. The old boiler from the steamboat. The spring and the still nearby." *Our children should have those things....* He killed the thought. But Day didn't want the River Inn; she called it a white elephant. In his eye, the place was a lady, a lady with her shoes off, lounging on the banks of a red river in one of those rare spots of wild country that might remain so for decades to come, because it was too hard for it to be anything else. He told Grace, "I'd love it to be our home. I don't know how much time we can spend there, but…'' His eyes met hers.

Grace was thrilled. They couldn't reopen the inn, but at least they could keep it. She said, ''I'll ask Day when we get back to Moab.''

Grace had brought a suit to wear to sit in the audience of ''The JoAnn Carroll Show,'' but Zac wanted to take her shopping for something new, so they ordered dinner from room service from the fine restaurant downstairs and showered while they waited for it. Forty-five minutes later, they rode the elevator down to the lobby to get a cab.

As the taxi carried them through the glittering streets, Grace looked out the windows. Recalling their old haunts—Jean-Michel's and their funky East Village walk-up—she felt no wistfulness. All she could think of was the day she'd left Zac there. And what had happened to him. Watching the passing lights play over his profile, Grace wondered if he was remembering, too. She put her hand in his and said, ''We have a different New York now.''

He read her thoughts, his own black. ''Yes.''

They went to a Madison Avenue boutique that was open late and found a three-piece Ben Rogan ensemble that suited Grace's figure and style faultlessly. Yellow bouclé jacket over a nautical black-and-white tee and black wide-legged pants. No alterations needed. While two saleswomen spent another half hour helping Grace choose accessories, Zac browsed the racks. Before they left, he asked Grace to try on a taffeta slip-dress with a full skirt and bustier top. It fit, too, and she liked it, and he had clothes, shoes and accessories sent back to the hotel. After that, they took a cab to a club called the Black-and-White Diner, where a jazz band was playing.

They'd been dancing for half an hour when the first strains of "Love Is Here to Stay" filled the club. Eyeing Zac suspiciously, Grace asked, "Did you plan this?" He'd been checking the newspapers before they left the hotel.

He smiled. "The first time I saw you."

As the saxophone wailed, serenading them, Grace felt the solidity of his body against her, heard him singing softly in her ear, noticed his arousal. Her lover. When the song ended, she looked up into his eyes and he said, "Let's get out of here."

They were leaving the dance floor when the band leader gave Zac a telling wink. Yes, thought Grace, he'd planned it.

Moments later Zac pushed open the door of the club and they stepped outside into the familiar smell of a Manhattan night. While Zachary searched the busy street for a cab, Grace watched some pedestrians approaching on the sidewalk. A group of women in evening black parted to pass a lone homeless man shuffling along the pavement. Suddenly disquieted, Grace stared at the figure.

As a cab pulled to the curb, Zac turned to help her inside, but Grace didn't move, except to open her purse.

"What are you doing?" he asked.

She slipped around him, holding out a twenty-dollar bill.

Then Zac, too, saw the man. Time stood still.

Meandering past them, his voluminous army surplus padding his body, the vagrant muttered, "Thick as thieves. The sinners don't know. Sinners are angels. Angels of repose.'' He stared at Grace, but didn't take her money, only walked on.

He reeked, and the smell seeped into Zachary's nostrils, an abysmal whiff of the past. Swallowing, he saw the man's red face, the cracks in his alligator-thick skin. Impressions bombarded him. Smells. Icy-cold feeling. Druglike haze. People who looked like animated clay figures. Like dough.

As the homeless man shambled on, Zac unwillingly recalled something he'd read in a book from the Santa Monica library. *Future generations will perceive the deplorable neglect of deinstitutionalized mental patients in the twentieth century as a horror worthy of the Dark Ages....*

''Zac?''

He started.

Grace had returned the twenty to her purse and was in the cab. Peering up at his face, half-illuminated by the lights from the restaurant, she saw the haunted look in his eyes. *I took up association with homeless people of unhappily like mind....* It was because of what Zac had told her that she had tried to give the man money. When she'd seen the vagrant, her mind had made an easy leap. It could have been Zachary.

With a last glance at the man, Zac joined Grace in the cab. As he closed the door and settled beside her, Grace noticed the taut muscles in his throat. She watched him swallow. She saw that his heart was racing.

He didn't meet her eyes but simply stared out the window with one of the bleakest expressions she'd ever seen in her life.

BACK AT THE HOTEL, they watched *Breakfast at Tiffany's,* from the hotel's offering of video classics and ordered frozen chocolate-mousse truffles and baked brie with garlic from room service. As they sat in bed sipping glasses of cognac from the room's bar and watching the last of the movie credits roll past, Grace thought about "The JoAnn Carroll Show." Setting her glass on the nightstand, she asked, "Are you nervous about tomorrow, Zac?"

Preoccupied, he interpreted her question in the broader sense. Tomorrow. The future. *Thick as thieves. The sinners don't know....* Again he saw the transient shuffling along the sidewalk.

Thinking of "JoAnn," he replied, "Somewhat." Zac wasn't keen on talk shows, but the exposure was good. He reached for the remote to flick off the set, but instead, he hit the button for the television.

Grace was looking right at the screen, and she saw his abdominal muscles, his fingers on the buttons of the jeans.

Zac saw, as well, and hit another button, which did nothing. He heard the music playing, sensed the strobe effect. The Ben Rogan ad.

Grace said, "My gosh."

He hit the power button.

"Zachary! I wanted to see it. They don't show it in Utah."

"Good." He set the remote on the nightstand nearest him, out of her reach.

Watching the play of muscles in his back as he moved, Grace said, "Why don't you want me to see it?"

Zac turned out the light and the room was cast into blackness. Grace felt his arms folding around her in the dark, and as she slid along the length of his body, he said nothing, just covered her mouth with his.

When she could she asked, "Are you embarrassed?"

"No. It's a job." But he didn't like the way the ads affected people. Strangers. Fame was a two-edged prospect. He feared it. And he wanted it. As he both feared and wanted Grace.

He put his hands on her, his mouth on her, taking her.

HE WAS PERFORMING on stage. Acting. He wasn't good; he could feel it, and when he looked out at the audience, people were leaving the theater. Desperation overcame him, and he began calling, "Don't go! Sit down!" As his panic rose, he looked back at his costar. It was Grace, and she was walking away, too, leaving stage right.

Anxiety welled in him. He went to the room backstage to stop her, but it wasn't a dressing room. It was a bedroom. A closed Tudor-style door. Silence behind it. Terrifying silence. He listened outside. He tried the handle, and it was locked. He shook it, calling...

He kicked it in.

The short cry awakened Grace. It was something between a moan and a scream. Opening her eyes, she knew where she was and turned to Zac, but he was already awake, his eyes wide in the dark. She knew he had cried out, that he must have had a nightmare.

Instinctively she reached for him, but at the first touch she realized his skin was cool—damp with sweat.

Feeling her hand, Zac said, "Sorry. It happens sometimes."

"To everybody." Grace stroked his body and his hair, and for a moment Zac closed his eyes, submitting. "What was it about?"

"Doesn't matter." He didn't want to talk about it. But this time, he hadn't awakened alone. He turned to Grace.

As they began to make love, Grace felt his tenderness, his automatic focus on her, his total presence. She returned the focus, the absorption, loving the sound of his voice as he said things that excited her.

But afterward, while he drowsed against her, drifting to sleep with the trust of a sated lover, the ghouls of three a.m. visited Grace. They'd been stirred by the nocturnal taxi ride through the city of her past and Zac's, and by the homeless man outside the Black-and-White Diner. They'd come alive with Zachary's cry in the night.

Now they paraded through her mind. They were her doubts. *What happened to you, Zac? Was it just a breakdown? Or something worse?*

THE NEXT MORNING Grace sat in the audience of "The JoAnn Carroll Show" and watched the famous blond talk-show host question Zac about *Kah-Puh-Rats,* then modeling, then his background. Skillfully, he steered the conversation away from his personal life and onto public ground—acting. His fame as a model had earned him this spot, but within two minutes everyone in the audience knew his mind was as fine as his body.

His understated British wit kept the audience in stitches. Grace laughed, too, but she was always aware that a camera might be trained on her face. JoAnn's guest was her own husband, and ten minutes into the show Grace was still trying to get over the wild reaction of the mostly female audience when he'd come out on stage. A coed directly behind her had stood up on her chair and yelled, "I want to have your baby!" And a

large tattooed woman two seats down from Grace was
wearing a tank top that read, "HIT THE SACK WITH
ME, ZACHARY."

Now, on stage, JoAnn was leaning toward Zac with a
curious smile, saying, "Would you mind— Oh, I hate
to ask." She looked at her audience conspiratorially,
winked at them, then turned back to her guest. "Would
you mind taking off your shirt?"

Women stood up, screaming and whistling. Grace was
afraid she was the only one still sitting. She was sure
the camera was on her and didn't know what expression
she was wearing.

Zachary said, "No, not at all."

The wildly enthusiastic crowd response made Grace
want to cover her ears. Zac stood up to unbutton his
blue silk shirt. His good-humored amusement and boy-
next-door charm had everyone eating out of his hand.
But Grace remembered how he'd turned off the Ben Rogan ad the night before. She knew he loved being in
front of an audience. And he was too good an actor to
show if he felt that doing this was even remotely demeaning. But how *did* he feel?

When his shirt was off, JoAnn walked around him
with her microphone, taking a good look and exchanging
glances with her audience. After a pregnant pause she
said, "Now, would you mind taking off—"

"Yes, I would."

The audience laughed.

JoAnn winked at the crowd. "Let's break for a word
from our sponsors, and then we'll take your questions
for Zachary."

After the break Grace sat impassively as strangers
plied Zac with questions that would have done credit to
the INS. Sexual fantasies. Birth control. Underwear.

Nothing was off-limits. He didn't always answer, but when the last inquisitor of the day asked him to describe his ideal woman, Zac said without hesitation, "My wife."

Grace smiled in case the camera was watching. But her thoughts flashed to a celebrity interview she'd read the year before, in which a popular actor had been asked the same thing and replied the same way.

A month later he'd left his wife of six years for an actress.

THE REST OF THE TIME in New York flew. Thursday evening Grace and Zac were back in Moab, and the next morning when he stopped at the production office to pick up his call sheet Zac saw that the infamous scene twenty-five would be shot that night. Meshach caught him in the hall as he was reading the sheet and said, "You and Ingrid will get it in a couple of takes, and then it'll be behind you."

Zac understood what he hadn't said—that if it wasn't effective, they would submit the script for more changes, trim his part again.

He was to report to makeup at four o'clock at the base camp near the Dewey Bridge, thirty miles up the river road from Moab. That afternoon they would film Powell coming to meet with Seneca and his brother, Captain O. G. Howland, to ask them to join the expedition. The meeting would take place at O.G.'s house, and then Seneca would return home to his wife, Melody, and tell her the news. The first scene would be shot at an old farmhouse along the river road, the next in another house ten miles north. Zac knew the schedule was tight, and he had to give strong and effective performances.

At midmorning he left the production office and drove

to Rapid Riggers. The day was sunny and dry, the forecast clear, and weather shouldn't interfere with filming. When he reached the river outfit, Grace and Day were on the porch talking. Ninochka was at Grace's feet, but she immediately trotted down to greet Zac. As he got out of the car, both women waved, then Day went inside, and Grace came to meet him.

Zac hugged her. "Come home with me. I have to be at work at four, and it's going to go all night."

Grace said, "Let me tell Day."

Minutes later she was closing her eyes in the passenger seat of the convertible. The husky climbed on her lap as Zac drove down the River Inn Road. Over the wind he said, "They're going to shoot scene twenty-five tonight. Do you want to come?"

The love scene. It was here. Her view of him blocked by Ninochka's fluffy tail, she said, "Whatever you want."

Zac kept his eyes on the snaking yellow line on the blacktop. "How about bringing a book and waiting in my trailer?"

Grace knew he wanted her close so that he could see her before and after. This love scene was a first for him as an actor, too. She put her hand over his on the stick shift. "I'd like that."

At the house Grace made an asparagus-mushroom quiche for lunch while he worked on an upstairs floor, correcting warps. Later, while they were eating at an iron patio table on the screened porch, a blue heron swept past, its rhythm as slow and even as the flow of the Colorado. Zac knew visitors would love the setting. He could imagine the inn as a retreat, like the finest hotels. A weight room in the downstairs northwest corner. A turndown service at night. Twenty-four-hour room service. He'd already seen where the croquet pitch could go, and he had a place in mind for a shuffleboard court. They could build a replica of the *Moab Princess*. Grace had the river permits....

Calling him back to this world, Grace said, "I asked Day about swapping the property. She was game."

"Great." But he sounded preoccupied. As they finished eating he said, "We have a couple of hours. Shall we go to the bookstore and find you something to read tonight?"

To take her mind off what he'd be doing.

Grace nodded, trying not to feel the threat to what was hers, trying to forget both Ingrid Dolk and the women in the audience of "The JoAnn Carroll Show." For all the love she and Zachary shared, one thing had never changed. He'd married her so he could do this job. Act.

He loved her.

But he loved his work most of all.

CHAPTER TEN

AT ELEVEN THAT NIGHT the stage was lit, and everyone was dismissed but the skeleton crew who would be filming the scene. In the dim light, Zac tried to tune out the other people, all but Ingrid, naked on the white sheets of the nineteenth-century high-post spool bed. He was too much a man not to admire her delicate shoulders and collarbone, her slim waist and her breasts, as perfect in their way as Grace's. She was a small, very beautiful woman.

She was not Grace.

As he came toward the bed, he felt the character of Seneca Howland sliding over him like a cloak. But he was also aware of himself. Of everything. Not just the scene they'd only talked through, not just this role, but how Ingrid was feeling. And how her character, Seneca's wife, Melody, was feeling.

Zac lay down with her, met her blue eyes and felt her warm skin and unfamiliar body brush his; a powerful uneasiness swept over him. He was aware of the camera's red light, of eyes watching, and he knew he was in no danger of arousal. But as he bent his head over Melody's—he was Seneca now—he knew he had never in his life walked so close to the line between right and wrong. He knew this was a place where any man could fall, and many had.

He touched Ingrid's cool lips with his, and he thought of Grace and of what he was trying to accomplish in the scene. He felt how strongly Seneca loved his wife, and he looked down at Melody and remembered that he was leaving on a dangerous expedition, that he might not return, that this woman needed him....

He began acting, playing it as it came, and so did Ingrid. And when he looked into her eyes, he saw Melody, a woman who didn't want to lose her husband. Ingrid was clinging to his shoulders, but he knew she was thinking what he was. *Let's get it in one take....*

CRICKETS WERE CHIRPING outside the trailer, but Grace didn't hear them. That afternoon Zac had bought her a new mystery novel by one of her favorite authors and she was swept up and lost, lying on the bed shivery-scared. When she heard the click of the door, she started, more in the book's world than in reality.

Zac stepped up into the trailer, and when he saw her he smiled, then closed the door and walked to the bed. He lay down beside her in his blue jeans and Oxford sweatshirt, his weight sinking the mattress. Seeing how far she'd plowed through the book, he said, "I bet you wish I'd go away so you can finish it."

That was true enough to make her laugh, but she laid aside the book and hugged him, remembering where he'd been. It was over. What she'd feared for so long hadn't been much worse than waiting for him at the dentist's office.

Zac saw her eyes and felt a purity inside him he hadn't known was there. He wanted to tell her how much he loved her, how sacred were the bonds between them, but he couldn't think of words to express the preternatural tingling of his body, the relief.

Because he knew that even the confidence he felt was dangerous, and that many married men had said, *It won't happen to me.* He was lucky. That was all.

Now he should renew his bond with Grace. If he continued to be lucky he would not be haunted by the feel and memory of a woman not his wife.

He said, "Let me shower, and we'll go home."

HE HAD ANOTHER BAD DREAM that night. Grace heard his scream, and in her own dreams she thought it was a child crying for its mother. When she opened her eyes, she saw Zac with his hand against his head. A gesture of apology. Ninochka had awakened, too. Front paws on the bed, she regarded Zachary with a worried expression.

Absently petting the husky, accepting her kisses, Zac looked at Grace in the moonlight shining through the French doors. "I'm sorry."

Recalling his nightmare in the hotel in New York, Grace said, "It's all right." She moved closer to him and found his skin and the sheets damp, as before. "That must be some dream." The last time Grace had woken up in a sweat, she'd had chicken pox. She asked, "Do you feel okay?"

"Sure. Down, Ninochka. That's a good girl. I'm fine."

His heart was racing. Grace asked, "Was it the same dream?"

"No." But close enough.

She watched him in the half-dark, waiting.

Zac sighed. "I...sometimes...dream about people I love killing themselves."

"That's awful," said Grace. "Did— Has that ever happened?"

"No."

Grace wondered if it was a reaction to what had happened to him in New York. She thought of the homeless man they'd seen when they were leaving the club. Zachary's response had been tangible. And he'd awakened with a scream that night. Grace's heart began beating as hard and fast as his, her mind locked in memory. *Don't leave, Grace....*

But she *had* left, and now Zac dreamed nightmares of the cruelest form of desertion.

The bed shook.

Zac said, "Ninochka—settle down. Nina."

As the fluffy dog insinuated herself between them, turning and squirming until she was comfortable and her people were not, Grace laughed. But she understood the husky's instincts. Something was troubling Zac.

Zachary coaxed the dog to the foot of the bed, and then he and Grace maneuvered around her until they lay skin to skin, holding each other close. Every fire of love sprang up between them, and the first kisses licked away the dark fears of the night. Soon, whispered sounds of lovemaking filled the air.

"Shh. *Gracie...*"

"Zac... I love you."

The puppy settled on the covers on the lower corner of the mattress and went to sleep.

THE NEXT DAY Grace was busy at Rapid Riggers. Though the Cataract Canyon launch date was still more than a week away, food had to be ordered, deliveries arranged. And river filming would begin in Desolation

Canyon in just two days. Though a caterer would provide meals there, Grace needed to help Nick and the other boatmen ready the rafts, jetboats and other equipment.

At about five-thirty Day came outside to the boatyard where Grace was working with Nick. "Zac's on the phone."

Pushing her hair off her forehead, Grace followed Day inside to take the call. She paused on the enclosed back porch to pet Ninochka, who was dozing on an old sleeping bag, then elbowed through the kitchen doors and picked up the phone on the reception counter.

Zachary said, "Hi. It's me."

Grace's heart pounded. "Hi, Zac." She was glad to hear his voice. What he'd said about his nightmares had unnerved her. It had haunted her all day.

"How's Ninochka?" Zac had left her at the vet early that morning to be spayed. Grace had picked her up.

"She's fine. Day said she'll watch her again while we're on the river." Grace paused. "When will you be home? What do you want for dinner?"

The timbre of the conversation became sexual. His answer had nothing to do with food, and Grace felt Day watching her from the door of the inner office. As she hung up the phone, she noticed her sister's odd expression.

"What is it?"

Day shook her head with a bittersweet smile. Then, suddenly, her face seemed to fall apart, and she said, "Dammit, you're really leaving. I'm going to miss you."

Grace went to her and hugged her, remembering an afternoon just weeks before when Day had embraced her, comforted her because she was divorcing Zachary. Now Day was crying and dabbing at her mascara, and she said, "Well, I've figured out how to get our commodore to stick around."

Nick. Day must have realized she would have trouble running Rapid Riggers alone.

Day said, "I think he'll stay if you sell him your half of the outfit. Then you can buy me out of the house."

Before Grace could respond, the swinging kitchen doors banged open, and the man in question looked in. Staring in astonishment at Day's tears, Nick said, "Day! You miss me already. That's why you're crying, right?"

Day rolled her red-rimmed eyes. "Why don't you go swim Cataract without a life jacket?"

Nick came over and hugged her.

Grace watched her sister submit for all of one second before she shook him off and said, "Leave me alone, deserter. I need a cigarette." But her eyes spoke to Grace, saying again that selling to Nick was the solution.

TWO DAYS LATER the Rapid Riggers boatmen and a fleet of rafts, mini J-rigs, jetboats, dories, and sport boats were assembled at the Green River put-in to Desolation Canyon at seven in the morning. The film crew arrived shortly afterward, and rigging took until nine. There was equipment to load and protect, dry bags to pack and label, and a wealth of coolers packed by the caterers to see the cast and crew through the day's shoot.

The morning was sunny and cloudless. The BLM ranger arrived and began checking boatmen's licenses and equipment. He would accompany the film crew on the river, making sure regulations were followed, protecting the natural resource. A park-service ranger would do the same when they filmed in Cataract Canyon.

There were several commercial trips launching that morning, and Grace noticed that the actors stayed out of sight in their trailers at the base camp near the put-in. A few of the cast, including Ingrid Dolk, had finished filming and returned to California.

Before launching, Nick and Grace and the other boatmen gave the film crew and actors an extensive safety lecture, including such topics as the health hazards of drinking river water and how to swim a rapid. Some of the points they would repeat over the next few days, and Grace knew the river guides' conversation on the water would be littered with anecdotes more sobering than any warnings.

When Zac finished with makeup, he came over to where Grace was rigging her raft, tying in two coolers with the help of one of the caterers. She made sure the lines were snug, then straightened and turned to Zac.

Dressed as Seneca Howland in a blue shirt, gray trousers, suspenders and knee-high boots, he looked like a time-traveler. There were too many people nearby for them to be alone, but they stole up the beach to exchange a few words, and Zac kissed her before they parted. When they put in soon afterward, Grace saw him rowing one of the dories, his stroke as strong and sure as that of any boatman on the river.

The day dragged, progress on the river slow. After lunch, they tried to film a scene in which George Bradley fell out of the boat. But Martin Place, rowing with one arm as Major Powell, took a big standing wave abreast and capsized the dory, cameraman and all. The actors were soaked and had to be taken back to base camp by jetboat to go to wardrobe and makeup.

While he waited for the others to return, Meshach set up cameras A, B and C on the shoreline and filmed Zac's crew running the rapid in the dory called *No Name*. Sitting with Nick on a rock ledge overlooking the river, Grace watched Zachary choose the perfect route.

Nick remarked, ''He's a good boatman. Your dad would have liked it that you married someone who could do that.''

Nick had been present at her father's graveside when Zachary was not. Grace was glad the guide had something good to say about Zac, but his comment evoked complicated feelings. She changed the topic. She had something to discuss with Nick, something she'd been putting off for two days.

''Nick, a while ago I told you Day and I weren't going to sell Rapid Riggers. But it turns out I need to sell my half.''

The boatman glanced toward the river and Zac, then back at Grace. He grinned, perhaps in understanding of the ways of love. Or maybe because he'd heard her offer. ''What do you want for it?''

She told him.

Meeting her eyes, Nick held out his hand.

As they shook on the promise, Grace felt as though she'd just sold her child. But she'd given Zac her vow. *Wherever you go, I will go. Wherever you lodge, I will lodge....*

FOR THREE DAYS they filmed on that stretch of the Green River. Then they moved downstream to Labyrinth Canyon and spent a day filming there. Afterward the crew moved back to Moab. Day and night they filmed. Zac's hours were erratic, but whenever he was done he went to Rapid Riggers to collect Ninochka, then returned to the house by the river, where he refinished floors and repaired the walls in the upstairs hallway. The dog followed him everywhere. She was the most loyal animal Zac had ever known—and the sweetest. They both forgot she'd ever been anyone else's.

Grace and Day and Nick began the paperwork to sell Day's half of the River Inn and Grace's half of Rapid Riggers. When both deals had closed, Grace would have money for renovations on the inn.

Though, of course, it would not be an inn.

At the end of the week they launched for Cataract Canyon. Because of the canyon's distance from civilization, cast and crew had agreed to camp on the river. A chopper would visit the set daily, bringing supplies, script changes and fresh ingredients for the meals Grace and her crew would prepare. Wine, seafood, fowl, meat, eggs, dairy products and fresh vegetables—far more variety than could be stowed in coolers on an average river trip.

The night before the launch, the Rapid Riggers crew transported their boats to the put-in at Mineral Bottom. From there they would start down the Green River through Stillwater Canyon to the confluence with the Colorado and onward to the white water of Cataract Canyon.

Zachary camped at the put-in with Grace. Once filming resumed, they wouldn't get to see much of each other, and both wanted the time together.

It was a precious night. The Rapid Riggers boatmen had the beach to themselves. After a casual meal around the camp fire, when the beach lay in darkness, Nick and Fast Susan set up an old survey tent to make a sauna. Grace and Zac collected the rocks for the sweat in a metal bucket, and they sat together by the fire while the stones heated in the flames.

Zac reclined in a low camping chair. With a beer in hand, Grace sat in the sand and leaned back against his shoulder and his chest. Listening to the sparks in the fire, the music of the river and the quiet sounds of insects in the air, she savored the smell of wood and tried not to wonder when she'd see the Green River again. She tried not to think of favorite campsites. Of rapids. Of friends she'd be leaving behind when she went away with Zac.

Dirty Bob's voice floated across the beach in the darkness. "Didn't somebody die in the Big Drop in '87?"

Fast Susan said, "Wrong year, wrong rapid. You're thinking of…"

Zac tuned in to the distant conversation. The white water stories were incessant, and he was beginning to wonder how much credence to give them. How much to fear the river. Certainly, this section of the Green was calm. But miles downstream, it joined the Colorado, increasing that river's volume. And then, the river descended more quickly…. A cataract.

Dropping his head back, he stared at the stars, more than he'd ever seen at one time, so many it was hard to find the bars of Orion.

Grace sat up. "The rocks are ready."

Zac stirred, started to slide into his shoes.

"Shake 'em out," Grace warned. "Scorpions."

"Saw one as big as your hand once at Spanish Bottom,'' contributed Nick, joining them. "Those rocks done?''

The river stories continued as the boatmen squeezed together in the sauna. Fast Susan poured water onto the rocks from an old coffeepot. As they sizzled and the dome filled with steam, Dirty Bob told Zac, ''Bet Grace never told you about the time she flipped in Stillwater.''

''Oh, shut up,'' Grace said, laughing.

''She didn't tie anything down—''

''There's no white water!''

''Which made that flip all the more *amazing,* Grace....''

Laughter. More ribbing. Zac heard the comradeship among them. The heat in the tent increased with the sound of the rocks hissing as someone poured on more water.

It was some time later, when they were all splashing in the shallows at the edge of the river, cooling off, that Dirty Bob turned to Zac and said, ''I guess there's no white water in Los Angeles, huh?''

''No.'' Zac stole a look at Grace, who was bathing in river mud in the moonlight. Her face coated with silt, she seemed to have become part of the earth and the river itself. Her eyes met his, then darted away. But not before Zac saw what it was costing her to leave.

When they had rinsed off a last time and were toweling each other on the beach, some distance away from the others, he mentioned it, and she looked at him in surprise and threw her arms around him.

''Oh, Zac, the happiest time of my life was in New York. With you. California will be like that.''

But she sounded as though she was trying to convince

herself.

They both knew nothing would be like that ever again.

THE MOVIE CREW and the park service escort arrived before seven, and the whole party put in. That afternoon, they stopped in Stillwater Canyon, where the size of their party forced them to camp on three different beaches. They set up one large kitchen, where everyone congregated for dinner, but snacks had to be provided for each of the three camps. There were peanut-butter-and-pretzel log cabins to build for appetizers, Cornish game hens to bone, morel mushrooms to clean, spinach miso soup to cook and purée. Every boatman worked on food preparation, and when Grace glanced up in a frazzle from adjusting the fire beneath a dutch oven she saw Zachary just feet away slicing artichoke hearts for risotto.

Joining him, Grace said, "You don't have to do that, Zac."

He hooked a finger in the waistband of her cut-offs and cast his eyes over her breasts in her cotton crop-top. His hand closed on her bare waist. "And leave you alone in the camp kitchen with Cute Nick and Dirty Bob?"

Grace whispered, "I love you."

His eyes echoed her words.

By dinner time, the Rapid Riggers crew had created twenty-one separate courses. Over a slice of frozen almond cappuccino dacquoise for dessert, Nort Stills remarked, "This is really something, you know? Chez River."

Hal Markley, spending a token night on the set, had understanding in his eyes as he told Grace, "You're a remarkable woman."

From the camping chair where he sat, Zac winked at

her with pride, and Grace longed to move closer to him and take advantage of the brief opportunity to talk together. But Hal was showing her his cellular phone, demonstrating that, indeed, it did not work on the river. And later, Grace was busy with clean-up, while Zachary had a night shoot that lasted until four in the morning. When he finally joined her in the ridiculously large tent the studio had provided, it was only to pull off his clothes and drop against her, his arm thrown over her, and fall instantly asleep. Barely an hour later, Grace left the tent to start breakfast and prep for lunch.

By day, Grace's raft carried much of the lighting gear, plus five members of the lighting crew. She enjoyed chatting with the technicians while she rowed. And during breaks, while the crew was filming on shore, she kneaded rising bread dough for dinner and mentally rehearsed lunch plans.

Overall, the film crew seemed cheerful, and Grace attributed that to their surroundings, good attitudes, good food and the Rapid Riggers guides. She saw Fast Susan drawing a hearty laugh from Martin Place, while Dirty Bob enthralled his passengers with river stories Grace knew were alternately hilarious and terrifying.

But when they reached the Confluence and the Green spilled into the Colorado, Grace's stomach began to draw into knots, and she knew the other boatmen were feeling the same thing. Everywhere they looked was an altered shoreline, with familiar landmarks submerged by high water. And there was no denying the sheer volume, the force of the water carrying them downstream.

What would Cataract be like?

FILMING IN the interim had been limited to a few calmwater and hiking scenes, and now excitement was high.

Zac glimpsed the white water from his seat at the oars of the *No Name* and he remembered Grace's instructions to him at their last stop, *Whatever you do, don't miss Spanish Bottom.*

He eddied out at the beach, and one by one the other boats did the same. The sound of the water was warning enough. *Hear me. Fear me.* And there was no missing the cautionary sign on the river just before the beach:

STOP

CATARACT CANYON

HAZARDOUS RAPIDS

200 YARDS AHEAD

At sunset Grace left her guides to serve steamed mussels and grilled quail to a crew who had already dined on appetizers—artichoke heart and asparagus salad and honey walnut bread—and she joined the park-service ranger, Meshach, Zac and Nick on a traverse over the boulders to scout Brown Betty Rapid.

Zac was two steps behind Grace, and he paused when she did, to stare down at the rushing mass of foam below, much bigger than he had imagined. His mouth went dry, and his legs felt like rubber.

Under the sound of the torrent, he heard Nick Colter, behind him, say, "I think I'm going to throw up."

Apparently, fear didn't fade with experience.

But as the director surveyed the rapid from above, his primary concern was the placing of cameras on the shore, and he plied Nick and Grace with questions about which route the boats would have to take—and whether a boat could take a different course to film the dories from another angle.

Together, Grace, Nick and the ranger fielded Meshach's questions and cautioned him with facts about the river. The biggest rapids were at the end of the canyon in the Big Drop, where the river fell thirty feet in less than a mile. The river was running at 80,000 cfs, and in 1983, when the number was 100,000, two dozen J-rigs, pontoon boats and dories had been stopped by the Big Drop. They'd huddled in eddies and eventually signaled for helicopters to carry their passengers to where they could be ferried back to Moab and Green River by jet-boat. This was very big white water.

Brown Betty was neither the most nor least difficult rapid in the canyon. But now the waves looked larger than Grace had ever seen them. She knew she would sleep badly.

Zac was silent as they walked back to camp. The fading sunlight cast bright shades of orange and brown and black on the riffles in the river and the rocks and sand on both banks, and Grace caught his eyes following a bluish Colorado River toad as it hopped near the shore. Glancing up at his profile, she said, "Zac, don't you want to use a stuntman?"

"No." His smile made Grace think of what Nick had said about her father. He was right. Sam Sutter would have liked it that she'd married a man who could row.

Others were less enthusiastic about the white water. During dinner and on into the evening, as Meshach gathered with Nort Stills and the crew, rumors flooded the camp. Which actors wanted to row, which didn't. Martin Place and Zac were the only ones interested in guiding dories, so Rapid Riggers boatmen were sized by wardrobe and told to report to makeup in the morning. Because there would be more boats than guides, and to facilitate additional takes, a chopper specially equipped with filters to protect it from the sand would meet them downstream at Cross Canyon and lift them back to Spanish Bottom to take more boats down the rapids.

That night, Grace and Zac climbed back to the scouting place, and she told him everything she could remember about the rapids ahead. Zachary listened attentively and asked the right questions, and later in their tent, they made silent, shaking love. And even when he was inside her, Zac could still hear the roar of the white water, could still in his mind see the white foam.

THE MORNING DAWNED GRAY against the ceaseless sound of rushing rapids. As she served breakfast, Grace heard Nort Stills grumble, "Could hardly sleep with that noise. It could make you go mad."

The river.

After breakfast Grace put on her wet suit in anticipation of the rapids. Rigging her boat, she was glad for the protection of the neoprene against the chill air.

Her only passenger would be the still photographer, who hoped to snap shots of the cameramen and actors in the dories. Anyone else not immediately involved with filming would remain behind at Spanish Bottom. There, her guides would serve lunch to the bulk of the crew, while Grace fed the others on one of the beaches downstream.

As Meshach hiked down from the rocks where he'd been helping to place a camera, Grace looked across the beach at Zac. The specially designed life vest he wore beneath the costume of Seneca Howland gave him only a little extra bulk, and Grace didn't trust it. Zac was all muscle and bone—highly sinkable. What if the vest didn't provide enough buoyancy?

At last she crossed the beach and joined him. His eyes

held a private look, a reminder of the night before, as he said, "Meet you in our tent at Cross Canyon."

She didn't answer, just patted his shirt, feeling the place where she'd used dental floss to sew the sheath holding his river knife to his vest. Zac's lips grazed her neck and her mouth and for a moment his hands locked around hers. A long look passed between him and Grace, private communication. *I love you.*

I love you, too.

Ten minutes later they launched.

Grace was in the second raft, with the *Emma Dean*, the dory named for Powell's wife, following. Nick rowed *Kitty Clyde's Sister*, and behind him was Zac at the oars of the *No Name*. The last crafts were the park-service boat and a J-rig carrying Meshach, a script supervisor and some other crew members. Rapid Riggers guides filled in for a few of the actors in the dories. Dirty Bob was with Zac in the *No Name*.

The whole fleet ran the first two rapids without incident and eddied out for a short break. As the boats gathered along the shore and crew members ran from boat to boat checking things, Grace could see exhilaration and triumph all around. Meshach's smile was the broadest. Noting the excitement in his eyes, Grace knew the director was thinking that the hardship of transporting the crew down the river had been worth it.

But the biggest rapids were ahead. While the camera loaders worked busily, actors and boatmen walked down the shore to scout. The third rapid had virtually washed out at the higher water level, and the next wasn't yet in sight. Everyone set out again, moving downstream. Soon Grace heard the white water and searched for a place to pull over and view the rapid. But when she glanced back upstream, she saw Meshach standing in the J-rig, waving everyone on like a general ordering his troops to charge.

Grace looked at Nick in *Kitty Clyde's Sister,* and he shrugged at her. These rapids shouldn't be that bad. They rowed on.

Larry, the photographer, suggested to Grace, "See if you can get over on the right so I can snap photos of the *Emma Dean.*"

Grace did as he requested, but as the first dory went by, Meshach hailed her from the J-rig and waved her down the river. While Larry snapped photos of the two dories following, Grace rowed toward the foam.

She saw at once that she'd made a mistake. The high water had changed the river, and the usual route was now a mass of standing waves. Clearer passage was over to the left, and she rowed hard to make it, but the rapid already owned the raft. Dead ahead was a frowning hole like the Mariana Trench. It had *keeper* written all over it.

Feet planted against a cooler, Grace pulled on the oars, but the raft still hurtled forward and poured down over the fall into the liquid chasm.

It was the worst white-water trouble Grace had seen in her life, and she rowed straight at the wave, determined to escape the hole before it caught the boat. But the wave was much bigger than the raft, and as the brown water rose up in front of her and the gray-and-yellow tube of her raft tried to climb it, Grace knew what was going to happen, and it did.

The raft flipped, and a wall of water slammed her, crushing her against coolers and ammo cans. Grace tried to get her bearings, but the raft was moving too fast, plunging, and she was caught on it, carried with it. She felt air and saw sunlight and gasped water, and then the boat jerked, moved up and flipped again. She felt her body bouncing like a puppet, felt her weight dangling from the strap on the back of her life vest as it buoyed her up under the overturned raft in a world where there was no air, only water pressing her against the sharp edges of the gear tied in the boat. Upside down, she felt the raft rise again, felt her body and neck twist awkwardly in an involuntary somersault.

God help me, she thought, throwing her arms over her head, preparing for the next impact. It was like one of those amusement-park rides when a person couldn't tell which way was up. But there was no safety code here. The wave slammed the raft down, and she was beneath it in a no-air world of brown. The boat dragged her.

Grace tried to fight her way up around the tube, anywhere to air, but the force of the river was too strong, and she could feel a line wrapped around her body. *Knife.* As she slid the blade from its sheath, the raft slammed an obstacle, a rock, and her body jerked. Her knife stabbed one of the tubes and slipped from her hand. The raft spun.

Air. Air. Grace tried to find the surface, tried to unzip her vest to free herself. *Got to breathe. Going to drown.*

In her mind she saw Zachary's eyes. *Lover,* she thought. She couldn't die. She couldn't die when she had so much to live for.

Her mind cried out for him.

CHAPTER ELEVEN

ZAC WATCHED the wave lift the boat a third time and smack it down. He was less horrified by the size of the hole than by the sight of Grace dangling against the raft, tossed in the waves like a dummy. She was trapped by a line threaded through rings on the tubes, and if the keeper kept pummeling the boat she would break her neck. As the raft rose up again, he saw it jerking her, saw her back twist.

Behind him Dirty Bob said, "She's caught on the chicken line."

Looking past the cameraman in the bow of the dory, Zac saw the route the *Emma Dean* had taken. He needed to go the same way—away from the keeper that held Grace's boat. He was rowing. There were other lives at stake.

His wife was dying.

Grace's raft plunged out of the hole and onto the tongue upside down, and Zac knew she was beneath it. He said, "Bob, take the oars. I'm going."

Dirty Bob said, "Do it." Rough, brown river-guide hands crowded Zachary's on the oars.

The dory was nearing the raft, and Zac stood up and jumped into the white water beside the rapid. He didn't feel the cold, only the pull of the river as it tried to suck him away from the gray-and-yellow raft. There were

D-rings on the upturned bottom of the boat, and he grabbed one of them and held on.

She was there, beneath the tube, twisting to try to reach the top.

Bracing himself against the raft as it bounded through foam, Zac unsheathed the knife she'd given him, her father's knife, and reached out a long arm for her. He sliced the white line stretched taut around her and severed the strap on her life vest. Immediately she bounced away from him like a corpse, disappearing under the boat.

Zac didn't see the wave, only felt the water pressing down on his head, tearing him from the boat, making everything gray-brown. When he came up there was only white water, cold around him. Then he saw the edge of the boat, the slick tube. A line swirled near him in the water, and he grabbed it and pulled himself to the raft. Crawling up on the underside as the boat hurled toward the next rapid, he looked all around the seething waves. No Grace. He slid back into the water and tried to go under the boat, but the river changed, became a mass of swirling, and there was nothing he could do but let it carry him.

In the chaos of tossing water, his mind went sick, and he saw things that had nothing to do with Grace. He saw nightmare images—the Tudor door, the shape on the bed—and he felt empty inside as the mighty river swept him along.

MESHACH TOSSED a throw bag from the J-rig, and Grace saw the white line spiraling through the air. She caught it and held it. As Fast Susan steered for an eddy, Grace let the pontoon boat carry her through the water until she felt silt beneath her feet.

Clinging to the line, she slogged through the mud, battered and ready to drop in her tracks. Suddenly she remembered the photographer who'd been in her boat. Still gasping, she called out to Susan, "Where's Larry?"

Susan pointed to the far shore, where the photographer was dumping water out of one of his wet-suit booties. Through the dripping tangle of her hair, Grace stared downstream after the dories, looking for the *No Name*. Zac would be worried.

Susan yelled, "Get on! We've got to go get Zac!"

Zachary! Grace's stomach plunged. Had Zac fallen out in the white water? He wasn't even wearing a wet suit. Hypothermia could set in fast, especially for someone as lean as Zac.

She scrambled toward the J-rig, and Meshach and one of the crew reached down to haul her aboard. As she settled on one of the pontoons, she gazed downstream. She saw the *No Name,* but Zachary was nowhere in sight.

Susan yelled as she gunned the outboard. "He jumped in to grab the raft. He must have cut you free, and then he went under..."

Grace felt sick. He had saved her life and she had never known he was there.

Zac, she thought, *where are you?*

ZACHARY HIKED up the shore as far as he could, climbing the rocks. Then he saw the dories coming toward the eddy, and he looked for Grace, but she wasn't there. She'd never come up.

The sun emerged from the clouds, but it didn't warm

him. Shivering, he peered at the raft on the beach. He'd turned it over himself to make sure she really wasn't underneath. One tube was punctured, slashed by a knife. His knife had found its way back into its sheath, but Zac couldn't remember when.

In the sun he leaned against a rock wall behind him, hardly noticing the red dust smearing to mud on his clothes and face and body. He remembered how Grace had looked under the raft and that maybe she'd already been dead. All he wanted was to find her body, and he made himself keep climbing as he stared down on the white water and the J-rig.

They were all yelling at him, and he squinted and thought he saw Grace, but it didn't seem real.

NICK, IN HIS ROLE as Emergency Medical Technician, insisted Grace sit down and be checked out before going after Zac. "Dirty Bob will get him."

Grace submitted to Nick's questions, then said, "I'm fine," and got up. She'd seen Zac standing over the river, and she'd known he was looking for her. Back aching from her pummeling in the keeper, she crossed the beach and started up the rocks. She wanted nothing but to touch her husband and let him see she was fine.

As she climbed the trail, she saw the two men coming down. Zac looked wet and wild. Unshaven. Dark. Like Heathcliff roaming the moors, only this was the Utah desert.

They met on the path, and he stared at her, then said, "Hi."

Grace reached for him and they held each other for a long time.

She needed to patch her boat, and Meshach was eager

to get on with shooting. The flipped raft had spoiled the scene, and he wanted another take. He told Zac, "You can talk to your wife for a bit. Then we'll go down to Cross Canyon, meet the chopper, fly back up stream and run the whole thing again."

Kneeling in the sand examining her raft, Grace wished she could protest. But this was why they'd come. They would film until they got the shots they wanted or ran out of boats. The director was already walking away.

Zac crouched beside her in the sand. "Are you really all right? Your neck isn't hurt? You didn't hit your head?"

"I'm fine." She sat back on the shore in her wet suit and looked at him. He was filthy, covered with red desert earth. "What about you?"

"The same." He shook his hair, and Grace saw him trying to get water out of his ears.

She gazed down the beach at Meshach and company. "I think they're ready. You should go and get dry."

Zac nodded. Her voice seemed loud to him, and he shook his head again, trying to return his ears to their normal equilibrium. Staring into her brown eyes, he said, "Don't go down the next rapids till we get back."

"I won't." Grace glanced up the beach to where the photographer was reloading his camera and hunting in his dry bag for other equipment. "Meshach's leaving almost everyone here. I'm fine."

"Okay." Zac kissed her, the first kiss since their swim in the rapid. He was aware of the shape of her lips, of their temperature, of everything. Even the day seemed to have become more bright, so bright he didn't see how he would make it down the river without sunglasses. But he had to. He said, "I love you," and then he got up and walked back toward the others.

Unsettled, Grace watched him go. A warning bell, a nameless fear, was tolling inside her, and she didn't know why. It was probably the shock of what they'd both just survived.

Her eyes followed Zachary as he got into the dory, and she felt her heart reaching out to his, trying to keep him close.

THE TIME PASSED QUICKLY. Trying to ignore the physical effects of her battering in the keeper, Grace set up the lunch buffet she'd carried in her boat. Two kinds of chilled soup, two salads, sandwich makings, whole-wheat currant rolls, poppy seed cake, slightly mashed raspberry cheesecake and chocolate espresso cookies, with a wide array of beverages in a cooler nearby. She was boiling water for washing the dishes when she heard the heartbeat sound of the helicopter and saw its shadow pass overhead, going upstream.

After clean-up, she turned her attention to her boat. Because any permanent patch needed twenty-four hours to dry, Grace decided to mend the tube temporarily, so the raft could make it through the remaining rapids to Cross Canyon beach.

Larry photographed her mending the tear, then scrambled up the rocks to find a spot from which to shoot the dories when they came down again. The cameramen had already placed their tripods where Meshach had indicated, and now they, too, were waiting.

When she had repaired the raft and inflated the damaged tube, Grace checked the gear that had gone through the keeper, then took a paperback out of her ammo can.

She put on some sunscreen, grabbed extra clothes, sunglasses and a water bottle, and hiked up the rocks above the rapid.

Sunbathing in her bikini, resting her sore, bruised body, Grace read three chapters of her mystery before she heard the helicopter returning, signaling the cameramen that the dories were coming. She put on her shorts and a red hooded sweatshirt and went to stand over the river to watch the boats.

The *No Name* was the second boat, following a J-rig, and Zac was rowing. From the bank, Grace admired his skill in the rapids. As he guided the dory toward the shore, she hurried down the loose rock trail to the beach. Reaching the boat, she grabbed the bowline and said, "Good run." Zac stared at her, then stood up indecisively.

Meshach, approaching on the J-rig, yelled into the hailer, "We're pulling over. Get out and stretch your legs."

Grace could see that the rest of the crew was now following from Spanish Bottom. The helicopter had flown downstream to the beach at Cross Canyon, where everyone would camp that night, and Grace knew it would make several trips back and forth, transporting actors and equipment. Not everyone in the crew was willing to face the white water, and Grace was sure news of her flip had made the rounds at Spanish Bottom.

Eventually Zac got out of the boat and stood on the shore. His new costume was soaked, as the first had been.

Grace said, "I love to watch you row."

Zac wanted to tell her not to talk so loudly, but he thought the problem was water in his ears. The thunder of the rapids was rock-concert volume. In fact, all his senses were heightened. The colors of the rocks seemed brighter, their shapes almost alive.

"Zac."

He blinked at Meshach.

The director clapped a hand on his shoulder. "Good job. You look good at those oars."

"Thank you." Why was everyone shouting?

He saw all the people coming down the rapids in boats, the crew calling out as the J-rigs plunged onward down the river, and it seemed more like a holiday than the making of a movie.

Meshach said, "Take a break, and then let's get those boats down to Cross Canyon. You're done for today, Zac. If you want to go with your wife, I think we can find someone to row that dory."

One of the J-rigs was pulling off into an eddy with an extra boatman aboard. Grace called to him, and Zac winced at the sound of her shout.

As Meshach moved away, Grace asked, "Are you okay, Zachary?"

He nodded, pounding his head as though to get water out of his ears.

Grace rerigged her boat and pumped more air into the damaged chamber using a hand pump. Eventually Zac nudged her aside and finished the job for her, but Grace was a little surprised at how long it had taken him to think of it. He must be tired.

When they set out in her raft, she offered him the oars and he took them with little reaction, but Grace saw he knew where to enter the white water. He had run this rapid earlier.

Zac's thoughts wandered. Why were they running the

same sections of river again? After a moment he remembered about the film. That was why. He turned to Grace. She seemed familiar and yet a stranger in her river hat and life vest. As she smiled at him, he stared at her brown eyes, and a grounding sense of time and place washed over him.

She was his wife. Sometimes they lived together in the inn by the river, and she snuggled next to him under the covers while their gray dog slept at the foot of the bed and crickets chirped outside.

The motion of the boat reminded him of the rapid. Returning his gaze to the white water, he found the tongue and followed it. Reading the river was second nature to him, though he found the raft clumsy after the sleek dory. As a wave dashed over the bow, soaking him, he looked back at Grace. The sun glittered in wet droplets on her suntanned thighs. She was like Persephone. She had come up from the "underworld"—ha-ha— and now it was spring.

"Zac! The rapid. Watch what you're doing."

He turned his head. One oar stroke saved them from a hole.

In a minute they were at the shore, and Grace jumped out and grabbed the bowline. Zac got out, too, and watched her haul the heavy raft up onto the beach. He was amazed by how strong she was.

But her dark eyes looked strange—almost suspicious—as she asked, "Want to pitch the tent?"

He considered her question. Should they pitch the tent? Or should they sleep under the stars?

("Pitch the tent.")

The thought startled Zac, it was so powerful. Almost more than a thought. More like...a voice.

A faint recollection came to him, a sense of something not good, something he should think about. His book, *DSM-IV*... Hearing voices. *Auditory hallucinations are by far the most common and characteristic—*

Grace said, "All right. I'll do it." She reached into the boat and began untying straps. A moment later Nick Colter came over and joined her, and Zac wondered why the river guide was helping.

Nick said, "How're you doing, Gracie?"

"Fine." She knew he was asking as EMT, as well as coworker. Her body did ache. Why was Zac just standing there? She could use his help.

Annoyed, she told herself he'd already put in a long day. It wasn't his fault that hers wasn't over. But it embarrassed her that Nick was helping now—and casting nasty looks at Zac. Nick respected people who did their share of work on the river and disparaged those who did not. Usually Zac was the first to help. But now he just stood watching. When at last he picked up the big sack containing the tent and trudged off toward an empty section of beach, Grace nearly sighed aloud.

Nick stared after him. "Are you two fighting?"

"Not that I know of." But Zac's strange behavior troubled her. As soon as she could, Grace took the dry bag containing sleeping bags and clothing over to the tent. He wasn't there. He must have gone to change out of his costume, remove his makeup.

In any case, she needed to start the evening meal. Guides were already setting up coolers and tables, and Grace began slicing fresh vegetables to grill. The dinner menu would include several Mexican courses, as well as barbecued chicken and cornmeal-crusted catfish served with snap peas and french-fried shoestring potatoes.

Preparations were comparatively easy, but as darkness fell on the beach Grace grew increasingly anxious about Zac. Where was he? At the first opportunity, she made another search of the camp.

Nick came and found her. "Zac's missing?"

Grace nodded. She was outside her tent, pulling on her pile cardigan. As she picked up her headlamp she told Nick, "I'm going to walk up the canyon and look for him. Will you please keep searching camp?"

"I'll get some help. Don't go too far on your own."

"I won't." But Grace was worried. If Zac had decided to go for a hike in the dark, he might have gotten lost or fallen on the rocks and been injured.

The canyon wound through tamarisk and between rocky slots on a little-known path that eventually led to the top of the two-thousand-foot cliffs. Grace couldn't imagine Zac hiking that far without water, especially not in the boots he'd worn to play Seneca Howland.

The canyon was quiet but for the sound of insects in the brush and water dripping somewhere. Nonetheless, even as she walked farther from the camp, Grace could hear the river.

She jumped as twigs brushed her in the dark, but the path was made of soft sand and easy to follow and she used her headlamp only intermittently. "Zac?" She shivered in the cool May night. She was going to feel silly yelling for him up in this canyon if it turned out he was back at camp.

But when Grace shone her headlamp on the ground she saw a fresh boot track. She was sure it had come from the boots he'd been wearing.

A chill swept over her, and she thought irrationally of

a mystery she'd read, a story of a madman hiding in a canyon and a woman who'd gone there and found—

Something rustled in the brush off to her left.

"Zachary?"

An enormous owl surged up in the darkness, wings flapping, and Grace gasped. But then it was gone, and she stood quaking in the brush, terrified. Voice tremulous, she cried, "Zac! Where are you?"

She trained her headlamp on the ground again, looking for more tracks. Eventually she found them. Using the light, she followed the footprints, but she was nervous, although she had no idea what was scaring her. This canyon was remote in the extreme. There could be no one up here but Zachary.

Where was he?

She flashed her headlamp through the brush lining the narrow, curved walls of the canyon. As the beam caught white cotton fabric and a human forearm, she started. *Zac.*

At once she was afraid.

He was crouched in a low alcove behind a cluster of scrub oak, peering at her from between the leaves. Just crouched there, in his Seneca Howland clothes. And it *was* Zachary, his long hair tangled from rowing the silty river. But for some reason he looked like a stranger, and Grace felt something awful in the pit of her stomach. An instinct told her to turn away, to go, to run back out of the canyon and get help, but she thought, *No, this is Zac. This is my husband, my love.*

She clutched her arms around herself, and he looked out at her. In the glow from her headlamp, which she trained not on him but near him, his eyes looked different than she'd ever seen them. She realized he was frightened.

What had scared him?

Grace glanced over her shoulder and up the canyon, then shone her headlamp along the path and against the nearby rock wall. Nothing. Turning off the light, she tried to see Zac in the dark. There were his eyes—two glistening things—and the slope of his nose.

She couldn't think why he'd be crouched there as though he was waiting for something. For a moment it seemed to her he was predator, rather than frightened prey, and then she thought how ridiculous both ideas were.

She said, "Zac, come out. I've been looking for you."

He didn't answer, and that sent another chill through her. Again she thought of leaving the canyon, going for Nick. Why did she feel this way? The man in the alcove was Zac, the person closest to her in the world...

But at the moment she felt almost as though she didn't know him.

I'm afraid of him, she realized. She took a step backward on the path, even afraid to let him know she was scared.

In the darkness Zac watched her. He thought it was Grace, but everyone looked so different, and he knew how good these people were with makeup. But why would they make someone look like Grace?

(*"What for?"*)

(*"I don't know, but if then, so what?"*)

Zac creased his forehead, trying to squeeze the voices away. They were soft, but he could hear them, and they annoyed him. He felt confused. Why was Grace frightened? Were they after her?

He whispered, "Grace, it's all right. Come here." Then it occurred to him again that maybe it wasn't Grace.

The light flicked on once more, and it was too bright. He decided to go out there, where she was. He folded his body out of the alcove and stood up between the rock and the brush. Branches rubbed his face and his shirt.

Grace said, "Zac, come out. I'm not going in there."

He paused, uneasy. Was it Grace?

("What for?")

("Beyond what?")

("And so on, then you can go, but don't sleep...")

He tried to listen to the conversation, but he couldn't follow it. And Grace had spoken too quickly.

Then, abruptly, came a crashing sound, like branches breaking, and a loud voice calling, "Grace? Grace!"

Zac crouched, hiding behind the shrubs.

In the dark Grace watched him. She was afraid to talk to him again, and she didn't know why. What was wrong with him? What was wrong with Zachary?

A shadow fell over her, and she jumped and turned. It was Nick, his long hair blue-black as a raven's wing in the night. He asked, "Did you find him?"

Grace said, "Uh, yeah." And then, because she knew intuitively that speaking to Zac wouldn't help, she gestured toward the shrubs.

She saw the alarm in Nick's eyes, and she knew he must think Zac was hurt—or worse. He shone his own headlamp into the bushes until it fell on Zac's frightened eyes, and then he instantly turned it off. He crouched on the trail and peered through the leaves at Zac. "How're you doing, Zac?"

Zac didn't answer. *Nick,* he thought. Could Nick be trusted?

(*"What for?"*)

He stood up and pushed aside the scratching bushes that seemed like live monsters. As he stepped out onto the trail, he saw Grace. She stood back from him, as though there was something wrong with him, a reaction that hurt at some point inside him beyond the voices.

(*"What for?"*)

(*"If so, then what?"*)

(*"Do not dream about such things in the black of night…"*)

Nick was watching him. "Zac, are you sure you didn't hit your head today? Do you have any bumps?"

Zac shook his head, trying to remember when he might have hit it.

"Dizzy?"

Zac considered. Was this "dizzy"? "No."

(*"What for?"*)

(*"Even though he said…"*)

"Think you can walk back to camp?"

What are they going to do to me? Zac thought. Standing on the trail in the grip of indecision, he looked at Grace. Beneath her messy braid, her beautiful arched eyebrows were drawn together. It was his job to protect her. Moving near her, he said in a low voice, "Let's go."

Grace glanced up at him uneasily. He wasn't looking toward camp. He was staring back into the canyon.

She thought of Nick's idea, that perhaps Zac had a head injury. That would explain his confusion. It might be an emergency. She looked up at him and shook her head. "You need to go back to camp. I think you hit your head. That's why you're feeling funny.'' And *acting* funny.

Zac glanced down at her. He was feeling funny. Maybe she was right. He said, ''Okay.''

IN THE TENT Grace shared with Zachary, Nick and the set medic, whose name was Colin, checked him over. They examined his head for lumps, shone a flashlight in his eyes, probed his neck, and asked questions.

''Who is the president?''

''Do you know where you are?''

Although Zac submitted, Grace could see him growing edgy. Every time the EMTs made an inquiry, his expression darkened and he grew more restless. He glanced frequently toward the tent flap, and he seemed to regard even her with suspicion. Grace wanted to talk to him, to ask what was wrong, but she knew she should let the EMTs complete their examination first. They asked him about his health and if he ever used drugs, and Nick asked if he'd picked up any Colorado River toads—the amphibians emitted a toxin through their skin.

Zac shook his head and regarded the EMTs with a look of profound distrust that Grace had never seen before. He seemed… She couldn't put her finger on it. Paranoid, maybe.

A memory surged through her like an electric shock.

I entertained the most florid delusions imaginable of persecution…

She blinked.

No.

Zac wasn't running around naked. He wasn't talking

about microscopic recording equipment in his clothing. He was hardly talking at all.

Grace looked at his face.

Something was wrong. She knew it. His pupils were even, but there was something about his expression, the way he was holding his face...

Grace asked, "Zac, do you feel at all like you did in New York?"

He stared at her for a moment, and then he seemed suddenly happier. "Yes," he said, and met her eyes. "But better. Immeasurably better. Everything's been better since—" He glanced at Nick and Colin and cut off the sentence. He told them, "I'm fine. I don't know why you're doing this."

Voice full of enthusiasm, he told Grace, "I want to go out and gaze at the stars with you. Let's go for a walk." He pulled on her hand.

Nick and Colin looked at each other, and Colin lifted his shoulders, as though to say *Why not?*

(*"What for?"*)

(*"Therefore, he is not to go..."*)

Zac frowned. "Does someone have a radio on?"

The other men and Grace listened, then shook their heads.

They left the tent, and outside Zac stared at the beach and the fires and the river and smelled the smoke in the air.

"How are you doing, Zac?" It was Meshach, pushing his glasses up on his nose. The director glanced at Colin. "Is he okay?"

The set medic smiled. "Seems to be."

Grace felt an uneasiness in her heart, and her eyes darted to Nick's. Did he think Zac was all right?

The boatman stuffed his hands in the pockets of his shorts. "It was kind of a hairy day. Swimming a rapid. Almost dying." He met Grace's eyes and shrugged.

Grace thought, *Maybe that's all. Stress.*

She looked up, wanting to touch Zac.

He was walking away, across the beach.

AS THE NIGHT WORE ON, Grace became convinced that something was wrong with him. He wouldn't change out of his costume. He seemed uninterested in having his smeared and dirty makeup removed. He didn't want to sleep. And Grace had only to talk to him for a few minutes to realize that he was at least disoriented and confused. At worst...

When they were alone, sitting on a rock by the shore, Grace questioned him. "Zac, remember what you told me about New York, after I left you?"

He stared at the water rushing by. He blinked.

("New York is gone.")

("Tell her to shut up.")

The voices pestered. They were sometimes querulous, sometimes simply annoying, always unpleasant. They made it difficult to think.

"Do you remember what you told me about *Leaving Hong Kong?*"

"I was Adrian. What are you talking about?" He frowned. "I don't want to talk."

Grace took his hand and sat silently beside him. After a bit she asked, "How are you feeling?"

"I feel wonderful." He looked at her. "Really, I feel touched by God. But sometimes it's hard to be chosen, because your senses are so acute. I'm special, because

I'm an actor, but I need to rest now, not have people pestering me with questions.''

(*"What for?"*)

"Shut up," he said.

Grace knew he wasn't talking to her.

Zac moved on the rock beside her and heaved a great sigh. "I'm going for a walk." He jumped down to the sand, faltering a little, as though something was affecting his normal agility.

Remembering how she'd found him in the canyon, Grace sprang down beside him, concerned. Nervously she glanced across the beach. Near one of the camp fires, Nick was in caucus with Colin, Meshach, Nort Stills and the park-service ranger. Grace wondered if they were talking about Zac or if they'd decided he was all right.

He definitely wasn't.

Worried as he started down the shore, Grace said, "Zac, I want some coffee. Will you come help me make it?"

He turned, frowning. "I wish you wouldn't talk so fast."

Grace looked across the beach, silently beckoning Nick. Miraculously the guide stood up and moved toward them. Zac saw him coming.

Panic swept over his face. His eyes grew wide, as though a group of terrorists with Uzis had suddenly emerged from behind the rocks. He ran. Fast. He headed downstream toward the base of the cliffs that walled the river gorge. Boulders were piled at its base, and in horror Grace watched him scramble up them without care. She could see his coordination was off. If any of those rocks rolled even once...

Zac.

She ran after him across the beach. Pausing at the base of the boulders, she stared up. He was still climbing.

Footsteps pounded behind her in the dark, and then Nick was there, watching Zachary scale the cliff face. The full moon illuminated his journey, and Nick said, "Don't worry. He'll get rimrocked before he gets too high. There aren't any cracks or toeholds after a while."

Grace hugged herself, eyes on Zac. *Don't fall,* she thought. *Don't fall.* She wanted to go after him, but she sensed that he was afraid, that he thought he was being chased.

Was this what he'd been like in New York?

Nick's voice startled her out of her reverie. "So what's wrong with your husband, Amazing Grace?" His eyes drifted toward hers, then stared back up at the figure on the cliff. "Does Zac have some mental health problems we should know about?"

Mental health problems.

The words were a puzzle piece fitting into place. Standing on the beach in the moonlight, with white water roaring beside her, Grace wondered why that had never occurred to her before. She and Zac had just…swept it under the carpet. A breakdown.

Mad.

She looked at Nick. "I guess so."

THE BEACH WAS BUSY all night. News of Zac's condition had spread among the crew members, and Grace saw people standing by tents, talking. Several came over to peer up at the rocky ledge where Zac had stopped his ascent. But the two EMTs persuaded people to go away and leave him alone.

Nick told Grace, "At least if he stays up there, we know where he is."

Meshach eventually turned in, while Nort Stills and Grace and Colin and Nick sat in camping chairs on the beach some distance from the foot of the rocks. The moon had gone behind the walls of the river gorge, and the beach lay in darkness, but a lunar glow still illuminated the ledge where Zachary sat. There was a wall of Precambrian schist at his back, and the effect was absurdly like that of a stage, with a spotlight on the actor. Who was still in costume.

Zac sat back against the schist with his knees drawn up, arms resting negligently on them, and occasionally he spoke to Grace and the others keeping vigil.

It wasn't Shakespeare.

Once he said, "Hi." Another time, seeing them all looking at him, he said, "I don't feel like acting now." And once he began speaking very fast, too quickly to follow, saying things that made no sense, and Grace realized he wasn't talking to them at all but to someone else. Someone who wasn't there. The realization was frightening, and she couldn't help thinking of the things he'd told her that night in the Anasazi Palace, of sleeping in condemned buildings with homeless people. Remembering the filthy man they'd seen on their trip to New York, walking down the street muttering to himself, Grace couldn't help but picture Zac in a similar condition. Alone and confused, because there was no one who cared about him.

She hadn't been there....

But she was here now. Watching him from below as he sat brooding beside the wall of rock that was as old as the earth, she thought of the past weeks, of the sun he had shone on her life with his love for her. She thought, *I will never leave you.*

In the shadows on the beach, Nort Stills said, "This is gonna play havoc with production." He asked Nick and Colin, "Can't you give him something?"

They shook their heads.

Nick asked, "When's that chopper coming tomorrow?"

"Four o'clock," answered Nort.

Grace huddled in her jacket, her sleeping bag around her legs for warmth. She asked Nick, "Don't you think he might be better in the morning?"

Colin's expression was doubtful. Both he and Nick had now heard the story of Zac's breakdown in New York.

Nick said, "It's possible he'll be better. But we need a contingency plan if he's not."

Grace's mind resisted the obvious. She said, "I could use one of the J-rigs and take him back up the river."

Nick looked at her.

Stills said, "If you could just give him something…he could finish filming and take a couple of days off." He gestured at Colin. "Isn't there *something* you can give him?"

Irritated, Grace said, "Maybe they can give *you* something."

Stills looked dumbfounded.

Nick cleared his throat. "I say we wake everybody before light and get the tents down and the beach cleared."

Oh, God, Grace thought. *Oh, God.* In her mind, she saw the orange life vests laid in an X on the beach. She saw the signal mirror flashing. She saw the helicopter with the red cross hovering overhead, descending to the beach.

Coming to get the man she loved.

CHAPTER TWELVE

"ZACHARY, YOU NEED a doctor."

Zac didn't look at her. In the dark he stared down at
the people on the beach, his handsome eyebrows drawn
together. He seemed to be deep in thought. Grace had
brought her sleeping bag up to the ledge, but he wouldn't
use it, so she did. The air by the river was damp.

She told him, "We're going to call a helicopter with
a medical team tomorrow."

"There's nothing wrong with me."

"You had a stressful day. Maybe something happened
to you in the rapids. Or when you saved me. You saved
my life, you know."

Zac's face looked off center. He seemed to be listening for something, and she wasn't sure he'd even heard
her. There were times when he spoke almost normally,
when she felt as though they were having a sane conversation. But then he'd say something strange, and it
was like falling into ice water. She felt silly for listening
to him. But she was also glad to listen, to be with him.
Because he needed someone, and she was his wife, and
she loved him.

But he had to be made to understand he was sick. She
told him, "I'm worried about you. You're behaving
strangely. Colin and Nick don't think you hit your head,

but we should find out what's wrong. So we're going to signal a plane to send a helicopter.''

Zac couldn't follow her. It was hard to understand anything because of all the talking.

(*"Never before done this way."*)

(*"After the fact, but before the present."*)

(*"What for?"*)

He looked at Grace, and he wondered if she could hear it, too.

But she was asking, "Would you like to come down and go to sleep with me?"

Zac blinked, the world clearing for a moment. Grace, her face against his chest, her fingers threaded with his. Drowsy warmth, drifting...

The vision clouded over. Gone.

Grace asked, "Did you understand what I said about tomorrow?"

Zac pondered her words. Tomorrow.

"Zachary, listen to me. Tomorrow, a helicopter will come with a medical team to fly you to the hospital in Grand Junction."

Hospital? thought Zac. He wasn't sick.

HE WASN'T SICK and he knew why they were sending a helicopter. To take him away. To deport him, except that wasn't what would happen. They had something worse in mind.

It wasn't light yet, and already the beach was crawling with people. He had to get away. He told Grace, "I'm going down."

Bad plan, Grace thought. In the past few hours she had climbed up and down the rocks several times, talking with Zac, reporting to Nick and Colin. Finally she'd asked the EMTs, "What if he won't get on the helicopter?"

The men had exchanged a look, and Colin, who'd spent years riding with an ambulance in Los Angeles, had said, "Oh, they'll get him on."

The words were ominous. In a straitjacket? she wondered.

Now Zac stood up, ready to go down to the beach. Although he'd been up all night, he seemed wide awake. Grace was weak with fatigue, her body battered by its ordeal in the keeper, her mind exhausted from trying to understand Zachary's.

Gathering up her sleeping bag, she handed it to Zac, thinking it might slow him, and they made their way down the rocks. As they descended, Grace scanned the beach under the lightening sky. With a feeling beyond gratitude, she saw that Fast Susan and Dirty Bob were already busy in the kitchen, starting breakfast. The other boatmen were moving dories to the far end of the beach and turning rafts upside down, stowing gear under them so it wouldn't be blown away by the propeller blades. Not all the tents were down. Five remained standing, and Grace saw Meshach beside one of them giving directions to a crew member.

Zac hadn't stopped the production, and Grace supposed that was good. Losing a day's filming would be expensive for the studio; as well, the shooting would draw attention away from Zachary. But although Meshach and Nort Stills made noises of concern, Grace sensed their underlying disesteem, as though Zac's worth in their eyes had lessened. The realization made Grace think of the homeless man on the street in New York.

If Zachary was regarded this way, what happened to the people who had no one?

Grace knew she should at least check in at the kitchen. But how could she cook and keep an eye on Zac?

As they reached the foot of the cliff and jumped down onto the sand, she asked him, "How about some breakfast?"

He squinted at her. "I think I have a call. At seven. What time is it?"

Did he really think he could work?

Maybe he can, Grace thought. He would need to use one of the solar showers to bathe. And he was still in his costume from the day before. Did she dare leave him to the crew?

At last Nick came over and Grace said, "I should see if Susan and Bob need me."

The guide said, "Okay," and she knew he'd look after Zac.

Unencumbered, Grace hurried to help the guides make breakfast. As she worked through a haze of exhaustion, preparing blue cornmeal and sunflower pancakes, bacon, French toast, rice pudding and fruit salad, she thought, *Maybe Zac will be okay. Maybe he's getting better. Maybe working will help.*

But as the cast and crew filed by with plates, getting their food, she looked past them and saw two boatmen laying life vests on the beach in two perpendicular lines to form a giant X.

As she poured orange juice for one of the crew members, he asked, "Why do you have to signal a plane? Why not use radios? Or one of the cellulars?"

"They don't work in this section of the canyon." Grace nodded toward the walls of the river gorge. The sun wouldn't rise above them for hours. "Those cliffs are two thousand feet high, and we're miles from the nearest town."

All they could do was wait for a plane to pass—or the helicopter the studio had hired to arrive at four that evening. When breakfast had been served, Grace slipped away to see how Zac was doing and bring him some food.

Miraculously he had showered and was in a fresh costume. Hoping things were improving, Grace brought his plate into the tent where the makeup artist was working on him. He frowned at the food but said nothing as she found a place for it on the table.

Grace studied his eyes and his face. He wasn't himself, but the fact that he was cooperating, trying to do his job, seemed hopeful. Leaving him, she went out to where Nick, signal mirror in hand, was watching the sky for planes. The guide looked as exhausted as she was. Like her, he was still in the same clothes he'd worn the night before.

Grace indicated the life vests on the beach. "Do you think we're going overboard?"

He glanced toward the makeup tent and shrugged.

"Maybe it was just reaction to what happened yesterday," Grace said. "He's under control now. Maybe he's getting over it."

Just then she heard a sound behind her and turned to see the makeup artist emerge from the tent. The woman came right over to them. "Um…" Her eyes darted between Grace and Nick.

Both of them looked at the tent.

"He's gone."

HE'D PLANNED it while he gathered things for his shower, stuffing everything in Grace's day pack. Two bottles of water. Clothes. Running shoes. Sunscreen. His river knife.

While Nick waited outside the makeup tent, he had put the plan into action. He'd cut a slit in the back of the tent and gone out.

He knew where they'd expect him to go. Back into Cross Canyon, back to the trail he'd seen the night before, the trail that led up to above. But that would make it too easy. He'd seen the faint switchback winding along the cliff face. They could pick him off easily there.

No, there was only one way out of here. First back into canyon, bluffing, and then... His dog. They might try to get to him through Ninochka. He had to go to Moab and reach her before they did.

What about Grace? he thought as he ran. Was she part of this?

What if they hurt *her?*

(*"Lies will tell in sleepless days..."*)

(*"Don't let him go up there."*)

(*"Why not?"*)

He stopped long enough to throw the boots in the shrubs and put on his running shoes. As he switched routes, climbing back along the rock wall to the beach, he tried to guard his thoughts. They might have thought-reading equipment. He wouldn't think about anything that mattered. He wouldn't think about his dog. Or about...her.

"HE HAS A PACK?" Grace asked when she'd heard the makeup artist's brief report. Her eyes scanned the beach. Zac must have gone back into the canyon. That was where he'd wanted to go the night before. Heart racing, she stared at the switchback zigzagging up the canyon wall, exposed for thousands of vertical feet. The trail was narrow as a brick in places. And Zachary's coordination was impaired.

Turning, Grace hurried to her tent, and Nick followed. After a quick glance inside she told him, "He's got my pack and the water bottles. And the knife of course. Who knows what else he took?" She looked at Nick, panic surging through her. "Do you have a pack?"

"You can't go after him, Grace. He's psychotic, and he has a knife."

Psychotic. That sounded a lot uglier than "mental health problems."

Grace said, "He's my husband. Believe me, he's less likely to hurt me than anyone else. Besides, he's a gentle person."

"He's not *himself.*"

She looked toward the canyon, where she knew Zac had gone. It was the only way to go, except the river.

The river.

She glanced first at the rafts overturned on the beach, then at the shore. *Zachary.* Disbelieving, she saw him pushing a dory away from the shore.

"Zac!" He wasn't even wearing a life jacket.

People on the beach stared at her as she ran. She heard Nick calling her, and she kept going, right to the river. Zac was watching her from the eddy as he fitted the oars in the oarlocks. Grace kept running—into the river, into the cold, turbulent water. The current sucked at her.

Tossing hair back from his eyes, Zac said, "I'm going."

She reached the side of the boat and grabbed the gunwale. "No, you're not."

"We can't wait! Get in!" His eyes, green irises in a field of white, roved the shore. Seeing Nick splashing into the shallows, Zachary pushed on the oars. "Goodbye, Grace. I'll find you again."

Grace clung to the gunwale, but the dory was twenty-one feet long and propelled by a strong man. Her feet dragged in the silt, then came out from under her as the dory swept out of the eddy into the current with her holding on, slipping down in the cold water, soaking her clothes.

From the shore, Nick yelled curses at them both. "Grace, you got shit for brains or what?"

Grace stared at the rapid ahead, then back at the shore. She'd already made her choice, and now she started hauling herself up over the gunwale as the water filled her tennis shoes, numbed her legs. Zac turned from the oars to help her into the boat. As his hands locked around her arms and Grace pulled a leg over the gunwale, Nick yelled, "Range Canyon! Got it? Range Canyon!"

Grace heard. The chopper could land in Range Canyon—which was well before the Big Drop. She yelled, "Ten-four, commodore!"

Zac steadied her as she scrambled into the dory, water streaming off her clothes onto the floor of the boat. In his face Grace saw confusion and illness, and her heart ached.

Oh, Zachary, she thought. *Come back.*

The white water roared near. Zac was at the oars, and it was too late to change places. Working to slow her pulse, Grace said, "Turn around and row, Zac."

Straddling the seat, he looked at her, then down at the space between them, the floor of the boat. His expression was terribly sad. But after a moment, he swung a long, muscular leg over the seat and took the oars.

Grace drew a breath. The dory was already tossing toward the white water. Like a good boatman, Zac rowed toward the V at the top.

We're going to be okay, Grace thought, feeling naked without a life vest. As she looked around and found a bail bucket, stowed beneath the seat, she began to plan. Range Canyon.

THERE WAS A STRETCH of calm water after the first set of rapids, but Zac kept rowing. "They'll come after us. They have other boats."

Grace hoped Nick would have the sense not to follow. He must know Zac was scared. She said, "Zachary, ship the oars. Just let us drift. I need to talk to you."

("Don't talk.)

("Liars in the alley. Don't drop the goose.")

Who was talking? Zac wondered. Letting the oars dangle in the water, he whispered, "Grace, can you hear them?"

Grace heard the fear in his voice, and she moved up to straddle the seat where Zac sat. She grabbed the left oar and pulled it into the boat. Her shorts and pile sweater were soaked, and she was chilled and eager to see the sun. Zachary's body heat would have to do in the meantime. Her thigh behind him, she reached her arm around him, under the backpack he wore, to try to grasp the other oar.

Zac pulled it in. She put both arms around him,

pressed her face against his shoulder. "What are you hearing, Zac?"

"They talk to me."

He had said he'd heard voices in New York. Grace rubbed his back gently. *Stay calm*, she thought. If she could just keep him calm until Range Canyon. If she could just persuade him to stop there.

"I can't think when they talk."

Grace didn't know what doctors did for someone in Zachary's condition. Could they make him better? Could they make the voices stop? She hoped so. She held him tight.

Zac moved so that he could see her. Grace. He was glad to have her along. He smiled, satisfied that they were together.

She wasn't smiling. She said, "Zac, do you trust me?"

He thought about it, then nodded.

"I want to tell you something." Her brown eyes were earnest. "You're putting our lives in danger right now. You don't realize it, because something's wrong with you. You need to go to the hospital. I want you to go. I love you. I won't let anyone hurt you."

(*"Bargains at five!"*)

(*"That's a real dollar value."*)

"We shouldn't be on the river, Zachary. There are very big rapids ahead, and we have no life vests."

Zac frowned. For a moment an image flashed through his mind. A raft rising vertically from the river, Grace dangling like a rag doll from a rope.

"Zac, remember the movie? Remember your work?"

His eyes grew fearful. He peered about the peaceful canyon. They were alone. Lowering his head to hers, he whispered urgently, "They're in this together. I don't know why."

Grace kept her eyes on his. "Zachary. What you're thinking is not real. What I'm telling you is real. Your mind isn't working right. You need a doctor."

Could she be right? *DSM-IV*. Was it published by the INS? Puzzling over it, Zac studied the river, the reflection of the orange walls on the water. The sun shone on the right side, reaching halfway down the cliff face.

He frowned and said, "Okay."

Grace thought, *Thank you, God*.

It was a brief reprieve.

Before the next rapid, Zac became agitated again. He nearly rowed them into a hole, and afterward, as Grace bailed, he resumed talk of escaping.

Knowing Range Canyon was approaching, Grace said, "Pull over at the beach on the right. Mile Long Rapid's ahead. We shouldn't run it without scouting." That was true, but Grace cringed at her chicanery.

Zac took her at her word.

He pushed for the beach, guided the dory into an eddy. Grace climbed up on the bow. The sunshine was hitting the shore, and it touched her skin as she leapt from the boat with the bowline.

Her heart pounded as she looked at Zac. She was going to have to be the actor now. "Pull up the oars." Glancing into the little box canyon, she said, "We'll need a big rock to put on the bowline."

Zac climbed out of the boat, stepping into the water. It swirled around his knees, and again Grace noticed his slight clumsiness. As he slogged toward her through the water, she pointed at a large rock some distance up the beach. "That one."

Zac nodded and started walking toward it.

Careful to let her feet splash the water as little as possible, Grace stepped into the cold river and began to move downstream, holding the gunwale of the boat. She could hardly breathe.

Past the eddy. Get out of the eddy.

The water on her legs felt like ice. She didn't look up. As she pulled the boat downstream, the current tugged at the dory. The stern swung out into the river.

Go, baby, go. Take it.

She grabbed the bow and shoved, and the dory swept out into the current, floating for Mile Long Rapid.

"WHAT ARE YOU DOING?"

His voice came from immediately behind her, and Grace jumped, shaking to her shoes. When she turned she saw Zac, inches away, eyes wide and intense, muscles quivering. "Why did you do that?" He was whispering now, his voice ragged. *"Why did you do that?"*

He was too close, too big, too out of control. As he stepped toward her, his eyes like a stranger's, Grace saw the muscles in his neck, in his shoulders and lean, sinewy arms.

"Zac—"

"You tricked me." His eyes narrowed.

Grace was afraid. She whispered, "Calm down."

"No! You lied to me! You're turning me in! *Why don't you love me?*"

Grace drew up, holding her ground, forcing herself to breathe. She tried to draw on a power inside her, something she knew must be there, the strength to confront any situation.

She stared at Zachary and saw the sun on his hair. She saw his smeared makeup, which had the effect of making him look more insane. But underneath she also saw the cleft chin, the jaw, the straight nose, the sensuous lips, the face she had kissed. The face that had kissed her in the most intimate ways. For a moment she remembered those times, the closeness, the love coming from him. The tenderness. This person in front of her was the same man.

Somewhere inside him, he was.

She forced herself to be calm, unafraid, even though his whole body was shaking, even though his face was so altered.

Even though he was psychotic.

She said, "I do love you."

Drawing a breath, she glanced at him one more time, then turned away and walked out of the frigid water, up the beach and into the sunshine. *Relax,* she told herself. *Relax, and he'll relax.*

She thought of the river knife and what Nick had said. Zachary probably shouldn't have it. Partway up the beach, she paused and looked back at him. He was staring at the boat tumbling through the froth, disappearing from sight. He seemed sad, but calm.

Grace knew it would upset him if she tried to take the knife.

She stood for a moment surveying the beach, which was bordered by rock and water. The box canyon was tiny, the walls vertical, impossible to scale without climbing aids.

She thought, *Good choice, Nick. Good choice.*

There was no way out of here.

Casting one last glance at Zachary standing beside the river, she collapsed on the silty shore, lay back and closed her eyes. And tried to stop shaking.

SHE DOZED, awakening only to the sound of the plane passing. It tipped its wings as it flew over, and she waved, knowing the pilot must have seen the signal on the other beach. The ranger had probably spoken to him by radio.

She sat up and looked around. Zac sat in the shade against the cliff wall, her day pack beside him. He'd taken off his clothes.

Grace closed her eyes and went back to sleep.

ZAC HEARD THE CHOPPER before she did, and he knew it was coming for him. As he stared up at the big white bird with the red cross on the side, emotion crawled up his throat. Rescue, he thought. The sight was comforting. *Take care of me*, he thought. *Someone take care of me.*
(*"Drink it up, Alice. Drink the last drop."*)

The sound of the propellers beating was loud, and he saw Grace coming toward him across the beach. Grace, who had pushed the boat down the river. She stopped and picked up his pants—Seneca's pants—and Zac's running shoes.

The helicopter was louder than the voices. It drowned them out. As the aircraft descended, Zac felt his hair start to blow. His heartbeat quickened. What were they going to do to him?

Grace stood in front of him and yelled, "Want to put on your pants?"

Zac stared down at the clothes she held. He nodded and reached for them.

Grace was relieved. Maybe this wouldn't be so bad. She touched his back as he bent over, sliding the pants on, his hair hanging in his face. He needed suspenders, but they were gone.

Grace said, "They'll stay up! It's okay!"

Zac focused on her eyes, his own blinking. He felt like crying. Why was this happening?

The whirlybird came lower. Zac's hair whipped all around his face, and the earth seemed to shake. His heart was throbbing in time with the giant white bird. What was happening? Why did he have to get on the helicopter?

Grace put her arm around him, smelling the salty sweat on his body. There was sweat on his upper lip, too, under the five-o'clock shadow. Scared sweat. But he stood straight and tall, his green eyes staring intently at the chopper as it came down and alighted on the beach.

Thinking of everything she'd learned about helicopter rescues, Grace told Zac, "Just stay back here! We'll wait for them." She knew the exhaust from the chopper was hot enough to burn them to a crisp.

The doors opened.

As uniformed attendants in light blue shirts got out, Zac backed against the rock wall. Grace saw two people bringing out a folding gurney, while a tall blond man with a bushy mustache, dressed in blue jeans and a polo shirt, jogged across the sand toward her and Zachary.

Zac's eyes were on the gurney. Grace felt his muscles tighten, felt him trembling. He slipped free from her grasp, pushing hair out of his eyes, and stared at the helicopter. Moving backward, he edged along under the overhanging cliff ledge, his eyes big.

The blond man reached Grace and held out his hand. "Dr. Jake Caruthers. I'm with Air Rescue. What's going on?" He glanced at Zac, who was creeping away.

As concisely as possible, Grace told him everything,

including what she knew about Zachary's problems in New York.

"Has he been violent?"

Grace hesitated, remembering when he'd yelled at her. "His moods swing. He's very scared."

"Has he taken any drugs? Is he on medication?

Grace shook her head. She turned to look at Zac. He'd disappeared.

The doctor said, "Don't worry. We'll find him. He doesn't have any weapons, does he?"

Grace remembered the knife. The pack was at her feet, and she picked it up, searched inside and found the river knife, the knife he'd used to save her. She drew a shaky breath. "No."

"Okay. We'll take care of him." The doctor gave her a reassuring look and strode back toward the helicopter to confer with the rest of the team. They peered up toward the canyon, and when Grace went over to join them, one of the men asked, "Do you know the terrain? Can he get out of there?"

"He can't." Grace wished she'd thought to reacquaint herself with the canyon earlier, but she knew it was small. Barely a canyon at all.

The doctor said, "Okay, we'll make a line and spread out. Find him, talk to him, see how he's doing, let him know what's happening. Grace, why don't you stay here? We'll probably have to take him down and give him some medication, and it's better if there's nothing else for him to worry about."

Take him down? Grace thought.

ZAC HUDDLED under an overhang at the base of the cliff wall. Beneath him was wet sand, seeping up between his toes; his head rubbed against silt from the rock. All around him, he could smell the canyon. Wet desert smells. Dry wet.

A group of strangers stood before him. The man in street clothes had crouched down and was talking to him.

"Zac, I'm Dr. Caruthers, and your friends up the river summoned the Air Rescue team because they thought you needed someone to take you out of the canyon. Your wife says you're not feeling well. Is that right?"

Zac felt his face quivering. "Don't touch me."

"No one's going to touch you right now. But we need you to take control of yourself. Can you do that?"

"I'm in control. I'm in control. I'm in control."

(*"Echoing harshness, acting by night in light of day."*)

He wished his body would stop shaking.

"Zac, see if you can calm down. We can walk out of here. You can get on the gurney, we'll give you some medication, and we can go to the hospital."

Zac shivered. He didn't want to go with them. He didn't know them. Why was he alone? Why did he have to be alone? What were they going to do to him?

Nearby a bush twitched, shivering in the wind, and he started. He stared into the leaves. Other canyon. Grace in her bikini. Kissing, taking off each other's clothes. That feeling when they held each other, when their skin touched, when he saw her eyes. Love.

"Zac?"

He jumped.

The blond man was looking at him. "Zac, let me tell you what we're going to do."

Zac couldn't follow the words. Why were they doing

this to him? Why was Grace letting them? He had to get away.

(*"Forevermore and not until."*)

(*"No, you may not use the WC."*)

Watching them, he ducked out of the alcove and started to stand.

They sprang at him, grabbing his limbs, pushing him down on his face, holding him.

Zac yanked against them, but he was pinned hard. There was dirt in his face, in his eyes and nose and teeth, and his chest pounded. He'd never been held so tight in his life, and he didn't know why it seemed good, good that someone was in control. But it wasn't him, and he started screaming.

Someone was pulling at his clothes. He shrieked.

"Zac, buddy, you're gonna feel a little sting."

He realized he was laughing hysterically. They stabbed him, and he yelled, "Stop it! Leave me alone! Don't do this to me! Help! Someone help me!" Laughing, eyes watering, crying out, he tried to twist his head, tried to see, but all he could find was the sleeve of a blue shirt.

A stranger's voice said, "You're all right, Zac. You'll feel better soon."

They were going to stuff him like a deer that had been shot. He tried to get up, but they were all holding him so tight.

He heard them talking, but he couldn't follow any of it, and then they were rolling him, and there was something beneath him. The faces of strangers looked down at him. A man in a blue shirt said, "Zac, you're going to be all right. We're going to restrain you so you don't hurt yourself or anyone on the helicopter."

Wide straps were going around him. He moved his head, reaching out, trying to bite an arm. If he caught someone he would hang on like one of those Gila monsters, bite hard... But no one was close enough, so he tried to break the straps. "I'm going to slap a malpractice suit on you! This is against the law! This is against any law! I'm a legal alien! I have a green card! There's a British Embassy here! You won't get away with this! I'm an Old Etonian and an Oxford man, and my father's an earl!"

A woman above him was smiling, as though he was funny. Who were these people? "Settle down, Zac. No one's going to hurt you."

("What for?")

("Never forget this.")

They were still holding him. A man was near him, and Zac spit at him. He spit at them all. Then he saw the woman, and he was too embarrassed to spit at her. Somebody said, "We've got to calm him down. We can't take him up like this."

He heard Grace's voice, but he couldn't make sense of the words. Someone was asking her questions. Zac knew they were going to operate on him, and he tried to scream again, but he couldn't make himself.

"Don't thrash." It was the woman. She turned and told someone, "More..." Instead of saying anything, she made a pumping motion with her thumb and fingers. Another shot.

Zac screamed at her. He was screaming for a long time, and he was hardly aware that they were carrying him.

"Zac?"

The eyes looking down at him were familiar. Brown.

Someone was stroking his hair. He felt a strange calm seeping over him, but he was still afraid. He watched Grace's mouth. One side moved more than the other, but he couldn't sort out which was which, only that it was her.

She said, "I love you."

"Don't let them..." But he was afraid to finish, to say it out loud, in case they hadn't thought of it. *Taxidermy.*

Grace stared down at his frightened face. She let her fingers slide through his hair, and she said again, "I really love you. Don't be afraid. I wouldn't let anyone hurt you, Zachary."

The feeling of calmness increased. It didn't feel natural, but it felt better. And it felt good to have Grace touching him. He couldn't follow her words, something about seeing him at the hospital, but he wasn't so afraid anymore.

CHAPTER THIRTEEN

FAST SUSAN SHOWED UP in the J-rig a few minutes after the chopper left. She'd been waiting farther up the river, and she told Grace the studio's helicopter would pick her up and take her back to Moab so she could be with Zac. The guides had known she couldn't ride with Air Rescue.

The studio helicopter arrived early, and by two o'clock, Grace was winging over the canyonlands, on her way to Zac. Day met her at the Moab air terminal to drive her the 120 miles to Grand Junction, Colorado. Thinking ahead, Day had gone to the house and packed clothes for Grace and Zac. As the Suburban carried them east through the desert on I-70, Grace told her sister what had happened on the river—and in New York.

She felt as though she was walking the brink of an emotional abyss. It was part exhaustion. Her muscles were stiff from rowing, her body sore from banging coolers and ammo cans, from twisting unnaturally in the keeper. It hurt to move, but it was the memory of Zac that kept her most on edge. She felt as though she'd been shivering for hours from listening to him, watching him, walking the convoluted paths of his mind. And her heart felt bruised, tender, because she realized how much she loved him, how much she wanted the real Zachary back.

And how much she needed to hold on to the parts of him she could still touch. He was in there. He would be normal again....

She was so lonely without him.

Day said, "Gosh, Grace, some of those mental illnesses are pretty bad. I saw a special about it on a talk show once. People Zachary's age get sick and never get well."

Grace clutched herself.

Zac...like this forever?

Day glanced across the seat and said, "Oh, God, I'm sorry." She pulled the truck over two lanes and onto a ranch road and stopped. Reaching for her sister, holding her, she said, "I'm sorry, Gracie."

Grace just cried, saying things that felt true to the deepest places inside her. "I love him. I'm never going to leave him." But through the blur of her tears, she saw Day's face and imagined what her sister might have seen on the talk show. That sometimes people *had* to leave.

IT WAS DARK when they reached the hospital. Grace felt as dirty as she was drained. Although she'd put on a clean T-shirt and jeans in the airport bathroom, the silt of the Colorado lingered on her skin and hair. She would find a hotel nearby and shower and sleep—after she saw Zac.

As Day parked in the visitors' lot, Grace realized how hard it would be to go into the hospital. This was where her father had died. This was where Nick and Day had told her he was dead. Wanting to protect her sister from the memories, Grace asked, "Would you mind going and finding a hotel nearby for me?"

Day gave her a look and pushed open the driver's door. "Yes, I would."

They went in together.

A receptionist at admissions directed them to the emergency room. There, a nurse told Grace they'd taken Zac to the "locked ward." Grace listened to directions, then turned to Day. Her sister was pale, and Grace knew the trip to the hospital was affecting her.

As they headed down the hall, Grace said, "Look, I don't think they'll let you in this place. I'd really appreciate it if you'd check me into a hotel." She opened her wallet to give her a credit card, but Day waved it away.

"All right, I'll go, and then I'll meet you outside Zac's ward. You want me to find a place with a kitchenette? You might be here for a while."

"Thanks."

Day smiled. "Tell him his dog misses him." Then, looking as though she'd been tactless, she added, "She misses you, too, of course."

Grace didn't mind being an afterthought. Ninochka was Zac's dog. She responded to no one as she did to him. At the sight or sound of the Austin-Healey, she always dashed out of the house or river office. *Like me*, Grace thought. *In love.*

After her sister had left, she found her way to the appropriate wing of the hospital. At the desk outside sat an athletic-looking redhead in street clothes. Noting the big locked door she knew must lead into the unit, Grace said, "I'm Grace Key. I think my husband, Zachary, is here."

The redhead showed instant recognition—in a way that made Grace wonder what Zac had been doing. "I doubt they'll let you see him, but let me check." She got on the phone. Hanging up moments later, she said, "Dr. Holyoak is coming out to talk to you. Why don't you have a seat?"

Grace sat in the waiting area, and soon she heard the door unlocking and saw a man come out. He was in his forties, tall and bearded, with thick mahogany hair that needed a trim. His khaki chinos and blue oxford-cloth shirt were wrinkled, and Grace liked his face, which was craggy and comfortable.

As she stood up, he came toward her and held out his hand. "Mrs. Key? I'm Dr. Michael Holyoak." The psychiatrist's manner was comfortable and reassuring. "I know you want to see your husband, and we'll do what we can in that direction, but let me fill you in first. After you see him, we can sit down and have a longer chat."

Hungry to see Zac but trying to be patient, Grace listened as the doctor told her they didn't know why Zachary was exhibiting psychotic symptoms. Tests had been run to assure that neither an organic problem nor a brain injury was causing the problem. He was refusing medication, and the period of time during which the hospital could give it to him without his consent had elapsed. Now, drug treatment could not be resumed without the hospital's proving that Zac was a danger to himself or others. As attending physician, Dr. Holyoak planned to petition the court to have Zachary involuntarily medicated. If Grace preferred, she need not be involved at all.

Frowning, Grace asked, "Can't we see if he gets better on his own?"

"I think the sooner he receives treatment, the more

quickly he'll recover.'' Before Grace could respond, the
psychiatrist delivered the next blow. ''He's in seclusion
now, and we don't encourage visits to patients there. It
tends to agitate them. But what I can do is let you look
at him through a window.''

Grace made an exclamation of dismay. She didn't
want to see Zac through a window. She wanted to be in
the same room with him. To touch him. ''Why can't I
talk to him? I'm his wife. I promised him I'd come.''

''We're trying to calm him down. I know you'd like
to talk to him, but our first obligation is to the patient.
This is what's best for him. And he has been violent.''

Grace wasn't surprised. Zac had been terrified when
they took him out of Cataract. Now he was locked up
by strangers. She said, ''I think it would soothe him to
see me. Maybe I could persuade him to take medication.''

The doctor smiled a little. ''It's pretty hard to persuade a psychotic person of anything.'' Without agreeing to her suggestion, he stood up. ''Let's go take a look
at him.''

Dr. Holyoak led her to the door through which he'd
come. He unlocked it, and they went through, and it shut
behind them, locking automatically. Then he opened a
second door. As that, too, bolted behind them, Grace was
acutely aware of the place in which they'd put Zachary.
Locked ward. She could go out. He could not.

She couldn't even talk to him.

The psychiatrist led her down a narrow hall. A man
in street clothes walked past, and Grace wondered if he
was a doctor. But as she and Dr. Holyoak reached the
nurse's station, she realized none of the personnel in the

wing were wearing hospital clothes. Probably uniforms upset the patients.

At the nurse's desk, a muscular black man sat writing. A voice was coming from a speaker somewhere nearby, and after a moment Grace realized it was Zac speaking, but she couldn't make out the words.

Off to her left were two rooms. As Dr. Holyoak led her toward one of them, the door opened and the tallest man Grace had ever seen came out. The door swung shut behind him with the snick of a lock.

The psychiatrist said, "How are we doing?"

The attendant smiled ruefully. "Ripping the place apart."

A phone rang at the nurse's station, and the call was for Dr. Holyoak. Before he left to take it, he said, "Leif, this is Mrs. Key. She'd like to look through the window at her husband."

Leif—*Lanky Leif*, Grace thought—smiled obligingly and led her to the door of the room he'd just left. He indicated the reinforced window and Grace peered through.

Zachary.

He was pacing the floor, wearing only pajama bottoms. Despite his condition—which was apparent in a glance—Grace was consoled to see him. Her husband. Behind her, she could still hear his voice from the speaker at the reception desk, and as she watched Zac through the glass he seemed to be talking to someone invisible, almost as though he was rehearsing. He looked wild. He looked what he was.

Mentally ill.

But Grace remembered his vulnerability in Range

Canyon, how he'd fought to free himself from the restraints, his green eyes wildly frightened, then calming on hers as the medication began to take effect. She felt a love for him so intense and overwhelming it was hard to recognize as the same love that glued them together in marriage. But it was the same love. This was the first time she'd known its power. It was bigger than she was. It was all she could feel. He was her husband.

She wanted him back.

Hugging herself, Grace surveyed the small room through the glass. The only furnishings were a sink, a toilet and a bare mattress. The mattress had been thrown over the sink, undoubtedly by Zac. She looked up at Leif. "There's not much in there."

Leif winked at her. "Don't worry. He's not bored." Then, sobering, he said, "Actually we can't let them have much. They kill themselves."

God, thought Grace. In the room Zac nervously inspected his arms and chest and ran his hands over himself, as though he had hives.

"We go in every ten or fifteen minutes and tell him where he is and what's happened to him and that no one's going to hurt him." In a serious straightforward way, Leif told her, "We're taking care of him."

After Cataract Canyon, Grace knew she could not. Not as he was now.

But he wouldn't be like this forever. He couldn't be. From the speaker behind her, Zac's voice intruded on her thoughts. She heard him say, "You must be silent, for I cannot think in the hell of your words. There are no answers here...."

Staring through the window, watching him, Grace felt reality slamming home.

Zachary was mad.

DAY WAS WAITING when Grace emerged from the locked area. Grace had answered many questions for Dr. Holyoak, relating all she had told the Air Rescue team and more. He'd seemed interested in Zac's problems in New York but didn't share his thoughts except to say, "We'll have to see how he does."

Day drove her to the hotel, which was just a block from the hospital and had a room with a kitchenette. After her sister had left for Moab, Grace lay down on the bed and tried not to think.

She knew she should call Zac's parents, but she'd hardly ever spoken to them—and not since she'd left him. What if Zac's mother was having one of her spells of depression? Upset, Grace consulted the clock and was relieved to find it was the middle of the night in England.

Without bothering to change clothes, she kicked off her shoes, got into bed and tried to sleep. But she couldn't, and she turned on her side, wanting him so badly that soon she was gasping tears into the pillow. She had never been so terribly afraid.

When she slept, she dreamed of the keeper and knew she was drowning. At the threshold of death, she started awake, and it took a moment to come back to reality. Where she was. Why.

A blackness deeper than the nightmare gripped her. She felt utterly alone. Zac was gone, as though he'd become someone else. And she wanted him back so much.

Why aren't you here? she thought, knowing the question was irrational. *Why are you never here when I need you most?*

"IF YOU LAY A HAND on me, I'll take you and this so-called hospital for all you're worth!" exclaimed Zac, advancing toward the phony doctor and his cohort. The second man was seven feet tall. Everyone here was large.

The man with the beard, the quack, said, "No one's touching you."

It felt as though someone *was* touching him. Someone or something. Zac had felt bugs crawling on him ever since he'd gotten to this place. Lice. He was sure of it. This wasn't a hospital. It was a medieval asylum. At any moment, they'd take him away for cold showers and electric shock. A lobotomy. Zac drew his emotions in line. "You do not know who you're dealing with. My father belongs to the House of Lords. I am the Honourable Zachary Key, and I demand my release."

"Zac, no one here is going to hurt you. You're in Grand Mesa Hospital. I'm Dr. Michael Holyoak, and I'm a psychiatrist."

For one moment, Zac wondered if what they'd been telling him could be true. If he was really in a hospital. If they were really there to help him. If he was...psychotic.

DSM-IV. He saw the book in his mind.

(*"Drink it up, now."*)

(*"Never too late."*)

(*"How much?"*)

Dr. Holyoak said, "We want you to be in control.

Someone has to be in control. It's going to be us or you, and we want it to be you."

Zac tried to grasp the words. In between each, the voices came.

(*"What for?"*)

(*"Have not said…"*)

He had to get out of here before they decided to operate. Brain implants. Lobotomy. Castration.

He eyed the seven-foot-tall man. Both he and the doctor were in front of the door.

Zac lunged toward them. The tall man shouted something, and the door flew open. More large people. Zac had met them before, and he sprang backward, yelling, "Back off! Keep your hands off me!"

They did.

They left, and he dove to catch the door before it closed. It wouldn't open, and he kicked it and pounded it with his fist and yelled, vaguely remembering another door that wouldn't open. He was trapped. And the bugs… He could feel their legs walking on his skin, everywhere, even on his genitals, and he cried, "Get them off me! Please get them off!" He tried to brush them away with his hands, but he couldn't even see them with his eyes, and he knew he was being tortured, and he prayed it would stop.

Someone make it stop!

GRACE DIDN'T GO to the hearing the next morning. She waited at the hospital, in the area beside the lockup, reading a new mystery. She'd picked it up in the gift shop on a glance, but now she regretted the choice.

The back-cover blurb read, "A dangerous psychotic is terrorizing the small Midwestern town of..."

A dangerous psychotic.

All her life, Grace had heard the word psychotic used only that way. Psycho. Norman Bates outside the shower curtain.

But Zac wasn't like that. He was afraid. Hearing voices...

No one would let her in to look at Zac without the doctor's okay, and the doctor had gone to the hearing. But at about eleven in the morning, Grace saw the psychiatrist coming down the hallway with a clipboard and several pieces of paper in hand. "Well, we got it." The court order. "We'll see how he does on some antipsychotic medication." Promising to come out and talk with her after he spoke to Zac—and of course wrote his orders—the doctor went into the locked ward. Soon three big men, nurses and technicians from other parts of the hospital, arrived and went inside, also.

Grace knew why they'd come. In her mind, she could still hear Zac's bloodcurdling screams filling Range Canyon, echoing off the walls, as the Air Rescue team restrained him. Now he was going through the same thing again, and Grace wished they would let her be there to tell him it was all right, to calm him afterward.

Almost an hour later, Dr. Holyoak emerged from the ward and joined her in the otherwise empty waiting area. Sitting down, he laid aside his clipboard and started to talk. They'd given Zac the medication and now it was a matter of waiting to see if it helped.

Grace asked, "Do you know what's wrong with

him?''

He shook his head. ''All I can tell you is that right now he's acutely psychotic. His CT scan was negative. This might just be a brief psychotic episode—a reaction to what happened on the river. But since you've said this has happened before, we need to look at other possibilities.'' He glanced at his notes. ''Let me ask you a couple of questions.''

They spoke for fifteen minutes, and finally he asked if she'd make an appointment at his office for the next day to tell him more about Zac.

Grace agreed, but before he could leave she asked, ''Is there a book you could recommend about mental illness?'' She wanted to understand what was happening to Zac.

The doctor looked hesitant. ''Well...yes. But please realize, Grace, that mental illness is complicated. Making a diagnosis can be difficult, and when we do make it, it's sometimes not as precise as we'd like. What I wouldn't want is for you to read a lot of books and decide Zac is schizophrenic or bipolar or what have you. That said—'' he took a pharmaceutical company notepad from his shirt pocket ''—there's a very good and popular book for families of people with mental illnesses. It provides a sensitive picture of the kinds of things a psychotic person may feel. It also deals with situations that may affect you. Things like what went on today. He refused medication. We had to go to court.''

Grace asked, ''When can I see him again?''

He glanced toward the door. ''Let me go see how he's doing. It takes a while for a shot to work.''

Several minutes later, Lanky Leif came out and escorted her back into the seclusion area so she could look through the window at Zac. He was still shirtless, and he sat against the wall with his knees up, brooding.

Grace stared at him, willing him to glance up. He did not. Her powerlessness terrified her, and her heart cried out to him, pleading harder than he'd ever begged her. *Come back. Dammit, come back!*

GRACE RETURNED to her hotel. She'd already called Zac's agent and explained what was happening. She'd also called the production office and talked to Hal Markley. Though eager to have Zac back on the set, the producer was understanding. "We'll shoot around him," he said. "Let me know if there's anything we can do to help."

Grace knew there was one more phone call she should make, and she dreaded it. She still remembered her last experience trying to reach Lord and Lady Key. *His Lordship is traveling, and Her Ladyship is unavailable. Who? Mr. Zachary Key no longer lives here. No, I can't tell you any more.*

Sitting on the hotel bed, Grace dug her address book out of her purse. She glanced at the clock. It would be after ten at night in England, but she shouldn't wait any longer.

When the phone began to ring, she held her breath. Although Zac had called them several times while he'd been living with her in New York, Grace had talked with his parents only once. They'd asked her about herself and made small talk, and all the time she knew they were wondering why their son had married a woman he'd known such a short time. She doubted Zac had ever told them the truth.

"Key here."

Grace's heart pounded. The earl's accent was much more pronounced that Zachary's, and Grace remembered thinking when they spoke the last time that he was hard to understand.

Trying to speak clearly, she said, "Your Lordship, this is Grace. Your daughter-in-law." She felt as though she'd stepped off a cliff.

"Who? Who is that?"

"It's Grace. Zachary's wife. Calling from the United States."

"*Grace?*" He sounded alarmed, and Grace knew he was afraid something might have happened to his son.

Reassured by his concern, she said carefully, "Zachary is in the hospital here. He's having some…mental health problems." Suddenly she wondered if she should have called. She really didn't know much about Zac's relationship with his parents. His father the earl. His depressed mother. Zac's brother, Pip, was several years older than he was, but Grace knew they were good friends, went rowing together on the river near Oakhurst when Zac was in England. Now, of course, they were an ocean apart.

Lord Key said, "Grace, I'm so glad you called. Please tell me everything." A woman's voice murmured in the background, and the earl answered, "It's Grace, calling about Zachary. He's…having some difficulty."

Grace heard the astonished response. "Grace?"

Grace thought of how she'd left their son, her husband, in New York. She remembered the homeless man shuffling down the street....

As coherently as she could, she explained what had happened to Zac. His mother picked up the phone, too, and Grace thought again of what Zac had said about her depression. She sounded fine now. Grace's heart flooded with warmth as the Keys repeatedly thanked her for calling. They asked for several numbers. Hers, the hospital, Zac's doctor.

Then his mother asked, "Grace, are you...are you with him, then?"

In a flash Grace saw the whole history of her marriage, most of all the last few weeks. Nothing mattered anymore except the love she and Zac shared, the vows they'd made. *In sickness and in health.* The words really meant something now. That she would be there for him.

But she knew she would be there because she loved him.

"Yes. We've...worked things out. We're, um, very married."

Lord Key cleared his throat. "Good." He rushed on to say that they would talk again very soon, and Grace had never been so grateful for the English habit of avoiding awkward topics.

BECAUSE DAY HAD GOTTEN her a room with a kitchenette, she decided to make a dessert to take to Zac. She walked to a bookstore where she found the book the doctor had recommended and from there to a grocery store. It was blocks away, and she was tired when she returned to her room, but she set to work in the unfamiliar kitchenette, sipping a glass of wine as she used the limited utensils to make a lemon meringue pie.

As she made the meringue, she thought of Zac in that seclusion room. And the Zac she loved. Running. Laughing. Coupons. She pictured him working on her house. Playing the piano. Befriending strays. Making love.

He'll be that way again, she thought. *He has to be.*

While the pie was baking, she called the hospital. Leif said, "Yeah. He's a little better. We just gave him another shot."

Grace asked him if Zac could eat a pie if she brought it.

"Let me check with the doc, but I think it's fine."

After hanging up, Grace opened the book on mental illness. The first thing she learned was that at any one time an estimated twenty percent of the U.S. population suffered from mental health problems serious enough to warrant care. But the percentage of people who sought care was much smaller, in part because of the associated stigma. Grace was stunned by the statistics. Until Zac, she'd never known anyone who was mentally ill. At least she didn't think so. But perhaps people didn't talk about it.

The scope of mental disorders was vast. Substance-related, schizophrenia and psychotic disorders, mood disorders, depression....

Depression. When Zac had told her about his mom, she hadn't perceived the problem as illness. Everyone got depressed sometimes.

Interested, Grace continued reading, acquainting herself with life from the point of view of a psychotic person. The book confirmed what she had intuited—that

Zac's mind was playing cruel tricks on him, creating a world whose demons ranged from the annoying to the terrifying.

She read about hallucinations of all kinds. Of sight and sound and touch. The voices heard by a psychotic person, she learned, weren't like thoughts. Rather, it truly seemed that someone—or several someones—was speaking. But auditory hallucinations could take a host of forms beyond voices. The sound of a beating heart, of rushing blood. Choirs singing. Meaningless babble. Nonsense sounds.

Zac must have been terrified to experience such bizarre phenomena without knowing the cause.

But how strange that he hadn't tried to find out. Zachary was a highly educated man. A man who knew the medical resources available to him, knew when it was appropriate to see a doctor. A man who used the library if he wanted to learn about something. A man who, had he looked into it, would have been alarmed by what he read about his symptoms.

Despite Dr. Holyoak's warnings, Grace grew worried as she read. With Zac's symptoms, he could have any of a number of awful things. And what Day had told her was true. A few of the illnesses mentioned came on when people were in their twenties—and stayed.

Oh, God, Grace thought. *What if he doesn't get well?*

ZAC LAY ON THE MATTRESS on the floor. Leif had just come in again to tell him where he was and what was going on and that no one was going to hurt him. Now he believed it. He didn't understand everything, but he'd been told that he was psychotic, that he'd refused medication, and that the hospital had received a court order to give him medication, anyhow.

He tried to piece it together. Cataract Canyon, the movie, Grace...*DSM-IV*. The thoughts filled him with panic, so he focused on the present. On what had happened since he'd come to the hospital.

He'd given people a lot of trouble, and the thought made him ashamed. Where was Grace? What did she think of him now?

Hearing a sound at the door, Zac looked up and saw a tall bearded man and the even taller Leif. He sat up sleepily, and the man with the beard said, "Hello, Zac. I'm Dr. Michael Holyoak. We've met, but I'm not sure you remember me."

Zac remembered. Embarrassed by his recent behavior, he said, "Hello."

"Do you know where you are and why you're here?"

Zac looked about the bare cell. He was caged like an animal. He knew it was because he'd behaved like one. Nodding, he said, "I'm in a hospital because I'm psychotic." But he felt only drowsy, and he wanted Grace. Where was she? Zac wished things were clearer.

The psychiatrist asked, "How are you feeling now?"

He couldn't think of anything to say. At last he shrugged.

"Hearing any voices?"

Zac stirred uneasily. How did Dr. Holyoak know about the voices? He shook his head. "I feel better."

"Good." The doctor nodded. "Would you like to see your wife?"

Zac peered past him toward the door. He couldn't see anyone through the window. "Yes."

"She brought you something to eat."

Eyes stinging, Zac buried his feelings. "Oh."

Michael Holyoak went to the door and Leif opened it, and Grace came in, wearing a pink cotton sweater and patched jeans and carrying a pie.

Grace's heartbeat picked up when she saw Zac. He looked groggy but much calmer than before. His long hair was uncombed, his beard rough, and Grace was embarrassed to discover she found him very sexy in hospital pajama bottoms.

But in his face, she saw illness. The drugs were just containing the symptoms. When he saw her he stood up.

Trying to ignore the others, Grace stepped toward him and hugged him with one arm. Warm skin and muscle under her hand. *Zachary.* He returned the caress—half-heartedly, she thought.

Zac felt as though they were on a date with chaperons. Did the men think he would hurt Grace? Hoping she didn't think so, he asked her, "Want to sit down?"

They both sat on the mattress, and she gave him the lemon meringue pie. She had two napkins and two plastic spoons. As they dug in, Zac felt his appetite returning. Soon Dr. Holyoak and Leif stepped out into the hall.

Immediately Zac set down the pie plate. Grace put both her arms around him, and they hugged tight, hard, the way they hadn't in front of the two men. She kissed him on the mouth, and he let himself kiss her back. But his eyes felt hot again and a little wet, so he stopped kissing her and just held her, his face in her hair.

Grace said, "I want you to get better so you can come home. I miss you." Remembering Day's message, she said, "So does Ninochka."

The dog. In his mind Zac felt her fur beneath his hands, saw her chasing her tail in the yard at the River Inn. The thoughts affected him like Grace's bringing the pie. He longed for home, for his life. Zac squeezed Grace tighter, not answering, and they were finding each other's mouths again when Dr. Holyoak came back in with a chair.

Sitting down, he explained that they would move Zac to a regular room in the same ward. Then he told Zac, "We'll start you on oral medication now. It should work as well as what we've given you. You'll probably still be taking it when you leave the hospital, and it's important that you do so methodically, even if your wife has to remind you."

Zac nodded. He hated taking even aspirin, but there was no choice. He didn't want to be psychotic. Remembering enough of his research to dread the answer, he nonetheless asked, "What are the side effects?"

The doctor said antipsychotic agents were among the safest drugs available in medicine. He named possible side effects—restlessness, diminished spontaneity, slurred speech, tremors of the hands and feet, impotence and tardive dyskinesia, a condition involving involuntary muscle movements. The last, he said, was generally a concern for people who were on antipsychotic drugs for a number of years; it was not a side effect at all of the drug Zac was taking.

When Grace looked at Zac, he had his head in his hands. She knew what he must be thinking. How could he be an actor with those kinds of problems?

Dr. Holyoak said, "I wouldn't think too much about side effects right now. From what you've said, Grace,

when this happened before in New York it subsided on
its own after a short time. Is that right?''

He was looking at Zac, and Zachary nodded.

''Do you know about how long?''

''Twenty-five days.''

Grace drew in a breath. *Zachary,* she thought. *You
worried alone.*

Dr. Holyoak studied him. ''I'm going to ask you about
that in more detail. Perhaps, when you're a little sharper,
you could write it all down—or ask Grace to help. It
might help us figure out what's happened to you.''

Zac thought of his mother and everything he'd read
in *DSM-IV*. He wasn't sure he wanted to figure out what
had happened.

He wasn't sure he wanted to know.

CHAPTER FOURTEEN

DR. HOLYOAK'S OFFICE was in a clinic adjoining the hospital, and Grace met him there at one the next day. They sat in a comfortable room with easy chairs, a couch and a bookcase, and for an hour she answered his questions about Zac.

The doctor told her, "Whatever you say here is confidential. Feel free to tell me anything about Zachary you think will help us get to the bottom of this. We all have the same goal. His recovery."

Grace told the psychiatrist about meeting Zac. Marrying him. Leaving him. As she spoke, she again felt a twinge of resentment that Zac hadn't been there for her when she needed him. Of course, on the river he'd saved her life. But when her father died... Telling Dr. Holyoak about her strange phone conversation with Zac after her father's death, Grace commented, "He sounded so self-absorbed. I guess he was hallucinating or something."

"Very possibly." Her underlying feelings must have shown because the psychiatrist watched her intently for a moment, then said, "You know, Grace, what's happened to Zac is not within his control. He was reacting to the trauma of your accident on the river. We see the same thing in soldiers under enemy fire, people who've been through a flood or other disaster. The mind can handle only so much."

"I was the one who almost drowned." *I handled it,* she thought.

The doctor said, "Seeing that this has happened before, it's probably safe to say Zac has some kind of genetic predisposition to this kind of thing."

Grace understood. Zac was sick and couldn't help it. It wasn't a matter of emotional weakness. It wasn't his fault—or hers. *Genetic predisposition.* Worried, she asked, "Is he going to get better? I mean, I've been reading that book..."

He smiled a little. "I think this is just a brief psychotic episode. It could be something worse, but he says the last episode didn't last long and he's been fine since. Can you tell me more about that?"

Grace repeated the story Zac had told her at the Anasazi Palace. Then she told the psychiatrist about his nightmares—dreams of people he loved killing themselves. "I've wondered if it's because I left him. He never used to have bad dreams when we lived together."

The psychiatrist shrugged noncommittally. "It could say something about his anxiety level. Also, it sounds as though he hasn't been getting a lot of sleep lately. In some people, that can trigger things of this nature."

Dr. Holyoak questioned her about Zac's moods, habits, social life and background. Grace told him what she knew. Prep school, grammar school, Eton, Oxford. Oakhurst. She said, "His mother's depressed. I just read about depression in that book you recommended. This probably sounds incredibly ignorant, but I didn't know it was a mental illness."

"It's not always. But it sounds as though what you're talking about with Zac's mother is. Tell me what you know about that. Is she on medication?"

"I don't know." Grace repeated what Zachary had told her. Frowning, she asked, "Could it be related to what happened to Zac?"

"Yes—which isn't to say it's the same thing. There's a lot we don't know about how these things work. It seems as though both of Zac's psychotic episodes were triggered by stressful incidents, in each case involving loss—or the threat of loss. Which resonates in interesting ways with what you said about his dreams." He looked thoughtful. "Tell me about his work."

She did. She told him about before she knew Zac, when he'd performed off-off-off Broadway. In back alleys, on a stage made from plywood boards laid across the counter of an East Village bar. She explained about the banned jeans ads and about *Kah-Puh-Rats*. "He's such a good actor I used to wonder what was real and what wasn't. In our personal lives. I don't feel that way now, but I still don't understand his emotions."

Dr. Holyoak answered, "With that kind of background—boarding schools, et cetera—he may have trouble expressing emotion. In the scope of things, channeling his feelings into acting is a reasonable response."

He changed the subject. "I'm interested in knowing more about his mother. His parents did call, but I haven't gotten back to them. I think I'll do that as soon as I can. What's the time difference between here and England?"

Grace told him. As the meeting ended and she got up to leave the office, her eyes swept the bookcase. Something on the shelf triggered a reaction in her, and she did a double take.

Dr. Holyoak, who had another appointment, moved toward the doorway, and Grace knew she should go. But she couldn't tear her gaze from the shelf. Among the other volumes was a large crimson book with saffron lettering on the binding: *DSM-IV*. Stunned to see it there, she read the subtitle: *Diagnostic and Statistical Manual of Mental Disorders*.

Her heart thudded. *He knew*. Zac knew he was sick.

Uncertain how to feel, she looked at the doctor, who was waiting at the door. She said, "Zachary has that book."

ZAC WAS SITTING on the edge of his bed in socks, blue jeans and a faded black T-shirt when Grace arrived for a visit. He stood up and kissed her, taking advantage of the minutes till Leif or one of the others looked in the door. They checked on him constantly, and when Grace was around they were even more vigilant.

Sitting down on the bed with him, Grace reached up to touch his face. "You shaved."

"Under supervision. I mustn't have 'sharps.'" Zac felt demeaned by the rule. He would never kill himself. Or anyone else.

But he'd never thought he would spit on people, either.

Grace thought of the *DSM-IV* she'd found in Zac's room. Dr. Holyoak had listened to her theory that Zac must have guessed the seriousness of his breakdown in New York and tried to discover what caused it. But the psychiatrist had said little in response, and Grace knew he suspected other possibilities. That Zac knew more about his condition than he'd ever said.

More than he'd ever told her, his wife.

Now she said, "Zac, I saw the *DSM-IV* in your room. I was collecting your laundry, and I didn't know what it was at the time." After explaining about noticing a copy in the psychiatrist's office, she asked, "Did you suspect you were sick?"

Zac knew the complex implications of the question and of any answer he might give—knew because he'd thought of little else during the past year. This was the green card again, only worse. He had to explain. "Yes. But listen, Grace..." God, it would have been so much easier if he'd told her earlier, when his mind was functioning properly. Now, even finding the words was difficult, and saying them was harder. He made himself try.

"At first, I thought it was something ghastly, like schizophrenia. But my symptoms had lasted just one month. I concluded it was a brief psychotic episode, nothing more. But I wanted to make sure I was really all right, so I stayed away from you for a year. If this had happened again, I wouldn't have come back."

Grace couldn't believe her ears. "You tried to diagnose this yourself? Didn't you see a doctor?"

"No. I was afraid of the INS. They don't want aliens with mental health problems, because they can become a burden to the state. I thought a doctor might report me. And by the time I felt secure about my green card, the episode was far in the past. When you and I started... When we became lovers again, I decided to see a doctor, but I didn't have a chance before this happened. If there was something seriously wrong, I wouldn't have kept it from you."

Their eyes met. Obviously there was something seriously wrong.

Grace's mind reeled. Reminding herself he was ill, she held her temper in check. But she felt betrayed. It was too much like Valentine's Day. Like hearing him say, *Don't do this, Grace. I need that green card.*

Not once in his narrative at the Anasazi Palace had he used the word "psychotic." Now she knew the omission was deliberate. Her accusation came out before she could stop it. "My God, Zac. How can I ever trust you?"

"I didn't want to worry you needlessly."

Grace pressed her lips shut. She didn't believe that for a minute. He'd been afraid. Of losing his green card.

But she saw a subtle difference this time.

This time, he had feared losing *her.*

THREE DAYS LATER Dr. Holyoak came to see Zac in his room prior to discharging him. While Grace and Zac sat in chairs near the foot of the bed, the psychiatrist perched on a stool, saying, "Zac, I think you've been experiencing a brief reactive psychosis—a brief psychotic episode triggered by a stressful event—in this case, the accident on the river. The last time this happened was just after Grace left. Also a traumatic time.

"But I have to say, my diagnosis is provisional. I'm troubled, because this has happened twice, and that's rare. We need to make sure this isn't a more serious recurrent disorder." Meeting Zac's eyes, he said, "Your mother's condition has made me wonder."

Zac's face was impassive, but Grace knew he was afraid. A recurrent condition could mean he would be on medication indefinitely. And already Grace had noticed something disturbing, something she was sure Zac noticed, too. The drug that was taming his psychotic symptoms had begun to exact its toll. Side effects...

Dr. Holyoak said, "Grace, I'd like to speak to Zac alone for a moment."

Curious but understanding, she got up and left.

When she was gone, the psychiatrist rolled his stool closer to Zac. "Look, I'd like you to talk to someone, get started in psychotherapy. There are mental illnesses for which drugs alone are the best therapy, but I think because of the nature of what's happened to you—and frankly, because of your family background—you would benefit by talking to someone. Sometimes things that happened to us when we were young affect our ability to handle similar situations as adults."

Zac drew back slightly. Medications with grim side effects were bad enough. He didn't need to talk to a stranger about his childhood. Anyhow, he'd had a good childhood. He said, "I wasn't abused." As he spoke he heard and felt the difference in his speech. Anxiety filled him.

Dr. Holyoak said, "It could be that something happened to you when you were young, something that had a painful effect on you—something you don't even recall. Or that you've never acknowledged was painful. It's possible something like that could make it difficult for you to confront traumatic incidents." The psychiatrist sat back in his chair. As though sensing Zac's resistance, he said, "It's possible that in a couple of weeks you'll be well and this will be no more than a bad memory. But twice, you've responded to threatened loss with psychotic symptoms. I think it could happen again. Wouldn't you like to do all you can to see that it doesn't?"

"Of course." But Zac's mind was spinning. *When you were young*... Keeping his counsel, he said, "You sound as though you think the cause is some trauma in my childhood. Is that it? Or is there something physically wrong with me? Which is it?"

"Well, I think it's safe to assume you have some kind of physical predisposition for this kind of episode. Perhaps some depression, in fact. It can manifest in many ways, and if that's all there is to it, medication can help. But the stressors that triggered both of your psychotic episodes were very similar. It makes me suspect that your childhood experiences might play a role, as well. So, to answer your question, my guess would be both."

Zac's chest felt tight. "You think it's genetic."

"In part. It's not clear how these things work. According to what your parents told me on the phone, your mother has had severe major depressive episodes with psychotic features."

His mother had been psychotic? Zac started to protest, but then he realized what the doctor had said. *According to your parents...* How could they not have told him?

"However," said Dr. Holyoak, "there are other issues at play here." He looked at Zachary. "You grew up with a mother who was often suicidal. That's a formidable burden for a child."

Zac stared. None of them ever discussed that with people outside the family. Even amongst themselves they avoided the details. *Your mum's having a spell.* His father would never have told...

But he had. And if his father had said that much, he would have said more. He would have told everything. Resigning himself to discussing it, at least briefly, Zac said, "Look, I remember finding her after the overdose, but it wasn't a suicide attempt. It was an accident. I'm sure you think it cruel that I was made to start prep school the next day, but that was my choice. My father had enough on his hands." Like Grace now. "I kept my chin up, and I was fine. Aside from the occasional bad dream, I've never had a moment's trouble coping with it."

The psychiatrist's ironic expression was eloquent. "Loss?"

Zac tightened inside, seeing the obvious. He had become psychotic. That wasn't coping. "I didn't lose my mother."

"You didn't lose your wife in the river. But I imagine that in both cases you thought you had." The psychiatrist changed gears. "There are good counselors at the mental-health clinic in Moab. I'll give you some names. The process will take time, but I think you'll find it's worth it."

"How much time?" He needed to get back to the set. *God. The film.*

"Psychotherapy can go on for months or years. Not always continuously, but it's a long process."

Months or years?

Thinking of *Kah-Puh-Rats,* Zac changed the subject, asking what had been on his mind all morning. "Can you reduce my medication? I can't work when—" He closed his mouth. The psychiatrist could see and hear.

He was slurring his words.

Dr. Holyoak sat back with a small sigh. His eyes were penetrating, and Zac knew exactly what he was thinking, exactly what was happening.

No, Zachary thought. *Don't say I can't.*

But the psychiatrist said only, "Let's wait for this to go away first, all right? If it's a brief reactive psychosis, you should feel better soon."

And if it's not? Zac thought. *What then?*

DAY AND NICK had brought the Austin-Healey to Grand Junction for Grace, and she used it to drive Zac back to Moab.

They put up the top to reduce the noise so they could talk. Zac's mind felt slow and he hated the sound of his own speech, altered by the medication, but he wanted to tell her about the conversation with Dr. Holyoak. When he did Grace seemed almost as shocked as he was.

"Your parents never told you your mother was that ill?"

"They must have assumed I knew. She was often depressed, but it was never discussed as an illness." He paused. "She used to threaten to kill herself."

Staring through the sunny windshield at the road ahead, Grace tried to hide her horror. "Your mother is suicidal?"

"Not anymore."

Grace remembered his nightmares. People he loved killing themselves.

She glanced at him in the confined space of the sports car, then returned her gaze to the road as Zac said, "I found her after she'd overdosed on sleeping pills. It was an accident, not a suicide attempt, but…well, of course I thought she was dead." Relating the story, he felt little. It was a dim twenty-year-old memory. Should he feel something?

Grace barely breathed. "You never told me that." There was a lot he hadn't told her. The green card. Suspicions he was mentally ill.

"It's not my favorite subject. But, anyhow, I'm supposed to go talk to someone about it.'' He'd rather have a root canal.

"Does Dr. Holyoak think it might make you better?''

"Well, obviously he thinks I'm screwed up.'' Again Zac heard his own words slurring, felt the slowed pace of his thoughts. He *was* screwed up. Royally. And he needed to tell Grace the rest. "He thinks it's genetic, too.''

"A predisposition. Yes, I know that.''

Zac said, "You want children.'' So did he.

"Did he say we shouldn't have children?''

"No.'' And Zac knew that brief reactive psychosis was not a chronic mental disorder, was not that serious in the long run. Recurrent episodes like his were rare. But was that all he had? His mother…

The rest of the drive home was quiet. When the car turned off the River Inn Road and down the drive lined with tamarisk, Zac felt a sense of dislocation and lost time. It had been only about two weeks since he'd been at the house, but since then the vegetation had come into bloom, the river had gone down, and the weather had become torrid.

The inn, however, was unchanged. When he saw the gables and chimneys, the French doors and curved balcony railings, Zac knew he was home. Here was the lady with her shoes off on the shore of the river.

As Grace parked under the cottonwoods, he heard barking and saw the silhouette of the dog jumping up against the screen door. Day had known they were coming. She must have brought Ninochka home. Eager to see the puppy, Zac told Grace, "Leave the bags. I'll get them later.''

He got out of the car and went up the steps to unfasten the latch. Ninochka bounded toward him, jumping up.

"Down." He crouched to her level, petting her, ruffling her fur, playing. Her tongue slathered across his nose and her madly wagging tail whipped his face as she jumped about, wriggling with excitement, beside herself. Zac said, "Look how big you are. You're the most beautiful dog in the world." Her markings had darkened since he'd last seen her, and her double-layered coat was thick and healthy. Grace joined him on the steps, and they sat there together, throwing an old pink Frisbee for the ecstatic dog.

Then Zac collected the bags from the car. Though he and Grace had been sleeping together in her room upstairs before they'd left for Cataract Canyon, he still kept his clothes in her father's old room. As Grace followed him and the husky into the downstairs bedroom, he said, "You need to go to work, don't you?"

Grace shook her head. "I'm out of a job. Nick and I are closing on Rapid Riggers this weekend. All I need to do is pack up my desk." Everything was changing at once.

She told Zac, "I'm going to make dinner. What do you want?"

Zac thought, *I want my life back. I want to be normal.* He forgot to answer.

Grace understood. Leaving him to his thoughts, she went out to the kitchen to see what was in the refrigerator. She needed to make a trip to the farmers' market to buy vegetables, but Zac... In the hospital, they'd taken away even his shoelaces. Nobody had said he was suicidal, but Grace didn't want to leave him alone at the house. Not after what he'd said about his mother. Not knowing what must be going on his mind. Genetic abnormalities. Slurred words. His career.

Grace worked in the kitchen for an hour, starting a loaf of bread and soup for dinner. Then she went down the hall and through the parlor to look in the door of Zac's room.

The French doors were open, and he was gone.

Trying to stay calm, Grace put on her sandals and went out onto the stone patio and into the heat. Zac was down by the river, near the boiler from the *Moab Princess,* throwing the Frisbee to Nina. Grace walked alongside the house and toward the shore to join them. She stepped on a twig as she approached, and Zac looked up.

Seeing her, he knew she didn't trust him to be alone. Angry—at his illness—he scooped up the Frisbee Ninochka had dropped and tossed it again. As the husky took off running, Grace reached him. She was wearing red cutoffs and a denim vest, and the sight of her body stirred him. At least he wasn't impotent, despite the meds. But there was a chasm between him and Grace, and he knew what it was.

Doubt. Every kind.

Ninochka bounded back with the disk, dropped it and stood waiting, poised to go again. Zac picked up the disc and threw it. Then he glanced at Grace. Her expression was probing and compassionate, but she seemed to know he wanted to be alone. She clasped his fingers briefly and turned to go back into the house.

Zac wanted her so badly the touch felt like fire. He watched her walk away, and when Ninochka brought back the Frisbee again, he said, "Enough, girl," and went to sit on a boulder near the shore. The husky came to sit beside him, and he scratched her ears and combed her fur with his fingers and accepted all her sweet affection. But it wasn't what he most wanted.

He hungered for his wife.

DINNER WAS QUIET. Afterward Zac helped Grace wash the dishes, but it took him a long time to think to offer. As they worked together, with him washing and her drying, Grace noticed his hands trembling, and she knew he saw it, too. Finally he put down the dishrag and said, "Excuse me," and left the room.

Grace finished the dishes alone, then went into her father's old room. Zac had gone outside again, but she could see him through the French doors. He sat on the patio steps watching the last colors of the sunset leave the sky.

Grace opened the screen door and walked out.

Hearing her, Zac was glad when her long legs settled beside him on the steps. In the dim blue light of disappeared day, his hand slid into hers, and he looked down, saw the difference between the two. His hand was muscular, long-fingered, big-knuckled, wood-colored. A man's hand. Hers was Graceful, paler. His fingers interlocked with hers.

Grace breathed shallowly. She wanted things to be as they'd been before Cataract. But everything had changed—just as it had when she'd left him.

Ninochka, who'd been snooping around near the foundation of the house, came up the steps and lay beside Zac. With his free hand, he petted her.

Grace waited, thinking, *Touch me.* She wanted more than holding hands. *Touch me like a lover, Zachary. Let me know you're really back.*

He might have read her thoughts. His hand slid from hers, and she felt it traveling up her spine, his fingers beneath her hair, stroking the back of her neck.

Grace looked at him, and that was enough. In the dusk that was turning to twilight, he brought his face near hers, looked into her eyes. Their mouths touched. Lips opened. Grace clung to his shoulders through his T-shirt, and then her hands wandered, too, to slide through his hair, to reach down the front of his body.

The low rasp of his breath reached her ears as she touched him through his sweat pants. Hard. Blood racing, she slipped her hand under the waistband, against his skin, reached down, and wrapped her fingers around him, felt his blood coursing. Zac grabbed her, pressed his mouth to her neck, fumbled open the buttons on her vest. Moments later they got up and walked the few feet to the door. In the downstairs bedroom, they pulled back the purple patchwork quilt and the blanket and top sheet and got in bed.

As they tossed their clothes to the floor, Grace whispered, "I missed you so much. I love you, Zachary."

He clasped her to him in a stanglehold. "I love you." He covered her mouth, kissed her with his tongue, felt her body pushing against his as their legs intertwined. Her love for him had never felt so tangible. So good.

Grace rolled over to slide open the night stand drawer. Aware of what she was doing, Zac lay motionless, sober, remembering what he'd managed briefly to forget. Mental illness. *Genes...*

He sat up, and took the packet from her, and she said, "Zac—"

Zac, let me do it.

Their eyes caught in the darkness, and Grace threw

herself into his arms. Zac didn't recognize the sound that came from his throat, didn't understand the fierce trembling of his body. It was more than arousal or need. It was love so strong it hurt.

Grace said, "Oh, Zac, I don't know what I'd do without you. I've never loved anyone so much."

Stoking the fire further was out of the question. Together, they hurriedly dealt with the condom and came together almost frantically, wishing there was some way to be even closer to each other. And never part.

Neither noticed when the husky jumped up on the mattress and lay down to sleep, and in the middle of the night Zac barely stirred when the dog moved over beside him and rested her head on his arm.

THE NEXT MORNING Grace and Zachary went for a run with the dog, and afterward Grace went to the farmers' market and the grocery store. She had finished her shopping at City Market and was heading out to the convertible with two bags of groceries when she noticed the flyer. It was posted on a message board outside the store, and she might have walked past had the largest words on the paper not stood out so boldly.

LOST: SIBERIAN HUSKY

Almost dizzy, Grace paused beside the board and read the entire flyer. A four-month-old gray husky pup named Jasmine had been lost on the Poison Spider Mesa Trail at the end of March. A reward was offered for her return, and two numbers were listed, one local, one with an unfamiliar area code.

Poison Spider Mesa, Grace thought. The Jeep trail led

from the River Inn Road up onto the plateau into a world of Navaho sandstone dunes. It was a popular place for mountain biking and hiking, but on top it was precipitous and desolate. No place for a puppy.

Still, her conscience smarted as she turned away from the notice. Ninochka must be the husky of the ad, and her owners cared enough to offer a reward. They'd probably be relieved to know that she was all right, that she'd found a good home. Maybe they'd let Zac buy the dog from them.

Maybe they wouldn't.

Grace stole another glance at the flyer. Without wanting to, she saw the local telephone number. It was easy to remember. Too easy.

Turning away fast, she strode across the parking lot in the hot morning sun. Ninochka was Zac's dog. They'd established a bond, and they needed each other. God, how he needed her now.

CHAPTER FIFTEEN

WHEN SHE GOT HOME, Zac was outside tilling a patch of ground near the carriage house. Ninochka lay nearby chewing a rawhide bone.

Turning off the tiller, Zac came to kiss Grace. In the slightly slurred voiced to which she was growing accustomed, he said, "I thought we should have a kitchen garden."

Grace's gaze lingered on his eyes. The sun was shining in them now, turning them the color of jade. Thick black lashes. Grace said, "I'm so glad I married you." However it had happened. Whatever else had happened.

Zac's smile faded. It was as though smoke had spread over the sky, dulling everything. They were standing very near each other as he said, "What if we can't have children?"

"If we decide we shouldn't, we won't." She kept her eyes on his. "But it's a choice. Let's make it when you're well."

Zac knew she was right. But he remembered what it was like when his mother wouldn't get out of bed. His father encouraging her, pleading with her, shaming her and finally lifting her just so that he could change the sheets. He'd never asked the servants to help. *If I get that sick...*

Turning away, he stared out toward the river. He

didn't want to tell Grace he'd tried to sand the floor upstairs and had gouged the wood with the sanding machine. He didn't want to admit that he'd tried to work on the porch at the northeast corner of the house but that his hands shook too badly to hammer a nail. He didn't want to say that he couldn't even play "Chopsticks" on the piano but could only sit and stare at Hamlet's mad girlfriend who'd drowned herself in the lily pond.

Instead, he told himself he would get better as he had in New York. Then he'd be able to do the things he always had.

At last he said, "May I use your boat this afternoon?"

Grace looked toward the Colorado. Clouds were reflected in the water. "You can't drive anywhere." Not on so much medication.

"I'll put in here. I can row upstream and back down. I thought I'd see if Ninochka would go."

The dog lifted her head at the sound of her name. Her tail flopped from one side to the other.

Grace said, "Okay."

Later that afternoon they put the dory in the river, and Ninochka eagerly joined Zac in it. Zachary had water for both of them and a dish for Nina, and Grace was glad the dog was going with him. As they rowed off, she returned to the house, trying not to think of the flyer or the phone number she couldn't forget.

TWO DAYS LATER they drove to Grand Junction for Zac to see Dr. Holyoak. He was so much better that the psychiatrist reduced his medication and said he could return to work whenever he felt able. He also reminded Zac about starting psychotherapy, and Zac promised to make an appointment as soon as the film was wrapped. Until then he had enough on his mind.

Though the producers had cut most of his remaining scenes, there were still several to be shot. Zac was glad the role had been shortened. The side effects of the medication were not disappearing as quickly as he'd hoped, and he dreaded returning to the set. The inn was his refuge. He'd begun working on the upstairs again… thinking.

Dr. Holyoak had warned him about avoiding stress and getting adequate sleep, and Zac knew that the career, the ambition that had owned him most of his adult life, was stressful. And it had caused him to make some bad choices. Marrying Grace hadn't been one of them, but how it happened was. Now, *Leaving Hong Kong* was only a memory—a bad one. But he and Grace had to live with the knowledge that he'd married her for a green card. Zac knew it ate at her. It ate at him.

He had done it for his career. And now, for the first time in his life, he wondered…

Was his career worth it?

THE NEXT MORNING a production assistant drove out to the River Inn to bring him a call sheet. At ten that night they would shoot the camp fire scene in which the Howland brothers and William Dunn decide to leave the Powell expedition. Zac was to report to the set at eight.

He and Grace left at seven-thirty in the Austin-Healey to drive to the base camp at Big Bend, upstream from Moab on the river road. It was a silent drive, and when Zac saw the trailers and the people, he was glad of Grace's presence. And ashamed of how badly he wanted her there.

As they got out of the car and crew members walked past, smiling at him awkwardly, Zac reflected on all Grace had done for him in the past weeks. Looking after him in Cataract Canyon. Visiting him in the hospital.

As he often had in the past few days, he thought about his parents—especially what they'd been like years earlier, when things were worse. His mother crying behind the door. His father beseeching, soothing...caring. Becoming angry and fed up. But always, ultimately, being there beside her.

Why don't you leave her, Dad? Pip had asked.

Zac had been about eight at the time, and he remembered his own paralyzing fear at his older brother's suggestion—and his relief when he'd seen his father's surprised expression. The earl had said, *Well, Pip, I love your mother. And she counts on me to take care of her.*

But Zac never wanted Grace taking care of him that way.

He could hardly stand the thought.

SENECA HOWLAND'S character had three lines in the camp-fire scene. Though Zac had repeated them a hundred times that day, he couldn't say them without slurring. Inevitably, when it came time to film, Meshach noticed.

The first retake didn't surprise Zac, but the second made him anxious. The third made him afraid. That time he knew he had enunciated more clearly than he had all day. And it wasn't good enough.

They changed lines.

They cut a line.

In the end the script doctor suggested giving him a flask and having him sip from it during the other parts of the scene, after which he was to appear drunk. That required retaking the part of the scene that *had* worked, the part during which he didn't have to speak.

Meshach said, "We'll make it work, Zac."

Zac was not comforted. He was trapped in a body that had become a demon. The body he'd always taken for granted. The body he'd always been able to control perfectly.

When he lifted the flask to his mouth, his hand shook.

Watching from a seat on a boulder some distance behind the cameras, Grace felt her heart clench and unclench. Why was he putting himself through this?

But she knew. Acting. He loved it and he needed it. The revelations that had come with his illness had made her understand how much. It was probably a way to deal with his emotions, especially pain.

Grace doubted it was the right way. Maybe if he found a better way, he would have no more psychotic episodes.

On the other hand, perhaps that was denial on her part.

Leaves crunched on the ground near her, and she looked up to discover Hal Markley slapping a mosquito on his neck. She hadn't known the producer was on the set. Smiling, he came over to lean casually against the boulder where she sat. He was dressed in duck trousers and a polo shirt, but at the moment he seemed surprisingly at home in the outdoors.

Nodding in Zac's direction, he asked Grace, "How's it going?"

Grace knew he didn't mean the filming. She was surprised by the inquiry, but she supposed the producers did have an interest in Zac's health. Particularly given his difficulties tonight.

Not wanting to say anything that could jeopardize

Zac's career, she replied, "He's getting better." It was true. But he wasn't off medication yet.

Markley nodded and stood there in silence for some time. Grace wondered why he didn't leave until he said, "Look, I want you to tell Zac we'll get this film wrapped one way or another. Don't let him sweat what's going on tonight. We see worse things on movie sets. Drugs. Tempers. Zac's a pro. If we have to shoot his scenes on the soundstage in a few weeks, we will. But I think he can finish this, and I'd like to see him do it."

Touched by the producer's kindness, Grace said, "Thanks. I will tell him."

With a faint sigh Markley said, "Yeah, everyone's bipolar in my family. Manic-depressive." Behind his horn-rimmed glasses, his eyes regarded Grace with empathy. "I know what you're going through."

She tried to hide her surprise, but he saw it and said, "Hey, there's a lot of people like Zac out there. And a lot of people worse off. Let me know if there's anything I can do for either of you. If you need any resources, I can give you some numbers. Legal information. Support networks. You're not alone."

You're not alone.

But despite Hal Markley's solicitude, Grace felt very much alone as she drove Zac home at two in the morning, after sixteen takes.

She told him what the producer had said, but he seemed not to hear. Grace knew he was preoccupied by his poor performance.

When they reached the River Inn, she went to bed in his room, where they'd been sleeping since his return from the hospital, but Zac didn't join her. He kissed her good-night, then went upstairs and walked through the halls with Ninochka.

As he contemplated the repairs still needed on the second floor, he thought about what had happened on the set and about the producer who had manic-depressive relatives, who was perhaps bipolar himself. He thought about the Ben Rogan ads and being on "The JoAnn Carroll Show" and being naked with Ingrid Dolk. He thought about running with Ninochka in the mornings and rowing the dory in the afternoons and about Grace working over her hot stove and coming to him in the night, her hair swinging against his face as she laid her body over his and moved against him like the river.

He thought of his parents.

He walked around and around the upstairs, thinking and thinking, and he felt shaken to the foundation of who he was.

THE NIGHTMARE CAME that night—with a difference. The paneled Tudor door became the reinforced door of the seclusion room. He couldn't kick it in, but he remembered the window, and he looked through...

A dog tongue slurped across his face. Paws pressed down on his chest. Jolting awake, heart racing, Zac immediately noticed the sweat-soaked sheets. *The dream.* Behind Ninochka, Grace was sitting up, her hair a sexy, uncombed silhouette against the starlight, her diamond earring flashing in the dark. Summoning the husky, she said, "Here, Nina. It's all right."

The dog looked at Zac, then moved and lay down on another part of the bed.

Zachary sat up and reached for Grace, folding her into his embrace, drawing strength from her presence. After a moment he said, "Go get in bed upstairs and go back to sleep. I'll change these sheets and join you."

Grace heard the steadiness of his voice under the words he couldn't utter with precision. She felt the strength of his body holding her. A tender embrace for her, not comfort for him.

She said, "Why don't you take a shower? I'll change the sheets."

Zac withdrew. "No."

He got out of bed, and Grace watched him pull on some sweatpants and leave the room. Hearing the door of the linen cabinet open and shut, she stood and began stripping the damp sheets from the bed.

Nightmares…

She started. Zac stood in the doorway. Even in the darkness, she sensed he was angry. "I'll do it, Grace."

She dropped the sheet and deliberately stepped back from the bed. Taking a seat in the rocker, she watched him change the sheets.

"Would you like some tea?" she asked.

"I can take care of myself, Grace."

She remembered earlier that night, when she'd had to drive him to the set. He couldn't take care of himself. Not completely. Not now. He certainly hadn't been able to take care of himself in Cataract Canyon. She said carefully, "Not that I think you can't get yourself a cup of tea, but what would be so awful about my taking care of you?"

He turned and stared at her in the dark, then tossed a pillow onto the bed. "Nothing." Everything.

"Isn't that what we do for each other?"

Zac didn't answer.

She sensed his strain but pressed, "Isn't that part of being married?"

Zac sat down on the corner of the mattress. She was still naked, and she looked beautiful there in the rocking chair. Strong. Womanly. He said, "I don't want you to be my keeper. You're my wife."

Grace stared at his broad shoulders, the silhouette of his body that was itself a definition of masculinity. She answered, "Helpmate? Friend? In sickness and in health?"

He tensed.

Grace thought of the times he'd met her after work at Jean-Michel's and ridden the subway with her. The labor he'd put into her house. How he'd saved her life on the river. They did take care of each other. Quashing a vision of her father's casket over his grave, she said, "I love you. You're the keeper, Zac."

Keeper. He'd heard her use the word that way in the past, once when she was talking to Ninochka. She'd called the dog a keeper, too. A good one, worth keeping. Grace loved him.

Like his father had loved his mother. Unconditionally. Zac said fiercely, "You don't understand how bad it is. You don't know what you're saying."

Her eyes pierced his in the dark blue starlight. "Who do you think got in that dory with you in Cataract, Zachary? Who listened to you screaming while they medicated you and took you away? I think I understand how bad it is."

"No. You don't."

Grace sensed he wasn't talking about himself but about his mother. "Zac, I didn't marry you expecting it to be a piece of cake." She *had* expected it to be for love, but that was moot now. There was love between them, and they were joined for life.

"You know, Zac, my dad used to tell me this. He said life is a river. There are calm stretches and rapids. Smiling holes and frowning holes. Those you can run and the ones that stop you. And the river wouldn't be as beautiful or interesting if it was all calm water."

Smiling holes and frowning holes, thought Zac. He remembered the past Christmas, his mother laughing. Laughing hard over some absurdity of Pip's. They'd all laughed. All been happy. That night, her mood had crashed. A medium-low—crying, but not as bad as she'd once been.

Yes, he understood smiling holes and frowning holes. Acknowledging, even celebrating, those extremes and the whole spectrum of human experience was what attracted him to drama. Comedy and Tragedy. But the last thing he wanted was for his marriage with Grace to become a vehicle worthy of the ancient Greeks.

Aware that he was on the verge of blurting out things too intimate to share even with her, he said, "I'm not obtuse. I know those things, Grace. I'll make the tea." Seeing her expression, a shell trying to hide the fact that he'd wounded her, Zac rebuked himself for deriding Sam Sutter's philosophy. He paused at the door and looked down at her. "Your father was wise."

In the kitchen, he filled the kettle and put it on the stove. Then he threaded his way to the living room in the dark, keeping the lights off so he couldn't see the painting of Ophelia. As he heard Ninochka coming across the floor and felt her settling near the foot pedals, he tried to steady his trembling fingers sufficiently to hit the right keys.

He played a shaky Chopin étude, then switched to blues, struggling through melodies as disturbing and dark as madness. He tried Cole Porter next. Rodgers and Hart. Gershwin. He started to play *that* song, but his chest felt too hot, and his eyes dropped to his shaking hands, to his wedding ring.

Abruptly he saw Grace watching him in the dark from the arched door to the foyer. She said, "The tea's ready."

Zac hadn't heard the whistle. *He didn't need a keeper.* But Grace said *he* was a keeper. Someone to keep. Someone worth keeping. Standing, he closed the cover on the keys. Careful not to let his gaze touch the woman over the mantel, he joined Grace. She had put on one of his T-shirts, and it hung around her thighs.

He pulled her against him. "I love you." They kissed with their tongues in each other's mouths, there under the arch. Her touch, and the things she'd said earlier, drew words from him. Confessions.

"My mother…she wouldn't even have a bath. It was as though she had no dignity—but she couldn't help it…." More spilled out in between, the uglier things. "She told my father she wanted to end it. I used to listen through the door. The door was always locked. I stayed outside and listened, because I was afraid she was killing herself. I wasn't supposed to do that, lurk outside her room. Pip showed me how to pick the locks. We weren't supposed to…"

Listening to his whispered words in the dark, Grace knew he was telling secrets. His secrets and those of his family. In her mind she saw a little boy hearing his mother threaten to abandon him in the most final way.

Finding her asleep in her bed. Unable to wake her. Certain she was dead. Not supposed to talk about it.

"She must have become depressed because I was going to school. I was her youngest. It happened the night before I was supposed to leave. They were to take me up early in the morning, and she took the pills so she could sleep that night. It was an accident."

Although she heard no uncertainty in his voice, Grace recognized an unspoken question. Had his mother really tried to kill herself?

"She's much better, now. I suppose she has better psychiatric help. Better medication. Things have changed in twenty years."

His voice trailed off, and Grace imagined what he must be thinking. Trying to understand how his mum could have wanted to kill herself when she had two sons. When she had him. He would never know for sure if she'd really tried that night.

Grace realized that his dilemma, though larger and more painful, was like one of her own—a question that had plagued her for more than a year. Had Zac married her for love or a green card?

Like him, she had to rely on the clues of her experience and the testimony of another—him. She must find the answer in her heart. Or learn to accept her doubt.

HE WAS OFF medication in a week, and the film was wrapped in two. As the studio pulled out of town, everything returned to normal, and Grace knew she and Zac had come to a crossroads. California. She knew that before they left she must call the owners of the dog.

Just as she knew that, if the owners had Ninochka's

papers, their right to the husky was indisputable. They could take her from Zac.

As the days wore on, she expected him to mention moving, but he never brought it up. Instead, he spent his time gardening, rowing and working on the upstairs of the house, and he made an appointment at the mental health clinic to talk to a counselor. He had two sessions in one week—the first with a psychologist, the second with a men's group. When he came home from the last, Grace found him in the kitchen with his shirt off. It was 105 degrees out, scorching summer. As he nodded hello to Grace, he lifted a beer bottle to his mouth with an unsteady hand.

Grace hadn't noticed his hands shaking for days, and the slurring had disappeared. She'd thought he was well. He looked well. She asked, "What's up?"

Zac took another drink and watched her, trying to block out the memory of the session. He hadn't spoken at all, but hearing other men discuss appalling traumas they'd suffered had been excruciating. He wasn't sure he could go back. But he knew intuitively that the pain was why he was supposed to go.

He told Grace, "Well, it was a difficult afternoon." It came out sharply, which he hadn't intended.

Grace responded to his tone. Impatient with keeping her distance, with letting him have his space, she said, "Zac, what are we doing? Are we going to California? I need to know what to expect from my life."

Energy shuddered through him. The tower shaking. Change. Instinct overwhelmed him. He knew it was the instinct he'd been fighting since the end of April, when he'd first come back to her, when he'd first seen this place. He said, "No. We're not going to California."

Grace's heart thundered. "What are we going to do?"

Zac swallowed some more beer so that he wouldn't say something sarcastic. Wouldn't say, *Well, dear, I'm giving you your way.* Because it wasn't her decision. It was his.

And it hurt.

"I don't know what we're going to do. Right now I'm planning to go rowing."

Grace eyed him suspiciously. Not going to California. Not, apparently, going anywhere. "Zachary, are you contemplating a career change?"

He met her eyes, and his looked like those of a person who'd lost a loved one. "Yes."

"Don't do it on my account."

He gave her a cold look and opened the refrigerator to get another beer.

"I never asked you to give it up."

"*Shut up!*" He slammed his hand against his face, took a breath and left the room. The dog, who'd been lying in the corner panting, got up and followed him.

Grace stood stricken in the middle of the kitchen, thinking of what she'd said. She knew she was wrong. She *had* asked him to give it up. In a hundred ways.

And it was the wrong thing.

Her emotions whirled. They had to go to California. If Zachary sacrificed his career for her, he would never forgive her. It would drive them apart. Anyhow, acting was the biggest part of him. She didn't want him to change. And *that* was one of the most startling revelations of her life.

California...

The dog.

She made herself do it.

As she dialed the number that had been on the flyer, she knew it was the right choice, but she felt as though she was betraying Zac in the cruelest way. She should at least break it to him first. But perhaps she could surprise him with Ninochka's papers, instead.

When she heard a woman's voice on the other end of the line, she almost hung up.

"I saw your ad about a lost husky."

"The dog? Have you found her?" The woman sounded genuinely excited.

Wondering if she was the owner, Grace forced herself to continue. "Yes. We found her about six weeks ago." Six long weeks. "We'd like to buy her." Zac would be thrilled. Surely he worried about the owners sometimes.

"Oh, I know she doesn't want to sell her. But she'd love to give you a reward. Where are you calling from?"

Grace's heart pounded. The owner wouldn't give up the dog. She thought of Zachary being wrenched from Ninochka.

Loss.

"Are you there?" said the woman. "I didn't get your name."

Shaking, Grace placed the receiver back in the cradle.

ZAC RETURNED in the dory at six o'clock, and Grace went down to the shore as he pulled the boat onto the beach. He looked suntanned and sexy, but Grace could hardly meet his eyes. She shouldn't have made that call.

As Ninochka made a beeline for the shade, Zac abandoned the boat and joined Grace. His arms circled her, his chest came toward her, and she felt his head against her hair as he said, "I'm sorry I yelled."

The phone call had almost made her forget the scene

in the kitchen. She told Zac, "I'm sorry I made you want to quit being an actor."

He pulled back so they could see each other's eyes. "You haven't. I'll always be an actor. I just want to do things differently." His hands went to her face, and he smoothed strands of hair into her braid as he searched her eyes. "Grace, would you like to turn this place back into a hotel?"

Grace opened her mouth but didn't speak.

"Tell me."

"Yes."

He kissed her. "Then that's what we'll do. I'd like it, too. Do you know you and I have always lived in hotels? Even our place in New York was a hotel once."

Was he giving up film acting? "What about your agent? I know he's been sending you scripts."

Zac kept his arm around her as he steered her toward the house. He spoke low, his head near hers. "I'll keep modeling. But no films right now. The psychotherapy is important. Our marriage is, too. Let's see if we can make this inn something special, all right?"

Grace felt as though she was dreaming. Her heart was racing, but she knew it wasn't just because Zac was holding her, saying those things. It was because of what she'd done while he was on the river. The phone call.

"Come this way." He led her around the side of the house toward the stone patio. His hand was on the small of her back, his fingers slipping into the waistband of her shorts. Subtle signs. He was going to get her into the shower with him, make love to her. Leisurely dinner, perhaps a movie on video afterward. Sweet companionship. Best friend.

She'd betrayed him.

As they walked around the corner of the house, he pointed and said, "Do you think we could have a croquet pitch there?"

Ninochka bounded past them, chasing a butterfly.

Grace said, "I found her owner."

"What?"

He stopped walking, turned and stared at her.

"There was a flyer at City Market." Grace repeated the contents of the ad.

Zac listened grimly.

"I called the number."

Zac felt his breath becoming strange, too shallow. He didn't know how to react. "Tell me."

She did, and afterward she said, "I'm sorry. I should never have called."

"Calling was the right thing to do. But you should have told me. Why didn't you?" When he saw her eyes, he knew. He was sick, and she'd been protecting him.

Taking care of him.

Across the slope, Ninochka investigated an animal burrow near the carriage house. Zac and Grace stood in the heat watching the dog.

"I'm going to phone her back," he said.

"The owner won't sell."

His expression made hers callow by comparison. "Of course she will. We just have to offer enough."

WHILE ZAC PHONED the woman in Moab that night, Grace sat at the kitchen table petting Ninochka and listening. What she could grasp from Zac's conversation was that the Moab woman was the owner's aunt and that the owner was from out of town.

As the conversation wore on, Grace saw Zachary's

face change subtly, saw him swallow, as though he'd heard something distressing.

When he hung up he looked at Grace for a few seconds before he said, "The good news is that the owner lives in Alaska and may not be able to come down here for some time to get her dog. The bad news is—" Briefly he stopped speaking, but then he went on as though his words were nothing of import. "She's a sled-dog racer. And she wants this dog back."

TWO MONTHS PASSED. They worked on the inn by day and made love at night. Zac went out of town three times on modeling assignments, and Grace occasionally filled in when Day and Nick needed an extra guide to row the Daily.

That was where she was the day the green Jeep Wagoneer came down the sandy driveway. Zac was working upstairs, in one of the rooms on the east side of the house. At the sound of the car, Ninochka trotted out onto the balcony to see who was coming. Zac followed.

The first thing he saw was two mountain bikes on a rack on the roof. The second was the Alaska license plate on the front of the vehicle. GTMUSHY. Zac's stomach rolled. He'd been dreading this visit all summer.

From the passenger door emerged a strongly built woman with a strawberry blond ponytail and a deep suntan that was peeling from her nose. Her sunglasses hung on a strap from her neck, so Zac could see her eyes as she squinted up at the balcony. She looked about his age, and so did the driver. He was big, with curly dark hair. Both wore shorts, tank tops and heavy hiking boots.

The woman nodded up at the balcony and said, "Hi. I think that's my dog."

Zac felt like he'd eaten lead. "I'll be right down."

As he slipped back through the French doors, Zac resisted the impulse to close Ninochka in the room to keep her from coming with him. There wouldn't be a problem. He could persuade the woman to sell.

And if he couldn't…Nina was hers.

Downstairs, he invited the visitors up to the screened porch. The woman was very interested in Ninochka and said to her companion, "She looks just like Tamar, doesn't she?"

"I'll say." The man crouched near Ninochka, touching her nose with his finger. "You're a pretty girl."

The woman asked, "What have you been calling her?"

Zac told her and watched as she tried out the name. Ninochka responded. The couple liked dogs.

Zachary wasn't sure what he'd expected. What he'd read about mushers at the library had been damning, and he'd gone back to read more when the Moab woman he'd called about the lost husky ad had told him the name of her niece, the owner. Betsy Jason was someone in dogsled racing. But over the years, she'd lost more than one dog during races. Running them to death.

To victory.

Now, meeting her was like seeing a part of himself— the part he'd recently discarded. Ambition. Or in Betsy's case, competitiveness.

They sat around a table Zac had salvaged from the carriage house weeks earlier. After inspecting the newcomers, Ninochka lay at Zachary's feet.

Betsy's boyfriend, Dan, remained silent while she said, "Look, I've brought you a reward, and I'd also like to reimburse you for vet bills, dog food, whatever you spent on her. It looks like you've taken good care of her, and I'm just thrilled to get her back."

Zac said, "I'd like to buy her from you."

Betsy exchanged a regretful look with Dan. Then she said, "My aunt told me that. I can't do it."

Zac felt it would be crass to name a figure so soon, so he said, "I'll pay whatever she's worth to you."

"Money doesn't matter. I have seventy-six dogs I've raised from pups. Ninochka's mother was one of the best. I lost her last year."

In a race. Zac was sure of it. But he was impressed with how readily Betsy had begun using Ninochka's name. Undoubtedly she knew it would be a step backward for the dog's training to do anything else.

Zac said, "She's been spayed."

Betsy shrugged. "That was probably a good thing for you to do." Her words implied she might have done something different.

Zac felt his way. Panic rose inside him, and he squelched it. "How did you lose Ninochka?"

Betsy threw Dan a killing glare.

Her boyfriend spoke. "*Mea culpa.* I took her mountain biking. We got separated."

Zac's hand slid down beside his chair and his fingers touched coarse hair, then downy undercoat. Ninochka licked his fingers. Meeting Betsy's eyes, hoping he could make her see, he said, "This dog and I have a relationship. She's the only pet my wife and I have. You have seventy-six other dogs."

"Seventy-five. This one is number seventy-six. And I assure you, I have a close relationship with every one of those animals."

Like an Indy driver has with the cylinders of his car,

Zac thought. He said, "I'll give you five thousand dollars."

Betsy's expression was compassionate. She said, "I'm glad Ninochka has been in the hands of someone who loved her. But I loved her mother. And I'm taking her back to Alaska. If you object, we'll have to call the sheriff."

There was nothing to do.

They were going to take his dog.

Betsy Jason's sled dog.

Zac looked at Betsy and said, "I'd appreciate it if you could leave her here now and come back tonight. She's my wife's dog, too. I know Grace would like to say goodbye."

CHAPTER SIXTEEN

HE SPENT THE HOURS till Grace came home playing with Ninochka, fighting feelings behind his face and his eyes, watery feelings. He felt dazed and frightened, aware of what was happening.

Loss.

It had set him off before. He had to keep it together this time. He had to stay sane for Grace.

Through the blistering afternoon, he played in the shallows of the river with the husky, then took her inside, where it was cool, and played with her there. He lay down with her on the bed, and Ninochka, smart Nina, knew something was wrong and kept licking his nose, giving him that "What's wrong?" look.

He told her.

THAT EVENING, Grace watched him gather Ninochka's things. Toys. Brush. The blanket from her bed. The dog knew. Her tail drooped. She lay down on the floor and watched them with worried eyes.

Grace was afraid.

What would this do to Zac?

His jaw was very tight, his movements deliberate but oddly relaxed. Almost rehearsed. Seeing him that way, seeing him pack the dog's things in a box, reminded her of another time he'd helped pack. Memories rushed at her. Leaving him.

Now Grace saw Zac through clear eyes. His emotionless features, the way he could walk around so casually when his world was falling apart, did not mean that he didn't love. Rather that he'd never learned how to show his pain—perhaps even how to feel it—and he loved too much to know what to do.

He had always loved her.

At seven, they heard the car outside. In the kitchen, Grace looked at Ninochka, then up at Zac.

His features even, he said, "Let's go, girl." He picked up the box, and Grace opened the door. They went out, but Zac had to call Ninochka three times before she would follow.

OUTSIDE, WHERE THE SUNSET made shadows shaped like cottonwoods, Betsy Jason removed Nina's collar and handed it to Zac.

He took it, not knowing what to do with it.

Betsy met his eyes. "She'll be happy. Really. These dogs are never happier than when they're running."

Zac held his tongue with effort.

Dan opened the back door of the Wagoneer. "Here, Ninochka. Here, girl. Come on! Come on!"

Ninochka looked at Zac anxiously and tucked her tail between her legs. After a moment Zachary started to walk to the Wagoneer to coax her inside, but Betsy held up her hand. "No. It's better if you don't. She should get used to my voice."

She walked to the car and said, "*Ninochka. Come.*"

Again the hesitation.

Betsy repeated her command.

The husky looked at Zachary. He looked at the ground, at the cottonwoods, anywhere else. He heard Betsy call her again, and he turned toward the river and watched the flow of the water. *Ninochka...*

When he looked back the dog was in the car. Betsy was praising her, petting her.

Taking her.

The doors shut, and Zac saw Ninochka looking at him through the window. As the engine started, Grace's hand slid into his, then her arm went around him. Dust choked the air as the Jeep turned and drove out.

Through the hazy orange light of the sunset, they watched the road resettle against the tamarisk, and then Zac turned to his wife, who was still there. Grace, whose brown eyes were frightened. Grace, who must be wondering if he would now go mad. She said, "I'm going to make some tea."

Taking care of him. Zac said, "Thank you." They went into the kitchen and he sat down at the table and stared at Ninochka's collar, still in his hand. After a moment he set it on the table, separating himself. It was going to be okay. He was just a little numb. Trying to think of other things, he asked Grace, "When we build the restaurant kitchen beside the Princess Room, how about if we put the sink against the west wall? Let me tell you what I'm thinking...."

At the stove Grace listened to his plan and tried to find an appropriate way to respond. She thought of their quarters, which would include the parlor, her father's old room and two others in the lower northwest corner of the building. She thought of the dog who had gone. There was nothing to say, and before the kettle whistled Zac suddenly got up and left the room. After the water had boiled and she'd poured it into the teapot, Grace went to find him.

He was in the living room, standing before the hearth, staring at the Waterhouse print in the dusk. He asked Grace, "Does this picture mean anything to you? Do you care about it?"

Ophelia.

Grace actually rather liked it, but it was just something she'd gotten at a garage sale. Nothing her family had owned. "It doesn't matter."

"'There's rosemary, that's for remembrance. Pray you, love, remember.'" Zac reached up and jerked the frame off the wall so hard the picture hanger flew across the room. "'And there is pansies, that's for thoughts.'" Holding the frame, he strode to the front door, opened it and went out. When the screen door banged behind him, Grace followed, onto the shadowy porch and down the steps.

He was headed for the river, but he stopped before he reached the shore. As Grace made her way toward him in the darkness under the cottonwoods, he turned the frame on its side and, with his man's strength, hurled it like a Frisbee out into the river.

It landed with a splash in the middle of the current, the glass winking its last in the falling light. Zachary yelled, "'Poor Ophelia! Divided from herself and her fair judgment, Without the which we are pictures or mere beasts.'" Still turned toward the river, he shouted, "'Your sister's drowned, Laertes!' Drowned! She should have taken her meds! She should have had some psychotherapy!"

But then he fell to his knees in the dirt and put his

hands over his face. Grace went to him and knelt beside him.

"Gracie." He turned to her, hugging her, and she combed his hair with her fingers, rubbed her cheek against the beard stubble on his.

He was shaking, and Grace held him tighter in the dark, in the night while mosquitoes whined in her ears. Hearing his quiet, gasping breaths, feeling wetness against her neck, she hugged harder, her head against his. "Shh, shh. It's all right. It's all right. I love you."

Zac could feel her soft skin and hair and smell the lemongrass, and it was comforting, but it made him feel more. This was what it was like to feel. Warm woman in his arms. Pain that wouldn't stop.

Holding him, Grace felt his sobs and caught the choked, almost unintelligible words of grief, words it hurt even to hear. "I want her back.... I want her back."

SUMMER BURNED ON, and he did not go mad.

His family came out for two weeks in late July, around the time of his birthday. While his father helped install ceiling fans on the screened porch, his mother visited with Grace, and Pip flirted with Day.

Day was a frequent visitor at the River Inn. The last time she'd come, to share the five-course dinner Grace had made for his family before they returned to England, she'd brought a yellow flyer, which now hung on the refrigerator:

AUDITIONS!
for a Moab Players production of
Suddenly Last Summer
by
Tennessee Williams

The auditions were in two weeks. Zac was glad. He wanted the distraction. The house kept him busy, but he knew he was mourning the loss of his dog. His dog, who was running somewhere on the tundra, maybe running too hard, running her heart out.

On a Monday in the second week of August, he and Grace awoke before dawn, took a long run, then came home and worked outside in the garden. Zachary wanted to expand the plot next year, perhaps landscape the periphery, but at least now they had fresh vegetables every night.

At 6:30 a.m., it was not yet too warm, and weeding the rows together was peaceful.

As Grace bent over, picking a pest from a squash vine, Zac watched her pale hair and her long legs. Since Ninochka had gone, the relationship between him and Grace had strengthened. Clicked. Zac knew he had simply loved the dog, but he also knew there was a part of himself he'd been afraid to show Grace. A vulnerable part it had been safe to feel with the husky, who would never reject him.

Straightening up, Grace said, "Don't you think it would look nice if we grew morning glories against the carriage house?"

"Would you like to get married?"

"What?" Grace stared at him.

She knew it was not a confused question. Zac was steady these days.

Grace understood him better than she ever had—both who he'd always been and who he had become. That he knew when to let the river steer the boat. When to push on the oars. When to pull. He'd been spending the summer learning how to stay out of holes, but they both knew the river was wild and unpredictable and it could catch him and keep him again.

He crossed the garden toward her, a muscular man in a pair of cotton rugby shorts and a tattered Oxford T-shirt. He needed a haircut and a shave, and he still made her heart stop whenever she saw him. His face near hers, he repeated softly, "I said would you like to get married? Would you like to marry me?"

Grace's heart quavered. "We are married. What are you talking about?"

His mouth hovered near hers. "I married you for a green card." He paused, watching her eyes. "I want to marry you for love."

Grace touched her lip with her tongue. Her gaze caressed his face. His chin. His mouth.

He said, "I'm so in love with you. I always was, but I really think we should fix this. I wasn't thinking of getting divorced first. Just getting married. Again. Will you marry me?"

Grace nodded. "I'd marry you again a hundred times, Zachary." Into her mind flashed the memory of his face when he'd been packing Ninochka's toys. When he'd been helping pack *her* things. She said, "I'd marry you a hundred times for a green card."

He lowered his face to hers and kissed her gently, then slipped closer, his mouth opening against hers. His arousal rose with the sun, and for a while they behaved like two people living in the middle of nowhere, not yet running a hotel. But eventually the ants, starting their day, began crawling on them.

As they stood up and adjusted their clothes, Zac said,

"It's up to you of course, but my idea was to pack sleeping bags and a tent, go down the river to somewhere secluded and make our promises to each other. Have a private celebration. Or if you like, we can invite Nick and Day. They'll have to bring their own boat."

"And find their own beach," Grace said, thinking of the sounds she and Zac made in the night.

They talked about their plans as they went inside. While Grace sliced peaches for a cobbler and rolled out dough for scones, Zac played the piano they'd finally had tuned. He was playing "Love Is Here to Stay" when the phone rang. Grace grabbed the receiver at once before he could stop the song.

"Hello?"

It was a woman on the line, and Grace listened carefully, her heart racing. She glanced through the dining room as she responded. Zac was still playing the song. "Yes... Oh, of course. That would be wonderful. Um...a plane ticket. That's no problem, but I think we might like to come and get her, instead. May I have your number? I'll call you back when I know how we want to do it, but yes, yes, we do. Definitely. Thank you so much."

She took down the phone number the woman gave her, promised to call back soon and replaced the receiver. Then she hurried out through the dining room and up the stairs.

ZAC WAS JUST STARTING a polonaise when Grace appeared beside him and set something on the piano's music stand. Still playing, Zac squinted at it. An airplane cocktail napkin. He ceased the song and reached for the napkin.

The honeymoon coupon he'd given her when they'd flown to New York together.

Grace said, "Since we're getting married, I thought we should have a honeymoon."

"Yes." He smiled and turned to straddle the bench, then pulled her down beside him. "Where would you like to go?"

Grace sighed. "It's so hot this time of year. I'd like to go somewhere *cold*. Like...Nome, Alaska." She met Zachary's eyes, and his face was tense. She knew he was afraid.

His brow furrowed slightly as he said, "Why there?" Then, softly, "Who was on the phone?"

"A sled-dog racer named Betsy, who wants to give you back your dog. She said Nina misses you, and...she wants to give you Ninochka and her papers. She said if we sent a ticket she'd put her on the plane, but I've always wanted to visit Alaska, and I thought if we could get married soon..."

Zac's arms slipped around her. "I'd be happy to honeymoon somewhere cold. You're all the warm I need."

And all the Grace.

EPILOGUE

Two years later
Love is here to stay...

ZAC OPENED the backstage door. Nick was outside in the shadows.

"Is everything ready?"

Nick nodded. "Aye-aye. How soon will you be out of here?"

"Thirty minutes."

"Okay. See you then. By the way, nice duds."

"Thank you. They're Siamese." Zac shut the door and slipped through the dark hall and back into the wings. He was on next.

GRACE SAT in the fifth row, her eyes glowing as she watched the musical rising to its climax. Day's sweet soprano blended beautifully with Zac's voice, and they played off each other well, always leaving the audience laughing.

Beside her Fast Susan whispered, "They gave him that part because of how he looks in those clothes. That little vest and no shirt. Does he dress up like the king at home?"

"He is the king at home. And I'm the queen. Shh," Grace said. "I love this song." She loved seeing Zac on stage. Every time. What he did as an actor was beautiful, and Grace realized that Zachary had made her perceive what drama, at its best, could accomplish. It could reflect life in a way that made those in the audience cherish their humanity.

With a smile in her heart, she watched and listened as Anna invited the King of Siam to dance.

AFTER THE FINAL CURTAIN call Grace went out the side door. She and Zac caught each other as he emerged from the back of the theater. He was sweaty and smelled like the stage. Framing her face in his hands, he kissed her on the mouth and said, "Give me five minutes to get out of this. Those flowers aren't for me, are they?"

"Of course not. They're for my sister. I have something else for you."

"Yes, you do." In the shadows against the brick wall of the theater, his hand slid to her breast. His tongue wandered in her mouth....

Five minutes later they were in the Austin-Healey, the warm spring night blowing through their hair as Zac drove toward the Moab Bridge.

Grace was eager to be home. She wanted to be alone with him so badly, to make love the way they did at night when the dishes in the restaurant kitchen were washed and the guests were in their rooms. They had good employees at the River Inn, trustworthy enough to manage dinner and guests so that Grace and Zac could slip out together for an occasional date. Or for her to see a performance, like tonight.

But being home was best. And lately lovemaking had become something more. Zac had been well for two years. Long enough. They were both good boatmen, and each knew when to bail for the other. They'd decided to try the rapids.

To try to conceive a child.

The sound of the tires changed as they crossed over the Colorado on the bridge. Then Zac slowed the car.

"What are you doing?"

"Stopping at Rapid Riggers."

Grace pulled her hair out of her face and looked toward the office. It was dark except for the security light. Why was Zac stopping here?

As he pulled into the lot, her eyes swept toward the river. The night was moonless, but she could see a large black shape on the water. Almost like a small barge. "What's that?"

Zac stepped out of the car and walked around to open her door. He was wearing his grizzly-bear shirt, and Grace touched him as she got out.

Taking her hand, he led her across the lot toward the river.

Grace could see the shape more clearly now. She could see the railing. The cabin. The paddle wheel.

Her heels were sinking into the mud, and Zac put his arms behind her and picked her up. Grace kept her eyes on the riverboat and saw the moment the lights went on. White lights surrounding the canopy. She could see that the craft had been specially designed to navigate the Colorado, and as Zac carried her out onto the concrete launch ramp, she read the name on the bow.

Sam Sutter.

She couldn't talk, only look up at Zachary. He'd been waiting to see her eyes. Then he kissed her, and the kisses continued when they'd climbed aboard, after they'd shared a champagne toast with Nick and Day, their partners in the riverboat venture, after Nick and Day had vanished into the wheelhouse.

The sound of the engine changed, and Nick, the captain, headed the boat downstream. As the *Sam Sutter* carried them home to the River Inn, Zac stood with Grace in the shadows. He sang to her, held her, whispered things that excited them both. Bowed his head over her breasts where they curved above the sweetheart neckline of the taffeta slip-dress he'd bought her in New York more than two years earlier.

As the lights of the inn neared, they saw their home from the water. Seeing the familiar details of the structure, Zac felt a sense of belonging that he'd never experienced anywhere else, even at Oakhurst. He and Grace had made the River Inn theirs. Zac hoped someday one of their children would want to run it, to keep it lovely.

After saying good-night to Nick and Day, who would take the boat back up the river to Rapid Riggers, Zachary and Grace walked down the gangplank to the boat ramp. When they reached the shore, two dogs rushed at them, tails wagging. Ninochka dropped a Frisbee at Zac's feet. "Not now." He crouched and petted her. "Coupon, don't jump on Grace."

Kicking off her shoes to walk up the sandy bank, Grace petted the second dog, a short-legged one-eared mottled-brown mutt whose face looked as though it had been hit by a frying pan. "Hello, Coupon." When she'd first seen the dog, she'd told Zac, *If you want to keep it, you'll need to use a coupon.* Now Coupon slept on her side of the bed at night. He was a darling.

She and Zac held hands as they avoided the front door and walked around to the stone patio. Grace poked her head into the restaurant kitchen beside the Princess Room. Jill, her sous-chef, saw her and said, "Everything's cool. Great night."

Zac was tugging on her fingers. Grace stepped back out into the night. Accompanied by their dogs, they slipped along the patio and through the French doors into their bedroom, and Zac closed the blinds in case any guests were out roaming.

He turned to her, his lips slightly parted, his eyes like coal. Grace lifted her face, reached for his shoulders...

The Romeo and Juliet bed was massive, made of cherry wood with panels on the sides and on the headboard and a wide ledge all around. Zachary had made it with love for her, aware every minute of what they would do on it, that it was the bed of their marriage. Lovemaking and sleeping and dreaming and a shared future. A life raft.

Now, on the bed, he made love to her, watching her, loving her, going in deep, with his heart and his body and his seed. Aware of what they both hoped would happen. A baby. Made in love. Grace clung to him, shuddering, and Zac felt her squeezing him, taking him with her as the walls of their private quarters absorbed their cries of love.

Afterward, as she lay in his arms and the dogs staked out their spots on the king-size mattress, Grace said, "You were so good in the play, Zac. I know you could be a star. A big star. I always knew it. If you ever want to leave here and be a professional actor again, it's all right with me. As long as I can go with you of course."

Listening to her, Zac remembered the praise he'd received for *Kah-Puh-Rats*. He thought of who he'd been when he'd married Grace for a green card. The changes in him were deeper than she knew. It was enough to do what he loved, as he had tonight. Look out on the audience. See faces smiling, laughing or simply responding to the performance, to whatever spoke to them. Now he saw greater peace and wealth in the home they'd built together and in the tradition they'd restored. In standing outside in the desert night. Here the air was thin and clear, and the ancient lights in the sky seemed only a moment away.

He held his wife closer, kissed her hair, watched Coupon snuggled against her leg on top of the sheets. He said, "Why would I want to be a star when I can be an ordinary man and hold heaven in my arms?"

Grace smiled. Zac would never be ordinary.

He was a keeper.

THE VERANCHETTI MARRIAGE
by Lynne Graham

The Veranchetti Marriage originally appeared as a
Harlequin Presents® novel. Six new Presents® novels
featuring men of the world and captivating women
in sophisticated international settings
appear each month to guarantee you passion,
glamour and seduction!

HARLEQUIN PRESENTS®

phone call over her. The chances of that cumulating were negligible.

Will a rather valiant effort, she tilted her chin. "I wanted to come to the airport."

Mr Veronchetti pulled us as set, his son surely to the door of your...

"I'm perfectly capable of driving my own child home," she snapped sharply and turned abruptly from...

CHAPTER ONE

NICKY CAME hurtling through the crowd ahead of his escort and threw himself into his mother's arms like a miniature whirlwind. "Missed you," he confided, burying his dark head under her chin where unmanly tears could be decently concealed.

Kerry's arms encircled him tightly. He had been staying with his father for an entire month. Kerry had watched the calendar through every day of his absence, resenting the unusual silence echoing round the cottage and the emptiness of her weekends. As she slowly lowered her three-year-old son to the ground, she noticed the two dark-suited men lodged several feet away. Nicky's escorts.

One of them stepped forward coolly to say, "It really wasn't necessary for you to come to the airport, *signora*. We would have brought Nicky home as we usually do."

There was a studied insolence to the roaming sexual appraisal of his dark eyes. Involuntarily, Kerry's magnolia skin heated. She knew that she shouldn't allow Alex's security staff to browbeat her. But she did. She was nobody of importance on their scale. The discarded ex-wife, who didn't even enjoy a semicivilised post-divorce relationship with their employer. They could afford to be as rude and superior as they liked. They knew better than anybody that Alex wouldn't even take a phone call from her. The chances of her complaining were negligible.

With a rather valiant effort she lifted her chin. "I wanted to come to the airport."

"Mr Veranchetti prefers us to see his son safely to the door of your home, *signora*."

"I'm perfectly capable of driving my own child home," she muttered curtly, and turned deliberately away, seeking a fast escape from a confrontation in the center of Heathrow.

"Until the little boy reaches home he's our responsibility." A restraining hand actually fell on her tense shoulder.

She couldn't believe this was happening to her. That she was being bullied by a hired security man, who treated her child like Little Lord Fauntleroy. Nicky was her son. He might be Alex's as well, but did she have to stand for such treatment? It was totally destroying Nicky's homecoming. She was aware of her son's brown lustrous gaze fixed anxiously to her strained face, and she strove to behave calmly.

"When I'm here, he's my responsibility," she stated with a forced smile. "Really, this is quite ridiculous. All this argument simply because I chose to meet him off the plane…"

The other man had stepped forward too. In one hand he carried Nicky's case. A fast exchange of Italian took place over her slightly bowed head. Murderous feelings were struggling for utterance inside her. The past four years had been very tough for Kerry. What she could never accept was that they should continue getting tougher. Alex was zealously trying to wean Nicky from her for longer and longer periods, and she had an absolute wimp of a solicitor, who was always sympathetic but equally trenchant in his view that her ex-husband was not a man to antagonise.

"Mr Veranchetti wouldn't be pleased." It was the older man who spoke now for the first time.

He talked as if Alex was God. Or maybe the Devil, she conceded abstractedly. People always employed that impressed-to-death tone when they referred to her ex. It had got to the stage where Kerry's blood chilled in her veins whenever he was mentioned. Alex had turned into a remote, untouchable figure of power and incalculable influence long before he had divorced her. It was humiliating to acknowledge that Alex's treatment of her in recent years had left her frankly petrified of him.

But today she suddenly found herself deciding that enough was enough. Nicky was hers and they were—believe it or not—on British soil. She didn't have to stand here being intimidated by Alex's henchmen. There was an angry flash in her copper-lashed green eyes as she stared at both stalwart figures. "Unfortunately, Mr Veranchetti's wishes don't carry the same weight with me," she murmured shortly, and stuck out her hand challengingly for her son's case.

After a perceptible hesitation it was handed over. The weight of it almost dislocated her wrist. She was a small woman and slenderly built. But, distinctly uplifted by her minor victory, she released a determined smile.

"Thank you," she said quietly.

"Why are Enzio and Marco cross?" Nicky hissed up at her in a loud stage-whisper.

"Oh, I'm sure they're not really cross," she replied cheerfully. "Give them a wave."

Nicky turned his curly dark head. "They're coming after us."

Well, if they wanted to waste time trailing in her wake out to the car park, that was their affair. She should have been firmer before now, she told herself bracingly. She shouldn't let strangers' opinions matter to her. But it was her conscience afoot, wasn't it? The fear that they knew why her marriage had broken up. That creepy, crawling and lowering fear that her sordid secret might be common knowledge among the higher echelons of Alex's security staff. It was that which invariably kept her silent: shame. Shame and guilt, even after four long years. *She* no longer felt she was worthy of respect, so she wasn't likely to be granted it by others.

"They're gone," Nicky said in some disappointment during their long trek to the van.

Kerry's tense shoulders eased a little. She lowered the case and changed it to her other hand. It was a cold, frosty morning, and her ankle-booted feet skidded on the whitened tarmac. She hunched deeper into her electric-blue cord duffle coat and quickened her pace to the blue van parked close to the fence. By the time she had got the case stowed in the rear and had settled in behind the wheel, she was beginning to notice how quiet Nicky was. Normally he was bubbling over with disjointed stories of where he had been, who he had been with and what a fantastic time he had had. For some reason his usual buoyancy was missing.

"Did you have a good time?"

"Oh, yes." He shot her a rather apprehensive smile as she reversed out of the space.

"So what did you do?" she encouraged.

"We went fishing 'n' swimming...and we went up

in the jet plane. Nuffin' special," he muttered, turning his small, serious face away.

No, she guessed it really wasn't anything special to Nicky. From no age at all he had been flying round the globe to rendezvous with his tycoon father. When he had been a baby, Alex had flown to London and a nanny had arrived in a chauffeur-driven car to collect Nicky and ferry him away for the day. But, as Nicky became less dependent on his mother and more familiar with his father, the day trips had gradually become weekends.

He was almost four now, an extremely bright and self-assured little boy. There was no nanny in attendance these days, and a phone call or a letter from Alex's London lawyer heralded arrangements for Nicky's sojourns abroad. Alex had unlimited access to Nicky. When Nicky had been a baby that hadn't bothered her. It had soon become clear that Alex did not intend to encroach too much then. The situation had changed quite rapidly over the past year, as Nicky left the toddler stage behind.

In infuriating addition, Nicky openly adored Alex. She had never been able to fathom that astonishing fact. Alex, so cold, so remote, so capable of sustaining implacable hatred for his child's mother...how could he inspire such trust and affection in Nicky? She could not imagine Alex bending to meet a three-year-old on his level. But it seemed that he did.

"Mummy, Daddy wants me to live with him."

Kerry's eyes were in the mirror, dazedly glued to the sight of the silver limousine nosing dexterously in behind the van. Her foot almost hit the brake as Nicky's statement penetrated. "What did you say?" she whispered sickly. "Say that again."

"He asked me if I'd like that," Nicky volunteered less abruptly.

Kerry let oxygen into her lungs again. What a sneaky, manipulative swine Alex was to ask that of a child Nicky's age! Just a conversation, though. Possibly the sort of conversation she might have had with Nicky had she been in Alex's shoes—the parent who got visits rather than round-the-clock privileges. It didn't mean that she had anything to worry about. After all, Alex hadn't put up a fight for custody when Nicky was born. Why should he now?

"What did you tell him?" she prompted carefully.

"Only if you come too. You see, I thought and thought and thought about it," Nicky assured her with subdued Latin melodrama. "And that's what I'd like the best of all, an' then I wouldn't have to miss you or Daddy."

Nicky's solution was touchingly innocent and hair-raisingly practical. He didn't understand divorce. How could he? He didn't even understand marriage. He had yet to see his parents in the same room together. Mummy and Daddy were entirely dissimilar people, who lived vastly divergent lives and with whom he did very different things. Her eyes stung with rueful tears, and she wished the limousine containing Enzio and Marco would stop crawling up her bumper. The van did not go at great speed up hills.

"And what did Daddy say?" she couldn't help demanding.

"Nothing. He looked cross," Nicky recalled unhappily.

Cross would have been an understatement, she envisaged with bitter humour. Was he trying to take Nicky away from her, or was she being paranoid?

"You still haven't told me what you did in Rome," she flipped the subject smoothly. "Did you go sailing?"

"Helena came too. She's nice. She's got lots of yellow hair."

"Oh." Kerry tried and failed to resist the bait. "Is she pretty?"

"Spectacular. Giuseppe says that. Does that mean pretty?"

She didn't ask who Giuseppe was. Alex had an enormous family of sisters and brothers and nephews and nieces with whom Nicky played when he was abroad. Veranchettis dotted the world. Milan, Rome, Athens, New York. So Alex had another ladyfriend...so what?

Alex had had one affair after another since their divorce. Vicky was very good about keeping Kerry up to date. Her sister had once been an international model. Although she had now retired and opened her own modelling agency, she still had a passport into high society circles, and in Europe Alex was pretty hot news. Helena...the name didn't ring a bell. She stifled the knife-like pain scything through her. It was bitterness and bile, not jealousy. Jealousy was what you suffered when you loved somebody, and Kerry had stopped loving Alex a long time ago.

She feared him and she hated him in equal parts. He had almost destroyed her. Alex didn't have a forgiving bone in his body. She might as well have beseeched compassion from a granite monolith! Her love had been beaten out of her soul, crushed just as he had crushed her with his distaste and his contempt.

The only good thing to come out of their marriage

was Nicky, but she had never doubted that Alex looked on Nicky's conception in a very different light because she was his mother. The fairy-tale marriage had turned into an unmitigated disaster. The dreams had finally turned to ashes, however, in her own clumsy hands. She attempted to dredge herself from her despondent thoughts and listen to Nicky's chatter. He had relaxed now that he had got Alex's question off his chest. He liked his world just the way it was. But would it always be like that?

"Daddy took me to the office and showed me Nonno's picture," Nicky rattled off importantly.

Kerry grimaced. Dear God, JR had nothing on Alex. Start 'em off young. Show him the empire. Show him the desk. She was darned if she wanted Nicky to become an industrialist like Alex. A sort of superior loanshark with a calculator for a brain and a heart which only beat a little faster in the direction of a balance sheet.

"That was nice," she said diplomatically.

"I'm going to be a fisherman when I grow up, like Guiseppe."

Not with Alex around, darling. Alex was a lethal mix of Greek and Italian genes, but they all had pedigreed beginnings. His mother had been a Greek shipping heiress, his father the son of an Italian tycoon. It was an explosive mixture, but not on the surface. Outwardly, Alex was twenty-two-carat gold sleek sophistication. Calm, concise, superbly controlled. Sometimes she wondered how she had ever been dumb enough to see other things in Alex. But eighteen-year-olds thought with their hearts and their bodies, not with their heads. They saw what they wanted to see. In her case, that had been a perfect world whose axis centred solely upon Alex. She hadn't seen to either side. She hadn't seen a single flaw. An amount of love which had bordered on obsession had blinded her.

It was starting to snow and she was getting angry about the persistent limousine still purring effortlessly along in her wake. Such nonsense! They had their orders, and like programmed robots they would go to ridiculous lengths to follow Alex's instructions to the last letter. Her shoulders ached with the tension of careful driving, and that monster rolling along on her trail was an added irritant.

It was a lengthy drive to the Hampshire village where she now lived. She owned a half-share in an antiques showroom there. Business had never exactly boomed, but she was within convenient distance of her parents' home. Nicky was very attached to his grandparents. He had strong ties here in England. Alex wouldn't find it that easy to sever those ties, she reflected tautly.

She rounded a twisting corner, still mentally enumerating all the advantages she had over Alex in the parent competition, and there it was. A big black and white cow stuck squarely stationary, dead centre of the road. A soundless scream of horror dammed up in her throat as she spun the wheel in what seemed a hopeless attempt to avoid collision with both the cow and the limousine behind her. On the icy road surface the van slewed into a skid. The hedge and the sky hurtled in a fast blur through the windscreen towards her. Something struck her head and the blackness folded in.

"NICKY!" Kerry surfaced with the scream still in her throat, the cry she had never got to make, except in her own mind. Firm hands pressed her back into the bed and her wild, unbound torrent of curly Titian hair flamed out across the pillow, highlighting the stark pallor of her features. "Nicky?" she croaked fearfully again.

"Your son is quite safe, Mrs Veranchetti." The voice was quiet, attached to a calm face beneath a nurse's cap.

The breath rattled in her clogged throat. She raised a hand to cover her aching head, and came in contact with the plaster on her temples. "He's really all right…?"

The nurse deftly straightened the bed. "He has a few bruises and he did get a fright."

"Oh, no!" Tears gritted her eyes in a shocked surge. "I must go to him. Where is he?"

"You must stay in bed, Mrs Veranchetti."

"My name's Taylor, not Veranchetti," she countered shakily. "And I want to be with my son."

The door opened. A tall, spare man in a white coat entered. "So, you're back with us again, Mrs Veranchetti," he pronounced with a jovial smile. "You've been unconscious for a few hours. You had a lucky escape."

"Mrs Taylor," the nurse stressed rather drily, making Kerry redden, "wishes to see her son."

"Your son's father is with him," the doctor announced. "You have nothing to worry about. Everything's under control."

"F-father…Alex?" Kerry gasped incredulously. "He's here?"

"He arrived two hours ago and your little boy is fine, Mrs…er…Mrs Taylor." He quirked a brow at the nurse, as if he was humouring some feminist display, and lifted Kerry's wrist.

Alex was here. Hell, where *was* here? She couldn't be that far from home. How could Alex be here? What time of day was it? Spock would have had a problem beaming up this fast! She sighed. Alex would have been informed immediately of the accident, with his own staff on the scene.

"Calm down, Mrs Taylor. I've told you there's nothing whatsoever to worry about. We intend to keep you in overnight purely for observation."

"I can't stay in...does that mean Nicky's ready to go home?"

"His father said he would take responsibility."

Something akin to panic assailed Kerry. Would Alex blame her for the accident? No, how could he do that? It wasn't her fault that she had been faced with a straying cow. Or her fault his wretched henchmen had been crawling up her bumper! But Alex, here in the same building...her blood ran cold.

"I think a sedative would be a good idea," the doctor murmured, as if she had suddenly gone deaf.

"I don't want a sedative." She started to sit up again. "I'm sorry, but I'm not ill."

"You're still in shock, Mrs Taylor."

Ignoring him, she wrenched back the covers. Her head was swimming. She ought to be with Nicky. She stilled. Not if Alex was there, too. She wasn't up to that. After four years, she would sooner face an oncoming train than Alex. Oddly enough, their last meeting had been in a hospital, too, staged hours after Nicky's birth. Her temples pounded with driven tension. Absently, she righted the bedding again in cowardice.

"Please lie down." The nurse's tone was softly soothing, implying that she was some kind of trying hysteric.

"You won't let him in?" She collapsed back heavily again, the fight drained from her.

"Who?"

"My ex-husband." She shut her eyes. She was both embarrassed and wretched. It wasn't adult. It wasn't normal to be this afraid of a mere meeting. But, nevertheless, fear was a wild creature within her. Nebulous, instinctive, illogical.

"If that's your wish." The older man met the nurse's eyes. Neither of them saw the point of telling the patient that her ex-husband had already been in for a considerable length of time while she still lay unconscious.

Kerry breathed again, although she was still trembling, wrenched by the knowledge of Nicky's distress and her own absence from his side. A needle pricked her arm and she shuddered in reflex reaction before her lashes slowly dipped.

"She's terrified of him," the nurse said in an avid undertone. "Did you notice that? I wonder what...?"

"Ours not to reason why, nurse," he parried drily. "And Mrs Veranchetti is obviously a very emotional woman."

The blonde staff nurse continued to study Kerry with overt curiosity. Her narrow-boned and slight body barely made a decent impression on the bed. She looked too youthful to be a divorcee, but the masses of flamboyant and beautiful hair and the delicately pointed face were undeniably stunning. Though Alex Veranchetti was equally worthy of remark, the nurse allowed with a reflective smile.

She had never met a more staggeringly attractive man. Those eyes, she recalled, that delicious growling accent. But she hadn't fancied him quite so much when he stood silently staring down at his ex-wife, not a muscle moving on his face, just staring in a set, uncommonly intent yet unemotional fashion, as if she was nothing whatsoever to do with him. Only when he had enquired if a specialist had been called had she noticed his pallor. But while he had consulted with the doctor he had studiously removed his eyes from the bed, and he had not looked back there again.

It was early evening when Kerry awoke. Light was fading beyond the uncurtained window high up in the wall. Memory came flooding back. Nicky. Alex. She glanced at her watch and found it missing, a patient's plastic identity tag clasped to her wrist in its place. This time she registered that she was in a private room, and she wondered how she would settle the bill.

Steven would be worrying about her, too. Her partner in Antiques Fayre was a furniture restorer. He used the workshop at the rear of the showroom, and by now, although time frequently had no meaning for him, he would be wondering where she was. She had promised to call in on the way home. A drone of voices could be heard beyond the door. She resolved to ask for her clothes. She had to get home, find out about Nicky…oh, a dozen things!

As the door opened she sat up, wincing at the renewed throb behind her temples. A light came on, momentarily blinding her before she froze in astonishment, the colour draining from her cheeks.

"I see you are awake," Alex commented, glossing over her incoherent gasp of shock at his appearance. He shut the door, and for several unbearably tense seconds he simply remained at the foot of the bed, studying her.

Dull-eyed and trembling, she dropped her head. He was etched in her mind's eyes with the utmost clarity. He looked so damnably beautiful. It wasn't the usual

word to describe the male of the species, but it was particularly relevant to Alex. He had the dark, perfect features of a fallen angel, and the lean, honed-to-sleekness
elegance of a graceful leopard. He was unchanged. He
hadn't dropped the remorseless, glittering stare which
looked right through her, either.

She could not help but relive their last meeting. "I
have made arrangements for you to return to England
with our son," he had delivered coldly then before leaving her again, impervious to the tears and the agony he
must have seen in her face as he destroyed her last hopes
of a reconciliation. Her hands clutched together convulsively. Pull yourself together, a little voice warned. He
had pulled her apart. She was still a heap of jittery and
torn pieces, unlikely ever to achieve wholeness again.
To do that, you had to forgive yourself first. You had to
like yourself. You had to put the past in its proper place.
And Kerry hadn't managed any of that.

The gleaming, amber-gold challenge of his gaze im-
parted one undeniable message. He hadn't forgotten. She
hadn't forgotten, either. How could she forget that she
had wrecked their marriage by doing something quite
beyond the bounds of forgiveness?

"I am told that you didn't want to see me." The
heavy silence buzzed back into her ears.

It was cat and mouse. Go on, snap me up, Alex.
You've done it before, you'll do it again. What's holding
you up now? She threaded a nervous hand through the
wild tumble of her hair. Accidentally looking up, she
caught his magnificent lion-gold eyes following the careless movement of her fingers.

"I hardly thought that you'd want to see me." She
chickened out of a direct attack. She didn't really have

the right to condemn. It was that sense of being in the wrong, that enforced acceptance of blame which had almost driven her to the brink of a nervous breakdown when she was pregnant with Nicky.

Alex strolled fluidly over to the window to stare out, presenting his hard-edged profile to her. "Naturally I wish to discuss the accident with you."

She shut her eyes on an agonising surge of bitterness. Of course, what else. Four years ago he had refused even to see her to discuss their marriage. He had denied her calls, returned her letters and made it cruelly clear to her that he no longer considered her as his wife. But... naturally...he could pitch himself up to the contaminated air she breathed now to request an explanation of an accident.

"You find something amusing in this?" Alex shot her a grimly implacable glance.

She went even paler. "No, there's nothing funny about any of it. It's quite simple really. I went round a corner and there was a cow in the middle of the road. When I tried to avoid it, the van skidded and went sideways, making it virtually impossible for the...car behind us to avoid hitting us."

"And this is all you have to say?" Alex prompted.

She had no doubt that he had heard a different story from his security men. A story which showed her in the worst of lights. Perhaps they had implied that she had been driving too fast on icy roads, recklessly endangering Nicky's life.

"Yes, that's all I have to say," she agreed heavily, pleating the starched white sheet beneath her hand with restless fingers. "I don't believe I could have avoided the collision."

"My staff did not mention an animal..."

Her control snapped. "Well, I can assure you that there was one, but I know who you're going to believe, don't I? So it would be a waste of time pleading my own case!" she threw at him bitterly. "Now, if we can cut the kangaroo court, perhaps you'd tell me how Nicky is."

Disconcerted by her abrupt loss of temper, his straight ebony brows drew together above his narrowed eyes. "I will not have you speak to me in such a tone," he breathed icily.

She hadn't intended to shout, but she found that she didn't feel like apologising. They weren't married now. The past could not permit them to be even distantly polite with each other. Alex had made it that way by shutting her out and communicating with her only through third parties. His unyielding hostility had killed the love she had once had for him. She had accepted the new order. He had no right to subject her to a face-to-face meeting now.

"There's nothing very much that you can do about it, Alex," she dared. "I don't jump through hoops when you tell me to any more, I don't..."

"Do continue. You're becoming extremely interesting," he derided softly, but his tone was misleading.

Kerry's voice had trailed away to silence under the smouldering blaze of fury she had ignited in Alex's eyes. Nobody talked to Alex like that. In all probability, nobody ever had. And certainly not the wife he had repudiated. Her fiery head lowered again. What had got into her? If her solicitor had been here, he would have been white to the gills over such reckless provocation.

"I've got nothing more to say," she muttered through compressed lips.

His gaze rested on her rigidity, then sank to her unsteady hands, and an expression of bleak dissatisfaction tautened his hard bone structure. "Nicky is with your parents. There was no need for him to remain in hospital."

"My parents?" Kerry echoed in dismay. "He's with my parents?"

Alex elevated a brow. "Did I not say so?"

"But...but that means..." She swallowed hard, but her face was full of unconcealed horror. "You must have gone there as well."

"Yes, and what a fascinating experience that was." Alex savoured the admission visibly. "You never told them the truth, did you? They have no idea why we are divorced. They also appear to be under the illusion that you chose to divorce me."

Her heartbeat was thudding in her ears. She had no defence against his condemnation, and could only imagine how her parents would have greeted Alex's sudden descent. They would have been polite and they would have been very hospitable. Her father was a retired vicar. Neither of her parents approved of the divorce, or of the fashion in which Nicky was being raised by parents who never even spoke to each other. They had never left Kerry in any doubt that they still regarded Alex as her husband. For better or for worse. Vows taken for a lifetime and not to be discarded at the first hiccup in marital harmony. Stricken nausea churned in her stomach at the idea of Alex and her parents getting within talking distance of each other.

"I couldn't tell them!" she burst out on the peak of

a sob which quivered through her tense body. "It was bad enough when I first came home. The truth would have shattered them."

"The truth shattered me as well," he delivered harshly, and turned aside from her. "But to return to the present...had you given me an opportunity to speak earlier, you would have realised that I do not blame you for the accident."

CHAPTER TWO

SUCH unexpected generosity upon Alex's part shook her. Surprise showed in her strained features, and his hard mouth took on a sardonic curve. "Nicky gave me his version of the accident. It matched yours. The men concerned will be dismissed," he revealed flatly.

"For...for what?" Kerry whispered, doubly shaken.

"You could both have been killed," Alex retorted harshly. "But, apart from that, I will not tolerate lies or half-truths from anyone close to me."

Or deception, or betrayal. There were no second chances with Alex; Kerry knew that to her cost. In the pool of silence, she was pained by his detachment, the almost chilling politeness which distinguished his attitude. She meant nothing to him, but Nicky did. Nicky was a Veranchetti, and Alex's precious son and heir.

"Your van is, I believe, beyond repair," he continued with the same devotion to practical matters. "I will have it replaced."

She bit her lip. "That's unnecessary."

"Allow me to decide what is necessary," Alex cut in ruthlessly. "Do you think I do not know how you live? Were it not for my awareness that Nicky goes without nothing that he needs, I would have objected to your independence."

She said nothing. She was infuriated by his arrogant

downgrading of the business she had worked hard to build up. He could keep his wretched money! She had never wanted it. It was a matter of pride to her that she was self-sufficient. And by being so she had won the cherished anonymity of reverting to her maiden name and finding somewhere to live where she was simply a woman living alone with her child. There were no headlines in Kerry's life now.

"I want to go home tonight," she told him.

"That would be most foolish."

She thrust up her chin. "I have business which happens to be very important to take care of tomorrow."

"You have a partner." There was an icy whiplash effect to the reminder. She reminded herself that Alex did not like anyone to argue with him.

"He'll be away tomorrow. In any case, I want to take Nicky home."

Alex viewed her grimly. "Nicky is in bed, and perfectly happy to be with his grandparents. Leave him there until you are fit again," he advised. "Even to me, it is obvious that you are still in a very emotional state."

A humourless laugh leapt from her lips. "And you're surprised?"

He lifted a broad shoulder in an unfeeling shrug. All of a sudden Kerry was on the brink of tears, and she wished that he would leave. So many times she had imagined what she might say to Alex if she ever received the opportunity. Not once had she dreamt that it might turn out to be so harrowing. A barrier the size of the Berlin Wall separated them now. Alex despised her. Alex, she sensed with an inner shudder, still believed that she had got off lightly, without the punishment he would have liked to have dealt her.

"You will be hearing from my lawyers in the near future," Alex said, consulting the slim, gold watch on his wrist, and she had an insane vision of legal reps leaping out from beneath her bed. "It's time that Nicky's future is discussed. He will soon be of an age to start school."

Dumbly she nodded, without noticing the intent appraisal he gave her. "Yes. I know."

"I am afraid I have an appointment in London now." He was looking at the door, and she had the peculiar suspicion that Alex, insensitive or otherwise, was suddenly very eager to be gone. "I have naturally taken care of the bill here. When you are home again, I will call on you there," he completed almost abruptly.

Her lashes fluttered dazedly. "My home? But why?" she demanded apprehensively.

"I will phone before I call," he responded drily, and then he was gone.

Had he suddenly accepted the need for consultation between them concerning Nicky? Dear God, she preferred his use of third parties now! Fearfully, she wondered what exchanges had taken place between Alex and her parents, and whether something they had said had brought about this surprising change of heart. She shrank from the threat of another distressing session with Alex. It was much too late now for her to be civilised. She didn't want Alex visiting her humble home, invading her cherished privacy and doubtless bringing alive again all those horrible feelings she had become practised at suppressing.

"Well, hi…"

Kerry glanced up in astonishment to see her half-sister

posing in the doorway, her tall, slender figure enveloped in an oversized fur coat. "Vickie?"

"No need to look so surprised," she reproved, strolling in. "I came home for the weekend. I got the shock of my life when I walked in and found Alex sitting there. When I realised he was calling back here to actually see you, I reckoned you'd need back-up. I've been sitting out in the car park waiting for his car to leave. He didn't stay long, did he?"

Kerry was very relieved to see Vickie. Her sister was the one person alive who could understand what she must be feeling now. Yet, paradoxically, they had never been particularly close. Kerry had barely been thirteen when Vickie left home, keen to escape her frequent clashes with strict parental authority. Since then fences had gradually been mended, but Vickie still remained something of a mystery to Kerry. Cool, offhand, not given to personal confidences and very much a party girl, Vickie had, nevertheless, become Kerry's confidante. But the secrets they shared had still failed to break down Vickie's essential reserve. After a brief phase of greater intimacy during her marriage, Vickie had once more become a rather patronising older sister with whom Kerry had little in common. They invariably met only in their parents' home. But the watery smile curving Kerry's mouth was warmly affectionate.

"No, he didn't stay long. He only wanted to question me about the accident."

Vickie tossed her pale golden hair, her bright blue eyes pinned piercingly to her younger sister's face. "And that's all?" she probed tautly. "He didn't touch on anything else?"

Kerry didn't pretend not to understand her meaning.

"Why should he have? We are divorced," she sighed. "But he still loathes me. I could see it in him. The condemnation, the disgust, the…"

"Oh, for God's sake, give it a rest!" The interruption was harsh, exasperated, as Vickie flicked a lighter to the cigarette in her mouth and inhaled deeply. "Why wind yourself up about it? With Nicky in existence, you were bound to meet sooner or later," she pointed out, and shrugged. "You know, I couldn't sit about at home any longer listening to the parents pontificating on the possibility of you and Alex getting back together again. The two of them are so naïve sometimes. Goodness knows what Dad was saying to Alex before I arrived. He's been dying for years to preach at him."

Guilty colour marked Kerry's complexion as she watched her sister pace restlessly. It must have been very embarrassing for Vickie to walk into such a fraught scenario. After all, she knew the truth behind her sister's broken marriage, and she had loyally kept that secret when she might genuinely have felt it her right to speak up. Kerry swallowed the constriction in her throat. She would never be free of her own conscience, as it was.

"Do you know what was said?" she pressed anxiously. Her father was a warm and kindly man, but her divorce had shocked him to the core. Her refusal to discuss her failed marriage had created a constraint between them which had not lessened over the years.

"Alex didn't drop you in it, obviously." Vickie made no bones about what Kerry feared. "They'd have been in need of resuscitation when I got there if he had! Stop fussing, Kerry. Their fond hopes aren't likely to be realised. Do you know why they're not here now? They knew Alex was coming so they decided to stay home. But he'll hardly be visiting again, will he?''

So relieved was she by her sister's assurance that Alex had not reviled her in any way that Kerry barely heard what followed. She slid her feet over the edge of the bed and breathed in. ''Will you give me a lift home?''

''Sure. I brought your handbag and your clothes. They gave them to Alex. I'll go out to the car and collect them. I wasn't sure you would be fit enough to leave.'' Vickie eyed her pallor consideringly. ''You don't look too hot.''

''I'll be fine after a night's sleep. Anyway, I've got that American buyer coming tomorrow. I can't afford not to be there for him.''

Vickie made no comment. She had never shown much interest in her sister's business. It was in no way as successful as her own modelling agency. But the dealer, Willard Evans, who regularly bought at Antiques Fayre, was a very important customer to Kerry. It might irritate Steven that Willard probably made a three hundred per cent profit on their finds back home in the States, but Kerry never looked a gift horse in the mouth. Since the building of the new bypass they had considerably less passing trade, and she was equally aware that, talented restorer or not, Steven was no businessman.

They were generally overstocked. Steven bought what he fancied at auctions, rather than what was likely to sell. Without the dealer's visits she believed they would have run into trouble over the poorest months of trading, although she had to admit that their bank manager had always been very reasonable when they had exceeded their overdraft facility.

She thought longingly of home, and wished she could go there, instead of back to the empty cottage. Unfortunately there would be too many questions after Alex's visit. She couldn't face those at a moment when she was wretchedly conscious of the mess she had made of her life. Confession might be good for the soul, but it would create great unhappiness for her parents. She seriously doubted that they would find it possible to forgive her. How could they understand what she could not understand herself?

She had been brought up strictly. Her mother had met John Taylor when she was already well into her thirties. He had been a widower with a three-year-old daughter and a busy parish to maintain. Many had saluted his second marriage as one of extreme good sense. Kerry had never been in any doubt, however, that her parents were quietly devoted to each other. Within a year of their wedding Kerry had been born. Her childhood might reasonably have been described as having been idyllic. Unlike Vickie, she had had few stormy encounters with their parents during the teenage years.

Vickie had left home to become a model. In no time at all her true English rose beauty had ferried her up to the top of the ladder. By the time she was twenty-two, Vickie was a success story, renting a small apartment off Grosvenor Place. The summer that Kerry finished school, Vickie had suggested that Kerry use her apartment while she was abroad.

"It's lying empty, and to tell the truth I'd prefer it occupied," she had admitted. "You'll look after my things. Isn't it about time you cut loose from the nest? If you don't watch out, they'll stifle you."

The Taylors had approved neither of Kerry's delight nor Vickie's generosity. But Kerry had been obstinate in her desire to spend some time in London. She had even managed to find herself a temporary job in a nearby travel agency.

"Just wait until you see the guy who uses the penthouse on the top floor," Vickie had murmured before she left, giving Kerry the lowdown on her neighbours. "He's devastating, but I'm never here long enough to make an impression. Anyhow," she had laughed, "I guess he's not really my type. He's as conservative as hell. I stuck my neck out once and invited him to a party. He passed, giving me the hint that I shouldn't have asked in the first place. Watch you don't make a lot of noise. He also happens to own this building."

Kerry had almost sent Alex flying on the day she moved in. She had come rushing full-tilt out of the lift as he was trying to enter it, and they had collided, sending the file in his hand skimming over the floor. With her usual sunny cheer she had scrabbled about picking up scattered papers and chattering about the amount of work he brought home with him. She had received the most glacial smile.

It had had no effect on her at all. She had taken her first proper look at him and her knees had gone wobbly. Devastating, Vickie had said rather scornfully. That combination of black hair and golden eyes had more than devastated Kerry. "Gosh, you'd make a marvellous portrait study," she had said crassly, getting abstractedly back into the lift with him.

"I assumed you were going out," he had drawled flatteningly. "Do you normally speak to strangers like this?"

"Oh, I'm Kerry Taylor, Vickie's kid sister...you must know Vickie. Tall, blonde; she's a model. She lives on the fourth floor."

"I do not," he had interposed drily.

She had reddened. "Well, I'm staying here this summer. I thought you might be wondering who I was. That's why I explained."

"Your floor," Alex had slotted into the nervous flood, stopping the lift on the correct level and making it impossible for her to do anything but remove herself.

His unfriendliness had been an unpleasant surprise. Kerry had been born and brought up in a small community where she knew everybody. The anonymity of city life had been a shock to her system. But in her inimitable way she had made friends wherever she could. The security men in the foyer had quickly got on to first-name terms with her as she flashed in and out, generally late wherever she was going or rushing back for something she had forgotten.

Alex had only used his apartment when he was at his London office. She hadn't known that then. Nor had she even begun to realise how wealthy he was. She had seen him regularly, stepping in and out of his chauffeur-driven car. And the women...Vickie had not warned her about the women.

She came in late one night from a party, and ended up sharing the lift with Alex and a svelte brunette. It had hit her that night that she was always looking out for Alex, and that the days she didn't see him were distinctly empty ones. Meeting him with the sort of mature woman she naturally could not compete with had turned her stomach over sickly. She hadn't been that naïve. She had known very well that he wasn't bringing a woman home in the early hours to play Scrabble. And it had hurt her. She could still remember standing in that lift, mutinously not speaking as she usually did, and feeling hatefully, agonisingly young.

"Goodnight, Kerry," Alex had murmured silkily, almost as if he knew what was on her mind.

She hadn't slept that night. She had paced the lounge, asking herself what kind of baby she was to let herself become obsessed by a male who didn't know she was alive.

A week later she had accidentally locked herself out of the apartment. The caretaker had been out, the security guard sympathetic but unable to help beyond offering to force the door for her. In her innocence she had imagined that Alex might have keys and, screwing up her courage, she had gone upstairs. His manservant had only allowed her as far as the hall. Alex had frowned the instant he saw her. "To what do I owe the honour?" he had demanded drily.

But he had laughed when she muttered about her hope that he had a key. He had asked her if she would like to join him for supper. While she ate he had dredged out her life story and her ambition to study Fine Art at university. His manservant had intervened to announce that the caretaker was now available, and Alex had appraised her disappointed face and said, "Would you like to dine with me some evening?"

"When?" she had breathed, making no attempt to conceal her delight, and he had laughed again. That was how it had begun.

From the start she had feared that Alex thought she was too immature for him. At thirty, he was already head of the empire his late father had left him. As the eldest in his family he had assumed weighty responsibilities at an early age. In comparison, Kerry had been between school and university, and as carefree and unfailingly cheerful as Alex was serious. It was an attraction of opposites. Her dippy sense of humour and her penchant for disorganisation had fascinated Alex...but much against his will.

Their short courtship had been erratic. Alex had tried to keep their relationship cool. Kerry had been wildly and quite frantically in love with him, and probably the whole world including Alex had been painfully conscious of the fact. The one strong card she had had then, without even realising it, was Alex's almost fanatical possessiveness. One afternoon her door had been answered by another man when Alex called unexpectedly.

Roy had been one of Vickie's friends. He had only come to collect stuff that Vickie had let him store in her guest room. Kerry had merely offered him coffee. Alex had misunderstood. By the time that was cleared up, all pretence of playing it cool was over. Alex was laying down the law like Moses off the Mount. Somehow he had started to kiss her, and not as he had indulgently kissed her before. Things had got out of hand and perhaps, knowing Alex, they had done so more by design than accident. He had swept her off to bed in a passionate and stormy mood. Afterwards he had looked down at her and murmured, "Now you are mine, and damn your age, we're going to get married."

It had been a breathless, whirlwind romance. Alex had bowled her parents over with his well-bred drawl and cool self-assurance. Kerry had not had a similar effect upon his family. She had soon appreciated that, behind the polite, cosmopolitan smiles, they all thought Alex was marrying beneath him and, what was more, choosing a female totally untutored in the talents required of a Veranchetti wife.

But, possessed as she had believed herself to be of Alex's love, Kerry had had no doubts. Their beautiful wedding had been followed by a fabulous honeymoon in the West Indies. Alex had then calmly dumped her in Rome with his mother. Athene had disliked Kerry on sight and nothing had given Athene more pleasure than when she was guilty of some social or fashionable gaffe. Within six months, even Kerry's even temper was strained. Confined as she was to an existence of idle ease, it had seemed to her that Alex had only married her to imprison her. He jetted back from abroad, swept her arrogantly off to bed and brushed aside her justifiable complaints with a maddening air of masculine indulgence.

He thought she was too young to run a household of her own. He didn't think she ought to travel with him. All the women in his family had always stayed very properly at home, awaiting their menfolk. The first cracks had come early in their marriage. Lonely, isolated by her poor Italian and family indifference, Kerry had been quietly clambering up the walls when Vickie took a job with a Venetian fashion house.

Against Alex's wishes she had gone to Venice to spend a week with her sister. Alex had flown into Venice and dragged her out of Vickie's apartment as if she was a misbehaving child. She had flatly refused to go home with him. She had not given way. As a result, Alex had labelled Vickie a bad influence.

Amazingly he had, however, agreed to buy them their own house shortly after that episode. They had moved to Florence, and while Alex had grudgingly said that

Vickie was welcome to visit, he had not been prepared for Kerry to visit Vickie in Venice again. The crunch had come over Vickie's birthday party. Alex had been in London when she phoned him to ask him to attend the party with her.

She had already been in Venice when she called, which had not precisely soothed Alex's ruffled feathers. "You realise that if you remain there you are putting our marriage in serious jeopardy," he had smouldered down the phone. "*Per Dio* I was wrong to marry a head-strong teenager, but do we have to advertise our differences to the world?"

He had also cast several unforgivable remarks on her sister's moral principles. Kerry had come off the phone angry and upset.

"I warned you," Vickie had drawled ruefully. "Foreigners are different. Alex would have given you a marvellous affair, but he's no fun at all as a husband. My God, he's locked you up and thrown away the key! He's made you pregnant because he wants to tie you down even more. Don't you see what he's doing to you? He's suffocating you!"

Sooner than cast a wet blanket over Vickie's enjoyment that evening, she had done her best to put up a sparkling front. She remembered little about the later stages of that crowded party. She did recall dancing with an American photographer called Jeff, and he had made her laugh. She must have had too much to drink. The next morning, Vickie had frantically shaken her awake and Jeff had been lying in the bed beside her. A split second later Alex had appeared in the doorway, and if she hadn't been pregnant, she honestly believed that Alex would have killed her there and then in the kind of crime of passion Latin countries understood. Without a single word he had turned on his heel and strode out of the apartment.

Jeff had beat an incredibly fast retreat. Kerry had simply been in shock, horrified that she had gone to bed with another man. Vickie had blamed herself for the whole scenario.

"I didn't give a hoot what you did last night," she had cried. "I thought it was time you got to let your hair down, but how could I have known that Alex was going to arrive at seven in the morning and practically force his way in?"

It hadn't been Vickie's fault. In a maudlin, depressed state of mind, Kerry had had to accept that she had fallen into bed with a virtual stranger. It was an unbelievable six months before she set eyes on Alex again. She had returned to their home in Florence to find that he had moved out. Within a week a lawyer arrived and served separation papers on her. It had seemed so important to her then to try and tell Alex that Jeff had not made love to her. A woman knew when she had made love, just as Kerry had known later that day when she calmed down enough to be sensible.

In response she had tried hard to trace Jeff before she left Venice, desperately grasping at the hope that he would tell her exactly what had taken place between them. Unpleasant as she would have found such an embarrassing confrontation, at least she would have had the proper facts. And at the back of her mind had lurked the rather naïve prayer that Jeff might have some mitigating circumstance to proffer, or even some innocent explanation which would turn the entire episode into a storm in a teacup.

But she hadn't even had a surname or an address to work on. Vickie had disclaimed all knowledge of him, confessing that she didn't even know who had brought him to her party, and voicing the opinion that it was a matter best left alone. In her unsuccessful efforts to find him, Kerry had clutched at straws, stubbornly refusing to see the point. That she had been touched at all would be sufficient for Alex. A kiss, a caress, a shameful frolic in the dark...it made no difference. It was not the degree of the offence, but the betrayal of trust.

Those months of pregnancy in Florence had been a nightmare. She had stayed indoors all the time, torturing herself hour by hour with guilt, and praying that Alex would eventually relent enough to visit her. He hadn't. His family had left her alone, too. Heaven knew what he had told them. She had finally had to face the fact that Alex had not been satisfied with his marriage before Vickie's party. Why then should he even be prepared to listen to her when she had broken her marital vows?

"We're here. Why are you so damned quiet?" Vickie complained.

Sprung back to the present, Kerry peered out at the gloom of her unlit cottage. Vickie dropped her bag on her lap. "Thanks," Kerry sighed. "Are you going home again?"

"No, I'm driving back to town." Vickie stared at her with disconcerting anger. "Honestly, you look practically suicidal. Alex isn't worth any more grief. He was a lousy husband. He was the most selfish, tyrannical, narrow-minded bastard I ever came across. I thought he was about to strangle you that day!"

"Vickie," she implored wearily.

"You can't still be that sensitive. So you went to bed

with another man! Do you think darling Alex spent all those business trips of his sleeping alone? You still have a lot to learn about rich European men,'' she condemned cynically.

Sometimes she had wished he *had* killed her that day. Instead he had deprived her of the one thing she could not live without then. Him.

REFUSING EVEN A CUP of coffee, Vickie drove off. Disappointed by her quick departure, Kerry tiredly unlocked her own front door. Empty. She felt so achingly empty. The cottage was freezing cold. She didn't bother putting on a light. Lifting the phone off the hook in the hall, she passed by into her room and stripped on the spot before sliding into the icy unwelcome of the bed. Ever since the divorce she had kept a strict control on her emotions, and it had worked. Nothing had ever hurt her since. It hadn't worked with Alex today. It would have been a wondrous gift to be frozen and emotion-free with him.

She fell into a doze around dawn. The doorbell woke her up. Her drowsy eyes fixed on the alarm clock, but it had stopped. She crawled out of bed, shivering in the morning chill. Yanking on her robe, she hurried to answer the door.

''I did attempt to phone when I realised that you had left the hospital last night,'' Alex drawled sardonically. ''But your phone appears to be lying off the hook.''

''Alex...'' Kerry curled back behind the door, much as if a black mamba had appeared on the step. Peering round the edge, she said, ''Could...could you come back in an hour?''

''Don't be ridiculous!'' His hand firmly thrust the door wider and he stepped in, flicking an unreadable glance over her. "I warned you that you should stay in hospital."

Alex could always be depended on to say, I told you so. She reddened, miserably conscious of being caught on the hop. He looked sickeningly immaculate in an expensively tailored dove-grey suit. "I'll go and get dressed," she muttered, and pressed the door of the lounge open reluctantly. "You can wait in there."

After a quick wash she pulled on jeans and a sweater. When she walked into the lounge he was standing almost on top of the electric fire with all three bars burning. She studied his dark, urbane face and clear, golden eyes from beneath the veil of her lashes. Tension hummed in the air in a tangible wave.

Abruptly she dragged her eyes from him. "Exactly why are you here, Alex?"

CHAPTER THREE

"I WANT to discuss Nicky with you."

Kerry sank nervously down on to an overstuffed chesterfield and studied Alex's hand-stitched shoes. Icy fingers of dread were clutching at her heart. "I don't feel so great today," she muttered apologetically. "Couldn't we leave this to some other time?"

Alex expelled his breath harshly. "No, we cannot."

"My throat's sore." She edged up shakily again on the limp lie. "I'm going to make coffee. Do you want one?"

"You're..."

She walked out of the room and slid down heavily again on to a chair in the kitchen. Alex was here to tell her that he intended to take Nicky away from her. It would be very like Alex to deliver the death-blow personally. It still astonished her that he had not sought custody when Nicky was born. In an Italian court, as a foreigner with a charge of adultery hanging over her, she would not have had a prayer of retaining her son. Last night she had not let herself think about what he might mean. She had blocked the fear out. But was it likely that Alex would condescend to visit merely to discuss nursery education? Who was she trying to kid?

"I don't want coffee," Alex said icily from somewhere behind her.

"I don't really care what you want or don't want," she admitted without even turning her head. "But you are not getting Nicky. I'll fight you to the death before I'll let you have him."

"This is scarcely a discussion."

"Look it up in a dictionary, Alex," she advised tonelessly. "You'll discover you have never had one."

He pulled out a chair opposite and sat down. He looked alien against the backdrop of her homely kitchen. In the pin-drop silence she studied the scarred pine table surface. Alex twice in twenty-four hours was too much to be borne. He should not have come without the prior warning he had promised. Overly conscious of her sleepy, make-up-bare face and jeans, she was mortified. It annoyed her to think that he was probably looking at her now and reflecting that he had had a lucky escape.

"Have you finished?"

She wanted to smash something. The derisive tone bit like acid. "Just get on with what you came to say," she prompted thinly. "I've got to be at the showroom for eleven."

The dark-lashed brilliance of his eyes clashed with hers. She was too angry to try and veil the loathing in her own gaze. His proud bone structure hardened. "I believe you know what I am here to...talk about."

She went back to scrutinising the table, her slight frame taut as a drawn bow.

"I'm no longer prepared to play so minor a part in my son's life. Once he starts school, how often will I be able to see him?"

"Holidays...weekends," she supplied woodenly.

"Apart from the fact that that is insufficient, I happen to live abroad. When he is at school he won't be able to fly hundreds of miles just for a couple of days. It is time that changes were made,'' he delivered in the same coolly measured tone. "Why should I suffer my son to become a stranger to me? It is not my fault that we are divorced. I remind you of that not out of any desire to be unpleasant. I merely state a fact.''

Kerry had gone very pale. Beneath her sweater a trickle of perspiration ran down between her breasts. He knew exactly how and when to insert the knife. Alex considered himself wronged. She was the sinner, but she was most unfairly the guardian of their son.

"What is this man Glenn to you?"

Her Titian head flew back in surprise. "Steven? What has Steven got to do with this?'' she demanded blankly.

Alex lounged back in the chair, perfectly calm, one brown hand resting loosely on the table. He might have been sitting in on a board meeting. "I asked you a question.''

"Well, you can go sing for the answer!'' she snapped lunging jerkily out of her chair. Suddenly she saw what Alex was getting at. If he took her to court, he would do whatever he had to do to put up the toughest fight. If that meant smearing her reputation to suggest that she was an unfit mother, he would not retreat from the challenge. When Alex went out to get anything, he put his whole heart in the venture.

Steven was a good friend and her partner. Occasionally he ate here. Sometimes he took her out for a meal when Nicky was away, but those social pairings took place with his girlfriend Barbara's agreement. A nurse with the International Red Cross, Barbara spent very little time in England. They had been in love since they were teenagers, but it was an erratic relationship, spiced by long periods of silence because Steven was reluctant to embrace the responsibility of marriage. He was content as he was, and too lazy to stray when Barbara was unavailable. But why should Kerry explain Steven's love life to Alex? It was none of Alex's business.

A hard hand spun her round. His fingers exerted pressure upon her narrow shoulder-blade. Tawny-gold eyes glittered down at her in a mixture of barely leashed fury and disbelief. In a sense she could sympathise with his incredulity. Four years ago she would not have dared to speak to him like that. But when she looked at the situation as it was, she saw no reason to hide her antipathy and her resentment. Alex would do what he wanted to do, regardless of how she behaved. He had proved that when he had ended their marriage, he had proved it continually in the years since.

"Let go of me!" she ordered, losing confidence as she collided for a heartstopping moment with his hard appraisal. Out of nowhere an odd breathlessness afflicted her, as if his fingers were squeezing her throat instead of her shoulder. "Alex, if you don't let go of me...I'll slap an assault charge on you...I've got nothing to lose!"

Dark colour overlaid his bronzed cheekbones, and an unholy flash of naked, seething anger lit his piercing gaze. "Shall I tell you what I am going to do?" His roughened demand was thickly accented as he stared down at her, releasing his hold upon her with a carelessness which revealed his contempt for her unnecessary threat. "I am going to do what I should have done when my son was born. Take you back and make you regret the day that you ever dared to forget who you belonged to..."

Kerry backed off against the kitchen cupboard, nervously licking her dry lips. "What on earth are you talking about?"

Alex cast her a hard, contemptuous smile. With the venting of that aggressive declaration of intent, he appeared to have regained his equilibrium. "Do you doubt that I can do it? I can't think of why I omitted to do it before. I can have my son in my home. He can even have what he wants. And Nicky wants his mother as well."

Dazedly she surveyed him. "But we're divorced."

"I could marry you again. I'm prepared to do that to get my son. He's still too young to be parted from you," he murmured shortly.

A brittle, stifled laugh left her lips. "You're crazy. I wouldn't marry you again if the survival of the human race depended on it!"

A black brow lifted, a ruthless smile slanting his beautiful mouth. "But what about your survival, Kerry? How would you cope if I told your parents why I divorced you?"

Parchment-pale, her strained features reflected immediate horror. "Why should you do that? You never see them. It doesn't matter to you what they think…"

"Yesterday it stuck in my throat to listen to your father talking about the sanctity of marriage," he whipped back in silken derision. "Oh, I know very well what they think. That it was I who strayed into other beds. No doubt you came home and complained at length about the frequency of my trips abroad. They reached their own conclusions. Why did I sit and listen politely in silence to your parents protesting that it is very difficult for our son to be divided between two households? I didn't owe you that silence. I owe you nothing.''

"Alex, I..."

He cut across her, "Last night I reached a decision. I will have my son and I will have you as well in the same house.''

She was trembling. Even hating him as she did, she could still appreciate that her father's well-meant interference must have dealt a stinging blow to Alex's pride. Alex had nothing to apologise for in terms of marital wrongdoing...at least nothing that could be proved and nothing major. His insensitivity towards her needs had not run to verbal or physical abuse. Dear heaven, she marvelled that he had remained silent about the real facts in the face of her father's innocent provocation. What was happening now she didn't really comprehend. It was too immense, too unexpected and too terrifying.

"I presume you understand me." Alex sent her still figure a fulminating appraisal. "We will remarry or I will tell your parents what you are too ashamed to tell them. Perhaps it is time they were deprived of their naïve illusions.''

Her lips parted. "You can't threaten me like that. It's blackmail...''

"Why not? If one may be blackmailed by the truth, let it be so." Alex failed to flinch from her shocked condemnation. "Why should I be deprived of my son? If I take you to court, I am unlikely to win custody. It is very rare for a mother to lose her child. If I destroy your reputation to achieve my own ends, I not only embarrass my family, I sentence my son to the possession of a mother he can only be ashamed to own to in later years. Mud sticks," he said succinctly, a fastidious flare to his nostrils. "I would be no cleaner than you if I began such a battle, and I have more pride in my family name. I will not dishonour it with lurid publicity."

She realised in stricken apprehension that Alex was not only coldly serious, he had mulled over the problem in depth. This was not an angry impulse to call her to heel. He wanted Nicky and he was not foolish enough to believe that he could separate his son from his mother without causing him a great deal of pain. In acceptance of the necessity he was prepared to take the two of them.

"Do you realise that my father has a heart condition?" she whispered shakily.

"I didn't know, but that is irrelevant to me. Perhaps you should have thought of that four years ago," he countered with chill emphasis. "I have more concern for my son, who is *my* family. To gain him I am prepared to use pressure, and let me assure you, *cara*, if you push me to it, I will carry through the threat. Why should I leave you to bask here in parental love and independence, raising my son as a foreigner in a..." Words appeared to fail Alex as he slashed a scornful glance round her kitchen. His mouth compressed. "My son should be in my home where he belongs, and he will be there soon if it is the last thing I do."

Kerry was breathing fast and audibly. Alex had her symbolically up against a brick wall. No matter where she turned, she could see no hope of escape. Until now she had not known the depth of his bitterness. She had his son when she had no right to such a privilege. He had suffered by the loss of Nicky when she was the one in the wrong. She had never even begun to suspect that Alex felt as strongly about the situation. But how could she have? They hadn't talked in all these years, and all this time Alex's indignation had been damming up. Yesterday it had reached new heights in her parents' home, and Kerry had foolishly given him the weapon. She had revealed how afraid she was of them learning the truth.

"You can't do this," she said weakly again.

Alex vented a humourless laugh. "Are you going to stop me? If you put your son's needs first, you would not need to be forced. You would see that for him to have two parents and the background to which he was born would be indisputably preferable to what he has now. Shuttled between the two of us like a parcel, confused by two languages, two completely opposing lifestyles!" he enumerated in savage repudiation. "How is he to know who he is?"

She did not need to have Alex throw the drawbacks of their divorce in her face. Did he regret the divorce now? Her soft mouth set cynically. He probably regretted the poor timing of her conception scant weeks before their break-up. Had she not been pregnant, he could have severed their ties for ever and remarried without a backward glance.

"So you have your choice," he concluded drily.

She bit her lower lip painfully. "You haven't given me a choice!" she argued furiously.

"You have until tomorrow to give me an answer." Golden eyes held hers with cruel mockery.

"You ruthless bastard!" she burst out unsteadily.

Lean-fingered hands enclosed her wrists. He jerked her up against his hard, boldly masculine body as if she was a rag doll. "I'll make you pay for every insult you give me now," he swore roughly. "In my bed... whenever and however I want you." Her darkened green eyes widened to their fullest extent. Alex's fingers pushed up her chin, savage amusement burning in his gaze. "I shall enjoy that. Using you as you used me. I loved you. I loved you beyond the bounds of my own intelligence," he confessed derisively. "I was so weak in the grip of that love that I was blind. But I don't love you any more. I don't need you, either. You have no hold on me now. You don't even have my respect. If I were you, I wouldn't incite my temper any further. You'll only pay for it at a later date."

The raw emphasis of the assurance left her boneless. His dark-timbred drawl had almost mesmerised her into complete paralysis. But, as his meaning sank in, her stomach somersaulted in violent rejection of his intent. A loud thump which she could hardly recognise as her own heartbeat was pounding in her eardrums.

"*Capisci, cara?*" With a cynical smile, he released her chin. "Tomorrow afternoon you can present yourself in my office in London. A car will call for you at two. You will leave Nicky with your parents and explain that you are attending a party with me tomorrow evening and staying overnight in London. I doubt if they will place any objection to the plan."

"Alex...you mustn't do this..." she whispered in absolute turmoil. "I have a life of my own...for God's sake, I can't spend the rest of it paying for..."

"One mistake?" The golden blaze of his bitterness lanced into her without warning. "It won't be for the rest of your life. It will be until Nicky is old enough to do without you."

He left her standing there. He let himself out. She stumbled over to the chair she had earlier forsaken in temper. She hadn't even realised that she was crying. But now her hands covered wet cheeks. She had been wise to fear Alex even when he was invisible in her life, for Alex hated more fiercely than she was capable of hating. He despised her utterly, and he hated her because once he had loved her and she had proved unworthy of that love.

Yet in all those months of their marriage he had not once told her that he loved her. Indeed, it had seemed after the honeymoon was over that Alex was more set upon showing her that he did not need her around constantly. He hadn't devoted much time to her. That primitive and fierce pride of his had seen shame in loving a teenager. Shame and weakness. Perhaps he had believed that it would give her too much power over him if she realised how he really felt about her. Instead he had slotted her into place and shut her out.

She did not doubt the veracity of his declaration of love. By making it, he had twisted something painfully within her. It all seemed such a waste. He had loved her and he hadn't liked loving her. In the end he would have overcome what he saw as a shortcoming. Alex was built that way. It might almost have been a relief when she blotted her copybook and he could rid himself of his despised susceptibility towards her.

But what she was realising now was that Alex had suffered too, and that, in punishing her, he had also been punishing himself. Even if he had relented and come to see her in Florence, though, she was still certain that he would have carried neither pardon nor clemency in his heart. He was hard and inflexible. His standards admitted no adjustments. Wrong was wrong in Alex's eyes.

And in her own. She might have lost her head when he threatened her, but still she saw his reasoning. She could understand his desire to have his son in his own home. She was less able to deal with the ferocity of Alex's desire for revenge. He wanted to make her suffer. He didn't know how much she had already suffered. Understandably, he did not believe that she had ever really loved him. What was she going to do?

Checking the time, she reluctantly put on her coat and set out for the showroom. Fortunately her home was on the outskirts of the village, and Antiques Fayre was on the main street. To her surprise, the showroom was already open. Steven was behind the counter, drinking coffee and chatting to a regular customer, who collected antique plates.

"I thought you had deliveries to make," Kerry opened ruefully.

He grinned. "I couldn't be bothered. Have you seen the state of the roads out there? Want some coffee?"

She nodded and watched his slim, golden-haired figure disappear into the back of the shop. Nothing worried Steven—falling trade and irate customers included. On the balance side, he was a non-stop worker with the furniture he loved. His problem was that he restored for personal pleasure rather than profit. In a normal mood she would have chased him out to deliver the completed pieces to the two customers awaiting the return of their furniture. But she was still in shock from Alex's visit.

"He's such a pleasant young man," the lady plate collector commented, taking her leave. "He advised me against buying that Spode plate. He's right, it wouldn't really fit my colour scheme."

Kerry silently gritted her teeth. At present, they couldn't afford helpful advice of that brand. The coffers were far from full. Steven reappeared, clutching a mug.

"So where did you get to yesterday? And what's with the plaster?"

Briefly, she told him about the accident. Immediately, he was concerned. "You should have stayed in bed today."

"Willard Evans is coming."

"Oh, profiteer day, is it?" Steven gathered drily.

"We'd be out of business without him." She spoke with greater heat than usual, and his blue eyes betrayed surprise. "Oh, never mind. Can I use your car later? I have to go and pick up Nicky."

"Do you want me to drive you? You look like death warmed up," he said wryly. "Is there something else wrong?"

She pushed her hair off her brow. "I saw my ex-husband last night," she confided tightly.

Steven shrugged. "No big deal, is it? What did he do? Land his private jet on the hospital roof?" He laughed lightly. "You should have touched him for some alimony, Kerry. I've never understood why you live like you do when you could be sitting in clover."

Her pale skin heated with colour. "I didn't want to be beholden."

"Old-fashioned word, that, and not very practical. You've got a kid to think of. Pretty soon he's going to be asking more questions and learning to enjoy his luxury stays with your ex more than he likes coming home."

"Leave it," she begged, looking away. "I'm sorry, I've got a lot on my mind."

At that point, Willard's hired Mercedes drew up outside. Steven took off, leaving Kerry to deal with him. A small, bespectacled man, he strolled silently through the showroom as usual before making his selections and negotiating prices with her. He never stayed long. He was taciturn for an antiques dealer. He had been coming to them for more than two years, and she didn't believe they had ever exchanged a word of anything that could be deemed personal conversation. It was one of the reasons Steven disliked him.

"There's just something phoney about the guy," he had said once. "He never talks. It's just in, out and off for another month."

"He's very businesslike," she had argued. "He doesn't need to make it a social call."

Today she was grateful for the dealer's undemanding brevity. As soon as he had gone she went out to the rear courtyard and got into Steven's vintage MG. During the drive to her parents' home, she looked back ruefully over the past four years.

She had come home to the vicarage from Florence. She had been shellshocked. Until Alex had walked out of that hospital she had still nurtured desperate hopes of a last-ditch reconciliation. Her parents had been appalled by the news that she was getting a divorce for, over the six months of their separation in Florence, Kerry had continued to write home as if there was nothing wrong. When she did arrive back there had been enough trouble without a confession of infidelity. She had not had the courage to tell them in the state she was in then.

And four months later her father had had a heart attack. Nobody had blamed her, but the shock of her divorce had certainly played its part. It was inconceivable that she now dredge up the murky truth. It was too late and too dangerous. It should have been done four years ago. But would her parents ever have spoken to her again?

Had they turned on her too, she really couldn't have coped at all. As it was, she had been under severe strain. For everybody's sake she had decided to move out and embrace independence. An enormous amount of money had accumulated in her bank account. Alex's money, paid monthly. She could have turned herself into a very merry divorcee. Instead she had withdrawn a comparatively small part of it and bought into a partnership with Steven. She had withdrawn the rest and returned it to Alex's lawyers with the information that she required no further payments. Several letters had followed, trying to persuade her into accepting the allowance. She had stood firm. Living as Alex's dependent was something she could not do, as the guilty partner. Thinking back, she realised that her obstinacy had probably antagonised Alex more, but that had not been her motivation.

The cottage was rented and furnished mostly from the contents of the vicarage attic. Despite her hard work and her appeals to Steven to be more professional, her income had never reached the level she had expected. Steven had needed a partner to stay solvent. He had happily handed over the reins of decision-making to her within the first months. Unfortunately the leopard had not changed his own spots. He still took what money he liked from the takings and lived rent-free in the flat above the shop. In short, Steven quietly went his own way much more comfortably than Kerry ever did.

Her mother was baking when she arrived. The spacious kitchen was full of the aromatic scent of fresh bread. Ellen Taylor had her daughter's build, but her hair was pure white. As Kerry came through the back door, she turned to study her anxiously. "How are you?"

"I've a slight headache still...that's all." Aware that she sounded stilted, Kerry went on to say, "Where's Nicky?"

"Out in the greenhouse with your father. Did Alex visit you last night?" Ellen prompted in a tone of eager expectancy.

Kerry nodded and turned away to remove her coat. Here, in this quiet house, her morning confrontation with Alex seemed unreal. She suppressed a shiver. She couldn't tell them the truth. It might kill her father. His rigid moral principles would come into direct opposition with his love for his youngest child. But she had no hope that Alex would withdraw his threat.

Alex was fighting for a worthwhile prize. Possession of his son. And Alex was very bitter. Nicky was more important to him than his ex-father-in-law's health. In any case, he blamed Kerry for the whole situation. The original sin had not been his but hers. As far as Alex was concerned, she had got herself into this.

"He came here straight from the hospital. I've never seen Alex so shaken," her mother confided. "Of course, you could both have been killed and he realised that. He loves Nicky very much, Kerry."

Her face set. "I accept that."

Her mother cleared her throat awkwardly. "Nor would I say that he was indifferent to you. Vickie said we were being silly, but sometimes a crisis can bring people together again."

A day earlier, Kerry would have laughed like a hyena at that suggestion. Alex could have come here and wept crocodile tears had she died. She had the sensation that

Alex would not feel that she had paid her dues until she slipped this mortal coil. Her eyelids gritted with moisture. The man she had once loved would not have employed blackmail tactics. What was she holding off on the glad tidings for? The minute Alex had laid down his demands she had tasted defeat. Alex could yank her back. Alex could do just about anything he wanted to do, because he had her trapped.

"And," Ellen hesitated, "he hasn't remarried. He told your father that he didn't believe in divorce..."

He believed in the institution fast enough when he had an adulterous wife, she reflected bitterly. But the grim and pointless retort remained unspoken.

"He wants me back." An edged laugh that was no laugh at all punctuated her abrupt announcement. "He wants Nicky, and he can't have one of us without the other," she gibed helplessly.

A pulsating silence had fallen. She glanced up warily. Her mother had stopped listening after the first crucial statement. She looked peculiar, her mouth wide, both brows raised in amazement. "He wants you back?" she echoed, recovering fast, and she was off in an Olympic sprint to the back door to call, "John!" down the garden so that her father could share in this wonderful news.

Evidently Ellen could not even imagine Kerry turning any such offer down. In common with Alex, her parents believed that Nicky came first. They had implied more than once that Kerry had walked out on Alex in naïve and selfish haste.

"You did say yes..." Ellen had her handkerchief out now and she was fiddling with it nervously, the unmentionable possibility of refusal belatedly occurring to her.

"Could you picture Alex allowing me to say no?"

Kerry quipped tautly, weighted down by double duplicity.

A beatific smile spread her mother's face and the tears came. "It'll have to be a register office…" she was lamenting as her husband came through the door.

The die was cast from that moment. John Taylor was not a very worldly man. He gazed at his younger daughter much as if the prodigal had finally made it back to the fold, and then settled down in an armchair by the Aga with an air of dazed and quiet pleasure.

"You were too young at eighteen," he sighed. "I warned Alex at the time, but he wouldn't listen. It will be different this time."

On the brink of hysteria, Kerry stood there, undeniably the spectre at a long-awaited feast, and alone in the trap of fevered and negative emotions. All she could feel was a mixture of fear and fury and disbelief. If somebody had told her yesterday that she would be marrying Alex again, she would have had them committed to protective care. But it really was happening, and all because of a stupid accident. If he hadn't seen her, if he hadn't spoken to her parents, if he hadn't endured the shocked realisation that Nicky might have died yesterday…none of this would be happening.

As soon as she could, she escaped. It was very difficult. They wanted her to stay. They wanted details. They seemed to be labouring under the impression that Alex had been so shattered by the sight of her in a hospital bed that he had flung his famed cool to the four winds and demanded that she marry him again because he could not live without her.

"You're doing the right thing," Ellen declared as she

saw her back out to Steven's car. "Nicky needs the two of you. Everything else will come all right. You'll see."

She drove off with a sickly smile. The tangled web of deceit seemed only to be getting thicker. She had explained about the party and, as Alex had forecast, they were more than happy to oblige. She hadn't got to take Nicky home at all.

"For goodness' sake, you'll have so much to do," her mother had protested. "Packing, sorting out business matters with Steven, getting ready for the party...you really ought to go to the hairdresser..."

Packing. The word had struck horror into her bones. What was she supposed to do about Steven? He couldn't afford to buy her out. Furthermore, who could tell what might lie ahead? But her logic advised her that, if she left Alex in the future, he would ensure that she did not take Nicky. In other words, marrying Alex a second time would be a one-way ticket, unless he changed his mind.

Steven laughed like a drain when she told him, and then said, "Fess up, you're pulling my leg, aren't you?"

She sighed, "No, I'm not."

"Come on, Kerry. Look at yourself. You don't look like an ex about to happily remarry her ex-husband. You loathe him!" he argued in exasperation. "What the heck is going on?"

She could not answer his question. What would be the point in dredging it all up? It wouldn't change anything. She assured him that she would remain a silent partner.

He shook his blond head. "You can't leave me in the lurch. I can't manage without you. Who's going to run the showroom?"

"You'll have to bring someone in. On the other

hand," she suggested gently, "Barbara once intimated an interest in the business if she could find a niche..."

"A niche?" he echoed in dismay, flushing, so that she knew that Barbara had dropped the same hints to him.

"Why not here, when I'm gone? She's a great organiser. I'm sure she could learn the ropes in no time. I did," Kerry pointed out, ignoring his total absence of enthusiasm.

"We get on better as we are," he muttered, looking hunted. "It's more stimulating this way."

When she finally reached home, she was exhausted. Steven had moaned and groaned until he had outrun her patience. He would have to learn to depend on himself again. Indeed, Kerry's removal from the scene might work to the long-suffering Barbara's advantage. Steven was likely to be very lonely.

She made a sandwich which she nibbled at without great appetite. She tried to phone her sister, but Vickie was out. She kept on trying to picture herself walking cold into Veranchetti Industries tomorrow. Her skin came up goose-flesh at the prospect, and her pride revolted at the humiliation underwritten in surrender.

CHAPTER FOUR

KERRY wished the receptionist would stop staring avidly at her. From the instant she had entered the building she had been aware of the ripple of curious eyes following in her wake. She wondered how many recognised her as Alex's ex-wife. The presence of a security man by her side had raised comment, by granting her a highly misleading air of importance.

"Mrs Veranchetti?" the top-floor receptionist had carolled in surprise. She had looked Kerry up and down, pricing her winter coat and boots, her attention lingering on the luxuriant fall of her hair. She could undoubtedly have accurately enumerated Kerry's freckles by the time Alex got round to seeing her.

His secretary came to show her the way. Alex's office was as she remembered. It was all sunlight and modernity, at glaring odds with the untamed darkness of its inhabitant. He rose from behind his desk, flashing her a brilliant smile. "Forgive me for keeping you waiting," he murmured, presumably for his departing secretary's benefit.

Kerry studied him nervously, her colour high. "Now what?"

He held out an assured brown hand. "Come here..." he urged softly.

She stayed where she was, glued to the carpet. A

treacherous, relentless awareness of him was quivering through her in response to the burning brush of his lion-gold eyes. Desire and satisfaction mingled there in heady combination. Trembling, she tilted her chin. "You can force me to come here and you can force me to marry you, but that's all you can force."

"Is it?" Alex strolled forward fluidly. Long fingers began smoothly to unbutton her coat, then he pushed it down slowly from her shoulders and let the garment drop to the floor.

"Stop it...for God's sake, stop it!" she pleaded, for the tension in the air sizzled over her raw nerves.

"Don't challenge me, then." His hand touched her hair and brushed against her cheek. "And stop behaving as if you are afraid of me. I don't like it. I've never hurt you."

Sometimes a physical blow could almost be kinder. She nearly told him that. As he had stripped that coat from her she had had the ridiculous suspicion that he planned to continue with the dress underneath. Now he drew her inexorably closer into the shelter and heat of his tall, powerful body.

"Alex...don't," she implored.

Her slight figure was alternately rigid and shrinking from the torment of his proximity. Something raw and blazing illuminated his narrowed gaze. His dark head bent and he brought his mouth down fiercely upon hers, forcing her soft lips to part for the thrusting invasion of his tongue. It was no gentle or patient reintroduction to his lovemaking. It was shockingly, shatteringly sexual.

His hand settled at the base of her spine, pressing her against his hard, muscled thighs. Heat coursed through her in a debilitating wave. The potency of his masculine arousal was no less overwhelming than the angry hunger of his kiss. A muffled whimper escaped low in her throat. An unbearable, completely unexpected tide of need was wreaking havoc with her sensation starved body. Excitement tore through her in a stormy passage, her mouth opening instinctively for his, her head falling back as his fingers wound into the tangle of her hair. His other hand was wandering at will over her tautening curves, cupping her breast, roaming over the firm swell of her hips in confident reacquaintance. The onslaught seduced her utterly. It had been too long since she had known Alex's touch—indeed, any man's touch. All the heat of desire which had once made her writhe against him in helpless need was controlling her now.

He suddenly loosed her swollen mouth and lifted his dark head. ''I could take you now…here, if I wanted.'' His fingers slid in derisive retreat from her. ''You have the soul of a wanton, *cara*. It betrays you when you least desire it to. Even with me, whom you profess to hate, you are eager.''

Kerry fell back from him, shaking like a leaf. Her nipples were tight, aching buds beneath her clothes. An ache was spreading within her, an ache she wretchedly acknowledged as a bodily cry for fulfilment. She had never hated herself as she did at that moment for surrendering to Alex when his sole intent had been to demonstrate his contempt. But she'd been woefully unprepared to discover that Alex's lovemaking still drove her crazy, regardless of all common sense. Once Alex had treated her as if she was a precious, fragile creature who might break if roughly handled. What she had lost, what she had destroyed returned to haunt her.

''I have made arrangements.'' Thickly lashed golden

eyes rested inscrutably on her hot cheeks and evasive gaze. "We will be married within the week. When you appear in my company tonight we will be announcing to the curious that we are together again. I ordered a selection of clothes to be delivered to the apartment. You will wear the blue evening gown tonight. I won't be back for dinner, so you'll be dining alone."

She should have guessed that he would take care of the clothing problem. Her wardrobe no longer contained couture garments. Bitterness assailed her that she should be as helpless in his hands as a child's toy.

"Sit down." He indicated the chair and lounged back against his tidy desk. "I have taken a precaution against any future desire you might have to conclude this marriage, too. You will sign a legal, binding contract, agreeing that you give Nicky into my custody if we should part again in the future."

"You can't ask that of me!" she exclaimed in horror.

"I am not asking, I am demanding," Alex contradicted with sibilant softness. "If you conduct yourself as a normal married woman and mother you will have nothing to fear from that contract."

She searched his harshly set features suspiciously. "You're planning to do this to take Nicky from me altogether," she accused. "You want to make my life so miserable that I'll want to leave."

His jawline hardened. "I would not do that to my son. It is natural that there should be storms between us now. But in time those will disappear. If you behave yourself, I have not the smallest intention of making your life a misery," he parried with a curled lip, as if the very suggestion of such behaviour upon his part was an insult.

"I'll be wretched anyway," she mumbled, on the brink of angry, cornered tears.

"Why should you be?" Alex demanded in a tone reminiscent of a whiplash. "You will have a beautiful home, your son, plenty of money, and all for what price? It is I who sacrifice pride in taking you back!"

"How the mighty have fallen…"

"*Dio,* don't taunt me!" Alex slashed back savagely but quietly. "You will sign that contract. You will sell out of your partnership with Glenn. We will make a fresh beginning."

Had she not had the memory of his loathing for her yesterday, she might have been taken in by this more civilised picture of a reconciliation for Nicky's sake. "I can't sell out and I won't."

"We'll talk about that some other time," he dismissed impatiently.

She took a deep breath. "Where are you planning for us to live?"

"I have not yet decided."

"I'm not living with Athene again!" she snapped in dismay.

An expression of icy derision tautened his strong, dark face. "Why would I take you there to live? You are no longer a teenager."

Her head bent in comprehension. "You told her," she muttered sickly.

"I told no one. But your sister…she was not so quiet. There were rumours," he admitted tautly. "Unsubstantiated, but damaging."

She refused to believe that Vickie had talked. But evidently word had somehow got out. Dear God, how humiliating that must have been for Alex! Lion of industry, betrayed by teenage wife.

"Naturally we will have our own home again," he stressed drily. "When we first married, I rather innocently believed that you would be happier living with my family and free of the responsibilities of entertaining. I didn't realise that my mother disliked you. It's not always easy to see fault in someone close."

"I did tell you."

"Yes, I know you did, but until I witnessed her barely restrained pleasure at the failure of our marriage, I didn't appreciate that you hadn't been exaggerating."

It was an admission of blame Alex would not have made four years ago, and it mollified her jangling emotions to some degree. She swallowed. "She...your family will be shocked by our remarriage."

"I am head of my family," he said with hauteur. "I will expect you and them to behave with civility and breeding when you meet again. I am answerable to nobody in my private life."

He bent down, swept up the coat he had stripped from her and extended it to her. "It's almost five. You will need time to dress for the party."

She dug her arms stiffly into the sleeves, and was extraordinarily tempted to lean back into the strong, protective heat of him and weep for what she had done in the past and Alex's inability to accept it. "You know...that night..." her tongue slid out to moisten her lips "...Vickie's..."

His hands suddenly rested heavily on her tense shoulders.

"That man...we didn't make love," she whispered

jerkily. "I know that. I don't remember much, but I know that."

Alex was intimidatingly silent, and then his breath escaped in a hiss. "It would be wiser if you didn't mention that night again."

She whirled round. But his embittered eyes made her bite back words of heated disagreement. Either he did not believe her, or she had surmised his feelings correctly. That she had got into the situation at all was sufficient for Alex.

"The car will be waiting for you," he prompted her departure shortly. "I will see you later."

The apartment had barely changed. It was all as she remembered, but for a couple of new paintings and a change of décor in the drawing-room. Umberto, Alex's manservant, might have seen her only the day before. He betrayed neither welcome nor surprise as he politely showed her through to one of the guest-rooms. He opened the wardrobe to display the selection of clothes hanging there. Matching accessories sat on the shelves, and several lingerie boxes reposed untouched on the bed. Alex's efficiency surprised her not at all. For Alex, such gestures were easy. He simply had to lift a phone.

She attempted again to phone her sister, who now lived in a flat in Chiswick which she had bought the previous year. This time, Vickie was home.

"Where the hell are you?" her sister demanded with unexpected shrillness. "I've been trying to get hold of you for hours!"

"I'm in London, in Alex's apartment."

"You mean it's true? It can't be, you can't be going back to him!" she argued. "You've got to be out of your mind after what he did to you!"

Kerry sighed. "Vickie, I..."

"I'll come over."

"No, don't." Kerry went on to explain about the party.

"I've got to see you!" Vickie flared. "You don't understand...oh, God..." Her voice trailed away.

Her sister's almost hysterical response to the news that she was returning to Alex surprised Kerry. Vickie very rarely lost control. "I'll see you tomorrow morning," she promised. "Before I go home again."

Vickie gave a curious laugh. "OK. I'll stay home for you. Nothing earthshaking is likely to happen between tonight and tomorrow."

Kerry came off the phone and went to examine the shimmering blue dress which Alex had mentioned. The light caught its glistening, iridescent folds. It was the sort of blatantly alluring gown which Alex would once have frowned upon. Pain snaked within her treacherously. Alex didn't look on her as an innocent any more.

She dined in solitary state. It brought back unwelcome memories of too many other meals eaten alone with one eye to the clock. But this time she was not awaiting Alex with the feverish and resentful impatience of a teenager in love. She was afraid, terrifyingly afraid of the insanity that had taken hold of her in Alex's arms, proving his point that she was ruled by her own physical responses. She had lied to herself all this time in telling herself that she hated him. It was her own self she hated for betraying him. In time, anyone could come to hate the reminder of a wrong. That was what Alex had become to her; an agonising reminder of that night and her own demeaning frailty.

She heard the thud of the front door while she was

dressing. The gown was more daring than anything she had ever worn. The swell of her breasts rose seductively above the fitting fabric which hugged from beneath her arms to her hips. The colour was breathtaking against her hair. Picking up the toning bag and the high-collared jacket, she could linger in the bedroom no longer.

Alex entered the drawing-room a few minutes behind her. His eyes swept in rampant appraisal over her. "Take the jacket off. I want to see you."

"No. Won't we be late?" she said breathlessly. But she took it off to prevent Alex performing the task for her, and stood there feeling like a slave on the block.

Dark colour had risen to his hard cheekbones. He made no effort to hide his masculine appreciation.

"You really have grown up."

The blaze of his sensual scrutiny made her shrug hastily back into the concealment of the jacket. He bit out a soft, grating laugh. "Surely not so shy? You're almost twenty-four now."

She was still a case of arrested development. She didn't date. She had never taken another man to her bed. She had spent all this time suppressing an essential part of her womanhood, and presumed that that was why Alex's hand on hers, even briefly, could send a shock of electrifying awareness through her. Frustration. That was all it was, and Alex was tormentingly familiar. She only had to look at him to recall the hard thrust of his all male body on hers, the feel of his satin damp skin beneath her caressing fingertips. Her complexion burnt up hotly, her pulses quickening. In bed there had never been distance between them. But there had been several women in Alex's arms since she had last rested there. Accepting that cruel reality cooled her fluttering senses.

Despite the divorce, Kerry had never learnt to stop thinking of Alex as her husband. He had taken his revenge in full the first time she lifted a newspaper and saw a photo of him in a New York nightclub with a glamorous socialite clinging to him. She had been sick with jealousy, but she had not been entitled to the emotion. They had been divorced by then.

The party was a glittering crush which contained not a single familiar face. Alex kept one arm round her the whole time. They were the centre of attention, and Alex seemed content to be on display. When a well-known gossip columnist approached them, he smilingly announced their marital plans.

"What have you been doing since your divorce?" she asked Kerry bluntly. "You disappeared right off the social scene."

Kerry tipped more champagne down her dry throat, an ignominious desire to giggle attacking her as Alex smoothly stepped in to speak for her, as he had done on several other occasions throughout the evening.

"My wife was living in the country."

"Selling plates," Kerry added brightly. "Atoning for my..." She collided involuntarily with Alex's dark eyes, and inwardly she collapsed like a pricked balloon. He made some witty remark, smoothing over her crazy outburst, and she studied the carpet, feeling like a child about to be put in the corner. Really, an ex-wife who had painted the town red would have been an intolerable threat to Alex's idea of what was decent. Without even trying, she had done what would have pleased most, she acknowledged bitterly. She had lived like a nun.

"Don't ever do that again," Alex growled as the woman moved away. "And don't drink any more.

You've had enough. I'm surprised you can even touch alcohol after..."

A chill ran over her flesh and doused the rebellion incited by an entire evening spent firmly beneath Alex's thumb.

His chiselled mouth compressed. "I should not have said that," he drawled curtly. "I apologise."

It was an apology of glacial and grudging proportions. Ahead of her stretched a lifetime of them. Her infidelity was as fresh as yesterday to Alex, and it always would be.

"You're never going to trust me again, are you?" she muttered sickly.

"I wouldn't trust you to the foot of the street," he agreed in a simmering undertone. "And it gives me no pleasure to tell you that. But since I believe that you are...genuinely sorry..."

"You mean, you really believe that?" Shame could not drown out anger. "You'd have been much happier if I put myself over a cliff somewhere, Alex. That's your idea of genuinely sorry," she whispered strickenly. "And you damned near succeeded in getting your wish. If I hadn't been pregnant I...I..."

He had lost colour. "Don't talk like that!" he snapped.

"No, you don't want to hear it, do you? All about the revenge you took then." Her tremulous voice was breaking. "How you let me crawl...I'll never forget that, Alex, and I'll never...forgive you either..."

He swept her out to the hall and sent a maid off for her jacket while smoothly thanking their hostess for her hospitality. She noticed the columnist covertly absorbing their departure and she reddened miserably, regretting her loss of control. But she could not for ever hang her head in remorseful silence, listening to Alex bestow pious comments. She was only human. The trouble was that Alex wasn't. Even loving her, he had given no quarter to either of them. He had meted out punishment with a ruthlessness which still had the power to make her shiver.

"You will never forgive me...ha!" Alex vented in the suffocating atmosphere in the rear of the limousine. "You wrecked our marriage. You went out like a spoilt, over-indulged brat and got drunk and gave yourself to another man while you carried my child. Am I to apologise for not having it within me to forgive you? I knew I couldn't. I stayed away for your safety, too. You were pregnant, you might have lost the baby. Perhaps I was hard upon you..."

Her teeth had bitten into her tongue, and the salty tang of blood had filtered into her mouth. "There is no perhaps about it. You nearly destroyed me. I loved you."

"If you had loved me, you would never have let another man touch you, drunk or sober!" Alex ripped back at her, all cool abandoned now that they were in private. "Do not talk of love to me. You were infatuated. Once the novelty had worn off, you wanted your freedom back."

"That's untrue...I was unhappy, but I didn't regret marrying you."

"Well, believe me," Alex breathed cruelly, "I regretted marrying you."

Dear God, what sort of relationship were they to have in the future? Alex tearing at her continually for a past she could not wipe out, and Kerry hating him for the grain of truth in every pronouncement. It was a vicious circle.

He sighed. "I don't wish to talk to you like this. I concede that I made mistakes too. Instead of giving way to my desire for you, I should have decided upon a long engagement, during which we could both have adapted to the differences between us. You were too young and insecure, and I was too selfish and intolerant," he conceded tautly. "I should have bought us a home in England. You would have had your own family then, and I would not have felt the need to play both father and lover. The combination does not work, and I disliked the necessity, but I asked for the problem."

His generosity surprised her afresh. There had been a time when Alex could not have admitted being less than perfect. But he had looked back, he had seen the distance which had forged them apart. "I did love you." She didn't know why it was so important that he accept that now, but it was.

Alex shot her a caustic and cynical smile. "For the last time, I do not want to hear you talk about love. It got us nowhere in the past. If it was love, it was a shallow and mawkish sentiment. All I want from you now is the outward show of wife and mother. That should not tax your ingenuity too much."

Deeply hurt, she turned her head aside.

"Do you want a nightcap?" he asked as they entered the apartment.

She shook her head. "I'll go to my room," she muttered tightly. "As they say, the show's over."

"On the contrary…" Black-lashed golden eyes met hers in glancing challenge. "It's only beginning."

Kerry retreated to her room and twisted angrily out of

the dress. She thrust it from her sight bitterly. Alex had dressed her as he saw her now. As a woman on offer to the highest bidder. A woman who could respond to his caresses as happily as she could respond to any other attractive man's. A woman who was easy sexually. Easy to seduce, easy to take. Dear God, that wasn't her! "That isn't me," she muttered in soundless despair to the mirror. If she had been like that there would have been a lot of other men since their divorce.

To think of Alex possessing her again with contempt and a hard desire to humiliate turned her stomach over queasily. She couldn't let that happen. She could go back to him, live with him, take whatever he had to throw at her, but she could not let him use her body. Whatever she had done, she was still an individual with a right to self-determination.

She slipped into bed and lay there. Alex was no rapist. He wouldn't force her to accede to his sexual demands. How could he really even want her? If she made it clear how she felt…oh, dear lord, Alex was the most Latin of men in that field. Even if he didn't desire her, he would go through the roof if she tried to bar him from her bedroom. She would have to be more subtle than that.

The door opened and she pulled herself up against the banked-up pillows, huge green eyes wide in the lamplight. Alex shut the door again with a decisive snap. He wore only a short black robe. A tangled mat of dark hairs showed between the parted edges. "Why should I wait for what I want?" he drawled softly, unperturbed by her obvious shock at his appearance.

"You can't…we're not married!" Wildly disconcerted by his unashamed intent, Kerry studied him in shaken disbelief.

Alex padded calmly over to the side of the bed, his long fingers already lazily loosening the tie of the robe. "We will be," he parried.

"Th...that's not the point! I don't want this!" she hurled at him wrathfully. "You can't do this!"

He shed the robe fluidly. "'Can't' doesn't belong in my vocabulary, just as 'no' does not belong in yours." Dark golden eyes held hers in fierce and obdurate purpose. "When I have made your body mine again, I will have obliterated other memories with my own. *Capisci, cara?*"

In Alex, twentieth-century female liberation had only ever received lip-service. Not an inch beneath the surface ran the hot-blooded buccaneering instincts of his seagoing forebears and the dark, domineering strength of a man who had absolute conviction in his own innate superiority over the female sex. It was the ice on the outside and the tantalising hint of the fire underneath which had first drawn her to Alex.

Dry-mouthed, in paralysis, she took in his lean, sun-darkened nudity. There was nothing shy about Alex in the bedroom. But Kerry had always possessed a girlish modesty which had in the past amused him. Something told her that there would be no such allowances made tonight.

"You can't," she whispered. "It would be wrong."

"Wrong?" He wrenched back the duvet and got in beside her with a harsh laugh. Her skin burned hot and tight over her bones as he gathered her into his arms, making no attempt to conceal his obvious arousal from her. "No, this is not wrong," he asserted arrogantly. "I will not be easy until I have known you again in the only fashion in which I ever knew you."

Rage shuddering through her, she endeavoured to evade his hold. He had planned this all along, and in her innocence she had trustingly agreed to spend the night, never suspecting the depths of Alex's determination to mortify what little self-respect she had left. "No!" she raked at him.

His hand closed on the bodice of her cotton nightdress and ripped it asunder. It was a gesture not of violence, but of sheer cool resolution. "Either submit or leave," he challenged her ruthlessly. "I gave you the terms before you came to me today, and you are still free to change your mind."

Her shaking hands drew together the remnants of the destroyed garment. She turned the pale curve of her cheek aside in anguish and despair. He had changed, and it wasn't only love that he had lost in the intervening years. He appeared devoid of tenderness and compassion, too.

"And you'll be content with submission, will you?" she muttered tremulously. "Knowing that you are humiliating me, knowing that I have no choice?"

"Yes, I will be content," he grated, his golden gaze skimming stormily to the revealed upper curves of her breasts. "I want you. God forgive me for it, but I want you on any terms, and I do not need you to preach on the subject of my fastidiousness. I am damned if I will deny myself what you could give to a stranger."

She shrank under the duvet with pained remembrance of what had rent both their lives asunder. He would enforce his mastery in this relationship. He would take her to prove that he was no longer sensitive to her infidelity. But in doing so, she swore, he would receive little satisfaction.

"Put the light out," she mumbled.

"No...do you know how many women have turned into you in the dark over the years?" His savagery flailed her. "But you are no longer special to me. I will satisfy myself in that tonight."

"I'll hate you for this until the day I die!" she hissed. "You're barbaric!"

"You made me that way." His powerful body was blocking out the light, shadowing her hectically flushed face. "Why shouldn't you taste the fruits of your own endeavours?" he demanded with seething bitterness. "But I will give you pleasure, even if it is only an empty pleasure. It ought to satisfy you. I wonder how many other men there have been to give you that same pleasure..."

"None; you turned me off men for life!"

His sensual mouth twisted. "I cannot believe that."

"I don't care what you believe, you savage!" she snapped back, outraged beyond all bearing by his insults.

The force of his mouth drove her head back against the pillows. The power of his hunger ravaged her. She lay completely still, a peculiar weakness overwhelming her. He would not use his superior strength against her. She was in no danger of a forced possession. Yet, even knowing that a struggle would drive him from her in aversion, she did not move a muscle. And even in the instant of questioning the inconsistency of her behaviour, a shaft of arrowing excitement seized her and drove her mind blank, as his hand moved expertly against her breast, brushing aside the ripped cotton, curving to the unbearably sensitive mound beneath. He muttered something thick and impossibly sexy in Italian, and she shuddered against the tautened length of his body.

I mustn't, I mustn't, I mustn't was rhyming in her subconscious, in a litany already becoming meaningless. His fingertips found the engorged bud of her nipple and he lowered his mouth there, employing his tongue and the edge of his teeth in a grazing, tormenting caress, while his other hand prepared the neglected twin for a similar onslaught. Her defence system flew down like a domino run. Her back arched. The blood was pounding in insane excitement through her veins, and the pleasure was breathtakingly all-encompassing. It had never been so intense or so powerful for her. Her fluttering fingers tangled with the blackness of his thick hair, and she was lost beyond reclaim in a physical world of sensation. A pervasive heat was building up agonisingly inside her. Her thighs parted at the brush of his fingertips.

"You want me...badly," Alex muttered roughly, his eyes brilliant with triumph. "Very badly."

She could not have denied him. Need was a burning, remorseless compulsion within her traitorous body, a dam-burst of hunger ignited by his first touch. As he explored her intimately, he captured her swollen lips again in an urgent admission of impatience. His weight came down on her as he slid between her legs and he took her in a sudden, passionate storm. There was a moment of unforewarned discomfort, followed by the torment of a passion rising close to assuagement. He thrust into her powerfully, conquering her brief spasm of withdrawal, and suddenly she was clinging to him in the grip of an ecstasy which was intolerable. It finally pushed her over the edge, and Alex jerked against her with a surging groan of satisfaction, driving his body violently into the pliancy of hers.

As the clouds of passion receded, Kerry was devastated by what she had willingly surrendered. She had never lost control with such utter completeness. Nor had Alex ever made love to her in a combination of savage passion and volcanic impatience. Desolation and shame over her own abandonment swept her in the aftermath of the empty pleasure he had promised. To have given herself unstintingly to a male who reviled her was surely the lowest level a woman could sink to. Tears clogged her lashes.

"You still belong to me," Alex murmured unfeelingly.

"You swine...I hope you're satisfied!" she said shakily, wrenching free of his relaxed body.

The light went out at the touch of his hand. "I haven't begun to be satisfied, *cara*," he contradicted silkily. He ran a taunting hand down over the naked curve of her spine. "That was for necessity...an exorcism, if you like. This time it will be for enjoyment."

"Don't make me hate you." Her whisper was choked.

"Hatred can be so refreshing," Alex fielded lazily, and reached for her again. "And you have an endless capacity for enjoyment. Why not accept the inevitable? I only ever play to win, and you're in the loser's corner. We know the worst of each other. At least there won't be any unpleasant surprises in the future."

His lips tasted hers. She was too weak and too shaken to resist. A tiny part of her seemed to think she deserved this treatment, just as Alex believed she had deserved it. She squeezed her eyes shut in the darkness. Within seconds delight and more delight, and the curious reflection that this was, after all, Alex, had intermingled, and she gave herself up to the ecstasy again.

CHAPTER FIVE

"SATURDAY." Alex delivered the wedding date with careless cool. "A car will pick you up from your parents' home at ten. I'll contact them today and invite them to join us."

Kerry mutely watched him embark on his third cup of coffee. Alex had eaten a very hearty breakfast. But he didn't have the demeanour of a condemned man. He was in an extremely good mood, dark golden eyes resting on her at least once every minute with veiled satisfaction. She was in torment. She didn't care that he had no plans to repeat last night before the wedding. It was too late to find comfort in the news.

Alex had achieved exactly what he wanted to achieve. He had subdued her. Her response had made a nonsense of claims of hatred and undying hostility. She felt as if she had been plundered by a Viking attack force. He had taken her in lust and revenge, and he had destroyed indefinably precious memories of the past. His act of exorcism had cost her too dearly.

"One of my accountants will sort out your business investment."

"No, they won't!" she picked up hurriedly. "Steven couldn't afford to buy me out."

Alex moved a nebulously expressive hand. "His problem," he said succinctly. "Throughout your association, he took gross advantage of you."

"What are you talking about? How would you know?"

"I have maintained an interest in your affairs, and that has not been to your disadvantage," he emphasised unsmilingly.

She tilted her chin, her eyes blank. "Meaning?"

"You really want to know?" Alex gave a shrug of almost rueful acceptance. "You could well have been out of business by now, were it not for certain measures I took. I informed your bank manager in confidence that I would guarantee any debts or loans."

Horrified, she stared at him. "How could you?" she whispered.

He sighed. "You haven't suffered by his understanding when you have been in difficulties."

"That's not the point. How dare you go behind my back?" she flared, her pride stung beyond measure. She had worked so hard at independence, and all the time Alex had been in the background, propping her up.

"Evans was also under my instructions." At her second arrested gasp, colour darkened his features. "I tell you this because deception is abhorrent to me, but you gave me little choice when you refused to let me keep you."

She was choking on a sensation of drowning now. Willard, too...she should have guessed the dealer was too good to be true. Always willing to buy, never failing to turn up, month after month. A paid employee of Alex's sent in to keep Antiques Fayre afloat. "How could you?" she said again helplessly.

His eyes were wry. "You are handicapped by your

partner's deficiencies, not your own. You worked for him as if you were an employee.''

''That isn't true. I ran the business!''

''Then why does he appear to benefit much more richly than you from the profits?'' enquired Alex drily. ''I thought you were having an affair with him. I could see no other reason for such generosity upon your part.''

She hated him for speaking cold, hard facts. She had never got over the feeling that Antiques Fayre was really Steven's. He had started the business up. She had been further restricted by his genuinely pleasant nature. Irresponsible and extravagant Steven might be, but should she ever be in trouble, she could find no better friend. Even so, she should have overcome her embarrassment a long time ago and insisted that Steven draw a wage and no more from the showroom.

''Kerry, had you not been hampered by your partner, I believe your business would have thrived. You shouldn't blame yourself.''

''I'm not blaming myself!'' It was the last straw to have Alex, from the pinnacle of his millions, soothing her wounded pride. ''I'm blaming you for interfering in my life and treating me like a helpless child! If I had ever needed help I would have written to your lawyers.''

''From your ditch?'' Alex enquired sardonically. ''We both know you would have sooner elected to starve than accept assistance from me. It was simplest to ensure that you managed with a little discreet help.''

''Thank you for nothing!'' She stalked out of the room.

He had taken everything now. Furthermore, it was obvious that Alex had kept her under close surveillance since their divorce. He had been spying on her. No wonder he had suspected Steven was her lover. There had been no other evidence of a man in her life. Last night he had learnt differently. He had it all now, right down to the ego-boosting discovery that she had spent four celibate years doing penance for her sins.

"Don't walk away from me, *cara*." His hand pulled her firmly round. "I did nothing wrong. I was responsible for you and Nicky. Had I been less generous, I could have decreed that you lived a very different life. I could have forced you to be dependent by demanding that you give my son a more suitable backdrop. I let you go your own way while Nicky was still a baby, but you have gone that road to its end now."

"Don't you dare come that prophet-of-doom stuff on me again!" she warned wrathfully. "I'm not one of the family yes-women you're used to. I've got brains and I've got just as much need for a life outside the home as you have! Do you hear me, Alex?"

"I should imagine the whole block can hear you," he said drily.

"Well, you were the one who taught me that a higher octave is the only way that you stop and listen! I nearly died of boredom the last time we were married..."

"Not in the bedroom..."

"You see?" she interrupted in a burst of anger. "You wouldn't talk to a man like that. You wouldn't humiliate a man by telling him that you had been bolstering up his business, either!"

He caught her fingers tightly. "I told you because I wanted no more secrets between us, not because I wanted to belittle your achievements. Can't you be grateful for the feeling behind the interference?"

"I've got nothing to be grateful for after last night.

You can stamp the account paid in full,'' she retorted bitterly.

"You wanted me."

"Not in cold blood," she muttered in deep chagrin. "Any respect I had for you died last night. Oh, don't tell me you didn't force me. You just pushed me to the edge and said jump. There's very little difference."

She spun away into the bedroom. He had not been with her when she awoke. Strangely enough, that circumstance had added to her sense of having been demeaned beyond the bounds of acceptance. She was in tumultuous conflict with herself. Yes, she had wanted him, madly, desperately. In the light of the day, the heated passage of the night only made her cringe. She had once expressed love sharing Alex's bed. What had she been doing last night? Submitting with pleasure? Reliving the past? Seeking redemption for her sins? Whatever she had believed she was doing, she had humiliated herself.

All through breakfast she had hardly been able to take her eyes off him. Habit was there, a terrible dangerous familiarity was there. But Alex was not the same man he had been four years ago. At one stage she could actually remember pretending to herself that he still cared about her. How pathetic could you get? While she had been pitifully deluding herself, Alex had been making her beg for his final possession. Alex had brought his bitterness into the bedroom, and her own wantonness had sunk her beneath reproach.

In less than four crazy days Alex had turned her inside out. She didn't know herself any more. Or perhaps she was afraid to probe too deep. Perhaps she preferred to believe that physical desire alone had betrayed her. Behind that lurked a bigger apprehension. She stared strickenly at her overbright eyes in the mirror. Suppose some of that old love still lingered…? Oh, lord, she mustn't even think this way. Alex would never love her again. To love him would be to sign her own death warrant, the final seal on his revenge.

A knock sounded on the door. She knew it was Alex. The knock was a positive joke after the fashion in which he had entered this same room last night. He was framed by the doorway, dark and devilishly controlled. "We can't continue to fight like this. It won't benefit our son to see us clawing at each other."

"Did you think of that last night?"

The golden eyes glinted. "Am I to hear of that for ever? We are not children. We were married once. In a few days' time we will be married again."

"You took advantage."

"I wanted you and I had the right," Alex stated with unequivocal arrogance.

She bent her head. "You didn't. We're divorced."

"I have never felt divorced, I have never felt truly free!" Alex sizzled back in a condemnation that suggested it was her fault. "I did not think of us as divorced from the moment I saw you again."

It made little difference to Kerry's feelings. As her hands laced tightly together, another fear occurred to her, and she went pale and then pink. She couldn't bear it if he had made her pregnant. It was no melodramatic fear. Her previous pregnancy she recalled as a ghastly ordeal. Once she had lost Alex she had had no pleasure from her condition. She had been sick almost continuously, and more depressed than any woman ought to be. Bitterly, miserably, she threw him a glance. "If last night has any...repercussions, I'm not having it. I'm telling you that now. I will never go through what I went through again...not for you...not for anybody,'' she swore.

Stark pallor slowly stretched beneath his golden skin. His facial muscles tautened. She assumed that he had not even thought along such mundane lines. A male bent on slaking his lust did not think of consequences.

''Then we must hope that there will be no repercussions,'' he replied harshly. ''I don't expect you to undergo something you found so objectionable a second time. Now, the lawyer will be arriving soon with the contract I mentioned. When it is signed, the car will take you home.''

She had the weirdest suspicion that she had cut Alex to the bone. Dazedly, she squashed the idea. He had his son. He didn't need any more children. Nor could he want another tie to her when he had already made it clear that he did not expect them to remain together indefinitely.

The lawyer was elderly. He opened his mouth to explain the thick document to her. Alex cut him off after one word. ''Just slash an X where we have to sign,'' he instructed drily. ''I have naturally explained the meaning of the contract to my wife.''

''But as an interested party...'' The older man flushed, probably thinking on the danger of offending so wealthy a client. He dutifully penned in the X. They signed. Alex then beamed with positive benevolence upon him. Kerry presumed that the contract tied her up in knots. Why else would Alex smile?

Umberto packed her new clothes. She put on a fine turquoise wool suit with a high-necked white silk blouse.

Once more she was Kerry Veranchetti. Kerry Taylor had vanished. If Alex had chosen the clothes, he had fantastic taste. Her own had not been half so elegant in the past. She had pursued fashion with teenage extremity. Her avant-garde appearance must have embarrassed him at least once, but a word of criticism had never passed his lips. With hindsight, she marvelled at his restraint.

VICKIE SWUNG OPEN her door and simply stared. Her eyes roamed in astonishment over the designer suit. "What was that I said about nothing untoward happening between last night and today?" she gibed with a contemptuously curled lip. "Funny, I did think you had more pride. Alex develops some crazy notion to marry you again, and already you're trotting about in fancy feathers. Anybody would think you can't wait to get back there!"

Kerry reddened as she followed her tall sister into the lounge. "I did try to phone you before I came to London."

"What happened?"

Kerry chewed her lower lip. When it came to the point, she couldn't tell Vickie everything. Somehow she felt that that would be stabbing Alex in the back. He had employed blackmail because he was desperate to gain custody of his son. And last night? She was equally to blame. She hadn't screamed the place down, had she? She hadn't thrown a chair through his triple glazing and threatened to embrace death before dishonour either, had she? No, far from it. Only afterwards had she had the decency to regret her behaviour.

"Why the beetroot-red blush?" Vickie straightened, slinging her lighter down and blowing a faint smoke-ring as she exhaled. ''Did he use sex? My God, he must have been desperate to get you any way he could!''

The high-pitched, venomous tone grated on Kerry's nerves. ''It was I who broke the marriage up,'' she said defensively.

''And you're going back out of guilt? Alex wants Nicky,'' Vickie guessed shrewdly. ''You don't still love him, surely?''

''Of course I don't.''

''He's about as lovable as a sabre-toothed tiger, and about as dated.'' Her laugh was harsh, her blue eyes intent on Kerry's perplexed face. ''Well, I can release you from the weight of your conscience. Would you like a drink?''

''Too early for me.'' She was uncomfortable with the strangeness of her sister's mood. In her opinion Vickie had already had a couple of drinks.

Vickie jerked a slim shoulder. ''You might change your mind in a minute or two. The…the night of the party…or maybe I ought to begin before that.'' Her strained gaze was oddly pleading. ''I hope that you remember that I didn't have to tell you this.''

''Tell me what?''

Vickie took a deep breath. ''When we were younger, I used to resent you…''

''Me?'' Kerry gaped.

Vickie sighed ruefully. ''You were always the favourite at home. You worked hard at school, steered clear of too many different boyfriends…you never put a foot wrong. Of course I resented you. But after I'd been away for a few years I felt bad about it. That's why I let you have my flat that summer. I was ready to play big sister.''

Kerry was completely motionless. She had often wistfully envied Vickie her glamour, her poise and her classic beauty. But Vickie wasn't confessing to simple envy. Vickie, she sensed, was talking about sincere and bitter dislike.

"I can hardly believe you never guessed. The parents certainly did. You see, I wanted Alex for myself." There was a crack in Vickie's stark and shattering admission. "I cast out every lure there was for him. I invited him to my parties and he never came. Every time he saw me, he acted like he didn't know me. And then you moved into my apartment, and in two months, my eighteen-year-old sister in her ragbag clothes had his ring on her finger, and my God, but I hated you for that!"

Chalk-white now, Kerry's face was filled with dawning horror. "You were in love with Alex?"

"No, not in love. But he was the man I had set my sights on." Vickie's voice wobbled, at odds with her shuttered expression. "I never got close enough to get thinking about love, but believe me, I chased him. Do you know how I felt when he fell for you? Humiliated. He never did tell you, did he? That I fancied him and made a complete ass of myself..."

"Oh...Vickie." On the brink of sympathetic tears, Kerry sprang up, ready to comfort her. "I had no idea, and I'm sure you didn't make a fool of yourself."

"Don't be kind, Kerry. I couldn't stomach that at this moment," Vickie snapped, her composed face contorting with strong emotion as she turned her back. "I took that job in Venice because I wanted to cause trouble. I hated him because he didn't want me. I wasn't good enough. I'd been around. Hell, so had he been...but the old double-standard was made by men like Alex." The words were pouring from her now in staccato bursts. "He wouldn't have married you if he hadn't been the first."

Kerry sank down again, thunderstruck by what Vickie had hidden from her. She recalled Vickie's pettish refusal to be her bridesmaid, Alex's unrelenting coolness towards the sister she admired. The facts had been there before her, the suggestion of something that did not ring quite true, but she had been so full of loving Alex, she had been blind. She bled for the pain she had unwittingly caused Vickie. It was one thing not to attract a man, another for the same man to marry a kid sister. And Vickie had never had any trouble in getting the men she wanted. She was a very beautiful woman. Alex's indifference must have hit her hard.

"I wish you'd told me about this a long time ago," she said unhappily. "I used to talk all the time about Alex. It must have upset you."

Vickie stubbed out her cigarette, and immediately lit another with an unsteady hand. "What upset me was the way he felt about you. He was besotted and it sickened me. But he had one Achilles heel. He was scared stiff your feelings were going to change and you were going to grow out of him," she continued jerkily. "That's why he was so jealous and possessive. He had worked out for himself that if you never got any rope without him or one of his sisters, you couldn't get up to much. The night of my birthday when you phoned him, I was listening on the extension...and I heard every dirty label he attached to me. Of course, can you blame him? Even after the wedding, I made it clear that I was available!"

Twin spots of livid colour burnt over Vickie's cheekbones. Kerry looked sickly away from her. Her sister spared herself no pride in the confession. She remembered Alex's blazing anger that night on the phone. He had succinctly summed up his opinion of Vickie's frequent and casual affairs. It must have been very painful for Vickie to listen to the character assassination.

"To give him his due, he had just cause. Alex is quick," Vickie conceded. "He knew how I felt about him, and he despised me for it. I was furious that night and very bitter. I had had a lot to drink, although I'm not using that as an excuse...Jeff had stupidly put something in your drink to try and brighten you up a bit. When I found out I was angry with him, but by then you had already collapsed. I hauled you up to bed before twelve and you were out for the count..."

"But you said I was up to all hours drinking..." Kerry whispered.

"It still hasn't sunk in yet, has it? I lied! I told you a pack of lies!" she extended rawly. "I never went to bed. I stayed up all night with the last of my guests. When I saw Alex's car drawing up down below, I decided to get my own back. I wasn't thinking of you or the future or anything. It was an impulse. It was Alex I wanted to hurt. Jeff was still drunk. I told him it was a practical joke. He tore into your room, threw off his clothes and got into that bed beside you. He was there all of two minutes before Alex arrived."

"No...it couldn't have been like that..." Kerry's tongue seemed too large for her mouth, the syllables of her dazed interruption dragging.

Vickie drew deep on her cigarette and stared at her. "It was. Jeff never laid a finger on you, not a single finger. I ran to the front door, threw it wide, looked suitably shocked and Alex leapt at the bait. I got the biggest thrill of my life watching Alex's face when he saw you and Jeff in that bed. It was pure farce, but it knocked Alex flat.'' She relived it without pleasure. Indeed, her voice was wooden. ''I didn't know he was going to go right off his head like he did. I thought he'd put it together for himself. He was always so damned clever about everything else. He should have smelt a rat the minute he got over the shock. But he didn't.''

In the grip of astonishment, Kerry was speechless. The sordid episode which had wrecked her marriage and nearly destroyed her had been a cruel, spur-of-the-moment practical joke! Nothing had happened. All these years she had carried round this soiled feeling of shame. And nothing had happened!

''How could I have known that he would walk out on you and wall himself up?'' Vickie demanded stridently. ''I didn't know what to do. I was scared. I would have ended up the family outcast. He would have ruined my career, too. All over his over-reaction to a crazy, childish joke! As if I'd have let him in if you'd really been in bed with somebody!''

''So you kept quiet.'' Kerry could not conceal her revulsion. ''You let me go through hell. In fact, you *watched* me go through it. I hated myself and I didn't even do anything!'' Her voice rose steeply.

Vickie collapsed down opposite, her eyes anguished. ''It all just mushroomed, it got too big for me to handle. But I had to tell you now, I had to get it off my chest. I couldn't see you going back to him because you thought you owed him the sacrifice...''

''Or did you tell me because you couldn't stand the idea of me being Kerry Veranchetti again?'' she countered in helpless suspicion.

Vickie flinched visibly. "OK, I deserve that and more, but I got over my jealousy and my infatuation a very long time ago. Don't you understand what I went through, too? I was terrified of telling anybody." Tears streaked her sister's face. "Once it was done I didn't know how to stop the shockwaves spreading."

But she had still protected herself. Kerry lifted her head proudly. "You have to go to Alex and tell him the truth. Do you hear me? And while we're on the subject, what about the mysterious Jeff, who so conveniently disappeared?" she stabbed grimly.

"Jeff?" Vickie's eyes slewed back to her in shock. "What's he got to do with it?"

Either her sister was very naïve, or this was sarcasm. Now she had the whole story, Kerry found Vickie's insistence that Jeff had been a stranger somewhat harder to swallow. "Did you really ask a complete stranger to take part in your joke?" she demanded uncertainly. "When I think about it, I find it hard to credit that you've neither heard of him nor seen him since. You know hundreds of people in the fashion industry, you're both in the same trade. Are you telling me that you couldn't track him down if you tried?"

"Track him down?" Vickie ejaculated. "What for?"

"Obviously in the hope that I could persuade him to back up your story for Alex. Jeff hasn't got any reason to lie, has he? Have you really never seen him since?" Kerry pressed less hopefully.

"Never...my God, it's a big world out there! He mightn't even be a photographer now, and even if I could...help, why should he risk life and limb to help you? Can you imagine the kind of revenge Alex would take?"

Kerry's brows pleated. "You're filled with amazing concern for somebody you don't know, aren't you? *What is his name?*" she prompted tautly.

"I don't know! I don't know a thing about him!" Vickie practically shouted at her, and it was obvious that for her this situation had got out of control. Kerry was talking about possibilities she had never foreseen, and suggesting taking the entire affair beyond these four walls, an affair moreover which showed Vickie to poor advantage.

"I don't believe you," Kerry admitted wearily.

"Alex wouldn't even believe me. Why try to drag anybody else into it? Even if I could find him for you, what good would it do? I'm damned if I would face Alex. He didn't trust you, that was his problem," Vickie argued vehemently. "Not mine. And the way he treated you afterwards showed you what Alex was really like. He's a bastard."

"You won't tell Alex, will you?" Kerry read the answer in her evasive gaze and experienced a spasm of sick disgust. "Well, may God forgive you, Vickie, because I never will. How could you have been such a cold, selfish schemer? What did I ever do to you?" she whispered.

Vickie just sat there, pale and trembling but silent.

Kerry got up, defeated but angry. "Let me tell you something else; you were in love with Alex. If you couldn't have him, you didn't want me to have him either. That's what it all came down to four years ago."

She walked out of the apartment, grimly and impotently convinced that Vickie was withholding information about Jeff. Four years ago, it had suited Vickie very nicely to have no Jeff available to refute her lies. Kerry's head was reeling dizzily. Vickie. To even credit that Vickie had saved her own skin and pride at the expense of her marriage devastated her. It was as if her sister had suddenly become a stranger to her. Kerry could not forget, forgive or even begin to understand how her sister could have remained silent when she realised Alex intended to divorce her.

Her sister just hadn't been able to hold on to the dark secret any longer. Her nerves had given way. Kerry remembered her nervous brittle manner at the hospital. Vickie had been scared that, if Alex and Kerry finally got together, her duplicity might somehow be revealed. How could it have been? Kerry had never understood why she should recall not a single thing between feeling drowsy and waking up. But she had never suspected that her drink had been doctored. Vickie had told her that she had over-indulged. Kerry had had no cause to disbelieve her, and Vickie had staged a very good act of sympathy that morning. Perhaps she had enjoyed seeing Kerry at the mercy of shock and horror. Kerry wondered painfully if she would ever be able to believe in anybody again.

WHEN SHE STEPPED OUT of the car at the vicarage, Nicky came running to her. "Can we go home now?" he demanded.

"Yes." Again she manoeuvred out of any long chats with her parents. They accepted that she had a great deal to do, and Vickie's revelations had made Kerry eager to be away from their unworldly contentment.

As Nicky chattered on the drive back to the cottage, a strange new lightness of heart began to lift her out of her introspection. The nightmare of her conscience had suddenly been banished. The shadows were gone. The guilt was gone. In a peculiar way, Vickie had set her free.

"Granny said that you and me and Daddy are all going to live together," Nicky relayed excitedly.

She tautened, sucked back willy-nilly to the present. How could she turn in her tracks now? She had no proof. Would Alex even believe Vickie, or would he think that Kerry was rather pitifully trying to cover up too late? A surge of savage hostility encased her then. The tables had been turned. She could hate Alex now without feeling guilty about it. He had judged her without a hearing. Suddenly she was in so much conflict that she couldn't think straight. She was sick and tired of being a victim. Vickie had made her one, Alex had followed suit with a cruelty foreign to Kerry's softer nature.

If she married Alex she would still be paying for a crime she had not committed. She had already paid a hundred times over. Dammit, why should she be victimised again?

Her fingers hovered over the phone to contact the driver and tell him to return her to the vicarage. She saw herself walking in and laying the whole story before them. Simultaneously, she saw herself destroying her family. It would still come down to her word against Vickie's. It would tear their parents apart to see their two daughters engaged in such bitter conflict. She couldn't do that to them. She couldn't risk her father's health, either. Her hand fell heavily back on to her lap. Alex had won, after all. Alex always won.

THE WEDDING TOOK PLACE five days later. Vickie took sick last moment, and phoned the vicarage to say she was down with gastric 'flu. Steven had spent most of the intervening period begging Kerry to tell him what was wrong with her. On several occasions she nearly broke down and spilt it all out: her ever-mounting sense of injustice. Four years, she kept on thinking, four wretched, miserable years that had practically crippled her emotionally because she had been enslaved by her own guilt.

She was like a statue during the brief ceremony in a London register office. They came out to a barrage of photographers. The Veranchetti rematch, someone quipped. Alex was all smiles, the two-faced swine that he was. Antipathy raced through her in a stormy wave, and as he met her eyes, his narrowed perceptively.

"What's wrong?" he enquired.

Kerry almost laughed. What's wrong? she thought wildly. Oh, there's nothing wrong, Alex. You forced me into this marriage, you're forcing me to share my son, you're forcing me back into a life-style I hated…really, Alex why should there be anything wrong?

"Are you feeling all right?" She guessed he could afford the solicitous look. He thought he had won. Well, he hadn't won. All hell would break loose if he dared to try and exert his marital rights.

He carried her firmly off into the car, away from the loud voices asking quite incredibly impertinent questions. "I have a headache," she lied.

"Stress."

What the heck would he know about stress? She turned her flushed profile aside. There was still the meal with her parents to be got through with a civilised show.

"Why didn't Glenn attend the wedding, if he was such a good friend?" Alex drawled softly.

"I try not to involve my friends in burlesque shows."

"I'm sorry that you feel that way about our wedding."

"What wedding?" Her green eyes flashed at him. Although she had promised herself that she would not start until her parents were safely off-scene, she could no longer control her ire. "You got me here at the point of a gun. Why the polite hypocrisy? I don't need it."

His lustrous dark eyes rested on her unreadably. "I don't want to argue with you today."

Why was there something special about today? Her contempt showed, and his aggressive jawline set. For the space of a heartbeat she thought Alex was about to lose his cool. But his thick, dark lashes screened his gaze. She admired his control. The limousine filtered to a halt in front of the hotel. She pinned a smile to her lips for her parents' benefit. Another couple of hours and the need even to smile would be over.

CHAPTER SIX

THEY WERE flying straight to Rome. It seemed that Alex could not wait to parade his bride to the family again.

"It will be easier if it is done immediately," he pronounced during the flight. He actually reached for Kerry's clenched fingers. "Believe me, no one will say anything to hurt your feelings."

His family could not afford to offend him; Alex either employed them or supported them. They would have had to accept Frankenstein's Bride with a smile had Alex made the demand! Her generous mouth thinned. Well, she wasn't the trusting and naïve teenager she had been on her last visit. Nobody would intimidate her this time.

"Is it the prospect of meeting my family again which is worrying you?"

She raised a brow. "Nothing's worrying me."

Nicky climbed up on her knee and planted himself bodily between them. "This is my mummy." There was a miniature Veranchetti stress to the possessive tone employed. Ever since Nicky had adjusted to the sight of his parents together, he had been growing increasingly less certain about whether or not he liked the combination.

"And my wife," Alex murmured.

"She's not." Nicky's mouth came out in a pout. "I'm going to marry her when I get growed up. You've got Helena."

Kerry forced a laugh. Alex surveyed her over the top of Nicky's dark, curly head in cool question. "I don't find that funny."

"It makes pretty clear sense to him. He's seen you with too many different women," Kerry riposted drily.

"Helena happens to be an eleven-year-old," he interposed. "And the women you talk about are at an end now."

She shrugged as Nicky slid down restlessly and crossed the cabin to play with the jigsaw she had set out for him. "I wouldn't speak too soon," she replied. "After all, I'm not going to share a bedroom with you again. Touch me and I'll disappear into thin air, Alex. I swear it. You can't have me watched all the time."

Long fingers tipped up her chin. "Don't utter foolish threats."

"It's not a foolish threat. It's what will happen," she informed him steadily, her eyes icy-cold. "You've got your son, you've got a wife who will behave like a wife in public, but in private, as far as I am concerned, the act dies."

"You realise that you are about to turn our marriage into a battle?" he raked in undertone back to her, his mouth taut. "*Dio*, when I was prepared to try and put everything in the past where it belongs, you begin to cause trouble. It won't work, *cara*, I warn you."

She swallowed with difficulty. "Content yourself with what you've got, Alex. It's all you're going to get."

Unhidden anger gleamed in his narrowed scrutiny. "Don't start it up again."

"You started it. You got us both into this marriage," she reminded him.

He sprang upright and strode up to the built-in bar, where he barked at the steward, who hurried to serve him. He looked ready to commit murder. Golden brown eyes arrowed piercingly over her coolly composed face, and against her will she trembled. She had had to tell him before tonight. Perhaps she had not employed particular tact. But there really wasn't a diplomatic way of telling Alex that he was barred from his wife's bedroom. He behaved as if he owned her body and soul. He always had. And he only wanted to exert his rights over her sexually in revenge. He had told her that with unforgettable candour. She was amazed that he could still behave as if she was the one being unreasonable.

"Daddy's cross," Nicky whispered when she got down to help him with his puzzle. "Did I do somefin' wrong?"

"No." She gave him a guilty little hug. Alex was emanating enough hostility to carry them to Rome without jet engines.

"Did *you* do somefin' wrong?" Nicky asked guilelessly.

Reluctantly, she approached Alex. "Nicky is picking up the atmosphere," she reproved tautly.

His fingers came down on her tense shoulder and she froze. His other hand splayed across her narrow back as he drew her firmly up against him. Deliberately taking advantage of her inability to struggle, he tasted her angrily parted lips. She stopped breathing, she was so busy fighting the danger of response. He laughed with throaty enjoyment against her lips, and merely deepened the pressure.

"Stop it!" Nicky screeched hurling himself at Alex's legs. "That's my mummy, leave her alone!"

Alex released her and dropped down lithely in front of their son. She had expected him to lose his temper, but he soothed Nicky and lifted him up, leaving her out of what appeared to be a man-to-man exchange. Annoyance snaked through her. It was the first time she had ever seen her child turn in his distress to someone else.

Nicky returned with enormous, hurt, dark eyes to stare at her.

"What on earth did you say to him?" she demanded of Alex.

"That I won't be leaving you alone. What did you expect me to say?" Alex enquired with a brilliant smile. "What he just saw he has to get used to. He's likely to see a lot of it in the future. That's a fact of life."

"Not of mine," she assured him through gritted teeth.

IT WAS POURING with rain when they landed in Rome. The Veranchetti home there was an enormous, impressive town house behind high walls. Kerry was quiet as the car wafted them through the gates. The courtyard was full of opulent vehicles. The family had evidently turned out *en masse*. Her own tension mounted another notch.

"It will be all right," Alex said gently. "I promise you that."

"I'm not worried. They're mostly a set of hidebound troglodytes with too much money," she parried wildly.

"What's a troglodyte?" In the echoing hall with its alcoves and tall Chinese vases, Alex bent his dark head teasingly.

She reddened. "It's not very complimentary."

A brown forefinger confidently brushed a straying strand of vibrant hair back from her cheekbone, and his breath fanned her cheek. "It's like a sunset, your hair. A glorious, multicoloured sunset," he growled half under his breath. "The very first time I saw you I imagined it cascading over white pillows..."

The tip of her tongue snaked out to moisten her dry lips. They had gone from troglodytes to sunsets to pillows. He lowered his head and ran the tip of his own tongue erotically along the same path, hunger burnishing his golden eyes, a devouring, smoulderingly sexual hunger which tightened his hard bone structure and sent Kerry into shaken retreat. "Later..." Alex practically tasted the word.

No, there wasn't going to be a later. Her colour high, she spun and recognised the tall, dark young man standing watching them. "Mario?"

"Kerry."

Alex's younger brother bent to kiss her cheek. While she had been away, he had grown to manhood from a lanky and boyish sixteen. He backed off again awkwardly, stuck for the verbal social niceties to fit the occasion. Nicky streaked past them. *"Nonna!"* he hollered at the top of his voice.

On the threshold of the crowded drawing-room Kerry stilled in surprise. Her son went hurtling cheerfully towards the thin woman with the patrician features seated in a wing-backed chair by the fire. His grandmother, Athene. He gave her an exuberant hug and grabbed her hand. "Come and meet my mummy."

Oh, my God, Kerry thought, feeling Alex's hand welding to her spine like a bar preventing retreat. "He's her favourite," he divulged.

But only next to her firstborn son, Alex. Athene looked upon Alex with a fierce pride which only dimmed when her eyes slid to the wife by his side. A cool kiss was pressed to her cheek. "You are welcome," Athene said graciously.

She was threaded through the gathered cliques. Alex was one of six children, with three sisters and two brothers. Between them they had about thirty offspring, or so it had always seemed to Kerry. Both the sisters and the daughter-in-law conformed in the Veranchetti clan. They maintained their husbands' homes and raised children and shopped as if there was no tomorrow...real exciting stuff, Kerry thought wryly. Entering this old-style family was like stepping back a century in women's rights to a time where the men were still men and the women were delighted they were. Alex's rule here was supreme. By some quixotic quirk of heredity, none of his siblings had an ounce of his drive and self-assurance. They followed him like a flock of sheep. His sisters adored him and his brothers admired him. His opinion was sought on the most minor decisions.

The general warmth of her reception surprised her. Athene's frosty smiles were the equivalent of a red carpet. It seemed that her supposed infidelity remained a secret within the family circle. Her discomfiture eased and Nicky bounced along beside her, showing off by introducing her to all and sundry.

"Nicky is so like you," Alex's middle sister, Carina, exclaimed.

"Me?" Kerry laughed. She only ever saw Alex when she looked at her son. His amber-brown eyes, black hair and lean, above average height all echoed his paternity.

"Your smile...he has your smile and your liveliness." Carina patted the seat beside her. "How does it feel to be back?"

But I'm not back, I'm only passing through...where? Dear heaven, where were they spending the night?

"A little strange," Kerry admitted truthfully. Yet there was a subtle difference to her own responses. She was no longer overwhelmed by the opulence and the formality which Athene insisted upon. It wasn't Kerry and it never would be, but she didn't feel a failure simply because she did not fit the family female mould. It was over four years. A woman did a lot of maturing in that time, she acknowledged.

"I am pleased that Alex and you are together again," Carina declared carefully. "Mamma was…er…disturbed by the divorce, and Alex cut himself off from the family for a long time. He…how you say…? Dug himself into work. Alex, he's like Mamma. Too strong…you understand?"

"No," she said frankly.

Carina moved a plump beringed hand. "He can't bend, he can't talk of what he really feels…you know? But where would we be without Alex to tell us what to do?"

Heaven? "I don't know," said Kerry dutifully.

"Alex is the clever one in the family. We were lost when he was too busy for us, but I think we learned that Alex had a life to lead of his own," Carina confided, her round, dark eyes resting ruefully on Kerry's face. "Before, if he was not at the office or abroad, you would find him having to help one of us…eh?"

Kerry nodded honestly. Alex had always been very much in demand. If they bought a new house, if someone was ill, if there was marital dissension or problems in business—they called Alex. In the past she had resented those constant encroachments into what little time they had together as a couple.

"I think you will find this has changed," Carina murmured, and her sincerity made Kerry feel uncomfortable, for the less she saw of Alex in their present relationship, the happier she would be.

After dinner, served in the lofty-ceilinged dining-room, Kerry inwardly accepted that they were obviously expected to stay the night here. Coffee was served in the drawing-room, and she found herself seated with Athene, everybody else steering a rather deliberate passage to leave them in privacy.

"We have had our differences in the past," Athene delivered with a regal inclination of her silvered head. "But you are Alex's wife again now and these must be set aside. I want you to know that I did not want the divorce. I begged Alex to reconsider. Our family has never had a divorce before, and you were expecting my grandson. In the light of your remarriage, it is clear that Alex should have listened to me." Before she could reply, Athene added smoothly, "We will not speak of this again."

The conversation became general, and Alex's other two sisters, Maria and Contadina joined them. As usual, all the men were on the other side of the room. Kerry's mind began to wander restively. She would have to share a bedroom with Alex tonight. Some wedding night it was going to be, she reflected tensely.

"You're in your usual rooms," Athene informed her later on, and Kerry's cheeks warmed.

She mounted the stairs, smothering a yawn. The resident nanny had marshalled Carina's children and Nicky off to bed earlier. It was comforting to find their bedroom suite changed beyond recognition. She felt less like a woman in a time warp. Then she had to admit that there was very little left of the happy, gauche and outspoken teenager she had been when she first came to this house. With hindsight, she disliked Athene less for the callous and cold snubs dealt to her behind Alex's back.

What a ghastly shock she must have been to Athene's snobbish and ambitious hopes for her eldest son! Alex's bride had been a chirpy teenager, who wore her thoughts and her feelings on her sleeve and hurled herself into Alex's arms when he came home, regardless of who was present. Her confidence had not lasted. She had lived on the periphery of Alex's busy schedule, and the shopping trips, the endless rounds of polite socialising which had filled his sisters' days, these had driven her up the walls with boredom.

"Alex...of all my sons," she had once heard Athene proclaim to a close friend. "Marrying a little nobody with no breeding and no background. She will always be an embarrassment to him. Wherever she goes she is late. Her taste in clothes is indescribable, and she gossips with the maids..."

In remembrance, a rueful grin lit Kerry's lips. How terribly lonely she had been here, and yet how afraid that the criticisms were just ones. But the memories no longer bit with venom. She had let her insecurities grow out of proportion, and Athene, still reeling in those early days from Alex's choice of bride, had received a vengeful pleasure from pointing out her failings. Once they had moved to Florence, Kerry had evaded every effort Alex made to draw his family back into their lives. It must have been very hard for him. Naturally he had thought she was being unreasonable. Athene had never dared to be malicious when he was around.

Why was she thinking this way? Why was she seeing her own faults and making excuses for his? He had neglected her. He had refused to see that she wasn't the rich idle wife type. When she had become pregnant the sense of being trapped had grown stronger, for Alex had used her condition as an excuse to keep her tied to the house in Florence those first few months. Vickie had had a strong influence on Kerry then. It had not been difficult for Vickie to heighten Kerry's resentment of Alex's possessiveness. But Alex had grown up with a mother and three sisters who automatically deferred to him. If he had loved her...how could he really have loved her? she asked herself cynically, irritated by the tenor of her thoughts.

He came into the room and shed his jacket. She kept on reading her magazine doggedly.

"This won't work," he breathed. "We can't live like strangers and hope to give our son a happy environment."

"You should have thought of that." His reasonable tone, the sombre cast of his appraisal were, however, disconcerting. She had expected a return of the anger and the obduracy he had briefly displayed during the flight.

"No." Cool fingers twitched up the magazine and tossed it arrogantly aside. "You should have thought of that before you shared my bed a few nights ago. We cannot for ever throw recriminations at each other. What is done is done. This marriage is a new beginning, not a continuation of hostilities. I will accept nothing less." The hawk-gold gaze rested calmly on her infuriated face. "That is all I have to say for now."

He strolled into the bathroom, leaving her a prey to temper. Alex had turned sanctimonious. At least in his contempt and anger and need for revenge that night at the apartment, he had been honest with her. But now he realised that he had been too honest and that she had more backbone than he had given her credit for possessing. Naturally, he didn't want a wife who loathed him. He didn't want the arguments, either. He could afford to be generous now that he had got what he wanted. Having taken her in lust, honour was now more or less satisfied. If he could convince her that he was now magnanimously prepared for a fresh start without retrospective glances into the past, what did it really cost him?

Alex could be very charming and very credible. Until she had offended, she had had no idea that nine-tenths of the real Alex was hidden beneath an indulgent and sophisticated surface. Having learnt painfully at first hand how merciless and hard he could be, she must never be taken in by pleasantries again. He couldn't possibly be practising sincerity. Not after the cruel intimidation and derision he had employed to get her to the altar. She had to admit that from the moment that ring went on her finger again, Alex had been extraordinarily civil. But then that was for Nicky's sake and his family's. No, she couldn't afford to trust him. At heart, he despised her still.

When he came to bed, Kerry was pretending to be asleep.

"Goodnight," he murmured softly, without coming near her.

In the darkness she grimaced. He certainly wasn't burning with desire for her! Anger and revenge had powered his previous hunger into a physical catharsis. Those fierce emotions slaked, only masculine pride would make Alex demand repetition. It would never happen again, she promised herself. Now that she was free of the shackles of the old guilt, she was her own person again, and self-preservation came first.

"GREECE?" she mumbled sleepily.

He had shaken her awake, and with difficulty. She had finally dropped off about four in the morning. Opening her eyes to Alex's leaping vitality and the intimacy of the bedroom scene sharply off-balanced her. He had further dismayed her by announcing that they were leaving this morning for the island of Kordos, which had come to Alex by inheritance via his Greek grandfather. "Greece?" she said again.

Alex shifted a broad shoulder sheathed in white silk. "We have to spend some time together."

"To satisfy convention?" she taunted.

His perfectly chiselled mouth firmed. "We need time to bridge the gap of years. Time to relax and become acquainted with each other again, if you like, and we certainly do not require an audience while we accomplish that feat."

"I don't want to go to Greece."

"That's unfortunate," he murmured drily. "We are going, and when we leave the island, we will return to our home in Florence. I still have the house there. You're going to be late for breakfast if you don't get up," he completed, sweeping up his jacket and departing.

Alex, you rotten, manipulative swine, she thought. He had saved it all up and delivered it as stated fact. A honeymoon in Greece and a return to Florence. It was a shock to learn that he still owned the house they had once chosen together. She had assumed that he would have sold Casa del Fiore.

She had to rush to get downstairs in time for breakfast, and Nicky was nowhere to be seen.

"Mario has taken Nicky and Carina's boys out for breakfast. He's also going to take them to the zoo," Alex supplied. "I explained to Nicky that we would be away for a while. He will have plenty to occupy him here."

As it sunk in that Nicky was not coming to Kordos with them, disbelief fired her almond-shaped green eyes.

"Alex and you need some peace," Athene ruled down the table. "And Nicky is too attached to you."

"How can a child be too attached to his mother?" Kerry enquired spiritedly. "We will talk about this in private," Alex threw her a warning glance.

"Mamma did not mean to offend," Carina soothed under the general cover of conversation. "But it is right that you should have time to spend as a couple before you become a family again."

Kerry set her teeth together. How dared Alex arrange to leave Nicky behind without even consulting her? Indeed, having foreseen her objections, he had simply chosen to go over her head.

"I hate to tell you this, but Nicky is becoming a spoilt little brat," Alex dropped when everybody else had deserted the table. "When he was with you he had all your attention, and when he was with me it was the same. I could not play the strict father then because I was afraid to destroy the relationship I did have with him. Everybody has spoilt Nicky because we were divorced."

"But that's going to change, right?" she gathered shakily.

"Gradually it will, as he adjusts to the presence of both of us." He refused to rise to her anger, and he sighed. "You know as well as I do that what I say is true, but the main reason I made the decision that he should remain here is that if it were otherwise, he would inevitably become aware of the conflict between us, and I will not have that happen."

Unwillingly she recalled Nicky's boisterous behaviour the night before. It was true that he was much too used to being the centre of attention, but she still felt that she was being punished through her son for standing up to Alex yesterday. How could she feel otherwise? She had no wish to develop a closer relationship with Alex. It was an impossibility, and in its own way a potential trap.

If she ever opened up to Alex again, he would hurt her, and she couldn't take that a second time. How did he even have the gall to imply that it was her duty to fulfil his expectations?

But she was forgetting that she was a second-class citizen in Alex's eyes. Remarrying an adulterous wife was no mean concession in his book. He undoubtedly thought that she ought to be eating grateful and humble pie for the rest of her days. Yes, sir, no, sir, three bags full, sir.

"Even had I discussed this with you, you would have said no," he continued. "Ask yourself how we can deal with Nicky when we are still at each other's throats? And then tell me I am being cruel to him."

Colour fluctuated wildly in her cheeks. "This is simply blackmail in another form," she condemned.

His eyes narrowed, his jaw clenching. "I would not use our son in that way," he contradicted icily.

"You used him in that contract, didn't you? You keep on forgetting that I am here against my will," she whispered dully.

Alex thrust back his chair and walked out of the room, rather than giving vent to his temper. Kerry went upstairs, feeling curiously empty of satisfaction. He hadn't liked the truth being hurled at him. And, much as it galled her to admit it, she had made a pointless reminder. She could talk about duress until the cows came home, but they would still be married.

"HOW LONG ARE WE to stay on Kordos?" she asked during the flight to Athens.

"One week…two." He eyed her with cool implacability. "When we return for Nicky we won't have this atmosphere between us."

"I never realised that you believed in miracles."

The sardonic look she earned washed pink into her cheeks. "You will make the effort that I am making. Neither of us could possibly be content in the mockery of a relationship that you appear to want," he asserted.

Her soft mouth moved tremulously. Oh, Alex, you really had it all once and you threw it away, she thought sadly. She had loved him very deeply. She had had him on a tall pedestal, and she had never ceased to marvel that he had chosen her. But he had broken her heart and her spirit. He had taught her how to be bitter.

Her hostility had ironically been exacerbated by Vickie's confession. Was it fair of her to feel that he should have given her a hearing? In his position, would she have? She doubted whether she could have walked away when denying Alex meant denying everything that was important to her. Thank God that it wasn't like that for her still, she allowed gratefully.

Kerry had never visited Kordos before. A trip had been suggested on several occasions, but business or family had always intervened. She watched the jewelled green speck Alex pointed out suddenly expand in size against the deep blue of the Aegean. A small and picturesque fishing village straggled round the harbour. The helicopter cast a long shadow over the dark pine trees which shrouded the steep hills behind the village. Up on the cliffs sprawled a long, white villa with a red-tiled roof. It was ringed on its rocky height by flagstone terraces. They dropped down on the helipad set into the level ground to the front.

The staff had emerged from the villa to greet them. Sofia and Spiros, who ran the house, and a gaggle of dark-eyed, giggly maids were duly introduced to her. But it was Alex who guided her into the shade of the house ahead of them and said, "I will show you to your room."

"I'm actually getting one of my own?"

"Why should I wish to share a room with you?" A satiric brow quirked. "I, too, like my privacy. I do not deny you yours."

It was a concession she had not expected and nor had Sofia, the housekeeper, who protested that the room was not properly prepared. He left Kerry alone, as she struggled against an unjustifiable tide of pain and despondency. Why on earth should she feel insulted? It was a step in the right direction, removing them from the dangerous intimacy she had feared. She stared out of the arched windows at the magnificent view of rock and sea and skyline merging majestically together.

Alex reappeared a few minutes later and insisted upon showing her around before she changed for dinner. She duly admired the clean, tiled floors scattered with priceless Persian rugs, and the air of comfort and tradition which adhered to the sparse furnishings in their plain, earthy colours. After that she took herself off for a short nap and ended up rushing to get dressed in time for dinner.

"You look rested," Alex saluted her mockingly with his glass. "Has it improved your humour?"

In exasperation, she stiffened. "There was nothing wrong with my mood. How am I supposed to react to a place like this? What are we going to do here?"

Alex burst out laughing, white teeth flashing against brown skin. "Do you really want me to tell you?"

It was a setting for lovers, not for two people who could hardly speak to each other civilly. "All *I* plan to do here is read some of the books I brought with me," she warned in dulcet dismissal.

He absorbed her mutinous face with arrogant amusement. "You want to punish me for persuading you into my arms before the wedding. But it was inevitable that the force of our emotions would bring us together. It brought me peace..." he stressed. "The past is over, *cara*. Why can't you accept that?"

Angrily, she began to eat. It had brought him peace. It had torn her apart. He had received the ego-boosting response he required from his recalcitrant wife. He had conquered his own distaste and her reluctance. He made no apology for the cruelty of his words to her that night. Why should he apologise? In his mind, he would always have the perfect excuse to employ that rapier tongue if she got out of hand. The past is over. No, he was wrong. The past had made the present for them both.

"I'm not sleeping with you, Alex," she asserted.

"Inevitably you will. You see, you want me." Golden eyes held hers steadily. "Why should you be ashamed of that?"

How could he ask her that after his admission that he despised her?

"How many times must I tell you that the past is finished?" His lean, strong features were harshly set. "You made one mistake, but we both paid dearly for it. Some day I will forget that other day, but I promise that I will never throw it at you in anger again."

Her mouth twisted. "And what are you doing right now?" she flared.

He slammed his wine glass down. "What do you think I am trying to do? I am trying to talk to you, I am trying to be civilised!" he gritted in the most uncivilised snarl.

"You're in the wrong century. I've had enough to eat." She rose with unhurried grace and left the table.

In her room she paced the floor. She had almost screamed her innocence at him. But she would only have demeaned herself in his eyes. He would never believe her and she had no evidence. Naturally he saw no good reason why she shouldn't abandon herself to pure physical gratification in his bed. In the depths of Alex's subconscious would always lurk the reflection that if she could do so with a stranger, she certainly wasn't in a position to deny a husband.

When she emerged from her bathroom later, swathed in a light cream satin peignoir, Alex was reclining fully dressed on top of her neatly turned-down bed.

''What do you want?'' she demanded.

He studied her tousled and damp appearance, the fiery hair tumbling round her heart-shaped face, the tight clasp of her fingers on the lace edges of the scanty covering. He took his time looking her over, a burnished glitter of desire brightening his dark eyes. A brilliant smile curved his mouth, making her vibrantly aware of the leashed sensuality coiled within his relaxed length. ''What do I want?'' he echoed softly. ''Only to kiss you goodnight for the servants' benefit. You will come to me the next time we make love.''

''There won't be a next time,'' she swore as he slid upright and folded his arms around her rigid body.

His lips feathered across hers, and she trembled long before the hard heat of his mouth properly engulfed the sweetness of her own. It was a taste of heaven and a taste of hellfire damnation all in one go. His hard thighs were imprinted against her softer curves as she leant inexorably closer to him, until he was holding her upright. She shivered violently in the unyielding possession of sensations infinitely stronger than she was, sensations that whispered and yet burned over every part of her.

With a husky laugh, Alex gathered her up and deposited her down on the bed before freeing her.

He stepped back, his smile mocking the confusion she could not hide from him as she swam back to reality again. "I do not think that you are cut out for the life of a celibate, *cara. Buona notte,*" he drawled with silken emphasis.

She groaned as the door shut. What was it about him, dammit, what was it about him that made him irresistible? Her hands curled into claws in the pillows. Her body had a blind spot where Alex was concerned. It was all this slothful eating and lying around and being waited on. Healthy activity was what she needed, and not of the kind Alex would suggest. There was no barrier there. It made no sense. She ought to freeze when he came close. But she didn't. The same powerful chemical attraction which had drawn her to him at eighteen was still there. Indeed, by some cruel twist of fate it had grown even stronger. She ought to be mature enough to handle Alex's sensual magnetism and see it for what it was: a hangover from her misspent youth, a symptom of frustration. Unfortunately, none of her frantic efforts to explain away her response to him made it any easier to get to sleep.

CHAPTER SEVEN

KERRY slid out of bed, irritably pushing her hair off her
damp brow. A tide of dizziness went over her and she
groaned. It was the heat. Alex would die laughing if he
saw her like this. Hot, harassed, sleepless. She curled up
in the basketwork chair by the tall window. It was their
fifth day on the island. From dawn to dusk, Alex had
been charm personified. He had broken the ice, in spite
of her determination to remain aloof. Somehow…heaven
knew how, her sharp, defensive retorts had begun to
seem petty. They were talking now without fighting. Of
course not about anything in particular. Safe things.
Nicky, the house in Florence, his business interests.

Her fingers rubbed at her tense neck muscles. She had
changed. She had changed from the moment Vickie told
her the truth. An inner strength had been reborn, a surge
of returning self-respect. It shook her to admit that for
four years she hadn't really cared about anything but
Nicky. She had just gone through the motions, even in
business, content to believe herself independent of Alex,
but too apathetic to employ the effort of will required to
lick Steven into shape. She could have made a go of
Antique Fayre. Instead, she had let it limp along, and
now there would never be another chance to prove her
own mettle.

Last night they had attended a wedding in the village

as honoured guests, and amid the jubilant mayhem of the celebration Alex had caught her to him, amber eyes rampant with impatience. "When...hmm?" he had muttered. "Why pretend? Deep down inside you must know what you want. Or perhaps you want to be told."

The chauvinist emerged around nightfall. Alex wasn't accustomed to waiting for anything he desired. His restraint over the last few days had been sheathed in a sardonic indulgence. The sexual charge in the atmosphere was like an electric current. After all he had done to her, how could she still want him?

The sight of Alex in a pair of low-slung, tight-fitting shorts and nothing else was lethal enough to stop her in her tracks. And he knew it. The torment was like a knot jerking a little tighter every day. She couldn't sleep because she ached for him. It infuriated her, it outraged her pride, but she couldn't deny it. Alex brought her alive as no other man ever had. An unholy and primitive pleasure sent her pulses leaping when he came close.

The clear, moonlit night beyond the glass was dancing dark reflections on the shimmering surface of the pool. It was three in the morning. Everybody would be asleep. The water glimmered a silent invitation. Leaving her room, she let herself out on to the terrace. It was the impulse of a moment to shed her nightdress and slide soundlessly down into the gloriously cool depths. With a sigh of relief she floated on to her back.

Alex would find himself a mistress. She could hug her inviolability to the grave. She turned over and began to swim. She didn't want him to have other women. She had her pride, too. It was the woman who looked the fool when her husband was entertaining himself elsewhere. She ground her teeth together at that humiliating reality. Lost within her own thoughts, she did not notice the ripples spreading on the water, signifying that she had company.

A pair of hands enclosed her waist. She gave a stifled gasp before Alex spun her round and pressed her back against the side of the pool, his hard, punishing mouth stealing her cry of bewilderment and fury. His lips roamed torturingly over her temples, her wet cheeks and down again to tantalise the corners of her mouth in a passionate barrage of burning caresses. Emerging from shock, Kerry planted her hands on his bare, muscular shoulders. "Where did you come from?"

"I saw you from my bedroom window." Alex dragged her small hands down and forced them to her sides. In the shadowy light, a hard-boned savagery clung to his taut, golden features. "You flaunt yourself...you go too far..."

"F...Flaunt myself?" she echoed incredulously, mortified to learn that she had had an audience. "You rotten...voyeur!"

His hands dug into the sodden mane of her hair. "*Dio*, I do not receive satisfaction from watching," he scorned. "But I'm entitled to take it when my wife plays at provocation." His mouth connected hotly with a hollow in her throat. "Your skin gleams like wet silver in this light." His hands skimmed down, not quite steadily, to the full globes of her breasts. "And I find that I am very much a man..."

"I never doubted it, but you promised!" she objected shrilly, a spasm of terrifying excitement shooting through her tremulous body.

"So I am human," Alex grated in unashamed excuse, involved in a scorching trailpath across her smooth ivory shoulders, pausing to nip at her earlobe before stabbing his tongue in a hungry thrust between her lips, and she quivered. Great breakers of anticipation washed over her in response.

The water eddied noisily round them as he pressed her closer still to his virile length. He did not have a stitch on either. A constricting pain tightened her stomach muscles on a wild, remorseless rush of pleasure.

"No..." She fought her own weakness in desperation. Her palms braced against his shoulders in a fleeting gesture of protest, and then breathlessly, mindlessly, her hands began moving down in slow connection with his damp skin, her fingertips tangling in the black whorls of hair sprinkling the breadth of his chest. With an earthy groan of approval he pressed her hand down over his flat stomach to demonstrate his need, and she capitulated without thought. She was starved of him, almost frantic in the cruel hold of the desire he had unleashed within both of them.

Suddenly he was sweeping her up and wading towards the steps. He cast her down across the bed in his own unlit room, lowering himself down to her again with primal grace. "When I saw you in that hospital, I knew it wasn't over. I looked at you," he cited in a husky, accented growl. "And I knew I had to have you again. You're in my blood like a fever and I'm in yours."

His fingers spread her wet hair over the white woven counterpane, and he ran his hot, burnished gaze over her ivory slenderness. She felt like a sacrifice of old. It was insanity but she was spellbound. There was a wild, womanly joy to the discovery that Alex was as entrapped as she was. It seemed to make them equal. And when he bent over her, her lips parted by instinct to welcome his.

KERRY HAD A THUMPING headache when she woke up. She crawled weakly over the bed to squint in dull-eyed

disbelief at the clock. She was back in her own room.
Her nightdress lay on the chair as if she had never put
it on, never taken it off. The curtains were firmly closed
on the brilliant light of midday. It was as if the whole
of the previous night had been a figment of her imagination. But the ache and the languor of her body told
her otherwise.

Had it been a dream that there had been something
magical about those hours? Why had she pretended to
herself that she could resist Alex? He had put the heat
on and she had scorched. She had burnt up in an inferno,
incapable of denying him.

Ahead of her stretched a never-ending roundabout of
falls from grace and morning-after attacks of conscience.
She swallowed hard as she thought about all the affairs
Alex had had since their divorce. Distaste rippled
through her. She was her own worst enemy still. Why
had she ever blamed him?

"Sleep well?" Alex lifted his blue-black head from a
perusal of a Greek newspaper and watched her walk
across the terrace.

"Yes." Her eyes searched his cool, dark features in
search of a smile, a greater warmth.

"Good." Alex went back to his newspaper quickly.
"Could you tell Sofia that I'd appreciate lunch soon?"

Disconcertingly, her eyes glazed over with tears. She
glanced down at the pale blue sundress she had carefully
selected from her wardrobe and, spinning, she went back
into the house. Last night Alex had slept with his wife.
What had she expected? A magnificent bouquet of flowers on her pillow? Some romantic, loving gesture? What
had happened might have been important to her, but it
wasn't to him. She ought to have reminded herself that
Alex's raw energy found a natural vent in sex. And, as

he had said, why should he not use her as he had accused her of once using him?

She mumbled to Sofia about lunch and mentioned a headache in the same breath, requesting a tray in her room. Her distraught reflection in the mirror there seemed to taunt her. How many times had she sought her soul in a mirror during the years since she had met Alex? How many times had she asked herself why her life was in such turmoil?

The pain and the anxiety had always melted down to the same source. Love. Such a cruel emotion to the unlucky. It was love which was stalking her like Nemesis now. She had never managed to kill her love for Alex. She had dug the weakness down deep and sought to bury it, but it had lingered, preventing her from finding peace even with herself. When had loving Alex ever caused her anything but pain? She did not marvel at her own reluctance to admit her vulnerability. Pride and simple fear had warred against the admission.

"Sofia tells me that you are not feeling well."

"It's just a headache. I'll lie down for an hour." Her voice emerged perfectly normally and she turned.

Alex was on the threshold, dark and tawny and compellingly masculine. Concern showed clearly in his narrowed, probing scrutiny.

"Leave me, I'll be fine," she insisted when he continued to stare.

"Are you in love with Steven Glenn?"

The unexpectedness of the quiet demand took her by surprise. His eyes were cool and level. The weather might have been under discussion.

"Why should you think that?"

His arrogant head tilted back, black hair gleaming in

the filtered sunshine. "I was curious, and it's wiser if we don't have any secrets between us."

"You've got everything else, Alex," she heard herself riposte drily. "I'm afraid you don't have access to my every thought too."

Fury glittered in his gaze. The illusion of cool was abruptly cast aside. "Then you will understand if I prevent you from returning to England in the foreseeable future," he delivered crushingly.

As he withdrew, the door rocked on its hinges. A sick tide of bitterness rose like bile within her. How could he think that she could love another man and still abandon herself to *him?* It certainly clarified Alex's view of her. As far as Alex was concerned, she was enslaved by her own promiscuous nature. Already he was suspecting his conviction that there had been no other men. He would have her watched like a thief when he was abroad. He would never trust her out of his sight. But she understood why he could live with her moral deficiency. It was her weakness, not his. Had his surveillance of her life included a photo of Steven? A humourless smile curved her lips. Steven was a very handsome man. Well, let Alex live with his suspicions! Steven was at a safe distance. If Alex had to distrust her, Steven was a harmless focus.

When she returned to the terrace after lunch, Alex was not there.

"Kyrios Veranchetti has gone fishing." Sofia answered her enquiry cheerfully.

She got a pair of binoculars and located him out in the bay.

"He with old Andreas like when he was a boy," Sofia burbled, sketching an impossibly miniature Alex with a workworn hand.

She could see two figures in the shabby *caique*. Sunlight glinted off a can of beer in Alex's hand. She put the binoculars away guiltily and spent the afternoon sunbathing. He came back just before dinner, angling her a flashing, sensual smile on his way past. "I won't take long to change."

He talked with animation over the meal. Their earlier conversation might never have happened. As she went to bed, she was wondering how she was to survive another decade of Alex's supreme self-sufficiency. He didn't care if she loved another man. He had her in body, he didn't need her in spirit, too. She was almost asleep when he came to her. Her drowsy, muffled protest was silenced by the tender caress of his mouth. If he had been storm and passion the night before, he was seduction and silence now. But this time she was agonisingly conscious of his withdrawal afterwards. He quietly removed himself back to his own room. Actually sleeping with her appeared to be an intimacy Alex could not bring himself to contemplate.

She woke up to the sound of the helicopter landing. When she walked out on to the terrace Alex was chattering in Italian on the phone, and two dark-suited men, one standing, one sitting, were with him. Her colour evaporated as she recognised one of them. The older one with the greying hair was Roberto Carreras, the lawyer Alex had sent to Florence with the separation papers. Just looking at the man brought back hideous recollections.

"Some coffee, *kyrie?*" Sofia bustled past, carrying a laden tray, and the men turned their heads, seeing her slim figure for the first time. It was too late to retreat.

Carreras immediately stood, his suave features betraying not an ounce of discomfiture as he politely spun out his chair for her. *"Buon giorno, signora,"* he said, and passed some meaningless comment on the magnificent view.

She was ill with mortification, forced to take the seat and smile in the man's general direction. Alex glanced up, an abstracted half-smile softening his expression. Sofia moved about, pouring the coffee, pressing Kerry for a breakfast order. But if she ate, she would very likely throw up, she acknowledged. She had been so distressed that day. The lawyer had remained coldly impersonal while she had begged him to speak to Alex for her, had begged him to convince Alex that he had to come and see her face to face. "That is not my client's wish, *signora,*" he had intoned expressionlessly.

In retrospect, she marvelled that she had survived that period. A shudder of fearful repulsion snaked through her as she surveyed Alex from beneath her copper lashes. "Excuse me." She got up on cotton-wool legs with a slightly bowed head. "I'll leave you to your business discussion."

Strolling into the house, she could feel Alex's questioning glance burning into her back. She went out to the terrace at the rear of the villa. How could she sit and make polite conversation with a man who had witnessed and played a part in her humiliation? It was too much to demand of her. But Alex was an unfeeling, insensitive brute. He probably didn't even remember that Carreras was the one.

There were too many cracks to paper over. This marriage could never work. Even her innocence could not wipe out the memory of a nightmare. Yesterday she had let herself float with the tide because she loved him and she had wanted to cling to the fragile hope that he had meant it when he talked about a fresh start. What a fool she had been!

She was standing by the sea wall, gazing down sightlessly at the waves crashing white foam against the rocks far below, when firm hands curved hard to her shoulders from behind. She flinched.

"They're gone," Alex drawled roughly.

So he had remembered...my God, how could either of them ever forget?

"You've got to let me go, Alex," she whispered. It was the only answer that she could see.

His fingers bit painfully into her slender forearms. "No," he gritted. "Why should you talk like this now?"

"You're hurting me."

His hold loosened, his thumbs rubbing soothingly over the indentations of his hard fingers. "I didn't mean to. I think I have bruised you. Forgive me."

An hysterical laugh bubbled up in her convulsed throat.

"I remembered too late to protect you from that embarrassment. It won't be repeated. It was an unfortunate oversight. You will not have to see him again."

The laugh escaped this time, high-pitched and unnatural. "What are you going to do? Tell him he's no longer welcome in your home because he once performed a certain task at your behest?"

"I will transfer him somewhere. He will not suffer by it. I can do no more. If you are so upset by the sight of him, I can no longer entertain him," Alex retorted with abrasive practicality.

She gulped. "I see. Are you planning to do that with everybody who might talk? The staff in the house in Florence, the security men, your secretarial staff in Rome who never put through my calls, the personal aides who ensured my letters were returned...what about the other lawyers involved?''

Spinning her round, he gave her a little shake. Perspiration gleamed on his hewn dark skin, lines of strain grooved deep between his nose and mouth. ''Stop this now,'' he insisted in a ragged undertone.

She turned up her tear-stained face in a movement of despair. ''You're not being logical, Alex. Athene may not descend to gossip, but a lot of your friends must be in the know. I know what a hotbed of gossip Roman society is, and the way rumours go, I should imagine that the word is that you walked into an orgy by now...'' She faltered out of all control and restraint. ''Doesn't it bother you that people are going to mutter and sneer behind your back?''

His hands sprung wide as he released her. He backed off several steps as if he could not trust himself too close. Slowly she shook her head, Titian hair flying about her in fiery glory. It had had to be said, all that Alex did not want to hear, for as those things happened she would be the one to pay the price.

''Don't you see that you will take your anger out on me?'' she pressed hoarsely.

''Cristo!'' The muscles in his strong brown throat worked. ''How can you believe that of me?''

Her arm steadied her weary body against the wall. ''You can't turn the clock back, Alex. You've got to see that. It was over for us a long time ago. You should have left me alone. You saw me in hospital and you acted on an ego-ridden whim. There is no going back. Let me go...''

He swung away from her, his brown hands clenching into impotent fists. She did not know whether his aggression was aimed at her for ripping the lid off the reality he ignored or aimed at all those faceless people who might dare to whisper. He punched one fist into his palm with a thud which tremored through the hot, still air. His golden gaze struck sparks from hers in an uncompromising refusal to yield.

"I believe I would sooner see you dead than let you go. I want you too much, and I am not afraid of gossip. Nor should you be, for who would dare to insult you to your face?" he demanded fiercely. "It will be a brave man who dares to offend me. This is between us and nobody else, don't you see that?"

"I can't take it, Alex," she said in a stifled whisper. "I was content as I was."

A black brow shot up. "You will be content with me. If you can accept me in bed, it is only a matter of time before you accept me everywhere else."

"Never! It's too late." Hectic pink searing her cheekbones at his blunt reminder of her weakness, she tried to walk away. The intensity of the powerful emotions simmering between them had exhausted her. Alex would never admit to a wrong decision. He would manoeuvre and manipulate and calculate to the bitter end in an effort to make it a right one. But when he talked of removing Carreras from the scene, he was touching the tip of an iceberg, and evading the issue. Carreras had only been an instrument, a highly paid professional man doing his job. It was the man behind the instrument who had driven her nearly crazy with grief.

Only black storm clouds loomed ahead. Alex was not omnipotent. He liked to think he was, though. He had been born into wealth beyond most people's wildest dreams. His Midas touch had transformed wealth into legend. Her supposed infidelity was probably the only situation that Alex had ever met which was outside his control. She had offended in a way no other living person would have dared to offend. He still regarded her as his, indisputably his, and no man and no woman could be permitted to take what belonged to Alex before he chose to discard it. She was the one slap in the teeth Alex had ever had, and with masochistic fervour Alex was seeking to redress that slur on his masculinity. How stupid she had been to believe Nicky his main motivation in this marriage!

"I wish I could go back and change some of the actions I took." The harsh confession was dredged from him. "But even if I could, I do not believe I could have behaved differently..."

An anguished smile twisted her pale face. How like Alex it was to lament and negate in one savagely candid statement.

"You were very young and I was hard, but I suffered too," he asserted roughly. "On three separate occasions I flew to Florence during those six months."

She stilled and whirled jerkily back.

"Once I got as far as the gates of Casa del Fiore before I told the driver to turn back." The dark eyes had no shimmer of gold. They were black and deep as Hades. "And you should be glad I turned back. I did not trust myself near you."

A picture of Alex flying into Florence and backtracking in triplicate frankly astonished her. Her imagination balked at the vision of Alex controlled by rampant indecision. But that he had tried to make himself approach her, that he had been drawn against his own volition, softened the dead-weight of resurrected bitterness which Roberto Carreras had aroused. Instinctively she moved back towards him. "W...What did you want to say?" Her voice was almost inaudible.

His jawline clenched rock-hard. "Why? Why, that is what I wanted to say. Was it because he was younger than I, better-looking, more exciting? Was it out of badness or out of need?" he selected in a savage undertone which froze her in her tracks with a sudden onslaught of throat-constricting fear. "Was he good? How often did he take you, how did he take you? That was all that was on my mind!"

His slim, beautifully shaped hands folded over the balustrade of the wall, the knuckles showing white. A surge of frightening anger had him in its merciless grasp. She was sentenced to appalled stillness by the horrific reality of how deeply Alex had been affected. She wanted to speak, she wanted to drag her sister kicking and screaming into his presence and wipe it all out. But common sense kept her quiet. In the mood Alex was in, the explanation would sound like fanciful nonsense. It would enrage him even more.

"And still sometimes it is on my mind. Because I never got my hands on him, and if I ever did I would kill him."

She trembled. "But...if you'd actually seen me, don't you think you might have had other...things to say?" she whispered.

"I knew you were not well. I was kept informed by your doctor. If I had come to you and you had lost our child, I could not have lived with myself."

It was not an answer to her question. But it had been a sentimental question. At no stage had Alex seen the smallest hope of a reconciliation.

"And that day at the hospital, after Nicky's birth, I looked at you," he breathed, "and I hated you for what you had done to us both. I never wanted to look upon you again, but I could never put you behind me where you belonged.''

Was that what this marriage was aimed at achieving? Deep down, was that what Alex was really seeking? He had called her a fever in his blood. He would secretly despise such a weakness in himself, but he would not admit to it in self-denigrating terms. She was suddenly convinced that, whether he appreciated it or not, Alex was hoping to look at her with perfect indifference at some time in the future.

''And you still believe we can make a new start?'' she queried.

His proud profile tautened. ''It is natural for us to drag up all the feelings that we never shared then. By doing so, we will lay them to rest.''

If more honest sessions akin to what she had just undergone lay ahead, a quick, merciful dive off a cliff would be kinder to her twanging emotions.

''I didn't deliberately seek to hurt you then.'' Alex looked down at the seas battering the rocks below and emitted a harsh laugh. ''I was not really myself. If it had been drugs, drink, illness…insanity, anything but infidelity, I would have stood by you.''

He stepped away from the wall. ''Do not ask me to let you go again. I don't like this view you have of yourself as a prisoner,'' he admitted. ''You have everything that any normal woman could want, and I take very little in return.''

He was daring her to disagree. His anger had gone, but he would have relished a good rousing battle to blow off the cobwebs. When she thought about it, she was the only person she had ever known who argued with Alex. ''You take everything,'' she contradicted painfully, and this time she did manage to walk away.

It was lunch before they came together again. Alex was back on the rails of cool, implacable good humour. He suggested they spend the afternoon on the beach and he wouldn't let her brood. "You see, you are not unhappy," he stated with arrogant emphasis the first time she laughed at one of his sallies. "You only think you are, and perhaps you want to be, but you are not."

"Were you very unhappy when I left you in Florence?" he asked, with a naïveté which could only astound, in the depths of her bed that night.

His limbs were still damply entangled with hers, his breath warming her cheek. In itself, the question was a miniature breakthrough in intimacy. Alex was normally edging away by that stage, making her wonder melodramatically if he hated himself in the aftermath of their passion. It was also the first time that he had ever made a personal enquiry as to her state of mind then.

"Scared," she muttered. "Lonely."

His lean body stiffened in the circle of her arms. His damp, silky hair brushed her brow as he lowered his head. "For him?"

"Oh, go to hell, Alex!" After an outraged second of disbelief that he could even think that, she yanked herself violently free of him. "How can you say that? I loved you, God, but I loved you!" She buried her contorted face in the pillows, her narrow back defensively presented to him.

"From love of so fine a strength, a man would surely take great comfort..." he raked back at her in cruel cynicism. "The love I got from you I bought. Your head was turned by my money and your body was ripe for a man's possession. Do not call that love!"

He slammed out of the room. Something went crashing noisily down in the corridor and she heard a groaned profanity. He had hit himself on the small table she had put outside to carry a vase of flowers. She sincerely hoped it had hurt like hell. If he wanted to play musical beds in the middle of the night and throw right royal rages, he deserved everything he got.

"I'M SORRY...how often must I say it?" Alex thundered across the table at lunch time the next day. "Yes, Alex, no, Alex, if you like, Alex! What kind of conversation is this?"

Sofia had almost dropped the coffee-pot. Out of the corner of her eye, Kerry noted her hasty retreat from the roar of Alex driven beyond endurance by silence. "I can't get very chatty about the idea that I married you for money and sex," she said bitterly. "Somehow you have twisted up our whole relationship. I didn't cost you a groat in comparison with anybody else's ex-wife. You got off really cheap," she pointed out coldly.

"I didn't want to get off cheap."

"Of course you didn't! If I'd ripped off every penny I could get, you'd have loved it. It would have proved that I was grasping." Breathing tempestuously, she settled back, wearing a baleful expression. She had hardly slept last night. She had been furious. On half a dozen occasions she had been tempted to wade into his room and bawl him out like a fishwife. Sorry wasn't always good enough.

"What do you want me to do? Get down on my knees?" he replied caustically.

"I'd kick you if you did, so I shouldn't bother," she responded tartly, catching the disorientating twitch of his mouth. Her own anger dissipated rapidly. They were squabbling like a pair of children.

He drove his fingers through his black hair and studied her. "Let's go for a walk," he suggested ruefully.

Beyond the house, he dropped an arm round her tense shoulders. "I lost my temper," he sighed. "And perhaps I lost it because what you said upset me."

He turned her round and dropped a kiss on the crown of her head. His careless action had the most outsize effect upon her. It was the first gesture of affection he had shown in an entire week. Up until now he had only ever held her as a prelude to making love, and last night she had angrily decided that that would happen no more. Now she was swerving again. Could a physical relationship bring them close? The lack of one would certainly drive them apart. But she suffered from the insecure fear that she was simply adding to his low opinion of her. Would he have respected her more, would he have been more inclined to listen to her if she had found the willpower to deny them both that outlet?

"I wasn't a very attentive husband then, was I?" he mused when they were on their way back to the house. "You must often have been lonely, even when we were living together. Why the hell didn't I go with you to that party in Venice?"

Her face shadowed.

"Shall I tell you why? It was so trivial. I was making a point. I was taking a stand. I worked late on into the evening, and then all of a sudden I got angry. I lifted the phone and ordered the jet to go on standby. I felt very self-righteous."

"Don't..." Should she try to explain? He seemed in an unusually quiet and approachable mood. As she hovered on the brink of an explanation that might well have

proved momentous in the face of Alex's candour, someone came out of the house and waved.

"Spiros. The post must have come in," Alex sighed.
"He remembers the workaholic I used to be."

that she was simply adding to his low opinion of her.
Would he have respected her more, would he have been

CHAPTER EIGHT

SOFIA HAD coffee waiting for them in the lounge. Alex, flicking through the envelopes, suddenly paused and strode over to her where she sat. "For you," he said.

He dropped the letter into her lap and she lifted it, recognising Steven's impossibly neat copperplate handwriting. She tucked the envelope in her pocket and collided with Alex's dark, intent scrutiny. She didn't realise what was wrong until he finally breathed, "Aren't you going to read his letter?"

He had recognised the postmark, of course. "Why, do you want to read it too?" she enquired in exasperation. "Honestly, Alex, Steven is my friend and my partner, and he has never wanted to be anything else."

"That has not been the impression I have received," he parried icily.

She had had enough, and he had barely begun. If Alex was even going to question her mail, what hope did they have? Could adultery be committed on paper? He really would not be satisfied until he had her locked away in a little cage. Warding off the urge to leap down his throat, she murmured gently, "You're going to have to learn to deal with your jealousy, Alex."

Even as she said it, she could have bitten out her tongue. She might as well have dropped a burning rag on the surface of something highly inflammable. He

went up like a Roman candle. "Jealousy?" he erupted
in raw rejection. "Of what would I be jealous?"

She paled. "Maybe possessiveness should have been
the word I used. I don't know. But I do know that there
is a problem."

"And shall I tell you what it is? My wife does not
have male friends. Either you sell out your interest in
the partnership or you give it to him. I don't care," he
grated. "But you will sever the connection completely."

For the second time he missed out on the coffee.
Kerry wiped at her damp eyes. The illusion of greater
understanding between them was destroyed. She no
longer wondered why he had brought her to Kordos. The
men in the village held Alex in the highest esteem. None
of them would have dared eye up his wife. He owned
the island, he was their benefactor. Whether Alex saw it
in himself or not, he really wanted to wall her up alive
and prevent her from coming into contact with other
men. What hope did she have of combatting his distrust?
Vickie, what did you do to us both? she questioned miserably.

She read Steven's letter. It was fortunate that Alex
had not tried to do so. "Feel like telling me the truth
yet? Remember this shoulder is always here. I make a
great wailing wall when I'm not wailing myself." It
chirped along much as Steven did, filled with personal
questions, casual endearments and entreaties to write
soon and tell him where she had hidden the spare keys
for the MG. An impending visit from Barbara received
a careless reference. "I can't cope without you, seriously
I can't," he completed. "Please dump him and come
home."

She sighed. No, he wouldn't be managing. He was
too disorganised. As long as there was food on the table

and petrol for the car, he would be happy. He had no ambition beyond that level, and he had depended on her heavily. If Barbara was half the woman Kerry thought she was, she would step into the breach. The business, properly run, would keep a married couple comfortably.

It was early evening when the call came. Spiros came into the lounge to have a discreet word with Alex. Kerry was lying on a couch reading an English newspaper and ignoring an atmosphere which positively pulsed with unspoken expectations. She had given Alex no reason to suspect Steven. The thought of lowering herself to further explanations stuck in her throat and a mention of Barbara now would probably strike Alex as highly suspicious.

"It seems you have a caller who refuses to identify himself."

Her head flew up. "I have a visitor here?" she said in amazement.

"A phone call," Alex contradicted.

She began to get up, but Spiros was already passing her the nearest extension. She swept up the receiver, fully expecting to hear her sister's voice. The voice she did hear shot her in a state of imminent heart failure back on to the couch.

"Kerry? If it's you, for God's sake say something," the New York twang implored. "I'm not much good at cops and robbers."

"It's me."

"I guess you won't have forgotten me completely. Jeff Connors?"

Had Vickie got hold of him, after all? It seemed conscience had finally won out. Dazedly, Kerry was practically digging the phone into her ear in case the voice travelled within incendiary distance of Alex. To her intense relief, he sprang up and left the room.

"I'm alone now. You can talk," she muttered.

"Vickie told me everything. You've got to believe me when I tell you that I had no idea you and your husband got a divorce. I just couldn't leave it lying so I came over…"

"Over where?" Her heartbeat had hit the Richter scale.

"Athens. I'm trying to rig transport over to this island of yours."

"Are you crazy?" she hissed in disbelief. "You can't come here, you mustn't come here. He'd kill you before you…"

"If your husband still feels that strongly, I was right to come."

"Have you got a death wish?" she murmured, thinking in a hurry, which was difficult when she was in a complete panic. "Don't come to the island. Wait until we get home to Florence and bring Vickie with you. That's essential."

"So you do want the story told?"

"Yes, of course I do." In her dumbfounded horror at the vision of Jeff stepping on to Kordos, she had not immediately picked up the significance of his willingness to redress the damage he had done. He really had to be a much nicer person than she had ever imagined if he was ready to take the trouble…not to mention the risk. Maybe he was just too stupid to realise what Alex was likely to do if he came across him. Alex would wipe him off the face of the earth before he even got his mouth open.

"We owe you and it will be straightened out," he promised. "I'll persuade Vickie by kidnapping if necessary. You see, I've got my own aspirations riding on this, too. I want to marry your sister.''

She came off the phone in shock. Vickie had told her so many lies. But her silence in London was now explained. She had been protecting Jeff. From Alex? Or from the knowledge of her own behaviour? After all, if Jeff, who existed in Kerry's memory as a lanky blond man with formless features, was talking about marrying her sister, his good opinion would not have been something Vickie wished to risk losing. Clearly they were very friendly and had obviously remained in touch. Having told all to Kerry, Vickie had evidently confessed to Jeff as well. Kerry shook her buzzing head to clear it. It was like a chain reaction, and if it kept on moving…dear lord, Kerry might just have a marriage with a future again.

''That was Steven. His idea of a joke.'' She lied without a blush, popping her head round the door of Alex's study with a wide smile.

He had a glass of whisky in his hand. His sombre features merely tightened, but she ignored them. A heady surge of hope was rising within her as she adjusted to the import of the call she had received. Alex could not deny both Jeff and Vickie, surely? Even for Jeff to face him was a revealing fact within itself. But it all had to be done properly. She sighed. ''Alex, please try to trust me.''

''How? Do I police you everywhere I go?'' he demanded scathingly. ''I almost lifted the phone to listen to your call. To even think along such lines unmans me!''

She drew in a long, sustaining breath. Had he been less self-restrained she would probably have been swan-diving off the terrace right now and striking out for the nearest patch of dry land. She inwardly thanked her guardian angel for Alex's principles. There was never anything sneaky about Alex in his dealings with her...aside of that business with Willard Evans and all the prying he had done. But she was in a good enough mood to concede well-meant intentions on those counts. Really, there was always a bright side to be found if you looked hard enough. And Kerry was suddenly seeing bright sides all around her for the first time in years.

Over dinner, Alex's silence passed over her preoccupied head. When she went off to bed, she slept like a log. The last agonies of the long nightmare would soon be over, she reflected cheerfully when she awoke the next day.

"I'm glad to see you so happy," Alex commented sardonically over breakfast.

Her nose wrinkled as she tasted her coffee. It had a curious sharp flavour, but Alex didn't appear to be finding anything amiss with his. She munched a piece of fruit to freshen her mouth. "Are we leaving for Florence soon?"

Dark eyes swept her unwittingly hopeful face. His thick lashes screened his gaze. "No. I am content here for the moment."

"You said a week, maybe two," she reminded him. "I miss Nicky."

"He can always come out here to join us." He shrugged with cool finality. "If you want to do some shopping, I'll take you to Athens."

"I do occasionally take my mind out of my wardrobe."

"And where does it travel then?" he murmured with a satiric edge.

Slowly she counted to ten. She still got up. "I feel

like some fresh air. I'll go down to the beach for a walk.''

"Don't go far. Carina and Ricky will be here for lunch,'' he warned her. ''They're leaving for New York tomorrow. He's taking charge of our public relations department over there.''

She managed a smile at the news. She liked Carina the best of Alex's sisters, but her mind was more intent on how speedily she could bring Alex and Vickie and Jeff together in Florence. Jeff had said that he would fly back to London today. Impatience shrilled through her as she went down the steep steps to the beach. She was terrified that Jeff would lose interest or that Vickie would persuade him against his plan. If he was in love with her, Vickie would have influence over him. Perhaps in the heat of the moment Jeff had flown out to Greece. Kerry had stopped him in his enthusiastic tracks. Suppose he gave up the idea? Vickie wanted to pretend that it was all in the past. She was afraid to face Alex. Her pride revolted against the concept.

Kerry wandered along the rocky beach, the sun beating down on her in golden warmth. She had been walking for some time when she came on the small cove where a yacht was moored. A bunch of sun-tanned young people were strewn out on the sand, sunbathing, while a stereo cassette pounded out Bruce Springsteen.

"You can't be a local!'' A dark-haired youth proclaimed loudly. ''Not with that gorgeous hair. I refuse to believe it.''

She grinned. ''You're English.''

Within five minutes she was sitting down with the group. There were two couples and one odd man out. They had rented out the small, shabby yacht to do a tour of the islands, and they were lively company.

"The people in the village aren't too friendly," Hilary, the curvaceous blonde complained. "We got flung out of the taverna last night because Dave got on the wrong side of one of the men. We got all this guff about this being a private island, and the local cop saw us off at the harbour so we simply shifted anchor. Are you staying at the taverna?"

Kerry was reluctant to admit who she was, for they had accepted her as one of them. She was enjoying the sound of her own language and the easiness of her welcome. "No, I'm staying at a private house. With my husband," she added circumspectly.

"You're married?" Dave, the one who had originally spoken to her, groaned in mock despair.

She laughed. "I've got a son of almost four."

"He must have stolen you out of the cradle. Rather you than me," the other girl, Ann, said feelingly. "Life's too short to get tied up young."

"It depends on the man," Kerry murmured, unperturbed, and the conversation moved on to the places they had been and where they were hoping to get before their restricted budget ran out.

"I'm gasping for a cold drink." Hilary gave her boyfriend a nudge in the ribs. "Go on, take a walk into the village. The shop's right on the edge of it."

In the end, two of the men went off. Kerry sat, crosslegged, talking about Antiques Fayre with Hilary, suppressing her regretful awareness that she was really describing a closed chapter in her life. Ann decided she was hungry and swam out to the yacht. Kerry rested back on the sand, letting the sun wash her upturned face and extended legs.

She must have dozed off for the next thing she knew, somebody was tugging playfully at her hair. Her eyes opened. Dave was bending over her, too close for comfort. "Where is everybody?"

"I persuaded Hilary to push off."

"Why?" she asked baldly, glancing simultaneously down at her watch. "Oh no..." she groaned.

He caught her arm and prevented her from scrambling up. "Oh, come on, you can't be leaving. You came down here for a bit of company, didn't you, and I'm more than willing to play ball," he told her with a thick, suggestive smile. "We could go somewhere a little quieter."

"Are you crazy?" Kerry snapped, her pleasure in the little friendly interlude now destroyed by Hilary's desertion and Dave's phenomenal conceit. The nerve of him, she wasn't looking for a toy boy!

Before she could pull free of him, his weight pinioned her down as his hand thrust at her shoulder and he made a rough, clumsy effort to kiss her. In sudden, frank fear, for he was considerably bigger and heavier than she was, she was trying to raise her knee when Dave went flying from her in a blur of movement. As he hit the ground several feet away, she pulled herself upright automatically, a gasp of stricken horror on her lips as she saw Alex dragging the winded Dave up with one powerful hand. Her husband's dark face was a mask of murderous fury. As his fist connected in a sickening thud of flesh on bone, she screamed, "Alex...stop it!"

All her life she had shrunk from violence. She wanted to end the carnage, but her feet were rooted to the spot by paralysed fear. The third time Alex hit him, the suffocating blackness folded in on her. She crumpled down on the sand as if he had struck her.

When she came out of the faint, she was lying on her bed and a whole row of faces were around her. "That boy…oh, my God,'' she mumbled as it all came back to her in a wave.

Someone's hand gripped hers. Somewhere at a distance Alex was speaking in a vituperative and vicious spate of Italian. "He's all right, Kerry." It was her sister-in-law's voice. "Ricky stopped Alex in time."

"I thought he was going to kill him…"

Carina came down on the edge of the bed, shooing off the female staff with sharp orders. The room cleared. She turned over the cool cloth on Kerry's brow. Kerry still couldn't stop shaking. She kept on seeing Alex wreaking havoc on an over-amorous youth barely out of his teens. Abruptly, she clutched Carina's hand. "You've got to get me away from here…" she muttered in despair.

"What is happening between Alex and you?" Carina was pale and concerned. "A young man tries to kiss you on the beach and Alex goes out of his head. I never saw him lose control before, but my brother would not harm you."

Kerry looked at her with desolation in her empty eyes. She was defeated for the last time. Alex had broken every bond he held her by. Her emotions had gone into the cold storage of shock. All she could feel was a tearing, desperate need to escape his domination. She didn't care any more about Jeff and Vickie and her airy-fairy hopes of their marriage surviving. It was a brief dream sequence she no longer had the heart to contemplate.

"We were walking along the shore to find you," Carina related. "You always forget the time. But Alex was laughing, you know…he was not annoyed…"

"I wish he had hit *me*." Kerry was not even listening to her.

"How can you say that? Alex would never touch you.

He thought you were being assaulted. Any man would have…no,'' Carina sighed unhappily. ''It was not right what he did. We saw one thing. He saw another. We saw the girl swim out towards the boat. It was obvious that there was nothing questionable. But Alex…Alex is crazy jealous of you.''

Kerry was enveloped in her own despair. She didn't hear Alex come in, but his wrathful, ''Who are you to keep me from my wife?'' penetrated. She shifted away in automatic recoil. She couldn't even bring herself to look at him.

''You animal,'' she whispered, unable to silence the reaction.

His flushed complexion lost colour.

She realised that he wouldn't leave her alone without an explanation. Woodenly, resentfully, she summed up a brief hour spent chatting to some young holidaymakers. It was punctuated and interposed by Alex's imprecations.

''Ah…you start talking to strangers, not even strangers from your own background,'' Alex gritted. ''Cheap tourists. Perhaps you forget who you are. You don't belong with such people.''

No, it was Alex she did not belong with. Once he had been a stranger. He would have remained one had she not possessed a bright, outgoing personality and the thick-skinned bravado of a friendly teenager. ''I spoke to you in a lift,'' she murmured helplessly.

To her surprise, he was quick to grasp the connection. ''That was different.''

No, it hadn't been different. She had always talked to people around her. She had always liked meeting new friends. Alex had been attracted by her vivacity, but he had caged her for the same trait. He chose to forget too that those cheap tourists came from a background of greater prosperity than her own.

"Is that how you met? In a lift?" Much intrigued, Carina was eager to lighten the brooding atmosphere.

Kerry's eyes were wry. "He practically cut me dead."

"Per dio..." Alex raked. "You go back six years to complain!"

She had still to look at him, though she didn't need to look. His lean, strikingly handsome features were permanently inside her head.

"I'll leave you alone." Carina escaped uncomfortably.

As the door shut, Alex planted himself where she could no longer avoid visual contact. "What is the matter with you? Hmm?" he demanded, dulled golden eyes pinned to her in derision. "You were flirting. How else did you get into the situation? They didn't even know who you were. My wife does not mix with people who trespass on private property. Have you no sense of propriety? No sense of discretion? Must I have you watched every place you go?"

Every harsh word lashed into her. She had no answers for him. A thick, impenetrable wall of glass separated them in understanding. She was only twenty-three years old, and just over a year of that time had been spent in the goldfish bowl of Alex's elitist society. But Alex had never granted her trust. She recognised how he had confined her with his family and vetted everyone she met. Her only escape route had been through Vickie. Alex had subconsciously behaved from the outset as if her betrayal was written into the stars. Somehow it helped to see that his excessive possessiveness had existed even then without just cause. She was not responsible for its birth.

"I want to leave with Ricky and Carina," was all she said.

Their relationship was impossible. The poison of distrust and jealousy infiltrated every corner of Alex's mind. A flirtatious glance, a little animated chatter with a man anywhere between twenty and fifty and Alex would be suspicious. It would only get worse. He would imprison her and suffocate her until only enmity and resentment lay between them.

"No!" Alex seethed on another feverish blaze of anger.

It hurt that she should know exactly what he was thinking. He was incredulously reacting to the news that he was in the doghouse when he had only done what any Greek husband would have done to a man making advances to his wife. He was furious that she had not made a more detailed explanation. He was outraged that she was not ashamed of herself. And at the back of it all, he honestly believed that she had encouraged Dave. That was riling him too. He had punished the perpetrator, but not the instigator. His own code wouldn't let him lay violent hands upon a woman. But for how long could that restraint hold out?

She slept for a while, her own constant lassitude nudging and not quite connecting with some nebulous recollection. Carina was there again when she woke up. "I'm staying for a few days," she announced.

Kerry sat up. "But you're supposed to be going to New York tonight," she objected.

Carina smiled. "Ricky can survive on his own for a few days. It's a service apartment and he'll be working all the time."

"You don't need to stay."

"Alex asked me to," she revealed reluctantly. "He's worried about you."

"He wants to make sure that you join me on my next walk along the beach, I suppose," Kerry gathered with bitter distaste.

"No, of course he doesn't." Carina pressed her hand in reproof. "He feels that you need a woman's company. Do you feel like dinner?"

She nodded. "Where's Alex?"

"Down in the taverna, getting drunk," Carina flushed. "Ricky left him there. You were shocked by what he did. Don't you understand how upset he is?"

Kerry's face shuttered as she got off the bed, keen to have a bath and a change of clothes. "It's not remorse, I'm sure. How was Dave?"

"He was all right," Carina repeated, a tinge of disapproval in her tone. It was heartless of Kerry to enquire a second time about her amorous assailant when her husband was drinking himself into oblivion down in the village. "His friends took him away. They were not decent young people, Kerry. That same young man insulted a fisherman's daughter in the village last night and started a fight." Gathering steam, she looked up. "And two girls and three men on a boat, none of them married. This speaks for itself. You are too trusting, Kerry."

In the privacy of the bathroom, Kerry appreciated how a few hours of grace had altered Carina's views. She could not see fault in Alex for long. Thus she had reduced Alex's violence by making the tourists into promiscuous troublemakers. Kerry was no doubt in the wrong for speaking to them at all, and excused for her over-familiarity by a gullible nature. Or were Carina's suspicions running parallel with Alex's now that her brother had done something so appallingly uncharacteristic as hitting the bottle?

He had to let her go now for both their sakes. On that beach, she had seen her naïve hopes for the future shattered by hard reality. Even if Vickie and Jeff did approach him, she seriously doubted that Alex would even give them a hearing. The poison had got too deep a hold in four years apart.

"Do...do you love Alex?" Carina blurted out over dinner, her plump face primed for a snub.

"Love's not always enough," she answered heavily. "He doesn't love me, but he has to keep me to prove something to himself. Letting go would be as healthy for him as it would be for me. We can't live in the past now."

It was too deep for Carina. She chewed her lower lip. "How can you talk about leaving him? You are only newly married again. Alex was happy when we arrived. Why are you so hard on him?"

MUCH LATER, Kerry turned over in her bed, and her lashes flickered up on the dark silhouette of the figure sunk in an armchair in the corner of the room. "A...Alex? Good lord, what time is it?" she whispered, shaken by his silent presence.

"Does it matter?"

She rested back again, shrouded by the same numb depression. "No."

"You should not be afraid of me," he breathed harshly. "Earlier you behaved with me as if I was...*Cristo!*" He sprang upright fluidly, his eyes glittering in the moonlight as he emerged from the shadows. "You are my wife, you are the mother of my child...what happened today? It was not my fault. For that to occur again—to see you with another man—naturally I lost my temper."

"Some day you might do it with me..."

"No!" He roared it at her in fierce rebuttal. "Whatever you did, I would not touch you. I am not a violent man."

But his passions were. They ran at gale-force turbulence with her. Everywhere else in Alex's life control and restraint ruled the roost. He was punctual, tidy, organised, immaculate in appearance. He carried enormous responsibility. He was a rock for his dependent and less able brothers and sisters to lean upon. He was in every other field a strong, principled and honourable man, worthy of respect. She was the fatal flaw that rocked Alex dangerously off balance.

"You've got to let me go," she repeated wretchedly.

The mattress gave under his weight. He leant over her. "These are teething problems. You are over-sensitive. All you can think about is running away. I do not run away from trouble. I face it," he said hardily. "And you will face it with me."

"We're poison for each other."

"*Dio,* such melodrama!" he growled. "And stop lying there as if I am about to attack you!"

Helplessly, she turned her head away. It was a mistake. His fingers laced into her hair and his mouth covered hers in hungry retribution. He found no answer in her. She was as inanimate and as empty as a waxen doll. He flung his dark head back, his ruptured breathing pattern breaking the stillness. "You can never be there for me when I need you," he condemned raggedly. "Why should I curse myself with a wife who has no love for me? Forgive me for forgetting that you are only here on sufferance. I will not disturb you again."

She knew then that the same process was working within him. Alienation. It would only be a matter of time before Alex let her go. He was too proud to hang on to a wife who could not respond to him in bed. It was the ultimate offence, and what a pity it was that she had not contrived the miracle sooner. Since she was seeing the hope of freedom again, she could not understand why tears should wet her cheek and why she should ache at Alex's roughened belief that she turned her back on him when he most needed her. He had never talked about needing her before. Why did he have to talk about it now?

THREE DAYS LATER, she was uncompromisingly sick the instant she got out of bed. One of the maids heard her retching in the bathroom and fetched Sofia. Sofia arrived to beam meaningfully at her while she clung to the sink, trying to subdue a second debilitating bout of nausea. Her pinched face had a greenish pallor and her eyes were haunted. She had woken up feeling sick, the last two mornings. She hadn't wanted to think about the fact. She had suppressed the awareness that there had been no comforting physical proof as yet that she was not pregnant.

Oh, God, please, no, was all she could think now. They were leaving for Rome this morning. Alex had been distant and civil for the past forty-eight hours. All the portents were that he was withdrawing from her, slowly but surely, with the rigid control of a reformed addict staving off the need for another fix. Steeling herself to kill Sofia's hopeful smile, she said, "Is there something wrong?"

The housekeeper frowned. "Is the *Kyrie* ill?"

"I don't think last night's fish agreed with me. I've been feeling unwell all night." Kerry tilted her chin.

Sofia retreated. Kerry splashed her face with unsteady hands. It couldn't happen, it just couldn't happen now. Her system could be upset by travel, the change in climate, the alteration in diet...by sheer nerves. But that night in London was all she could think about. One reckless night at the wrong time. The nausea, the dizziness and the lassitude were all horribly familiar. Alex had impregnated her and she wanted to scream blue murder. It wasn't fair, it just wasn't fair when she was already practically at her last gasp.

"Are you feeling well?" Carina enquired over breakfast. "You seem very pale."

"I had a restless night." She studied the table. She felt like a plague carrier. She felt as if someone had painted a cross on her forehead. She was too self-conscious, too petrified to look anywhere near Alex. But in another sense she wanted to rage at him for his rotten potency. All she could think about was the horrendous misery of her months carrying Nicky, memories inextricably interwoven with what had been going on in her life simultaneously. The mere threat of repetition bereft her of all rationality, and if he found out he would never let her go.

How she got through the helicopter trip she never knew afterwards. It was mind over matter. She had suffered dreadfully from travel sickness, even in a car, when she was pregnant with Nicky. But air travel was the worst of all. On the flight to Rome, mind over matter was no longer sufficient to subdue the churning in her stomach. She spent most of the flight in the washroom, or so it seemed. Concealment had become impossible.

Carina hovered, muttering worriedly about food poisoning. Alex was pale and suspiciously silent after the receipt of one single glance of burning reproach from Kerry. The whole event might have been masterminded by fate to reveal her secret. The only time Alex had ever seen her airsick she had been pregnant. It did not take a lightning bolt of amazing perception for him to suspect the cause.

He insisted on carrying her off the plane. He had recovered his colour, but he looked guilty as hell. It gave her a malicious pleasure that he should understand exactly how she felt. A doctor was waiting for her at the townhouse. Carina helped her into bed. By then, the penny had dropped with her, too.

"I was never like this. No wonder you are miserable," she soothed sympathetically. "It is very hard to be pleased when you feel so ill."

"One swallow does not make a summer," said the doctor glibly. "No pregnancy is a blueprint of another. There may well be small similarities, but with rest and calm you could enjoy excellent health this time."

Kerry saw nothing but misery ahead. As soon as he had gone and Alex's sisters and Athene had given up offering advice, she turned over in bed and wept inconsolably. The axe had fallen. Her body wasn't her own any more. How easy it was for the uninitiated to talk about the redeeming joys of motherhood when they did not have eight months of purgatory stretching in front of them, and a marriage that had already stopped being a marriage beforehand.

CHAPTER NINE

"THE DOCTOR wants you to stay in bed for a few days."

Kerry emerged from beneath her hair. "I hate you!" she screamed.

Alex's black hair was ruffled, his tie was loose and his strain was palpable. She went back under her hair again, racked by the cruel injustice of it all. He didn't love her, she was going to be dumped in Florence again and left to suffer well out of Alex's radius. That doctor didn't know what he was talking about when he told her that things would be different this time around.

"You realise—you *must* realise that I cannot agree to an abortion," Alex delivered, knotting the rope, did he but know it, round his own throat. "I...I couldn't live with that. I wish I could, but I couldn't. Perhaps it will be a false alarm." He sounded very much as if he hoped it was.

What sort of man was he to even think of such a solution? Horror darted through her in wrathful rejection. But desperate straits demanded desperate measures, she decided. When Alex was adapting to a strategic retreat from the battlefield of their marriage, fate had sprung a rear attack on him. Once again he was being condemned to fatherhood with a woman he didn't love, couldn't respect and couldn't live with.

"I'll never forgive you for even mentioning the possibility," she mumbled feverishly. "How could you even think about it for a moment? How could you even say that?"

"I?" Alex unleashed, suddenly springing free of his unusually quiet manner and doing so loudly enough to make her look up in dismay. "I..." He pointed to himself in raw, flaring Latinate emphasis. "Not want my own child? *Dio*, I am jubilant!" He slung the assurance at her, stressing each syllable so that the words rolled off his tongue in fluid provocation. "And I'm not about to apologise for it, either. This time I will be able to watch my child grow. This time I will not be on the outside!"

It was eleven that evening before Alex reappeared. Having run the gamut of her emotions and vaguely appreciated that, no matter what stance Alex took, she would still be unreasonable, she was very quiet.

"I am taking time off to see that you look after yourself," he announced aggressively in the darkness. "If I could suffer for you I would, but I can't. I just don't want you to think that I am leaving you alone."

He gathered her resistant body close with determined hands. His fingers spread protectively over her flat stomach in a movement which was uniquely revealing. "How soon will we know?" he prompted impatiently.

He was holding her, at last he was simply holding her. But the baby had inspired the warm attitude of concern. He really was pleased, she realised. He had switched his possessiveness from her to the life inside her womb. So might he have patted an incubator. All of a sudden, everything else took second place. She sniffed. The numbness had faded again. Of course it had. Loving Alex was a life sentence. It really didn't matter what he did. It would always be the same.

Over the next three days he drove her scatty. She was deluged with fancy nightwear and the latest books, and adjured not to move a muscle. He seemed to be stocking her up to spend the next twenty years flat on her back. One of his sisters did him the cruel disservice of presenting him with a book on pregnancy. By the time Alex emerged, much stricken from its overly informative depths, a headache would have had him rushing her to the nearest hospital.

"Are you dying?" Nicky whispered from under her arm one afternoon. "I heard *Nonna* say Daddy thought you were dying?"

He rocked her with laughter. He made her see the funny aspect to Alex's over-zealous attitude. When the doctor called, she asked him to speak to Alex. Otherwise Alex was never going to believe that she was fit to travel to Florence.

It was an hour before Alex appeared. "You don't look healthy to me. Have I been making a fuss?" he prompted tautly.

It was her fault he had been, she acknowledged guiltily. How many times had she referred to previous sufferings? Had that been to punish him for his absence then? She did not like the picture. He was sincerely worried about the baby, and she was not an invalid.

"I think the doctor was right. It's not going to be as it was before, and even then there was no danger of a miscarriage," she pointed out.

Alex stiffened. "Why does it have to be like this?" he drawled in weary bitterness. "All I ask of you is that you have this baby and love it, even though it is my child."

She blinked back stinging tears. "You don't have to say that to me, Alex. Don't you understand? I panicked, my nerves probably made me feel sick!'' she teased shakily. "You don't have to feel..."

"Guilty?'' His eyes were dark and sombre. "I took no care of you that night. I thought only of my own needs. This did not need to happen.''

She frowned, cursing the childish recriminations she had hurled. "Alex, I'm an adult too. I didn't think either, and it's not...it doesn't have to be a disaster. We both want this baby, don't you see? That's something we can share.''

His ebony brows pleated. "It will be all that we share. We will live separately in the same household. That is what you wanted from the very beginning. It was unreasonable of me to demand anything else.''

Shot from shock to the unalterable discovery that what she had once believed she wanted was now as far removed from her present feelings as Alex appeared to be, she searched his face dazedly. "Unreasonable?''

"Yes, it was. You saw more clearly than I. We must hope that we make better friends than lovers,'' he quipped smoothly. "It will certainly be less explosive.''

Her fingers knotted into the sheets. "Friends?'' she parroted to herself.

Alex vented a humourless laugh. "I see the prospect confounds you, but why not? How else may we live together peacefully? When I forced you to marry me, I asked the impossible from us both. I have accepted that.''

"Yes.'' She saw that he had reached that acceptance. He had dug down to the roots of his desire for her and exorcised it. If he no longer viewed her as a sexually attractive woman, he could banish his jealousy. Friends. Her mind boggled. She didn't want Alex as a friend, she couldn't suddenly switch off now. It was too late.

He smiled at her ruefully. "So you see, there will be no further distressing scenes between us. I feel a lot happier knowing that."

It was just as well somebody was in the mood to celebrate. Kerry wasn't. Didn't he see that those days on Kordos had been a necessary period of adjustment? Before that ghastly scene on the beach had erupted, a new and fragile understanding had been under formation, in spite of his jealousy. His behaviour had shattered her that day, and perhaps, she grasped now, it had shattered him too. He was really acting quite predictably. He saw a fault in himself. He rooted it out. After all, she might be the cause of the fault, but he was truly stuck with her now. Alex had brought logic to bear on their problems, and Alex's cool logic had never been less welcome.

APART FROM a little nausea during the flight to Pisa airport, she was fine. The closer they got to journey's end, however, the more tense she became. Casa del Fiore had been her prison during their separation. She associated the eighteenth-century villa with unhappy memories. But evidently sentimentality had no such hold upon Alex.

The house was on the outskirts of Florence, set in the lush, rolling hills of the Tuscan countryside, which was already blossoming with the softening green veil of spring. The day they had viewed Casa del Fiore, it had been surrounded by an overgrown meadow of wild flowers, its dulled and neglected façade gleaming a faint pink in the dying sunlight. After the agent had gone, Alex had tumbled her down and made love to her among those flowers. She reddened and paled again with self-loathing. Memory looked like being her sole comfort. He had got tired of her even before that fight, she was convinced of it. When had Alex ever denied himself anything he still wanted?

"Welcome home," he murmured as the limousine swung between the tall, eagle-topped pillars at the foot of the long driveway.

Casa del Fiore seemed to drowse in the blaze of the noonday heat, the soft yellow walls of the rambling villa complemented by the terracotta roof tiles. The arrow-shaped cypresses lining the avenue cast thin shadows in the car's path.

She had chosen this house, not Alex. Her enthusiasm had been undiminished by the mountain of improvements required inside and out, and Alex had let her have her way. She had flung herself into transforming the drab interior, struggling with Italian workmen brought up to *"Domani"* and forever going over her head to talk to Alex, who had never had the time or the interest to deal with them. When he had left, she had stopped decorating, leaving only a few rooms complete.

Nicky scrambled out of the car first, eager to explore. Alex had never brought him here. He had closed the house up with only a caretaker. The staff were all new, smilingly grouped in the front hall. The ghastly cherry-red carpet she had mistakenly chosen for the floor still darkened the entrance.

Lucrezia, the housekeeper, beamed at her cheerfully and, as soon as the introductions were over, Kerry forgot about Alex and went off to explore. It was like moving into a timeslip. Everything was exactly as she had left it. The kitchens were still untiled. The rooms she hadn't touched were still empty and shuttered. An incredible medley of styles reigned supreme wherever her immature taste had lingered. The rear sitting-room still rejoiced in lamentably quarrelsome floral fabrics.

"I gather you didn't use the house at all," she remarked, hearing his step behind her. "It's pretty hard on the eye, isn't it?"

"I like it. It's bright, warm," he replied almost abruptly.

Upstairs, her throat closed over in the doorway of their bedroom. For once her efforts for a cohesive scheme had come together. But the pale lemon-washed walls, the abundance of gorgeous fabric at the windows and over the bed made her turn away. How could he bring her back here? Didn't he have any sensitivity at all? Everywhere she looked she saw a frail, drooping shadow of herself in the past. Welcome home, indeed!

Brown fingers linked slowly with hers. "Was it a mistake to bring you back? You loved this house."

Irritably she rammed back her own eerie spectres. Alex suffered from no such imaginative qualms. "Where will we put Nicky?" she asked, walking down the wide, sunlit corridor to glance into empty rooms. She had furnished one guest-room. He hadn't changed that, either.

"I'll use the dressing-room off our bedroom," he replied as if he could read her mind.

She gave a brisk nod, colour rising to her cheeks. Project one was evidently to furnish the room through the communicating door for Alex's occupancy. "I've got a lot to do," she mused.

"You mustn't overtire yourself," he ruled. "I will be here. Ask me to help with anything you wish."

Unexpectedly, she laughed. "Alex, the last time I showed you a wallpaper book, you spread a file on top of it."

"I must often have hurt your feelings," he remarked with unsmiling gravity. "It won't be like that again."

"I'm not expecting you to immerse yourself in household trivia,'' she said dully, recoiling from his sacrificial attitude.

Later she watched him from the bedroom window. Nicky was kicking a ball towards him and throwing a short-tempered fit when Alex kicked it back past him. Shorn of his jacket and tie, his black hair tousled by the breeze, he looked remarkably relaxed as he scooped his son up and hugged him with an unashamed affection which jerked her own heartstrings with envy. He looked happy. He had put a wall between them that she didn't want, and he looked happy. He had only battled with his pride when he decided that they should opt for a platonic marriage.

When she was in bed, she thought of him lying in the narrow confinement of the single just through the wall while she tossed in more space than she could find comfort in. You'd better get used to it, she thought, Alex never changes his mind about a decision.

When she slept, she dreamt that she was locked inside a house without windows or doors. Everywhere she ran in her frantic need to escape she came on another stretch of blank wall. Her eyes flew open, a sob on her lips. Alex was bending over her. "It's only a dream... hmm?" he soothed, and the fear went out of her. "Do you want me to bring you a drink?"

Drowsily, she shook her head. She bit her lip, and then said it anyway, "Don't go..."

Alex stilled at the foot of the bed, already in the act of leaving her. Stark embarrassment flooded her as she registered his surprise and reluctance. But the slither of his silk robe marked his agreement. "Go back to sleep," he murmured as he slid quietly into the other side of the bed.

When morning came, his head was against her shoulder, his thick hair brushing her chin, his arm lying heavily over the swell of her breasts. A mixture of hunger and tenderness gripped her as his dark lashes lifted and she merged with slumbrous gold. Immediately, he shifted away from her warmth. "I don't think sharing a bed is a very good idea," he murmured sardonically. "The next time something goes bump in the night, I shall leave a light on for you."

She forced a laugh and watched him depart, but she was stung to the quick, almost certain that he had seen the helpless invitation in her eyes. Her energies, it seemed, would be pinned more rewardingly to the house. Alex no longer found her an unbearable temptation.

The next few weeks were both tranquil and busy. She had the hall carpet lifted to reveal the beautiful pale pink Gavorrano marble beneath, and she engaged an interior designer. Alex was talking about setting up a branch of Veranchetti Industries in Florence and shifting his staff from Rome. She was astonished, but gradually came to appreciate that the concession was in keeping with an Alex determinedly taking an interest in every detail of the household upheaval and prowling round baby boutiques in her wake. At every opportunity Alex was proving that she could have no cause to complain of neglect. His enthusiasm and his good humour were daunting, but then he never did anything by halves, and, had his efforts to please led him into her bedroom, she could have been ecstatic. Unfortunately, Superhusband went to his own bed every night, and did not appear to be finding it a strain.

They came home from a shopping expedition in Florence one afternoon and there was another letter from Steven awaiting her. Alex passed it to her with a brilliant smile. "He likes to keep in touch, doesn't he?" he quipped. ''Perhaps you will want him to visit with us this summer.''

Leaving her pole-axed, he strode off into the library. Had it been her imagination that he was jealous of Steven? What a lowering admission it was that the hint of a dark, brooding scowl from Alex on the subject of Steven would have made her day!

The same post included a letter from her mother, who wrote that she was rather concerned about Vickie. She had not been home since Kerry's departure. ''She's very strained over the phone, not like herself at all,'' Ellen wrote. ''Do you think there's a man involved? I hoped that she might have confided in you.''

Kerry hadn't heard from Vickie, nor did she expect to. She assumed that Jeff's appeal to her sister had failed, and that with it his desire to unlock the past had waned. It was now almost four weeks since he had called her from Athens. Sooner or later, she would have to write to Vickie. She didn't want their parents upset by the discovery that their daughters were mysteriously at loggerheads. But it was still too soon for Kerry to face penning that letter. Her anger had subsided, and much of her bitterness, but she was still paying the price of that morning through her marriage.

The following morning, Lucrezia brought her breakfast in bed. Alex came in with Nicky, her son bouncing up and down with exuberant excitement. Still half asleep, she surveyed them.

''It's your birthday,'' Alex said drily.

She blinked, for she had completely forgotten. ''Happy birthday!'' Nicky cried, thrusting an envelope on top of her cup of tea and settling a luridly coloured box beside it.

''Happy birthday.'' Alex pressed cool lips to her

flushed cheek and presented her with a card. It was all very restrained and polite.

His card was one of those ones with no message. Admittedly, he would have had to sack Florence to find a card with a blurb suitable to their association. What it did have, though, was an enormous key taped inside.

Kerry looked at him hopefully. The key to the communicating door between their bedrooms, she thought wildly, for the lock was empty on both sides.

"It's a surprise," he proffered with an oddly tense smile. "We need to go out to fit the key to a door."

Disgraced by her own imagination, she nodded. Eating breakfast was impossible after that. Nicky was left at home and Alex drove them into Florence. He parked by the Arno and took her walking through the narrow, crowded streets.

"Am I going to like it...the surprise?" she prompted doubtfully.

"I hope so...I think so." The cool, sensual mouth curved into an almost boyish smile as he guided her off the Via Tornebuoni. "I thought of it in Greece."

He had been thinking of her birthday that far back? She could only be complimented. He grabbed her hand impatiently. "Close your eyes," he instructed, and his arm folded round her to move her on another few steps before turning her round. "Now you can open them."

"Am I supposed to see something?" she muttered, gazing at the green and gold decorated windows of the apparently empty shop in front of them.

He sighed. "Look up to the name."

What she read in flowing gold script immobilised her. Antiques Fayre—Firenze. While Alex employed the key in the door she tried to crank her jaw shut. Alex had bought her a shop?

"Aren't you coming in?"

She stood inside the enormous interior on the dusty floor which was littered with packing cases and rubbish. It was easily four times the size of what she had left behind. "How...how did you get it? It's so central. It must have cost a fortune...or is it rented?"

Alex looked pained. "It belongs to you. I made the previous owner an offer that he could not refuse. At the price, he might have removed the rubbish," he complained grimly.

"You want me to go into business?" Kerry wished there was a seat somewhere around. Her legs were wobbly. She was afraid there was a catch, and this was some gigantic misunderstanding.

"That was the idea, but..."

"I knew there was a but."

"The baby," Alex reproved and spread his expressive hands wide. "I didn't know there was going to be a baby. Do you think you could wait until after its birth to start this place up? I am afraid it would be too taxing a project to begin now, but when the baby is born we can get a nanny..."

She sagged. The but had not contained the tripwire she feared. Silence fell. She was in the trancelike hold of astonishment. Alex had opened the door of her gilded cage.

He expelled his breath. "I know you like to be busy. You have so much energy. When the house is finished, Nicky at school, what would you do with yourself? I suggest you hire a manager so that you are not too tied to the business, but that is up to you."

She wanted to cry. When Athene heard about this, she would think her son had gone crazy. "You thought about this in Greece?"

"I know how bored you were before at home. You needed more stimulus. This time I want you to be content in our marriage, and here you will have your own challenge, you will…"

"Alex, it's the most wonderful thing anybody's ever done for me!" she interrupted extravagantly. In buying her this business, Alex had overcome his need to lock her up. She could see in his dark, set features that he was still questioning his own decision and was somewhat ambivalent about his own generosity. But what mattered was that he had done it for her despite his own fear of giving her this amount of freedom. She reached for his hand uncertainly. "You won't ever have cause to regret this."

His ebony brows pleated. "I have to trust you. You were right when you said that. The problem was mine," he stated tautly. "That day on the island, I shocked myself. It will never happen again. I promise you that."

Her bronze lashes veiled her stinging eyes. How like Alex it was to force himself into the very opposite of what he wanted when he realised that he was behaving unreasonably. She could have applauded his determination on a much less extreme show of trust than this, and suddenly she could see hope for them both, without Vickie or Jeff. Surely it was possible that, when Alex had dealt with his own gremlins, he would come back to her in every way?

Five days later, Alex flew to Rome. He was due home for the weekend, but the afternoon passed without his appearance. Early evening, Kerry was perched on the window seat in the salon, wondering why he hadn't phoned, when a little yellow Fiat came bowling noisily down the driveway. A tall blond man extracted himself awkwardly from the driver's side and straightened.

Vickie strolled round the bonnet and grasped his hand. Kerry froze. They had actually come. A minute later, Lucrezia showed them in.

"Alex is in Rome, he isn't back yet," was the first thing Kerry said.

In the uneasy stasis, Jeff stuck out his hand, a dull flush of red lying along his broad cheekbones, his other arm planted round her strained sister. "I don't expect you to like me, but I'm four years older and wiser now," he said wryly.

"I guess you've been wondering what was going on," Vickie said very quietly. "Jeff never knew that you and Alex split up that day. I don't want you to feel he's equally to blame. It was over two years before we ran into each other again. I started seeing Jeff, but I had to keep quiet about it. I couldn't take him home, I couldn't tell you about him. It was poetic justice, I suppose. I was caught in my own trap."

"I had absolutely no idea why Vickie was holding me at bay. If I had done, believe me, I wouldn't have let it lie," he stressed levelly.

"The day you left me...I was upset," Vickie muttered. "I phoned Jeff and I told him everything."

"And I flew off half-cocked to Athens, without really thinking the whole thing through. Your reaction when I called made me appreciate that it was going to take more than a few words," Jeff admitted.

Vickie took a seat stiffly, still watching Kerry's anxious face. "As you've probably guessed, I refused to come initially. I'm not proud of that. It was unforgivable. I don't win any badges for courage. I couldn't have done it without Jeff's support. I did love Alex, Kerry," she faltered and looked up at the man by her side. "But never the way I love Jeff. I'm glad it's over, you have no idea what a relief it is..."

Jeff cleared his throat impatiently. "I think right now Kerry has to be more interested in hearing that we've seen Alex."

"You've seen him," Kerry echoed. "But how?"

"I thought it would be wiser if we saw your husband at his office, and didn't involve you until we saw how it was going to go," Jeff supplied.

Kerry shut her eyes, rocked off balance to learn that the deed had already been done. "What did he say?"

"It was...ghastly," her sister said shakily. "He went all quiet. It was like the whole thing just suddenly sunk in on him. One minute he was raging, the next he sat down."

"But did he believe you?" Kerry pressed in exasperation.

Jeff drove his fingers through his untidy hair ruefully. "Oh, I think he believed us all right. I'm not sure he would have if we hadn't both been there, though."

"You said he went quiet? Pleased quiet? Angry quiet?" Kerry prompted in desperation.

"He was appalled...stunned," Vickie answered reluctantly.

"But he hasn't come home."

"He does have a lot to think about." Her sister looked at her guiltily, unhappily. "He divorced you. Finding out the truth now, when it's too late to really do anything about it..." Vickie hesitated. "You see, I never thought about how it was going to be for him. Telling him the truth wasn't really giving him anything to celebrate. That's the best way I could put it..."

Kerry viewed her in blank incomprehension. Alex ought to have been jetting home in haste to...to what?

Fling himself at her feet and apologise? Like Vickie, she had never thought beyond the moment when Alex would know the true story. She had never questioned how Alex might react.

''I think it's time we left,'' Jeff said bluntly. ''We're booked into a hotel, and the last thing Alex needs is to find us plonked here when he does come back.''

''Do you think if we held off getting married for a few months, you and Alex would come?'' Vickie whispered uncertainly.

''Frankly, I think your sister has got more on her mind right now.'' Jeff's tone was dry and Vickie reddened.

Kerry gave way to her sister's red-rimmed eyes and gave her a brief hug. The ice was broken, but she still could not have looked Vickie in the eye and told her that she completely forgave her. The cost had been too high. She managed to smile as she saw them off. It was difficult. Alex's delayed return was worrying her increasingly. She phoned the family house in Rome to speak to Mario, who was presently working as one of Alex's aides. She learnt that Alex had left the office before lunch time. By the time she got off the phone, she regretted calling. Athene had come on to the line to ask if there was anything wrong.

At two in the morning, she finally went to bed, and anxiety had been replaced by anger. How could he do this to her? Didn't he realise how worried she would be?

CHAPTER TEN

IT WAS NOON the next day before Alex arrived home. He was as sleek and immaculate as ever, but he looked as if he had been up all night. Aside from the faint pallor, the etching of strain round his mouth, Kerry could not have read a single emotion in his shuttered dark gaze. He stared at her and sank down on to a sofa. For a moment his glossy head was bent, and then he lifted it again and the air of vulnerability was gone.

"I should have phoned, but I should imagine that is the least of my sins," he began.

"Vickie and Jeff came here last night. I know you've seen them," she interposed.

A wintry smile firmed his mouth. "I almost made a derogatory comment about them both, but you have a saying about people in glass houses..." He paused, his bone structure prominent beneath his bronze skin. "I spent the night in the car. I didn't know what to say to you then. I needed time. Your sister informed me that she had told you the truth before you married me. Why didn't you tell me?"

The impatience had drained out of her. A curious foreboding was clenching her tight now. "I didn't think you'd believe me."

He bit out a harsh laugh and studied his linked hands. "You know me too well. I shouldn't have asked the question. A more caring and less intimidating husband might have invited confidence. I don't blame you for keeping quiet. Jeff...it was he who phoned you on the island? You were very happy that day," he drawled in the same measured, carefully unemotional tone.

"Of course I was...after all this time, I finally saw a hope of it all being cleared up," she replied.

"It is now." Releasing his breath slowly, he stared across the room at her. "An apology, no matter how deeply it was meant, would be another insult to the many I have already offered you. In my desire for revenge, I have done you incalculable harm. Nothing I could do or say would make up for the pain I have caused you."

Her eyes were haunted pools in the ashen pallor of her face. Her fingers curled tightly over the back of the armchair in front of her. She felt sick because she was afraid. If he loved her, there was plenty he could do, but he did not love her. Faced with his own mistrust and misjudgement, all Alex could feel now was the heavy burden on his conscience, the impossibility of finding adequate words to express his regret for all that had happened between them since that day in Venice.

"You said that the clock could not work in reverse," he reminded her. "You were correct. Even before they came to see me yesterday I had already seen this. I had also come to appreciate that a...loving husband would not have behaved as I did four years ago. I might have seen that if my wife did end up in another man's arms, my own behaviour had undoubtedly contributed to the betrayal. But then I was not capable of seeing that..."

"Alex...I..." she faltered, torn by his pain but held back by his icy control.

He rose abruptly to his feet and moved a silencing hand. "No, don't tell me not to say these things. I must say them. I fell in love with you because you were so full of life, and then I proceeded to crush it out of you," he breathed contemptuously. "Worse," he continued before she could argue that his faults had not been so severe. "I didn't even notice I was doing that to you."

Her fingernails bit into the velvet beneath her hand. "It wasn't so bad as that," she protested weakly.

The dark head flung back. "Do not be so generous to me," he grated. "When was I ever generous to you? Had I left you in the life you were contented with, I would feel less like some Dark Ages tyrant now. But no, once again I had to come into your life and make a mess of it, even to the point of making you pregnant again. And why did that happen? Because I blackmailed you into bed. I might as well have raped you."

Kerry was trembling. So much of the understanding she had once longed for had been locked up inside him. It must have existed before yesterday. Alex could not have put all this together overnight. But what she was hearing was too extreme, too terrifyingly linked with a hard, bitter finality for her to receive any comfort from it.

He drew something from his inside pocket. "This is the contract I forced you to sign." He tore the document violently in half and cast the pieces into the grate. He straightened again, pale but controlled. "Now you have no restrictions. I will leave you to lead your life as you choose to lead it. If you do not want me to see Nicky," his voice roughened and dropped low, "this I will accept, too."

Shock was coursing through her in waves. Dear God, it was happening all over again! Only this time he had had the decency not to send a lawyer to do the dirty work. A searing memory of the letters she had written and the calls she had once made sealed her lips rigidly on any protest. If he was leaving, she would let him leave. Why should she tell him that she loved him, when her feelings weren't returned? She refused to make the smallest move to argue his decision.

"You married me just to get revenge, didn't you?" she accused with stark eyes. "And once you'd got it, it was worthless, wasn't it?"

His dark eyes flamed golden. "Yes…worthless." His low-pitched response was wry. "And I know that to give you your freedom back when it should never have been taken from you is poor recompense. But it is all that I have to give."

All that he had to give. The statement rippled through her slight body, burning and wounding wherever it touched. It took her anger away. It numbed her. "And what am I supposed to do now?" she asked woodenly.

"You do whatever you want. I will do nothing. You can have a divorce, a separation, whatever you choose. Where you live is also your decision," he laid out tautly. "Naturally, I will leave this house…"

"That's very generous of you, but I can be generous too," she assured him shakily. "I'll pack for you!"

"I have already asked Lucrezia to take care of it," Alex murmured tightly. "This is what you want, isn't it?"

"Of course it's what I want. My God, Alex, you don't think I'm about to argue, do you?" she gibed, half an octave higher.

A tiny muscle jerked in the corner of his compressed mouth, as if her venom had thrust fully home. In a torment of blind rage and despair, she watched him leave the room. She listened to his steps ringing up the stairs, and it seemed no time until they came down again. Still she had not moved. The slam of the car door echoed through the window. Unexpectedly, the door opened again.

Alex hovered there, shorn of his usual cool poise. But then, the last time he had walked out, he had not had to tolerate an audience or a conscience. She observed him with cold eyes. "Did you forget something?"

Alex, you bastard, how could you put me through this again? But she didn't speak. As he turned on his heel, she crammed a shaking hand to her wobbling mouth and bowed her head over the chair which was still supporting her. Why was it that no matter what she did he could still walk away? Here she had been, expecting at first guilty discomfiture upon his part but inevitably the same release she had experienced after Vickie's revelations. But the one salient fact she had overlooked was that Alex did not love her. Alex had reacted according to his principles. He had forced her into this marriage. In apology, he was removing himself from her life again. She was fiercely glad that she had let him go thinking that she was delighted to see the back of him. Once before, loving him had humiliated her. It had not done so this time.

A quiet like the grave settled over Casa del Fiore. The staff seemed to creep about. Lucrezia, full of enormous Florentine compassion, looked upon her with great, tragic eyes and endeavoured to tempt her flagging appetite. At the end of a week, Kerry was emptied of tears. Her misery had stirred Nicky into rampant insecurity, and she had to pull herself together for his benefit. After the strain of smiling all day, she ended up ringing Steven late one evening. It was a long call, and forty-eight hours later Steven arrived on the doorstep.

Nicky greeted him boisterously and, under Lucrezia's

dazed scrutiny, Kerry threw her arms about him too. "That'll have to be some shoulder," she sniffed.

His classic features pulled a clownish grimace, and his blue eyes were rueful. "It's one of the very few things I'm good at."

"WHY DIDN'T YOU tell him how you felt?" he asked later, when Nicky was in bed.

"There was no point." Her tone brooked no argument.

"I've never met Alex..."

"Aren't you the lucky one?" she muttered, blowing her nose. "He was a jealous, suspicious toad the first time around, but you know, this time he was worse...he was so nice all the time, it was like living with a saint over the last few weeks. Not my idea of Alex at all."

Steven looked understandably a little at sea, and tried to be constructive. "My gut reaction is that in clearing out he thought he was doing the decent thing, like somebody out of one of those ghastly melodramatic plays they enjoy in Greece."

Kerry was unimpressed. "If he hadn't wanted to let me go, he wouldn't have. Let's talk about something more cheerful. He's gone and that's it, and I never, ever want to see him again. Do you hear me?" She snatched at another tissue and wiped at her overflowing eyes.

Steven stayed only for three days, and mentioned that he would be selling up the business. Barbara had convinced him that he would cope much better with a simple workshop in a town where there would be more demand for his services, and she was thinking of looking for a job closer to home. Kerry had to quell the unpleasant feeling that everybody else's problems were working out, while her own simply increased in complexity.

She let the workmen back into the house. Her life wasn't going to fall apart again, she assured herself. She had got by without Alex before, she would do so again. She kept herself busy and she fell into bed every night exhausted. Alex had been gone exactly three weeks when Athene arrived without so much as a polite call to advertise her intent.

Kerry, surprised with a scarf round her head, wearing a pair of jogging pants and a stripy rugby shirt Alex had once worn, stiffened as Athene strolled in, her cool, dark appraisal sweeping her in obvious recoil. "Perhaps I should have warned you that I was coming."

Kerry showed her into the small sitting-room, since the salon was being redecorated. Athene shed her coat and inched off her gloves. "If it is not too impertinent a question, may I ask who the young man was that you had staying?"

Off-balance, Kerry stared back at her.

Athene quirked a silvery brow. "Your housekeeper is related to one of my servants. Such news travels fast," she remarked drily.

Kerry reddened. Athene in this formidable mood could only be compared to the iceberg which sank the Titanic. She found herself hurriedly making an explanation, and alluding carefully to Barbara's existence in Steven's life.

Athene's Arctic cool melted slightly. "Ah," she nodded. "This makes greater sense. You don't look to be thriving upon my son's absence."

"That's a matter of opinion," Kerry parried proudly.

"I am not quite in my dotage," Athene fielded, and her thin lips almost smiled. "This outfit you wear can only be an expression of grief." She paused and then looked up. "I did not come here easily. You and I have only Alex in common, and I have come for Alex's sake.''

"Alex left me…'' Kerry began spiritedly.

Athene waved an imperious hand. "But not, I think, willingly, and I have no need to receive details. I knew from the first moment I met you six years ago that you and Alex would have a stormy relationship. Given your personality, it was only a matter of time until the trouble began…''

"*My* personality?''

Athene frowned irritably. "You are too defensive. Will you let me speak?'' she demanded thinly. "If Alex had married a quieter girl, content to fit with his expectations, the marriage probably would have lasted as yours did not. You were outgoing and lively, and Alex was stifling you because he could not bring himself to trust you. The fault was his. Perhaps I could have stopped it then by speaking to him. I chose to conserve my own dignity. I did not interfere, and when I would have done, it was too late.''

Kerry sighed. "I'm afraid I don't see what you could have done.''

Athene smiled grimly. "Yes, you have noticed that Alex and I are not close. Did you ever wonder why? Alex was my firstborn and my favourite, but I believe his first loyalty always lay with his father. Nevertheless, when he was a child, we were close until a certain episode occurred.'' Her voice was becoming taut and hesitant. "I lost my son's respect. Has he told you of this?''

Puzzled by the increasingly personal tenor of Athene's words, while marvelling that Athene could ever have done anything to fall foul of Alex's high principles, Kerry murmured gently, "Alex wouldn't have told me anything of that nature unless there was a need for me to know.''

Athene sighed. ''It was not a need he would have acknowledged, and it is an episode he has done his utmost to forget. That I have always been aware of,'' she conceded, almost as if she was talking to herself. ''When I married Alex's father, Lorenzo, I admired him very much. I was only a teenager when I understood that it was my parents' dearest wish that I should marry the son of their oldest friends. It was not arranged, you understand, but it was expected.''

''Were you unhappy with Alex's father?'' Kerry prompted in surprise.

''When I fell in love, for the first and last time in my life,'' Athene stressed looking her almost defiantly in the eye, ''then I was unhappy.''

As Kerry's face tightened in astonished realisation that Athene was admitting to having loved another man, her companion's lips compressed tightly.

''Why not me? None of us are born saints. I had been content with Lorenzo. He was a good man and a faithful husband, and he still loved me on the day he died. He never knew that for a few short weeks of our marriage I carried on an affair with another man, and it would have caused him great pain to discover that secret. He had always awarded me unquestioning faith and trust,'' she admitted heavily.

Mottled colour had suffused her powdered cheeks, making Kerry sharply aware that this confession of frailty had cost Athene dearly.

''We met quite by accident,'' she continued expressionlessly. ''He was a businessman, but not wealthy. For me, it was a kind of madness. I counted no costs when I became involved with him. Every moment I could steal from my family, I was with Tomaso, and inevitably we were found out." Her voice had sunk very low. "I wanted desperately to be with him somewhere where we could be alone. We used to have a summer place outside Cannes. Alex was at boarding-school then. He was to spend his half-term there with me. There was illness in the school and they let him leave early. He crept into the house to surprise me, and he discovered me in Tomaso's arms. He was only thirteen, and I was terrified that he would tell his father. I realised too late what I had done. I sent Tomaso away and I never saw him again. I had my children and my husband to consider. Alex remained silent. He understood that nothing could be gained from any other course but his father's pain and disillusionment."

As the implications of the sad, reluctantly advanced confession swept Kerry in a stormy flood, she swallowed hard sooner than betray a sympathy which would be fiercely rejected. Athene might have strayed in the madness she described, but for a strong woman of deep, religious convictions her choice had been completely in character.

In the heavy silence, Athene took a deep breath. "He didn't betray me, but I lost the son who loved and respected his mother that day. He never alluded to the incident again. How else could he behave?" she appealed tiredly. "His love for his father tied him to silence. He grew up that day all at once. He learnt that appearances could be deceptive. Now perhaps you may understand why Alex would find it very hard to trust a woman."

And why he divorced me and why he wouldn't come near me, Kerry added in inner anguish. He had been afraid to end up in the weak position he probably believed his father had held throughout his marriage. He had cut her out of his life sooner than risk that danger. "Why have you told me this?" she asked.

"For Alex. The settlement of a debt," Athene emphasised, looking every year of her age. "Now perhaps you will go to him and tell him there is no other man in your life."

The edge of her contempt stiffened Kerry. "It's not as simple as that. Alex doesn't love me."

"Does that matter, if he needs you?" Athene turned on her like a lioness defending a cub. "If there was a cure for you I would have given it to him! You are Alex's one weakness. I don't know how he kept away from you for four years. And you say, 'he doesn't love me'," she mimicked in a die-away echo, but her lined dark eyes were suspiciously bright. "Do you think I came here easily to ask for your help? He is on the island, and when I saw him last week he was exceedingly drunk. While you are painting your walls, my son is going to pieces!"

As Athene stalked back out to her car in high dudgeon, Kerry was picturing Alex standing in the doorway as he had that last day. Alex without words, simply taking a last look at her. Does it matter what drives him if he needs you? "You can never be here for me when I need you." The ragged condemnation he had uttered weeks ago thickened her throat. It was three steps to the phone, and she got there in one. If there was something wrong with Alex, she would go to him. Just once more she would put her own pride on the line. Athene would not have approached her lightly.

By the time she lurched out of the helicopter late that evening, and the pilot tucked Nicky's limp, sleeping body into her arms, her adrenalin-charged rush to Alex's side seemed a little excessive. Nobody was expecting them. Kerry had purposely not phoned. She had not wanted Alex to have time to prepare himself for her arrival.

Sofia hurried towards her in a dressing-gown, with Spiros in her wake. Kerry settled Nicky into the manservant's arms with a relieved sigh. She had been prepared for Alex to appear, looking his usual smooth self and embarrassingly curious about her uninvited descent. But he didn't appear, and Sofia fussed round her, trying to persuade her to go to bed. A thin bar of light was burning below the study door. Seeing it, Kerry turned from Sofia and opened the door.

The shutters were drawn, the air rank with the pervasive fumes of whisky. Alex was slumped in a chair, and she no longer needed to wonder why he had failed to come and greet her. He hadn't had a shave in days. He was haggard, his cheekbones protruding sharply to emphasise his unhealthy pallor. Her sleek, beautiful Alex had gone skinny, and he was viewing her with unfocused dark eyes much as a drunk uncritically accepts the presence of a parade of pink elephants.

"Oh…Alex, how could you do this to yourself?" she whispered painfully.

She threw open the shutters and the windows to let in fresh air. Something crunched under her shoe. She bent to lift a crumpled black and white photo of herself, a stolen photo taken when she was unawares some time in the past. She was emerging from the showroom, talking animatedly to Steven.

Alex muttered something incoherent. He closed his eyes and opened them again. "Kerry?" he slurred uncertainly. "Don't go away again."

He pulled himself up in the chair and she stood over

him with folded arms. "Do you love me?" she demanded shakily, surmising that she was most likely to receive the truth in the condition he was in, and if she was taking advantage, too bad.

"You'll disappear if I say yes," he mumbled accusingly.

"No, I won't. You've got that the wrong way round," she protested.

He pushed unsteady fingers through his tousled black hair. "Yes."

Her eyes watered. "Say it, then."

His mouth curved into a shadowy smile, the sort of smile a pink elephant might inspire. "I love you," he managed, and then, "Much too much to hold on to you."

"No...no!" She could have kicked him. "I didn't want the qualification. That's just so typical of you, Alex. You can't even say three little words the way I want to hear them. I've waited six years, and in six years I got it thrown at me in the past tense once, and now I get it with a qualification. If I had any pride at all, I wouldn't be here ready to tell you that *I* love *you*..."

She retreated, shocked by her own loss of control. But Alex had finally been sprung from his lethargy. He stood up, swaying slightly. "Hallucinations don't shout."

"I didn't mean to shout," she answered shakily.

His hand lifted to touch a strand of her gleaming hair. "I'm not fussy," he muttered hoarsely. "Did you mean it?"

"Yes." She watched him breathe again, watched a gleam of vitality spark in his dulled eyes.

"And I have to be drunk." Red washed his sallow complexion. He backed towards the door. "I need a shower...I need a coffee. Don't go away."

She wiped her eyes as he left the room. She had seen in his face what no counterfeiter could have copied. The same pain, the same fear, the same loneliness, and she was ridiculously tempted to sit down and have a good cry. If he had left her, it had not been because he wanted to leave her. It was almost an hour before he reappeared. Either a miracle potion or simple shock had sobered him up. Shaven, his long, straight legs encased in tight jeans matched to a clean white shirt, he looked like Alex again, only not quite so confident as was his wont. He strode out of the bathroom impatiently, and then wheeled round in surprise to find her seated on the end of his bed.

"I thought you'd got lost," she said, hot-cheeked.

"And I thought you were with Steven," he drawled tautly.

She told him quietly what she had told Athene earlier in the day.

"He cares for someone else? How is this possible?"

"They've known each other since they were teen-agers, and sometimes they don't see each other for months on end. He's a friend," she hesitated, "I wouldn't have been attracted to him in any other way, in any case; he can be a real pain..."

His strained mouth curved helplessly with humour. "A pain...all I saw were those golden looks of his...for months." His smile ebbed with discomfiture.

"I saw that photo. You must have spied on me. Why?"

"Is there always a sane explanation for the things we do?" he countered tautly. "I told myself that I had a right to know what you were doing when you had my son. But when you began to go out socially with Steven, I couldn't bear it and who knows what goes on behind closed doors? I was afraid you might marry him. Then, when I saw you again, everything I had spent years denying came alive again. For a few days, I was like a man possessed. I didn't care what I had to do to get you back, I didn't even ask myself why I was doing it.''

A tender smile softened her lips. ''You're forgiven. If you hadn't used pressure, we wouldn't be here together now.''

The topaz eyes narrowed. ''How can you say that? *Per Dio*...I behaved like the savage you said I was.''

''I love you, Alex.''

He moved closer, his dark features clenched taut. ''I realised that I still loved you the first time we made love again, but I believed that you cared for Steven. At best you seemed to tolerate me, and then after that incident on the beach, you were cold in my arms. I had even killed that,'' he emphasised with hard self-derision.

''I was upset, frightened by your jealousy,'' she argued warily, wondering why he had yet to put his arms around her.

''I know.'' In shamed acknowledgement, he looked at her guiltily. ''But I still could not have let you go. I couldn't face losing you. In the end, I was even relieved that you were pregnant. It was another way of holding on to you. It didn't matter that I couldn't make love to you any more, it didn't matter to me that you cared, as I thought, for another man. I still had you, and that was sufficient. When they came to me and told me the truth, everything came apart...'' His hand sketched a movement of defeat. ''Before, I believed I had rights, and I made excuses for myself. When I couldn't any more, all I could do was let you go, and it was hardly enough in the circumstances.''

Her patience was wearing thin. Did he plan to stand

here for the rest of the night, unsmilingly endeavouring to persuade her that he was an undeserving cause? She could have walked on water after seeing the love in Alex when he was too low to work at concealment. Now she did something far less dangerous. She closed the distance he was carefully maintaining from her. Her hands cupped his hard cheekbones, her green eyes clinging to his. "I didn't want to be let go. I love you. But I wasn't going to beg you to stay."

The dark gaze positively shimmered. "But..."

"No buts." Her fingertip brushed his tense lower lip softly.

He searched her face torturously and then, with a groan, he locked her tightly to him. He trembled against her, and Kerry hugged him close as he buried his face in her hair, his voice muffled and gruff. "Do you know what it was like to have to leave you? I hope you know what you are doing now. I could not leave again."

For a long time he kept her imprisoned in his arms, and when he moved it was to back her down on to the bed with a husky sigh about the convenience of the setting she had chosen. "I should tell you something," he confided then, abruptly. "There has never been another woman."

Her lashes flew up in bemusement. "I don't think I..."

His dark visage split with sudden amusement, the momentary and rare embarrassment she had seen there dissipating. "I had this...er...complication." His fingers toyed with the buttons on her blouse as he loosed them one by one. "Every time I got that close to a woman, I would always think of you, and the desire...it would recede. Didn't you notice how desperate I was that night in London? Four years is a very long time to feel that you are only half a man because you do not want to admit that you are still in love with your ex-wife.''

A slow and beatific smile was building on her lips.

Alex grinned. ''It was not very funny.''

''Serves you right.'' Her hand roamed possessively over the hard thrust of his thighs evident beneath the tight jeans. As she realised what she was doing, she blushed, and his golden eyes clung to her adoringly.

''Yes, it served me right.'' He rolled her back into his embrace. ''But I wasn't sorry when I got you back. We always belonged only to each other. I need very badly to remind myself of that now,'' he whispered raggedly, and branded her mouth with the fever of the fierce, raw hunger that spoke for itself.

''WHAT MADE YOU come to me?'' he prompted when she was still languorous with the exquisite release of their lovemaking.

She hid her expression against his shoulder, and her arms tightened convulsively round him. ''Athene visited me.''

He tensed, his dark, dishevelled head lifting up.

''Yes,'' she confirmed. ''She told me, and it hurt her to tell me. She loves you very much, Alex.''

His breath escaped in a hiss. ''She didn't love my father, did she admit that? He adored her. I could never bear to watch him dance attention on her after that day. I was afraid ever to be like that with a woman...yes, it influenced me when we were first married, how could it not? I could never accept that you could love me as I loved you,'' he completed roughly.

''But I do,'' she stressed, smoothing his cheek gently. ''And loving me isn't a weakness, Alex.''

Hard fingers caught her chin, a rueful smile slanting

his lips. "But I am weak with you. My life is hell without you; how could it be otherwise? All those years wasted because I was too proud to come to you...what a bloody fool I was!" he swore fiercely. "Nothing was worth what we both went through apart. So much unhappiness, so many mistakes."

Her heart leapt in her throat as he looked at her. The dark-fringed golden eyes were unguarded, nakedly vulnerable for a split second as he wrapped her firmly against him again. "But this time I will love you always, no matter what the future brings. Perhaps I will never have the words to express how much you mean to me," he sighed regretfully.

"I don't know. Superhusband wasn't doing too badly on actions," she teased. "I was very slow on the uptake."

"Super...husband?" Alex growled.

She grinned. "All that boundless bonhomie..."

A reflective smile removed his frown. "It wasn't easy. I was hoping to convert you from Steven. But patience...it is not my strong point. I don't know how I kept my hands from you; it was a torture to do so." The husky confession was feelingly reminiscent of the deprivation he had endured, and already his natural assurance was reasserting its sway. "Never again."

She rested back invitingly. "I second that."

"Why is it that you always have the last word?" But he won silence by his own nefarious means, and laughter shook her slightly before she gave herself up, without a care in the world, to Alex's mastery.

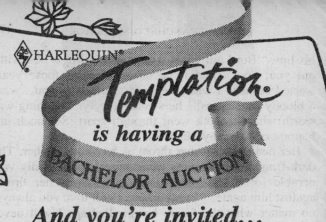

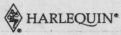

HARLEQUIN®

Escapade

A SPECIAL COLLECTION OF BOOKS FROM FOUR HARLEQUIN SERIES.

If you enjoyed these titles you are sure to enjoy more of what Harlequin has to offer.

More titles are available at your favorite retail outlet.

---

50 cents off!

the purchase of any

HARLEQUIN INTRIGUE, HARLEQUIN TEMPTATION, HARLEQUIN SUPERROMANCE or HARLEQUIN PRESENTS series book.

PHE50US

HARLEQUIN®
Makes any time special.™

Coupon expires December 31, 1999. Valid at retail outlets in the U.S. only.

5 65373 00050 2 (8100)0 10582

Look us up on-line at: http://www.romance.net   PHE50US